SIKANDER

To Atiya Raza &
Tariq Khan
Enjoy the story! ☺

Salahuddin

8/8/2010

SIKANDER

By

M. Salahuddin Khan

First American Edition

KARAKORAM PRESS™

KARAKORAM PRESS, Lake Forest, IL

SIKANDER IS PUBLISHED BY KARAKORAM PRESS

SIKANDER copyright © 2010;	KARAKORAM PRESS
Cover art copyright © 2010;	M. Salahuddin Khan
Interior maps / illustrations copyright © 2010;	M. Salahuddin Khan

Published in the United States by Karakoram Press, an imprint of QMarket Corporation

Edited by Pamela Guerrieri

Library of Congress Control Number: 2010904104

ISBN 978-0-578-05288-5 (paperback)

ISBN 978-0-9828511-0-4 (hardcover)

Printed in the United States of America

First American Edition; July 2010

www.sikanderbook.com

KARAKORAM PRESS, Lake Forest IL

In the name of God, the Beneficent, the Merciful

To "human beings," wherever they may yet remain,
To the ones whose humanity has withstood conflict,
and
To the memory of my ever-loving parents.

M. Salahuddin Khan

Preface

Whether we like it or not we live in a complex and often dangerous world in which cultures often brush against each other. Diasporas and migrations fuel such effects and the assumptions grounded in one culture frequently fall apart when naïvely applied to another. I'm a product of a diaspora. I was born in Pakistan. I moved to England at the age of four, spending the next thirty-two years growing up and receiving an education there. In 1988 I moved to the United States. From my earliest years, I've found myself thrust into an outsider's perspective of never quite belonging to the place where I've lived.

SIKANDER is a human story. It follows a young man's coming of age and subsequent growth through adversity. He finds himself more than once having to deal with loss, which brings him to the recognition of the ultimate and relative value of his own humanity and his relationships with people.

Sikander is also a citizen of the species. He belongs nowhere in particular and everywhere in general. In spirit, he transcends cultures while being a product of his native culture. Sikander's religion is a matter-of-fact aspect of daily life, informing decisions from the mundane to the seismic. Being a part of his daily existence, his religion is neither hanging in a closet only to be worn on Fridays, nor is it is a manic permanent resident of his frontal lobes.

SIKANDER also allows the reader an in-depth immersion into the "ordinary" nature of most of the world's routinely lived Islam, which is far removed from the misconceptions sadly prevalent in much of the non-Muslim world. The story does not, however, intend an apologist perspective. Neither does it suggest that we have a simple "east-versus-west" narrative to consider. It simply forces us to step into the ordinary lives of everyday Muslims while allowing us to be aware of the textured, varied, and nuanced hues of such life from rural Afghanistan to urban Pakistan and to a lesser degree for diaspora Muslims in the USA. All of this is still within the mainstream camp, without venturing into radical or heretical renditions of the religion which also obviously exist.

Sikander's personal growth as a man involves working through the cultural differences in the practice of mainstream Islam and the conflicts between it and the "fringes" of the religion without making him be a religious fanatic of any stripe while doing so.

An additional theme was to examine the veneer-like quality of what we call civilization. Seen frontally, it projects depth and substance and seeming durability. We use words like "institution" to help us consolidate such sensibilities into our collective psyche. But turned on its side it reveals its true lack of depth and fragility. After all, civilization has only existed for a few millennia, which is but the blink of an eye against the vast ocean of time that has shaped *homo sapiens*, the animal that lies beneath. We should not be surprised to see how readily any human being is capable of descent into unfettered inhumanity, under the sanction of higher authority. It also reminds us why we have governments, laws and rules and why "minor" losses of liberty, while alluring in their seeming role of safeguarding physical security, can so often lead ultimately to disaster, and in a very real sense, increase the risks to physical security.

Lastly, in *SIKANDER* I wanted to weave the thread of an individual life through the fabric of world events that shape it. When today we hear about casualties and soldiers' tragic deaths in conflicts such as the post-9/11 Afghanistan war or Iraq, the human interest focus is upon the lives and families of the fallen. We want to know what defined them as people, how they grew up, their military career, family and so on. All these things quite properly help us to look into their essential humanity and feel empathy for such a tragic loss. *SIKANDER* has been squarely aimed at doing something similar but from the viewpoint of the equally ordinary people of Afghanistan and Pakistan, whose lives have been touched by conflict and its fallout, but whose deaths are sadly often just statistics. The story attempts to remind us to re-examine how this rendering of "otherness" upon such lives causes us to fail to see *their* no-less-essential humanity.

I would also like to clarify that the story's setting in Afghanistan, Pakistan, and the USA is secondary to its core focus being that of an examination of human nature and behavior across the boundaries between cultures. For a sense of realism, much effort went into researching historical events and the geography of the regions involved. This does not make this book a work of reference about either the events or the geography. The purpose of the research was to provide as realistic a context for the narrative as possible. But at the end of the day, it's a work of fiction. As for a source on the nature of Afghan and Pakistani culture, I would like to believe that the included glossary is both accurate and substantive and would strongly recommend the interested reader study its contents.

A word about spelling and pronunciations. *SIKANDER* is written so that pronunciations made by non-native speakers are spelled accordingly. A good illustration is "Qunduz" versus "Kunduz." Please take the time to examine the glossary section which provides not only meanings and context but also some guidance on pronunciations.

I hope you enjoy the story.

Table of Contents

Chapter 1

Difficult Times

THE LATE AUGUST SUN had passed its peak in the northwestern sky, transforming the light in Aftab's classroom from its previous drab gray to a blazing orange yellow hue. The light and shadow contrasts from the starkly lit scene outside attracted the attention of two of his students sitting nearest to the windows. University Public School was in session for its first week after the long summer break and the boys were still adjusting to being back. Rich memories of summer freedom left them struggling to pay attention to Aftab as they waited with fidgety anticipation for the bell, its metallic trill heralding the end of class and the start of the weekend that Thursday afternoon. With it would come Aftab's stern release to signal their permission to stand up and leave. Until then, he would not permit himself, nor his students, the slightest acknowledgment of the approaching end of class, much less the week.

His students referred to him as "Mr. Aftab," and it was his job to impart upon them a knowledge of the English language and the ability to read and critically interpret English literature. For this school term, it was to be Shakespeare's *Julius Caesar*. Aftab began the term intending a single reading through the play to be followed by more critical analysis over the subsequent several weeks. He had intended to cover one act per day, but he was already falling behind and had yet to start the fourth act as the first week neared a close.

While Aftab was not a physically strong person, he more than made up for it with his icy will; when he said "no," that was the end of the matter. Discipline was important to him and he intervened without hesitation at the slightest hint of it slipping. As the boys by the window had drifted their attention from the all-important subject he was trying to teach, an intervention was inevitable. Aftab launched into the distracted duo, a largely disinterested Anwar Haque and the daydreaming Sikander Khan.

"Sikander, pay attention if you please!" Aftab called out, while casting a modest scowl—whose purpose was immediately served—at Anwar. The scowl notwithstanding, Aftab's statement skillfully combined command and plea, betraying something of the conflict in his mind about handling his young charges. They were all from a well-off layer of Pakistani society, consisting of mostly business and military families in the provincial capital, Peshawar, of Pakistan's North West Frontier Province. These privileged families lived in the more affluent neighborhoods and being influential, they were not to be trifled with. Living in up-and-coming Hayatabad's Phase 2 development, Sikander's family was certainly no exception. A teacher had to be careful of being overly harsh, as parents might otherwise complain to the headmaster, which often ended in dismissal. Aftab knew that his excellent teaching skills, his reputation, and his experience of English-speaking foreign lands made such dismissal less likely than in most cases. He was simply a hard man to replace. Nevertheless, it would be foolish to subject such a theory to needless tests, so Aftab had developed something of a skill for admonishing his students.

Sikander had been peering in the direction of the north playground. Beyond its low wall streamed the east-west flow of traffic on Peshawar's Grand Trunk Road with its incessant horn blowing, including the puny buzzing of the rickshaw horns that accomplished with numbers what they failed to do with individual decibels. Trucks and buses had the most "colorful" musical air horns with annoying melodies proclaiming their presence and, no doubt, the earnestness with which they intended to occupy the road. In Pakistan without use of vehicle horns, a serious collision was virtually assured, and to blow the horn was an act of courtesy to reveal one's presence instead of the harsh critique of driving ability that it conveyed in much of the developed world. Thankfully, though, at a distance of a hundred meters the noise was diminished to form almost a "music of life" in Sikander's daydreaming yet troubled mind.

Having heard his teacher's rebuke, Sikander was now firmly yet politely gazing back at him. "Sorry, Mr. Aftab, sir!" he said. The apology was delivered as a formality and largely drained of any real meaning. If anything, his eye contact contained even a hint of challenge.

An independently minded young man, Sikander was partly buoyed by the knowledge that his family had some standing, and partly by the fact that with his solid build he was now developing into an imposing Pathan. Sikander would soon turn eighteen, and though he could be a typically adolescent handful at times, he was no bully and often exposed a deep, pensive, and intellectual side. He had allowed himself a lapse in attention in Aftab's class as he was especially skilled in English. He read English works voraciously and was fond of the many American TV programs, usually Westerns, movies, and sitcoms syndicated without dubbing or translation into Pakistani TV. He was equally delighted to pick up old, unsold, and often used copies of Reader's Digest in the Hayatabad book stores.

Sikander's appetite for things American mirrored the revived interest in the USA then in full bloom in Pakistan. Since the Soviet invasion of Afghanistan more than six years earlier, and especially so more recently, everything had changed. Ronald Reagan was at last coming through with more serious measures than anti-Soviet verbal lashings or a boycott of the Olympic Games. There was meaningful military aid and it endeared America to virtually every layer of Pakistani society. The burgeoning Pakistani diaspora in the US and the links that were thereby growing between the two countries at the level of the common middle class also made a significant contribution. This was in no small measure reinforced by expatriates remitting billions of dollars in hard foreign exchange back to their homebound Pakistani relatives each year.

"Now, as I was saying," Aftab resumed, buying a moment to re-assemble his thoughts. "When you return on Sunday, I would like you all to have read through the fourth act of *Julius Caesar* and be ready to discuss how Brutus and Cassius quarrel and reconcile before the Battle of Philippi."

Discussing Shakespeare's feuding characters was the last thing on Sikander's mind as his attention returned to the sprawling setting outside the dusty windowpane. He hankered to leave Pakistan. He wanted to see more of the world and was certain he would be doing so before long, given his coming of age and his parent's relative wealth. He had even been given an appetizer for his wanderlust when he and Jamil had accompanied their father, Javed Wahid Khan, to Dubai less than three weeks earlier during the summer break. While unusual for such business trips, Javed had known about the need to travel as long ago as June and had decided it would be a good idea to take his two sons with him.

Sikander was trying to work through his feelings about Javed. There was much about his father to admire and respect. He was an imposing, burly figure at forty-five, and a generally successful businessman. In Pakistan, nutritional deficiency was widespread. As a result, the traditional cultural perspective toward larger, swarthy people was to consider them "healthy." A strong correlation existed between such people and their relative financial standing. In Pakistan, Javed would be called healthy and sure enough, there was no denying his prosperity.

But especially more recently, Javed was also a disappointment to Sikander. At the superficial level, to Sikander's schooled sensibilities, Javed's simple garb of qamees and shalwar seemed needlessly ragged, given his command of a flourishing business. He had chosen the informal attire of the Pakistani common man and it rankled with Sikander as an embarrassment when he compared his father's appearance with what he saw as the more appropriate suit-and-tie dress sense exhibited by his class fellows' parents. But that was merely cosmetic by comparison with the other issues Sikander was having.

The Dubai trip had been Sikander's first ever outside Pakistan, and he had been taken aback by the pace with which things were moving there. Even Pakistani migrants seemed to be doing pretty well. He had been proud of his ability to put his English to work while visiting the grand city. Having transcended its classroom academic feel, the language had demonstrated its practicality in helping him engage with people there and exercised his mind in a way not possible with the more passive experience of watching English language TV and cinema. Sikander had noted the euphoric sense of empowerment that followed successful communication. It was as if he had built a machine according to the instructions and turned it on for the first time only to watch it, half-unexpectedly, work as intended.

Upon returning from Dubai, he had been so enamored with his experience that in a very real sense Sikander could not simply let it go. His passport served to remind him of the venture and he liked to carry it with him, though he was occasionally embarrassed at being caught peeking at acquired travel stamps.

In the rush of enthusiasm from the Dubai trip, he had recently suggested an operational improvement for the family business to his father. But Sikander was mortified in front of his mother, Sofie, and fifteen-year-old brother, Jamil, by Javed's dismissive ridicule of his proposal as naïve. Like many fathers, Javed did not give much credence to his son's inexperienced offerings. This occasion had differed in the extent of his father's insensitive laughter, the witnesses, and Sikander's inner adolescent convulsions. Silently, Sikander fumed, as all rules of culture and religion denied him any demonstration of frustration or irritation. Now, unless something very distracting was occupying his mind, it would invariably return to processing this lingering issue.

Sikander's only available emotion had been to sulk about the matter. But this had not gone unnoticed by Javed and it had irritated him. He had even struck Sikander with a light slap to his mop of hair to convey his displeasure—which only increased when Javed received a scolding from Sofie for being insensitive after the ridicule incident.

As far as Sikander was concerned, Javed's inclination to extinguish Sikander's views was endemic. Their arguments over Afghanistan often served to illustrate this to him. Sikander was in favor of deeper involvement by Pakistan. Despite Pakistan's provision of unfettered refuge for Afghans within its borders and channeling of American military aid into Afghanistan, to Sikander, it was all inadequate as long as the Soviet occupation remained to harass the Afghans. Moreover, Sikander felt his opinion had the legitimacy of the research he had carried out on the subject for an English debating session at the end of the prior school year. He was recognized by everyone as effective with his research and the delivery of his argument. Everyone but Javed.

Embroiled in this recent father-son challenge, Javed was reluctant to concede any ground to Sikander. After all, what did Sikander truly know of the world? On this specific debate, however,

Javed was genuinely more circumspect. While he appreciated the fact that the refugee problem certainly benefited his own business, he was not happy that the Afghans were given freedom to wander all over Pakistan. The country was awash with drugs and weapons to the detriment of Pakistan's own fragile social fabric. For Javed, President Zia-ul-Haque was far too liberal and had not thought through the consequences of such policies at all adequately. His natural instincts suggested that any assistance should have come with more restrictions. Sikander's views merely hardened his opinions and a seemingly inescapable cliché of father-and-son challenge had ensnared them both.

The school bell finally rang, jarring Sikander out of these thoughts, and the whole class became poised to disgorge from the classroom waiting only for Aftab's permission. Aftab sat down, pausing as he always did before any pronouncement, and in a firm, amused, but cynical tone he uttered, "Hence! Home, you idle creatures get you home!" as he peered over the top of his eyeglasses, quoting from the opening lines of Shakespeare's *Caesar*. He smiled at the boys filing out of the classroom, his eyeglasses demanding the assistance of his forefinger. These boys would be the class of '88, he reflected, recalling his familiarity with the way it was described in America.

"Hamid! Come on yaar!" bellowed Sikander to his friend in his native Urdu. "I have to get home quickly. We're going to my aunt's this evening and I need to get ready." Sikander's tone made it clear he was in a rush more from the wish to avoid being in further trouble than anything like enthusiasm.

"Hang on, Sikander. I'm coming," replied Hamid as he struggled to catch up with his friend after both had left their lockers.

Hamid was an introspective and intelligent youth, with the simple ambition of getting a Pakistani Air Force commission after high school. As if to telegraph this to others, he was cultivating the wisps of a square mustache while being otherwise clean-shaven, emulating the look that had become popular among PAF pilots. He had no trace of doubt about this ambition and was determined to be relentless in its pursuit after high school.

Sikander and Hamid had been neighbors since Hamid's family had moved into Hayatabad just three years earlier, and the easygoing teen was generally happy to follow Sikander's lead. Of the two, Sikander was more impulsive and assertive, and he could always be relied upon in the event that things got tough in the almost neatly trimmed streets of Hayatabad. Beyond the boys' friendship, their families interacted on friendly enough terms. Their fathers would have described themselves more as social acquaintances but their mothers were the best of friends.

Sikander and Hamid strolled briskly home to the peaceful precincts of Hayatabad's J-Block. Having done very little during the summer break, Hamid was keen to hear about Sikander's experiences during his Dubai trip. Sikander was happy to oblige and the conversation made the walk feel completed in short order.

As Sikander finally reached his own home, the hazy Peshawar sky had turned a gray orange pink. In that light, the now sympathetically colored but otherwise large cream stucco wall defined the outer perimeter of his residence. The building itself grew out from behind the wall like a giant red-brick tree being of the unusual design that its upper floors extended beyond the lower ones. Behind the façade, the dwelling was arranged with a large front block and a rear two storied courtyard. On the upper floor flanking the open U-shaped courtyard were most of the family's bedrooms. With the exception of its unusual vertical development, it was not especially different from most well-to-do Pakistanis' homes.

The black-painted solid metal double-gate was wide enough to admit a car or SUV, and in one of its halves, it had a second hinged door-within-a-door which allowed for convenient pedestrian access. It was here that Sikander waited having pressed the door buzzer.

Pakistani municipal facilities were never very advanced even in affluent areas, so a wealthy home often resembled an island of relative inward prosperity in a sea of unkempt chaos formed by the network of residential streets in which it was immersed. Hayatabad was a better suburb in this respect than most, but the contrast was still noticeable. This juxtaposition of the tranquility and structure within those walls and the largely unmanaged nature of the outside world simply underscored why the homes had boundary walls and why they stood so high.

When Sikander arrived, he briefly noted that there was more calm and quiet than usual. He buzzed the outer gate again when Jamil, whose class had finished earlier that day, came out of the house to let him in. Once past the gateway, Sikander penetrated the premises swiftly, almost pushing Jamil out of the way, with a mind to head straight for his room. Hurriedly following him, Jamil seemed to want to say something but before he could, Sikander cut him off saying, "I can't chat now," as he raced on upstairs.

He entered his bedroom, lay down his books on his modest desk, and changed into the more comfortable but on this occasion, slightly dressy qamees and shalwar. His hurried buttoning of his qamees was arrested, however, when he thought he could hear a soft sobbing sound from elsewhere in the house. It was clearly not from a child but far enough away to require confirmation as to what it was and from where it was coming. He hurriedly completed his change of clothes, and curiously stepping out of his room, he followed the sound, arriving before long downstairs to the kitchen where Javed and Sofie were sitting. Sofie was the one doing the sobbing while Javed's chin rested on the palm of his hand with his elbow firmly planted on the kitchen table bearing what seemed like a heavy burden. Ordinarily, Sofie was comfortable with command and held herself that way, but some areas of her psyche were definitely vulnerable and as Sikander could see, whatever was unfolding at the moment was plainly assaulting one or more of them.

Hesitatingly, Sikander managed to utter the customary "a...assalaamu 'alaykum!" but he could see that this was not an occasion when he would receive the customary reply. His father briefly glanced at him, again dismissively, as far as Sikander was willing to interpret. His mother who had paused her sobbing upon seeing him, returned to doing so with renewed energy as his presence underscored the challenges she was processing at that moment. Sikander could not remain patiently waiting for someone to say something so he ventured to his father the obvious questions.

"What happened? What's wrong?"

Sikander once more recalled the cooling down of his relationship with his father following their recent exchange regarding Sikander's business suggestions. The issue lingered between them, and Sikander was wary of the present problem being related to the family business, with the potential to draw him into yet another clash with his father arising from yet another potentially "stupid suggestion."

"It's the business," said Javed to Sikander's infinite dismay. "We've been dealt a blow by one of our suppliers. I...I had just put too much faith and confidence in them from all my past dealings. Didn't think it would be a problem." He shrugged as he shook his head.

"What?" asked Sikander, treading carefully between appearing callously unconcerned and becoming too quickly vested in the problem. He also had to resist helping Javed see his own fallibility after their latest tussle. "What problem?"

"We've been swindled out of five million rupees," Javed sighed, barely able to contain the lump in his throat. "The Kabeers in Dubai. I'd given them a large payment, most of it from borrowed money, to supply us with electrical parts."

This was certainly not normal procedure, since transactions of this nature ordinarily went through irrevocable performance-specific letters of credit. However, Javed had been there and had been given a proposition for a large shipment of electric motors to come to him directly from Taiwan. The Kabeers could give him that shipment with an extra eight percent discount, but only if he paid them first by direct wire transfer. He had looked them in the eye believing he had a measure of their reliability and trustworthiness. He was wrong.

The Kabeer Brothers Trading Company of Dubai had been suppliers of his for specialized products, bringing items in from other parts of the world to the free zone of Jebel Ali in the United Arab Emirates. From there, shipments could be efficiently broken down and shipped to nearby countries exempt from any Dubai taxes. Javed had been doing business with the Kabeers for over six years up to that time so he felt he knew them pretty well. Tragically, however, they had been evading Dubai taxes for their "in-country" shipments throughout the Emirates and now they were being sought by the local police. There was little hope of recovery of Javed's five million rupees, which in 1986 calculated to over three hundred thousand US dollars. Such a large loss would certainly result in severe change in their lives, and Sofie was extrapolating those more specifically.

At seventeen, Sikander wasn't quite able to grasp all of the ramifications to the business, although he could certainly understand that the loss of so much money would mean an inability to meet commitments. But at seventeen, Sikander was also a little too ready to see things in over-simplistic terms which made him feel that there was surely some way to solve this problem.

"What are we able to do?"

"I wish I knew!" Javed heaved, avoiding eye contact with his son. Although an extended family might have been helpful at a time like this, Javed was uncharacteristically an only child. His cousins lived in Lahore and Rawalpindi and they had not been in touch for years. His wife's relatives were a little more near to hand but far too aloof, at least to him, to be considered a source of help in such a crisis. There was no way he could see himself getting their attention and certainly not to this degree. "We're going to have to sell things," muttered Javed. "Including the house."

To Sikander in terms of friends, schooling, career, and countless other consequences, this could only be considered a serious blow. He was sure that something could be done and was insufficiently wise in the ways of the world to realize that just about all of those things had already been considered by his father. Sikander was barely aware of uttering, "Can't we re-arrange things? Collect from people who owe us, and that sort of thing, Abba-jee?"

"Of course! But that won't be enough," snapped his father, more testily and with the tone of exasperation usually emerging from those weary of responding to well-meaning tones of the "how can I help?" variety. Sikander understood that this was probably far enough for him to go, for now at least. Pathans as a rule had something of a reputation for being irascible and his father was not a worthy exception. Even Sikander had become more short tempered in his adolescence though not yet, at least, at the level of his father.

Knowing that Javed had himself been forced to intervene in his own father's business crises, Sikander speculated he could leave school to save money and to help with the business, even though this could squash his dreams of leaving the country and making something of himself. The sound of footsteps echoed in the hallway. It caught Sikander's attention and with a glance behind him, he saw huddling near the staircase Jamil and thirteen-year-old sister Sameena. They were equally on edge, no doubt wondering what they might do and what this development might mean to them. Sikander felt their worries, which further fueled his sense of urgency to do something—if not immediately then very soon.

"If we don't come up with something then God forbid there'll be a neelam on the house," reflected Sofie sadly. The neelam, a

Pakistani form of public auction, meant about as much neighborhood embarrassment as one could ever wish to avoid. "We won't be able to live anywhere near here!"

Waves of realization came crashing, one after another, onto the shore of her consciousness as each new consequence presented its own unique brutality. Sofie struggled to hold herself together against the onslaught.

Javed's approach was to meet these challenges with stoic silence. He continued to consider his options, sometimes seemingly coming up with something that might work, only a moment later to realize the fatal flaw and move on to another futile idea. Between attempts at solutions, Javed could not help recalling his mortified stupidity at trusting the Kabeers with such a critically large sum of money and one which he could certainly not tolerate being without. The image of a jackass was stubbornly unwilling to be evicted from his mind.

For now, though, he knew that between himself and Sofie, they had to wear a brave face and try to negotiate their way through some of their own obligations, sell whatever assets made sense to liquidate, and try to find for themselves a new, lightweight existence until things improved. He also knew that Sofie could be strong once she quieted down and took a moment to focus on the practicalities of life for at least the immediate future. She was the kind of person who could handle adversity much more readily than uncertainty. She just needed time to work through the present situation and her way of dealing with the unknowns was to extrapolate each consequence as best she could. Indeed, by now, only ripples of realization remained to register with her, allowing the sobbing to pause and more of the usually steely Sofie to show through.

"Well," she said, staring infinitely into the marble floor in front of her and raising her left eyebrow. "We have to spend some time organizing what will have to be done and...uh, going over to Naghma's place right now doesn't seem to be the right thing to do."

She was regaining her focus and began taking charge again. "I'll call her," she said as she arose, adjusting her dupattha as if to signal a semblance of normality in whatever she was projecting to her husband and children. She picked up the phone and called Naghma to let her know that there had been an unforeseen development and that a trip into the Cantt area was not going to be possible that evening. Like Sofie but unlike Javed, Naghma and her husband Nadeem were part of a wealthy Yousufzai landowning family that had been in Peshawar since long before the creation of Pakistan.

As Sofie was leaving the room, Javed turned to the children.

"Look, for now, let's not all go about with long faces. Try to behave normally. Alright? We might work something out so let's just wait and see," he said, with as much conviction as he could muster. It was more command than encouragement, thought Sikander.

With a nod and having little else to do, he went to his room. *If we're to behave normally* he thought to himself, *I might as well change into simpler clothes and get the homework out of the way.* He lay on his bed with his Shakespeare open and thumbed through to the fourth act. He began reading and, despite his strength in English, was grasping most but not all of the arcane language. Before long, he came to the point at which Brutus, overruling Cassius's advice over preparations for battle, proclaims to him:

> There is a tide in the affairs of men, which taken at the flood leads on to fortune.

His eyes arrested by the words, Sikander took a moment to pause. He had heard these words many times before, recalling their frequent use by Mr. Aftab. Their origin was now registering with him, but at that moment, there was a new resonance to them in relation to the way the family's situation would likely play out for himself. The passage made him think about life's turning points and the present circumstances were about as easy to imagine being a turning point as any. Whatever the outcome, maybe at that time, at that place, he was meant to head in a different direction and the family's misfortune, however challenging it might appear, might simply be the trigger, the flood tide for his life's boat to be launched into whatever destiny awaited him. Sikander's optimistic nature was inclined to see all changes as opportunities and the present circumstance was sure to be the largest "opportunity" he would confront for some time.

If I don't leave school voluntarily, surely it'll be only a matter of time before the cost makes it necessary anyway, he thought. Like many thoughts whose wisdom emerged from repetition, the wisdom in this one grew and the thought began acquiring legs. He imagined himself minding the more routine affairs of the business office while his father focused on extinguishing the financial fire. Given his lack of information about the specifics, there was little point in Sikander worrying about how to begin resolving that crisis. But taking the burden from his father for routine business operations was surely a different matter.

There's less than two years schooling to go anyway, he justified to himself. *I could always resume education once the family gets back on its feet.* Before long he was extrapolating how it would feel to be resuming classes with the presently more junior boys in the school and how his present class fellows would be out in the world pursuing their careers while he still had another year or so to go. Hamid would be in the PAF and no doubt flying jets or at least learning how. Eventually, one thought blended into the next and he fell asleep.

An hour ahead of the rising sun, the azaan came blaring over the loudspeakers that Friday morning. In the greater Peshawar area, masjids were somewhat densely concentrated which meant that azaans could be heard approaching progressively from the east, each three-minute azaan overlapping the next in a growing westbound sonic montage until finally, and necessitated only by ritual, the Zarghooni masjid's own loudspeakers would signal that this one was for real as far as Hayatabad was concerned, with the montage meanwhile moving on, its sound progressively diminishing as it proceeded west.

The Zarghooni was built specially for Hayatabad's Phase 2 development and was the nearest and loudest of the masjids to Sikander's home. After rising for the fajr prayer, Sikander went back to bed. He was tired and there were a couple of good sleep hours left in the morning.

Shafts of streaming sunlight coursed through the large gaps in his bedroom window drapes and with them falling on his eyes, Sikander stirred awake. The normal feeling of ease associated with any Muslim Friday-to-Saturday weekend greeted him for a moment, but it wasn't long before the events of the previous evening resumed their grip of his consciousness. The intervening night's sleep had done nothing to diminish the pressing reality of his family's situation, and that made him afraid.

Following the Jumma prayer, his father began the firefighting task in earnest. Initially he took to the roads of Peshawar going from one customer's home to the next. After exhausting local possibilities he started making calls all over the country to people who owed him money. It didn't help that he was bothering them on a weekend. In some cases, the money was not actually due and in others it was really an advance on trust for the next ninety days of supplies. All the same, the best that Javed could do was to identify a million rupees that might or might not all materialize. Getting their promises of assistance was one thing, but when it came to fulfilling those kinds of promises, people were notoriously unreliable. Depression threatened as the day wore on and nothing of a meaningful nature seemed to be emerging. The more that Javed struggled, the more stressed he became and that would only worsen his ability to succeed in smooth talking the next person.

Sikander, who traveled with his father after Jumma, looked on feeling helpless. It was hard to watch what was happening, and feeling his own paralysis to affect the situation, he wanted to get away. That evening he decided to walk over to Hamid's place. He swore Hamid to secrecy as he told him most of what had happened over the last twenty-four hours. Hamid was shocked and naturally wanted to know what Sikander would do.

"That's really serious, yaar. Where do you think your family will go? And what about school?" he asked with genuine anxiety at possibly losing a friend to distance.

"I've no idea," replied Sikander resignedly.

Neither Sikander nor Hamid realized that Hamid's sister, Rashida, had been in the house upstairs, and at just the wrong moment she had picked up the conversation where it made sense to her not to reveal her presence. Rashida was thirteen—an age too young to understand how lives can be transformed by the tiniest of indiscretions and too old to let interesting neighborhood facts go to waste.

Later that evening, Rashida let her mother, Rubina, know what she believed she had heard but most particularly about the Khans having to move and somehow or other being in trouble. Deeply concerned for her friend, Rubina thought long and hard about what to do. Hamid's family was relatively well off and they might be able to help. Sofie had not shared anything with her, so the situation demanded guile to uncover the truth without damaging a good friendship.

By Saturday morning, not realizing the nature of the problem facing the Khans and certainly not its scale, Rubina decided that it would be simply unacceptable for Sofie, Javed, and the family to be forced to move without so much as a finger lifted by their friends. After all, that was what friends did. Determined to do something, she donned her dupattha and a light jilbab and strolled over to the Khans' place. The Khans' maidservant let her in, and after the customary salaams, the two friends sat down in the living room and began to chat about the usual meaningless things. Throughout their discourse, Sofie managed to hide her inner feelings very well and Rubina almost felt that perhaps the whole story was an embellishment by Rashida of something probably far more innocuous. It would be embarrassing to bring up her knowledge of a problem that might have been blown out of proportion. After a second cup of sabaz chai, Rubina decided to launch into her mission.

"Sofie?" she began cheerily. "I uh, was thinking we might go into Peshawar and shop at the Meena Bazaar and maybe after that go to Andarshah. I hear that some fine new jewelry has arrived for this weekend and we really should go and check it out. Who knows? Maybe we'll be able to pick up something really nice for Rashida's and Sameena's jahezes, and well, it's always fun to bargain those poor jewelers down to the bone," she said, chuckling nervously.

While there was some legitimacy to Rubina's proposal, it would serve as a ruse to test the accuracy of what Rashida had told her.

Sofie didn't flinch. No careless loss of eyebrow control nor wavering of the corners of her mouth would be allowed to give away her inner tumult. Had she known how to play poker and been uncaring as to the religious injunction on gambling, she would have been masterful and independently wealthy.

Without doing so too quickly, she beamed. "Indeed? Well, give me a few moments to take care of my hair and put something on and we can go now." The part of her that loved to shop and more particularly to haggle for jewelry was in any case engaged, so the bluff was not too difficult. Yet the more deeply troubled part of her had begun formulating a strategy. In front of Rubina, she would feign dissatisfaction, offer a deeply insightful critique or haggle for unacceptably poor terms with shopkeepers, to carry on a more convincing act.

Sofie excused herself to escape to the refuge of her room. As she sat in front of her mirror, she fought to compose herself. Sofie was a frail woman, regal in appearance, holding her head just a little higher than normal, driven in part by a subconscious feeling of inferiority in being married to a nouveau-not-so-riche husband. She had been married by arrangement to Javed as his father's business had made the family more prominent and acceptable to the higher echelons of Peshawar society. Sofie was not arrogant; rather she had a warmth and loving quality as much as a concern for her sense of place in society, and while she might have had misgivings about the kind of family she was marrying into, she had been far from disappointed with Javed's physically magnetic appeal.

Despite its generally modest success, the family had been through several ups and downs. In the wake of such inconsistency, Sofie had often been left to fight to hold the family unit together as Javed's natural inclinations focused on doing the same for the business. She had focused on the household needs, the children's educations, and their general physical and emotional health, and though she believed Javed deeply loved his children, it grated on her how little time he spent with them rather than attending to the business.

Brushing her hair, she lost herself for the briefest moment in the anticipation of having a little enjoyment and company with Rubina but with the moment's passing, the pressing family crisis came coursing back to dominate her consciousness. She stopped brushing and gazed at her reflection. New tears welled up inside her at the pretense she was about to project upon her dear friend. Years of social interaction had given her the ability to put on her guard when in company and all the more so with close friends. She would need to call upon that ability once again, she realized, as she forced herself to mop her cheeks and repair her makeup. With her mask now ready, she came down to put on her jilbab and ushered Rubina to join her in their new Toyota Corolla with the family driver, Jehangir. While not exactly a prestige car in most of the world, with import taxes at three hundred percent, a Toyota Corolla in Pakistan was a reasonably good indication of social standing. Jehangir drove them into Peshawar city to the far east side where the bustling Meena Bazaar was located.

With the range of attractive fabrics that had come in from Korea, at every turn, Rubina tried to get Sofie to reveal something through her unwillingness to spend any money, and at every turn Sofie would not oblige. Some fabrics were too bright, some too dull, and yes, others too expensive but nothing was said out of the ordinary. Sofie also managed to put in about the right number of smiles and frowns as well as the pretense of really wanting the occasional item, haggling intensely for it while rejecting it when the seller would not cave in to her impossible demands.

After a short lunch break, they drove to the jewelry stores at Andarshah Bazaar and again Sofie put on her act. Often she would offer words of encouragement to Rubina to go ahead and buy some bangle or necklace but refrained from doing so herself. At least that way the trip would be seen as worthwhile for Rubina and if pressed, Sofie would put it down to mood, headache, or that she herself just hadn't seen any "must-buy" product.

They returned and now Rubina, realizing that her ploy had proved inconclusive, decided to take a different path. As the last of the shopping bags of her purchases had been removed from the car and she sat down for the next round of tea drinking, she mulled over her approach. Sairah, the maidservant carried in the tray of tea and set it down on the finely carved wood and glass coffee table. As they each sipped from the dainty cups, Rubina looked down, shook her head slightly and let out a chuckle.

"What?" asked Sofie, smiling innocently.

"Oh! It's...uh, it's nothing" said Rubina.

"Rubina? What's up?" pressed Sofie sensing possible mischief but maintaining an air of joviality that betrayed her total lack of knowledge of Rubina's awareness of anything untoward.

"Well," said Rubina, "it's funny really. You know I heard something from Rashida yesterday and I really couldn't imagine it being true."

"Oh? What would that be?" asked Sofie confidently and with whatever curiosity she could spare in her present state.

"It's probably nothing really, but it was about...you and...uh, Javed bhai and the family," Rubina went on.

"About...the family?" Sofie pretended, blood draining from her face as she strove to hold her smile in place.

"Yes," said Rubina. "It's ridiculous really, I mean...well, Sofie, you know how children can be? Rashida had said she overheard Sikander talking to Hamid about you all—moving away?—and something about selling the house? I mean, why would you suddenly just up and leave?" She chuckled again, leaning a little forward, looking for affirmation but this time more nervously. Sofie paused and eyed Rubina with a steely gaze and moved not another muscle of her face or body.

She was at a crossroads. She could press on and hope she could fend off this inquiry or break down and tell all to her dear friend. She held on a little longer, drawing energy from the brewing volcano of fury that had taken shape at the matter having leapt out of the family confines so soon and in such an out-of-control manner.

Somewhere between the surprise, the fury, and the forces now losing their battle to hold her face in place, Sofie broke down and cried. Rubina, having expected to learn some bad news when she first came that morning, had been gradually convinced otherwise throughout the day. Now she too experienced shock and surprise that something serious, perhaps more serious than she had at first suspected, was going on.

"Sofie? Oh Sofie...my poor dear. What? What is it? I'm sure we can do something," she offered as she got up to sit next to her friend. Sofie put the facts across to Rubina in a rough patchwork of comments.

"We'll have to sell our house!" she bawled. "We're going to need to move," and "It's Javed...The Kabeers...Dubai...it's a business problem!"

Occasionally Sofie paused, overwhelmed. Rubina asked a clarifying question or two and eventually the story was fully assembled in her mind.

Rubina was truly sorry for her friend and uneasy about how her initial sense of being able to help had now given way to helplessness at the scale of the problem. But this wasn't the kind of problem that a neighborhood could solve. "Look, Sofie, if there's anything we can do...please don't be shy about asking," she offered politely, but appropriately vaguely.

"Oh...that's so nice of you Rubina, but really...I can't imagine how anyone can help." Sofie sobbed as she thanked her friend, not for

the possible assistance but for sharing in her sorrow at the situation and listening to her ramblings. In the end, Rubina knew that Sofie needed to be left alone. She picked up her things and saw herself out, and as she walked back home, she marveled at how well Sofie had worn her mask earlier that day.

Sikander had been up in his room completing his homework while the scene with Rubina had played out, and toward him, Sofie was of a much less vulnerable disposition than she had displayed to Rubina moments earlier. She was livid at having witnessed their affairs spilled out in her own home by her best friend, and in her ire, she didn't lose a moment to call Sikander down and let him have an earful. Sikander, who had been trying all day to deal with his own handling of things, was utterly shocked that his words had leaked out and offered a vigorous defense. He protested that he'd been discreet with Hamid and that he hadn't known that Rashida was listening. Unmoved by his appeals, Sofie remained totally implacable about Sikander's poor judgment.

In the face of Sikander's instincts to sacrifice himself on behalf of the family, Sofie's attacks were too much for his young sensibilities. After his defense came offense. He lashed out at his mother.

"Well, perhaps it's all because you're too proud and pretentious and maybe Allah saw fit to visit this punishment on us for being that way…Did you consider that?" challenged Sikander.

"Sikander, how…how *dare* you speak to me that way!" retorted Sofie, utterly shocked that her own son would say such a thing, but feeling the sting of a possible grain of truth.

"But it *is* something the family deserves. It *has* to be!" Sikander declaimed, shouting his challenge back at his mother, as he overshot even his own thoughts. Fueling those thoughts was the simmering resentment at his father's lack of judgment in his dealings with the Kabeers.

Sikander's counter-attack was ill-timed, as just then his unsuspecting father stepped into the room amid the yelling, hearing only Sikander's most damning accusations without any redeeming context from the earlier exchange between mother and son. His entry abruptly brought the yelling to a halt.

Of all the things in Pakistani society, the monarchic status of patriarch and matriarch was among the least violable. It was simply not done to shout at one's parents or be short-tempered or angry with them in any way. Even the Qur'an had its own divinely revealed injunction against such behavior, and the Ten Commandments' "honor thy father and thy mother" held deep meaning for Muslims.

Enraged by Sikander's reference to the family deserving its misfortune, but even more so at Sikander's tone toward Sofie, Javed immediately unleashed his wrath on his son.

"Sikander!" he uttered with a seething, menacing softness. "You know, that's no way to speak to your mother. Don't you ever speak to her in that fashion again." Javed's tone changed abruptly as he finally exploded with, "You talk that way and you're no son of mine! Do you hear me?" as he stalked forward to less than half a meter from Sikander, continuing to scowl at him. Javed had been through two of the most trying days of his life and was himself in despair when he had returned home. The exchange between his tearful, angry wife and his son had simply pushed him over the edge.

In the interaction between father and son, there was something primal. It came hot on the heels of Sikander's earlier issues with his father before any of this crisis had broken. For a moment, the son uttered no words but simply glared back at his father. The father knew he was probably admonishing his son this way for the last time, as his son was now of age. With his inability to speak out against his father, Sikander's frustration mounted. Despite his willingness to sacrifice his education for his father's mistake, why was *he* now the focus of irritation for his parents? He exploded fiercely.

"Well, it's true! We've been too proud with our success! And now with one moment of stupidity—" The sharp smack of Javed's large hand landed at about the same spot as on the previous occasion but this time with all the vigor that Javed's fury could muster. He didn't say anything. His slap eloquently arrested Sikander's angered utterances.

With what remained of his rapidly depleting capacity for rational thought, Sikander now most wanted to be alone, away from them all. As if reading his son's thoughts, Javed pushed him physically on his shoulder as he shouted, "Go! Get out my sight!"

Leaving a worried Sofie looking on, Sikander stormed up to his room, gasping with rage and committed to leaving them all to themselves and in his indignation, "being one less person to bear" for his mother and father. Sofie wanted to chase after him as clearly the situation was beyond any expectation of her earlier rage. But the fuming presence of her husband filled the room with paralysis.

As Sikander packed a few belongings, he came across his passport. He looked up and gazed at his bedroom window. He imagined that Allah was simply putting him through this experience as a way of preparing for a significant moment in his life. The moon was out that night and he had no idea what he would do next, but he wanted to leave without making a scene or facing any protestations that he should stay, unlikely though that might be, thought Sikander, with his own simmering sensibilities far from exhausted. At least those were rationalizations he was comfortable with. He was less comfortable with his inner voice telling him he was simply running away from a problem and that escape might be cowardly.

Sikander packed away his passport and put on a slightly warmer shalwar and qamees over which he wore a sleeveless jacket with a few pockets in it. Even though it was August, the nights could sometimes get cold so he did not think twice about also taking a light overcoat with him. He took what money he had, a not altogether small sum of about eight thousand rupees rolled up into a wad with a rubber band, well hidden behind a long cherished volume of Iqbal on his busy bookshelf. With that squeezed into his jacket pocket, and his meager belongings in hand, he crept out of his bedroom window, over the railings of his veranda and onto the top of the outer wall. From there it was a drop of less than three meters to the sandy street surface below before he walked away, knowing no one would have heard him leave.

Although he was filled with inner conflicts about leaving or returning home, he felt that the option, while he was cooling down, was still available for him to do either, especially as he hadn't let on about his intentions and the family was, at least for the moment, unaware of his departure. His first thought for a night's sleep was in no doubt, however. He would go over to the Zarghooni masjid and spend the night there sleeping on its plushy carpeted floor. That would require a short walk out of J-Block into Lalazar Avenue and up to the corner of Phase 2 Road. Masjids were often frequented by people spending a

night or two lying under their own robes or a blanket so this would not seem out of the ordinary. Moreover, in the morning there would be some sort of food offering which would at least help him avoid running away from home on an empty stomach. Since it was now long after the isha prayer, he knew he was unlikely to run into any friends or acquaintances.

Sikander walked through the entrance courtyard of the masjid into the main hall and at first, motivated not to draw too much attention to himself, he quietly sat on the floor and took out one of the many widely located copies of the Qur'an that were on the low bookshelf clusters surrounding the bases of each of the masjid's great pillars. He began reading its verses quietly to himself. It was probably a better time than most, he thought, to be consulting its pages.

After a few moments reading, his attention drifted to a far corner of the masjid, where he noticed a group of what looked like Tablighi Jamaat types wearing turbans wrapped with the characteristic trail of spare cloth running about half a meter over one shoulder. He was too far to be able to discern any conversation and besides, it wasn't done to be calling out across the prayer hall in a masjid. Hayatabad was near the southwestern edge of Peshawar so Sikander imagined another possibility was that they might be from one of the sprawling refugee camps around the west side of the city at Nasir Bagh. It was either that or the Tablighi Jamaat.

Typically, the Tablighi Jamaatis would go out in groups of from three to fifteen people and invite fellow Muslims to rediscover the path of Islam and to re-energize their beliefs. The organization's adherents were known for their persistence much as Jehovah's Witnesses were viewed among many Christian communities.

Whoever they are, they'll probably be gone in an hour or two, he thought as he lay down by one of the masjid's beautifully decorated pillars. Curled up under his overcoat, Sikander went to sleep for the four hours or so that remained before the dawn azaan.

Chapter 2

Mujahideen

THE AZAAN WAS UTTERED and Sikander felt himself being nudged, gently at first but then more forcefully. His slowly opening eyes were greeted by the image of a large man with a mostly dark beard tinged with the unmistakable dark orange of henna dye, interrupted in places by an occasional spirally gray hair. The beard was about twenty centimeters in length. The man had a kindly, though weather-beaten appearance as he leaned over Sikander and urged him to wake up in the good Muslim tradition of not letting friends sleep through a call to the dawn prayer. With such urging, it was not too hard to regain his consciousness in a moment or two and as he did so, Sikander became more fully aware of the man's now broadly grinning presence.

"It's time for fajr salaat," the man urged in his coarse Pashto, still grinning. That alone was enough to suggest that this person was probably from the refugee camps. He was fair in complexion and had gray-green eyes. Visible at the top of his turban of white and blue striped cloth was a green cap, and what was left of the cloth that did not seem necessary to continue wrapping around his head lay hanging over his right shoulder. Under a gray sleeveless jacket was a dark beige qamees and shalwar. Confident he had done his good deed, the man then moved on to join his companions as soon as he could see that he had committed Sikander to stand up and go off to perform the wudhu. When Sikander came back ready for prayer, he noted the strangers

standing in the third row back from the front and instinctively moved over to join them, but as the imam was beginning the prayer, speaking to them was out of the question until the prayer was over. By now, the numbers in the hall had swelled and Sikander grew anxious that someone who would recognize him might show up. This was not that likely as although the masjid's azaan was loud and clear for the wakeup call, his friends and family generally did not bother to go out to the masjid except for the Jumma prayer or on major days such as 'Eid-ul-Fitr or 'Eid-ul-Adha, but almost never for fajr which would more typically be performed at home.

Salaat-ul-fajr drew to a close as the imam performed salaams by turning his head to his right and left uttering "assalaamu 'alaykum wa-rahmatullah" in each direction. Sikander arose to try to strike up a conversation with the strangers. Although generally Sikander's family spoke Pashto, they conversed mostly in English or Urdu—or the unique blend of the two that belonged to Pakistan's upper societal echelons. Being more than a little proud of his cultural heritage as a Pathan, Sikander could handle himself comfortably in Pashto.

Pashto was always a requirement for someone to be acknowledged a Pashtun, since so much of the Pashtun code of Pashtunwali, as it was known, was wrapped up in the language. Instinctively, Sikander guessed that speaking Pashto would gain him some degree of acceptance by this group and though each of the four young men and the older one, who was evidently their leader, were imposing figures, there was a certain living warmth on their faces that drew him to seek admission.

As the group was turning away, he approached the apparent leader and offered his salaams. The customary response of "wa-alaykum assalaam" was not long in coming and did so in chorus from the five-man troop. Although a salaam would generally get anyone's attention in this part of the world, and more particularly so in the precincts of the Zarghooni masjid, it also required some kind of follow-up to establish a dialogue or discourse. Sikander began with, "I'm Sikander Khan" as he held out his hand and smiled.

The older figure was taken by this otherwise evidently Pakistani youth's clean and largely accent-free delivery in Pashto. Grinning broadly to reveal a fine set of miswaaked teeth, he uttered, "Ah! And my name is Abdul Latif Khan. These are my sons Abdul Rahman Khan and

Abdul Majeed Khan, and these are my nephews Ejaz Khan and Saleem Khan."

There was a shaking of hands and customary hugging and as the ice between them began crumbling rapidly, Sikander felt that it was safe to ask them their purpose.

"We're here to resupply ourselves," said Abdul Latif. "I come here about four to six times a year to take back supplies to aid in our effort against the accursed Russians back home."

"You...you fight?" asked Sikander, realizing that this might be too direct a question but a little too late to prevent himself from asking it.

"W'Allahi, of course we fight," said Abdul Latif. "Are we not Pashtuns and do we not have the obligation to rid the country of those accursed Russians?" Abdul Latif could not bring himself to say the word "Russian" without attaching some form of denigrating epithet, but "accursed" was a clear favorite. "What about you? What do you do?" he asked.

"Until yesterday I was living here in Hayatabad, but I've determined that this is no longer for me. I angered my mother, and my father asked me to get out of his presence," offered Sikander, shrugging.

When pressed to tell Abdul Latif what exactly he had done, Sikander related the previous day's episode and that as he had been rejected by his father, it was time, at least for a while, to go out on his own. Abdul Latif stood deep in thought, uneasy with the father-and-son nature of Sikander's issue. His own two sons had been listening intently with disturbingly empathetic nodding, as if they could relate to Sikander's experiences.

Abdul Latif's fatherly instincts were leading him to knock some sense into the boy and send him home. It would be a good example to show his own two sons. But at the same time, he sensed something of a determination in Sikander and felt that perhaps it was indeed time for Sikander to become a man and return a wiser person to his family. Besides, pressing Sikander to contact his family might drive him away from the group with no saying where he might end up. Having judged Sikander's character as firm, if a little misguided, Abdul Latif finally opened up and said, "Sikander, come with us. We'll take some early morning green tea and it'll help us all think more clearly at this hour."

The six of them proceeded out of the grounds of the Zarghooni masjid along the short distance to the Civic Center of Hayatabad, which was commonly referred to as the Jumma Bazaar, but more officially, Itwar Bazaar. In its recesses lay the Rahman Coffee Shop, a place as familiar to Abdul Latif and his troop as it was to Sikander. Instinctively on the way to the Jumma Bazaar, Sikander put his hand into his jacket pocket and confirmed that his wad of money was intact. Although these seemed like religious people, it was probably premature to trust them just yet.

Minutes later, Abdul Latif came back from the counter with two cups of green tea in hand and his two sons followed him each with their own two cups. Saleem and Ejaz brought up the rear, each with a few bakery rolls in a bag. The six of them sat down to a decent, if not rich, breakfast.

About now, Sikander thought, his parents would be stirring and thinking about the day ahead. It was Sunday and his father had probably already left the house without even thinking about Sikander or the previous night's tirade. Sikander was unwilling to forgive him for that, and as for his mother, he was sorry he had upset her but the exchange with his father would have to be resolved in his own mind before he could re-engage with her. It would probably take his mother another hour or so to discover that he was not home, and even then she would assume that because it was Sunday, and Jamil was also probably already out of the house, Sikander was naturally with him at school. It would not be until the end of the day that she would start to wonder where he was. His thoughts were interrupted by Abdul Latif who asked him what he thought he would do now.

"I don't really know." Sikander shrugged. "I can't go home now. My, uh...bridges are burned there," he said, "and I...I can't just wander the streets of Peshawar."

"No," replied Abdul Latif, solemnly. "You can't. In fact, the way I see it there are really only two choices. Go back home and deal with what's going on or come with us and join a struggle that by the grace of Allah will be worth fighting for. We can help you. We can protect you, feed you, clothe you, and train you to be a useful soldier in this jihad. We are mujahideen and w'Allahi, we can use all the help we can get!"

Sikander felt the seismic nature of the words coming from Abdul Latif's lips, and a rock the size of a coconut had seemingly materialized

in his stomach. He had spent many hours opining with his classmates, and his father for that matter, on the worthiness of the mujahideen cause in forcing the Soviets out of Afghanistan and reminding them how heroic those poor villagers had been who had seen their villages destroyed, their homes demolished, their fields and crops reduced to barren land, and their children maimed by land mines mistaken for toys. Now he was confronted by real people living this real experience; it was no longer an intellectual exercise. Then there was that moment of pause he had experienced the previous night as he had been packing his things in his school backpack and considering his future. Perhaps *this* was the half-expected sign and these seemingly warm and genuine people were indeed to be trusted and were simply in a roundabout way, Allah's method of sending him a message.

"I...I need to think about this Khan sahib," said Sikander, buying a little time to gain mastery over the myriad conflicts racing through his consciousness.

"And we would not expect any different," Abdul Latif agreed.

His sons and nephews grinned knowingly, looking upon Sikander as someone closer to them in age. They knew what he was going through and hoped that their demeanor would encourage him to make the "right" choice. Abdul Majeed was the first to make the case.

"Look, Brother Sikander," he began. "The way I see it, you're a Muslim. We're Muslims oppressed in our own country and it's as simple as that. What is there to think about? If you have decided to leave home, then w'Allahi let it be for a purpose that will allow you to return to your family as one worthy of your father's ancestors!"

The sophisticated urgency of Abdul Majeed's reasoning coupled with the simplicity of the words he had chosen proved to be an arresting combination, and just as Sikander was digesting his growing sense of compulsion, Saleem joined the fray.

"Brother Sikander, it won't be so bad, you know. There will certainly be danger, but we know the area like no one else and we don't often lose many of our own people. We cheer when we hit a Soviet tank and reduce it to a burning wreck or drive it into a ravine. We cheer when we send the enemy back out of our valley, cowering until they see their helicopters coming in to rescue them!"

Abdul Latif chuckled as he knew to a certainty how the conflict would work itself out in Sikander, but it was nonetheless entertaining to see the different stages of realization arriving on Sikander's face. All the while, Abdul Latif would offer a slow head nod, aiming his chin slightly downward while peering straight ahead into Sikander's eyes with his infectious smile. It was as if he might with these gestures encourage the emergence of the only possible conclusion from within Sikander's psyche. And when it came, he greeted it as one might the arrival of a newborn child into this world.

"W'Allahi! Alhamdulillah!" proclaimed Abdul Latif and the other young men gathered round Sikander to pat him on the back and hug him welcome into their fold. The decision had been harder to make than to live with. Sikander, being the impulsive young man that he was, began rapidly reinforcing his choice with an avalanche of rationalizations as to why it was the only one possible, and with that, formed his own broadening grin. For good or ill, he was now committed. Besides, it was time he made his own contribution for the cause he had done so much talking about. He would prove himself and vindicate his running away from home to himself, his siblings, and his parents.

"So what do we do now?" he asked.

"We have to go into Jamrud Bazaar. We'll need to pick up some supplies and get them back to our temporary house, not far from Jamrud Fort, about seven or eight kilometers to the north of here. We'll be spending one or two nights there awaiting our ISI brothers who will inshaAllah have more information about enemy positions from the Americans. If we're lucky, we will also be picking up some weapons to take back with us. There will be more to tell you once we get to Jamrud. And Sikander…mujahid, welcome to our cause."

Sikander nodded in acknowledgment and felt genuinely honored to accept Abdul Latif's assignment of such a title to him.

"You know, of course, that Sikander is our name for Alexander the Great?" asked Abdul Latif.

"Yes, I do know the origin," replied Sikander, and at that moment his back straightened involuntarily. In himself he felt now more of a soldier and he needed all the more to live up to his illustrious name

as he gestured forward with outstretched palm giving concession to the leadership of Abdul Latif, with a simple "Let's go."

They walked out of Hayatabad along Lalazar Avenue before heading north toward Takht Baig Chowk. As they walked, Sikander asked curiously, "Brother Abdul Latif, why were you in Hayatabad of all places last night?"

"Because we had been to a meeting with a captain of Pakistan's ISI. They are our friends and they're helping us by delivering information that they in turn are receiving from the Americans. We assume that the captain has a home somewhere in the Hayatabad area, but we can't be sure because he usually asks to meet us right by the Jumma Bazaar. He calls himself Captain Junaid, but we don't really suppose that's his real name or title. We were with him last night before coming into the Zarghooni masjid for isha prayer. We thought we might as well spend the night there and w'Allahi, that same night you were sent to us!"

Sikander and Abdul Latif continued chatting as they walked and before long they had arrived upon Takht Baig Chowk. From there they turned onto the Grand Trunk Road to head west to Jamrud.

Centuries before motorways existed and rivaling the best traditions of Roman road building, the emperor Sher Shah Suri had decided to improve the routes in his empire covering much of northern India. He built the "Sadhak-e-Azam"—literally, "the greatest road." It was built over a trade route that had existed since antiquity and was progressively extended beyond his short reign, but it remained the enduring legacy of that reign. In the modern era it stretched for almost two and a half thousand kilometers, linking Kabul in Afghanistan in the west to Sonargaon in Bangladesh, passing through the Khyber Pass, Peshawar, Rawalpindi, Gujranwala, Lahore, Amritsar, Delhi, Agra, Aligarh, Kanpur, Allahabad, Varanasi, and Calcutta in between.

As they strolled along the GT Road, Sikander got more inquisitive about his companions. "So which city do you live in, Brother Abdul Latif?" he asked, feeling proud that his school debate research had given him more than a smattering of geographic knowledge about Afghanistan. Abdul Latif could not hold back a chuckle when he heard the question.

"Not a city!" he declared, containing his amusement. "It's a small village to the south of Jalalabad called Laghar Juy. It's—" Abdul Latif mulled over how to describe its location but gave up and thought to himself, *The lad will be going there anyway, so why not let him find out by experiencing the journey?* After all, with travel in the country being far from simple, knowing the whereabouts of a place did nothing to communicate what it took to get there. He shrugged. "You'll see where it is."

For now, though, the going was fairly easy along the GT Road and before long they arrived at Jamrud Bazaar, a bustling and chaotic place with all kinds of vendors crammed into a tiny area, each vying for the meager rupees that bargain hunters generally spent there. In plain sight, a little further down the road from where they loitered for a brief pause, was the famous Baab-e-Khyber or Khyber Gate, a limestone brick structure imposingly spanning the GT Road while promising the Khyber Pass to the west ahead. They were not going to pass through it that day, but they were going to be headed that way eventually. On a vast mound to the north side of the GT Road beyond the Baab-e-Khyber lay the old Sikh-built Jamrud Fort, a massive fortress made from large red sandstone blocks and looking every inch impregnable.

What a spectacle any battle might have presented in the taking and losing of that place! thought Sikander.

Strolling around Jamrud Bazaar was enjoyable, if not for the buying of goods, then at least for the shade it provided from the hot August sun. At that particular time, Sikander felt a little idiotic carrying his coat over his shoulder, but as there was nowhere else to put it, there was no point dwelling on it.

They picked up a few provisions, then stopped at a small local masjid for zuhr. By early afternoon they sat down at a local roadside dining place serving a dish of chickpeas and Peshawari naan. When they went back into the bazaar, Abdul Latif opened up to Sikander.

"Aren't you going to spend any of that money?" he asked. Sikander's face reddened. He had been careful about it all day long but now he guessed that maybe Abdul Latif had checked him out while he had been asleep on the floor of the Zarghooni masjid. It was a clever way of disclosing his integrity to have left it where it was. "It won't be of any use in Afghanistan," he said. Abdul Latif was generally reticent to use the name Afghanistan. He did not identify with it politically and saw

it as way of separating his Pakistani Pashtun brethren from those on the other side of the border. But there were times when it was quite frankly the only reasonable way of referring to the place.

Sikander had not so far needed to spend his money. He was the guest of his Pashtun hosts, which meant that his needs would be theirs to meet. According to Pashtunwali code, covering such needs extended to personal protection and no one was going to touch Sikander without first exposing themselves to the considerable wrath of Abdul Latif and his sons and nephews. This was a binding obligation upon any Pashtun host with anyone under his protection, even if such a person were up to that moment his sworn enemy.

"Then let me buy our food while we're here in Pakistan," Sikander offered. The shopping continued until they were unable to carry any more. The thought crossed Sikander's mind more than once as to how exactly this group was going to get into Afghanistan and how, furthermore, they were going to make any headway with their accumulating baggage.

By early evening, tired and more than a little hungry, Sikander marveled at the stamina of his hosts. Though he was strong for his age, lugging around his share of the bags of supplies along with his coat wore him down. He had been on his feet most of the day. Finally, at around seven in the evening, the group approached the intersection of the GT Road and the Warsak Dam Road. They were originally supposed to meet their ISI contact there an hour earlier but were obviously late.

"Abdul Latif!" cried out a man in his thirties standing about ten meters away, making sure his voice would be heard over the blaring traffic. "Where've you been?" asked the voice. "Arif and I have been worried about you. You were supposed to be here at six!"

"Assalaamu 'alaykum, Junaid! No need for alarm," reassured Abdul Latif as Junaid approached him. "We got a little sidetracked into a recruitment operation that seems to have...um, worked out pretty well." By this point Junaid had moved up much closer until he was standing within a meter of them all.

"Recruitment?" asked Junaid. "What recruitment?"

"Meet our most recently added mujahid!" exclaimed Abdul Latif, who went on to relate the story of the encounter that same day at dawn. Junaid raised an eyebrow as he leaned to the side to look past his

friend and gazed upon Sikander, examining him from head to toe as in a military inspection. "Hmm," he observed, "mashAllah, he's healthy." Turning to Sikander, Junaid asked, "What's your name, son?" Junaid used the familiar Pashto word zwey to mean "son," which was at once endearing and clarifying of the social standing Junaid was claiming for himself. He was an officer of the Pakistani army but was understandably not dressed like one here in Jamrud for a mission such as this. The Russians no doubt had spies and there would be no sense in telegraphing a presence unnecessarily.

"My name is Sikander Khan. I'm from—"

"Nice to meet you," interrupted Junaid while making barely perceptible sideways glances to assure himself that neither he nor the rest of the group was being watched. "Come!" he said. "We have to go this way." He gestured toward the Warsak Dam Road leading north from the GT Road. "It's about three kilometers from here," he continued as he held out his hand to relieve Sikander of some of his burden.

"Where's Arif?" asked Abdul Latif.

"He went on ahead," explained Junaid. "He should be waiting for us there. Let's hope he has something to eat; I'm famished!"

The group broke up into three with Abdul Latif and Junaid at the front, Sikander and Saleem as a second group about twenty meters behind, and Abdul Majeed, Abdul Rahman, and Ejaz bringing up the rear. They strolled, stopping occasionally and browsing for short spells at some roadside stores on their way, comfortably overtaking each other if the need arose, so as not to draw attention to themselves as a single group. About an hour later, Abdul Latif and Junaid came upon a larger than average house where they walked around to the rear entrance to be received. As each of the following travelers arrived, they likewise approached from the rear.

Arif Saiduddin Khan was a portly fifty-three-year-old Pathan landowner in Punjab who also maintained this particular house just north of the GT Road in Jamrud. He was reasonably well off but did not care to show it. Having been kidnapped for ransom—almost a routine fact of life in these parts—once before about eleven years earlier, at least while he was visiting this particular home, he would not be ostentatious. Around the back of the house was a mud-covered Mitsubishi Pajero, the inexpensive vehicle of choice in the North West

Frontier Province of Pakistan being as handy off the roads as it was on. To Sikander, as he began walking past the vehicle while approaching the rear entrance of the house, it hardly seemed in a functional state. When he instinctively gave it a closer examination, however, with the moonlight coming through, it was actually pretty clean inside. Perhaps it wasn't so old, he mused.

As they were admitted into the back of the house, they were informed that Arif was occupied with another matter and all except for Junaid—who had needed to talk to Arif before rejoining the group— were taken downstairs into a modest basement room. Abdul Latif and the rest of his group, of which Sikander was increasingly feeling like he was a part, sat around a large table. It had spread out on it a map of Afghanistan's Nangarhar Province. This was one of the provinces bordering Pakistan's North West Frontier Province, or NWFP, and in particular, the NWFP's Federally Administered Tribal Area, or FATA.

The FATA was where a virtual administrative stalemate between Pakistan's central government and the tribal rulers was the norm, with neither side interested in disturbing the arrangement. The central government didn't have the resources to govern the area in a conventional sense—not at least while India's forces were a threat on the eastern border—and the tribal rulers had absolutely no ambitions upon the rest of Pakistan. As long as they could come and go across the border into Afghanistan (or in the south, into Iran) they would not bother anyone, except of course for pursuing the income generated by kidnapping for small ransoms any visitors who had not sought their protection.

Around the edges of the map, holding it in place, were a few empty plates and a bowl of fruit. The fruit bowl was well stocked with apples, apricots, plums, and a few carrots, while another smaller bowl was filled to the brim with almonds. Sikander's stomach grumbled in anticipation, but he didn't want to be the first to move. He tried to steal a glance at Abdul Latif but blushed as a smiling Abdul Latif was already ahead of him and had seen Sikander longingly gaze at the fruit. Neither of them moved to be so ill-mannered as to attack the food in the absence of their host.

Soon afterward, a conversation between Junaid and Arif began arriving down the stairs before either of the two men were visible. About

two seconds behind the words came their speakers, who were in deep discussion about the evening's priorities.

"—safe route, where to drop off the truck, the Hind, and T-62 concentrations and even perhaps when those Stingers will be available. That sounds like what we have to discuss tonight," said Arif as his large form began to materialize feet first from the dimly lit staircase into the better lit basement room. "Oh! And the money," he added as he was now fully downstairs and looking back over his shoulder at Junaid's form appearing behind him.

"Assalaamu 'alaykum wa-rahmatullahi wa-barakaatuhu!" exclaimed Arif with all the joyful body language of a twenty-year reunion as he turned away from Junaid to greet the people in the room. It was not customary to convey this fully extended form of greeting unless it was a truly special occasion, or, as in this case, it was just the personal habit of the individual offering the greeting.

Everyone in the group paid their counter salaams and the meeting almost began. "Before we begin," said Arif, "we should make du'a for the success of your venture."

No one was going to disagree with the need for du'a, given their impending return to the dangerous world of the Afghan resistance, so Abdul Latif, being arguably the one with the longest beard, instinctively stepped in to lead a small quiet recitation and supplication for success.

"Alright," said Arif as he picked up the fruit bowl, offered it to Abdul Latif, Junaid, and then Sikander, put it down again, then gestured to the remaining young men present to pick from it as they pleased. He plucked an apricot, took a good-sized bite from it, and gestured the rest of it toward the map.

"This is Nangarhar." It seemed like a simple enough statement. However, in these times, maps were a surprisingly rare sight. If anyone ever took out a map and opened it up, people gathered around it as a curiosity. It revealed their intimately understood world but from a perspective never seen and rarely imagined. Abdul Latif, his sons, and his nephews knew just about every hill, valley, cave, and stream between Peshawar and Jalalabad, but they too were intrigued to see a tenth of their knowledge diagrammed in this fashion.

"We've recently secured a new safe house for taking mules across," began Arif. "Here's how you will be crossing the border. You'll

need to proceed up the N5 Torkhum Road for about twelve kilometers. At the point where the road splits to either side of the river, there will be a trail leading to the southwest and it will lead through a compound all the way up this hill where there is a large, low house. That's where you'll be emptying the Pajero and you will be met by our people. They'll be Afridis and will have five mules for you behind the house. They'll be bringing the...Pajero...back...here." Arif began running out of steam as he looked at Abdul Latif and then around the room, landing his gaze finally at Junaid before saying with a mildly annoyed yet quizzical look, "I was told there would be five of you."

"Uh...yes," said Junaid. "We don't need to go over the whole story right now but it seems Abdul Latif's picked up a new young mujahid! We didn't introduce you but this young man," he gestured to Sikander, "is going to be fighting fi-sabeelillah!"

"Really!?" exclaimed Arif in a drawn out delivery. "And what is your name, zwey?"

"Sikander, sir."

"Ah, Iskander!"

"Er...no sir, my name's not Iskander, it's Sikander,"

"Hmm...yes...yes," said Arif, dismissively. "But it's all the same, you know?"

"It isn't to *me*," responded Sikander, who had not meant to be as defiant as he sounded.

"What do you mean?" demanded Arif with a rapidly brewing frown on his previously cherub-like face. "Don't you know that they're both versions of Alexander the Great's name?"

Sikander was puzzled by this seemingly innocuous correction causing so much grief with Arif who until that moment had been highly amiable. He thought for a moment but pressed his position with a little more force. "Sir, my name is my right. It was given to me by my parents and may not be taken from me against my will to be done with as someone pleases." Sikander surprised everyone but most of all, himself, with the lucid, yet assertive manner in which his response was delivered.

Arif's frown deepened into a slightly terrifying scowl and the two stared at each other while Sikander felt that it might be a good

moment for his new friend Abdul Latif perhaps to step in to diffuse the tension. In a few seconds, though, the frown vanished magically as Arif burst out laughing. Once he did so, the others in the room began to follow suit, though with considerably less sincerity. "Son," he said, "you're going to be dealing with some pretty bad things out there and well, I can see you have some steel in you!" he remarked. "Oh—and well said about your parents naming you. Very good...very good!"

Now that this little issue had been dealt with leaving everyone's dignity intact, Arif returned to the matter at hand. "As we're using a new safe house this time, we're going to have you do a slightly different zigzag to get to Laghar Juy."

Abdul Latif studied the map with a mixture of amused interest and earnestness. "Which path do you have planned for us to use?" he asked. Out of deference, the rest of the group had the confidence to know that if a question needed to be asked, Abdul Latif was going to ask it, and if not, then he would not be wasting time satisfying simple curiosity with questions.

Arif began the detailed explanation. "At the house on the hill, there'll be a stash of light arms, including six boxes of ten RPGs and four RPG launchers. Together with the supplies you'll be taking from here, that should come to about two hundred kilograms. From the house, after you've packed the mules, you'll be taking a western route down the ravines until you turn north right here toward Chenar Kalay. There are some caves in the hills to the south of the village, which is where you will have to sleep for the night. Sorry," he said, apologizing for the poor accommodation that was to be afforded the men. "After fajr, proceed north and then west...here, then south again right here. His thick calloused finger pointed to various spots on the map. "From there you'll be in a steep climb up into Showlghar Kalay. That should get you to late afternoon right here." He gestured to a point on the map well to the south of the main highway heading toward Jalalabad and in country where the trail switchbacks as indicated on the map could only mean steep climbs and descents.

"Once you've rested in Showlghar, you should still have time to make it before nightfall to Baro. It's heavy going, but it can be done. So far so good?" asked Arif.

"If we go through Baro, it means we'll need to go through Morchal and that obviously requires getting across to Takhto Kalay. I

know it's August, but at this time of year at that altitude we could have difficulty with rain," said Abdul Latif. "But if we can pass Taktho Kalay, then it should be easy getting down into Chineh. After that, we'll have a straight run to the west and I know a little-used gap next to the more obvious main one which will get us into the next valley to the west over here. From there you can see Laghar Juy about eight kilometers away and we can even make that at night if we have to," he explained.

"I've seen weather charts from the CIA," said Junaid. "There isn't any rain for at least the next four days, so this should be a good time."

Sikander was impressed at the command of the landscape that Abdul Latif demonstrated, and with this impression he found himself feeling increasingly secure being around the man. Whatever lay in front of them, as long as Abdul Latif was with them he felt certain they would get through it.

"That's about the measure of it," responded Arif. "Once you get to Laghar Juy, the next part is down to the Soviets and where they'd like to be when you hit them!" he joked.

"So...what about that?" asked Abdul Latif as he turned his attention to Junaid, who until now was mostly listening with fascination and a tinge of envy for the young men following Abdul Latif into the enemy's backyard. Although he was a member of the ISI, four years earlier he had spent part of his military career with the SSG mountain unit, one of just six commando units in the Pakistani military at the time he had been with them. During his training period he had been sent to the US to train with the First Special Operations Detachment Delta— more commonly known as Delta Force—right after its creation. He had also done a stint with the Strategic Support Branch of US Special Operations Command, which was a combination of CIA and DIA units, where he had learned much of his intelligence basics. These days, the ISI had a special Afghan Section headed by Colonel Mohammed Yousaf, and "Junaid" was one of Yousaf's best officers.

The ISI was heavily supported by the CIA and they could be relied upon to give him up-to-date information about Soviet troop concentrations and anticipated movements. They also provided reliable information about re-supplies brought in by the Soviets with major equipment such as the commonly used T-55 and T-62 main battle tanks,

and that nemesis of the Afghan mujahideen, the Mi-24 helicopter gunship.

"Our information is that sometime between five and ten days from now, a full Soviet brigade strength force will be heading out down the road from Jalalabad in the general direction of Torkhum near the border," Junaid began. "We expect them to split up somewhere between Batawul and Hazar Now. If they do split up, then look for about two thousand of their troops supported by T-55s and more than a squadron of Hinds to come rolling south toward Laghar Juy and its nearby villages. In order to prepare for that offensive they will be assembling their tank units in Batawul, which they can keep an eye on from their base in Jalalabad. You and the other forces of the Hezb-e-Islami Khalis could, inshaAllah, inflict some heavy damage on them if you can carry off an ambush as soon as the cavalry unit has completed its assembly and before it is out of Batawul. It'll mean keeping a close watch on Batawul," explained Junaid.

"We may be able to keep some spies in the closer villages nearer to the road," said Abdul Latif. "We have some that we can station at Anarbagh Village at least for a short while. Also, there's some high ground to the north of Ashraf Village at Mar Koh, which would get us within a thousand meters of the road near Batawul and we could try watching from there at night, but the accursed Russians are not such idiots as to let that happen without being tipped off. We'll have to see how things progress closer to the time."

At this point Saleem and Ejaz exchanged a glance and Ejaz pointed out that his uncle—a brother of Abdul Latif's sister-in-law—lived not far from Mar Koh, so when the time came, he could be relied upon.

"Very well then," said Arif. "Sta na shukria! Brother Junaid, I think we are done for the night and it's time for these mujahideen to retire for the evening." All eight of them stayed together long enough to complete the isha prayer, after which Junaid promptly stood up to leave.

"Let me see you to the door," Abdul Latif offered, as he too rose and both of them disappeared up the stairs and out of the basement. Shortly afterward, Abdul Latif came down again, yawning and looking like he was about ready to drop down anywhere.

Meanwhile, Arif took Abdul Rahman and Abdul Majeed around to the back of the house where the dirt-covered Pajero was parked. "We've had it cleaned up inside," he said, "but we didn't want it to be too attractive on the outside. We don't want the thing stolen before you even get going!"

As they looked over the vehicle, Arif pointed out the list of issues with the mechanicals. "The steering has quite a lot of slack, so be especially careful when you take that last trail off the N5 highway," pleaded Arif. Although he hadn't actually paid for the vehicle—the ISI people had provided it—he had grown somewhat fond of it and its stellar performance in the rough country around Peshawar. He also pointed out a couple of secret gun-stashing compartments in the back in case they needed some "insurance."

With the vehicle inspected, the three of them re-entered the house to join Abdul Latif, Saleem, Ejaz, and Sikander for a good night's sleep before the long trip ahead. As Sikander rested his weary head, he felt a wave of remorse at the fact that he had left everyone at home with no sign of where he was going, and by now, his parents, brother, and sister must have been distraught at his absence and failure to have even attended school. He had occasionally gone off with friends after school until relatively late into the evening, so they might not have been alarmed until now, but he knew that the worry would be building rapidly and his father would start calling around.

As the minutes slipped by, Sikander was consumed by thoughts of his father and the state in which he had left him, trying to protect the family while now having to deal with the new crisis of the disappearance of his son. Sikander resolved to see if he could call his mother and let her know something of his plans and hopefully learn from her that something might be coming together for his father's business problem. But there was no question of him backing out of this mission now that he had committed himself to Abdul Latif. These were tough times in Afghanistan and he drew strength from this fact to bolster his conviction about his decision to leave home.

Chapter 3

Khyber Nights

T HE TROOP AWOKE IN TIME for the dawn azaan the
following morning. Time did not permit them to go to any
local masjid, so they formed their jamaat in Arif's home. They
went to sleep as usual for a couple of hours after that and
awoke for the day around nine o'clock.

"We need to go back into Jamrud today and bring back lentils,
chickpeas, and rice for the village," said Abdul Latif. "Meanwhile, Arif
will help you three load up the truck and make sure that it's properly
oiled and fueled," he directed toward Saleem, Abdul Majeed, and
Abdul Rahman. "Ejaz, Sikander, and I will go into Jamrud and we
should be back by around eleven-thirty or so. After that we'll get going
so that we can get to the drop-off point before maghrib."

The young men nodded in acknowledgment and after a short
breakfast of fried eggs and bread slices grilled on an upturned tawa, they
headed toward the vehicle. Abdul Latif, Sikander, and Ejaz left the
house and proceeded down the Warsak Dam Road toward Jamrud
Bazaar. They picked up sacks of chickpeas, lentils, and rice, for which
Sikander, under no pressure from Abdul Latif, decided to pay. Also at
the bazaar, Sikander spotted a dark beige hooded nylon rain jacket and
a pair of short hiking boots that would be much more suited to what he
thought he might face in the coming days than his present counterfeit
Nikes. He had particularly liked his purchase of the boots, which
seemed pretty new, but was surprised when, upon re-examining them

after buying them, he turned one of them over and saw what were unmistakably Russian characters in the arch just ahead of the heel. Abdul Latif explained to Sikander how Soviet soldiers would sometimes buy their way out of trouble by offering their would-be captors items such as these and indeed on many occasions, weapons. Such items were simply too valuable to consume so they frequently found a profitable outlet in the markets on Pakistan's side of the border.

The Pashtun way was oddly comfortable with the notion of captivity, ransom, and release, and as long as it was all reasonably affordable, all it did was keep tribesmen on their toes and encourage them to move around in bands to avoid capture. Thus, if a Pashtun was unlucky enough to be captured, he would be ransomed for the equivalent of fifty or a hundred dollars or something of comparable value and then let go. It didn't much matter if the captive was fellow tribesman, clansman, or sworn enemy. By the same token, however, in keeping with the tradition of melmasthia or "guest protection," if a stranger, or even an enemy for that matter, was voluntarily to "go in" to the house of a Pashtun, then it would be like a request for protection and treatment like a guest, which would result invariably in both being provided without hesitation. So even though Soviet soldiers did some pretty despicable things, the culturally ingrained familiarity of the hostage-and-ransom experience was enough to allow enemy soldiers to buy their freedom, albeit with much of their clothing missing along with all of their weapons. The incentive for the Pashtuns to let them go was often no more than an avoided cost of keeping prisoners and most Pashtuns did not routinely indulge in murdering even Soviet prisoners.

The three of them were walking back on the Warsak Dam Road toward Arif's place, when Sikander felt the need for Abdul Latif's honest opinion. This pressing urgency became all the more acute as the moment of truth was fast approaching and before long, all of them would be putting some distance between themselves and Peshawar.

"Brother Abdul Latif?" asked Sikander. "You know I've been gone from home for two nights now and I'm feeling worried about my family."

"Yes, I had been thinking of the same thing," noted Abdul Latif, being at once reminded of how young the age of seventeen was despite this fit young man's apparently strong and mature physical state. "What do think you should do?" he asked.

"I'm not sure," replied Sikander, concerned not to suggest that he was having second thoughts about his commitments to the men.

"Well, how would it be if you gave them a phone call from Arif's place?" asked Abdul Latif. "You could at least let them know you're safe, find out how your father's progressing with his issues, and at the same time let them know you've committed yourself to a worthwhile purpose. You wouldn't need to reveal where you are and there isn't any way for your family to learn that, so it would be pointless for them to call anyone, including the police," he elaborated.

Abdul Latif's simple analysis of the situation captured all the key issues and was actually quite workable, which impressed Sikander. Still, something didn't add up when Abdul Latif mentioned that calling the police wouldn't do much good.

"The police?" asked Sikander. "Why would calling them be pointless? I mean, I understand that they would still need to know where to look, and...yes, they are the butts of frequent jokes about ineptitude, but...for serious things like this, surely they're worth talking to?"

"I, uh...spoke with Junaid yesterday when seeing him out of Arif's place," replied Abdul Latif. "I had mentioned to him that the police might be contacted by someone from Hayatabad claiming that his young adult son had gone missing." Abdul Latif paused for a moment. "Junaid didn't think it would be a problem," he said simply, without saying any more. He knew full well that Sikander would have understood that given Junaid's ISI credentials, his intervention in something like this would be both discreet and effective in making the police work with less than complete vigor toward locating him.

Despite the struggle with lugging the sack of rice over his back, Ejaz allowed himself a chuckle as he overheard the exchange between Sikander and Abdul Latif, realizing of course that Abdul Latif had thought through all the angles—a thoroughly typical attribute of the man.

Ejaz and his brother Saleem were both quiet young men. They had lost their father, Abdul Latif's younger brother, Abdus Sami, earlier that same year in the second battle of the Zhawar caves in Paktia Province. He had been a commander with Younus Khalis's Hezb-e-Islami Khalis forces under the nominal command of Jalaluddin Haqqani. Tragedy struck as they had been defending the Zhawar caves. Initially

units of the puppet Democratic Republic of Afghanistan—or DRA—forces mounted an offensive to recapture the caves. When their DRA clients could not make headway, the Soviets brought in their own forces and air power under General Valentin Varenikov in early March. It had taken them until the middle of April to dislodge the mujahideen forces, but not long afterward, the caves were retaken by the same mujahideen.

Upon his death Abdus Sami was celebrated as a great "shaheed." His wife Noor, two sons, and a daughter, Rabia, had survived him back in Laghar Juy. As Abdus Sami's surviving older brother, it was now Abdul Latif's duty to take the family under his wing.

The three of them arrived at Arif's house where they could see the Pajero, still dirty as ever and packed with their supplies but not to the hilt. Arif was there and he welcomed everyone back. "It's all fueled, oiled, and ready to go!" he said as he handed the keys over to Abdul Rahman who would be doing the driving. While he could drive if pressed to do so, Abdul Latif had not been particularly fond of it and usually avoided it. Given his history with vehicles, no one would have disputed that it was in everyone's best interests that he not make that day an exception.

"Before we leave, may we use your telephone, Brother Arif?" asked Abdul Latif.

"Of course," replied Arif. Abdul Latif beckoned to Sikander to follow him into the house. Instead of retreating back into the basement, Abdul Latif took him into a living room on the first floor where, on a small side table in the corner, there was a telephone.

"I'll leave you alone and will be outside with the others," said Abdul Latif. "Just come on out when you've finished," he added as his raised eyebrows accompanied an empathetic smile.

Having thanked him, Sikander waited for him to leave. He thought for a moment to rehearse what he would say for virtually every point or response he imagined might be made by his mother or father and then dialed the number to call home.

The phone barely rang once and it was Sofie who answered. "Hello?" The croaky voice revealed her exhausted but anxious state. Sikander took a moment to form his thoughts and again she filled the vacuum with her plaintive "hello," this time with more urgency.

"Assalaamu 'alaykum, Ammee-jan," said Sikander slowly.

"Sikander! Oh! Ya Allah tera shukr hai!" exclaimed Sofie heaving a great sigh. "Sikander, where *are* you? Where have you been? We've been going out of our minds with worry!" Slowly as she registered that Sikander was obviously safe, Sofie's tone shifted into mounting anger. "Sikander, why aren't you at home? Why? Your father and I have been so very worried and distraught! He even called the police! Have you no concern for what you've done to us? Sikander?" Unable to sustain her anger, she ended the barrage of questions in tears. "*See* what you've put me through!" she cried.

"Ammee-jan, look, I'm really sorry for raising my voice to you the other evening. I...I shouldn't have done that, but what Abba-jee...said to me...it made me think about what I have to do. I'm going to be gone for a while." His response caused an immediate cessation of the crying.

"Gone? How do you mean...gone!?" she asked, stunned at the absence of a simple apology and a promise to return home immediately.

"Yes...gone, but only for a while, Ammee-jan," he replied and then proceeded to explain how he had found Abdul Latif and his entourage and how he was going to do what he maybe should have done at least a year ago.

"But...but Sikander, have you forgotten the trial your father is going through right now? Do you have no thought for how troubled and pained he's been? What about school and...and the family and everything else?" she asked. "And what about Hamid and your other friends? Will you just abandon them? Oh, Sikander, bettha! Come back home...please!" she pleaded, realizing that this was no time for anger.

"Look. Ammee-jan, I really *do* love the family and I wanted to let you, Jamil, Sameena, and...and Abba-jee, know that I'm fine and inshaAllah will make you proud of your son and not feel so ashamed at what I had done in sharing our problems with Hamid, even...even though I did my best to keep it just between us."

"Sikander, that was no reason to up and leave! Your father and I, we...we were very...troubled!" she sobbed. "Come back. Please come back, now bettha!"

"Ammee, I promise I'll be back but it won't be within a few days. I need to do this now. I...I can't just come back and go to school anymore, and I know how I wanted to finish my schooling so that I could try for—anyway, that will all have to wait. Besides, an American college might now be impossible with the business being in trouble. Right?"

Sofie could see that she was getting nowhere with her pleadings and began to calm down a little in order to try to find some angle which would persuade her headstrong son, when she realized that she hadn't told him about some of the good news during his absence.

"Sikander," she said, holding the tears back, "your father has managed to buy some time. He's convinced three of his customers to give him advances on the next six months worth of business, which will leave him enough profit to take down a quarter of what he's lost with the Kabeers. He's managed to borrow another third and inshaAllah, if he can make two of his larger creditors wait for four months, we will be able to pull through. We may...we may still be selling the house and moving into something smaller, but really, Sikander, please come back, bettha. Please, please come back."

Her pleadings weighed heavily on Sikander as he sighed. But a serious burden on his mind had now been significantly reduced. Ironically, Sofie's words had backfired as they emboldened Sikander to continue with his newfound purpose with at least some assurance that life wasn't about to implode back within the family home.

A point Sikander did not appreciate, though, was the blow that his leaving school would deliver to his father. Javed, having himself dropped out of school to look after the business after his own father, Shahnawaz, had suffered a major illness, had been anxious that Sikander should not miss out on this important and defining part of his life. Moreover, he felt slightly inferior whenever dealing with his in-laws because he knew that his wife was better educated than he was. *That shouldn't happen with my children*, he had determined to himself.

"Look, Ammee-jan, I won't be able to come back right away, but tell Abba-jee I'm sorry he had to see me behave that way to you and tell him I'm really very relieved to see that he might be able to deal with the Kabeers issue and potentially manage things. Tell him I want to be back, but I want to make him proud of me. I don't want him to...to wish me out of his sight like the last time we were together." Sikander

paused, finding nothing left to say. "I uh, have to go now, Ammee, but I promise as soon as I get the chance I'll call again. Give my love and salaams to everyone and my salaams to you and Abba-jee." Without waiting for another plea from his mother, Sikander lowered the handset to its cradle, turned to leave the house, and rejoined Abdul Latif and his companions.

The rice, chickpeas, and lentils were neatly pushed down into the back compartment of the Pajero and after bidding Arif farewell and his bidding the travelers "fi-amanillah," the six of them piled into the vehicle. Although it was much later than planned at two in the afternoon, they set off down the Warsak Dam Road toward the GT Road turning west through the Baab-e-Khyber, past the Jamrud Fort toward Landi Kotal. Not long after passing the fort, the road abruptly changed its identity to become the Torkhum Road as if to put away all things related to the sedate nature of the GT Road and prepare travelers for the fearsome passage through one of the greatest gateways on earth and among the most difficult to traverse—the Khyber Pass.

Steep vertical cliffs rose on both sides and at its narrowest point, the pass was barely three meters wide. Through here had come invaders from the ancient Aryans, Persians, and Greeks, to the medieval Arabs, Tartars, and Mughals. The British, though not having invaded through the pass, had spent much blood and treasure in making it more traversable to support their own less than successful adventures in Afghanistan.

The Pajero, a 1983 model, was one of the earliest five-door seven-seaters in this model line made by Mitsubishi. The base vehicle had won many grueling rallies in the world, but there were probably few tests of the Pajero's guts as demanding as the Khyber Pass. Once the GT Road had become the Torkhum Road, it initially feigned innocence as it ran reasonably smooth and straight into the first set of guardian hills to the west of Jamrud. These were the easternmost members of the Safed Koh, an Urdu term for White Mountains, running from south of Peshawar a hundred kilometers west and defining the border between Pakistan and Afghanistan along the westernmost and tallest seventy-five kilometers. In Afghanistan they took the not surprising name of "Spin Ghar," being the Pashto for White Mountains.

From the Safed Koh hills, the road took on a new and more menacing personality. About two kilometers into the climb, the

switchbacks were upon them and the conversation, which had afforded the luxury of some of Abdul Rahman's attention and had proceeded with joviality until then, suddenly died down. Everyone's eyes fixed firmly on the road while Abdul Rahman's arms and hands went into overtime negotiating the switchbacks and dealing with the awful slack in the Pajero's steering that Arif had warned him about. The afternoon sun descended lower but was not low enough to be hidden by any but the most nearby mountains in the deepest ravines. Having crossed into the western half of the sky at that time of day, it shone in the travelers' faces for most of the trip.

I suppose it could have been much more intense if we'd needed to proceed all the way to Landi Kotal at the top of the pass and then down into Torkhum, pondered Sikander. Eventually, they came to the point where the Torkhum Road split into two with uphill traffic on their left and downhill on the far carriageway to their right. Shortly thereafter, they found the small open compound on the west side of the road. The compound looked abandoned but for the odd item of rusting equipment and machinery. Sikander had no idea what it was, but it did not seem to matter. At the far end of the compound, they saw the opening into the trail leading up the hill to a modest elevation where there stood a small house awaiting their arrival.

The vehicle slowly made it up the switchbacks to the house. As soon as they rounded the last bend, the land contours flattened off considerably and to his right a long way down Sikander could see the Torkhum Road with its relatively light traffic headed up into Landi Kotal. In front of the vehicle it was now apparent that there was also a large shed next to the house.

The Pajero was parked and turned off, and the passengers and driver spilled out onto the small apron of gravel that was the house's front yard. By now several young men had come out to meet the new arrivals.

"Assalaamu 'alaykum!" called out Abdul Rahman, closing the driver's door behind him. The customary replies came along with all the requisite hugs and mutual handshakes. The six men went into the house and four young men sprang into action to unload the Pajero, completing the task in less than five minutes.

"I'm Khurram Afridi," said a man who seemed to be their leader. "Your mules have not arrived as of yet, but you're supposed to

leave tomorrow anyway and we're expecting them to come in later tonight. Don't worry, they aren't coming from far away and they'll be fresh," he assured.

"Abdul Latif," said Abdul Latif in his briefest of self-introductions. He gestured to Khurram to lead the way into the house and, half turning to his companions, likewise gestured to them to follow him in.

The house was nothing special. It seemed it was used as a staging point for such expeditions as this and did not appear otherwise inhabited. A single light bulb hung from a crudely installed holder in the ceiling as did two ceiling fans. It was approaching sunset and with so many mountains surrounding them, darkness came quickly. The hosts had been down into the Torkhum Road area before the travelers had arrived and brought back hot lamb kebabs wrapped in Peshawari naans. This was a welcome meal for them all, and after the meal and the maghrib prayer, the troop sat on the floor and chatted about their different experiences in the aftermath of the Soviet invasion of Afghanistan.

Khurram and his fellow helpers hailed from the predominant Afridi tribe in the Khyber area. Abdul Latif and his followers were Shinwari Pashtuns. Sikander was a Yousufzai and with his upbringing in Peshawar was less sensitized to the often complex nuances of Pashtun tribal rivalries and alliances. One thing he did know was that the Afridis seemed to have a virtual lock on the opium traffic passing out of Afghanistan through Pakistan to many parts of the world. Just thinking about this, Sikander had no trouble imagining this group of Afridis using the house as a drug distribution warehouse. They would surely have no difficulty procuring mules as one of the preferred forms of transport for their opium.

When drugs were not preoccupying the Afridis, chances were that they were busying themselves with making guns. The Afridis were well known for their mastery of the thriving cottage industry of firearm manufacture. This was particularly true for the Adam Khel or "Clan of Adam," referring to a long deceased ancestor. Anything from scrap metal, old cars, tools, and a host of other things from which the metal could be recovered would be fair game for turning into an unlicensed copy of a Lee Enfield or a Browning pistol. AK-47 Kalashnikovs, which were rare prior to the Soviets arriving, had started to appear as they had

been captured or sold, and had crossed into Pakistan where the Afridis promptly set to work copying them. The best of Afridi workshops could now turn out a functionally highly comparable rendition of a typically captured master weapon, which would be relegated, upon such capture, to the demeaning role of template for the mass production of replicas.

Directly after salaat-ul-isha, the travelers sprawled out on the floor and, with blankets or coats to cover them, fell asleep. After all the walking earlier in the day, they had little difficulty embracing slumber.

♣

Just as on the day that Sikander first met him, Abdul Latif's grinning face greeted Sikander as he stirred into consciousness. It was time to get up for fajr, have breakfast, and be on their way.

As much as Abdul Latif was comfortable in the hilly terrain and not one for driving a vehicle, Sikander had never been off the roads in the mountain country to the west of his home. His family had been up out of Peshawar toward Landi Kotal before, when his father had combined the need to deliver some switches with a long day's outing for the family. Now it was to be mules and traveling on foot. He was pleased he had bought his rain jacket and boots the previous day, and while he was gamely looking forward to traveling into Afghanistan, he had to admit, though only to himself, to being apprehensive about the perils of the journey.

The short breakfast of Peshawari naan with sabaz chai was quickly done with, after which the group stepped outside to be greeted by Khurram, his companions, and five mules. Three of them were grays, one was a roan with a slightly bluish tinge, and one was a gray-black mix. Given the rock colorings in this part of the world, these colors were ideal for camouflage.

Having introduced Abdul Latif's troop to the mules, Khurram and his people proceeded back into the shed next to the house where it was clear they were laying out the materials to be packed. Abdul Latif and his men followed them in. Against one wall, the rocket propelled grenades were stacked together with their launchers. A dozen AK-47s— or perhaps good copies of them—were laid out next to them together with a box of two dozen ammunition magazines, each containing thirty rounds. The supplies that Abdul Latif had brought up with him from

Jamrud were grouped into four piles on the floor. Other boxes were stacked three or four high against other walls of the shed.

"We have to group these into ten roughly equal piles and bind them up with these ropes," Khurram instructed, pointing to the weapons and sweeping his outstretched hand toward the piled supplies. "The supplies can be put onto two of the mules and the remaining three will have to take the RPGs and the launchers. We're going to give you six of the AK-47s and the box of ammunition. All of these will be wrapped up in the wool blankets and then we'll mount them on the mules."

"Keep the rifles and a few ammunition magazines out so we can carry them while we're walking," Abdul Latif ordered, before re-entering the house to take another look at the map which he'd brought back from Arif's place. At that point he made a command decision and would not be following Arif's prescribed route, at least not at the beginning. The clear weather conditions looked as if they might be holding and that would enable them to save a day if they took a slightly different route that was only feasible in good weather.

With AK-47s in their hands, Abdul Latif and his sons and nephews finally felt as if they were fully clothed. The Pashtuns were widely known for their relationship with their weapons. Being without a firearm was analogous to wearing a suit and tie but no socks into a New York business meeting. One wouldn't be stared at for nakedness, but the attire could hardly be described as complete.

The packing took about an hour and a half to finish. Walking out in front, Abdul Latif had his men take hold of the bridles of each of the mules, as the troop said their salaams to Khurram and his people. Turning away from the general direction of the Torkhum Road, they climbed up a slight ridge behind the house and then along the trail doing rapid switchbacks to descend into a ravine on the northwest side of the house. "This will keep us lower and allow better passage toward Chenar Kalay," explained Abdul Latif.

Sikander wrapped his nylon rain jacket around his waist and enthusiastically wore his boots. There weren't many clouds dotting the sky and rain seemed highly unlikely. At this elevation the sky was also noticeably less hazy than in the streets of Peshawar and Hayatabad.

Sikander's mule was the roan and he had the ammunition and two boxes of RPGs with him, which had the mule hauling about sixty

kilograms of dead weight. A remarkable animal, both curious and intelligent, while inheriting more strength than either her horse mother or donkey father, Sikander's mule was all of these things and seemingly well trained. He liked her distinctive pattern of colors with their bluish tinge, and based on that simple observation, Sikander named his mule Neela, which in Urdu meant "blue." This was less inspired than it might have seemed since he had already called the gray-black mule, Kala, the Urdu for "black."

The sun was practically overhead when an hour and a half into their journey they reached the bottom of the ravine where there was a fast flowing stream. The group stopped for ten minutes, sampling the water, which was all the more cool and refreshing for the heat of the afternoon. The mules welcomed the opportunity for rest, though there was plenty more stamina in them.

After that short break, Abdul Latif paused for a moment and looked up at the sheer cliff to his right. "We need to keep this mountain on our right and as we go round it we'll begin climbing again to that ridge line you see in front of you," he said. "Once we're on top of the ridge you'll be able to see on the other side there'll be a descent into a valley, which will open up into a small plain. Leading out of that plain is another valley which, if we stay to the right of it, we'll be able to continue along for about eight to ten kilometers into Chenar." Everyone nodded in agreement and Sikander saw no reason not to follow suit. All he knew was that the rest of them seemed to know what they were doing, and as if to sense what Sikander was thinking, Abdul Latif went on to explain that they would stop for the night in the plain he had mentioned, where there were several tiny villages whose names were not known to him but he was pretty sure they would find shelter in one of them.

For a while the trail widened and Ejaz gestured to Sikander to move up alongside him so that both mules were on the outside and both men on the inside. This was a simple basic rule to give protection in case anyone was to attack them. They would be shielded to some degree by the animals and that might buy them the precious few seconds to get organized and deal with the threat.

As they were hiking in this fashion, Sikander decided to engage Ejaz in more conversation, and it was along this route that he learned of much of the Afghan resistance, experienced through Ejaz's eyes and

ears. He learned of the sad tragedy of the loss of their father and how Ejaz was now the nominal head of the family though, of course, he routinely deferred to his more experienced uncle who had, after all, also lost a brother.

Ejaz was a thoughtful individual who spoke, if anything, rather lyrically. From the way he expressed himself and the imagery he created when describing life back in Laghar Juy, Sikander wondered if Ejaz might, in other circumstances, have joined the ranks of the many Pashto poets from the Shinwari tribe such as Amir Hamza Khan Shinwari about whom even Sikander had read a great deal. Ejaz described the abundant fields, fed by the stream flowing out of the nearby mountains—fields that had been there before the Soviets had arrived—and how these days many of the same fields were now bombed out and barely arable. He also described the stunning beauty of the Spin Ghar and how the mountains formed a wall which often sheltered the Laghar Juy region from the more aggressive winds coming out of the south, making it a pleasant place to live.

Sikander asked him how his brother, mother, and sister had coped with the passing of his father. Ejaz was still pained by the loss but visibly brightened up with pride when describing the details of his father's death in the battle of Zhawar as related to him by the several survivors of the skirmish that had been part of the Hezb-e-Islami Khalis. He related how his mother always beamed with pride when talking about her late husband, but in truth, her grieving lingered more intensely than she let on. She was often given to bouts of lonely silent crying, typically in the night after isha. Although she plainly hadn't intended for her children to feel her pain, she was not very successful in hiding it.

Ejaz also spoke of his sister, Rabia, who was almost sixteen, four years his junior, and how she always looked up to him. She was intelligent and well read, though only in Pashto. Some of the men in Laghar Juy had frowned on the notion of girls doing anything but producing children, cooking, cleaning, and sewing. Neither Abdus Sami nor Abdul Latif had shared this view. Theirs was not so much a modern gender equality concern but more a case of their belief in a strict interpretation of Islamic teaching in which the practical integrity of society could only occur if well-educated women could pass their knowledge on to their children before the pressures of generating a

livelihood would be upon those children. From this perspective, therefore, literate girls and women were a must. Periodically this would cause tensions in the community but it was never a crisis issue.

Tired and more than a little hungry, Sikander, who had now fallen back behind Ejaz owing to the trail's narrowing, brought up the rear with Neela. The mule had begun to show signs of tiring but they had, after all, been climbing for the last half hour up the trail switchbacks. Sikander could see that they were headed toward a saddle feature on top of a ridge. It was terminated on its left side by the ridge, which proceeded to their east for over a kilometer. To the right of the saddle was an incline consisting mostly of crumbled, frost-shattered scree and then a rock face that rose almost two hundred and fifty meters. The saddle was the best place on the ridge to reach for and it was therefore no surprise that the winding trail led to that one point.

From below the saddle, they were still relatively high and where Sikander presently stood, looking back toward their point of departure, he could make out in the distance the hazy, dusty air over Peshawar and the meandering Torkhum Road coming out of Jamrud. The house where they had spent the night was not visible as it was now hidden by the mountain wall on his right, around which they had been climbing. However to his left, the view was quite breathtaking. The fact that he knew that somewhere in the haze was his home town of Hayatabad, left Sikander with a gnawing feeling that triggered memories of his mother's impassioned pleas of the previous day. Sikander earnestly hoped that Javed would get over the remorse that he was sure his father must have been feeling, and focus instead on solving the family's crisis. It didn't take long for Sikander's feelings to spill over into emotional upwelling and he cried softly, knowing that with all the noise coming from the several pairs of feet and hooves up ahead and the mules' heavy breathing from having to climb up the slope, his emotional lapse would be quite adequately inaudible.

The group coalesced at the top of the saddle and now the mountain shadows were long and looming over them. As promised, the location provided an excellent and, for that matter, quite scary perspective of the downward slopes into the plain in front of them. Sikander had to admit that he had no idea of how such a descent was even possible, but he had complete trust in his companions who even

now were practicing their code of melmasthia and being extra careful to be sure his needs were being met.

Melmasthia was a curious concept in which the hospitality extended to the guest was its own form of status symbol for the host. The opportunity to be presented with the needs of a guest followed by the impeccable fulfillment of them were all the hallmarks of honor for a Pashtun. There was a well-known saying among them that food eaten alone was destined to become crap, while food shared with a guest was destined to become flowers for the spirit. The Pashtuns had many colorful sayings.

After a brief rest allowed them by Abdul Latif, they were on their feet and moving again, beginning their descent into the plain. As they continued descending, the ridge behind them permitted one final glance back toward Peshawar before eventually blocking off any further view of the city. When that moment unfolded, it filled Sikander with a sense of severance, wondering when he might again lay eyes on his home and family, along with an anxious curiosity about what lay ahead. They stopped twice for a brief rest before completing the descent by about four in the afternoon. Now, the going was a lot easier as they were on a high plain in the middle of which ran a narrow river that they followed for about a kilometer until they reached a small village.

The villagers were Aka Khel Afridis—feud-rivals of the much larger Adam Khel—and they were only marginally hospitable to people emerging from Adam Khel territory, but Abdul Latif knew one of the Aka Khel senior chieftains of the entire area, Khan Jehangir Sultan, reasonably well and if he could invoke his protection, he was sure these people would not hold against him that he was emerging from the territory of their rivals. Besides, he, being a Shinwari, had no particular feud with the Aka Khel. To everyone's relief, Jehangir was well known in the village and once this was established, the villagers shifted from their hesitant posture to a more welcoming one, although still showing a disturbing amount of interest in the weapons.

Only by reminding the villagers of their shared hatred of the Soviets, invoking Jehangir's name, making a thousand-rupee "gift" from Sikander's intact stash, and speaking with the firm and forceful voice that conveyed the confidence of someone unafraid of their situation did Abdul Latif manage to achieve security for the group.

"Above all," whispered Ejaz to Sikander, "it's important not to communicate the fear of becoming victims to these people.

Everyone followed Abdul Latif's lead. By the time he was done, they were so welcome that one of the members of the village jirga took the step of offering them an empty home to stay for the night and inviting them to dine with him and his family, which all but sealed their protection. Abdul Latif had handled the situation as well as any career diplomat and had only to give up a thousand rupees of Sikander's money in return.

Still, thought Sikander, *at least I now hold a new obligation upon my fellow travelers. They owe me.*

Beyond speaking the language, Sikander was beginning to think like a Pashtun. What he had articulated to himself was one of the cornerstones of Pashtunwali, known as "badal," a form of compensatory exchange or redress. Seeking vengeance was simply one form of badal, and the one seeking it was at liberty to take it equitably but no more than that. There could be no gratuitousness.

The group arrived at their rest stop, unpacked, and took a brief rest after a combined zuhr and asr prayer. Immediately after maghrib, Sikander decided to step out for a stroll. As the evening drew on, and the sky darkened, Sikander grew aware of the night's dazzling array of stars. He and his companions were at least seven hundred meters higher up than in Peshawar and there was not a hint of dust in the air. It was as if Sikander was discovering the true nature of fresh air, having breathed in the exhaust fumes of Peshawar's incessant traffic for a good part of his life. But it was the clarity of the night sky that most struck his inquisitive mind as he could see so many more stars than ever before. The land cooled down quickly after sunset up here, and though it would be getting much colder later, at this time it was very pleasant for Sikander as he strolled out in the open.

Just before eight o'clock, the group went to the home of the village elder, a man of fifty-five years—but who appeared to Sikander to be ten years older—called Yaqub. Yaqub introduced the men to his three sons, one of whom, Aurangzeb, was about the same age as Abdul Majeed and Sikander while the others were much younger. The two younger ones, Nadeem and Sohail, looked quite similar to each other but Aurangzeb looked nothing like them. As Sikander began to think about this, Yaqub called into the room behind him where Sikander had

become aware of the presence of the women of the household. They had prepared the meal, but he had tried not to draw attention to himself with too many obvious glances in their direction. His seventeen male years did their best to hinder his self-control. Through a succession of such discreet glances, Sikander had assembled a picture of a young girl of about eighteen, an older woman of perhaps thirty-two or thirty-three, and another older woman more like Yaqub's age. The back room was dimly lit with oil lanterns and details were hard to make out.

"Hinna, come out and bring in the food!" said Yaqub. "Our guests are hungry and tired."

The girl carried out a large plate with lamb kebabs and another with rice. She was not veiled in the sense of the head-to-toe burkha but had a shawl over her brown hair and a long red and blue tunic dress which was colorfully decorated. Sikander could see her natural beauty and clear complexion, but above all else her eyes were her most striking feature and impossible to ignore.

A dance of stolen glances ensued. While Sikander discreetly examined her, the girl's own blue-green eyes darted around the room dwelling briefly on Ejaz and then on Abdul Rahman, each of whom quickly looked away, slightly embarrassed that she had caught them almost staring at her. As she set the plates down on the floor where everyone was seated cross-legged on a large blue and orange wool Bokhara rug, her eyes met Sikander's and then Saleem's but then back again to Ejaz. She smiled nervously as she withdrew, and it was hard for Sikander to retract his gaze, but his sensibilities drew him away from such an offense.

Uncharacteristically, Yaqub smiled as he observed the young men in Abdul Latif's entourage. As Hinna was reversing out of the room, Yaqub felt compelled to reveal that she herself had woven the rug on which they were sitting, in response to which, while Abdul Latif complemented Yaqub on having such a fine and skilled daughter, the retreating Hinna visibly blushed. It would have been quite improper for any of the young men to have offered the comment. Besides, most of them hadn't been able to focus on Yaqub's words.

Close on Hinna's heels came Yasmeen, the woman in her early thirties, with a large tourine of lentils and a plate piled high with goat-buttered naan bread. She was likewise dressed in a tunic with a little less decoration and also wore a shawl drawn over her head but with a

large overhang almost burying her face. Even so, curiosity got the better of Sikander as he managed to glimpse her smile and responded in kind. As she too retreated into the rear of the house, it dawned on Sikander that Yaqub was probably married to both the older woman—whose name never came up—and Yasmeen. Yaqub's oldest son and Hinna must have been the older woman's children, while the two younger boys would have been Yasmeen's. This was not pure speculation on his part, as he could see a resemblance between Hinna and Aurangzeb along with a resemblance between Sohail and Yasmeen.

As the conversation unfolded over dinner, it became clear that Sikander's surmise was correct. The night drew on and the hosts and guests chatted about things in Pakistan and the war and life in general. Each time a new course of food had to be served, Hinna would bring it in and collect the empty dishes. Yaqub made several more references to his daughter's skills and other fine qualities without sounding too much like a salesman but making it increasingly apparent to Abdul Latif that Yaqub was hoping for a potential proposal. In these parts, no clock ticked faster than for a daughter who had come of age and getting her married as soon as possible was a parental duty. The evening's invitation had not been without such a motive.

Clearly, Yaqub had guessed at the eligibility of the young men at Abdul Latif's "disposal" and was hoping that providence would move its hand in Hinna's favor that night. From Sikander's point of view, looking at Ejaz, it might have. But that would have to wait, at least for now, until their mission was accomplished and the Soviets were driven from Afghanistan. When weariness settled among them, the guests finally asked their host's permission to leave.

The men were led back to their rest house outside of which the mules that had been brought under Yaqub's protection were sleeping like babies, tired and well fed.

Among the dreams that Sikander experienced that night, the most memorable was both vivid and pleasant. He saw himself standing in front of a large black shiny granite wall, confronted with the challenge of having to climb it. All around him was barren sand, a blue sky, and this wall. He looked up and saw that it seemed to go on for at least a hundred meters. With no support or other tools, he instinctively put one hand upon the wall a little higher than his head and was immediately surprised to feel it grip the shiny surface, much as a lizard's

foot might do. Slowly but with impossible ease, he managed to scale the wall and when he reached the top, it was as if he had managed to climb onto the top of a large cube. He could now stand and walk upright on the cube's top surface.

Once there, however, the hitherto black shiny surface transformed into a beautiful green pasture and in front of him was a fast flowing stream. The smell of clean air was palpable and he found himself dwelling on each breath to savor its sweetness. A small boat moored to the stump of what was once a large bush floated visible on the stream and he approached it. As he neared, he became aware of a stunningly beautiful girl standing on the other side of the stream. She seemed to be about his own age or possibly younger and was dressed in black from head to toe, but her dupattha and qamees were trimmed with a silver embroidered design. The dark outfit contrasted with her creamy face, and as his eyes connected with hers, she held his gaze while making a barely perceptible bowing gesture with her upper body, all the while, her eyes locked on his.

Still bowing slightly, she beckoned with her right arm by gently holding it out and bringing it in toward her chest. As she completed the gesture, she stood back upright maintaining eye contact as she smiled demurely, looking hopeful for his next move. No intelligence was required to decide what that should be and Sikander made it into the boat, loosening the mooring while shoving off toward the girl. As he did so, he noticed the boat taking on water. His focus shifted to avoid it sinking and while adjusting his position, the boat capsized. Yet he didn't seem to feel the need to struggle even though he could feel his lungs take on water. He saw the girl's head above him looking through the surface of the water upon his submerged face and could now hear the soft, beckoning voice, "Sikander...Sikander...Sikand—"

At that moment, he found himself being woken by Ejaz, calling out to him in a loud whisper, "Sikander!" and nudging him heavily to get him to stir.

"Uuh? What? What is it?" Sikander muttered softly, as he stirred, disappointed with the lack of reality of the experience of the last few moments but pleased with its content.

"Wake up," said Ejaz.

"What...time is it?" asked Sikander, rubbing his eyes.

"It's three o'clock."

"Why...why are you waking me at three in the morning?!" whispered Sikander loudly while observing the implicit contract of relative silence between the two of them so as not to stir any of the others, all of whom were sleeping soundly.

"I'm having difficulty sleeping," said Ejaz. "I...uh, I can't stop thinking about Yaqub's...Yaqub's daughter. Did you see her eyes and her golden hair? Huh! W'Allahi, she's cast a spell on me. I'm lost to her!" he went on shaking his head from side to side forlornly.

"Mhmm...I know what you mean, Ejaz," acknowledged Sikander, still in a loud whisper. "Look...uh, let's go outside and talk," he offered. Sikander could see Ejaz's head nodding in the darkness silhouetted against the faint light coming through a window and quietly he got up, picked up his blanket, and wrapped it around his shoulders. The two crept out of the house into the thoroughfare outside. They could talk more openly now.

"So, what do you think you want to do, Ejaz?" asked Sikander feeling a little out of place as he was at least three years the junior of the two and hardly in a position to dispense advice. It was no doubt a measure of Ejaz's less than competent state of mind that he thought Sikander might help think through his situation and feelings. Moreover, Sikander was beginning to feel slightly annoyed at this being the reason for Ejaz transporting him from such a delightful scene as his erstwhile dream into Ejaz's reality.

"I will tell my uncle that this is an eligible girl and I...I am an eligible young man and he'll intercede for me with Yaqub," elaborated Ejaz, still developing his idea.

"Then what's your problem, Ejaz?" asked the now puzzled but more irritated Sikander.

"Well, what if she doesn't want to marry me?" he asked. Sikander was slightly surprised but impressed at the question, since it was hardly typical in tribal custom to be considering the girl's wishes and yet here was Ejaz who could think of this as his only obstacle.

"Ejaz, why do you worry about this if her father will consent?"

"It's his consent without hers that I worry about," he replied. "She's obviously lived mostly under her mother's wing until now and

what could he possibly know of her wishes, to be handing her over to a stranger like me?"

"Well, we're in no position to solve that problem right now, are we, Ejaz?" began Sikander. "I mean, we are about eight to ten kilometers behind where we should have been right now as far as I can remember from Arif's instructions and this...this distraction is hardly something we can afford. I can't imagine Abdul Latif getting sidetracked by this while we have to continue back to your village."

"*I* can..." came a voice from behind, startling the two of them. "But not for long." Abdul Latif had awoken, heard the talking outside, and stepped quietly to the door mostly out of suspicion that someone might be trying to disturb their cargo or steal away the mules. He had heard enough of the conversation, though, to feel for poor Ejaz and had an idea that was now gathering enough force in his mind to elicit a wry smile on his face.

"Uncle!" uttered Ejaz, in a mixture of surprise and embarrassment. "What...uh...what exactly do you think you can do?" This was a question as much aimed at discovering how much Abdul Latif had overheard as it was an attempt to learn what might be done.

"Ejaz, you're a young man and I was there last night and I understand the mind of someone like Yaqub perhaps a lot better than you do," he responded, being sufficiently cryptic to entertain himself a little longer with Ejaz's unclarity as to Abdul Latif's own understanding of his conundrum. "Oh, come on, Ejaz!" he continued. "Let's get to the point. You want to ask for Hinna and Yaqub wants you to ask for her. After that, will you like her? Will she like you? Allahu a'alam!"

Ejaz nodded with interest.

"Look, Ejaz. Who likes whom is one of life's unfathomable mysteries, but remember this—you won't remain who you are and she won't remain who she is, at least not for long. You will affect who she'll become and she you. So, the way I see it, what matters is not so much what is true now, but what you both do in life together with each other and for each other, to make true tomorrow."

"What do you propose to do, Uncle?" asked Ejaz, and as usual Abdul Latif was way ahead of him.

"Well, the way I see it, it would be quite proper for me to approach Yaqub with the proposition. He seemed interested last night anyway so he won't be surprised. However, I'm also going to suggest that he seek his daughter's permission to accept her father's recommendation because, in our family custom, we think it's bad luck not to consult the bride-to-be." He chuckled triumphantly.

"Uncle!" exclaimed Ejaz who could then say little else being thus overwhelmed with delight at his uncle's characteristic beneficence, understanding, and intellect.

"Now you've ruined a night's sleep since it's almost time for fajr and we have a long day in front of us," said Abdul Latif in closing. "Do you suppose we can get back to bed for the hour or so we have left? Hmm?" he added pointedly.

The three of them went into the house and slid back under their blankets. As they lay there, Sikander recalled the brief passage he'd read in his Shakespeare homework and thought to himself that here was Ejaz, who had taken the tide at its flood alright and understood exquisitely Shakespeare's reference to losing "our ventures."

Morning broke and the usual duties were performed. The mules had had a chance to rest from the prior day's climb and now it was time to make sure they were fed and watered before taking a quick breakfast to get going once more.

Yaqub was not about to let his reputation for hospitality be sullied by such ill manners as allowing the travelers to come to his door. He had already ordered up some food and told his two younger sons to take over the breakfast to the travelers' quarters. He also instructed his oldest son to tend to the mules.

After breakfast, as Abdul Latif returned to Yaqub's house he broached the subject of Hinna and Ejaz.

"Brother Yaqub," he began. "You have been a most gracious host and indeed attended to our every need since we have been here. Reluctantly, we must now depart, but before we do, I must confess that having seen how richly endowed you are with your...uh—talented— daughter Hinna, we would be most honored if you would accept to seek her permission to be...to be engaged to my nephew, Ejaz."

Delighted at the proposition, Yaqub had to hold himself back from overtly revealing this sentiment, though both men knew of its existence. "Indeed?" declared Yaqub. "And what have you in mind exactly?" It was Yaqub's tangential way of referring to mehr. In these parts, the Muslim concept of mehr was more entrenched in that it was for the bridegroom to furnish to the bride as her property to do with as she wished. This was contrary to the inverted notions prevalent in mainstream Pakistani society, which entailed the bride's family coughing up a substantial figure to pay the groom's family for accepting their daughter as a new burden—the so-called "bride price" or jahez. Though a small jahez was a widespread custom, it had in many cases truly become a bride price and would often break a girl's parents financially. As such, it was completely out of keeping with any provision of Islamic origin. Indeed, the mehr was, in such circumstances, often a paltry figure representing the groom's obligation to the bride—a further inversion of authentic Islamic rules.

"This will need to be determined no doubt more precisely," offered Abdul Latif, "but Brother Yaqub, you might consider that Ejaz is an upstanding man and the surviving son of the legendary shaheed Abdus Sami, my brother who valiantly fought and died protecting the mujahideen at the caves of Zhawar. Will she not have honor enough by being the wife of such a one as he?"

"Of course, of course!" uttered Yaqub who had heard this for the first time and who was by now really warming to the idea. His concept of asking his daughter's permission was ironically about as strong as that of Ejaz, so Ejaz had lost a couple of hours of sleep for no good reason.

He gestured to Aurangzeb to retrieve his mother, who had the right to give her daughter away in marriage, so with her dupattha drawn forward over her head, Shahnaz, Hinna's mother, stepped silently into the room. She offered her salaam greetings and was respectfully acknowledged in like fashion. Yaqub began describing the proposal from Abdul Latif as she absorbed it all through her veil without any words or body language. Hers was also a concern about the mehr and she too had her own tangential way of addressing the subject.

"Brother Abdul Latif," she began calmly, "look, you know Hinna is as close to me as my own liver...and...and I have sheltered and clothed and fed this daughter of mine for almost twenty years and

would not allow her to be harmed in any way. We have heard of the ways of the Shinwari and have understood you to be a good people, and we respect your brother's shahadah that he died fighting so bravely and for such a cause as that. But how can I be certain that my daughter will not be abused?"

"Upon my word of honor, your daughter shall be our daughter. Is it not said that a daughter is but a guest in her parents' home and that her true home lies where her destiny might take her with the family into which she marries? I commit that if my nephew so much as harms a hair of her head, he will answer to me for it and will be happy to pay the mehr which will not be less than—fifty?—thousand rupees, upon demand to her. And if he fails to live up to this condition then w'Allahi, I will have him brought to your door to answer for it."

The point was not lost on Yaqub and Shahnaz, and at that moment they decided that they would ask their daughter for her permission. A face saving option was thus created in case they changed their minds. They could put it down to their daughter's lack of interest and no one would be slighted or accuse the other party of reneging on an understanding.

Hinna was asked and only after the briefest of pauses did she nod in agreement. In doing so, she drew her dupattha further over her face in shyness at the proposal and directed her gaze downward as befitting a girl in her situation.

"Then it is settled," said Abdul Latif. "And my warmest mubarak to you and your family! Of course, we will need to go on today, but we will be back inshaAllah with the full baraat when you are ready for us. We will send a ring to you as soon as we have given the good news to Ejaz's mother and also obtained her consent."

This was satisfactory to Yaqub who was delighted at having landed a match for his daughter and with such honorable people, as far as he could judge.

Abdul Latif emerged from the house beaming. He approached Ejaz and let him know, upon which Ejaz was quite beside himself with joy while the others looked on in amusement and heartfelt happiness for him. Sikander could not help also feeling intrigued as he reflected upon how such a scene might ever play out on his own behalf. He wondered what his wife-to-be would be doing at this moment and what kind of a

life she might have had up to now, whoever she might be. One thing he did acknowledge to himself was that it would not be so bad if his wife resembled the mystery girl of his dream the previous night.

Abruptly, this particular thought was arrested as Sikander realized that while he earnestly wanted to do so, he couldn't recall the dream girl's face. It was as if his dreaming mind had been so swamped by apprehending her beauty that nothing of his mental capacity had remained available to form a cognitive image. Still, he thought, the experience *was* tangible and even if he couldn't remember what she looked like, he would at least remember the dream as a whole.

Indeed that previous star studded night—with its small village of the Aka Khel, the mountains of the Khyber, and the girl of his dream—was one he would surely remember until his dying day.

Chapter 4
Laghar Juy

WITH A BRIEF BUT COLORFUL celebration of the engagement behind them, Abdul Latif motioned to his companions to wrap up and check the fastenings on all the straps and ropes on their mules and cargo. Finally ready to depart, Abdul Latif bid salaams to Yaqub and his family. The women came to the front of the house and, with their dupatthas drawn but faces largely visible, were unable to conceal their evident happiness with the new developments. Ejaz and Hinna were allowed to exchange more than simple glances toward each other, now that their status had been transformed into fiancé and fiancée, nominally at least, until Ejaz's mother approved of the match.

Yaqub offered escorts for the men to the edge of the village, which was not an offer to refuse, especially in light of the newly established bond. Two villagers were assigned to them, and leading their mules, all eight proceeded out of the valley toward the northwestern end of the plain where the mountains revealed a certain menacing beauty, warning all travelers passing through them to take them for granted only at their peril.

The early morning sunlight had by now lit up the valley floor from its presently shallow angle into a glorious blaze of emerald fire walled off by glowing dark red mountains to the west, with pink and orange snow topping the tallest of them.

The toughest part of their journey lay ahead. Having arrived at the northwestern end of the plain, they picked up the path of a stream. The creek bed led them through the mountains, causing the troop to swing around to the west and then southwest in order to remain in the lower elevations. This was as far as the escorts were able to take them and having given their salaams, they turned around and disappeared, heading back to their village. Abdul Latif's group continued through the stream's valley until it opened out into yet another plain, much larger than the previous one at almost eight kilometers across.

Energized by his enchantment with Hinna and the prospect of being her husband soon, Ejaz's step never wavered. As he was crossing the larger plain, taking in its beauty, he could not help but roll around in his head, poetic comparisons of the scene with his fiancée's captivating beauty—comparisons made all the more easy as everywhere they looked, the vista was indeed enchanting. To the south, on their left lay a long straight line of mountains not quite tall enough to be snowcapped this time of year. Shaded from the low morning sun, they formed a gray-green wall leading into the beautifully green vale, which was mostly a combination of fallow grassland and cultivation.

To their right, now more brightly lit by the low sun, was a solitary hill rising some three hundred meters like an island, with the plain passing around either side of it. Behind it, along the far northern and western periphery of the plain stood taller mountains with gaps wherever a river or stream came through to drain into the large plain. The planned route via Chenar required them to take one of the gaps about halfway along the mountain wall. However, given the excellent weather, Abdul Latif toyed with the idea of going directly to Showlghar. A higher climb would be involved, but it would shorten their journey by no less than ten kilometers. Instead of climbing into the Chenar gap, they would have to proceed to an opening farther down near the western corner of the plain, just before the point of convergence of the northern and western mountains. Several scattered settlements, most notably Khwar, Chena, and Halwai, dotted the plain and each was a potential source of trouble; but armed as his group was, Abdul Latif felt confident that they would not be bothered. He decided to head directly to Showlghar.

Occasionally they came across a villager or two, but all remained cordial. Ejaz and Abdul Latif strode out in front at the head of

the group. Behind them were Saleem and Abdul Rahman, traveling together in the usual formation of mules on the outside and travelers on the inside. Feeling safer than on the previous day, the two men walked slightly ahead of the mules instead of hiding between them. Abdul Majeed and Sikander brought up the rear.

Abdul Majeed was about twenty years old, Sikander guessed. Exact ages were not all that important to the people living in Laghar Juy, so even Abdul Majeed himself had only a rough idea. Although relatively quiet, he seemed to Sikander like a more intense individual than his cousins, or his older brother Abdul Rahman, for that matter. His dark beard hung almost as long as Abdul Latif's and a patch of skin was clean-shaven above his upper lip. His eyes were brown but narrow. He was a striking young man and most people would have considered him handsome.

Over his gray qamees and shalwar Abdul Majeed wore a black buttoned sleeveless jacket but always left it unbuttoned. Headgear consisted of either a creamy white pakol or a black turban worn in traditional frontiersman style with about half a meter of cloth left unwrapped and hanging loose over his shoulder. On this day it was the turban. At a hundred and eighty centimeters tall, he carried himself in a highly dignified manner without seeming arrogant.

"What about you, Abdul Majeed?" asked Sikander, who until then had not interacted very much with him, though when he had done so it had always been friendly. "When do you think you'll be married?" he inquired half-jokingly. On the heel's of Ejaz's provisional engagement, the subject of marriage had been foremost on the travelers' lips all morning.

"Allahu a'alam," declared Abdul Majeed with his usual miswaaked grin.

"Alright," said Sikander, "but Abdul Majeed, is there someone in your mind or heart?"

"Maybe." Along with his signature brevity, Abdul Majeed waned inscrutable.

Sensing a possible unease, Sikander changed the subject. "SubhanAllah! I never thought a place could be so beautiful. Don't you agree?"

Abdul Majeed nodded and this time being more open, he volunteered that he had been through these parts more than once with his father who knew the area quite well. "We sometimes used to come here to pick up mules. They have some particularly strong breeds and they can be as large as horses, only much stronger. I always enjoy coming up the mountains into the Akal Khel's area, although last night was my first in that particular village. We've normally traveled to and from the Torkhum Road taking a more southerly path via Sara Garhi."

Sikander was curious about the risks of traveling through the remote terrain. "Don't you find it dangerous, Abdul Majeed? Have you ever been injured doing this?"

"It certainly is dangerous and we have to be careful because there can be rock slides in the spring and summer and sometimes that can get so bad that we can't recognize the landscape in those ravines." He gestured ahead and to his right. "The ice in winter forms in the cracks in the rock and widens the weakest of them. When it thaws, it loosens the rocks and they come crashing down, especially after heavy rainfall. It shouldn't be so bad right now, though, as the last of the rains passed a few weeks ago with it being almost September. And as for injuries..." remarked Abdul Majeed as he glanced down and by so doing, directed Sikander's gaze. He raised both eyebrows and his left shalwar leg to reveal a twenty-centimeter scar running up the length of his shin. Sikander took one look and winced, eliciting a grin on his companion's face.

Abdul Majeed's commentary about the valleys made them seem from this distance like mysterious portals into an unknown realm leading from the wall of mountains.

Eventually the wall was reached, and at the appropriate ravine defining the gap for heading up to Showlghar, the travelers turned into the mountains. They had made good time crossing the large plain in about two and a half hours, while slowing down at each little stream or brook. The sun had begun to get serious during their walk across the plain and as it was now noon, the shade from the steep valley walls was more than welcome.

Along with the shade came a feeling of foreboding, however. The valley slopes were devoid of much by way of vegetation while the boulders, rocks, and rubble in front of them had a sharp, jagged, and

altogether unforgiving appearance. A mountain stream drained out of the ravine onto the plain they had just been crossing.

Deftly, Abdul Latif led the way over the rocks, knowing instinctively where the footing would be sure and where it would be questionable. Periodically, he would look up to check if he was taking too much of a chance with the way the rock was hanging over the path in front of them. *This is no country for wheels*, he mused. But for feet and hoofs it was ideal and it was here that the mules demonstrated their real mettle.

The day wore on and the group made slow but steady progress over the roughly four kilometers of climbing and winding up into the pass. Having crested the pass, the going became much easier as they began their descent into Showlghar Kalay.

Afghanistan had embraced them and it was five in the afternoon.

As it was also enemy country, a direct run to Laghar Juy was out of the question. Instead, their route would have to hug the slopes at whatever elevations were feasible. They would proceed to their west but make a large arc around the northern edge of the mountains stopping briefly at Baro Kalay and then on to Takhto Kalay. Indeed, a route taking them back into Pakistan before turning north once again to re-enter Afghanistan not far from Laghar Juy was also a distinct possibility. That was all still ahead of them, however; for now, it was time to greet some fellow Shinwaris, spend the evening with them, and relax.

Showlghar was a small village but many of the people who had heard of the brothers Abdul Latif and Abdus Sami were pleased to see the seasoned warrior with his young troop, and more pleased to see fresh weapons being brought in to help with fighting the Soviets. The head of the village was a substantial man of forty-five by the name of Akhtar Ali Khan. He received the visitors warmly.

"It was either the DRA or the Soviets. They've been flying their helicopters over this area most of the day. They must be looking for you people. Perhaps you were seen and given away by those Afridis. Huh! They only seem to care about money, guns, and opium!" Akhtar Ali didn't much care for the Afridis—and was none too hesitant to show it—although there was no specific dispute or feud going on.

Being engaged to an Afridi, Ejaz was distinctly uncomfortable with Akhtar Ali's tone and he glanced at Abdul Latif to see if he could elicit an appropriately tactful intervention from his uncle. The discomfort registered, and the ever-astute Abdul Latif didn't take long to deflect the subject into a new direction.

"Perhaps it was just a routine patrol. This is, after all, a fairly loosely managed border and there's plenty of back-and-forth illicit traffic. It's hard to believe they've singled us out."

Quite apart from Ejaz's subjective concerns, Abdul Latif could not imagine the problem being Yaqub or Khurram Afridi, though one or more of Yaqub's fellow villagers could not be ruled out. Abdul Latif reflected on how his choice of not coming via Chenar Kalay might have been luckier as well as wiser. He had only mentioned Chenar as a destination when outside Yaqub's house. If there had been any informants or, more likely, opportunists looking for some ready cash, they would have directed the Soviets toward Chenar.

After the day's trek, Abdul Latif's group simply wanted a good hot meal, a bath, and a night's sleep. All of these were provided. The bath was a large closed off room into which some of Akhtar Ali's people had brought in large buckets of hot and cold water and a metal jug. Bathing involved dipping the jug into the hot water bucket, adding some cold water from the other bucket and pouring the contents of the jug over the body. If the mixing wasn't precisely to the right degree, the experience was...invigorating.

Thus invigorated, Sikander slept that night a deep and restful sleep. He longed to know how his enchanting dream of the previous night might have concluded. It lingered in his waking mind, but asleep, there was no such luck, and any dreams he had were forgotten when he awoke the next morning to an especially loud but, noted Sikander, unamplified azaan from somewhere in the village.

As soon as Sikander awoke his first thought was to raise his mentor. This time he'd be ready for Abdul Latif who had obviously needed more rest from the prior day's journey. Shaking him vigorously while grinning, Sikander managed to stir him into consciousness. Abdul Latif was not slow in awakening. His eyes opened abruptly as he gathered his senses—a survival instinct born of the troubled times. He looked at Sikander, and emitted a soft, sighing chuckle, acknowledging

the essential payback in the question of who would be the human alarm clock for whom that day.

Fajr was performed with about another thirty villagers, and without going back to sleep for the usual couple of hours, Abdul Latif's troop gathered their mules and proceeded downhill from Showlghar to the west followed by a trek along another slowly rising ravine.

Abdul Latif wanted to use the low light to his advantage and now the terrain at the northernmost edge of the harshest of the mountain country was a lot more passable. Having come through the ravine, they made good progress toward Baro. To their north, the sun began to light up the gently sloping plains that led all the way to the Jalalabad-to-Torkhum road about fifteen kilometers in the distance. Light dust trails could be seen from truck convoys moving back and forth between Torkhum and Kabul. The mountains behind the travelers to their south kept them in the shade for a considerable while longer as the peaks cast long northwesterly shadows over the plain almost as if to point in the direction of Laghar Juy. Abdul Latif used the opportunity to bring Sikander alongside him and point to one of the shadows.

"Take a look at that peak's shadow, the uh…fourth one from the right. Do you see the shadow's tip? That's where we live and where we're going to be inshaAllah tonight."

The thought of finally being back home filled Abdul Latif's voice with a noticeably upbeat tone, but he wasn't about to abandon his instinctive caution.

"It'll be too dangerous to make a straight run for it," Abdul Latif noted. "Not with these weapons and mules. But at least you can see it now and keep it in your sight most of the time while we head in that general—"

Abruptly, Abdul Latif lifted up his right hand directing everyone to stop. All of them followed suit. He paused for a moment, on the heels of which was a transformed look on his face. Instantly, he urged everyone to move deeper and higher up into the slopes as he was sure he had heard the dreaded, unmistakable chopping sound of a Shaytan-arba, or "devil's chariot"—the mujahideen name for the Mi-24 helicopter gunship.

Sikander had heard nothing. *Surely he's only imagined it*, thought Sikander. *Perhaps after all that talk last night.* But he also knew

that although it would mean a little straining, he probably ought not to be the only one to ignore Abdul Latif's order.

"Quickly!" said Abdul Latif with a sternness that didn't need to be shouted. The warning infused an extra level of energy into Sikander's step, but he could see how his companions adeptly climbed up the shadowy slopes while, despite his youth and relative fitness, he lacked the stamina to keep up with them at this altitude.

Leaving Kala with the others, Ejaz instinctively came back to help him, taking charge of Neela, while freeing up Sikander to climb more easily. Indeed, their newest mujahid recruit found his footing and quickly managed to join the rest who were by now in a deep crevice in the mountainside. Ejaz followed behind with Neela when a piece of rock that had promised more gave way while failing his right foot. Despite his best attempts, Ejaz tumbled and lost his grip of Neela's bridle and of about fifteen meters of mountainside before he could arrest his sliding. A meter long streak of blood painted the mountain slope, culminating in Ejaz.

Saleem immediately sprang from his hiding point to rescue his brother while Abdul Majeed went on to pick up Neela from where she had been let go by Ejaz. Abdul Latif meanwhile looked on as all of them could now hear the sound of the chopper.

Like all other Soviet aircraft, this one had a NATO designation which, for all helicopters, began unimaginatively with the letter "H." The Mi-24's NATO codename was thus the "Hind"—a name that had found its way into mujahideen usage through their interaction with the Pakistani ISI, who in turn had picked it up from their CIA contacts.

Always harbingers of destruction, the five giant titanium rotor blades produced a characteristic sound. In the distance coming from their east about three kilometers away was a visibly growing black dot low in the sky following an east-west track roughly parallel to the edges of the lower slopes of the mountains.

Abdul Majeed had taken control of Neela, whose gray-blue color was luckily a perfect match for the particular rocks surrounding them. He quickly brought her up the rest of the slope into the deep crevice to join the others. Saleem helped a limping Ejaz to his feet while keeping low and moving slowly to avoid creating a focal point for attention against the vast stationary backdrop of the mountain slopes.

However, both brothers knew that they had to get far from the potential telltale streak of red that would all but direct the airborne death-dealer to them. Crouching, the two of them limped a little higher up the slope and further west.

The mules are all under cover. The best thing that can happen is for Saleem and Ejaz to stay put and hide behind those large boulders until the gunship flies past them, thought Sikander. By the way the helicopter was flying, if they could escape detection, it would actually miss them by about forty meters further out from the mountain than they were.

The Hind was built like a flying tank and against its armor an AK-47's 7.62mm rounds would be about as useful as blow darts. This much was clear to Abdul Latif. It would take at least a 23mm round to penetrate the helicopter—even the cockpit glass. *If it could fly past us and present a blind spot to us*, hoped Abdul Latif, *then I'd be able to try something*. So far, albeit unwittingly, the helicopter was cooperating.

The gunship continued on its path without veering. Inside, the pilot and gunner were chatting without focusing too hard on the scene in front of them, and as nothing untoward seemed to be going on, they continued obliviously forward. Fortunately for the mujahideen, at that level up the slopes, the frost-shattered rocks and boulders presented a "noisy" visual scene to the crew, and it would take much more attention than this crew seemed willing to dedicate to discover the hiding travelers.

It must be a routine patrol, thought Sikander. *If we can wait it out, we'll be fine.* He was new to the ways of this war.

Wasting no time, Abdul Latif untethered one of the RPG boxes, flipped it open, and pulled out a grenade while unstrapping a launcher and readying it for firing. Sikander was puzzled. When they were coming into Afghanistan, they had talked about the weapons they were carrying. Abdul Majeed had told him that the RPG was only effective against APCs or tanks.

How can Abdul Latif be thinking he can use it now? Sikander wondered. He put it down to an act of perhaps misguided improvisation on Abdul Latif's part.

Saleem and Ejaz did as Sikander had hoped. Crouching behind a large boulder, they constantly adjusted their position to remain out of

view to the helicopter crew as it flew by, its flight path clearly indicating that the travelers had gone unnoticed. As it was now about five hundred meters further to the west, Abdul Latif gestured to both Saleem and Ejaz to hurry back to the crevice as he loaded an RPG into the launcher, stepped out to an area of the slope where he could give room to the jet blast from the back of the launcher, and waited.

Sikander looked on with continued puzzlement and wondered what could be gained by alerting the authorities to their presence by attempting a futile attack with such an inappropriate weapon. But in the tension of the moment, he was not about to interrupt Abdul Latif.

When the helicopter was about seven hundred meters away, Abdul Latif found a natural hole in the rocks on the ground behind him and taking very careful aim, he fired the RPG toward the helicopter. The grenade immediately created a blast jet behind the launcher, scorching the rocks at the far end of the hole as it hurtled skyward. Abdul Latif had been lucky with the calm air and his aim proved accurate.

The grenade exploded just before it reached the helicopter. The engine sputtered. One of the blades seemed to shed about a third of itself, visibly falling away from the aircraft. In a split second a bright orange flash erupted from the engines, followed by two or three much larger flashes, seemingly from within the helicopter. Almost three seconds later, the sounds of the explosions arrived as a belated accompaniment to the visual scene. What used to be a helicopter was now a cloud of fragments, each fragment hurtling earthward to traverse the three hundred meters that lay between it and the ground. The crew had no time to radio any message and it was a clean kill.

The last piece of debris fell streaming a trail of thick, black smoke behind it. It was the burning torso of the pilot, fused by the heat to the back of his seat. This detail, however, was not visible to the mujahideen from almost a kilometer away. What had a moment earlier been engaged in idle chitchat while flying a routine patrol mission, was now a ghastly lump of charred and smoldering fabric, aluminum, plastic, flesh, and bone.

"Allahu Akbar!" came the cry from Abdul Latif, followed immediately by his companions as Sikander joined in to the tail end of their proclamation just in time to seem to be in unison.

He pondered the events of the last thirty seconds. There had been a primitive, almost simian quality in the tone of Abdul Latif's takbeer—a primate's victory cry, oddly wrapped in the esoteric recognition of God's supremacy; a sound that Sikander would not readily forget. Unable to continue processing the human dimensions of the moment, Sikander unconsciously switched to mere curiosity about the more comfortable subject of its technical essence.

Based on what he had understood of the grenade, he continued to be puzzled by the now obviously effective tactic, and as the group sat down to focus on Ejaz's injury, Sikander ventured the question to Abdul Latif as to how he had managed to use an anti-tank weapon against a helicopter. With the poise of a mentor, Abdul Latif took a calm pleasure in explaining.

"If you set the grenade to self-destruct, it'll do so as a safety feature after about nine hundred meters from launch. The feature prevents unexploded RPGs from simply lying around dangerously. But when it destroys itself, it behaves like an anti-aircraft weapon and as long as this is done carefully, it can work, especially if you can get its airburst to hit something near the back of the engine or near the rotor hub. That Hind was armed with ground anti-personnel attack weapons but didn't use them. That means they hadn't seen us, so I waited until it was possible to take a shot. If I'd missed, it would possibly have gone unnoticed by the crew. Even if it had been noticed, they would only have seen an airburst with no immediate sense of where it had come from. Of course, if I hit it, the helicopter was pretty likely to come down, as it did."

Sikander's awestruck expression pleased Abdul Latif as he continued seeing to Ejaz's injured ankle. There was not an ounce of remorse on his face as to the fate of the crew—only the pleasure of knowing that the Soviet devil incarnate had taken another blow. But he wore this fulfillment only on his face. It was impossible for a man of Abdul Latif's inherent humanity to be completely unaffected by the act of killing, even if he had seen plenty of it. Those sentiments, however, would take their time to play out.

Whatever satisfaction Abdul Latif might have drawn from downing the helicopter, he knew it wouldn't be long before it was missed. There was probably not more than an hour before a search mission would be assembled with perhaps another hour before they

would be scouring the region with who knew how many helicopters as long as any were available. Abdul Latif and his entourage had to hurry to put a lot of distance between this event and themselves. They needed to climb to higher elevations, and passing through the hamlet of Baro was out of the question now. Even Takhto Kalay might be a problem if they wished to remain undetected.

He decided that five kilometers was a minimum for the next two hours so he devised a plan which would have them all descend to lower elevations to make the going easier until the last forty minutes, and then start climbing back up into the craggy mountain slopes to evade whatever forces might be coming. No longer were the mountain shadows available, as the sun had climbed and began to illuminate the slopes. Abdul Latif needed to look for every inch of cover he could find. Successfully evading a counter-response meant that a deeper penetration into the mountains would be necessary just to add a margin of safety, and they might need to wait up there for that night before venturing to come back out to make a final attempt at Laghar Juy.

Ejaz's ankle was wrapped with an improvised bandage torn from his qamees which allowed him to move with relative ease. He remained with Abdul Rahman while Abdul Latif took charge of Kala.

A wave of guilt swept over Sikander. It was he, after all, who had faltered in his attempt to catch up with the others and prompted Ejaz to come to his aid. If he had been a little quicker, things might have been different. Now he owed Ejaz and he felt the obligation gnaw at him as he saw the slight limp in Ejaz's gait.

Sikander duly expressed his "uzr," his regret that he had been the cause of the problem, and he thanked Ejaz profusely for having instinctively come out to help him.

"You're my brother in jihad," explained Ejaz wearing the slightest hint of a frown along with his smile. "Please don't discuss it anymore." Ejaz's perspective was not one of etiquette. He had genuinely needed the subject to be dropped as this would only increase his feeling of counter-obligation and in his own sense of badal, he did not want his creditor status diluted by such apologies.

The plan of descending to lower ground proved effective and they progressed about five kilometers in an hour. They had not seen any kind of response as of yet, looking in the distance sometimes toward

Jalalabad and sometimes toward Torkhum. No more gunships appeared to be flying out.

Perhaps they don't have any idea of the size of our force and they want to investigate the "incident" before mounting a forceful attack, thought Sikander. *Hopefully they'll think it was some kind of accident.*

At that point, Abdul Latif directed the men to climb back up the slopes. He was satisfied that they were now far enough from the wreckage to be able to evade detection. About twenty minutes after they had started their climb, they could see a Mi-8, "Hip," and another Hind nearing the point at which they had lost contact with the downed helicopter. A pillar of black smoke had erected itself where the wreckage had fallen so it was not hard to locate. While the Hip was landing to disgorge its troops, the Hind continued to hover maintaining a watch over the scene. Abdul Latif could not make out how many troops had emerged from the helicopter, but he guessed it might have been about eight to ten. Whatever their number, they moved first to examine the wreckage and then spread out into three groups to secure a perimeter, remove parts of the wreckage, and check the local terrain.

"Alhamdulillah!" exclaimed Abdul Latif, "Sikander, young man, you seem to be lucky for us. It seems the Soviets are being careful. They either don't know at this time what they're up against or they think there's been an accident. They'll want to investigate the crash and not risk any more aircraft without knowing more about what happened. If we're lucky, they won't see that we hit them with an RPG and they'll see no bullet holes or any other sign of combat. The explosions that disintegrated the helicopter came mostly from their on-board munitions. If I were their commander I'd want to know what brought it down before committing a large troop force and that's going to give us more time. Besides, he's probably going to radio back to his commanders before making a move."

They climbed to higher ground while remaining in the mountains, not venturing back into the gentler slopes below. Abdul Latif wanted to keep the Taktho Kalay option open so he led the group back toward the Pakistani border. Maybe it would mean another night away from home but he also knew that this would be the best route for them.

As they headed west, the peaks to their left, running on for about sixty more kilometers ahead, were a continuation of the Spin

Ghar. This part of the range was significantly taller and had snowcaps at about four thousand meters. Abdul Latif led his mujahideen troop around to face the more nearby mountains and headed them back into higher ground, making the usual switchbacks to gain altitude. The more elevation they gained, the more they were at an advantage to spot any offending Soviet threats from the air. Threats from the ground would be even easier to spot and were much less likely. The sun was now high over the plains and they were in a well-lit position so they could made good progress into the mountains back toward Takhto Kalay.

Takhto was a small village consisting of mud houses dotted among steep terraced hills, which were farmed largely but not exclusively for subsistence by the villagers. It was five in the afternoon when Abdul Latif and his entourage walked into the village from the north. He knew the village fairly well as it was not that far from Laghar Juy, and although Laghar Juy lived off its own agriculture, some of Takhto's more exotic produce was often brought down from the mountains by mule into the small markets in each of the many villages, including Laghar Juy, in the gentler slopes below. Apricots were among the exotica that seemed to sell well in lower level villages.

In those villages that were dotted around the landscape between the Spin Ghar and the main Jalalabad-to-Torkhum road there were long stretches of time in the aftermath of any of the frequent Soviet attacks that would reduce much of the agricultural land to little more than a lunar landscape. Likewise, village homes, such as they were, would also be demolished by the bombing, and while rebuilding everything, villagers would often look to Takhto as one of the sources of supplies that would afford them a means to survive.

Over the years, this frequent interaction created new relationships and one of these was between Abdul Latif and his good friend, Azam Ahmed Khan, of Takhto. But Abdul Latif hadn't been up there in some months so he didn't completely recall his way around the area. The layout near and around the last of the switchback trails was somewhat different from what he had remembered and as the group hiked up into the central cluster of mud-brick houses, he asked the villagers that came out to greet them to point them to Azam's house. Azam's son Humayun was home, but Azam was out in the fields although, according to Humayun, probably on his way back.

Humayun knew Abdul Latif and welcomed the group into the house while arranging to move the mules to rest up around the back. The mules were duly unpacked and the supplies and weapons were hastily shuffled into an adjacent outdoor compound surrounded by a mud-brick wall.

Now that they had the chance to sit down, eat, and rest, a certain tension filled the air reflecting the unexpected skirmish that had engaged them earlier that day, and the serious threat to their own safety that had occurred due to Ejaz's loss of footing and Sikander's lack of acclimation to the altitude. The uneasiness mirrored the transcendent truth of the elimination of lives that day, regardless of who the victims were. Everyone grew somber and not particularly inclined toward chatter. There was a minor break from this melancholy spirit when Azam Ahmed Khan did finally arrive home and Abdul Latif and Azam hugged each other—Abdul Latif a little more tightly than Azam had a right to expect. They exchanged a few kind words and Azam's wife asked him to ask Abdul Latif if he wouldn't mind taking some fruit and vegetables to one of her friends, Aamina, down in Laghar Juy.

Abdul Latif led the maghrib prayer in a solemn tone. Abdul Rahman and Abdul Majeed stuck themselves in a corner of the main room of the house and read from the Qur'an while Sikander remained seated, imagining how barely five days earlier he had been studying Shakespeare, watching TV, and engaging in thought-provoking debates about Afghanistan and the Russian occupation. Ejaz nursed his grazed and twisted ankle, which was slightly sore but obviously healing, while Saleem could do little more than wander outside the house thinking about how close he and his brother had come to dying and how that would have affected their mother and sister. No one wanted to discuss any of these thoughts in any depth and they all preferred their own particular ways of handling the experience.

The morning brought a new day, and for the feelings occupying the men the prior evening, a new day was what it would take to return to their normal selves. Instinctively, Abdul Latif took the lead to build back their spirits and he began to talk about reaching home that afternoon. Once again after fajr, there was no sleep for the usual couple of hours. The group had to make their way down the slopes to the edge of the mountains and depending on what they saw, they would either continue descending into the plain or else remain in the mountains,

cutting across each small brook and stream gulley until they could approach Laghar Juy from its "rear" following the stream's valley into the village proper. In any case, over the years, the village had progressively retreated to higher ground as a result of bombing from time to time, as this made it easier to reach the mountains and caves where villagers could take cover.

The men packed their mules in the usual fashion. After bidding salaams to Azam and his family, they were once again on their way, about half a day later than planned, despite cutting out the Chenar leg of the journey.

The descent from Takhto was relatively uneventful. They discovered no signs of nearby Soviet presence and the group had a fairly easy time of it once again under the protection of the Spin Ghar shadows in the early morning. However, Abdul Latif had no desire to repeat the encounter of the previous day, and ever watchful for the possible emergence of helicopter gunships, he and his troop moved cautiously along at a modest elevation following the mountain contours until they arrived at the headwaters of the stream whose path would lead them directly into Laghar Juy. They rested for about an hour before resuming the descent until finally, in the early afternoon, the village houses began to be discernable.

Soon, the group was within sighting distance of the lookouts on the south side of the village. The village men who had been posted there came out to greet Abdul Latif and his entourage. Not only were they pleased with their kinsfolk returning, but the lead lookout gave a defiant cheer of "Allahu Akbar!" when they saw the several mules carrying nothing but weapons and some much needed supplies. Abdul Latif gestured to one of the lookouts to take charge of the mules and supplies and move them into the village safekeeping store where other such weapons were being kept.

Reluctantly, Sikander gave up Neela's bridle. He hadn't said much during the trip about it but he had grown fond of this mule, being particularly taken by her docile nature as well her hardiness. His impression of mules had been generally negative until this experience, and he had certainly expected more difficulty with getting Neela's cooperation, but she had been a gamely animal and had endeared herself to Sikander through her remarkable intelligence and skill when it came to negotiating the rough and rocky terrain.

Before long, Abdul Latif and his troop ventured down the slope and entered the village carrying their weapons over their shoulders as they casually marched in.

As he strolled deeper into Laghar Juy with his companions, Sikander could see the randomly distributed remains of ruined mud-brick houses or partly destroyed walls amid what looked like simple, intact, and occupied mud-brick homes. Several families came up to greet him as an obviously "extra" mujahid and he acknowledged them warmly. He was heartened to see such acceptance from people so hard-pressed by the times and, as was plainly obvious, so often set back to have to rebuild their albeit simple homes not once, but maybe two or three times, after successive bombing attacks.

Thoughts of Hayatabad came flooding back when he considered these things, and for him, apart from the burning desire to contact his own family, he felt the occasional sting of guilt at how oblivious he had been to the plight of the Afghans, how superficial and pretentious his own family life now seemed, and how, despite the very real stress of his family's economic situation to his mother and father, it all seemed so inconsequential. Another guilt often came over him when he had been on the journey, a guilt that he felt once more now. He realized how different was the experience of actually living this war by comparison with the comfortably intellectual debates over its nature and conduct, in which he had often engaged with class fellows. Now, his ignorance had been dented by his albeit brief encounter thus far with the war's harsh realities.

Razya was a stoic. She had begun the day like most others and was preparing the charcoal for cooking something for herself, her sister-in-law, and her niece, whom she expected to arrive later that day. The charcoal was soon ready and she began to build the fire.

The war against the Soviets had been going on for almost seven years and prior to that, things had not been very peaceful under the Afghan communist regime for over a year since the Saur revolution. Since then, there had been nothing but war and death. Razya's response had been to grow thick skin and pray each day for nothing to happen to her precious husband or sons. However, she had resigned herself to hear one day an awful revelation, and in her own mind, without ever

discussing it, she had rehearsed her reaction to such a calamity. It was just her way of preparing for the worst.

This was not to be such a day. Eventually the troop arrived at Abdul Latif's house. As they entered, Abdul Latif called out Razya's name and a wave of relief came over her as she muttered under her breath a thankful prayer for his safe return and then more vocally, "Khan, you're back, alhamdulillah!"

There was no frenzied excitement of embrace. Razya acknowledged the men's arrival, smiled joyfully, and felt as if she could return to breathing again after a stifling twelve days of her family's absence.

Abdul Latif gazed at his wife and sighed. He had borne the brunt of the responsibility for his sons and nephews and was pleased to be relieved of his burden. He allowed himself a moment or two of rest and a glass of water, before promptly rising to his feet with the realization that he had become so familiar with Sikander's company that he had not recognized the need for an introduction. "Razya, we have a new mujahid. Come. Meet Sikander Khan."

Sikander politely introduced himself, fleetingly looked at his friends, and then back at Abdul Latif. Abdul Latif acknowledged the glance and turned to the two sons of his brother saying, "Saleem, Ejaz, we need to get you both back to your home. It's been long enough. Sikander, you can come too if you like."

It was only proper for Abdul Latif to see to it that Saleem and Ejaz were reunited with their mother and sister who, after all, had no husband or father returning to them. That would do nothing to dampen their clear delight at seeing the two young men back safe and sound, whenever they might show up.

Out of respect for Abdul Latif, Saleem and Ejaz had likewise not simply marched on over to their own house, as they wanted their uncle to be the one to escort them home.

"Abdul Rahman and Abdul Majeed, go up and help our people to offload the mules and give those things we picked up in Takhto to your mother. Tell her they're for her friend Aamina. See to her needs and I'll be back shortly," he said.

"Come on." Abdul Latif continued, turning to Sikander, Saleem, and Ejaz. "Let's go and break the good news to your mother!"

"Good news? What...good news?" came the question from behind him. Sikander briefly saw an expression on Abdul Latif's face that he had never seen before—fear.

As Abdul Latif explained what had happened with Ejaz and Hinna, his wife let out a joyful shriek and as it faded came the realization prompting her to frown and ask, "Khan! You were going to go to Noor's house and let her know without telling me?"

She knew of course that it would be completely unacceptable to dishonor Abdul Latif with anything like a scolding in front of his own sons, particularly in front of a stranger like Sikander. However, she did aim a narrow-eyed gesture to her husband that seemed to achieve the same goal, and then promptly began with a whole new tactic.

"Khan, I think that such matters are really best discussed between women, and...besides, whatever Noor thinks of this arrangement, she's unlikely to reveal her true feelings to you. Don't you agree?"

Abdul Latif nodded sheepishly, leaving his head hanging as he shrugged.

"Why then, let me go with you and I'll be the one to explain—" she offered as she looked past Abdul Latif into the eyes of Ejaz, cocking an eyebrow with an expression blending sternness and pleasure, "—how auspicious such a marriage might be."

Ejaz had no option but to study the smooth dirt floor when her eyes met his as he allowed himself just a single nod to let his Aunt Razya know that she was indeed being wise.

"Well then, Abdul Rahman, you and Abdul Majeed had better come with us too," Abdul Latif declared, as a look of relief mingled with resignation came over his face. They were happy to oblige. The seven of them proceeded in the general direction of Noor's house, no more than fifty meters away.

Coincidentally, Noor was readying to accompany her daughter Rabia to Razya's house so that the two of them might help Razya with preparing dinner and chat with her about various unimportant matters. They proceeded out of the house when Rabia darted out in front of

Noor who in turn extrapolated Rabia's trajectory to find her sights landing squarely on the group of seven figures walking down what approximated to a street in such a village. Noor became immediately aware of both her sons among them and was overwhelmed. The scene made her recall a day, barely nine months earlier, when such a troop as this had returned from the Zhawar campaign without her Abdus Sami, initiating in a single moment a whole new course for her life as a widow. Combining this thought with the joy of seeing her returning offspring caused her to weep and smile at the same time. Though her boys had not been away much more than ten days, every such trip was perilous.

The group came together and after the usual expressions of salaams, all of them turned and headed in the direction of Abdul Latif's home where preparations for dinner would resume, but now at a substantially larger scale.

When the hubbub had settled down and they had regrouped at Razya's house, Noor observed Saleem and asked him to come closer. Saleem moved toward her, his head lowered in respect, while she said a prayer in silence and she stroked his still-lowered head gently. The same was done with Ejaz and as he approached her, the slight limp became more obvious, prompting her to ask about it.

Abdul Latif and the young men exchanged looks, conscious that no one had bothered to suggest a rehearsal of how the incident might be described to the people back at the village. After that event, it had become an obviously unspoken truth that no one really wanted to talk about it.

"Ejaz...uh...lost his footing in the mountains," said Abdul Latif with a slight chuckle. "And you would have thought that he'd never been up there the way he was handling himself with his mind so preoccup...pied." He uttered most of the last word without realizing where it would land him until it was a just a little too late and his eyes darted toward Razya's who returned the look with her own unique glare.

"Noor," said Razya, gathering her thoughts and smiling at her sister-in-law. "Let's go into the back and chat. These men are tired after so many days coming across the mountains. Let them rest a while right here and we can go into the back courtyard and start preparing dinner. I have much to discuss anyway."

Noor, Razya, and Rabia proceeded to the rear of the home where the open-air charcoal preparation on a makeshift stove of mud bricks had been interrupted. Around the stove were one or two small sitting planks or patthras. They were about ten centimeters high off the ground and that was enough to create a workable seating posture while cooking.

"Noor," said Razya, "as you know, Ejaz is now, mashAllah, a fine young Pashtun and I think it's certainly about time he was with a wife. Don't you?"

"Why, yes I...in fact, I'd been thinking abou—" Before she could finish Razya continued, having confirmed the all-important affirmative.

"Well Noor, Allah moved his hand as he wills, and Abdul Latif had to lead the men through a different route than they usually use. They came through a village in the Aka Khel area. You know—where Khan Jehangir lives?" she asked, looking for acknowledgment.

Noor nodded slowly but intently, indicating to Razya to proceed.

"Noor," continued Razya, "when Abdul Latif was going through that village, he and his men met with a very respectable family headed by Yaqub Khan who invited them all to his home for dinner before they moved on. Well, by chance while they were there, Yaqub's daughter, Hinna, was asked to serve the meal. When he saw her, Abdul Latif felt that this girl would be a perfect match for your Ejaz and he was sure you would understand his concern for Ejaz's well-being and future, so he put the question to Yaqub." Razya managed to get this much out and felt that a pause would be appropriate for Noor to digest what was being said to her.

"I see," said Noor, encompassing all that was either possible or necessary at that moment.

Razya beamed. "Well, you can imagine his delight when Yaqub said he thought that such a relationship would be most auspicious and would help to increase the bonds of kinship between the Afridis and the Shinwaris, you see?" By now, Razya felt as if she was making real progress.

"Yes...yes, I do see," said Noor, who had adopted a vacant look while uttering the words, and with Razya gazing at her, the glint of sunlight reflected off the watery edge to Noor's eyes as she began, without so much as a sob or other sound, to stream tears down her face. An ordinary emotional moment would have seen Noor pick up slack in her dupattha and wipe her face with it. On this occasion, though, she was too immobilized to deal with her appearance and the glistening tears running down both cheeks continued while she sat and listened.

Ever since her late husband had been killed in Zhawar, Noor had become contemplative and reclusive. She rarely said much and if she did, it was only after a lot of introspection. At this moment, she imagined her husband coming home with such news. She imagined him feeling proud of his son's stepping up to the next phase of his adult life to marry and bring forth children to carry on the family and the clan. Imagining them was all that she could do when finally, she let out a soft whimper and leaning her head into Razya's shoulder, she wept inconsolably.

Razya could often appear so stoical as to seem to be heartless at times. This was not one of those times and she needed no explanation of precisely what feelings must now have been running through Noor's mind.

"Noor?...Noor," she soothed. "This is a time of joy for your Ejaz, not sadness." She sensed as she said these words that nothing more need be said and she sat with Noor, knowing her feelings completely. Having thus let herself go to Razya, Noor took a minute to regain her composure.

"Razya," she said sniffling. "My husband's brother is my brother and my children are as his children. I consider myself today to be thankful to the Almighty that he decreed for me to bear two sons and that they fight in his name with Abdul Latif. May Allah grant him a long life and may he bless your husband for his kind consideration for my Ejaz." She paused to take in a much-needed breath and continued, "And Razya, where would I have gone? What would have become of us if your family hadn't been there for us? No. If Brother Abdul Latif has seen a girl he believes is fitting for my Ejaz, then w'Allahi, I'm content with it."

She rose from her patthra to go into the main room of the house to greet Abdul Latif flanked on either side by the five young men.

"Brother Abdul Latif," she said looking beyond him to stare into the eyes of Ejaz, "it seems you have...procured an addition to our family?" She paused as Ejaz picked up on the reference and broke eye contact with his mother. "Ejaz, come here," she beckoned in her most motherly tone and as he responded, he instinctively bowed his head for her to bless him, not saying anything as he smiled in the knowledge that the news-breaking to his mother had now been "handled."

The rest of the day was spent in describing more about the group's recent adventure and enlarging on Sikander's introduction to the women in the household. One such introduction was to Rabia. She had been intrigued with the stranger's arrival and, never having been to Pakistan, found his brief introductory description of his life there to be most fascinating. She was about a year younger than Sikander, yet for her station in life, she was among the better educated people in the village. Until his death, her father had been particularly concerned with obtaining reading material for his daughter—though all of it had been in Pashto—whenever he made one of his trips into Jalalabad.

In the quiet of the late afternoon, Sikander found time to step outside briefly. While wandering around, he began absorbing the sights of the children playing, the men sitting around in small groups drinking chai, and the women generally going about their business looking after the smallest children and doing normal housework.

There was an air of contentment with life, despite its many hardships, which contrasted with the higher-paced existence of Hayatabad where the psyche seemed more attuned to acquiring yet more possessions while dedicating no small amount of energy toward the protection of all that had hitherto been acquired.

But here before him in this tiny village of Laghar Juy, amid the adversities of ordinary living compounded by a patently asymmetric war, Sikander could see and feel a sense of simplicity and truth in its unpretentious existence. He was wholly unprepared for its seductiveness. Nevertheless, seduced he was.

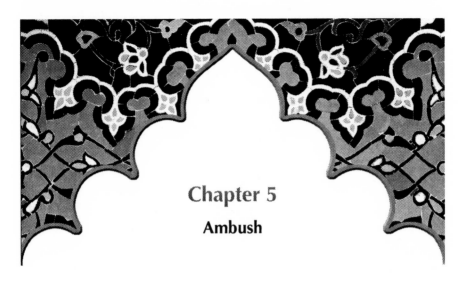

Chapter 5

Ambush

A
WEEK PASSED FOLLOWING Abdul Latif's emergence from the mountain trails into Laghar Juy. Each day the village lookouts maintained a vigilant watch for any activity by either units of the DRA or of the Soviet forces that could signal an impending attack. Abdul Latif and his fellow village elders grew concerned at the possibility of a surprise attack from Jalalabad or Batawul. The Laghar Juy villagers had managed, however, to enlist some trustworthy lookout volunteers up in Anarbagh Village who would have an easier time of watching the Jalalabad-to-Torkhum road, especially near Batawul.

Meanwhile, Jalaluddin Haqqani arrived at Laghar Juy to discuss the plan to ambush the tank force that had begun accumulating on the southeast side of Jalalabad near the airport where at least a dozen Hind gunships were also stationed, much as Junaid had predicted back in Jamrud.

Haqqani, a slender man, wore an overly large turban while his long beard showed signs of frequent dyeing with henna that resulted in the grayer hairs of the beard coming out in a bright tangerine color as the dye began to wear off. He wore a bandolier of the ubiquitous 7.62mm caliber food for his AK-47 assault rifle, though he rarely used it now. Haqqani had made a name for himself under Maulwi Younus Khalis by leading with great tenacity those forces placed under him and he rarely yielded to retreat from DRA or Soviet counter-attacks. He

frequently traveled to and from Pakistan, maintaining both a residence there and a strong tie to the Inter-Services Intelligence people as an effective funnel for weapons and money to help the mujahideen fight the Soviets.

Haqqani came to Laghar Juy and called together the local jirga and a few of the other senior mujahideen to go over the approach to the impending ambush. Abdul Latif was one of the jirga members and had brought along Abdul Rahman, Ejaz, and Sikander to share in the planning. Haqqani's force for this operation consisted of about forty men and he was counting on Abdul Latif to be good for five to ten additional fighters.

"Alhamdulillah! Our spies in Jalalabad are reporting that the tank buildup near the airport is very real. We may need to change our plans to make an ambush on this force much closer to Jalalabad before it gets too large," said Haqqani. "Their intention seems to be to take them towards Hazar Now, which will allow them better defense of a garrison that they intend to build up at that location, and once they do, they'll present a much bigger threat to the villages to the south. It will be harder to escape any direct attack except up the mountains. InshaAllah, we'll attack them before they can do this and if we succeed, we'll also have weakened them."

Abdul Latif listened intently before proposing an approach.

"Brother Jalaluddin, what if we were to let them stream out of Jalalabad and even get as far as Batawul? There's a place on the main Jalalabad-to-Torkhum road where there are enough small buildings and other natural obstacles that they will really have no choice but to move in a column. We could surprise them with a hit on their trailing tank followed immediately by their lead tank. It would put the rest of them in some confusion but remaining largely immobilized by being boxed in by the wrecked first and last tanks and the natural obstacles to their left and right. If we can force them into such a fix, we should have the advantage to strike and destroy them almost at will."

Jalaluddin paused for a moment. "Hm…that *would* be my approach, too, Abdul Latif, but their helicopters? Even if they're not escorting the column, their middle group will no doubt report the attack and we'll have problems avoiding them, won't we?"

Abdul Latif had already anticipated Jalaluddin's question. "It's a possibility, of course, Brother Jalal, but if we could create a nuisance barrage of RPG fire toward any helicopter cover, they'll be drawn to respond or move out of range, rendering them largely ineffective. We'd station our primary force on high ground on either side of the Jalalabad-to-Torkhum road. In fact, if we could use the hills to the north and south of the road at Mar Koh near Batawul, we could create a killing zone on the road. Small arms fire can then be directed toward any escaping soldiers or we could capture them for ransom. If the helicopters do withdraw to higher altitude, or move out, we can redirect our attack force more squarely on the tanks and if the helicopters remain engaged, then w'Allahi, we'll bring them down."

"Bring them...bring them *down?*" questioned a startled Jalaluddin, wondering what his clearly seasoned mujahid captain could possibly offer next.

A gleam materialized in Abdul Latif's eye as he continued. "Yes indeed. I'd previously heard of RPGs being used with the self-destruct setting to explode near a flying helicopter and that it would behave almost as if it were an anti-aircraft weapon. Like you, I was skeptical, but on our way into Laghar Juy, we had just such an encounter with a Hind and we fired from behind the helicopter. It took shrapnel to its rotor and engine. That shaytan-arba disintegrated. Now, it isn't easy. But I think it can be taught to our people and if we attack in groups of two or three while our main force hits the tanks, the helicopters can be neutralized."

"SubhanAllah! Brother Abdul Latif. Do you think you can teach this skill?"

Abdul Latif nodded, grinning.

Jalaluddin paused for a moment to consider how he would deploy his men to take maximum advantage of the proposed tactical plan. His eyes didn't take long to signal that something had begun crystallizing in his mind.

"Let's have sixteen men focus on helicopters and twenty to hit the tanks. For the tanks, I'd like to further split the twenty to have six at the rear of the column, four at the major intersection in Batawul between the river bridge and the Mar Koh hills and ten at the hills themselves. The groups at the rear and on the hills should be split

evenly to have half on the north side of the road and the other half on the south. The four at the intersection should attack from the south side. The rear groups should lie in wait under the river bridge and come out to attack the rear tank as soon as it passes. The hit will be the signal for the group at the intersection to knock out the most nearby tanks and that will signal the men on the hills to take out the lead tank.

"For air defense, we'll use the same hills at Mar Koh, but Abdul Latif, you will place your men higher up the hills. Focus only on their helicopters. Keep six men on each side dedicated to those helicopters with two on each side to create a rearguard in case we get attacked from the east or their helicopters try circling back around us. All my remaining men will provide small arms support against any escaping DRA or Soviets as well as blocking escape routes to the east."

It was about as amusingly improbable as an eighty-year-old grandmother parallel parking a Ferrari. *This rustic, rag-tag Pashtun seems to have a really comprehensive grasp of military tactics*, thought Sikander as he listened to the unlikely wizened commander. He also noted how the man was a full-fledged "maulwi" or one well versed in Islamic theology, adding to his awe of the man.

Sikander's thoughts shifted to the plan itself, and for the briefest of moments his sensibilities, focusing on the technological dimensions of it all, had been made numb to the amount of killing that it would likely entail. But reality soon came rushing in to fill his temporary vacuum of conscience. This was no armchair newspaper article, TV commentary, or one of the many American war movies he had seen at home. This was real. He was now on a path to witness and participate in real slaughter.

Sure, he could think of it in terms of tanks, helicopters, and grenades, but there was no getting away from the people. His body began to tremble, which he found difficult to bring under control. Each time he seemed to have done so, it took only a moment for it to resurge, and again Sikander would have to fight to regain control. He had never found relaxing to be such hard work.

Looking skyward, Jalaluddin noted the sun's approximate position and gestured to one of his young stalwarts. "Omar, please go up to the roof and say the azaan for the midday prayer."

The whole troop, minus four lookouts, conducted the prayer, with Jalaluddin performing the duties of imam. Following the prayer, he gathered his entourage and bid salaams to Abdul Latif and his men. "We'll send word of when the tank column is supposed to move out and until then, make sure to train at least twenty men for that helicopter attack, Abdul Latif."

Abdul Latif nodded affirmatively, and taking care not to move in a single large group, Jalaluddin Haqqani moved himself and his people out of Laghar Juy back up to higher ground.

A few kilometers to the west of Laghar Juy up in the mountain slopes were the caves of the Spin Ghar. With CIA help they had been fortified and could be relied upon to store arms, supplies, and other equipment. Of these, the caves of Tora Bora were the preferred place to hide whenever it became apparent that Laghar Juy might be attacked. It was exceedingly difficult to dislodge an enemy from those caves and such a move was known by the Soviets to be potentially foolhardy since the occupants would quickly disperse and regroup after any such offensive. Going after each enemy fighter would be an impossibly risky and expensive task, so the Soviets preferred to let the battle come to them or hit the mujahideen in their villages.

Haqqani and his force would be relatively safe in those caves and could easily cross the short distance into Pakistan in the face of any large enough threat.

Abdul Latif stood pondering for a moment, weighing the task he had taken upon himself, but it didn't take long for him to be clear about exactly what he had to accomplish. He scanned his boys and when his eyes settled on Sikander's, he gazed at the young man, and with his characteristic wry grin, he uttered, "It's time we got you equipped and trained, my young mujahid."

Sikander caught the sense of a hidden message in the tone and wondered what lay in store for him and the training to come. He was about to find out very quickly.

Abdul Latif beckoned to his younger son, telling him to take Sikander to the highest ground in the village where Abdul Latif normally arranged to have his men practice with small arms fire. The rest of the village, which continued down the slope following the contours of the stream, would provide adequate cover for the noise. Sikander was to be

trained to use the Kalashnikov AK-47. Abdul Majeed and he walked up the hill to the designated spot.

Looking across to one of his other mujahideen friends, Abdul Majeed asked him for his rifle. After being reassured that it would be returned to him, the young man handed it over. "Take this," said Abdul Majeed to Sikander. "Let's go round to the back of that abandoned house ruin and start. I'll set up some targets and will show you how to make the best use of this weapon."

The two of them disappeared behind the house and Abdul Majeed picked up some small rocks, perching them on the meter-high rubble that formed about two thirds of the back wall of the ruin. He returned to Sikander and began with the most basic instructions.

"Sikander, take your rifle and this empty clip." He handed Sikander an empty clip. "The clip holds thirty rounds and here..." Abdul Majeed pulled out several rounds from his bandolier and started inserting them in the clip, continuing, "this is how you insert them. You try."

Sikander found it to be surprisingly easy.

"Once the clip is full, you insert it like this." He demonstrated pushing the banana-shaped clip into the underside of the weapon with its lower end curving forward. The clip slid in snugly and latched. Once this was done, he pulled back the slide to load the first round.

"See?"

Sikander nodded as he hadn't found any of this challenging, except embracing the lethality of each of those rounds and what it might mean as the terminal entity in a hapless soldier's life.

Abdul Majeed continued, "The clip's loaded so we'll practice by trying to hit the rocks and knocking them off that low wall. When you do that, be sure to aim so that the back sight here—" he gestured to the rear V-shaped sight, "holds the front sight in the middle. Now, if you're close to your target, be sure to aim for a body shot."

"Why?"

"Because the recoil is enough to lift the barrel slightly, which will give you more of a chance that your second shot will be a head shot. If you do well, then both will hit the mark; if your first shot isn't lethal, then the chance of your second one completing its mission is still

higher than if your first was pointing only to the target's head," explained Abdul Majeed patiently.

Sikander marveled at the nuanced understanding that nearly seven years of battling the Soviets and their DRA puppets had delivered to the mujahideen. He resolved to be a conscientious mujahid himself. Firmly gripping the rifle he lay on his belly, took aim at the first rock, and squeezed the trigger gently. The rifle let out three rounds in what seemed an instant. The rock didn't budge and from what they could see, evidenced no encounter with a bullet.

"No, no!" Abdul Majeed chided. "You didn't take time to aim and you held that trigger too tightly. Huh! You'll lose a lot of rounds too quickly if you do that and won't hit anything...except maybe your own friends!" he added with a scathing grin.

He's enjoying this! thought Sikander as he watched Abdul Majeed schooling him on the use of the most basic of weapons.

Soon the world's easiest-to-learn assault weapon had claimed its latest adherent and Sikander was knocking rocks the size of small melons off their perches from fifty meters away. He was able to control the delicacy of his trigger finger's touch to let off just one or two rounds.

When this basic level of skill had been reached, Abdul Majeed walked over to a part of the boundary wall that was about two meters in height. Picking up a small pebble, he scratched out the approximate outline of a human form with the head centered at about the correct height off the ground for a standing adult. Within the outline, he drew a rough circle corresponding to where the heart was expected to be and another on the face.

"Now we're going to practice controlled fire on one specific part of the body. You choose, Sikander."

Sikander made it clear he wanted to go for the head and so committed them to work first and foremost on heads. Abdul Majeed picked up the rifle, took aim, and fired. The first shot made its mark just below the chin line in the place corresponding to the neck, and the second shot hit just inside the upper edge of the face circle. "Not bad," Sikander muttered.

"Now you try."

Sikander picked up the weapon and lay down on his belly. He felt the weapon's weight and balance and took aim as he'd been instructed. The first shot just missed the right ear but the second one was where the nose might have been. "Very good!" lauded Abdul Majeed, gleeful at the marksmanship and Sikander's clear effort to manage the recoil. He didn't seem to mind a bit that Sikander's second shot was better than his own.

"Alright now, most of the time the targets you'll want to be hitting will be moving. That means just as you had to lift the gun slightly to handle the bullet's dropping along its path due its weight, you'll also need to aim slightly ahead of the motion of the target so that by the time your bullet gets there, the target will be there too. That's something to judge but I'm going to try throwing up some large sized stones so that you can get a feel for this."

The two of them continued practicing until finally Abdul Majeed acknowledged, "Sikander, there's really nothing more that I believe I can explain to you that you wouldn't now learn better by practicing with the weapon. Let's hope you'll survive the practice!"

Pleased with this endorsement of his ability with the weapon, Sikander allowed himself a cheerful grin as they strolled down the hill back to Abdul Latif's home after returning the borrowed rifle to its original owner.

As had been commonplace in those days, Noor and Rabia were over to engage in talk and to help around the house. Saleem and Ejaz were clearly not at home and Sikander assumed they must either be working the field or on another mission.

Sikander's standing as a new mujahid recruit was established, and he found himself transitioning from the status of a melmasthia guest in Abdul Latif's household into more of an accepted family member. This was true in most respects with one important exception. Noor visibly took pains to keep Rabia from much interaction with Sikander. Rabia was her only daughter and she did not want any hint of scandal or compromise in the rules of etiquette relating to such interactions. No amount of acceptance of Sikander would ever constitute his becoming a blood relative mehram, and as long as that was the case, Sikander would just have to maneuver himself around awkwardly in Abdul Latif's house whenever Noor and Rabia were there. For her own part, Rabia, who was a characteristically independent teenager, simply glanced

downward or away, or pulled her dupattha a little further forward when Sikander was present but showed no other hints of shyness.

During the seemingly endless wait for the enemy tank movements, a delegation of two mujahideen arrived from Pakistan having come through Yaqub's village, bringing yet more weapons, among them several more AK-47s. Sikander was pleased to see the delivery as no doubt he would now become the proud owner of at least one of them. The visitors' names were Aamir and Yassir Khan.

Unusually among the items brought in by Aamir and Yassir were gifts from Yaqub's family and, as this was a Pakistani Aka Khel delegation, they did little to conceal their expectations of the confirmatory ring along with other engagement gifts for Hinna. They had reliably transported the gifts to Abdul Latif, his wife, and sister-in-law so they could certainly be trusted to take gifts back with them.

Sometime previously, after a day trip to sell farming produce in the markets of Jalalabad, Abdul Latif had obtained the ring. However, it still awaited an appropriate opening to be transported together with a recently sewn engagement outfit for Hinna. Other gifts for her parents and brothers had also been readied.

Abdul Latif had expected to be done with the ambush before now and it was one of his mounting frustrations that the matter of the engagement-sealing exchange of gifts had yet to take place. He would now have to deal with the embarrassment of receiving gifts before formally sending those from his family's side to the girl's family. He would, moreover, have to make sure they were all the more attractive as part of his own inimitable sense of badal.

Once Aamir and Yassir arrived and had been seated, they were served refreshments and food and given all other customary courtesies including a place to stay the night. The following morning after breakfast, the guests were formally handed the bride's ring, the engagement dress, a few small items of gold jewelry—the absence of which would have constituted a gross insult to her parents—and a small cloth wrap containing two hundred dollars.

One of the intriguing aspects of life in these parts was the use of currency. The Afghani was a rapidly inflating currency and exchange rates with the Pakistani rupee weren't reliable. Both Afghans and Pakistanis accordingly often found it useful to deal with each other in

American dollars. Abdul Latif had about two thousand dollars, which had been obtained from selling captured commodities from Russian soldiers into the bazaars in Peshawar, where he could readily demand dollars for whatever he was selling.

There was virtually no possibility of the travelers absconding with the gifts, as this would have been an open invitation to be hunted down and killed using some of the worst and most painful killing methods ever practiced in this part of the world. Besides, Abdul Latif had a nose for untrustworthiness and neither Aamir nor Yassir fit such profiles.

As Sikander watched these proceedings, he gestured to Abdul Latif to speak to him alone.

"Brother Abdul Latif, I've been wondering if it might be possible to get a message back to my family that I'm well and unharmed and performing inshaAllah a worthy mission. These people are returning to Peshawar and I'd very much like my message to go back with them."

"How would you propose to get it delivered?"

"Well, I think if you were to send a note back to Junaid for your own purposes and put my note to my father and mother inside the note to Junaid, then perhaps—"

"Perhaps Junaid, who would know your address in Hayatabad, would be able to deliver your letter physically to the mailbox and not reveal his identity or your location?" Abdul Latif completed the sentence, nodding.

"Something like that," Sikander agreed, impressed with his mentor's grasp. "And Junaid, to whom I had given my address once we had arrived at Arif's place, as we had discussed in Peshawar, has enough pull with the police not to be seen with suspicion in case there is some kind of watch on our house."

After only the briefest of pauses to process the request, Abdul Latif approved. "Please...bring the letter you wish to send or write it now." He gestured toward a small rough table bathed in daylight which would be ideal for composing a letter.

Sikander moved quickly to avail himself of the opportunity. The letter was written, handed to Abdul Latif, and examined for any security-related concerns. Having no such issues, it was placed in a sewn silk

envelope and handed to Aamir for Junaid's attention. Aamir duly placed it into his qamees pocket. Suitably laden with gifts for the bride and her family, sufficient provisions, and Sikander's letter, Aamir and Yassir readied their mules and headed back to Pakistan.

A day after the visitors had left came word from Anarbagh that some two dozen tanks were to be coming out of Jalalabad the following morning and were headed on their way toward Hazar Now. As this had been expected, Omar, Jalaluddin's apprentice, was dispatched to Laghar Juy to signal the launch of the now highly rehearsed ambush plan. After dismounting his horse, Omar immediately sought out Abdul Latif and told him it was time to gather his men and get going. Abdul Latif motioned to Abdul Rahman to withdraw the women and children from the village and head toward Tora Bora. Having made sure they were safely tucked away in the caves, he was to circle back to join the main force heading in the direction of Batawul. Thankfully, most of Jalaluddin's men had been waiting in Anarbagh so they had no need to race to an attack position with the same urgency as Abdul Latif, coming as he was, out of Laghar Juy.

There had been plenty of time to teach Haqqani's mujahideen the self-destruct ruse with the RPGs, and Abdul Latif was confident that most of the mujahideen in each of the air defense groups were knowledgeable about setting the grenades to deliver the required lethal airburst impact.

On the morning indicated for the tanks to be passing through, the mujahideen dispersed as planned. Six men tucked themselves under the designated bridge to the west of the built up area in Batawul. They would emerge three each on the left and right side of the bridge to its east. From there they would be in a position to fire their grenades to the rear of the last tank as soon as it had crossed the bridge over the river, which in these times was really a riverbed. The four that were to attack the central tank as soon as the rearmost tank in the column would be hit, took their positions under cover by some nearby shops on the south side of the T-junction intersection in the center of Batawul.

Two hill formations lay on each side of the east-west road at the eastern edge of Batawul in Mar Koh. The larger formation, reaching almost two hundred meters above the surrounding terrain, was on the north side of the road and the other much smaller one, at less than a hundred meters, was almost directly across on the south side. Near the

tops of these hills were stationed the air defense forces intended to engage helicopters, all led by Abdul Latif.

About halfway up the same slopes, another ten mujahideen were stationed, five on each hill. They would focus on the lead tank and, like the group at the road intersection, were to strike it as soon as the first explosion was heard, signaling a successful hit on the trailing tank. If they could disable the lead tank quickly, they would direct their attention to the next in line and move on down toward the rear, descending from the hills as they did so. They were to meet up with their colleagues coming from the west having attacked the rear and both groups would end up somewhere near their fellow fighters at the intersection. Ejaz and Saleem were among the men on the eastern hills, while Abdul Majeed was assigned to the group at the road intersection.

Ten seconds were all that could be hoped for before any surprise element in the ambush would be whittled down to a non-issue. For the mujahideen to succeed, they would have to act in their practiced, well-oiled manner. Rapidly.

The job of Abdul Latif's men was to remain focused solely on any helicopter activity and to fire upon the helicopters as incessantly as possible. It would be sufficient to keep the helicopters distracted so as not to interfere with the anti-tank operation. It would be stupendous if one or two helicopters were to be hit and brought down. Only if the helicopters withdrew would it be acceptable for Abdul Latif's small group to join in the engagement with the tanks.

At the far eastern end of Batawul, the balance of Haqqani's forces, a squad of another twelve mujahideen—armed with plenty of ammunition and their Kalashnikovs—were to be deployed to catch escaping soldiers. Sikander was to be among them, having now taken possession of his own weapon with which he had already formed a bond, and which he was certain he would be keeping for the rest of the war.

About forty minutes after the mujahideen had settled into their positions, the first of the T-62 tanks came rumbling through Batawul. About two hundred meters above the ground, a flight of four Hind helicopter gunships tracked the slowly moving formation, as ready as they could possibly be to respond to any attack. The tanks were in a widely spaced column formation a little more than three kilometers in length. As soon as the last of them had crossed the small river bridge to

the west of Batawul, the six hiding mujahideen waited until the trailing helicopter had also passed before springing from under the bridge. They waited for the trailing tank to reach about seventy-five meters down the road in front them before opening up with their RPG launchers.

Two grenades were launched, followed immediately by a second salvo. A third salvo was held in reserve to allow sweeping up for any mistakes as well as readiness for the tank in front of the trailing one when it would assuredly stop. The T-62's armor was notoriously weak at the rear of the tank.

The first two RPGs came screaming into the last tank in the column. Two large orange flashes preceded a deep, black, billowing cloud of smoke as the vehicle came to a standstill, with its engine disabled and no one conscious inside.

For a moment at least, the remaining tanks continued moving as if nothing had happened, their commanders unaware of an issue to their rear. As soon as the smoke became visible to Haqqani's men at the road junction, they launched their attacks on the nearest approaching tank. At the same time, the attackers on the eastern hills opened up on the lead tank. Amid respective volleys of RPG fire, three vehicles were immobilized.

With the tank column in confusion, it was a straightforward matter for the east and west attacking forces to move systematically along the column from the rear and the front toward their fellow fighters in the central group, taking out the intervening tanks one by one, knowing that the helicopters would be preoccupied with defending themselves, at least for the time being.

Pandemonium ensued as the column began to form two separately compressing halves, each consisting of tanks bunching up as they closed in on the immobilized tank in front of them. Inevitably, all of the tanks came to an abrupt halt. The position of the column severely limited options for a lateral breakout by any of them so their commanders were left with no choice but to fight from within the column and hope that the helicopter gunships, which were extremely well armed, could strike back effectively.

Once it had become clear to the Hind pilots at the rear of the flight that there was an offensive against their charges below, they radioed to their fellow flight pilots to locate the source of the enemy fire

and eliminate it. Just as this was about to happen, Abdul Latif's troops from higher up the northern hill let loose their RPGs on the helicopters. Of the six that had been fired, his RPG created the airburst as had been intended and promptly set that helicopter, almost a kilometer away, on fire and useless. In about ten seconds, it was out of control and came crashing to the ground not far from the tank column. The other three members of the flight split into two. One group of two helicopters remained over the now paralyzed column while the remaining solitary helicopter was dispatched to fly round the far side of the north hill and come back to approach the hills from the east.

The pilots of the two gunships hovering over the tank column had determined where the RPG fire aimed at themselves was coming from. Until now, in accordance with Abdul Latif's instructions, no one on the southern hill had fired at a helicopter as of yet. One of the two Hinds was facing the north hill squarely while the other began veering to its right to aim toward the source of the separate RPG fire directed on the tank column and coming from halfway up the south hill.

Abdul Latif was ready for them and signaled to the group on the south hill to open up while his fighters made a move to a different spot on the north hill. This would add to the enemy's confusion for a few moments longer and potentially shake their confidence that a response might even be possible, let alone effective.

All the while the fighters lower down the hill remained fixed on their tank targets and had already begun to leave the hills to pick off the remaining tanks. Those mujahideen who had attacked the trailing tank used its wreckage as cover to fire on the next one along in the column, now with no air cover as all helicopter activity had shifted focus onto the head end of the tank column. As the lead helicopter above the column began swinging to its left to take aim at the north hill, a second salvo of three RPGs came from across the road on the south hill from a little under a kilometer away. Realizing now that they too were in a killing zone, both pilots hastily tried to adapt to the unfolding situation. The pilot who had begun to swing for the north hill was already committed and managed to fire off some rockets. Immediately two of them came screaming out of the helicopter. Unknown to the mujahideen, they were equipped with flechette warheads which burst just before impact releasing several flechettes—small steel darts with tailfins which produced horrible flesh injuries. Typically the head of the

flechette would bend on entry and the tail would break off producing a second, debilitating injury.

One of the warheads had been properly timed and went off, injuring two of Abdul Latif's troops slightly just as they had been maneuvering to take cover. Hot on their heels, a third, non-flechette rocket exploded after impacting a rock outcrop on the hillside. Rocks flew in all directions near the tail end of Abdul Latif's troop. This time, one of his fighters was literally torn to pieces and another killed by rocks flying into his head. A third mujahid appeared to have taken a small stone close to his right eye as he struggled to function with blood streaming down the right side of his face. Abdul Latif now had two dead and three injured on the north hill, leaving him concerned at the sustainability of these losses with just three able-bodied fighters remaining, two of whom were still on rearguard duty looking out for helicopters approaching from the east.

Moments later, the sound of another airburst was apparent from somewhere close to the very gunship that had launched the rocket attack. Briefly, it was awash with flames before exploding in the air as onboard munitions were ignited. The RPG that had attacked it had come from the south hill, eliciting a relieved grin on Abdul Latif's face.

The remaining helicopter over the tank column let loose a salvo of rocket fire toward the anti-tank group that had left the Mar Koh hills to proceed west to attack the rest of the column, when it, too, came under attack from the south hill. His remaining colleague was about ready to make an appearance on the far eastern side of the north hill in preparation for a rearguard attack on the mujahideen troop that had been raining RPGs down on the tank column from halfway up the north hill. From their detour around the hill at low level, the crew of that helicopter hadn't been prepared for the mayhem that was developing and the loss already of two of their fellow crews, with the third crew all but doomed.

Now the focus of RPG fire from Abdul Latif's forces on both sides of the road at the tops of the hills was firmly on the one remaining helicopter over the tank column, which did not take long to succumb, leaving the last helicopter crew that had flown around the hills to approach from the rear, to fire on the mujahideen on top of the south hill. However, having seen the fate of their colleagues on the north hill, the south hill mujahideen had already taken cover lower down on the

hill and were well on their way to joining the men leading the tank attack. The rocket fire hit the area around the top of the hill with no consequence.

The sole surviving helicopter swung back to face the north hill and was about to pull in closer to Abdul Latif and his troop when a burst of RPG fire from across the road caused a large airburst to the left of the helicopter, sending shrapnel in all directions. A large piece tore through a rotor blade, weakening its titanium integrity, and in about three rotations it parted company from the rotor assembly, flying off sideways and striking yet another rotor blade, which also lost part of its tip. Missing a whole rotor blade and part of another, the helicopter shuddered violently from the imbalance of forces to which it was now being subjected, rendering it uncontrollable. The gunship plunged earthward just south of the tank column, exploding on impact.

The air defense mujahideen were now free, for the moment at least, from the need to worry about helicopter support. This left the full force of their firepower available to crisscross the road from their elevated locations with RPG rounds that were tearing up the tank column like ducks in a shooting gallery. Not only were they exposed from the rear, but Soviet tanks were also especially weak against attack from higher elevations. Before long, Abdul Latif and all of the anti-tank squads from both hills joined up with their colleagues on the ground.

As the outcome of this skirmish seemed inevitable, figures began emerging from the tank wreckage driven by the fear of onboard explosions from the poorly protected munitions, which created a very real threat. As they disembarked, they made sure to let it be known with their arms straight in the air that they were surrendering.

A single line of surrendering soldiers took shape as they emerged from the killing zone largely unharmed and saw, on the road ahead, Haqqani's troops ready to open fire at the slightest chance of a break from their surrender posture. They marched with their hands high above their heads, as Sikander, who now held a loaded weapon aimed straight at the oncoming figures, wondered what he'd do if his threatening stance was not respected by any of the enemy soldiers. He would have to kill them. He didn't have to think about it for too long.

The commander of the third tank had disembarked to talk about surrender terms with the twelve mujahideen that had been tasked to capture any escaping soldiers. The men coming out of these tanks were

regular DRA soldiers and not Soviets—judging by their fluency in Pashto—and soon, twenty men were all seated cross-legged in two rows on the ground waiting to learn what would happen to them.

In fact, the attack had resulted in twenty of the twenty-four tanks being disabled and all but four of the tanks' crewmembers dead. The remaining four tanks were intact. Their sixteen crewmembers rounded out the total prisoner count to twenty. None of the helicopter crews had survived. The surviving tanks seemed to Sikander to be in fair shape and no doubt capable of being captured as a part of the spoils, since, with so many DRA defectors over the years, the mujahideen were well aware of how to operate the Russian T-55 and T-62 tanks.

As the crews were lined up sitting with their hands on their heads, Jalaluddin, who had by now arrived from an observation post a little further east of most of the action, made a seemingly conciliatory speech to them.

"My Afghan brothers, fortune has not been kind to you that you have chosen the path of attacking your fellow Muslims. We know that many of you have been forced to do this by circumstance. Surrender yourselves to our cause and we'll help to clothe and feed you and your families, and together we'll rid this country of ours of the Soviets. Ultimately, inshaAllah, they will suffer a great loss. A loss of face and a loss of power as they will surely leave only in humility. Think then. What will become of you?"

Jalaluddin had few illusions, as did the prisoners. If they didn't join the mujahideen, then they were truly the worst of vermin in Jalaluddin's eyes and they needed to be annihilated. If they did elect to join, then they would go through intense preparation and an equally intense watch to be sure that they were genuinely deserting the DRA. The mujahideen had seen great success in past skirmishes with defections and there was no reason to suppose that on this occasion things would be different. Among them they had established special groups of desertion handlers who prepared such recruits to the cause.

From somewhere among the DRA soldiers came the cry of "Allahu Akbar!" as clearly Jalaluddin's message had penetrated his particular consciousness. A second later came another cry and another until the whole scene cascaded into a rousing cacophony of men interested in changing sides.

As this took place, Sikander was met by Abdul Latif who had returned from conferring with Jalaluddin, having also told him of the loss of his men and the one with the injured face. It was young Omar. It seemed he might be losing his right eye.

Jalaluddin ordered six of his troops to round up any of the small arms they could find and march the prisoners away toward Anarbagh. He knew that after numerous skirmishes the unspoken truth was that the Soviets and DRA largely kept to the major cities while the mujahideen held the countryside. He judged that it would be unlikely that a retaliation would occur until at least a few days had passed, and then it would likely be another of the Soviet airborne attacks on one or more of the villages outlying Jalalabad. Sustained evacuation of the villagers was therefore important and would have to remain in place for a few days until things settled down.

Meanwhile, Haqqani ordered two mujahideen per tank driver to join each of four tank drivers from the defecting troops to maneuver the captured T-62s slowly out of the column, pushing aside the dead hulks of the burnt out vehicles, and to join him on his own journey into southern Nangarhar and Khost. On his orders, his troops disbanded roughly along village lines and Abdul Latif gathered together his men including Abdul Majeed, Saleem, Ejaz, and Sikander. Abdul Rahman had not had time to join the skirmish and met up with his fellow mujahideen just south of Anarbagh as they were on their way back toward Laghar Juy.

"Abdul Rahman, do you have the village families secure?" asked Abdul Latif.

"Yes, I left them near Tora Bora. They knew how to reach the caves from there. We should all go up there until after any attacks on the villages have died down."

The expected response to the ambush came within the week when a flight of Hinds and two Mi-8 Hips came rolling into Laghar Juy's valley. They began by firing their Gatling guns and rockets into the mud-brick buildings. But their real mission was to be performed by their bombs. Each helicopter carried ten 100-kilogram bombs and each pilot unloaded his deadly payload over his own designated part the fields

outside Laghar Juy and its adjacent villages. The pilots knew that this would have the longest lasting effect.

The villagers had been in hiding more than twenty kilometers away up the mountain side from where they could see in the distance the Hinds proceed with impunity to tear up their villages. Most people had seen this kind of attack on their homes and fields more than once before, and by now, no one was materially vested in amassing prized personal possessions in a place like Laghar Juy.

When the dust settled and the last of the helicopters could be seen disappearing in the distance toward Jalalabad, the villagers came out of the caves and started leading their livestock and packed mules back down the slopes into the villages. Sikander accompanied his friends as usual, staying close to Saleem and Ejaz and their mules. Noor and Rabia rode together on one of the mules while the other was packed with a few belongings that personally mattered to Noor. Razya was likewise on a mule being led by Abdul Latif, with Abdul Majeed and Abdul Rahman walking out in front.

After four hours, the villagers were in the upper reaches of Laghar Juy and were able to examine the damage firsthand. All forty of the 100-kilogram bombs had exploded, which while being a curse considering the damage wrought was also a blessing that no one would be exposed to an unexploded device.

Further down the slopes, the villagers were able to see many of the mud-brick homes affected in some fashion or other, but owing to the focus being on the fields on this occasion, there were quite a few homes that had come through virtually unscathed. Noor's was one of them. Razya's was not. It had been flattened. Razya had to gasp, not so much from shock—few things could evoke such a reaction these days—but rather from imagining how accommodations would be handled.

"What will we do?" asked Sikander of Abdul Majeed. Abdul Majeed looked over to Ejaz as they exchanged shrugs. Turning back to Sikander, Abdul Majeed observed the obvious, telling him that Noor's household was going to get larger for a while.

Abdul Latif, leading Razya, approached the group of young men minding Noor and Rabia, both of whom were still on their mule. "We'll have to move in together with you, Sister Noor," he explained, telling her nothing she didn't already know. "It will be only so long as we have

to build our own replacement home, which of course we'll begin immediately," he added.

Noor was not happy about the prospect of three additional young men gathering in her home with her sixteen-year-old daughter, but she understood what the priorities were and nodded meekly without a word. This was a time of war, which admittedly had existed for about half of Rabia's life. It called for exceptions to cultural norms, but its abnormalities were still exceptions in Noor's mind.

Razya gave only a hint of emotion when she gazed upon what used to be her dwelling. She was not exactly devastated at the loss of so little, but it was impossible for her genetically innate nesting instinct to be immune from all sense of setback. Being the ever-optimistic Razya, however, she put a positive spin on things. "Noor, since this is the only possibility for now, we can at least work together on preparations for Ejaz's wedding, don't you agree?" Given the circumstances, Noor nodded and couldn't hold back a rare chuckle as she considered the comedic notion of a wedding among all the rubble.

As the conversation wound up and the family group began to accept the idea of living together for a while, Tahir, a villager from further down the slopes, hastily made his way to Abdul Latif who stood now with his AK-47 perched over his shoulder like a yoke, resting both hands on it, having nothing particular to add to the discussion of weddings and accommodations. As far as he was concerned, the important facts had been communicated and that was that.

"The fields! They've destroyed them completely," exclaimed Tahir with a quiver in his voice and gasping for breath after his sprint.

"And the grain store?" asked an unsurprised but disappointed Abdul Latif.

"About two thirds of that too," Tahir replied, heaving. "We don't have enough for a complete replanting even if we do manage to level the fields and fill in the craters." A look of considerable despair began to overwhelm him as he shook his steadily lowering head.

Sikander watched the expressions on Abdul Latif's and Tahir's faces, and as he looked around he could see how out of step he was with interpreting just how bad that news had been. In the short time he had spent with his Afghan friends, the one quality he had seen permeating their demeanor was a strongly forbearing nature. Almost no

adversity seemed great enough to form a basis for mental collapse or wringing of hands, despite them having seen more adversity than most in the world would see in a lifetime. "Wh-what does this mean?" asked Sikander to Ejaz—who stood closest to him—in a low voice while not wishing to reveal his own disconnect to everyone.

"It means we have to find more wheat from somewhere soon or face starvation during the winter and that...that might mean we have to go back to Pakistan to get it," he explained somberly. "But we also have to build your home and get the fields readied quickly or else the autumn planting will be missed, so as you can see, it won't be a quiet period."

Abdul Rahman sighed adding, but not wishing to, the unstated but obvious additional consequence. "It also means the Soviets will have forced us to focus on these things and that'll deny us the ability to organize any new attacks on them. That in turn will allow them to build up forces and attack us again."

This setback would require the people to repair the field surfaces and replant the wheat from grain reserves, such as they might now be, and hope that the planting would take hold. If not, they would have to increase the space allocated to poppy planting and hope that they could use the cash to buy wheat. Poppy planting would not be required immediately since planting season could be delayed even until late October or early November. However, that would do nothing to supplant the grain reserves lost in the attack.

Abdul Latif was the youngest member of the village jirga. Their involvement was clearly necessary on this occasion as virtually everyone was affected. Hurriedly the jirga met to discuss options. A plan emerged that required the villagers to organize into three groups. As this was a matter of survival, everyone would have to make their contribution. The first group was to head up to the higher mountain villages like Takhto, Showlghar, Baro, and Chenar and persuade each to sell about a quarter to a third of their reserves to the Laghar Juy delegation. The second group was to repair the fields and ready them for planting, while the third group would be dedicated to reconstruction of the homes. Meanwhile, any family having lost its home would have to be housed by a family with an intact home, until a replacement house could be built, much as had already been arranged within Abdul Latif's extended family.

Thankfully the enemy had no capacity to shut off the main stream running through the village, providing irrigation as well as the water that would be needed for mud-brick making, so a key commodity was still plentifully available. Sikander was assigned to the group charged with rebuilding homes together with Saleem and several other young but strong men whose stamina would be important to this task. The women and girls were to help in forming and baking the bricks to be used.

Abdul Majeed and Abdul Rahman were assigned to field repair while Abdul Latif led the delegation to secure grain from the mountain villages. Ejaz accompanied him along with five or six other village men. Gathering as many mules as they could muster, they set off for the hills.

The following days were filled with toil. Sikander and Saleem got to work on the reconstruction. Their first order of business was to cut a channel about eighty meters long from the main Laghar Juy stream to a point much closer to Abdul Latif's home site. At that location, Noor and Rabia took the mud from its edges and mixed it with chopped straw or mule hair. The mixture was poured and tamped down into a simple wooden mold to be left out in the sun, and once the mud started to dry the mold would be removed with the resulting brick left to dry out completely. Once the bricks hardened, it was down to Sikander and Saleem to put up the walls as close to their original position as possible.

Sikander spent considerable time with Razya, Saleem, Rabia, and Noor as the reconstruction progressed. Rabia's quick wit became increasingly apparent as Sikander noted that her relatively quiet and shy demeanor was melting away in her attitudes to him, given that he had almost become a member of the family. Saleem and Rabia would occasionally quarrel with each other and Sikander's adjudication would be sought on such occasions. From Sikander's viewpoint, Rabia could make a compelling case and he was impressed by her seemingly effortless ability to cover the entire range from caustic to charming within a single argument.

Despite his role as judge in these matters, it was not uncommon for Sikander to find himself drawn into argument with her. If it seemed he was losing, he would sometimes tease her with derisions delivered in Urdu or English while smirking at her inability to grasp what he had said. Rabia had studied neither of the two languages, but she was sure he had insulted her—achieving Sikander's desired effect—and it would

elicit a glare from her, often culminating in a playful smile and a slight narrowing of her eyes as almost immediately her mind would be busy planning a devious retribution.

On one occasion, after being teased by Sikander, Rabia decided to leave some of the straw and hair out of the mud being used for the bricks. Sikander and Saleem, none the wiser, managed to build at least five courses of a wall and were standing back as they sometimes did to take a rest while admiring their work. Rabia, with a gleam in her eye, joined in, feigning her own admiration, when the weight of the wall initially caused an ominous bowing out of the freshly laid bricks, which was followed shortly thereafter by their total collapse into a pile of mud crumble.

The two young men exchanged looks and, to Rabia's infinite delight, wore priceless expressions. Horror, puzzlement, and understanding swept over their faces in succession, assisted in the latter case by a now unrestrainable Rabia who, unable to contain herself any longer, pulled out a wad of straw in her hand, making sure they saw it. She burst out laughing and dashed away from them as they gave chase.

Saleem was genuinely mad at her, at least for fifteen seconds, as he had been the "innocent" bystander on this occasion. Sikander, however, the ostensible target, could see the humor and once he was past the issue of the wasted effort, he had to laugh. In these somber times, such humor was itself of value so he'd been inclined toward letting her go with a simple admonishing about the seriousness of the reconstruction effort. But first she had to be caught, which, although a foregone conclusion, was not a completely trivial mission.

When they finally did catch her, Saleem, feeling none of Sikander's leniency, moved in to pluck her right ear. Gripping it for dear life with the same cautionary zeal as he might have applied to holding his arms around a crocodile's jaws, he marched her back home. Sikander brought up the rear as Saleem presented his case to his mother and Razya. Noor admonished her daughter appropriately. Privately, she had to admit to being pleased at seeing Rabia taking on more of a personality and entertaining herself in a more usual girlish fashion. Rabia had spent much of the earlier part of the year coming to terms with the passing of her father. As it was now September, Noor noted to herself that Rabia must be seventeen years old, though the precise date

was uncertain. She knew Rabia had been born after the planting season in 1969.

Rabia had studied at school until the end of the past July. It had been her father's wish that she become a doctor. She had been one of the more accomplished students at the local village school and now that he had become a shaheed, she was determined that if she should ever be given the opportunity, she would strive to fulfill his wish. The school had long since been demolished by bombing and hadn't been properly reconstructed given the difficulty in obtaining anyone to teach under such circumstances. When they weren't fighting or arguing, Rabia would routinely revisit the subject of life in Pakistan with Sikander but especially about his schooling.

Once, as the three of them were resting after several hours of construction work, Rabia began probing. "Tell me more about the schools in Peshawar, Sikander."

"What more would you like to know?"

"Oh, you know, how did you come and go? How were the classes?"

"Well, we'd sometimes walk to the school, which is in a large area of land just to the south side of the GT Road. That's the road that continues into the Khyber Pass and through Jalalabad to Kabul."

"Hm…how many boys were in your school?"

"I'm not sure. Probably over four hundred. We'd be in classes of between fifteen and twenty and study all kinds of subjects."

"What was your favorite?"

"I don't really think I had a favorite but I did like English and geography. Sometimes our English teacher, Mr. Aftab, projected his slides from his travels and that would be interesting. He had a lot of material on America. I also liked reading English books." He began to recall some of his most recent studies and the dreams he had about traveling to America and what he would most like to see and do there.

About as interesting to Rabia as the schooling in Pakistan was the way people got around. She knew about all the modern modes of transportation but had never experienced any other than the mule and the horse, with the exception of a brief jeep ride with her late father once. "What about the cars?" she asked. "How do you feel when you

travel in them? Don't you feel the bumps on the ground when you go so fast?"

Sikander patiently answered her questions, all the while increasing her appetite for more information until it would be time to get back to work or to finish the meal or resume whatever else had been pressing at the time.

Rabia was sufficiently aware of the outside world to have more than a smattering of knowledge, but it was unique in the village for someone like her to have direct access to a person with experience of having lived elsewhere. He would tell her about the kind of things he had learned and enjoyed playing English teacher, translating for her the names of things like the grass, the river, the mountains, and all sorts of everyday objects found in their environment.

Two weeks after the bombings, Abdul Latif's home was complete. It was built slightly larger than previously on account of Sikander's presence and the boys lost no opportunity to make other minor improvements that might ease their living, given the situation. Three days before completion, Abdul Latif and Ejaz returned from the hills and the glow on Ejaz's face betrayed that they must have needed to travel even farther back into the mountains into Hinna's village. Indeed, Abdul Latif had brought back with him a few simple gifts for Noor and her family, as well as confirmation of preferred dates for the wedding.

With the departed groups returning reasonably well supplied with grain seed, the fields repaired, and the homes rebuilt, life could continue in Laghar Juy with some semblance of normality. The shortage of grain was still meaningful, but there was enough to make it through an average winter. Regardless, they would now have to plant poppy seeds, as it would be a waste to allow the repaired fields to go fallow for want of wheat grain.

Now that the family was safely back in its new quarters, Sikander had more time on his hands, and though he pitched in like everyone else for the planting, he would often take the time to stroll into the southern and higher elevations of the village and look back away from it toward the high mountains, contemplating life back in Peshawar and how it might be unfolding. Sikander was homesick.

Chapter 6

Applecross

IT WAS THE END OF SEPTEMBER and most of the destroyed homes from the attack at the beginning of the month had been repaired or rebuilt. The villagers of Laghar Juy were settling in for what they anticipated would be a usual winter. Lower down the slopes the weather was fairly mild, but at the upper elevations it could get harsh, especially during the prolonged period in the day when the sun was blocked by the mountains to the south.

Abdul Latif had imagined that once again, as in prior years, the war with the Soviets and the DRA would likely shift to a lower key mode as the weather would inhibit some of the more adventurous initiatives by both sides. He would be wrong.

In the first week of October, the two men who had visited the previous month, Aamir and Yassir Khan, were back in Laghar Juy with more weapons to be stockpiled for the offensives that would no doubt be coming with the break in the weather in spring. As before, having visited Yaqub Khan, they brought word that all preparations were underway for a wedding in late February, a time that could usually be relied upon for good weather. Noor agreed to this date and a certain level of modest preparation became an ongoing fact of life in her household. Rabia had taken an interest in her big brother's soon-to-be big event and was eager to lay her eyes on the girl that was destined to be her sister-in-law.

As was customary, the two travelers were afforded all the hospitality demanded by melmasthia. They were put up in Abdul Latif's house and temporarily Sikander and Abdul Majeed were asked to bunk over at Noor's place.

One evening, Noor invited Abdul Latif and his family to dine with hers and to bring the visitors with them. The group sat on the floor in the usual cross-legged style for a large dinner gathering, and the meal was served on a cloth placed over the durree in her main room. As Rabia, Noor, and Razya did most of the serving, the men began talking about the war and what might eventually transpire.

"Brother Abdul Latif, your role in devising the attack strategy on the tanks last month was reported by Jalaluddin to Younus Khalis and stories of your bravery and intelligence have now traveled quite far among the mujahideen," gushed Aamir.

Abdul Latif grinned modestly and did the required thing of declaring "Alhamdulillah!"

"Indeed," said Yassir, "the RPG tactics have been noted, Brother Abdul Latif, and the men you trained in preparation for that engagement that returned with Jalaluddin have now been training other men."

"I can't say I invented it, but I'd heard of this technique having been used by Massoud's people up in the Panjshir Valley though I hadn't ever seen it in action before I tried it myself on my last trip back from Pakistan; but you know, brothers, I know that the Americans have finally started sending their Stinger missiles into Afghanistan, alhamdulillah. I hope we start seeing them soon in Laghar Juy."

The two men exchanged knowing glances as Abdul Latif paid attention to forming a mouthful of rice and lentils in his right hand. Sikander watched intently, expecting to hear some relaying of a rumor or two, but was taken by the depth of understanding that seemed to be traversing the space between the two visitors without also entering the rest of the room.

"We...uh...we've heard the same about Stingers being used by Gulbuddin Hekmatyar's men, and at the end of last month there was a spectacular success, which downed three shaytan-arbas in a single skirmish!" noted Yassir.

"Really?" asked Abdul Latif. "So have you learned anything about how we might receive and be able to use these remarkable weapons Brother Yassir?" he went on.

"As far as we've heard, the Pakistanis have been trained in their use and are training Hekmatyar's men right now. In fact, some ISI men have been over to America this past summer to be trained and as far as I know, they've started training people."

"W'Allahi we have to get our young men skilled in their use!" Abdul Latif remarked impatiently as he moved on to discussing how the weapons might be getting into Afghanistan, how big they were, how mules might be adapted and so on.

After dinner, the men arose and washed their hands.

"It's a pleasant evening outside; Yassir and I are just going out for a stroll. Brother Abdul Latif, we'll walk over to your place when we're done. Any idea when you'll be back there?" asked Aamir.

"We'll be over soon. We're just going to help pick things up here and clean up and then we'll be coming back. Please go ahead."

Abdul Latif, his wife, and Abdul Rahman prepared to help Noor and her family to pick up the large floor cloth and clean up after dinner. Sikander stayed back to help for a while but needed to go out to relieve himself after the meal. When he finished he was on his way back into the house when he was stunned to hear something he hadn't heard in quite a while—English.

"...to make sure Haqqani's people also get the missiles and get trained," said Aamir in a low voice.

"Yeah, the men have to be selected carefully. There's only going to be a limited number of missiles initially and we don't have a lot of time," Yassir noted. "Do you think Abdul Latif will make a good trainee?"

The dim flicker of lamp light peered through from the window openings of a few nearby houses. The silver light of the moon's last quarter was also low in the eastern sky casting long shadows but still allowing Sikander to make out their silhouettes in the darkness. Visual contact was in any case unnecessary as Sikander had already recognized the not quite soft enough voices.

Aamir nodded affirmatively and remarked on what a good leader Abdul Latif had shown himself to be. "But it'll create a problem in this area if we take him away for that long. They need him here to coordinate the defense of the village and mount any further attacks if the Russians build up too quickly again."

Sikander was stunned at the discussion on which he had eavesdropped from the rear of Noor's home and as he was transfixed in the pitch black of the house's shadow cast by the moonlight, the two men rounded the back corner where he stood near the latrine. Instinctively, Sikander stepped out of the shadow to confront the men but all he could think of was to mutter the single word, "English," in a low voice conveying surprised curiosity more than question.

Yassir and Aamir looked at each other and back at Sikander. Until now they had not seen or heard Sikander speaking English, as he had never had the need except on isolated occasions with Rabia, which they had never witnessed. Having always assumed from their brief interactions that Sikander was a local, they had not thought to consider his possible grasp of their native language. A few more words were exchanged and it became clear to the two men that their cover had been compromised. It took a moment for Aamir to recover his composure and start revealing more of the truth about himself and his friend.

"Sikander, my...my name's Andrew, and this uh...this is Simon. We're British military officers and we've been traveling between Afghanistan and Pakistan for the last eight weeks now. We've been supplying you mujahideen and we're here to help your cause. However, it's important that we don't get caught as British soldiers so we've maintained these disguises and as you've obviously seen, we're also trained to speak Pashto without any accent."

"I'm-I-I don't know what to say!" Sikander uttered in his own English. "I am so surprised to see you speaking like Pathans and yet be British soldiers," he rambled. "What...what are you going to do now?"

The two men looked at each other for a moment and then again at Sikander. "Well," remarked Simon, his eyebrows raised, "we probably need to discuss this with Abdul Latif, don't you think?"

Dazed, Sikander nodded and motioned to the two men to walk on in front of him. Unsure of what to think, but having decided that

there was probably no danger, he was increasingly pleased in some way by the fact that he would be recognized for having "outed" the two of them.

They arrived at Abdul Latif's house and as they walked in, Abdul Latif acknowledged "Aamir" and "Yassir" but noted the incongruity of Sikander's presence, as he was supposed to have remained at Noor's place. "Sikander? What are *you* doing here?"

"Brother, er...Aamir and Yassir have something important to tell you."

"Yes, yes alright," Abdul Latif replied as he called out to his wife. "Razya! Make three more sabaz chais, will you?" She called back her acknowledgement from the rear of the house. While his two sons were seated on their durree, with their backs against the wall, eyelids heavy and longing for sleep, Abdul Latif began unraveling his turban to relax and walked over to his metal wardrobe cabinet to put it away, giving the visitors his divided attention.

"Brother Abdul Latif," started Andrew. "Please sit down as we need to tell you something important."

Abdul Latif heard the earnestness in Andrew's voice, scrutinizing him quizzically before passing his attention to Sikander and Simon as he sat down on the floor. Once he was seated, the two British officers began a lengthy explanation of their true identities, or at least the names they were authorized to reveal, with Sikander making it clear that he was the one to have found them out.

As the explanation unfolded, Abdul Latif looked across the room at his two sons, then at Sikander, and back to the two men, as if he was fishing for someone in the room who could make sense of this. When it was over, Andrew and Simon remained silent and waited for him to respond.

"Brother...Undrew?...Endrew?" Abdul Latif began, not quite knowing what to call the man sitting across from him.

"Please, call me Andy," interjected the officer.

"Hm...Andy?" said Abdul Latif nodding slightly. "Can you...uh...prove your claims?" he asked with more than a hint of suspicion. "And, more importantly, what is your mission with us?" All

the while Abdul Latif's instincts were on full alert as he grew concerned speculating about the purpose of the men's presence.

"We cannot absolutely prove who we are," said Andy. "We're not allowed to reveal our real names but we can assure you we wouldn't be willing to share even this much if we were intending any harm. You know if we're British, then we're very much on your side in this war. If we'd been Russians then we wouldn't have been using English in secret. Your friend Sikander had surprised us when we thought we were alone and he, quite frankly, also surprised us with his knowledge of English!" said Andy, frowning slightly as he looked back toward Simon, then Sikander.

Abdul Latif paused to think about what Andy had explained and it was hard to argue with such reasoning. He was, however, still dealing with the inherent nature of the deception to which he had been subjected and his own ego was still somewhat wounded for having not been entrusted with this truth.

"I'm inclined to believe you, Andy, but your...your deception has been dishonorable and I'm disappointed by your unwillingness to share the truth with your own host."

"Brother Abdul Latif," responded Simon with soothing apology in his voice, "indeed we are ashamed of the deception, but it was necessary for us to maintain this in case any of us were captured; and then you wouldn't have been any the wiser, which would have helped to protect you. We've been sent here to find good people to take with us for training on the new Stinger missiles. In May, President Reagan approved the delivery of these weapons into Afghanistan. Zia-ul-Haque, who was reluctant at first for fear of Russian retaliation, only just agreed to take them and deliver them through the ISI, but there isn't sufficient training support in Pakistan and it can't be done with secrecy, so we're looking for people to take outside of this country into Europe for training."

"But why not the Americans?" Abdul Latif queried, not quite settled down after the revelations of the last few minutes.

Andy and Simon looked at each other. They were resigned to complete revelation now and didn't see how any more damage could be done. "The CIA doesn't want its operatives captured in Afghanistan and they don't wish to be directly associated with Stinger deliveries to

the mujahideen," responded Simon. "They've asked the British government to provide training and that's why we've been sent."

Mists were beginning to clear in Abdul Latif's mind. He was a seasoned warrior and was trained by many years of war and hard experience to think ahead and read situations before they became fatal. His survival was a testament to this. Yet here he was, being surprised on this occasion. It was an uncomfortable feeling to have been so close to a possible assassination yet unaware of it. *What if these men actually had been Russians and I'd been fooled by them?* he wondered.

Nevertheless, Abdul Latif was sufficiently in command of himself to separate such insecurity from the facts being presented, and to evaluate them on their own merits in a way that didn't let feelings make unwarranted inroads into judgment. At least that part of his survival instinct was still working. There was an uneasy silence as the men looked on, which was broken by Razya coming through the back room with tea and the men trying hard to take on a demeanor to conceal the tension of the moment from her.

Having completed her last chore, Razya bid the visitors a good night and went to bed. Abdul Latif became more convinced that they probably were in fact there to help and that he should move the discussion forward.

"Andy," he began. "We'll keep this between the—six?—of us and I—"

"Brother Abdul Latif," Andy interrupted, "we would request that you open up at least part of this information to one of your nephews as we will need him to cooperate also."

"How?"

"Well," started Andy, who by now had made it quite apparent that he was the senior officer, "after our previous trips we'd seen how well these young men had handled themselves and were convinced of our ability to train them but now that we've also seen that Sikander here can speak our language, we think he should also join us as he'll make an excellent interpreter with the other mujahideen."

Already basking in the pride of being responsible for uncovering the operation, Sikander was left feeling slightly embarrassed for being the object of such praiseworthy attention.

"We'd like to take Sikander with us but—" said Andy, pausing.

"But what?" asked Sikander with a little too much concern.

"Well, we're only able to take three trainees with us."

Abdul Latif, his two sons who had remained largely silent until now, and Sikander glanced at each other then back toward Andy. "So, who do you have in mind?" Abdul Latif asked.

"Ejaz is due to be getting married and we don't want to interrupt that process. Meanwhile, Abdul Rahman, you're the older brother and more ready for a leadership role when you return, so we were thinking now we ought to be taking you, Saleem, and Sikander. That will also leave Ejaz to look after Noor and his sister, while you'll have Abdul Majeed here to help you."

"I see...and how should Rabia, Ejaz and the two mothers be told of this? How long will the boys be gone? How will you take them back with you?" The questions were beginning to form a pile and overwhelm Abdul Latif's own mind.

"We can't say any more than that we're going back to Pakistan for about a month," explained Andy. "You can say that the young men have to do another supply pickup which will require them to go beyond Peshawar anyway," he said, developing the appropriate deception for the rest of the family. "At least it will be the truth even though not all of it."

"It will be a month? That will be it?" asked Abdul Latif to be sure that he would know how to lie to his own people to explain the absence of the boys.

"Yes," replied Simon, being more familiar with the training process. "And as it's Sunday today, we'll need to leave the day after tomorrow in the morning if we're to be at our pickup location on schedule no later than Thursday in Pakistan," he explained. The immediacy of the mission caught everyone by surprise and Andy again felt the need to elaborate.

"Our original goal was to spend a month longer here and we'd have revealed our mission to you much later, after completing our assessment, but uh, well, you know what happened. Instead of next month's training, we believe we might as well move things up and take

the most immediate program, which is due to start next weekend. We'll radio news of the change to our ISI friends once we reach Peshawar."

Abdul Latif paused to absorb everything before pronouncing, "So be it. We're about to perform isha now and I suppose you're not actually Muslims, so uh...do as you please," he uttered with finality, feeling awkward over their earlier religious pretense while he, his two sons, and Sikander proceeded with isha as the two erstwhile imposters went to bed. With isha complete, Sikander walked silently back to Noor's place beaming with anticipation at this unexpectedly exciting development in his imminent future and his role in precipitating it.

When everyone arose the following morning for fajr, Abdul Latif made clear to Razya that Sikander and Abdul Rahman would be leaving for a month. She was a little surprised but not overly so. She put it down to a more complex mission than usual and that was that. Razya was nervous of reading too much into missions, being concerned about such information grating on her mind and fearing she would be unable to bear the anticipation and waiting that would follow. No, this would be better for her to accept it and let it go.

Noor was altogether more anxious and wanted her many questions answered until Abdul Latif stepped in, explaining that Saleem's mission was pivotal to the mujahideen cause and that she should bless them all for it.

Taking Saleem and Ejaz to one side, Abdul Latif told them that the mission was a more complex one than usual, and that Saleem would get the rest of the details after they left for Peshawar with Sikander, Abdul Rahman, Aamir, and Yassir. The rest of the day was spent preparing for the trip with five mules rigged for riding. This would help them remain on schedule. Razya helped Abdul Rahman prepare for the trip and Rabia did the same for Saleem and Sikander.

The preparations added a certain reality to the mission that was just beginning, and while Sikander had certainly been homesick for Peshawar, having now seen both hardships and victories with his newfound people, his sense of nostalgia for the impending separation from *them* began registering with him.

The following morning, with all preparations complete, the group set out on their mules directly toward Chenar and then across the rugged mountains over to the point south of Landi Kotal where Sikander

had remembered leaving the Pajero several weeks earlier. He reflected on how different he had become in those short weeks, and how much he had done. He had received an education in every respect as meaningful as his schooling in Peshawar, and the thought brought his family and school friends to mind as he longed to share his exotic experiences with them.

Riding the mules allowed them to make rapid progress through the mountains. The Pajero awaited them as they arrived at the same house where it had been parked previously. There was no telling how many times it might have made the trip back and forth between the house and Arif Saiduddin's place. The travelers dutifully dismounted, transferring their light cargo over to the vehicle to take them on to Jamrud.

By early Wednesday evening, they were all safely at Arif Saiduddin's house where they were to spend the night. As before, they were met by Junaid and Arif to be sure they understood the arrangements for the following day.

That night the five travelers, Arif, and Junaid headed down into Arif's basement. Saleem had so far been calling the two friends Aamir and Yassir and, as instructed, Sikander and Abdul Rahman were not to inform him until they were given approval. Upon walking in, Arif in his usually jovial fashion saw Sikander and gave him a welcoming hug.

"Welcome back young...Is...Sikander!" he exclaimed as he almost stumbled with Sikander's name once more. "Hmm...I see you now have a small beard taking shape, mashAllah. Perhaps you will be looking like a maulwi the next time," he joked.

Sikander patiently acknowledged the joke and looked across to Junaid. They exchanged knowing glances as Sikander was seeking some indication of his message having reached his parents. Junaid's body language seemed to convey that it had.

"Alright," began Arif. "It's very simple. Tomorrow morning you'll be leaving right after fajr for Sargodha. I have a home there on Fatima Jinnah Road not far from the bus station. You'll be staying the night, and from that point onward you'll receive further instructions. On this occasion, Junaid bhai will be taking you and explaining a little bit more en route, so you can all rest on the long drive."

Sargodha, thought Sikander. He had known that Punjabi city was famous for many things, among them, its important Pakistan Air Force base. His exhilaration mounted.

With this simplest of briefings over, the group performed salaat-ul-isha and retired to bed. The following morning, directly after fajr, while they began packing their belongings, Sikander approached Junaid.

"Junaid bhai, I think from the way you were looking at me last night that I can assume that my note made it to my family?"

"Sikander, I took it personally as far as the street where you live and paid a young boy fifty rupees to drop it into your mailbox. From the street corner, I watched him take it to the correct mailbox and once I saw he let go of the letter, I was on my way."

Before Sikander could say much more, Junaid already posed the next question. "Would you like me to take another one?"

Sikander nodded. "When will you be able to do that?"

"On Friday afternoon, when I get back from taking you to Sargodha, I'll do the same thing as before. You can take your time to think about what you'll write and let me have the letter to examine it in the morning just before I leave you all."

Sikander thanked Junaid saying he hoped to repay the favor one day.

"You're already doing that, Sikander. We're all proud of the work you've done so far in Afghanistan. Many mothers or fathers in this country could not say that about their own sons."

Sikander had always found Junaid to be a likeable fellow who was clearly intelligent and well organized. His knowledge of Junaid was, of course, only superficial. However, as he had lived among strangers for so many weeks and shared many hazardous and enjoyable experiences with them, Sikander, still feeling like something of an outsider, had quickly learned to sharpen his already keen skills in observing people. For Junaid, he had felt a fraternal bond and the sense that this man would do anything to keep a promise—not an altogether common quality in Sikander's experience.

The credit inherent in this bond was also called upon for Junaid's next request of the visitors. "Brothers, it's time to leave the

weapons here. They'll be kept here for safekeeping, but we can't travel beyond this province very easily with them and there's really no need."

Though difficult to swallow, the point was understood and Abdul Rahman, Saleem, and Sikander reluctantly set their weapons down against the wall behind them, taking off their bandoliers, and feeling highly undressed. Sikander didn't lose the opportunity to pick up Saleem's knife and scratch a squiggle on his AK-47 so that he at least might identify it on his return. His sense of incompleteness without the weapon was itself complete.

Shortly, the travelers were packed and back inside the Pajero. Junaid drove while Abdul Rahman sat in the front passenger seat. Sikander and Saleem took the next row, with "Yassir" and "Aamir" in the rear along with some basic provisions for the journey ahead.

The Pajero left southbound on the Warsak Dam Road to the GT Road and from there on its way out of Peshawar east toward Rawalpindi. Between Peshawar and Rawalpindi was a broad plain to the south of which were some imposing mountains, none of them snowcapped but sharply contrasting with the intervening plain. Sikander, being in the second row on the right side of the vehicle, was well placed to view the mountains about ten kilometers away. He couldn't help recalling his recent journey into Afghanistan, but more especially, the essential mystery of mountains to which the journey had exposed him. They were the walls of nature, making it difficult to reach out and touch a neighbor or to see the strange ways that people, cultures, and life in general had evolved on the other side, beyond the wall.

He also reflected on how strange the sense of time and distance could be when walking, riding a mule, being in a Pajero, or flying in an airliner. His mind could only grasp long distances in terms of travel time, yet changing modes of transportation as he had been doing, upset that natural relationship, turning distances themselves into something mysterious.

Turning to look into the vehicle, Sikander's gaze landed on Saleem sitting next to him. Though not a very talkative individual, having only ever been as far as Peshawar, Saleem was clearly fascinated by the beautiful backdrop. Seeing him made Sikander feel a sense of pride about his own country. Saleem returned the look with an acknowledging grin.

He doesn't yet know the real identities of Aamir and Yassir; he has no clue as to what's being asked of him. He only knows he's on yet another mission which his uncle has asked him to perform, Sikander reflected. Saleem appeared all the braver for it in Sikander's mind as his thoughts now drifted to the future and what they would be encountering in the larger world outside Pakistan and Afghanistan. With the imposition of secrecy, Sikander and Abdul Rahman would have to act as surprised as Saleem would no doubt be when the appropriate moment came. But that was some way off, and Sikander turned back to look outside the vehicle and admire the scenery.

The GT Road continued out of Peshawar until it finally met up with the Kabul River, which it broadly followed passing through Nowshera and on to Attock. Approaching Attock, it veered to a southerly track, continuing to follow the line of the Kabul River. Attock, the city formerly called Campbellpur by the British, was located at a point where the ravenous Indus coming out of the northeast of the country, drank the Kabul in an incessant gulp at this junction. Over the river, the road bridge turned them sharply to the east again as it passed the base of the imposing overlook of Attock Fort, no doubt constructed for the sole purpose of safeguarding the integrity of the crossing. The challenging nature of such a mission was evidenced by the several large caliber pockmarks—from skirmishes long forgotten—in the massive fort's walls. It was almost forty years ago that the British had left and who knew how much earlier than that when this fortress had last seen a fight? In any event, its purpose seemed to have been well served, but clearly no longer necessary.

As they headed into Rawalpindi, they stopped at a roadside eating place for naan and lamb kebabs, and in the fine autumn weather, with the beautiful plain and mountains in the distance, Sikander's pride could no longer be resisted as he quizzed Saleem on the latter's thoughts about his native land.

"Don't you agree that this is a beautiful country, Saleem?" asked Sikander upon reading Saleem's face, betraying the obvious wonderment from absorbing an inspiring scene experienced for the very first time.

"I do," said Saleem, drawing comparisons in his own mind with his experiences in Afghanistan. "Though you must agree that Afghanistan is also very beautiful, yes?"

Sitting next to Saleem, Abdul Rahman emitted a chuckle.

"Yes, yes it is, Saleem," acknowledged Sikander patiently. "But what do you think are the differences?" he asked, attempting to tease out of Saleem the compliment he was looking for.

"Well, I think the people look different, a little darker perhaps than anyone in our group. I think this food is different, in some ways more flavorful," he noted, in a reluctantly deferential nod of acknowledgment toward Pakistani cuisine. "I like the easy roads which allow us to move much more quickly than in Afghanistan. Would you like me to continue?"

"No!" laughed Sikander, with understanding.

After zuhr and a short phone call by Junaid, the group got back into the vehicle heading toward Rawalpindi, which they passed through quickly. It was apparent to Sikander that both Abdul Rahman and Saleem were now seeing a different side of Pakistan, a country that in its own way was in the upswing of one of its periodic but unsustainable economic booms, but which were virtually unknown in Afghanistan. The roads were bustling with as much traffic as in Peshawar, and Saleem began imagining a Jalalabad sometime in the future perhaps looking like this.

Leaving Rawalpindi, they followed the GT Road southeast toward Lahore. South of Gujar Khan the road crossed the northern edges of the Salt Range hills, which also dropped them into the river basins of Punjab. Two of those rivers were the Jhelum and the Ravi. Following them but capturing them anyway was the Chenab, which itself was consumed by the ever dominant Indus about a couple of hundred kilometers down river.

When they reached Wazirabad, it was time for asr. Stopping at a small roadside masjid, they again took a break. Not long afterward, they left the GT Road to head in the direction of Pindi Bhattian on a much smaller road, and from Pindi Bhattian, proceeding northwest, they made Sargodha by nightfall. Once there, Junaid had to leave them, letting them know that another driver would be picking them up in the morning and that in his phone call earlier in the day, he'd confirmed arrangements to stay with a cousin overnight before heading back to Peshawar. As this was a slight change of plan from the earlier conversation, Sikander quickly set about writing to his parents, letting

them know that he was back in Pakistan but couldn't say where, that he loved them, and missed them, but hoped to see them soon. Junaid took the note, examined it, and finding no issues, he folded it into his breast pocket. He gave the look of assurance to Sikander that like any other mission, he would give all due attention to the task of delivery. The Pajero was left at Arif's house on Fatima Jinnah Road and Junaid hailed a taxicab.

The following morning, the five travelers awoke and completed fajr. Preparations prevented them from sleeping again and they sat down for an unusually early breakfast as the sun began its ascent in a clear sky. As Arif's house servant, Fuad, was under strict instructions to see to their needs, he dutifully laid out a rich breakfast fare of grilled bread, eggs, halwa, pooree, and slices of fresh pound cake on a table in the large living room. With breakfast done, Fuad picked up the dishes and faded away into the back of the house. As soon as Andy could confirm they were indeed alone, he gave Sikander the acknowledging look to indicate that the rest of the plan was about to be revealed.

"Brothers, we have to brief you on the rest of this mission."

Andy looked at Sikander, Abdul Rahman, and Saleem, as Simon, who had been pacing the room slowly while drinking his tea, took a seat.

"My friend and I, we are British soldiers with the Special Air Service and we've been in Afghanistan to gather worthy mujahideen such as yourselves for training to learn to use the Stinger missile system. It will potentially make a huge difference to your ability to defend against airborne attacks. We can't tell you our real names but you can call me Andrew, or Andy, and this is Simon."

Simon nodded, wearing an impish smile.

"We had already met the three of you and your brothers, but when we heard of your brave fighting last month, we knew you'd make excellent trainees for our program. You're brave. You're intelligent. That makes us convinced you'll be able to teach your brothers and friends when you get back. This program is going to make a big difference to help you against your enemies. They're our enemies too." Andy paused for a moment to let them digest the news.

Saleem, his mouth agape, swung around to face Sikander who was feigning surprise as best he could. His eyes darted to meet Abdul

Rahman's, who was wearing his look of surprise rather better than Sikander. Saleem's heart raced and the slightest hint of Sikander's relatively less concerned look led him to ask, "Did you know this?" Sikander shook his head from side to side in vigorous denial.

"Where will you be taking us for the training?" asked Sikander, realizing that his ignorance of the answer would improve his chances of seeming ignorant of everything.

"We've gathered together fifteen of you and six of us to go to the PAF base here in Sargodha. This is the second group that's being trained and we're keeping the group sizes small until we know we can scale up the program effectively. There'll be a PAF C130 Hercules which will fly us all the way to Doha in Qatar, and from there we'll transfer into a Royal Air Force C130 taking us to Rome, where we'll refuel and go on to Scotland to do the training. The flights will take most of today, but as we have little time to lose and we need you back before the winter makes it too difficult to return, we'll begin training immediately the day after we arrive."

Sikander was taken aback at the scale of the investment being made to assist the mujahideen. He had just been given a glimpse of it and he was proud to be one of the few people selected, sure in the knowledge that his English would prove invaluable when it came to being instructed in detail. Gazing at a dazed Saleem, Sikander tried to ease him past the effectiveness of the deception, encouraging him instead with the same reasoning that helped himself feel positive about the mission. Abdul Rahman kept pretty much to himself, adopting a look of brooding curiosity as his own particular way of continuing his act.

"Brothers," urged Sikander. "We've been chosen alhamdulillah! Shouldn't we be pleased to return fully equipped with the weapons and skills we're supposed to be acquiring? We'll have the chance of making a real difference and...and just think. We could become celebrated heroes of the jihad, like your father, Saleem."

Emerging from his daze, Saleem quickly regained his faculties and having heard Sikander speaking was just as quickly coming to a similar conclusion. A smile slowly took shape, more rapidly transforming into a grin, accompanied by a frown of intrigue as he finally landed on the message being given him. This mission did seem intriguing and exciting. He would give everything to do it well.

Meanwhile, continuing his "silent surprise" response to the supposed revelation by Andy, Abdul Rahman simply nodded while adopting a look of realization and agreement for the benefit of Saleem.

Succumbing to a moment of pride, Sikander felt the need to show off his use of English as he turned to ask Andy, "When do we leave?"

"In ten minutes," came the short reply. It was in Pashto, so that both his companions would understand and Sikander's cockiness might be deflated a little.

The group reached the airport in the Pajero and handed the keys to a man who seemed to be expecting them. He was dressed in PAF uniform but Sikander guessed he was probably ISI. They walked over to one of the smaller buildings near the tarmac apron that was adjoining a hangar. Against the far wall were several lockers. Andy and Simon went to one of them and took out some large rucksacks, which they opened and removed what looked like clothes. Proceeding into an adjacent bathroom, they changed into their British Army uniforms and marched out. Without their Pathan garb and turbans, they looked like slightly long-haired, bearded soldiers, but they did look like soldiers and, thought Sikander, *now they look British.*

"Let's go!" called out Andy to the three of them, leading them out through the small door at the far end of the room which in turn opened out onto one of the many aprons of the airfield. Sikander was able to see the other mujahideen together with their escorts, and as they converged on the aircraft that was to take them, he experienced a growing sense of purpose. At that moment, all feelings of homesickness lay buried under the full weight of his anticipation of the mission ahead.

The Hercules C130 of the PAF's Six Squadron based at Chaklala near Rawalpindi waited on the ramp ready to roll. The rampant antelope insignia at the front of the aircraft gave away its pedigree. It belonged to Pakistan's oldest air squadron and the only one for tactical air transport operations such as the one being undertaken that day. It had landed barely an hour before, and now that it was nearly nine in the morning, was already fueled as it awaited its cargo of fifteen mujahideen and six SAS officers.

The group climbed the loading ramp into the back of the cavernous aircraft. Neither Abdul Rahman nor Saleem had ever flown

and despite their typically casual Pathan attitude toward most life-threatening experiences, they felt sufficiently lacking control of this one to be exhibiting a little nervousness, but with no shortage of excitement. Sikander had traveled with his father by air already. This time he was in a completely different space than an airliner and he wondered how this, the next in a hopefully long line of life's first-time experiences, would feel. He didn't have to wait long but he had to admit to the slight sense of pleasure at his advantage over his companions. They had routinely had the upper hand in Afghanistan with it being home turf and now it was his turn. He too had been around and seen or done things with which they might be unfamiliar. They might learn a thing or two from him.

Once the mujahideen were seated and strapped in on the metal benches lining the walls of the cargo hold, the massive ramp door was closed and the lights in the rear were turned on. The airframe juddered as the engines began to wind up and as they finally spun into self-sustaining action, the noise became a ninety-seven decibel roar. The British officers sitting nearest the cockpit of the aircraft opened a bin from which they withdrew ear protecting muffs and passed them out to the rest of the passengers as they put on their own. The passengers followed suit without hesitation.

Sikander and Saleem sat next to each other. With their backs to a window, which was to the right of Sikander and to the left of Saleem, neither was able to resist the temptation to swing around somewhat awkwardly on his perch and observe the scene outside. Abdul Rahman was on the opposite side of the airplane facing them. Something about the unnatural notion of being suspended in the sky in a large metallic object made him reluctant to peer outside.

After taxiing down to runway 14—Sargodha's longest—and completing a few final checklist items, Squadron Leader Omar Amin pushed the combination throttle forward. A brief initial lurching jolt was quickly followed by the aircraft beginning to roll smoothly down the runway. Its oversized wings hauled the aircraft aloft, climbing rapidly while presenting a spectacular view outside.

Sitting on the left side Saleem and Sikander could see much of Sargodha retreating beneath them. Finally, however, the haze over the city got the better of the view and there wasn't much to look at. Maintaining runway heading for almost half an hour, the aircraft

climbed to over six thousand meters. Off on the distant horizon to the northeast, the snowcapped mountains of the Karakoram stood with their shoulders above the haze layer like a row of distant, white giants guarding a mysterious fairy-tale land behind them, with sharply pointed craggy white peaks, at once alluring yet dissuasive to all but the foolhardy.

Finally the aircraft made a large sweeping turn to the south and then the southwest as it established cruise heading toward Qatar on a course that would keep it well to the south of Afghanistan's airspace. The rest of the flight was uneventful, if a little bumpy. At that time of year, the big convection systems from the summer and monsoon seasons were over and the air was ordinarily settled but could occasionally become choppy. It was choppy that day.

Cruising at seven thousand meters and absent the normally oncoming wind for this route, they managed to make almost six hundred kilometers an hour, which enabled a landing in Doha just before noon local time. When the engines finally shut down, everyone removed their ear defenders and the big ramp door was lowered.

A sudden rush of heat and the blinding noonday light burst into the otherwise dark cargo bay and the mujahideen had to strain briefly as their eyes rapidly adjusted to the full force of the day's brightness. By the time the ramp door had completely opened, three dozen Qatari soldiers had lined up to flank each side of the ramp all the way to a building entry door in front of the disembarking mujahideen. Two British Army officers stepped forward to meet and greet the travelers.

The whole troop was led into a small building at the other end of the lineup and was ushered quickly inside where each of them found a seat. Andy and Simon came back to where their three charges were sitting, offering them drinks and light refreshments. Out of courtesy they stuck to their Pashto, which looked decidedly odd coming from the mouths of two uniformed British Army officers in the middle of Qatar.

Everyone took advantage of the food and drink as the flight had dehydrated them. They also took bathroom breaks and made their prayers in a chapel off to one side of the main hall. It was a very well appointed room. *Probably some kind of VIP lounge*, Sikander observed silently, and by the way Saleem's and Abdul Rahman's heads were constantly swiveling, he guessed the same thought was also going through his friends' minds.

After an hour of resting and walking around the room, picking up the occasional magazine—which Sikander could see offended the sensibilities of some of his fellow mujahideen with their pictures of uncovered female faces and tight clothing—the troop was asked to make one last visit to the bathrooms as the next flight was to leave in half an hour.

Eleven men got up to go, including Sikander, and as soon as they had all returned, they were led out of the building past the lineup of Qatari soldiers, into the cargo hold of what seemed initially to be the same aircraft but was in fact a type C-3 Hercules from Royal Air Force Lyneham's Forty-Seven Squadron. It was in slightly better shape than the PAF aircraft, and once again everyone took up approximately the same seating positions as before. On this occasion newer ear protectors were handed out to the passengers.

The engines were started, the familiar rumbling began, and after taxiing out to runway 16, once again they were airborne. Rising into the sky, the aircraft almost immediately entered a steep climbing turn to the right to establish a northwesterly course taking the Hercules over the Arabian Peninsula in the direction of Alexandria, Egypt. About four hours after takeoff, the airplane was making its passage eight thousand meters above the grand sweeping arc of Alexandria's bay, where it turned onto a more northerly track, making the Mediterranean crossing directly toward Italy and a landing in Rome.

Sikander and Saleem were tired but as the aircraft was on the last few maneuvers coming into Rome, they still managed to steal a glimpse of the city from below the light cloud cover. For Sikander, Rome was mythical. He had read so much about it and had thought himself fortunate to be asked to study Shakespeare's *Caesar* at school. There were many place names he'd read about, and his curiosity trumped his weariness as he strained to look through each of the several breaks in the clouds to see the city's old but majestic face presenting itself. Every so often, several easy to spot landmarks like the Colosseum could be seen, which, until then, had only been seen by Sikander as pictures in his history books back in Peshawar. The landing took place about six hours out of Qatar and eleven from Sargodha, at five in the afternoon local time.

In Rome, the mujahideen passengers were led off the aircraft to wait in a lounge for one last time. As it was around sunset, the maghrib

prayer was performed and one of the older mujahideen led the congregation. Since they were traveling, they were able to avail themselves of shortening and combining their prayers to "qasr," for maghrib and isha.

Another light meal on remarkably clean plates with gleaming cutlery was brought out before the troop. Their Muslim sensibilities were not offended, as the staff at the lounge had obviously been forewarned about dietary issues and had prepared a light fettuccini alfredo which was quite filling for most of the passengers, once they got the hang of the hanging fettuccini.

An hour later, they were again airborne, heading northwest for another four hours when finally the engines were throttled back and the Hercules descended to complete the last leg of its flight. It was too dark to see outside as it was almost nine in the evening local time. In sharp contrast to the scene over Rome on their departure, Sikander noted the absence of lights on the ground as the aircraft made its final approach to land.

Broadford was a small airfield on the Scottish Isle of Skye. The C130 demonstrated its ample skills as it came easily to a halt on the short and narrow ribbon of a runway, approaching the airfield's solitary building before the pilot finally cut the engines and opened the cargo ramp. They felt the rush of fresh air but this time it was much cooler. It reminded Sikander of Laghar Juy's air but without the more natural "livestock" smells he had become familiar with in the Afghan village.

Tired and sleepy, the mujahideen were quickly ushered out of the Hercules and marched over to a nearby HC2 Chinook of the RAF's Eighteen Squadron. All of them filed in, found seats, and once again were airborne for the brief ten-minute flight. They were now at the SAS training facility at Applecross in Scotland, whose existence was little known to most people and, naturally, not at all to the mujahideen.

The men were led out of the back ramp onto a windy tarmac surface from which it was a short walk of less than fifty meters to a large cabin into which they were directed. Well lit, warm, and of metal construction, it had bunks running perpendicular to its windowed walls. Each double bunk stood between each pair of windows.

Without ceremony, the weary travelers took off their shoes and began dropping on whatever beds to which they could each lay claim.

Sikander asked Saleem which bunk he wanted. Saleem took the lower one. Sikander climbed to the top. He lay down feeling drowsy, as it was now around three in the morning in Pakistan. Abdul Rahman was on the bunk to their left and he had already drifted off. Above him was an older mujahid, a fellow by the name of Hamza Ali, who had led the prayers in Rome. In the bunks to their right were two relatively young men.

None of the visitors slept for long. By three in the morning local time, Sikander's eyes were wide open as were many of the mujahideens' and they began milling around, wondering what to do next. The entire SAS training compound was secure, so locking them up in the cabin was unnecessary and it gave the men a sense of greater freedom to wander about. The local terrain was a reasonable proxy for their own home country and would provide an ideal environment in which to learn Stinger operations. All of those men who did go outside remained close to the cabin in the pre-dawn darkness while taking in the fresh sweet Scottish country air.

The first hint of daylight made itself apparent casting a dim, pink glow through the small window in the door at the end of the cabin. It was easily visible with all the cabin lights turned out. Comparing it with what he could see through the remaining cabin windows, Sikander noted that this must be the southeast source of the autumn morning sun. Given he was in Scotland, he could form a good sense of his bearings for the Qiblah. This was always a significant thing for traveling Muslims. Proceeding to one of the bathrooms at the far end of the cabin, he waited in line to perform the wudhu. When he was ready he came out and joined the others who, having also noted that the door was facing the Qiblah, laid out their blankets on the floor to perform salaat-ul-fajr facing the door. Others had either already done so and were back asleep, or were still asleep due to tiredness.

As the morning established itself and sleep was out of the question, back at their bunks, Sikander and Saleem began making some new introductions with their fellow mujahideen as the airplane ride had been too noisy to be conducive to communication and they had been too tired. One of the two younger men on their right, a twenty-year-old, sat on the edge of the lower bunk facing Sikander and Saleem while above him was another slightly younger boy of eighteen.

"Assalaamu 'alaykum! I'm Irfan," offered the mujahid on the lower bunk. Sikander and Saleem responded with the appropriate

greeting and introduced themselves. "We're from the Khost area," explained Irfan, rolling his eyes upward toward his companion. "He's my brother, Usman."

"Waziri?" asked Saleem, seeking instinctively to understand tribal origin.

Irfan shook his head in smiling denial. "Ghilzai Pashtun."

Saleem smiled back as Abdul Rahman came over to join them.

At around half past nine that morning, the SAS officers arrived and started banging on the cabin's walls to stir everyone awake. The cabin's largely metallic structure made this technique effective in getting the few sound sleepers to stir. Like most of the others, Sikander was wide awake from being on Pakistan time. He wondered where Andy and Simon might be.

Those who had returned to sleep after fajr arose for the second time that morning and before long were piling into the bathrooms to prepare themselves for the day. About then Simon entered the cabin and Sikander eagerly walked over to him.

"Good morning, Simon. What's happening now?" he asked.

Simon calmly told him to go back to his bunk and await instructions from the SAS officer who would soon be arriving. Meanwhile Simon and four fellow junior officers had brought in several boxes. Opening them, they immediately started pulling out polythene bags containing fresh dark beige qameeses and shalwars with quilted green body warmers, fresh underwear, and black woolen socks. From other boxes several pairs of black boots were retrieved and laid out on the floor.

"Her Majesty's government is pleased to welcome you all." Simon pronounced in clear Pashto. "Please put on these new clothes which are a gift from the British people to the courageous mujahideen of Afghanistan."

Sikander looked at what he himself was wearing and found no difficulty complying with the request. He was the first to come forward and as soon as he did, the rest followed suit. He quickly found clothes and shoes that would fit him and after a brief detour to the bathroom to change, he returned freshly attired to his bunk to show off his new

outfit. Saleem, Irfan, and Usman lost no time in retrieving theirs with Abdul Rahman a couple of steps behind.

Half an hour later, another SAS officer, a little older than Simon, walked in and pronounced another order, in English. "Today, we're about to begin a four-week intensive program to help you use the Stinger missile effectively," he said. "I'm Captain James Laing, and I will be in charge of your training." The man's voice sounded hard-edged and before Simon had delivered his translation, Sikander had already leaned over to Saleem's ear to let him know what had been said. From this, Sikander reasoned that everyone at least spoke Pashto and were therefore probably all Pashtuns or Pashto speaking Uzbeks and Tadjiks, although no one exhibited the slightly Mongolian features typical of the latter two ethnicities.

Captain James Laing let it be known that today their training would begin and that each day, they would need everyone to be awake by dawn so that a full day's training could be completed. There was a lot to learn in order to make the Stinger weapon system effective. While it might be an easy weapon to fire, it was not so easy to fire successfully, without training.

He also laid out the camp rules. There was to be no travel outside the camp perimeter as the entire operation was to be a secret. They were free to exercise and play games or worship as they wished and materials such as for reading or writing would be provided. All food was strictly halal having been brought up from Glasgow, where a thriving Pakistani community had been established over the previous three decades with a highly developed infrastructure for halal food preparation and distribution already in place. Several other minor rules of housekeeping were clarified, as was the reason for not asking the visitors to wear Western clothing. They were to be trained in the comfort of their normal attire while using the missile system and if this policy was to expose any issues, the training would be a good way to discover them. Captain Laing wrapped up his short introduction and the group was free until after lunch when the first set of lessons was to begin.

After a substantial buffet lunch, the group was led into a hangar-like building that had been set up with classroom seating. At one end was a raised platform with three small steps and a podium. Behind that was a large white screen. The visitors were asked to be seated by

Captain Laing and once the lights were dimmed and the drapes drawn across the windows, he opened the proceedings.

"The Soviet 40th Army has been occupying Afghanistan since December, 1979," the captain began. "In that time, they've supplied the puppet government of Afghanistan, which calls itself the DRA, with deadly helicopters in the form of the Mi-24 Hind and the Mi-8 Hip, which you all are quite familiar with unfortunately. The Soviets have also often flown the helicopter missions themselves. They have indiscriminately attacked your villages, your fields, your crops, and your livestock. Many of your innocent women and children have been killed or badly wounded by these attacks. What we are about to train you to use is the FIM-92A Stinger missile system. Sometimes you will hear the word M-A-N-P-A-D-S. In English, this stands for the Man-Portable Air Defense System and refers to several small but deadly missiles. The latest of these is the FIM-92A Stinger."

As he spoke, on the wall behind him, Laing's comments were supported by simple but powerful images of the infamous helicopters and the horrific effects that had been perpetrated using them. He also showed a diagram of the Stinger system being held over an operator's shoulder suggesting how it was to be used. As everything was being translated into Pashto, Laing moved along at a fairly slow pace but remained watchful to be sure that his audience absorbed what he was saying.

"My dear mujahideen friends, you've been selected for this important mission because you've been observed to be both courageous and intelligent. Both these qualities are critical for you to be successful. Our objective, when we finish this training program, will be to turn you all into deadly users of the Stinger missile and bring the Russian helicopters down so that they no longer pose a threat to you. If we can help you succeed, you will be rid of the Soviets from your country and a great victory will have been achieved...inshaAllah." Although Laing didn't understand Pashto, he knew enough to utter the Arabic invocation of the name of God for the mujahideen whenever predicting a positive future.

The audience perked up as the translation came through and one of them shouted the word "Takbeer!" to which the rest responded in a loud chorus "Allahu Akbar!"

Laing continued, "We are passing out these books that contain the lessons we wish to convey to you."

As Simon translated, two other lower ranking soldiers picked up a large pile of ring binders in which the training course had been translated from its original English version, a 194-page tome entitled:

"Introduction to Man Portable Air Defense Weapon System: Sub course No. AD 0575, Edition A—US Army Air Defense Artillery School, Fort Bliss, Texas."

"We have three main lessons to give you in which will be several learning activities; each activity will consist of both a lesson portion in this room and a practical portion. We'll ask you to use training versions of the full weapon and as you become more capable, we'll also ask you to fire at least one live missile at our firing range. The first lesson, which is an introduction to the overall system, will have the following learning activities." Laing began listing the activities as he illustrated each of them with 35mm slides.

"First, we will cover the mission capabilities of the system. Second will be a detailed description of the different components of the system. Third will be familiarization with handling procedures. Fourth, the operation of the Stinger weapon. Each of these learning activities will have an accompanying set of one or more exercises that we'll ask you to perform. The exercises are designed to make your knowledge complete and, in time, your usage of the weapon both fast and flawless. Please be sure to read these documents as we go through the lessons." Laing paused for a moment to gather his thoughts before resuming.

"Now, we know that some of you aren't...uh, able to read. This shouldn't be a problem as we're going to be arranging you in groups of three and we've made the selection so that you will have at least one person in each group who can read the documents and explain them to the others. Does anyone have any questions?"

Simon's translation came on the heels of Laing's speech and as he too wrapped up, the room was filled with silence as no mujahid was looking to embarrass himself with what might seem to be a stupid question. Standing up and in his best English, Sikander asked, "Thank you, sir. How long do you expect this lesson and these four activities to take?"

Laing had not been briefed on Sikander's use of English and was at once surprised and pleased that this young man had stood up in front of his fellow mujahideen and neither been embarrassed to ask the question nor to do so in English. As the Pashto translation came through to the men, Laing began looking around the room and could also see that Sikander had for many of the men become a source of pride—something of a bulwark against possible patronizing on the part of the instructors, he seemed observant and well-educated.

"That's an excellent question, young man," Laing responded, raising his eyebrows and allowing himself a brief grin. "Assuming things go according to our plans, we'll take ten days to get you through lesson one."

Laing looked around the room as Simon translated to see how people were gauging the implied depth of subject matter to cover four learning activities. He paused a moment longer not asking for more questions but leaving just enough time for someone to raise his hand or stand up. Relieved to see that no one did, he returned to his presentation.

"Once we've completed all the learning activities in lesson one, we'll deliver lesson two, which will focus on how to operate as an efficient crew for using the Stinger. It will consist of the following learning activities:

"First will be how to detect, interrogate, and identify aircraft. Second—general engagement procedures. Third—methods of engaging aircraft. Fourth—team operations. Fifth—team radio operating procedures. Sixth—early warning methods. Seventh—relations with fellow combat units supported by the Stinger. Eighth will be mobility and combat loading, and ninth will be system support capabilities."

Laing continued, supported by illustrations of each of the learning activities of lesson two with simple visuals to help communicate the points as Simon maintained pace with his translations. Again Laing asked for questions.

Gripped by jet lag from their tiring trip of the previous day, no one ventured any questions.

"Alright. After these two lessons are complete we'll deliver lesson three, which will be concerned with familiarizing you with training devices which you'll later be using to increase your practice

time with this weapon system. But there'll be plenty of time to go over the materials during the rest of your stay. We'll now call out your names to arrange you in groups of three and when we do, please go over to the man holding up the placard with your group number on it," explained Laing, pointing to different parts of the hangar and giving the cue to each of the soldiers holding placards to hold them high in the air for all to see.

"Group One—Fareed Mirza Khan, Ghulam Ahmed Khan, and Akhter Mujahid Malik. Group Two—Irfan Karim Khan, Usman Khan, and Ahmed Ghani. Group Three—Abdul Rahman Khan, Saleem Khan, and Sikander Khan. Group Four—Jamshed Ali, Dilawar Hussain Khan, and Shahid Waheed. Group Five—Massoud Ahmed Khan, Wali Khan, and Hamza Ali Khan."

The names having been called, each of the mujahideen got up and walked over to the SAS officer holding the applicable placard.

"Andy!" exclaimed Sikander as he recognized the man holding a placard with a large number three painted on it. His companions followed suit and were equally happy to see him. They asked him where he had been, but even though he was clearly pleased to see them, he declined to answer. Still, it was good to see him back. Sikander could now understand the limitation of no more than three trainees that Andy had explained back in Laghar Juy.

The following ten days were long and grueling. Over the course of this period, Andy was the main instructor for Abdul Rahman's group, but in contrast to the cozy relationship they had with him when they knew him in his role as Aamir in Laghar Juy, he was no friend when it came to driving them hard and challenging them to avoid mistakes. Anyone could pick up a Stinger and with only a little training could fire it toward an enemy aircraft. However, to have a strong chance of success required practice, practice, and more practice together with an intimate knowledge of how the system worked.

By the time the ten days of lesson one were over, Sikander, Saleem, and Abdul Rahman were able to name all of the key components of the system. They knew how to handle the weapon, including the grip stock assembly and the secondary missile round. They had become familiar with the battery coolant unit, or BCU, which was used to emit high-pressure argon gas into the infrared sensor area to cool it enough to create a contrast between its own temperature and the

heat signature from a target in flight. At the same time, the BCU provided electrical power for the entire system until missile launch.

One part of the weapon they did not need to focus on to a great extent was the Identification-Friend-or-Foe (IFF) System, whose role was to emit an interrogation signal to a target and invoke a coded response from it. If the response was correct, it signified that the target was a friendly aircraft. In Afghanistan, there was no such thing.

After each learning activity, the groups answered test questions and only when each of them received at least a seventy percent score could the group proceed to the next learning activity. Sikander scored an eighty-five percent, Abdul Rahman likewise, while Saleem scored ninety percent on lesson one.

When the groups were not in intense training, they were free to roam around the camp during breaks or in the evenings. At these times, Sikander loved to go out and sample the air. He couldn't get over how air could "taste" so different from one part of the world to another and how sweet that taste could be.

Applecross had to be one of the most beautiful places on earth. To be sure, the Swat and Kaghan valleys, and the mountains like Nanga Parbat, the Baltoro peaks, and K2 of northern Pakistan were, by any measure, stunningly beautiful. Likewise, the sheer white peaks of the western Spin Ghar and the Hindu Kush of Afghanistan were undeniably breathtaking. Yet here in this serenely quiet little corner of Scotland was a place that didn't so much clamor for attention to its beauty like a Hollywood actress, but rather as a less glamorous yet equally alluring girl next door, Applecross made an innocent appeal to be appreciated, and through tranquil humility, reached more deeply into the human spirit than simply to stir the taste buds of the eyes.

The SAS training facility grounds at Applecross reached right up to the banks at the water's edge and Sikander would often stand by the chain-link fence at its boundary, embrace the breeze in the early morning or evening, and gaze out over the peaceful autumn water. As the sun rose, the hills across the water about a dozen kilometers away on the islands of Scalpay, Raasay, and Rona were brightly lit while behind them even more majestic were the rolling furry mountains at the southern end of Skye. In the evening, the setting sun would shoot shafts of orange light through the gaps in those mountains before being walled off by them, giving each a heavenly red halo and then disappearing only

to return the next day. Sikander had no idea of the names of these places, and their obscurity only increased their enchantment.

One evening, after a long day in the classroom, he stood at his favorite spot overlooking the islands and hills across the water. The thought of their anonymity crossed his mind and in it he saw an ironic parallel. He was in this nameless paradise having come to learn how to kill people whose names he'd never know, who would be trying their best to kill him without knowing who he was, for reasons at best only vaguely understood by them, but largely to avoid their own deaths. And it wouldn't end there. Who knew how many disasters would be spawned by any one of those deaths? Or, for that matter, by that same death not occurring?

As Sikander grappled with such impossible questions in the full grip of the slowly shifting light of the vista before him, a voice called out from behind his right shoulder. "Beautiful, isn't it?"

Reluctantly but only briefly, Sikander turned to see who it was. "Ah! Irfan, assalaamu 'alaykum," he acknowledged his new friend as he returned to the scene, anxious not to miss even a moment of its captivating and dynamic mystery.

"Wa-alaykum assalaam, Sikander. The British soldiers have arranged for a volleyball net so that we can get some exercise after all these classroom lessons. I'd like to play with you on your side, if you're interested in playing, that is," offered Irfan tentatively.

Irfan's request took only a moment to register with Sikander. Not wishing to move his head, he permitted himself to lower his gaze for just a moment as he experienced the briefest of flashbacks of the volleyball games he had played at the University Public School in Peshawar from time to time. He reflected on how he had been unrelentingly competitive, sometimes arguing with the referee in a manner that would get him dismissed for "not appreciating why the game was being played." He turned around to give full attention to Irfan, and as he uttered the words "of course" he saw Irfan's face brighten with delight at his simple response. The thought of school nudged his mind into thinking about his family.

"Irfan, tell me, I bet you're missing your family back home just as much as I am, aren't you?"

Sidling up to the chain-link fence, Irfan considered the question, adopted a wistfully distant look, and turned to gaze at the shimmering water about half a kilometer beyond the fence, before replying bravely, "Sikander, I...I only have Usman, who's here with me. My father, mother, two brothers and sister were killed in a helicopter attack in 1982." Long resigned to such a tragedy, Irfan smiled weakly in acknowledgment of his powerlessness over a fate that had thus chosen to shape his young character.

Sikander's train of thought dissolved into a train wreck. "Irfan! Oh I...I'm so sorry." He realized the indelicacy inherent in any casual reference to family with a fellow mujahid. How could he have been so insensitive to the probability of lost loved ones among the mujahideen, after so many years of war? Sikander apologized as he embraced the realization of why indeed they were in this place learning what they were learning.

The volleyball net was erected inside the main hangar where most full group briefings normally took place. It was a helpful release to be able to play, and before long the visitors had mastered the rules and, more importantly, the game. Two teams were established, each consisting of six men, and as three of the mujahideen were not interested in playing, the numbers worked out.

Saleem, Sikander, Abdul Rahman, Irfan, Usman, and Ahmed formed the first team and Fareed, Ghulam, Akhter, Dilawar, Shahid, and Hamza Ali made up the second. The rest of the men watched and cheered, mostly for the second team. Irfan and Sikander turned out to be the strongest players in the whole group and before long were forced to play on opposite sides despite their clear enjoyment from being able to trounce the opposing team when on the same side.

With playtime over, lesson two of the Stinger training commenced, directing their focus on successful operating procedures. This lesson was easily the more hands-on so far. It involved physically working with practice missile launchers and missile rounds with special reference to the numerous precautions and safety features that the Stinger incorporated without which it would either not operate, or be lethal to the wrong people.

As the process of lesson two continued for two more weeks, the bond between Sikander, Saleem, and Abdul Rahman grew stronger as did their collective attachment to Irfan, Usman, and Ahmed Ghani, who

was an extremely quiet and shy individual. However, between Sikander and Irfan, a special friendship had begun to take shape and flourish.

At first, the members of group three from Laghar Juy were inclined to blame each other for any shortcomings, especially as the group couldn't progress to the next learning activity until everyone scored above seventy percent on the prevailing activity. Although Saleem had been the top scorer for lesson one, Sikander edged ahead of him throughout most of lesson two, though Saleem in turn was significantly ahead of Abdul Rahman. Eventually they grew to understand that taking responsibility meant collectively accepting the blame for a failure as much as the credit for a success. They also learned how to act reliably and instinctively through the surprisingly many steps needed to ready a weapon or reload a missile round and fire it accurately for an effective hit.

Nowhere was the need for teamwork more demanding than in setting up for recognizing, interrogating, and aiming at a target. Using a Stinger was a two-person task and the groups were composed so that the three different available pairings could all work in each of the roles. In the case of group three, the strongest pairing turned out to be the one with Sikander and Saleem followed by Sikander and Abdul Rahman.

At last, lesson two drew to a close at three and a half weeks into their training. Once again, the mujahideen were reassembled into the hangar and Captain Laing began a presentation about what awaited them.

"Fellow mujahideen, we've now been here for over three weeks and you've trained long and hard, in classrooms and with your practice equipment. You've learned how to work reliably and quickly. That's going to be your situation when you need to use these weapons in earnest facing the real foe. Now comes the last step, which is to fire the actual weapon. We're going to ask the top two scoring pairs from each of the five groups to fire a live missile. To do this we'll take you by helicopter into the mountains to the southeast of this camp where a firing range has been set up. Here are the firing pairs."

Laing proceeded to call out their names and when he reached group three, he pronounced, "Group Three, pair one—Saleem Khan and Sikander Khan, pair two—Sikander Khan and Abdul Rahman Khan—" After all pairs had been thus named, Laing concluded the firing roster announcement.

Sikander was to be in two live firing sessions and was thrilled. He tried to keep his demeanor to a dignified modesty but wasn't helped by warm congratulations from both Abdul Rahman and Saleem.

With the briefing about the firing range complete, Captain Laing went on to describe the procedure in more detail but finished his description with something of a surprise.

"Everyone, I know you've now spent almost a month inside this camp and you must be feeling, well, like prisoners!" He emitted a nervous chuckle. "It isn't our intention to treat you that way, and we know you understand the requirements for secrecy and security. However, we've obtained permission to take you on a bus tour of these remarkably beautiful islands tomorrow. This is an excellent time of year to appreciate the scenery. We'll be taking our food with us from the camp and won't be stopping in any kind of shop or village community. Also, to keep your identities as mujahideen undercover, we're going to ask you to wear British Army uniforms so that anyone who might look into the bus will not notice anything...um...extraordinary. Now, we know that most of you have long beards, which are generally longer than we give permission for in Her Majesty's armed forces. We're therefore asking you to...well, trim your beards. Not to shave them off, mind you. Just to keep them to...a few inches. We've inquired of religious experts in Sunni Islam and have been told that this is acceptable. If any of you still feel you don't wish to do this, then I'm afraid you'll be required to remain in the camp and we'll understand and respect your wishes."

Simon translated with his own independent hesitancy mimicking that of Laing. Sikander had learned by now how Simon was more than simply a speaker of Pashto. He was really the unit's cultural officer who had familiarized himself with many detailed nuances of Pashtun and Muslim life. He had sensitized his captain on the question of the beards and strongly argued to have the road trip. Even so, as Simon was translating the part about cutting beards, a rumbling began to emerge from the seated mujahideen. Simon was clear at that point that mere translation of Captain Laing's words wasn't going to do the trick. Remarkably, he offered a glimpse of his true grasp of some of the often complex intricacies of Islamic jurisprudence when he began describing many hadiths and the rulings of the eighth-century Imam Abu Hanifa who had declared that there was no harm in trimming of a beard

from the sides while the end had to be at least a fist size in length. Any shorter would admittedly be problematic, but Laing wasn't asking for that. For anyone left with the conviction that any trimming was haraam, they would be allowed to stay in the camp as explained by Captain Laing. Needless to say, many in the room were quite taken aback by Simon's comments and only now were the mujahideen beginning to understand that they were being assisted by truly dedicated and special people.

Those with the problem beards who wanted to take the trip were directed to one of the mujahideen who had volunteered to do the trimming. Twelve of the men emerged as either having taken the decision to trim or who already had beards that were acceptably short.

That evening Andy came over to see his three friends from Laghar Juy and revisited all the preparation necessary to complete the firing range practice successfully and to know how to remain proficient thereafter. Only when he was satisfied that his protégés would do him proud did he leave the cabin, offering a parting acknowledgment of the following day's trip and proclaiming that he was looking forward to it.

The bus arrived at seven o'clock the next morning and twelve "plausibly British" soldiers, with Andy and Simon as chaperones, climbed aboard. With short drapes over each window to hide the immediate context of their present location, the bus departed. The tour was extensive, beginning with a drive north along the coast of the Applecross Peninsula, then southeast over the hills toward Tornapress along the Bealach na Ba or "Pass of the Cattle"—in parts, one of the steepest roads in the UK. It was en-route to Tornapress that Simon and Andy systematically drew back the drapes.

Having reached Tornapress, the bus lumbered along on the main road south leading eventually to Strathcarron and on toward Auchtertyre where they joined the much faster A87 road to get across to the island of Skye from Kyle of Lochalsh. After the crossing, the bus drove past Broadford airfield, which Sikander thought he recognized from the prominent but simple building near one end of the runway—a vague recollection from their initial landing that first night, more than three weeks earlier.

The rest of the trip took them around the edges of Skye keeping on the A87 until reaching the tiny village of Borve. This was the northernmost point of the road and was where they stopped just after

leaving the village, to absorb the views and eat their lunches. The road at this point had become once again a little tighter but prettier as the bus took the western route around the island to rejoin the A87 at the southern end of Loch Sligachan. At this time, the sun was past its zenith and, even though October was almost over, the weather was otherwise spectacular. The mountains to the south of the road rose sharply to their highest point on Skye and presented a beautiful backdrop to the green rolling landscape on the other side of the road.

Whatever he might do with his life, Sikander determined, he would do everything in his power to come back to this heaven on earth, assuming he could ever discover where it was. He tried to memorize some of the place names from the road signs he saw along the route, but they were numerous and not easily pronounced by a young Pathan from Peshawar.

After the day of respite came a flood of energy to resume their training. Immediately after fajr the following morning, the mujahideen were ready for the final test—the live firing of a Stinger. No time was lost to have them airlifted by Chinook all the way over to the mountains southeast of the camp. But for the weather and flora, the terrain was about as perfect a replica of the Afghan hills as could be realized in Scotland.

The layout of the firing range suggested an elaborate planning and setup process. Captain Laing took the official role of the officer in charge, or OIC, and had several people to assist him. There was an officer in charge of safety, a senior non-commissioned officer focused on the range firing, and an ammunition officer to ensure that all the weapons were delivered and stored properly awaiting firing. Five weapons rounds and five additional missile rounds had been delivered, along with five dummy rounds.

The weapons rounds each consisted of the grip stock, IFF antenna, BCU, the aiming sights, and all the connections needed to hook up to an IFF processor, together with the missile itself in its sealed tube. The replacement missile round merely consisted of the missile in a separate sealed tube together with several ancillary consumables, such as fresh BCUs.

Also stationed at this location was the target detail officer who had responsibility for the target launch and control area from which remotely controlled targets were to be flown.

Out at the far end of the range, five firing stations had been prepared, from which the missiles firings would take place—under Andy's coaching in the case of group three. Behind these were five tracking stations whose purpose was to track both targets and missiles and report on performance. Behind them was a tower for the OIC, Captain Laing, and to either side of this arrangement were several auxiliary stations such as for maintenance, firefighting, or medical aid along with their staffs.

Directed to their respective locations according to their groups, Sikander and Abdul Rahman were asked to go to the third one from the left to join Andy who was already waiting for them. The non-firing trainees, which on this occasion included Saleem, were asked to remain in the tracking positions to the rear of the firing positions. This enabled them to practice tracking the same target that was being fired upon by their firing colleagues up ahead. To Sikander and Abdul Rahman's left was Irfan with his younger brother Usman, both eager to demonstrate their new skills. To their right were Shahid and Dilawar, likewise eager.

Based on all their training, the two-man teams each had to acquire, interrogate, recognize, track, and shoot down a radio controlled 1/6th scale target with proper allowances made for scale effects between the model and full scale. A 1/6th scale model doing 30 meters per second at a mean distance of a kilometer, presented the same targeting challenge as a jet fighter six times farther away doing 180 meters per second, or almost 650 kilometers per hour. The exercise further entailed demonstration of proficiency in removing a spent missile tube and readying a fresh missile round for the next firing. The second pair in the team would then make the second firing, again removing their spent tube and readying the weapon for another firing—in that case with the dummy missile round—and the test would be over.

All the grading factors associated with their training tests were applicable on this occasion, which itself was to be separately graded. They would have to show that the gunner could properly shoulder and prepare the device, detect the aircraft at maximum range at the direction of his partner, assume a proper stance, interrogate the aircraft using IFF, interpret the response, determine the class of the aircraft, range the target, activate the weapon, track the target, positively identify the target, recognize indication of infrared acquisition of the target, uncage the guidance gyro, apply super-elevation aiming to compensate for

gravity, apply lead to anticipate the aircraft's direction of motion, fire the weapon, remove the power source, remove the spent tube, and ready the next missile round on the grip stock assembly.

The tests began in earnest with each group going in sequence. Group three's turn arrived and Andy, as the firing coach, called out "Activate!" Sikander slid forward and latched down the safety actuator switch. He instinctively recalled the steps, tracking his target in a sweeping but steady arc and with his left forefinger depressed the uncage switch while his right forefinger hovered over the fire trigger.

Once there was positive confirmation for "Weapons Free!" called out by the firing coach, based on the OIC's clearance, all discretion was in Sikander's aim and his right forefinger. After he acquired his target, he gently but firmly squeezed the trigger. He would now have to keep aiming the weapon for the next few seconds as the launch sequence was initiated.

A cracking sound heralded the sequence as the launch tube's rear cover broke away, resulting from the launch motor's activation, spewing out a small jet blast toward the rear. Hurled forward, the missile immediately shattered the front infrared sensor window and drew out the lanyard, which would become taut and pull away from the rear of the missile when it was nine meters in front of Sikander. The launch motor fell away on cue, and as the lanyard pulled away also, it ignited the combination of the boost rocket and sustainment rocket. Without hesitation, the missile, which had thus far displayed an unimpressive nine meter hop from the launch tube, acquired a new and deadly personality as it sped away accelerating to almost 750 meters per second in the blind, relentless pursuit of its quarry. Almost immediately the boost rocket shut down leaving the missile in "sustained propulsion mode." Within ten seconds the Stinger found its mark and exploded, terminating all evidence of the target's existence, owing to its small absolute size relative to the missile.

Briefly paralyzed by what he had just accomplished, but after only a second, Sikander let out a shriek of delight as the moment's reality surfaced in his consciousness. He sought visual approval from Abdul Rahman who had helped him set up the weapon and acquire the target. Abdul Rahman was likewise visibly delighted as he was well on his way to readying the next round. In the same moment, Sikander's mechanical memory caused the spent missile tube to be removed and

the new round to be latched in place. As soon as this was done, the weapon was set down on the rack to await its next angry moment.

The tests continued largely with the expected levels of performance owing to everyone's high degree of preparation. Most of the actions requiring the trainees' focus were by now second nature based on all the repetitive training effort that had taken place leading up to the range firing. When the firings were finally over, the mujahideen were once again lifted out by Chinook and returned to their camp in Applecross, feeling quite confident in themselves.

The following day was to be the mujahideens' final briefing day and their last in training before returning to Pakistan for their trek back into Afghanistan. As they filed into the hangar for this last full group briefing, Captain Laing, Andy, and Simon as well as the other commissioned and non-commissioned officers formed a line against the front wall of the room. Laing began in his usual briefing style.

"Mujahideen. Yesterday you all demonstrated your proficiency with one of the most advanced and effective weapons systems in the world. Not only have you done so, but also in…most cases,"—he threw a glance in Sikander's direction— "you've done this with little or no formal education and have shown that you can be a well organized, disciplined, and deadly air defense fighting force. The Soviets and DRA are continuing to devastate your homeland and with this weapon system you will finally have your chance at neutralizing their one advantage in this fight so far; their airborne weapons. Together, we've spent the last month getting you familiar with the Stinger, and we've become familiar with each of you. To us, whose true identities must remain secret, you're like members of our family and, I know…" he hesitated as he began to choke a little on his words, "I know that for many of you, this might well be the only family you have now after the losses of this terrible conflict. Tomorrow you'll be leaving us and we will, in all likelihood, never meet again, but we want you to know that we'll never forget you, nor your dedication and commitment. We'll always value the bond that's brought us all together. This bond allows me today to consider you to be brother SAS soldiers and with your permission, for us to be your brother mujahideen! We wish you God speed, fi-amanillah, and farewell."

When the speech was over, Abdul Rahman stood up and shouted "Takbeer!"

In unison came back the chorus of "Allahu Akbar!"

Again he shouted, and again came back the same chorus after which the whole room cheered as each person standing up, greeted and shook the hands of the ones nearest him. When they settled down, Andy stepped onto the stage and gave his own moving statement while informing the mujahideen that at the back of the hangar were their completion certificates for the program. Though it did not have the same meaning as in an advanced and modern army, and most mujahideen would have been hard-pressed even to find a picture frame to mount and display their certificates, they nevertheless picked them up and held them as prized possessions. After the briefing was over, Sikander, Saleem, and Abdul Rahman, with heavy hearts, went to greet Captain Laing, Andy, and Simon. The latter two had been friends of theirs for more than two months now and would be sorely missed.

"Will you be coming back with us to Laghar Juy?"

"Yes, we will, Sikander," said Simon. "But we'll only be making sure that the first batch of Stingers arrive safely into Laghar Juy and then we'll have to move further west near Tora Bora and south to Khost and Kandahar, where we expect to find more mujahideen to recruit and repeat this program at a larger scale. Let's hope that they can match your outstanding skills," he added as he scanned each of their eyes.

The rest of the day was free for the mujahideen, who were no longer referred to as trainees. They were still not granted exit from the camp for security reasons, but they were able to roam it freely and take in their last day of the Applecross air. The fresh October breeze would be imprinted on their memories for the rest of their lives and they all sensed it.

The night came. Most of the men could not sleep in anticipation of the long journey back to Afghanistan. It would be at least five or six days for the return trip since they would be moving much more slowly with their mules packed with Stinger systems. Lying in his lower bunk across from Sikander, Irfan was in a contemplative mood.

"Sikander, are you awake?"

"Hmm?…Yes."

"Do you suppose once we've returned to Afghanistan that we'll…see each other again?"

Sikander thought for a moment and came back with his best speculation. "We might, Irfan. If our people come across to Khost or you come up to Tora Bora or any of the villages in the hills to the south of Laghar Juy, or—" he paused. "But then again, probably not."

"Well," said Irfan, "you know Usman and I are the only family to each other and we're both honored to know the three of you. If, if anything—may Allah forbid—should happen to either of us, I'd like to know that the other could seek you out in Laghar Juy and seek your protection. You know, life isn't very kind to orphans in Afghanistan and—"

"Irfan, you and Usman are our brothers. I myself have been taken in by Brother Abdul Rahman's family and his parents are truly fine people. If you could only meet Brother Abdul Latif and his wife, you'd know how true it is when I say he'll make sure that any of you would be most welcome in his village. Especially after—Allah forbid—something like that."

"Sikander, I'm lucky to have found a friend in you. InshaAllah I won't worry what happens to Usman if...well, you know."

Sikander didn't want to continue the discussion. The topic made him feel awkward and he simply embraced the words of confidence and affection from Irfan in an appropriately courteous manner, excusing himself to get some sleep. Irfan understood. Sikander didn't sleep.

Churning in his mind were Irfan's words. He had yet to get over the effect on him the day he had discovered that a single moment had transformed these two boys' lives and terminated those of so many loved ones around them. That thought soon led to others about his own family back in Hayatabad. Rolling all these thoughts, together with memories of the last two and a half months, around in his mind was more than enough to keep him awake until fajr.

The morning came and after fajr, which was led this time by Abdul Rahman as imam, the mujahideen made ready for their long trip home. They were packing up their few possessions, but most especially their army-issued clothing and boots along with their certificates, when Andy sauntered into the cabin. The SAS had long discovered that reveille served no purpose, as these people were naturally wide awake before sunrise anyway. As he briefly opened the door to enter the cabin, the air outside could be heard being chopped by the twin rotors of their

familiar Chinook. Following Andy's gesture to the visitors to proceed out to the helicopter, they left the cabin reluctantly and for the last time, strolling across the tarmac toward the open ramp door of the helicopter, they filed silently in.

Before stepping inside, Sikander took a last look back at the cabin, the camp, and in the distance by the hangar a solemn looking James Laing who was saluting them. Instinctively, Sikander waved back before turning to face his colleagues already taking their seats. The ramp door was sealed and the giant machine took to the air.

The atmosphere inside was somber, as contrary to the circumstances of their arrival a month earlier, the mujahideen were alert and taking with them all the imagery their eyes were able to absorb, for as long as they possibly could.

Near the horizon, the low bright pink morning sun snuck in under the cloud base, painting the bottoms of the clouds a loud gray-pink while illuminating the emerald landscape below. It cast long, sharp, edge-defining shadows from every bush, tree, and dry stone wall while here and there, like the occasional stray gray brushstroke, the morning mist appeared to smudge the painting beneath. As if to entice them not leave, nature had organized one last spectacular gesture of farewell from Applecross to its most recent exotic guests. To many of the men, having missed it for so long in their own lives, this was what peace looked like. It was seductive.

Still, Andy and Simon and their counterparts from the other trainee groups were on board, and that was some consolation. The helicopter continued to climb.

It was already one o'clock in the afternoon when the PAF C130 touched down in Sargodha. Of all the moments that would be difficult, everyone knew that this would be prominent among them. Sargodha was where each of the mujahideen would bid farewell to their recently formed friends, going their separate ways across the rugged landscape back to their respective provinces in Afghanistan. After the aircraft landed and came to rest, the cargo door opened and the mujahideen disembarked holding on to their turbans as the massive turboprops were still running. They filed into a dispatch building as was being gestured for them to do and once inside, many traditional hugs were exchanged

along with promises of remaining in touch, which everyone knew would be impossible to keep.

"Time to go," said Andy to his team, and his four companions took his lead to depart the building and be on their way. As they came out onto the parking lot outside the dispatch building, like an old but loyal dog, their familiar dirty Pajero was the first thing to greet them. Standing beside it and grinning was the second—Junaid. Seeing his friends, he greeted them warmly while, in a business-like fashion, he urged them to hop aboard for the trip back to Jamrud. Once they were on the road and leaving the airfield behind them, Junaid turned his head, keeping one eye on the road, and asked the most obvious of questions.

"Well? How'd it go?" Before anyone else could speak, Andy jumped in. He didn't want Junaid to be compromised with too much information. While Junaid was familiar with the overall parameters of the men receiving Stinger training in Europe, he had no specifics on the location and Andy wanted to keep it that way. Indeed Junaid didn't even know, at least not yet, that Aamir and Yassir were in fact Andy and Simon.

"It went very well. Very well."

"Well, that's good. Because the Russians are hammering away at our mujahideen and we have to do something quickly. I'm pleased that the Americans are stepping up their weapons supply. Really pleased!"

Idle chitchatting about other aspects of the support operation ensued with most of the travelers napping in the vehicle from time to time given the long flight and the short night they had just experienced. The plan was for Junaid to take them to Jamrud, leaving them at Arif's place.

By nightfall, he did just that.

Chapter 7

Stinger

THE MUJAHIDEEN GROUP had to wait an extra two days in Jamrud for the arrival of their first battery of Stingers. The shipment arrived. Enclosed in green painted aluminum containers were eight weapon rounds combining missile and grip stock assembly. Four replacement missile rounds, each containing just a missile in its tube together with three BCUs, came packed in thin plywood containers. There was thus a total of twelve distinct firing opportunities. A set of two proficiency practice systems were also in the shipment. The missiles had been flown into Peshawar and trucked over to Arif's place where all five of the men were staying. As before, Sikander managed to dispatch a message to his family but was crestfallen to learn he would be unable to hear back from them as the lines were temporarily down in Jamrud, leaving Arif's phone out of action. Time was simply not available to wait around indefinitely until phone lines were operational again. They had to return to Laghar Juy.

No Pajero this time, thought Sikander—a thought made meaningful by every bump and hollow seemingly amplified as the ten-ton troop carrier, doubling in this case as transportation for both the missiles and the travelers, wound its way up the Khyber Pass, leaving it for the familiar house where they would be transferring to the mules. Another night's stay at that place and they readied the eight mules to ferry everything back to Laghar Juy.

Sikander was delighted to discover that Kala and Neela were both among them and he staked his claim on Neela before anyone else. She had been a dependable and skilled animal on his first trip and Sikander was half convinced she recognized him when she took a couple of steps in his direction as if also to be laying claim on him.

Trekking over the mountains was much more arduous on this occasion. Although the missiles were not heavy, their elongated cases presented challenges. Each mule could handle one on each side, and like splints attending a broken limb, strapped lengthwise, they greatly limited the mules' ability to bend their torsos to the left or right. This was important for making the numerous turns up and down the switchbacks in the hills. On several occasions, the mules lost their footing and struggled to remain on all fours, but the more they traveled, the more impressed Sikander became with their hardiness, intelligence, and above all else, loyalty.

The loss of two days in Jamrud fueled the urgency of their need to return to Afghanistan, so with the moon in its full phase, they continued until well after dark before resting. As Sikander crossed the mountains with his companions, this time with significantly more confidence than on the first occasion, he couldn't help recalling how different from Laghar Juy his experiences of the past four weeks had been. A yawning gulf stood between the realities he had been exposed to in less than half a year. His mind constantly revisited his rapidly accumulating recent memories as if to make sure that none of them would somehow fall off the edges of his consciousness like the contents of some ill-managed, overcrowded desktop. He thought of Peshawar and Dubai and spending the nights in the Khyber Mountains, and the beautiful hills and water of Scotland where they had trained at a place whose name he didn't yet even know.

Sikander realized at that moment that all these memories weren't simply experiences to be stored and retrieved by his separate persona. Rather, they were part of the landscape of his very being, shaping who and what he was becoming. As he gazed up at the crystalline moon and stars that night he felt extremely small, but with the cargo and the skills they were taking back into Afghanistan, he did not feel insignificant.

Upon returning to Laghar Juy, the men were welcomed with excitement and relief after such a long absence. Among the welcoming

villagers, only Abdul Majeed and Abdul Latif had any idea of what was in the oddly long containers strapped to the sides of each mule.

A day after arriving at Laghar Juy, the moment finally came for "Aamir" and "Yassir" to leave for Tora Bora, Khost, and Qandahar, moving on to continue their task of recruiting more weapons trainees. For Sikander, Abdul Rahman, and Saleem, it was not really feasible to display to the rest of the villagers the strength of the bond of friendship that had now been formed with the SAS officers, so the three of them, together with Abdul Latif, Abdul Majeed, and Ejaz, offered to escort the two men up the slopes until they were effectively out of sight of the village. At this point the parting would truly be in a manner more in keeping with their friendship.

"You know," said Andy remaining in the character of Aamir, "you three were in the first group of Haqqani's men that we put through that program and you came through it better than Hekmatyar's men did! Frankly, you surprised our people back in the training camp and they're all now trying to see how to make it tougher for the next lot!" he joked.

Andy was careful not to elaborate on any location names or give away more than necessary. "In any case, we're both really proud of how you handled yourselves, and we...we wanted you to have these." He pulled out a pouch from inside one of the wrapped up bundles strapped to the side of his mule and presented Abdul Rahman, Sikander, and Saleem each with a British Army standard issue Cabot Watch Company automatic wristwatch, explaining to them that this was what full-fledged British Army soldiers were issued. "You've earned them, fellahs!" he said while neglecting to remain in Pashto, then glancing across at Sikander, he winked, becoming slightly embarrassed by the moment.

Ejaz looked puzzled at the unintelligible words he'd just heard and when his eyes met Saleem's, the latter briefly closed his eyelids, smiled, and allowed a reassuring nod to convey that an explanation would be forthcoming soon.

Simon cut in, "We'd like to believe we're professionals who focus on the mission and follow orders, but you know, we do care about what you're trying to accomplish here. We're going to remember you and the other mujahideen, and the uh, time we shared with you." Simon paused. "Anyhow, Allah Hafiz! God will be with you in your struggle against those murderous killers occupying your country, and

don't forget now—" he drew in a little closer to Abdul Rahman and with a friendly prodding on the chest, drove home the point while lowering his voice, "in a few months we'd like to be reading the newspapers about how the Russians were driven out of Afghanist—"

Simon couldn't continue without letting his voice waver. He gave up and simply repeated "Allah Hafiz!" before turning around and walking up the slopes with Andy and their two mules.

Abdul Latif, Ejaz, and Abdul Majeed looked on as their investment in this relationship had clearly not matched those of the other three, but they too were moved to see the sadness on all sides. Andy and Simon trekked up the hills into the distance and the six escorts turned around to return to the village with Sikander, Abdul Rahman, and Saleem lost in wistful reflection, comparing their identical gifts with each other. Ejaz sidled up alongside Saleem.

"Saleem, what was that?" he asked, casting a tone of curiosity over a layer of complaint in the way that normally follows the discovery of knowledge hitherto benevolently concealed by a friend. His eyes darted between the other two returnees looking for a revelation of some sort. "Saleem?" he pressed.

"Aamir and Yassir aren't who they appear to be," responded a giddy Saleem.

"Oh? Who were they?"

"They were British military officers, Ejaz, and they are very good at what they do."

"English, you mean?" asked Ejaz, feeling like he wasn't getting very far with his brother.

"That's right," replied Saleem. "Imagine our surprise when we first learned of this as we traveled with them."

Abdul Rahman, Sikander, and Abdul Latif exchanged knowing glances at that point, though the latter put on a less than convincing show. The troop proceeded down into the village with Ejaz finally getting the explanation he was looking for. He felt slightly envious at what he'd missed, but mostly he was pleased that his brother had made it back together with his cousin and Sikander. Ejaz was more than a little sensitive after his father's failure to return from Zhawar.

October drew to a close so those fields that were designated for the purpose had to be planted with poppy and that year, with the damage created by the earlier bombing and the loss of grain seed, the villagers had to adapt by dedicating more land to opium. The crop was, after all, extremely hardy and could easily survive in weedy and rough soils. Besides, November was about as late as the seed could be planted reliably, so although their sensibilities understood something of the negative effects of addiction to the refined heroin that came from their opium, the villagers gave it little thought, seeing it as a necessary cash crop.

November rolled into December and life in Laghar Juy was mostly calm, punctuated occasionally by the distant sounds of fighting. The Soviets and the DRA were clearly not interested in trying to invade and hold territory in the rural areas, preferring to hold the larger cities and the main routes between them. Yet that did not stop them from going out and attacking villages where their own reconnaissance had shown mujahideen resistance building up or in reprisals against whichever village their own intelligence suggested was responsible for the most recent ambushes. Likewise, the mujahideen maintained a close watch on arms or troop buildups—which were by nature concentrated at a few locations in and around Jalalabad—and would typically try to ambush them when the opportunity presented itself during a force movement. With winter closing in, there was a lull in the fighting and Abdul Latif used this brief time of peace both to continue rebuilding in the village as well as to train his villagers to be more effective in tactics and the use of weapons.

Sikander began to grow increasingly proficient with his AK-47 and was outshooting Abdul Majeed—the acknowledged marksman of the family—about half the time. He finally grasped some of the more nuanced behaviors of his weapon, which he had retrieved along with the others back in Jamrud before returning to Laghar Juy. It had a slight tendency to pull to the left for which he was able to compensate while he had also mastered the super-elevation requirement to compensate for gravity, but he was still working on leading with his aim on moving targets. As he practiced, he was joined on occasion by the "brothers," whereupon the activity would shift to practicing the procedures for a Stinger attack, though of course with only the training hardware. They had been given specific instructions about practicing to keep proficiency and they enjoyed doing this to demonstrate to the others,

including Abdul Latif, Ejaz, and Abdul Majeed, the skills that they'd mastered.

The women of the extended family busied themselves with slow but steady progress preparing for the wedding. Everyone agreed to postpone the date until May. There was too much effort required to make up for the last attacks on their fields and besides, Hinna's family was slipping behind in its preparations, so a delay was a welcome relief. Due to the fact that Rabia was the only girl available of supposedly similar build to that of Hinna, she was easy prey for modeling the new clothes now being made for the bride. Ejaz was also called upon to model those being made for him and he enjoyed critiquing both, always in hood humor, but often to the annoyance of his mother and aunt.

More than once, Sikander happened to be present during such modeling exercises and had to be discreet in his own reactions to Rabia as an emerging young woman whom he had to admit he was growing more and more fond of. This fact was not lost on the keenly observant Razya, who was routinely at Noor's place, working with Noor on the sewing, and for now, at least, she remained simply that—observant.

To an Afghan woman of Razya's age in particular, it was a major achievement to have arranged a match between a young eligible boy and girl, adding significantly to her prestige. To some extent, Razya had been disappointed at having been robbed by circumstance of that possibility for Ejaz, for whom, being his aunt, it would have been perfectly appropriate to have arranged the match.

It was December 13th when a man from Anarbagh village came hastily by horse to Laghar Juy. He sought out Abdul Latif bringing news for him from Jalalabad. It was Tahir Ali Khan whom Abdul Latif knew fairly well.

"Assalaamu 'alaykum, Brother!" greeted Tahir as soon as he reached Abdul Latif who was walking back to his own home from Noor's. Abdul Latif was a caught a little by surprise as he turned to see who had called out to him.

"Wa-alaykum Assalaam! What news, Tahir?"

"The DRA people are readying another attack on this area. They haven't forgotten the pounding you gave them and their Soviet friends in September. They don't think their last attack was an adequate payback.

Knowing you'd probably switch to poppy, they've been waiting for you and now you've planted it, they'll be looking to get their complete badal. Do what you can to prepare yourselves."

It was intriguing for Sikander to note how comprehensively the notion of "badal" in the Pashtunwali code was at work, even inside the Afghan army, and unless a retribution felt equitable, those seeking revenge would be left with the gnawing sense that more should have been done while potentially also having to live down likely ridicule from friends and family.

"I see," noted Abdul Latif, stroking his rusty beard. The stroking stopped and gripping it as if he might in preparation for tearing it off, he asked nervously, "Tahir, do you have any idea when this might be happening?"

"Our best information? Probably three days from now, but that isn't very reliable. It could be tomorrow or if they're watching the weather, they may simply be waiting for the best opportunity."

"What kind of attack force?"

"Their focus will be on the village's fields, especially the poppy. I'd say it'll likely be a helicopter attack. I don't think they have any relish for a close combat engagement. It costs them too many defections," Tahir snickered. "But, Brother Abdul Latif, Anarbagh has a ghundi alliance with Laghar Juy as do other villages in these parts, so let us know if you need us to come."

Defections were a serious matter. If the enemy soldiers from the DRA forces were treated well in captivity or managed to "sell" their weapons in exchange for security and protection, word would spread that such treatment was going on and encourage more widespread defections without unnecessary loss of life. If the defection could be made to stick, it would present more debilitating consequences for the enemy as the transfer would both subtract from their forces and add to the mujahideen—always a much better outcome than a simple enemy loss. In many cases, the only thing preventing defections was the knowledge that the government would retaliate by harming a defecting soldier's family.

Abdul Latif pondered the situation for a moment. Obviously the jirga would need to be informed, but he already had in mind what to do.

"Brother Tahir, JazaakAllah for the information. We'll prepare to evacuate the village by tomorrow evening and post lookouts on high ground to the south. In the meantime, you're welcome to stay with us before heading back to Anarbagh if you'd like."

Tahir accepted the kind offer, based on which, Abdul Latif's house was naturally to be the place of stay. By now it was routine that whenever guests stayed at Abdul Latif's place, Sikander would spend the night with Noor's family, which he didn't mind doing as it was barely fifty meters away. That night was to be no exception, but before he went over, Abdul Latif asked Abdul Rahman and Abdul Majeed to join Sikander, meet with Ejaz and Saleem, and discuss how they would ready themselves for a probable helicopter attack on the fields. It was late afternoon and if the attacks were to be within the next few days, the only people trained to operate the Stinger were the three young men who had just returned, so it would be down to them to devise the appropriate plan and to do so quickly.

The two young men marched across to Noor's home, explaining the situation about Tahir's staying over and Sikander's spending the night at Noor's place. Noor had become used to this routine as much as Sikander and barely raised a remark. They proceeded into the open yard at the back of the house and began discussing their preparations for Stinger usage. All three of them were eager to demonstrate their new skills in more than just the slightly childish make-believe way that proficiency sustainment training had required. Again, they took out the training weapon system for at least two of them to practice how to engage the approaching aircraft, start up the electronics, lock onto the target, and fire.

In spite of their earnestness in proficiency practice, the young men appeared for all the world to Rabia like overgrown schoolboys playing battle with sticks for swords or guns. More than once she secretly looked out through the square opening that was the kitchen's window into the backyard and had to cover her mouth to conceal the occasional irrepressible giggle. Unknown to her, Sikander had noticed but hadn't let on—preserving his own dignity as much as anything else.

Abdul Latif consulted with the jirga to arrange an orderly evacuation procedure that he felt needn't be executed unless the lookouts had a confirmed sighting of the enemy's helicopters. Based on Abdul Rahman's suggestion, from that point forward, the Stinger was to

be carried on its sling strap by both Sikander and himself. The replacement missile rounds would be slung-carried by Saleem, Abdul Majeed, and Ejaz. Meanwhile, the BCUs, including the spares shipped with each package, were to be carried in improvised bags strapped around each of the latter three's waists. This would allow for five firings in short order and though Abdul Latif could hardly imagine the enemy dedicating five helicopters to the attack, even if they had more, the remaining pilots would surely "bug out," he reasoned, if enough of the rest of them were dropping like dead flies out of the sky at the hands of such a new weapon. This meant that given the Stinger's four-kilometer effective range, they could engage as soon as the first helicopter was within two kilometers of the village which would trap the oncoming helicopters in a killing zone from which escape would be all but impossible.

The following day the clouds rolled in and it rained heavily but briefly. It had the beneficial effect of removing virtually all of the haze that had built up over the past few weeks of dry weather, which in turn made the lookouts' jobs easier. It also meant that the helicopters weren't coming just yet.

The day after the rains was both spectacularly sunny and clear, quickly drying out the mud that was everywhere from the previous day. Many villagers had just re-awakened after the usual post-fajr sleep at around half past nine. The lookouts were still at their posts and as the morning shift was just about to take over, there was a shout from one of the upper level lookouts.

"Hinds!" he proclaimed. "Maybe half a dozen! I can't be sure," he shouted. "And they appear to be headed in this direction. I don't see the formation drifting to the left or right. They look to be about fifteen to twenty kilometers away."

It took less than a minute for word to travel back to Abdul Latif's place. "Start the evacuation!" ordered Abdul Latif as soon as the sighting had been confirmed. "Abdul Rahman, Abdul Majeed, get Saleem, Sikander, and Ejaz. After that you know what to do. *Hurry!*" he prodded when he saw everyone scramble out of their dwellings.

The two men ran down to Noor's house, quickly stirred the other three, and the five of them bolted with weapons slung over their backs toward a cluster of mud-brick homes about halfway downhill into the northern part of the village as villagers noisily rushed past them up

the slopes in the opposite direction. Sikander gestured to Abdul Rahman pointing at one of the taller homes with three floors, suggesting they climb to the rooftop. Abdul Rahman nodded in agreement and before long, they had slipped into the house, climbed the steep mud-brick steps, and reached the rooftop.

"Sikander," called out Abdul Rahman, "you and I should stand together here. When both missiles have gone, we'll turn to Ejaz, for you, and Abdul Majeed, for me." Turning to Ejaz and Abdul Majeed, he ordered each of them to prepare ready rounds with Ejaz on Sikander's right and Abdul Majeed on Abdul Rahman's left. Each of the two men had at least practiced preparing rounds in the few days since the other three had returned from training.

"Saleem, you stand in between Sikander and me. You'll need to do lookout duty for both of us. Don't worry, they're helicopters and we'll have the time for you to work with both of us. Sikander, I'll aim at the second helicopter but I'll fire first. The lead pilot won't be able to see any more than the missile trail and it'll surprise him. You take the lead pilot with your missile and then we'll attack whoever comes closest. May Allah remind those haraamzadas of their cowardice when we destroy one of them!"

And their stupidity when we've taken four! prayed Sikander silently.

In reality the Stinger gunner lookout role wasn't required on this occasion, but it offered a reflection of the training that was instinctively drilled into them, which drove Abdul Rahman at this moment. Sikander glimpsed in the man some of Abdul Latif's style as he busied himself preparing for the launch.

Four heavily armed Hinds in line astern formation and one on each flank creating an overall diamond pattern barreled in toward the village, and by now the lead helicopter was a little less than two kilometers away with the next one about fifty meters further back and about five to ten meters lower. The remaining two in the line astern formation were likewise separated both vertically and horizontally. Their approach was such that the entire flight presented some of its left side to them as they were more directly headed to the fields to the right of the men on the rooftop than approaching them in the village.

"Now!" exclaimed Abdul Rahman as he and Sikander shouldered the missiles and screwed in their BCUs, unfolded the antennae, removed the front protective covers from the missile tubes and raised the open sight assemblies on each of their weapons. Abdul Rahman and Sikander started tracking their designated targets. Abdul Rahman pressed his impulse generator switch and immediately the BCU's chemical charge and electrical power sprang into action, bringing online the weapon's IR sensor and guidance electronics together with the guidance gyro. Simultaneously, the BCU's argon gas coolant filled the IR sensor body, rapidly bringing down its temperature. He now had a little less than a minute before the BCU would run out of power and coolant.

For the Stinger missile, targeting a helicopter was among the easier things to do since there was no lead required due to a helicopter's typically slow airspeed and low maneuverability. The missile was, after all, designed to hit fast flying jets and was easily capable of handling a helicopter's evasive maneuvers. It would remain locked on target with little difficulty. All they really needed was for the enemy to come within range. About six seconds into the startup sequence, the IR sensor emitted the tone indicating a lock on the heat signature of Abdul Rahman's target, the second helicopter. In English, he instinctively shouted, "Weapons free!" and pressed the uncage button followed by the firing trigger.

Abdul Majeed looked on in amazement as the rear cover burst open and the blast from the launch motor hurled the Stinger forward through and shattering the IR window. The missile continued for nine meters before the attached lanyard had been completely pulled out of the launch tube, promptly forcing it to disengage from the rear of the missile, initiating the ignition of the rocket's boost-sustain motor. In a long smoke-trailing arcing trajectory, the missile reached out and closed in on the target helicopter. About a second before impact, the missile's internal guidance switched over from its heat seeking infrared to the target adaptive guidance circuit, modifying its trajectory away from the heat source toward the main body of the helicopter. The inevitable impact followed. The missile exploded, destroying the second helicopter and setting off its on-board munitions.

Sikander had already made it past the BCU impulse generator switch, spun up the electronics, and as the first missile exploded, he

pressed the uncage button and the firing trigger. The same launch sequence ensued.

The weapon's deadly contents dutifully pursued the lead helicopter. Its pilot had already banked sharply to the left to steer away from the village fields, but as Abdul Rahman had correctly anticipated this move, they were too far into the killing range of the missiles for any amount of maneuvering to enable an escape from the next salvo. As it banked, the lead helicopter was hit from the rear by Sikander's missile and as before, was destroyed, killing the three-man crew. Flying into debris, the third helicopter sustained some damage from the blast of the one in front, which had suffered at the hands of Abdul Rahman, and its pilot also began banking sharply left to avoid being the next victim.

Abdul Rahman had meanwhile loaded and latched in a third missile round handed to him by Abdul Majeed, while Ejaz passed his round to Sikander to mount and latch on his grip stock assembly. Again Abdul Rahman fired. His missile sped swiftly in an arc to his left and hit the rightmost helicopter in the formation. Its pilot had decided to bank to the right instinctively away from the explosion in the middle of the formation from a few moments earlier.

Sikander was about to hit his impulse generator switch once more, but as it became clear to the Afghan pilots that with a three out of three hit rate, it would be a bad idea for them to take on this new weapon, they abandoned the run at the village. Sikander held off from depressing the impulse switch and unshouldered his weapon, saving the BCU in the process. Conserving these valuable missiles was clearly important and it would be better to wait for the next impending threat than simply to take out yet another helicopter.

As he lowered the weapon, he was overwhelmed by a great sense of accomplishment but also awe—and then terror. The best he could do at that moment was to join in the chorus of "Allahu Akbar! Allahu Akbar!" that had begun emanating from behind him among the villagers below and which was now being uttered by his four companions on the rooftop. Even so, as he shouted the words, he felt strangely detached from the scene. As if outside himself looking at himself, his mind settled on the terrible fact that this time he had now actually killed somebody when just several weeks ago he'd been a Shakespeare-reading student at Peshawar University Public School.

Why that particular comparison was running so vividly through his mind he couldn't say. He couldn't even dedicate the attention needed to pose such a question consciously to himself. Indeed, though unable to articulate it, he had experienced a momentary severance from the human race and where he was right now, in this eerily slow-motion inhumanity, had its antipodes in his most human self-image being that of the student in Peshawar. Consciously, he could only marvel in horror at the comparison itself. This time it wasn't the same as watching his friends attacking in Batawul or being with Abdul Latif improvising with a rocket propelled grenade. This time *he* had pulled the trigger and those few millimeters of index finger movement had changed who he was. Forever.

Something inside Sikander snapped him out of this terrifyingly lucid moment. Perhaps it was, after all, the rousing sounds from the villagers or perhaps simply an inbuilt mechanism to avoid the insanity with which he felt he was flirting. Either way it didn't matter because by now the villagers had surrounded the house and were cheering all five of the young men on the rooftop. He had to join in as they each came carefully back down the steep mud-brick steps to be greeted by their village brethren. They had been saved from attack. At this point, Sikander acknowledged the surreal but cruelly simple transaction.

The villagers and fields had to be saved. The helicopter crews had to die, he thought, in a moment where such logic was all that was available. He began catching up with the scene and felt as if he was re-entering his own body. Just as he was doing so, he caught Abdul Latif standing in the churning crowd like a rock near a seashore. He stood motionless, looking straight at Sikander with a penetratingly meaningful stare, as if by such a stare he could throw out a line to Sikander to say, *I know*; to say, *Now you understand and now you're one of us. Not just a mujahid, but one of that tiny band of all human beings who have ever lived, to have also willfully take another person's life. Know that this is a band you can never leave.*

As if to recognize the young man's need of the moment, Abdul Latif formed a smile as he continued to fix his stare at Sikander, but then the smile assumed more warmth as his eyes' innumerable creases went into action and he shouted out, "Allahu Akbar!" without shifting his piercing gaze from Sikander. Instinctively Sikander was drawn toward

him, as if he might find some reassurance that he had indeed remained human, despite his sense of irreversible transformation.

When he finally approached Abdul Latif, the man grabbed him around the waist, gave him a huge hug, and lifted him off the ground while grinning. He did the same to the others and they to each other. The elation was not simply for the downing of three helicopters, though it certainly merited such celebration. This was for what that day's events represented for the future of the war.

At last, Sikander felt himself experience some semblance of normalcy. When the hubbub had died down and the villagers felt it was safe to return to their own homes, Abdul Latif finally called out to Sikander as he walked alone.

"Sikander!" he hailed, just barely shouting. "Just remember...the second time is always the hardest!" Sikander needed no further clarification, as he knew exactly what Abdul Latif was referring to.

The families converged on Abdul Latif's home and when they neared it, Tahir met up with them. "That was the most amazing thing I've ever seen!" exclaimed Tahir. "Did you see how the missiles just turned? It was...it was like the helicopters were pulling them in...like they were fish on a line being reeled in from a boat."

"Indeed they were," said Abdul Latif. "And, mashAllah, did you see how my boys performed? Alhamdulillah!" he countered. He was proud and impressed at their quick thinking and in particular with Abdul Rahman's tactics which had placed the first attack on a helicopter in the middle of the pack and thereby dispersed the remaining ones to maximize confusion and make them easier to attack. Abdul Latif thought for a moment about what to do next and turned to Tahir.

"Brother Tahir, go now and return to your village. Make sure that everyone hears of what happened and that they too spread the word. It is important to do so that we can lift the spirits of our mujahideen brothers!"

"On this day? I'll be delighted to be the messenger," cried Tahir. He packed up his horse and rode off toward Anarbagh as quickly as he could. News traveled fast in these times anyway and Tahir was anxious not to be trumped.

That evening, Razya invited Noor and her family to come over to dinner. It was something of a celebration of the victory and when the family members arrived, they were welcomed in and asked to sit around the durree that had been spread on the floor for the food.

"This was a remarkable day, Brother Abdul Latif," said Noor. "Those weapons...they behaved as if they were alive, didn't they? Abdus Sami would have been very proud, as I am now, if he had seen what his sons and nephews had done. Rabia and I were amazed. Simply amazed!"

Sikander glanced at Rabia with a newfound confidence in his demeanor. His eyes met hers directly and communicated that no longer could she treat the practice sessions that the young men had engaged in as "childish." Returning the fleeting glance, she almost pouted with a barely perceptible, grudging smile, accepting that his earnestness in training had perhaps been valuable after all, before she cast down her eyes, embarrassed at being so accurately interpreted. In her usual but attractive way, she drew her dupattha forward, shrouding her face with its little greater overhang.

It was too unsafe to abandon the lookouts and Abdul Latif guided the village elders to continue with round-the-clock watches, though he had been so impressed with the performance of these remarkable weapons that he knew the DRA forces and probably the Soviets would be re-evaluating their strategy. The perceived advantages of the helicopter gunships that had for so many years acted with virtual impunity and kept the mujahideen at bay were now in question. Those advantages had thus far allowed the DRA and Soviets to force the mujahideen to dedicate more attention to protecting their loved ones, tending to their wounds, or repairing their fields than to retaliation, but now that the Stinger was available, the tide of the conflict had turned decisively and both sides knew it.

As the winter drew on, the skirmishes did indeed wind down as usual, but the Soviets' newfound caution also informed their decisions. In the relative lull, the mujahideen forces likewise regrouped, determining how best to leverage the new balance of power. Word had arrived from Jalaluddin Haqqani's men and Younus Khalis's larger Hezb-e-Islami Khalis that, all told, the Americans had supplied some three hundred Stingers as well as several of the French anti-tank Milan-2 wire-guided missiles. Better still, the word was that several more were

on their way and the results that Laghar Juy had experienced were being felt more widely around the country as more and more weapons-trained mujahideen were returning to the fight with their knowledge in turn being imparted to their fellow fighters.

As the weather improved, the skirmishes began once again, but with the Stinger response in the air and the even simpler-to-use Milan-2 against tanks on the ground, the Soviet initiatives in 1987 were much more circumscribed than in any year previously. A fragile, implicitly understood peace was in place and it seemed like the ideal time to be getting Ejaz married to Hinna.

By the end of April, all preparations had finally been made for the wedding and the time had come to collect the small wedding party representing the groom and his family to go across to Pakistan into Yaqub's village. The weather had been dry and clear for most of the month so the mountain passes were quite traversable. It would take barely a day and a half to get to the bride's village.

Traveling with the groom were Noor, Saleem, Sikander, and Rabia together with Abdul Latif, Razya, and Abdul Majeed. Abdul Rahman remained behind in the village to take charge and to field at least one competent fighter with air defense if it were needed in the family's absence.

Having modeled all the bridal clothes that had been made for Hinna, Rabia was filled with anticipation to see her sister-in-law to be. Her excitement was infectious. From time to time, she would strike up conversation with Sikander, always, of course, under the watchful eye of either Noor or Razya. As they were leaving the large open plain before entering Yaqub's village, Sikander teased her for being so talkative.

"Tell me, Rabia, why have you suddenly taken to chattering so much?"

Rabia displayed her insulted look, understanding fully that this was only "banter" on Sikander's part.

"Hm? Why not chatter? Must we all pass our lives in the brooding silence that *you* seem to be exhibiting of late?" she countered. Indeed, Sikander had become a little more withdrawn as he himself had still not fully come to terms with killing the helicopter crew a few

months earlier, and although he was not given to brooding, he had become noticeably more pensive.

"Well," said Sikander, "I'm sure when you have your new sister-in-law back home with you, she'll want to be far from you, driven away by your ceaseless conversation!"

"Sikannnnder!" said Noor. "Please stop teasing Rabia. She's naturally excited by the wedding and looking forward to meeting Hinna," she declared before muttering, "as am I," then looked askance at Abdul Latif and Ejaz, each of whom pretended not to notice her or her acerbic remark. Rabia meanwhile had the studied appearance of indignation and was more than happy to have her mother defend her against Sikander.

"Rabia," offered Sikander wearily, "do please continue."

"Yes," she remarked, with her annoying tone of victory, "well, I was going to talk about these beautiful mountains of ours and ask you how they compare with the ones in Scotland where you trained to use those missiles, but it doesn't matter now." Rabia feigned yet more injury to her dignity and this time more than anyone could accept, including her mother.

"Rabia," chided Noor, "if you must continue with that tone, then you might as well indeed be quiet and let us all get a moment of peace on this trip."

Sikander began to feel prompted to assist quickly and throw out a line to Rabia. "No, no, it's alright" he intervened heroically. "Actually, I don't mind answering that. Rabia, the way I see it, each place...each thing...has its own beauty and there isn't a single kind."

"Hmm...I suppose that sounds like it might be true, Sikander, but what exactly does it mean?"

"Look, there's no doubt that the mountains of Afghanistan and Pakistan are glorious. They...they're magnificent. But what I found in Scotland was a less intense yet somehow more appealing beauty."

"Less intense...and more beautiful?" Rabia sounded puzzled.

"Well I...I suppose I can't really say how. Perhaps it's just the tranquility of people being peaceful and not at war that was affecting the way I saw it."

Sikander realized as he said it, the probable truth of what he had just uttered. Being at war had truly taken something out of the otherwise beautiful places they were traversing at this time. If beauty was indeed in the eye of the beholder as he recalled Mr. Aftab recounting, then these beholders, himself included, could not truly see what was there, while struggling to have the eyes that a country at peace might have offered them.

Seeing his contemplative expression, Rabia decided simply to close the subject with "Hmm," and to ride along for a few more minutes before opening up again.

The marriage entourage finally arrived at the village that Hinna had until now called home and were received with all due ceremony. Customarily, they were put up in a home other than the bride's and the celebrations began. Gifts, primarily of clothing with a little jewelry, were exchanged. Hinna was decorated on her hands and feet with beautiful henna dye patterns amid singing and attans.

The following day the ceremony took place. Hinna was adorned in the bridal outfit of a creamy white lehenga and bodice each embroidered heavily with rich floral patterns of sequins and gold threads. Razya and Noor had busied themselves the night before making final adjustments to reflect the small differences between Rabia and Hinna.

Gazing upon Hinna, Rabia felt a stirring. Decked out in the bridal outfit, she was naturally a beautiful young lady. *Hinna's plainly doing it more justice*, thought Rabia while she couldn't help thinking about a time in the future when such an experience might befall herself.

The qazi was brought in to conduct the wedding, asking first the bride three times for her acceptance of the groom and the amount of the mehr, and signing on papers, with two witnesses, one representing the groom and the other her "advocate," in this case Yaqub, both present. The qazi then marched the same witnesses over to a separate room where the groom, also decked out in his wedding garb, was asked for his acceptance of the bride and his obligation of the fifty thousand rupee mehr, also three times. All were relieved when the groom completed his acceptances and made his mark upon the appropriate papers.

The qazi declared the nikah to be complete and offered a du'a in which the wedding guests also participated. With the official

ceremony being thus concluded, the rest of the day was left to more singing, attans, and food. Sikander's take on the celebrations, which were like nothing he had experienced even in traditional Pakistani weddings, was actually more focused on the oddly incongruent merriment set against the war and destruction that was taking place in these times. Such a sentiment made him feel more respect for a people willing to defy their circumstances in this way, daring to enjoy themselves and the occasion.

Everyone stayed in the village for two days. On the third day it was time to take the new bride to her permanent home and family in Laghar Juy. Tearful parting salaams took place. Hinna leaned and cried on Shahnaz's shoulder, then Yaqub's and junior mother Yasmeen's. She finally hugged Aurangzeb, Nadeem, and Sohail and was taken to where the groom's entourage was waiting to set off for Laghar Juy. The lull in fighting these days meant that the journey back was uneventful.

Upon arrival, the groom's extended family and local guests were invited to participate in the second half of the ceremony, the walimah, which though normally was the responsibility of the groom's family, on this occasion with Noor being a widow most of the arrangements were left to Abdul Latif and Razya to organize.

Noor enjoyed having another young woman about the house and at now a quite mature nineteen, Hinna was better than ideal. Sikander also imagined getting to know Hinna a little better and hoped for her to shoulder some of the burden of meeting Rabia's insatiable intellectual and conversational appetites.

Chapter 8
Arghandab

I N THE SOUTH OF AFGHANISTAN the mujahideen had already established well-fortified positions up and down the Arghandab Valley to the west of Qandahar. From time to time they sought opportunities to mount an offensive to capture the city. Early in 1987, they had finally made a push, first by striking at Soviet and Afghan State Security Ministry positions as a diversion, then going after other outposts defended by government-friendly lashkars. Three of these militias were the Jowzjani Uzbeks under General Abdul Rashid Dostum, Meri Baluchis' Baluch militia, and the Achakzai militia under Esmatullah Muslim. Although the city didn't fall in the attack, all three suffered at the hands of the mujahideen.

It had been no ordinary skirmish and worried the government immensely. Removal of the mujahideen from Arghandab, partly for the strategic threat to supply lines between Qandahar and Herat, and partly because of the desire for the ever-demanded badal, had now become a priority.

By early April, the mujahideen militias were also aware of preparations for retaliation for the earlier attack and were bracing for it. They began sending out requests for reinforcements. Among those asked was the inimitable Jalaluddin Haqqani.

It was the middle of the Ramadhan month of fasting in May of 1987 that Jalaluddin returned once again to Laghar Juy. The village was

by that time well supplied with fresh stocks of Stingers and Milan-2s. Haqqani brought word to Abdul Latif that Younus Khalis had been working with other mujahideen militia to send help in support of the defense of Arghandab as the government counter-offensive appeared increasingly likely. He usually visited Abdul Latif on matters such as this and the Qandahar campaign was an important one to discuss.

"Brother Abdul Latif, the new situation with the weapons that the Americans have, by the grace of Allah, sent to us is helping us to move the war to a new level. We don't need simply to be engaging in skirmishes or village defense. We've received word that Mullah Naqib of Jamiat-e-Islami and Abdul Latif, the...uh...the one who leads the National Islamic Front of Afghanistan, have their militias in the Qandahar area. Younus Khalis also has Lala Malang and his men in the same area, and we keep learning from deserters that a large attack is being prepared against us by the government forces, so he's asking me to supply more people to Lala Malang."

"Yes," said Abdul Latif, "I'd heard that Qandahar was becoming a priority. So what do you have in mind, Brother Jalal?"

"Well, as I'm being asked to send people to support Lala Malang, mashAllah, I can think of few better than you to lead one of the groups from here and a few of the other villages surrounding here."

"Brother Jalal, I'm ready to go if that's your direction," said Abdul Latif. "However, Qandahar is far from here and we'd be wise to leave our weapons stocks together with a defensive contingent in the villages. We could go back over the mountains to Peshawar to obtain fresh weapons from the ISI, which we can transport by truck down to Quetta. From there we can re-enter Afghanistan near Spin Boldak and come into Qandahar from any direction that the situation might dictate."

"Agreed. My contacts in the ISI won't have a problem furnishing fresh weapons as they're now coming in pretty large quantities. They should also be able to transport our people down to Quetta while they can have the weapons delivered into the local PAF base. The details will be worked out but please prepare to get the men together, Abdul Latif. How many do you think you can assemble?"

"I'd imagine about thirty or so. People have become a little more confident with the new weapons and we might be able to increase that number."

"How long will you need to get going?"

"I think perhaps three or four days, but give me five and whatever I can put together I will. What about mules?"

"Yes…we can arrange for more to be brought in from Tora Bora; we now have a fairly good stock. How many do you need?"

"I would say thirty right here, which can be distributed to the outlying villages. We'll group together at Takhto Kalay to cross into Pakistan. We could ride them with light provisions if we're to be supplied out of Quetta with our main weapons. That'll make the most sense."

"Very well, Abdul Latif. It's settled," said Jalaluddin. "I'll make my own appeals in the local villages and ask those people to get word to you about where to meet for the crossing to Peshawar and a few other details. Meanwhile I'll also start to coordinate things with the ISI people. InshaAllah, this year could be very decisive!"

With his business concluded, Jalaluddin bid salaam to Abdul Latif, hastily leaving Laghar Juy to do as he had promised. That same night after breaking fast at iftar and performing isha, Abdul Latif asked his sons and Saleem to make the appeal for six or seven other mujahideen to go out to trusted people in the nearby villages, organize multiple bands to gather up at Takhto Kalay, and wait for Abdul Latif and his band, which would be the last to arrive. From there they would proceed to the safe house near the Torkhum Road before being driven across to Jamrud at Arif's place. The ISI would bring a large troop transport and take them to Quetta while air-ferrying a large stock of Stingers and Milans to meet them there.

Each village was to leave a contingent of two Stinger-equipped and trained men if at all possible. If not, they would need to post lookouts and create an evacuation plan in case of attack. Ejaz was allowed to remain in Laghar Juy while all this was going on, as he was a newlywed. However, as each man had to perform his duty and Ejaz had missed out on the Stinger training, he very much wanted to take part in the upcoming Arghandab campaign. Abdul Latif had no disagreement. The same could not be assumed for Hinna, at least not until she was

sold on the idea. Ejaz's mission, while his brother was out persuading other men to join them, was to remain in the bedroom persuading his new bride.

"Hinna?" began Ejaz. "Hinna, we're married and…and I know we barely know each other, but do you know, from the minute I first saw you bring in the food in your father's home, you had my heart pounding, and I felt this…this strange pain when you left the room. It was a beautiful, sweet pain. I couldn't let the moment pass without doing anything. Huh! You cost me that night's sleep! Allah be praised for my uncle. The following morning we were engaged. Hinna, I know it hasn't been long, but truly, I…I don't have the words to tell you what you mean to—"

Hinna gently placed her fingers over Ejaz's mouth. "Ejaz, my love," she interrupted as she lowered her hand again, "I was just silly, and shy, at the time I first met you. Hm! I was thinking how amusing it was to be asked to serve the dinner. But you know, when I saw you again after I learned of the proposal, something went through me too. I felt myself changing inside and I…I too was feeling the way you mention. And *I* couldn't tell anyone."

Ejaz nodded, continuing his woefully rambling attempt to break the news to her of his likely absence. "So Hinna, it's difficult to imagine being away from you for even a minute or two. But you know the realities of these times and you know we're routinely being asked to fight for what we believe in. Hinna, I need to go with Uncle Abdul Latif to Qandahar. We…we're winning this fight and our forces outside Qandahar are facing a critical—a really critical—threat from the Russians and the Afghan army. We have to go down there to help them and maybe win this whole war. Gorbachev has already committed the Russians to pulling out. This will force them to be serio—"

"You mean…you'll be leaving me? Here?" interjected Hinna, sounding more disappointed than angry. Ejaz hung his head low and nodded, avoiding her gaze. Hinna's love for Ejaz continued to grow with her discovery of him. It was the kind of love that lacked all confusion. His own struggle to break the news to her was a palpable but pale measure of his love for her. His eyes found the courage to re-engage with hers and she lowered her head to one side while looking on at her husband with a fascinated curiosity, but above all else, pure and simple love. She frowned warmly. The frown quickly turned into a

friendly pout, dissolving any remaining resistance Ejaz might have had. If she wasn't convinced by now, his mission was doomed.

"Ejaz, I...I know how hard this must be for you. You don't need my permission," she offered wistfully. "Certainly not if you believe you do. Go. By the grace of Allah, go and come back by his grace safe, well, and with a victory—but right now, come. Come closer and hold me in those strong arms of yours, will you?"

Ejaz obeyed, and as she laid her head against his chest, she cried a solitary tear. His eyes found hers once more. Seeing the wetness in them, he kissed her lips softly in the knowledge that his mission had been accomplished. She responded in kind, but with the full measure of her loving spirit as the two of them melted slowly onto their bed.

Saleem, Abdul Rahman, and Abdul Majeed went out and spread the word among their contacts while Sikander stayed behind with Abdul Latif and Razya. After four days, the task of gathering up mujahideen was complete and each small band made its way discreetly out of its own village toward Takhto Kalay.

At last, the time came for Abdul Latif, Abdul Majeed, Ejaz, and Sikander to bid their farewells to their women and leave Abdul Rahman and Saleem with them in the village, much to the disappointment of the two cousins. However, they were a proven team with the Stingers and could not be spared for this new expedition. Hinna, for all her seeming fortitude at the moment of learning about the mission and Ejaz's impending absence, finally broke down and cried quietly but uncontrollably as the men began to leave. Standing between Noor to her left and Rabia, she instinctively leaned on Noor's right shoulder as she took her own right arm and wrapped it firmly around Rabia. The three of them blended into an almost single melancholy being while Razya was left next to Abdul Rahman and Saleem standing more stoically firm, but whispering prayer upon prayer for the safe return of the men.

Abdul Latif and his companions disappeared into the distance and up the slopes to the southeast of Laghar Juy until they were eventually lost among the rocks and boulders comprising the backdrop at the feet of the imposing Spin Ghar.

After reaching Takhto, they were met by thirty-three mujahideen who had gathered there as planned. They spent the night in different

places with Abdul Latif and his immediate family bunking up with Azam's family. Over the following four days, in bands of eight or so at a time, they made their way across the mountains and back to the Torkhum Road outside Peshawar. The mules were returned to Takhto by other mujahideen who were still ferrying weapons into Afghanistan and this relay process went on until all the men made it into Pakistan. Each day, as each band of eight arrived, they would be taken to Arif's place, rested, and if not fasting then fed and driven across to Peshawar's PAF base where they were housed in barracks designated for the ISI.

By the fourth day, Abdul Latif himself took his own band across and as usual they were ferried from the Torkhum Road into Jamrud to stay with Arif Saiduddin, who was waiting to welcome them in his customarily ebullient fashion.

"Allahu Akbar! Abdul Latif, welcome friend and welcome to all your boys!"

"Greetings and salaams to you too, Brother Arif!" proclaimed Abdul Latif.

With the greetings suitably out of the way, Arif launched into a description of the plan. "We have a transport coming later today for you. The good news is that we won't be risking a long road trip to Quetta. You're all going to be driven to Peshawar PAF base and Six Squadron will be taking you down. Your weapons will be shipped with you."

"What happens when we get to Quetta?" asked Abdul Latif.

"Actually, you're being flown into the PAF base at Pishin. The Hercules can make it in, especially with less than forty of you. You'll be met by Junaid who's already there and he's arranged for all of you to be staying at Pishin on the base until nightfall."

"Pishin? Is that far from the border?"

"No. Closer than Quetta, actually. At about midnight tonight you'll be trucked down to Yaru Karez and from there the road leads all the way to Chaman at the Afghan border. However, as usual, the truck will navigate you off the road a little before then and you will be put up for the night at several homes in a small village about two kilometers to the northwest of the northern exit of the Khojak railway tunnel."

"Mules?" asked Abdul Latif.

"They'll already be there, but do understand that by then you will have crossed the most difficult of the mountain terrain already, so it should be easier than your trip here, for example. We have friends at that village who will meet you and help. You'll be able to take the mules to carry your weapons going north from the village following the edge of the Toba Kakar Mountains, keeping them to your east. You'll then need to go to the west once you are due north of Chaman. Keep going until you enter Spin Boldak and you will be able to meet up with more mujahideen from there."

"Spin Boldak is under our control?" asked Abdul Latif, feeling that he would probably have known if that were the case as this was an important border town.

"Control? Who can say control these days! But we have strong mujahideen presence and it should be under their control. If I'm right then you'll be able to rest there. If for any reason Spin Boldak looks to be too dangerous, you'll need to keep going west until you enter the Arghandab Valley to the northwest of Qandahar. However, make sure to come around the north side of the Dahla Dam and its lake because the Soviets and DRA have the eastern side of the Arghandab to themselves."

"I see. Anything else, Brother Arif?" asked Abdul Latif.

"No, I think we've covered everything."

Having covered every detail of the plan, Arif glanced at Sikander and with a broad grin asked the one question that Sikander was hoping for: "Would you like to use the telephone? It's working."

"Oh yes...yes, I most certainly would," said Sikander, heaving a sigh as if he'd been holding his breath all this while for just that moment.

"Please—" Arif motioned to the stairs from the basement up to the ground floor passageway leading to his living room, "but do remember, limit your conversation to family matters and do not discuss specifics," he warned.

From the time he had left home all those months earlier, Sikander had begun this journey in his life by being indiscreet. Few people could advise him now, better than he could himself, on how not to make such a mistake again.

He made his way to the living room to make his call. It was four in the afternoon and it was a Friday. He supposed his mother would probably be at home preparing iftar. It was a warm, comforting thought that helped him rehearse the overwhelming number of things he wanted to say to her—most prominent among them that he loved his family, that he now had in a very real sense an understanding of the meaning and value of a family, which his previously sheltered existence had largely denied him. He also thought about the several written messages he had already sent and was concerned to avoid repeating himself as time was precious.

Sikander dialed the number. The call didn't connect. He cursed. Unreliable electromechanical switchgear often caused the telephone system in Pakistan to disappoint. On the fourth attempt, his call connected and the phone rang. Once...twice...

"Hello?" said a female voice. His mother. "Hello?" she said again.

"Ammee...it's me. It's Sikander." He paused as all his rehearsed thoughts flew out of his mind, like birds from an open cage, overwhelmed by the moment.

"Sikander!" said Sofie. "Bettha! Where are you? Are you in Pakistan?" she managed to get at least these questions out before succumbing to her emotions.

"Ammee...Ammee-jan!" said Sikander, trying hard to keep himself together. "Ammee-jan. I'm in Pakistan. I'm alright, but I've been living in Afghanistan and fighting as a mujahid for the past several months. Ammee, the Americans have been helping us and I've been trained. I was trained in Europe on how to use their best weapons. General Zia has committed Pakistan to helping us by—"

"Sikander, are you eating properly? Are you well, bettha? Not sick, are you?" asked his mother as she regained her composure. "Can you...can you come home at this time?" she asked in a somewhat subdued tone, knowing that entreaties would not be effective now.

"Ammee-jan, I...I can't begin to tell you how much I want to see everyone at home. I want to share so much with you all now and I, I promise I'll be back...I promise. But I'm on an important mission. I...I can't leave everyone to come ho—"

"Sikander, we received your notes but had no way to reply," interrupted Sofie once more. "How can we speak more often with you?"

"Ammee, where I stay there aren't any telephones and whenever the chance arises I do try to contact you one way or the other, but no chances have been available for several months now. I wish I were home! I so much want to see everyone. How's Abba-jee? Is he still angry with me?" asked Sikander.

"Who can remain angry for so long, Sikander? At first he was very disappointed. You...you had abandoned him. Then when we started receiving your notes and understood that you are doing what you are doing, he was more at ease. In fact, bettha, speak to him, he just walked into the house. Javed? Javed, please come! Hurry, it's Sikander!" she called out as Javed walked through the door.

Sikander's heart skipped a beat and he wound himself up for a potentially difficult conversation.

"Hello? Abba-jee?" Sikander asked tentatively. There was a moment of silence and then his father picked up the phone.

"Sikander!" said his father. "Bettha...bettha, where are you? Where are you calling from?"

Sikander sensed a subdued tone in his father's voice, which was not at all what he had expected. As if they had formed a huge wall, his defenses—which were ready for any onslaught—instead caved in from the unexpected force in the meekness of his father's tone.

Sikander cried, straining to hold back the bawling sound but revealing nonetheless his own inability to speak. Javed would not be deceived.

"Sikander. Bettha. Don't cry, bettha. It's alright. We're all well here and...I know what you are doing. I was wrong to drive you away like that but you know sometimes Allah will work in his own way, and who are we? Sikander?" he called out Sikander's name but Sikander's silent weeping was still in full flood as he vigorously wiped his face to make way for more.

"Abba-jee, I'm here. I'm here. I do love you. I miss you, Abba. I'm so sorry about leaving the way I did but I...I'm doing something that I'm hoping will make you proud of me." Sikander clung to his coherence by a rapidly weakening thread.

"Bettha," said Javed slowly. "Look, if it's worth anything, I wish I was with you and doing what you're doing. May Allah give you the strength to prevail and come home. I only ask that you keep contacting us and...don't worry about us. Alhamdulillah, we've been getting back on our feet with some good government work at the refugee cam— well...let's just say we're fine."

To Sikander, Javed was a transformed person and it made Sikander reflect upon how transformed he himself might have seemed to his father.

"Abba-jee, I have to go now. I can hear the others calling for me, but please, look after yourself and don't worry about me. I'll call or write again as soon as I can. And oh...Ramadhan Mubarak and Allah Hafiz!"

"Ramadhan Mubarak! Allah Hafiz!" said Javed, hurriedly wiping at a threatening tear.

"Sikander!" came the call from downstairs. It was Arif. "Sikander, please come on down now," he called politely, not wishing to rush the young man.

Sikander took the steps with heavy footfalls. When he walked into the war-room that he'd now seen many times, he sat down among his friends and studied the map that had been the basis of the most recent discussion with Abdul Latif.

Abdul Latif, his sons, nephews, and Sikander managed to get in both zuhr and asr prayers before a small truck appeared outside Arif's house. The men squeezed into it, tucked their lightly packed belongings into the back beneath their legs, and were soon on their way to PAF Peshawar.

When they arrived, they were greeted by the rest of the men they had last seen three days earlier in Takhto Kalay. Once they were together, a man in PAF uniform came into the barracks asking them to gather their belongings and assemble outside in half an hour. He and an assistant also began handing out food packages so that the mujahideen could perform iftar, as the sun would soon be setting.

It wasn't hard to prepare for travel as the men had only their rifles, some ammunition, and a meager sack of personal items each,

including fresh clothing. Being a newlywed, Ejaz had the freshest change of clothes in his sack.

Outside the barracks, the sky darkened as the men were led by the PAF officer who had met them a few minutes earlier and they ambled in two abreast formation up to the gaping rear of the C130. Sikander hadn't remembered the tail number of the aircraft he had used to go to Europe more than six months earlier, but in all other respects this aircraft seemed identical. The benches were in their familiar places along each side of the fuselage, but in the middle was a fixture that was a rack of some sort; in it were several familiar green aluminum Stinger missile cases along with some sixty of the now equally familiar Milan-2 anti-tank weapon cases coupled with six Milan-2 launch post cases.

Sikander felt a little superior at having now been aboard such an aircraft many times and he succumbed to the need to fuss over his fellow travelers, but none more so than Abdul Latif, to show him exactly how to strap in and put on the ear protectors. Abdul Latif looked back at him and observed Sikander in a way that Sikander was all too familiar with. *I know what you're doing*, spoke his eyes.

As the aircraft droned aloft into the evening sky, it reminded Sikander of the trip to Scotland, triggering a brief wave of nostalgia for the company of Abdul Rahman and Saleem. They flew due south for about forty minutes and then made a straight run for Pishin over the next two hours, touching down finally at around eleven in the evening. Long before Pishin's runway 24 was exhausted, the pitch on the four Allison turboprops was hurriedly reversed, arresting the giant bird in short order. When the ramp door opened, the hot dry air of Pishin greeted the travelers as it filled the cargo hold and before long the men were pouring out of the aircraft.

"Assalaamu 'alaykum!" came the familiar voice on the ground. Everyone instinctively gave the customary reply. Abdul Latif had been looking down minding his step as he emerged from the cargo bay when the familiarity of the voice he'd just heard prompted him to lift his eyes.

"Junaid! How are you? You...rascal! I haven't seen you in months."

"Likewise, likewise, Abdul Latif!" Junaid exclaimed as the men hugged each other. Abdul Majeed, Ejaz, and Sikander followed suit. "Sikander, you and your friends up in Laghar Juy have made quite the

name for yourselves. People still speak of the three helicopters that you took down last year."

"Really?" asked Sikander, slightly surprised but genuinely skeptical. "Let's hope we can make a difference in Qandahar."

"It's why we're all here!" declared Junaid cheerily. "Anyhow, we have time to talk on the road as we have a good distance to cover. About fifty kilometers in the dark mountains tonight."

The men piled into two ten-ton troop trucks while some of their weapons were loaded in with them with the remaining weapons packed into a third truck. *This'll need a lot of mules*, thought Sikander.

Once everyone was clear of the aircraft, the convoy trundled down the rough road out of the airfield and headed south to Yaru Karez. The village was little more than a road junction at which they turned right heading northwest toward the mountains and Chaman. The mountain ride was a truly terrifying experience. On more than one occasion the truck made sharp veering maneuvers, and with everyone inside and no visibility except for the occasional moonlit view through the split in the canvas back flaps into the valleys and sheer drops outside, each of these normally fearless warriors, in the cramped space at back of the every truck, was gripped with fear of not knowing what might be the cause of their demise among these mountains that night. Eventually, the trucks came to a rest and by now the men were very drowsy. They hadn't crossed the border but they had crossed the worst of the mountains.

As soon as the engines were silenced, the back flaps opened up and to everyone's immense relief, they were able to step out to stand on firm ground. Heading the group, Junaid called over one of the tribesmen from the village to confirm the mujahideens' arrival and their need for the mules to be prepared. In less than twenty minutes, seven mule teams, each with four mules, were produced and the men began packing them. Meanwhile, the local villagers had already prepared their homes to bunk the travelers for the night.

It was approaching three in the morning when the packing was complete. There were sixteen Stinger weapon rounds and a further eight missile rounds. These were bundled onto twelve of the mules, with one case on each side to maintain balance. Five were used to carry six Milans on each side and one launch post. A further seven to pack up the

men's belongings and ammunition with between four and six mujahideen to a mule. Four more animals were kept in reserve in case of injury. The seven mule teams were organized in bands of four to six mujahideen according to how the corresponding personnel and ammunition packs had been distributed. In that way, each team of mules had at least one personnel pack animal and three weapons pack animals, thus forming a self-contained weapons-equipped team. AK-47s were shoulder carried by the men themselves. After the long journey and with the packing complete, it wasn't hard for the men to sleep that night.

The following day, after the usual duties of eating for suhur followed by the fajr prayer, the men sat together in an open courtyard, partially shaded by one of the mud-brick walls of the house in which Abdul Latif and his troop, together with Junaid, had stayed. All of them were there for one purpose—to discuss their routings into the Arghandab Valley.

"Is it still going to be Spin Boldak?" asked Abdul Latif.

"Too dangerous," noted Junaid shaking his head. We think that the government forces could attack Spin Boldak any time now and if we get bogged down there, we risk failing to arrive in time to help our Arghandab brothers against a DRA attack. Arghandab it is, I'm afraid."

"Well then, we'd better get going. We've no time to lose," responded Abdul Latif.

The plan was now for the mujahideen troop to proceed in small groups at one-hour intervals and fan out with each troop in a slightly different but generally northeasterly direction remaining close to the feet of the Toba Kakar mountains to their right. They would then have to turn west to head through some relatively easy country for a further fifty kilometers until reaching the main Kabul to Qandahar highway. They were to cross it under the cover of darkness, after which they would head toward a point well to the north of the well-guarded Dahla Dam. From there, they would come around past any DRA or Soviet troops that might be there, and once on the eastern side of the valley, southwest of the dam, they would be traveling in friendly country. It would be a simple matter to hike the few kilometers southwest following the west bank of the Arghandab until they arrived at Sokhchala—their rendezvous point with Lala Malang and his forces.

Abdul Latif kept Abdul Majeed, Ejaz, and Sikander with himself and the four of them took the lead team. He also took one spare mule to ride, which would be taken in turns on the long walk. Making a reasonable four kilometers an hour, they arrived at their first rest point in the early evening and after a simple but much needed iftar, they made ready to sleep in the open at the base of the mountains by the banks of a small brook that drained to the west coming out of the mountains. As travelers, the fasting of Ramadhan wasn't obligatory during such times and the men resolved to suspend their fast for the rest of the journey, as dehydration was a real threat.

The night was bearably cool under the clear sky. As they lay there, Sikander, who hadn't said much during the day, was in the mood for talking now and with Ejaz nearest him he simply opened up.

"Ejaz? Ejaz, are you awake?"

"Mmhmm," mumbled a tired Ejaz.

"Ejaz, do you remember when we first met Yaqub and his family?" asked Sikander.

"Uh! Of course...why?" came Ejaz's softly chuckling reply.

"And I don't suppose you remember how—smitten?—you became that night?" asked Sikander. "Hinna had quite the effect on you, didn't she?

"Mmm...you *know* I recall, Sikander," sighed Ejaz. "Why?"

"What was it like exactly, Ejaz? What did you feel?"

"Hmm? Well, I'm not exactly sure how to describe it. I suppose it actually felt like...like an ache, in my stomach. But not like an ordinary stomachache. It was as if I'd have to suffer this until I saw her again, and that somehow seeing her would fix it, yet it felt strangely—good, yes, good—to have that ache, I mean. Have you had such an experience?"

"Uh...no..." replied Sikander. "Well, not exactly," he qualified before elaborating. "Ejaz, I've sometimes had this feeling for...for Rabia and well, you felt this way once and came to me asking what to do. How would you help me in my situation now?"

"Sometimes?" asked Ejaz. "Why only sometimes?"

"I...I don't really know. I think it's because when I want to talk to her...with someone else present, of course, it usually turns into an argument. But then somehow...I don't know, I feel like her fighting with me in that way...makes me feel more attracted to her. Does that make sense?"

"Ha! Sikander, you're not going to find sense in how you feel about a girl! But if you do feel this way, then we should talk about it when we get back. But tell me, what brought this up now?"

"Oh, just lying here I suppose, under the open sky, seeing the stars, and cooling off from the hot day. I was just reminded of that time when you met Hinna, and I'd just been having this dream when—Ejaz?"

"Mmm..." Ejaz grunted from within a snore, as he drifted uncontrollably off to sleep.

In the open mountain air, they slept a little too well and it was down to Abdul Majeed to wake up his companions with the dawn. With the usual wake-up cues all but absent, he shook them vigorously. The mountains to their immediate east made seeing the sunrise virtually impossible and they were far from anything resembling a masjid to be able to hear an azaan.

Fajr was quickly completed as was the short breakfast of rations brought from the village where they had begun the mule journey. Drawing water into their flasks from the brook, they set off to the west as soon as it was light enough, allowing the brook to lead the way.

After some four hours of trekking, the brook, which had by now become a stream, underwent a large bend to the southwest as it fed upon several other sources making it about three to five meters wide. Following the bend for about three kilometers, they found a dry riverbed leading up the hills to their north. Abdul Latif motioned to the men to cross the stream, taking more water while the opportunity presented itself. With the water collected, Abdul Latif took the lead up the riverbed, which made a convenient though at times steep path up the slope. When they were almost at the top of the climb, they came upon a small clutch of mud-brick homes and were warmly received by the villagers, where they asked the occupants for shade and drink and to rest for a couple of hours before moving on.

One of the villagers, a man by the name of Sarib Durrani, lived alone, being a widower, and seemed especially keen to assist them.

Directing them to follow him into his simple home, he offered them pomegranates and bread, both gleefully accepted as the men were by now ready to eat anything.

"Qandahar?" he asked.

Abdul Latif nodded.

"You bring weapons, yes?"

Abdul Latif again nodded, instinctively judging the consequence of acknowledging what was impossible to hide on the mules as being acceptably small.

"Good. Good. It's time those haraamzadas were kicked out of Qandahar! They killed my wife last year when we were coming back from there. Huh! It almost seemed like a sport to them. To hit us with the gunfire from their shaytan-arbas. We were out in the open! There wasn't anywhere to hide or take cover. What could we do?"

"I'm not sure we'll get them out of Qandahar, brother. It's well defended. In fact, we have to keep them from reaching out of there to destroy our people to the west in Arghandab."

"Hmm...well, I know it's a tough proposition, but inshaAllah, one of these days...one of these days."

Abdul Latif again nodded politely. Everyone else was tired but no longer hungry and no one seemed interested in building on the conversation. Abdul Majeed glanced at his father who picked up the message in his eyes.

"Brother, if you'll excuse us, you already know our business here and we must really be on our way. We thank you for your hospitality and the refreshments."

Having taken the welcome opportunity for rest, they moved out of the small village in the hills continuing west toward the Kabul-Qandahar road.

The going was not too challenging though there were a few small streams and many brooks to cross, but eventually in the early evening they came upon one of the two major rivers flowing into Qandahar. It was the Tarnak, which ran parallel to the main road at that location about fifty kilometers to the northeast of the city. The men decided to rest just before reaching the Tarnak at one of the small

clusters of homes where friendly locals of the region would take them in if need be. Virtually everyone from these parts was from the huge Durrani Pashtun tribe and were no friends of the communists.

Early the next morning, beneath a blanket of darkness, the group moved on to cross the major road which was in some disrepair but still often used by government forces and the Soviets to move supplies and arms up and down the country. About every hour or so, a convoy would pass, so it was important to have an excellent view in both directions before attempting to pull a team of mules across without being detected.

Once the crossing was made, they continued on to the high ground to the northeast of Qandahar, and by daybreak they were descending into the area north of Dahla Lake, the artificial body of water northeast of Dahla Dam. Keeping a good distance from the well-guarded dam, they came round the lake's north side and on to the west bank of the Arghandab River. As they entered the river valley south of the Dahla Dam, the air acquired a new fragrance.

"What's that?" asked Sikander.

"Pomegranates," replied Abdul Latif. "It's a pity they're not in season right now but what you can smell is the full bloom of the flower and here in the Arghandab Valley there are tens of thousands of pomegranate trees."

As the group approached the green zone where the pomegranate orchards and open fields were now clearly visible, a small band of armed mujahideen approached, quizzing them about who they were and whose militia they belonged to. Though passable, Abdul Latif's explanations were not nearly as effective as the Stingers and Milans packed on their mules. The troop was allowed to continue into the valley.

"There are six more teams coming through this area, so please be on the lookout for them," said Abdul Latif as he and his companions marched on with their mules and deadly cargo. Proceeding as directed by the guards, it didn't take them long to arrive at Mullah Lala Malang's headquarters in the leafy settlement of Sokhchala.

Lala Malang's first noteworthy skirmish with the Soviets was at a place called Deh Khwaja, not far from where he was presently dug in. He had ambushed a Soviet supply column attempting to resupply their positions in Panjwayee from Qandahar's air base. That was back in

1982, and owing to his fearsome reputation for handling captured opponents, his name was at once terrifying and reviled among Soviet and Afghan government forces. But to his mujahideen brethren he was welcoming and generous, though without mercy to those he was convinced were traitors. Abdul Latif had never met Lala Malang.

"Assalaamu 'alaykum! Mullah Malang," greeted Abdul Latif after being shown in to see the commander. He extended a warm hand to the young man who was to become his commander for this mission. "I'm Abdul Latif and I have almost forty mujahideen coming in with me from Jalaluddin Haqqani's force out of Nangarhar. We've been asked to provide assistance in preparation for a possible Soviet attack in this area."

"Wa-alaykum assalaam! Brother Abdul Latif." Malang chuckled briefly, commenting, "You know, we have another Abdul Latif here. He's the commander of the NIFA forces. We should be sure to avoid confusion, don't you think? Maybe we should call you by a different name?"

Abdul Latif did not know Malang well enough to know if this was a joke, a test, or Malang being serious. He played it safe.

"Whatever you consider will be helpful in winning this war is acceptable to me." Abdul Latif held a suspended shrug before letting it go, ceding the conversation to Malang.

"Well, it's not a pressing matter and we'll get by for now with your real name. So, what have you brought by way of weapons and men?"

"As I said, Brother Malang, we've almost forty men. They should be coming in throughout the day. We walked from near Chaman with almost thirty mules and we have twenty-four Stingers and sixty Milans along with our own light arms. The Milans can be fired from a total of six launching posts and I have sixteen launch systems for the Stingers."

"Hm…very good!" said Malang. "Why not rest for now? We can go over plans tomorrow when all of your men are here and properly rested too."

"As you wish, Brother Malang. I—"

"Sorry to interrupt you, Brother Abdul Latif, please call me Lala. Jalaluddin and Younus Khalis both call me by that name."

"As you wish, Bro…uh…Lala, I'm certainly interested in resting. When would you like to convene tomorrow?"

"Let's do it at—ten?—in the morning. Here."

Abdul Latif understood and walked out of Lala Malang's command headquarters feeling if anything, a little under-appreciated after his tiring trek from the border. He rejoined his boys who were waiting outside and asked to be directed to quarters for them all. The men were taken to another building nearby, which was really a group of inter-connected brick buildings that looked like they might have been used for storing pomegranates in season. The men from Nangarhar were all to be housed there.

The mules were unpacked and the men moved their weapons and materials into the rooms assigned to them.

"Well?" asked Ejaz, aiming his question directly at his uncle.

"We're supposed to bunk here and meet Lala Malang in the morning. I'm tired, so that's what I'm going to do. I suggest we all do the same."

There was an uncharacteristic tension in Abdul Latif's voice, as if he had been uneasy with the meeting with Lala Malang or that it had somehow not proceeded as expected. Ejaz was not going to press the matter with everyone tired, but it grated with him. In any case, everyone settled down and took a couple of hours to sleep after their long trek.

Sikander continued absorbing the sharp difference between this place and the more open hilly country he'd been across as well as the familiar Nangarhar. This was heavily tree-lined and the powerful yet invigorating fragrance of pomegranate blossoms seemed out of place for a war-torn part of the world. *At least both sides in the conflict seem uninterested in destroying it at this point*, he thought. It didn't play on his mind for long, as he too drifted off to sleep.

The group awoke after a few hours well rested, and after completing a combined zuhr and asr prayer, Sikander together with Ejaz decided to go for a stroll among the leafy orchards. Abdul Majeed remained in their quarters and relaxed.

"So, Sikander…my sister, eh?" laughed Ejaz. "You know, there was a time when all a man had to do was throw a cloth over the woman

he wanted to marry and pay her father an agreed price. If he did that, she would be his."

"And if the father was no longer alive?"

"Then the oldest male relative would normally suffice." Ejaz smirked.

As he realized he was being teased, Sikander stopped pressing his friend any further. He would just take in the air and the scenery.

They returned for maghrib and by now all but one of the mujahideen teams had come in. Sikander was still overwhelmed with the pleasant scent of the place, which at sunset seemed to go into high gear. It made the night's iftar dinner all the more flavorful in his mind. He took a moment to close his eyes, losing himself in the place, shutting out the war, and allowing his mind to embrace the redolence to build whatever sensory picture he could from it.

Morning came and after the usual fajr and nap, as promised, Abdul Latif, Sikander, Abdul Majeed, and Ejaz arrived at Lala Malang's command post. Somehow, Malang seemed in a more jovial mood and welcomed all of them, inviting them to examine the maps on his table.

"The government forces of about six thousand men are located here, here, and here." Malang gestured to different locations dotting the Qandahar area. "From what we can determine, against us we have units of the Fifteenth Division and the Seventh Tank Brigade near Zhare Dashteh. That's about six kilometers to our north. They're supported by the Fourteenth and Seventeenth Divisions and they have militias from all over the place, including Kabul. It doesn't look as if the Soviets are truly committed, but they do have Qandahar air base and units of the Seventieth Motorized Rifle Brigade. Likewise, the DRA are equipped with armored personnel carriers. Mostly farm boys these days. Not well trained. I really feel for them." Malang shook his head sideways, sighing at their prospects.

"I suppose the Soviets must remember their embarrassment at Deh Khwaja," said Abdul Latif, at which Malang's eyebrows perked up while grinning. He peered across the table at Abdul Latif, meeting his gaze squarely.

"Ah! You've *heard* of that?" he asked with more than a little glee.

"Directly from Jalaluddin Haqqani," responded Abdul Latif, returning the smile.

"Hm, in any case, I don't think we'll be so lucky as to have them totally out of the picture, but you could be right." Malang wore the look of fond reminiscence, while he projected the possibilities of direct Soviet participation in any upcoming attack. He began thinking aloud.

"I don't think they feel this is their fight like the DRA do. We gave them a bloody nose at the beginning of this year and almost took Qandahar. It's now late May and they're itching for their badal! I'm guessing they'll probably push to time their offensive for victory by 'Eid-ul-Fitr a week from now."

"So, Lala, what's your proposed defensive plan?" asked Abdul Latif.

"Well, let me ask you, what would you do, Brother Abdul Latif? I've heard only good things about your own adventures against the DRA and Soviets in Nangarhar. Any thoughts?" responded Malang.

Abdul Latif hadn't expected such a question, but he looked at the terrain and thought for a moment before opening up.

"Brother Lala, I have seen and walked around the valley on the way in yesterday. The irrigation ditches are very deep, which means that to avoid falling into them, the heavy armor of the enemy will have to follow specific pathways. On the other hand, we can take deep cover in those same ditches. You also have well camouflaged bunkers where I can set up our Milan missile launch posts and arrange them to crossfire into any arm—"

"Yes, yes, Brother Abdul Latif, but how do you propose to handle a whole division of Soviet tanks? We could be looking at eighty or more. I know they won't be able to come into the orchard area and we've already been using the channeling tactics you mention, but they'll try fighting from the edges of this green zone and landing their shells onto us."

"Brother Lala, if the orchards are impassable for the tanks then they'll use their tanks like ships against shore positions to soften up our forces while moving their APCs to get infantry in among us. I suggest we dig in to the bunkers while shelling persists and place just a small force

of lookouts at strategic locations just in case the tanks try to break through."

"And from the air?"

"Well...they'll no doubt try to pound us with helicopter and Sukhoi jet attacks before the tank shelling. In any case, the main point is that I'd expect them to send in their infantry after believing they've softened us up, however they choose to do that. But I think we can be ready for an air assault with our Stingers and we do now have the new Milan-2 missiles which will be effective if we place them along the deep ditches at the edge of the green zone. That'll force the Soviet tanks to keep a distance or go further down the valley to find an opening."

"All good points, Brother Abdul Latif. It's been our experience that the regular Afghan army is of poor morale and if we can get a high kill rate and block their remaining vehicles, they'll either pull back or surrender."

"Yes, I agree that's likely, but as long as we treat their deserters well, they will desert in great numbers."

"And the helicopters—how many Stingers did you bring?"

"We should be able to take down at least a dozen with just the missiles we have with us. That would be if we hit half our targets. If the Soviets are providing the air cover, either they'll bring up reinforcement or they'll see our success and want to keep their helicopters from harm. If they keep coming, we won't have an answer, but Brother Lala, what about the other militias in the area? How are we working with them?"

"Mullah Naqib's dug in further down the valley on the west bank at Chaharqulba and Abdul Latif—the uh, other one—has his force to the north of Pir Paymal downriver from here. They've got exceptionally good bunkers so I'm guessing they can hold up well enough. Naqib has a solid supply of RPGs and I'm not sure but I think he has just received Stingers. If they get attacked by tanks, it'll be the same story, as there isn't much open ground so the Soviets would be risking channelizing their tank pathways. The tanks will be vulnerable."

"They'll have to pepper the helicopters with RPGs if they don't have Stingers," warned Abdul Latif. With that, Abdul Latif's guidance to Malang was to hole up in the bunkers and place the Milan units along the northwest edge of the green zone. The Stinger teams would be taken

up to higher ground on the west side of the riverbank but farther south, from which they could offer support for both Malang's and Naqib's force from air attacks out of the southwest, the north, or even Qandahar. "It's in our interests obviously to offer maximum protection to Naqib's people because the air and land offensives will have to get past him to get to us. We can do the same for him with the tanks."

"Based on that reasoning, Brother Abdul Latif, I'd say the best location for the Stinger people would be about three quarters of the way up the hills about a kilometer southwest of here. It can cover all access pathways into the valley, particularly from Qandahar air base through the Baba-e-Wali gap."

The men agreed and parted. Abdul Latif rejoined his men and prepared them for the plan. Lala Malang was pleased with the discussion. Both points of view had made for a better plan and that was what was important as far as he was concerned.

The plans were implemented and all the mujahideen could do was to wait. It would not be for long.

Two days after their arrival, Sikander was practicing his procedure with the Stinger missile system and had been giving Abdul Majeed some guidance on how to prepare the missile rounds and where to stand to assist him as gunner as well as to avoid jet blasts and chemical discharges. They were at their designated position up the hillside. Likewise, in the valley floor, Ejaz was working with Abdul Latif down in the ditches at the northern edge of the green zone, training other mujahideen to work the Milan system.

The Milan was a remarkably easy weapon to use. All that was required was to clip the nearly seven-kilogram missile to the launcher post and then aim at the target. However, it was not a fire-and-forget weapon, as it was wire-guided to a two-kilometer range. This required maintaining an aim on the target along with the obvious need for more open spaces where trees and brush would not interfere. Any penetrating APCs that did manage to get past this defense would be attacked by RPGs launched from well-defended positions in any of the irrigation ditches.

At about eleven in the morning as Abdul Latif and Ejaz were working with their trainees, a loud boom rudely interrupted them. It had clearly originated from the green zone to the south.

Up on the hillside, Sikander's head spun. "What was tha—? Over there!" he shouted, answering his own question and pointing to a flight of eight Hind gunships on their way toward Chaharqulba. "Naqib's position! They're going after his bunker and ditches."

The helicopters were clearly too far to be attacked with Sikander's own battery of Stingers, but he could see concentrated RPG fire pummeling them. Moments later, one of them fell and exploded on the ground among the pomegranate trees. Sikander clenched his fist and stiffened his forearm in a gesture of satisfaction. He felt the urge to join the fray, but his good sense kept him from doing so. He and Abdul Majeed had been stationed on those slopes to provide protection against air attack over Sokhchala, and there they would have to stay. Abdul Majeed looked over his shoulder. Noting two other mujahideen climbing up the slopes to get closer to where he and Sikander were standing, he stretched out his arm with his palm down as if patting the ground to tell them to hold fast for a moment before waving them up toward him once he was sure that the Stinger gunners weren't under threat from the Hinds.

Down in the valley, Abdul Latif knew that he needed to act quickly before the tanks moved away from the missile operators' locations. "We have to intercept these tanks!" he shouted to Ejaz and the other mujahideen who were with him. "Remember, when you aim the missile, keep the target in your sights until it's hit then run to the next spot. Don't stay put or you'll be turned into pink dust by those tanks. Wait for my signal. That way we'll launch a few together just to confuse them and worry them about how many firing locations we have."

"Let's go, Uncle!" called Ejaz as he ran to take up his firing position. Abdul Latif followed suit, then arranged for the gunners to be separated by between eighty and a hundred meters each.

Half an hour after the rocket and bomb attacks on Chaharqulba began, the tanks at Zhare Dashteh started moving southwest, paralleling the edge of the green zone toward a location from which they could begin pounding the spot where Naqib's forces were stationed. As they moved closer to Abdul Latif and his men already waiting in ambush, Abdul Latif gave the signal.

Five missiles went rushing to their targets and despite the sandbags, the Soviet T-62 and T-55 armor was simply too thin to remain

protected. Four of the missiles made contact with their quarry. Each target tank appeared to explode from within and come to a rest amid a cloud of billowing white smoke that quickly turned black. As soon as each of the four tanks had been hit, Abdul Latif motioned to his gunners to move about fifty meters to the southwest all the while remaining in the irrigation ditch. The tank columns were gathering speed, though, and it was hard for Abdul Latif and his people, despite their spread out positions, to remain fully engaged with the main body of the tank force.

From their vantage point on the western valley slopes, Abdul Majeed and Sikander were able to watch the unfolding scene down the valley to their left where Abdul Latif and Ejaz had engaged the tanks and to their right toward Chaharqulba where a heavy firefight was underway. The DRA forces had advanced with APCs hoping they would find sufficiently softened up mujahideen, but were met instead by a hail of AK-47 fire and RPGs which made easy prey of the armored personnel carriers.

Those of the emerging men from the APCs that did not immediately gesture surrender were shot down by the mujahideen who, sensing themselves gaining the upper hand, came out of their bunkers to take them on.

"Most of the enemy is pulling back!" exclaimed Abdul Majeed with glee. In the distance he could also see several of the infantry now moving forward but with their hands in the air surrendering.

Meanwhile, despite moderate tank losses inflicted by Abdul Latif's sustained Milan fire, Naqib's positions were still taking a pounding from the advancing tank column from Zhare Dashteh as well as from Nagahan much further to the southwest of Chaharqulba and well beyond reach of anything out of Sokhchala.

Unable to imagine himself in their position, Sikander was filled with a sense of dread at what it would take to stand and fight in the face of such an onslaught. *Those people have real courage,* he thought as he saw himself falling short in a moment of involuntary self-comparison with them.

Despite the earlier progress with the APCs, the mujahideen in the valley at Chaharqulba were clearly unable to make the headway needed against the tanks. Able to penetrate tough armor and devastate a tank, the RPGs proved inadequate to the task of penetrating both

sandbags and tank armor with much lethality. However, Sikander did note that the tanks could never get sufficiently close to destroy the stronghold as the orchards, those blessed pomegranate orchards, were too thick a barrier to penetrate.

"They don't seem to want to push it," observed Sikander.

"No. They're being forced to move along the edge of the green zone and won't come into the open areas where they'd be chann—"

A deafening roar came from nowhere initially and then from just over their heads as two Sukhoi Su-25s screamed past the two air defense gunners, descending into the valley to their northeast. They were flying at no more than thirty meters above the downward sloping valley wall but only a moment later leveled off as they readied for a bombing run.

"It's a ground attack on Sokhchala!" shouted Sikander. "They came from our side. We see their rear ends. We're firing!" he continued, more annoyed than afraid. Sikander and Abdul Majeed turned to indicate to their fellow Stinger crews to follow suit. Just as Sikander was about to return his attention to the jets, he noticed approaching another Stinger team about eighty meters away. They were coming from the direction of Chaharqulba.

Alhamdulillah! They do have Stingers, noted a relieved Sikander. However, as attention was in short supply, he had to refocus on the two Sukhois. Sikander shouldered his weapon, went through the routine, and felt relieved that the aircraft were doing all the right things for him by moving directly away, slowing down for their bombing run and holding altitude. Within six seconds he fired. Four seconds later a second missile was on its way from somewhere to Sikander's right about fifty meters away.

Sikander's Stinger had been fired at about the lowest angle possible but made it cleanly out of the tube, ignited its boost-sustain motor, and pursued the aircraft with the determination of a greyhound chasing a racetrack rabbit. Having intercepted its quarry less than five seconds later, the missile erupted in a huge fireball where, a moment earlier, an airplane had been flying in the sky over the orchards of Arghandab. The fuel in the Sukhoi and its complement of explosives combusted while fragments rained down on the trees below. The second Sukhoi instinctively banked away from the explosion, though the pilot might have improved his odds by doing the opposite, using the

fireball to confuse any second missile's IR sensor. Luckily, he hadn't and the missile in pursuit of his aircraft would not be persuaded to abandon the chase, visiting the same fate on the airplane. The second pilot, however, did manage to eject.

Sikander stared at the parachute descending into the mêlée below. He was taken by the oddly beautiful color and the graceful way it floated, which seemed so out of place among the rest of the battle activities. The hypnosis was short-lived.

"Sikander! Sikander, we have to move from here!" shouted Abdul Majeed. They had no time to cheer on this occasion, and neither had Sikander the time to digest the words of Abdul Latif when he had made his first kill in Laghar Juy. Abdul Latif had been wrong about the second kill. There hadn't been time to hesitate. Somehow, the killing just happened. It wasn't a matter of easy or hard. It just was.

Sikander couldn't dwell on this complex thought, however. Eight more helicopters emerged from behind the hill heading to a point over the northern tank column with which Abdul Latif was now making serious progress as the column had slowed down to focus on Chaharqulba. One of the Hinds, however, was not tracking to the same course and, it seemed, was heading for them in the telling posture of impending attack.

Coming from somewhere behind and to his far left Sikander caught a glimpse of a white and orange streak heading straight for the helicopter. The helicopter's gunner had managed to get off one rocket round, readying for a second, as realization of being counter-attacked forced the pilot to try to evade the oncoming Stinger, futile though that was. Like some self-fatal bee sting, the doomed helicopter's rocket landed less than fifteen meters to Sikander's right and he felt himself being thrown to his left and landing hard on the ground, six meters from where he'd been standing. He was dazed and barely conscious. But he quickly came back to his senses as a moment later came a loud explosion. The offending helicopter was heading in pieces down to the valley floor having maneuvered hard to his right away from the slopes, thus increasing the distance to fall.

Still shaken, Sikander lifted his torso enough to turn his head and look upon the Stinger gunner who had saved him from further rocket fire and probably saved his life. Had there not been the other Stinger ready and aiming at that helicopter when it was, Sikander's own

weapon could certainly not have been readied in time to avoid many more rockets and Gatling gun fire blowing him up or gunning him down. Gasping for breath, with his jaw dropped but in a noticeable grin, Sikander conveyed his appreciation. The grin broadened when he saw who had done him this favor.

"Irfan! Usman!" cried Sikander to the young mujahid and his brother trudging up the hill toward him. He tried to get up but saw that he was bleeding from his right ankle. A small rock the size of a golf ball had struck him, but at least he had been lucky enough to be near a large boulder which had stayed put and protected the rest of him from the rocket warhead's blast.

"Sikander! Alhamdulillah, we do meet again!" cried out Irfan. His expression lost some of its beaming when Sikander rolled over to reveal the blood streaming from his foot. "Are you alright?"

"Yes...yes, I think so!"

Sikander used his weapon as a crutch to help himself up and hopped on his good foot for a moment. He looked down and could see a patch of red about the size of a quarter where his right ankle should have been. A chunk of bone had been sheared off along with the skin covering it. He gently let down his right foot to shift weight on it. The adrenalin was doing its job and he couldn't feel the pain he expected to feel. But the adrenalin had only loaned its analgesia. Payback would be later.

"We have to wrap that up," said Abdul Majeed gazing at the wound and he tore a piece of Sikander's qamees to bandage the injury after washing off the dirt and debris with the water from his flask. The water stung but Sikander was otherwise in working order.

"I can still shoot," said Sikander.

"We're counting on it," replied Abdul Majeed as he helped his friend to his feet while deflating a little of Sikander's self-appreciating sense of heroic fortitude.

"Irfan...ha! Irfan, you, you...Only Allah could have known you were needed here today. How are you, brother?" asked Sikander.

"We are both very fine. Very fine!" Irfan grinned while saying his last two words in English. He acknowledged the truth of Sikander's observation and the blessings of Allah for his training. "We're here

down from Khost to help with Mullah Naqib's defense of Chaharqulba," he explained and described how he had been sent to the valley slopes to protect against helicopters pounding Naqib's bunkers.

"Abdul Majeed, this is Irfan and...Usman!" said Sikander as he made his best attempt at a hug for each of them. Abdul Majeed followed suit and introduced himself.

"Ah! Abdul Rahman's brother!' exclaimed Irfan knowingly as Sikander followed the introductions with a little more elaboration.

As they wrapped up the reunion and introductions, two tell-tale Stinger streaks of white smoke drew trails over the valley floor as they headed to their targets, and again bright orange flashes were followed by burning debris falling to the ground. From the remaining helicopters a salvo of Gatling gun fire and rockets headed back across the valley. One of the farther helicopters had now been targeted by another missile coming from much further south across the gap and as it too was hit, it was clear that the Soviet pilots had not been prepared for this diversity of firing locations.

The adrenalin had numbed more than Sikander's sense of physical pain. "There's a couple closer to us that we can go for!" In that moment he felt as if he was owed something. His injury needed revenge and someone had to pay. Quickly hobbling toward the boulder where he'd been standing in the first place, he leaned against it and motioned to Abdul Majeed to bring him the grip stock of his launch weapon and one of the readied missile rounds that Abdul Majeed had previously prepared. He latched it on and nodded over to Irfan and Usman as well as their other gunner team colleagues several paces behind them while pointing to the rearmost helicopter on the left. He planned to take the one in front of him to the right. It was firing at their fellow gunners lower down the valley.

The left helicopter was hit first while Sikander wound up his missile which he quickly fired. His target, however, was gaining altitude and as it did so, Sikander could see the missile wasn't adapting to the maneuver. He briefly wondered why when he saw the Stinger heading out just above the middle of the helicopter formation where it exploded without hitting anything.

The sensor's malfunctioned, he thought, *or maybe it was the motor*. It didn't matter. Having taken place in the midst of the helicopter

formation, the explosion had sufficiently jarred the Soviet pilots that they felt it was time to withdraw. Their commander hadn't seen the sense in a "badal" mission anyway.

No more jets came.

Seeing their advance brought effectively to a halt, all but about a hundred of the DRA forces elected to retreat as did the tanks, despite thus far having remained largely undaunted, though Abdul Latif's team managed to take out two more near the tail end of the column as they caught up with it. Among the DRA forces, those who did not retreat simply downed their weapons with their hands high in the air, hoping to be accepted as yet more defectors. Most of them were, though no officers were captured. It had not been a good day for the Afghan army.

With the withdrawing tanks clearly visible from the valley slopes, Sikander, Abdul Majeed, Irfan, and Usman, together with their fellow gunner teams, cheered loudly "Allahu Akbar! Allahu Akbar!" and after about half an hour, when it became clear that a follow-up attack was looking decidedly unlikely, they started walking—and limping—down the slopes back toward Sokhchala.

Lala Malang's men regrouped that evening to review their performance of the day, with Abdul Latif and Ejaz being in a position to describe the situation on the ground and the assistance they had provided Naqib's men in Chaharqulba. Their own casualties had been light with the loss of two men and about twelve injured, mostly from flying wood shards after some tanks had fired back at them and hit nearby trees.

"They once again underestimated our weapons and our natural advantage in this terrain," began Lala Malang.

"Yes they *have*," replied a slightly perplexed Abdul Latif, raising his eyebrows at what he felt was a clear poverty of intellect demonstrated by the Afghan army on this occasion. "They let themselves get too confident about our weapons and felt it was safe to come in with sandbags on their tanks. Our RPGs initially helped them to believe that but now that they know about the Milans, they must be adapting their strategy."

"Certainly I would be doing that," acknowledged Lala Malang as he began discussing possible responses. "The Soviet air cover and

motorized rifles didn't seem to be very committed today, don't you agree, Abdul Latif?"

Abdul Latif nodded. "Yes, they must know, at least for now, that they don't have a good response to our Stingers and probably believe this is not a fight worth losing helicopters and pilots for. Their Sukhois weren't effective either. But I wouldn't rule them out just yet."

"Agreed," said Lala Malang. "Tomorrow will give us a better indication. They might perceive we have an open weakness at our rear toward the dam up river. They could also bring troops over the hills by dropping them from Mi-8s on the crests of the hills to our north or they could come in from the southern opening in the valley and fly in low, which I believe is a problem for the Stinger. Is that correct?"

"Sikander has more knowledge among us about that," replied Abdul Latif as he called out for Sikander who dutifully hobbled over, leaning on Irfan's shoulder.

"The Stinger can be fired successfully from the valley slopes. We did it today and took out two Su-25s. That was with aircraft just about level with our horizon," Sikander explained.

"Good! At least we know we can handle that, so you gunners are to remain on the valley slopes but much lower down than before, and I want to keep you concentrated in the same areas as today but also post lookouts up and down the valley as well as toward the Baba-e-Wali gap," said Lala Malang. Everyone agreed and the day was done. The time came to break the fast and a large collective iftar was spread out for them in the local masjid.

As they sat for the meal, Sikander was delighted to introduce Irfan and Usman to Abdul Latif and Ejaz who in turn warmly embraced the two young men for having helped save the life of their newest mujahid.

Although the following day they were ready for a repeat attack, only minor skirmishes took place, mostly with APCs advancing with poorly trained DRA troops. The effect was to swell the number of defectors who would then be taken to Pakistan for interrogation and potential orientation to join the mujahideen.

From the defectors it was clear that yet another DRA offensive much closer to Naqib's stronghold was being made ready. Abdul Latif

suggested to Mullah Malang that it would be highly appropriate to come to the aid of Mullah Naqib because Chaharqulba was closer to the important Baba-e-Wali gap from which most of the enemy resources were being launched. Reluctantly, Malang agreed and three days after the first skirmish Abdul Latif's troop, now including Irfan and Usman, set off to the southwest toward Chaharqulba.

They were warmly received as Abdul Latif arrived with more Milans and Stingers, adding to those in Naqib's possession.

"Those crazy DRA commanders! Their boys have no skills and still they are being sent to attack us!" remarked Naqib in disgust. "We just had an APC captured yesterday and told the infantry commander to go back and tell his own commanders that they should stop before more of our Afghan sons are killed! All he could do was to tell us his...his sorry story about his wife and children in Kabul and how he couldn't ask his commanders to withdraw or his family would be punished severely. Haraamzadas!" he uttered, shaking his head with visible disgust.

"Where would you suggest we place our Stingers and Milans?" asked Abdul Latif.

"Over there for the Stingers." Naqib pointed to a small clutch of largely ruined village homes on a more gently sloping part of the west valley of the Arghandab than the one they had been using previously. "From those positions you can take cover and you should be able to attack helicopters coming from most directions into here. They typically come in flights of four or eight, so it will be a good idea to get eight gunner teams up there. We have the Stingers, and Sikander, I've heard good things about your skills from Irfan. Let's see how you fare taking charge tomorrow," he added.

Sikander could not suppress a slight stiffening in his posture as he felt the pride of being asked to lead the air defense team, as Naqib continued: "Meanwhile, for their tanks, I'd suggest the irrigation ditches on the western edge of the green zone. From there you have adequate cover and can hit tanks coming in from Zhare Dashteh."

"That's pretty much what we were doing earlier this week," noted Ejaz looking at Abdul Latif.

"We'll make sure that happens," said a voice from the doorway of the bunker where Naqib was situated.

"Ah! Akhtarjhan, come in...come in." Naqib beckoned with a wave of his hand. "Akhtarjhan, this is Abdul Latif and his men from Nangarhar. They're here to assist us with defense against tank and helicopter attacks, and...apparently, his best gunner is a friend of our illustrious Stinger brothers!"

"Welcome! Jazaakumullah for your support," thanked Commander Akhtarjhan with an appropriately deferential smile respecting Abdul Latif's age, regardless of rank.

Abdul Latif returned the thanks and the two men began discussing the air defense plan in more detail. Abdul Latif had heard of Akhtarjhan from other people and was familiar with the tragic story of his becoming a mujahid at the age of twelve when his older brothers had been killed in Babur Village. Now in his early twenties, he was probably no older than Abdul Rahman but he had become something of a legend for his daring and bravery in a number of attacks and ambushes against the DRA and Soviet troops.

The following day, at about nine in the morning, the Stinger teams walked the six hundred meters to the general area that Naqib had indicated. Several bombed out and abandoned dwellings awaited them, so they had their pick of ruined walls to create a number of covered positions from which to fire. The location was also ideal for protecting Sokhchala where Lala Malang had prepared his defenses. Once they were together, Sikander proposed that they split into two teams of four gunners along with their partners. Each would be separated by about fifty meters and train their missiles on any attacking helicopters. At that distance they could still make intelligible hand signals while being well separated.

A pattern had become established where at around eleven o'clock in the morning, the aerial bombardments would begin followed by enemy ground force advances supported by remote shelling from tank columns which remained in open ground on the southwest and northeast of the strongholds all along the plain, west of the river.

That morning was to be no different and at about quarter to eleven, the first flight of Hinds rolled in, flying a hundred meters above the orchards. The Stinger teams were ready and only had to initiate the BCU gas release to arm their weapons, which they held off from doing until the helicopters were within roughly two kilometers range. They would continue to hold their fire if the helicopters were far from the

stronghold of Naqib's bunkers, as the pilots would be wasting their bombs and there was no need to give away the Stinger positions prematurely.

The DRA and Soviet pilots knew all too well the location of Naqib's bunkers and were on their way to soften them up. There wouldn't be any bomb wasting.

Sikander organized the Stinger teams to have all eight ready to fire but wanted to keep the initial salvo to just four of them. If a helicopter force was to turn on them having discovered their location, the second group was to fire. He assigned a young mujahid called Zahir Mirza to lead that group, asking him to set his men about a hundred and fifty meters from the first group.

"Sikander, I think we should do it now," urged Abdul Majeed.

"Agreed." Sikander nodded in the direction of Irfan to his left and the other gunners to his right and rear. In a few moments four white, smoky snakes, each with a missile for a head, wound their way to their designated targets. One failed to go off and three made direct hits, but only two achieved immediate destruction. The damaged helicopter withdrew limping in the sky. The pilot struggled to maneuver but eventually lost control as his machine failed to respond. With its tail almost wagging, he flew it into the ground where it exploded on impact.

As this was happening, two helicopters approached the source of their first two friends' demise. Sikander searched for Stinger fire from the second group to counter the helicopters but initially, at least, nothing came. In that split second, Sikander looked into the distance at Zahir and noticed him fumbling with his launcher.

Why aren't they firing!? Sikander was gripped with dread at thought of the inevitable consequences. He and his fellow gunners were sitting ducks and the least they could do was to stop sitting. His command was simple.

"Run!" Sikander screamed, pointing to the southwest. Immediately, the Stinger teams began sprinting away from the approaching helicopters coming in for their kill. Sikander was the laggard, being far from fully healed with his ankle injury. He cursed the injury and then whatever devil had intervened to paralyze Zahir.

Those helicopters not pursuing them proceeded to drop their 100-kilogram bombs over the bunkers and fired rockets into the irrigation ditches wherever they saw RPGs being fired at them.

Though he was supposed to fire at the advancing helicopters in a second salvo, Zahir had temporarily lost focus, unable to get his own weapon going as he had not screwed on the BCU correctly, leaving his impulse switch inoperative. Instead of asking his other group members to fire, he panicked as he continued struggling with the obstinate BCU.

By now, the first Stinger team hurried to relocate as it was taking Gatling gun fire as well as rockets. A full ten seconds later than necessary, Zahir's fellow gunners, who had been pre-occupied by the distraction of their leader's difficulties, finally broke from him and set upon the advancing helicopters. Two streaks lunged at the Hinds which were each less than a kilometer away by now in hot pursuit of the first Stinger team. Both were instantly arrested as their flaming remnants came crashing into the barren ground north of the green zone.

At last, Zahir was able to get the BCU connected and shouldered his weapon as the one remaining team member who had not fired joined him in the attack. They managed to score direct hits with two of the remaining four helicopters that were harassing Naqib's bunkers without much effect, before the two surviving helicopters withdrew in haste. None of the eight-man group had latched a second missile round and held off from doing so as they saw the enemy withdrawing.

"That was close!" gasped Abdul Majeed to Sikander. He was keenly aware of how close to death he had just been. The awareness filled him with an inexplicably eerie euphoria.

"It certainly wa—" began Sikander when he abruptly stopped transfixed by the contortion on Abdul Majeed's face. All the euphoria of a few seconds earlier had vanished, as he had disengaged his eyes from Sikander and looked beyond Sikander's shoulder hoping to exchange the same sense of relief with Irfan and his brother.

"Irfan? Irfaaan!" came the plea from Usman as he lifted Irfan's limp torso. Blood was streaming out of Irfan's left side and head. The young mujahid didn't seem to be moving. Sikander ran across—as best he could with his slight limp—to check on the youth that had been his gunnery class fellow and only three days earlier, saved his life. He could

see the extent of injury was severe. Irfan had taken more than one hit squarely in the right side from the back and had a grazing, but severe hit to the left side of his head.

"Irfan!" Sikander emitted a harrowing moan as he attempted to evoke a response from the young mujahid. Irfan's eyes opened slowly and he began coughing up blood, looking up at his brother and Sikander.

"We'll get you back down to the village," Sikander spoke in a soft voice which transformed instantly to a bark as he turned around and shouted "Over here!" to the other gunners to come to his assistance.

"N...o...oh!" said Irfan struggling to get out the single word. "I'm done...not going to—" He stole another gasp of air as he began to utter the kalimah "La...ilaha...illallahhhh" in a low voice and then continued moving his lips without making a sound as if he were completing "Muhammadur-rasulallah!" to himself. A moment later the air vacated what was left of his lungs and his soul vacated his eyes, never to return.

"Irfaaaan!" Usman's plaintive cry came as he nestled his brother's head to his own breast and rocked to and fro with it in his arms. In a gesture of comfort, though he could hardly spare any, Sikander laid a hand gently on Usman's shoulder, while he succumbed to a twisted, anguished expression. *Why!? Why him?*, he pondered bitterly as he gazed skyward. The war had exacted yet another heavy price from this hard-hit family and had whittled it down to just one sole survivor, left to mourn them all. He was consumed by grief and began sobbing with Usman, joining heads with the youth.

"We...we can't stay here," urged Abdul Majeed as tactfully as he could. "Sikander, we can't stay. We need to move. I think another flight's coming in from over Baba-e-Wali."

Abdul Majeed alternated between looking back at the battle in the valley and forward to the dead Irfan and the two young men mourning him. Finally he laid his own hand on Sikander's shoulder and without saying any more, squeezed it tightly.

Sikander understood and got up, picking up his launcher and missile. He asked Usman to do the same but the request proved futile at that moment.

A part of Usman didn't care if he lived or died now. *If it's God's plan to finish off the family then let it be this day*, he thought. Explaining he'd be back, Sikander arose and turned to get closer into the valley, indicating to the remaining gunners to latch their second missile rounds onto their launchers "And this time, be ready to fire!" he screamed in a rare moment of unbridled anger as his glare fixed on the mortified Zahir.

Irfan's words from Applecross came pouring into Sikander's consciousness and it took all of his energy to concentrate as he struggled to focus on the black blobs silhouetted against the gray sky. Six helicopters were on their way in the general direction of where the Stinger teams had been gathered near Irfan's body.

"Spread out!" he screamed again to his fellow gunners. "Let's get them!"

Abdul Majeed helped him latch the next round and Sikander inserted the BCU, initiated it, and aimed. He would take his time on this one. The moment the IR sensor tone indicated a lock, his missile was unleashed. Three more followed suit after which the gunners immediately ran, looking for cover among the bombed out ruins. The helicopters hovered three kilometers away and their pilots managed to see where the gunners had run to, but they had already begun maneuvering desperately to avoid the streaking missiles heading for them. The only thing lying between them and destruction was a possible missile malfunction. The missiles did not oblige. Another three fresh streaks of orange and white smoke leapt in quick succession toward the remaining three helicopters which were by now in full retreat. One of them, took a hit while the other two escaped injury as the missiles missed them, exploding in the air after the seventeen-second self-destruct sequence had completed. The gunner teams regrouped.

"They won't be back today," said Sikander, wanting to be amused by his own quip. Instead he felt a sinking feeling in his stomach as he was drawn unrelentingly back to processing Irfan's death when he remembered to utter the ayah from the Holy Qur'an, "Inna lillahi wa inna ilayhi raaji'un." This was the customary utterance when learning of the death of a fellow Muslim, meaning, "Indeed we are from God and to him shall we return."

Strangely, after saying that, Sikander found himself dissecting the words from different perspectives. While they represented to him a self-evident truth, he was trying to understand why these were the words

to be used for such an occasion over all other possible references in the Qur'an. Though he was no Muslim scholar, something inside him made him feel that maybe they simply meant that when any calamity in ongoing life occurred, it was all nonetheless—in life. As such it held no significance in after-life. If Irfan had been wealthy, poor, comfortable, or hard-pressed, it didn't matter when it came to dying. No worldly calamity or manifest success would have meaning next to the ultimate absolute of a return to God and, he guessed, on such an occasion, reciting this ayah was a way to remind himself of this truth. The Quranic utterance was for him, not the deceased.

Carefully, Irfan's body was brought back into Chaharqulba accompanied by Sikander and Usman on either side. Abdul Majeed explained the situation to Ejaz and Abdul Latif, who had also sustained a minor wound. It saddened them both to learn of the loss of the young man whom they had only just come to know.

"Mullah Naqib will help to complete the proper preparation for burial," suggested Abdul Latif as he offered words of solace to Usman.

"Usman...this is truly shahadah, you know?" Abdul Latif's eyes creased as a smile came on his face. "Your brother has an assured place in heaven. His heart was true and he knew what he was fighting for. He wasn't concerned with removing Soviets from this country. He was fighting to keep its Muslim character so that you and he could live in peace as Muslims and raise a fam...a family." Abdul Latif looked across at Sikander making it clear he should pick up the task of providing whatever solace might be possible.

Sikander approached Usman and offered such comfort as he could to the youth. "Usman, your brother had mentioned this possibility to me when we were in training. He told me that you and he have had no other family but each other." Sikander paused to take in a breath, which became unexpectedly difficult. "He told me that and asked that I...we," Sikander glanced at Abdul Latif, "we should take you in as one of us. As a brother."

Abdul Latif laid his hand gently on Usman's shoulder, as Mullah Naqib walked in.

"Hmm! Inna lillahi wa inna ilayhi raaji'un!" he pronounced, slowly shaking his head and wearing a wistfully solemn look. "A shaheed!" Naqib turned to Usman. "We must humbly thank Allah for

forgiving him all his sins as he now carries the mark of the shaheed. He has all the more reward for fighting and dying while fasting in this the last week of Ramadhan! Truly Usman, I'm envious of your brother's fate. Come, we must bury him right here in Chaharqulba, where he earned his shahadah."

Usman was unable to offer much by way of opinion or decision about such a thing as burial. He felt horribly empty. His only surviving connection to the past was now gone. His gunnery class fellow and cheerful soldier companion—well beyond biological brotherhood—was no more.

The preparations were made. The body was bathed, perfumed, and wrapped in a white cloth brought in from the village, and then buried as everyone looked on, offering their own prayers and throwing their own handfuls of dirt over the grave.

Over the next several days, Sikander made many efforts to bring young Usman closer to himself, but Usman needed to work through his own grieving in the best way he could. At the time, the best person to understand his experience, though, was Akhtarjhan and Sikander asked the commander if he would also try to help Usman through the process.

"We can't rush that," explained Akhtarjhan. "He does need reminding of his brother's martyrdom, but it will take him time to come through. You people have been generous to take him in and I know I would have felt much more strength if the same had been done for me when I lost my brothers but..." he sighed raising his eyebrows, "we have to go on."

The skirmishes came and went and the mujahideen did take more casualties. At one point when they had become dispirited at being unable to make much headway against the DRA's armored weapons, over the objections of his commanders, Mullah Naqib demonstrated the reality of his envy of Irfan's shahadah, taking a weapon and striding out alone into the fray arguing: "This is their last battle and will decide the battle between them and us. They've tried to conquer this place for years and this is their last throw!"

The move rallied his commanders to join him.

After almost seven weeks and now well into July, the DRA offensive seemed to peter out as the DRA forces and Soviets abandoned their revenge mission, returning to a status quo of occupying Qandahar

while leaving the western Arghandab Valley to the mujahideen. However, their losses were severe. In the entire attack, they suffered at least five hundred dead and between a thousand and two and a half thousand defections. They lost a hundred vehicles, tanks, and light transports as well as over a dozen helicopters or aircraft.

By sheer losses, the Arghandab counter-attack was a disaster for the enemy. The mujahideen had perfected a clever approach of using terrain to dig in and defend against attacks, and when not being attacked, to make highly targeted, well-orchestrated ambushes. They were also effective in speeding up defections and desertions from which they derived much intelligence and morale-boosting value. On top of all this, they had virtually perfected the art of attacking a withdrawing force if there was any weakness or lack of cohesion in its rear.

On July 20, 1987, less than three weeks after Arghandab, the Soviet Union announced its intent to withdraw from Afghanistan and General Gromov, commander of the 40th Army, drew up the plans.

At the end of their expedition to Arghandab, Sikander had sustained a minor injury to his right ankle. Ejaz had likewise been hit in the left arm by wood shards from a tank shell exploding in a nearby tree. Abdul Latif had been hit in the left leg with a small piece of shrapnel. But despite the battle wounds and death toll all around, he had now gained yet another new "mujahid son."

Chapter 9

Rabia

WITH THE WITHDRAWAL BY the enemy troops from Arghandab back into Qandahar, there was little else to do for the visiting mujahideen that had come in to assist. Abdul Latif and his group of now thirty-four mujahideen needed to return to their homes and families. They had been away during the very important month of Ramadhan and missing the festival of 'Eid-ul-Fitr made returning all the more necessary as soon as circumstances permitted—and that, by all accounts, seemed to be now.

Abdul Latif made the customary request for permission to take his leave of his host Lala Malang, who gave the customary permission without hesitation. The group, freshly supplied with rations and mules, was soon on its way back toward Chaman.

The return route was virtually a reverse of their entry to Arghandab, and in three days, they had regrouped at the same small village just north of the Khojak tunnel where they had first received and packed their mules. From there they sent a message into Quetta whereupon the ISI came to collect and transport them to Peshawar. Returning to Peshawar was both easier and more difficult. On the one hand, they were not traveling with bulky weapons systems—just their own AK-47s. On the other hand, flying by C130 was not deemed necessary, so the troop went in two ten-ton troop carriers by road up through the remote towns of Zhob, Dera Ismail Khan, and Kohat, before

finally arriving in Peshawar. This took the better part of two days when at last the troop re-camped at Peshawar's airport. From there they were taken in small vans and pickups in groups of five or six, much as they had arrived almost two months earlier via Arif's place in Jamrud.

Abdul Latif had held back to lead the last group to leave, and upon their arrival at Jamrud, Arif greeted them heartily.

"Brother Abdul Latif, your courage and action in Qandahar are causing a stir among the ISI as they've been interviewing the many deserters that have been brought back here. Alhamdulillah, it sounds like it went well, but I'd really love to hear it from one who was there." Arif was hungry for stirring tales of daring and valor.

Abdul Latif did the best he could to relate the experience and as he finished in his all too brief and dry a summary, he shrugged wearily wafting his hand in the general direction of his young band. "Brother Arif, you'll get better details from these brave young men."

"Abdul Majeed, Ejaz, oh, and...Sikander?" asked Arif quizzically as he gazed upon Sikander's now ten centimeter long dark brown beard and mustache trimmed back above the lips.

Sikander nodded acknowledgingly. "Arif bhai, I'd like you to meet Usman. His elder brother became a shaheed in Arghandab just before 'Eid-ul-Fitr...he died in Usman's arms," reported Sikander as he sucked the energy out of Arif's appetite for information.

"Oh, Inna lillahi wa inna ilayhi raaji'un...Assalaamu 'alaykum Usman!" said Arif. A look of genuine sympathy came upon him as he lost his characteristic smile while sensing the discomfort caused by Sikander's brief explanation. Usman returned the salaam quietly and politely but didn't say much more. "Well," uttered Arif resignedly, "perhaps we can discuss your experiences later."

Returning his gaze toward Sikander, Arif became aware of the elevated standing projected by the teenager. He was no more the young lad who had been brought before him, having to defend the pronunciation of his own name just under a year earlier. He was battle hardened and ready for anyone and anything. Sensing the somberness of the group, Arif decided he would make the customary offer of the phone call to Sikander, now that he was back in Peshawar. Sikander gratefully acknowledged the offer, taking the stairs up to the living room to make another of his rare calls home.

"Hello?" came the voice. It was his brother Jamil, whose voice sounded a little deeper than Sikander remembered. *He'll turn seventeen soon*, thought Sikander and for a moment, he held in his mind the thought of rewinding his life to the day before he left home when he too was seventeen.

"Jamil?"

"Bhai-jan? Oh, bhai, at last! It's so good to hear from you."

"Jamil...yes, it's me...it *is* bhai-jan. How are you? How's Sameena? Are Ammee-jan or Abba-jee home?"

"No, bhai-jan. They're not here right now. Abba-jee is out somewhere and Ammee-jan has taken Sameena to the doctor. She won't be—"

"Sameena? What's wrong with her? Is she alright?"

"They don't think it's anything serious, but she needed to see a lady doctor. They should be back in about an hour or two."

"Well, give her my love and salaams and likewise to Ammee and Abba-jee. Wish everyone 'Eid Mubarak. I'm sorry I couldn't be with you for this 'Eid. I would really like to have come home for a while. It just couldn't be right now. But I do promise, I promise I'll be home before too long."

"When, bhai-jan? *When?* It's been almost a year now and we haven't seen—"

"Jamil, we're making progress with all these new weapons! The Russians are readying for a withdrawal. Can you *believe* it?"

"Bhai-jan, I wish I could join you too, but no one will even entertain the thought. Abba tells me I have to finish my schooling and he's—"

"And he's right. Jamil, he's *right!* School's extremely important. Trust me, Jamil. Seriously...for both of us, yaar, you have to study hard. Don't disappoint Abba or Ammee like I must have done. Look, I...I have to go now, Jamil. I'll write if I can, or send notes. Alright?"

"Bhai-jan, it's...it's just not the same without you. Please! Come back soon!"

"I will, Jamil. I will, I promise. I'll try contacting you again as soon as I can. Allah Hafiz."

Hanging up the phone, Sikander stared at Arif's beautiful rug for a few moments, as he pondered life in Hayatabad and how it was probably unfolding without him. He prayed silently that Sameena was not in any serious health trouble before proceeding back down to Arif's war-room.

The group didn't do much in preparation for the trip back, spending the night in Arif's place to be ready early the following morning once more to take the now familiar route to Laghar Juy.

That trip was largely uneventful. But as Hinna was now a part of the family, an en-route stopover with Yaqub and his family was obligatory. Yaqub and Shahnaz, for their part, fussed over Ejaz and provided the men with the customary gifts to be taken to their daughter's "new" family.

Two nights later, the men were descending the slopes from the south into Laghar Juy. It had been almost nine weeks since they had left and as they came in from the mountains, the July afternoon heat became increasingly noticeable and hard to bear. They made many stops to rest and take a drink and mercifully, a plentiful supply of snowmelt coursing through timeworn brooks and streams left them with no shortage of water.

The early evening saw them ambling into the upper slopes of Laghar Juy, eventually walking into the area of Abdul Latif's home, and as usual, with no prior word of their imminent arrival. Mightily relieved and excited to receive them, Razya began immediately to organize a belated welcoming, combining celebrations of 'Eid, their victory, and their safe return, all mingled into a single event. But that would come later. For now, Ejaz also needed to return to his home and the others decided to accompany him. Abdul Rahman already happened to be at Noor's conferring with Saleem about taking delivery of fresh supplies of Stingers when the returning travelers strolled in from Abdul Latif's home.

Abdul Rahman and Saleem hugged the returning men with great relief and delight and Rabia practically enveloped Ejaz with her greeting, while Noor hugged him as she whispered a prayer of thanks for his safe return. Once Rabia was over her own relief at the return of her big brother, she began unleashing her usual onslaught of inquiry and probing upon all of the returning warriors. Everyone except Usman, to whom she presented her alter ego of the shy young lady until it would be time to open up. Usman, like Sikander, was to be put up at

Abdul Latif's place, sharing a tight squeeze with Sikander, but given special treatment as the brother of a recent shaheed.

"Brother Ejaz!" began Rabia almost immediately. "I've known Sister Hinna for longer than you have. Isn't that absurd?" she chided as she looked askance toward her brother, with a glint of mischief in her eyes.

Ejaz smirked and nodded, acknowledging the essential truth of Rabia's comment before retorting, "And I've known *you*, Rabia, for far too long!" He laughed for the first time in many days. Ejaz was amused with his quip but more with the fact that he knew about Sikander's emerging interest in her. He had an advantage over his sister, which was far too rare to be left unsavored. However, the important business at hand for Ejaz was to seek out his beloved Hinna.

"Where's is she?" asked Ejaz not needing to say who, but a little anxiously nonetheless. Since there hadn't been any way to alert the villagers to the impending return of the warriors, it wasn't exactly reason to be worried but he looked around and couldn't see her.

"Can't wait to see your sweetheart again...hmm?" goaded Rabia. Ejaz paid the briefest attention to his sister's little taunt and continued looking for only a moment longer.

Hinna was out in the back seated on her patthra and working the small stove, having been so engrossed with starting a flame that she hadn't registered the commotion going on in the front of the thick-walled mud-brick house. With the flame started, she stood up to select a cookpot and as she did so, she immediately registered the image of her husband simply standing and staring at her with the setting sun illuminating his face like a beacon.

"Ejaaaz!" she exclaimed, almost lunging toward him for a giant hug. Ejaz was equally eager to embrace his wife and as soon as she was clear of the stove, they moved away gripping each other in silence. Hinna couldn't help but weep quietly for joy at the return of her beloved. Words were in neither of their minds to express what needed to be expressed.

After everyone was done with reunion greetings and people began to settle down, buoyed by his own euphoria at returning to his love, Ejaz decided he would also discuss Sikander's comments more fully with him and if it appeared Sikander was more than just infatuated,

he would ensure that the proper procedures were followed so as not to spoil the possibility of a match through some faux pas in Afghan etiquette on Sikander's part. Besides, they were both young enough for no one to be in a particular hurry, and in any case, Rabia's wishes had yet to be discovered. Who knew? Perhaps she had someone—or type of someone—completely different in mind for herself. For Ejaz, although an exception to cultural norms, knowing her wishes was important.

Meanwhile Razya had her own eye on the situation and was ever watchful for any sign that might surface during the 'Eid-cum-homecoming celebration that she had organized. The results proved inconclusive in themselves, but the shrewd Razya had a keen insight and began detecting something of a stirring in Sikander whenever he was in Rabia's presence. Either he would become a little more cocky or fumble for words, both of which were in Razya's calculus the kinds of signs she was watching for. But for now, she would keep things to herself.

It had been about a year earlier that Mikhail Gorbachev had made the first non-specific pronouncements of a start of Soviet withdrawals from Afghanistan. After the stepping up of arms sophistication being supplied to the mujahideen and with the cost of remaining in Afghanistan, the Soviets had no stomach for a prolonged stay. They needed a way to prop up a regime that would enable them the luxury of a graceful withdrawal. On the heels of Arghandab, General Gromov had begun to work out the details, but in the meantime the fighting continued, though with a difference.

Outside the major towns and villages there was little to gain by engaging the mujahideen, as it would mean either unnecessary loss of men and assets or the additional defection of DRA forces. Neither of these could possibly advance a Soviet cause, so the fighting took on a noticeably lower tempo. The mujahideen for their part had no current interest in making an onslaught on the major cities and roads. They preferred to dig in with extremely well-defended positions and if the DRA or Soviets made the mistake of moving large numbers of troops or hardware, then ambushes were among the favorite responses.

Life in Laghar Juy had therefore settled into something of a peace long forgotten. People farmed and rebuilt their homes. During this period people even began to engage in minor recreation. A favorite

among the villagers involved heading up into the gentler, lower slopes of the Spin Ghar for a leisurely walk or an outing to see the snowmelt streams and rivers.

❧

In late July, less than a month after the men had returned from Arghandab, Noor decided to organize a small family gathering in honor of her son and daughter-in-law. The appointed location was to be out on the slopes by Laghar Juy's main stream which flowed down to the Kabul River east of Jalalabad. They would cook up a slaughtered lamb and make kebabs and steaks out in the open. At this time, with snowmelts in full force, the stream flowed more like a river with its unusually high volume. It needed to be approached with some caution, so the family gathered near the shade of a cluster of walnut trees about fifty meters from the bank of the stream.

While Abdul Latif and his two sons slaughtered the lamb, Ejaz and Saleem buried into the ground a makeshift clay pot that they had brought with them, with the intent to fire it up with wood to create the heat necessary to form a primitive but highly effective tandoor. Once the lamb was completely cooked, Noor and Hinna had the task of preparing the meat in dishes combined with fresh vegetables and coarse bread. Meanwhile, Usman, Rabia, Saleem, and Sikander took a stroll toward and then along the edge of the stream.

Having shed her initial stranger-shyness in front of Usman, Rabia, as usual, did most of the talking.

"Brother Usman, you know I tried to get Sikander to say something about those wonderful places you went to in Scotland, but he's been less than forthcoming with me. I had heard from him, though, that you and your brother, may Allah grant him peace, were also there. Perhaps you can tell us more?"

"Well," Usman began, taking in a deep breath followed by a sigh, "it was—what? About nine or ten months ago now?—but it seems very much like a dream, Sister Rabia."

"I'm sure it was indeed beautiful. Can you tell us more about it, Brother Usman?" she asked sweetly, trying not only to enlighten herself but also to help Usman come out of his shell.

"We arrived in total nighttime darkness not knowing what to expect, you see. We were taken into a cabin and spent the night there,

but when we awoke in the daylight, we had a good-sized window next to our bed and I looked out. I was amazed to see such a scene..."

"Yes? Please go on."

"It was a large expanse of still water about half a kilometer out in front of us, but small islands with hills dotted the water while behind those were even bigger ones. The sun would set by sinking behind those islands and each sunset was truly beautiful. Sikander, Irfa...Irfan, and I would go out after asr to see the sunset and it would glow behind the mountains and...Irfan, he'd walk around the compound with me, telling me more about our family. He was three years older than me and I was only ten, when our family was killed by the Russians." Usman stopped.

"Hmm...did you ever get to the water and the mountains?" continued Rabia, attempting to nudge him past the moment.

"We did once, when we'd almost completed our training. The soldiers took us in a bus and those of the group with long beards were asked to have them cut so that they could be dressed to look like local members of the regular army." He paused again to chuckle. "Some of the men would never allow that. No. Huh! Never. But some of us didn't have much of a growth yet to be cutting it back and others had acceptable beards to begin with, so I wouldn't say it bothered too many of the men and in any case, they were itching to leave the camp after so long behind the fence. Hm! I remember sitting inside that bus. It took us through such beautiful country." Usman wore a reminiscing grin.

"What was it like to fly in a helicopter?" asked Rabia.

"Rabia," interjected Sikander. "I think you'll lick his poor mind clean with your questions! See what I mean, Usman?"

Saleem, Usman, and Sikander laughed as Rabia pouted but from no real annoyance.

"Well, I don't mind discussing it," said Usman. "It's a great feeling, Rabia, if you've never flown. It...it's like the ground simply gets further and further away and at some point it doesn't seem like you're really moving but just floating. The best part would be if we ever passed through the clouds and looked at them not from below but above. Just like when we're really high in the mountains, but even higher."

"Mmmm...Brother Usman, I think you have a wonderful way of describing your experiences. Certainly you—aghhh!" Rabia shrieked as

her left foot was consumed by large piece of muddy soil that had given way and, complete with her foot, slipped into the flowing water, dragging the rest of her with it. Although listening to her, everyone else's attention was elsewhere at that moment and no one managed to notice Rabia's unfolding situation rapidly enough to intervene.

"Heeeelllllp!" she screamed as she was carried downstream by the water. It wasn't really deep, but in these slopes its speed was sufficient to make it hard to retain footing. In the short time that she had screamed, the mud had all but washed away from her trapped foot, but this did little to alleviate Rabia's new predicament of being swept away. Beyond Sikander, Usman and Saleem, her screams could be heard by the rest of the group that was largely attending to the preparation of the lamb, but almost immediately Ejaz and Abdul Latif dropped their work to see what was going on. Abdul Majeed's gaze was fixed in the general direction of Sikander in a state of bewilderment, still grasping precisely what had happened.

God! She'll drown! thought Sikander, his mind racing to think of what to do.

"Hellllp!" cried Rabia once again and this time, without much thought, Sikander jumped into action, removing his turban and outer jacket and running down the bank, being careful not to lose his footing. He broke off a small branch of a nearby tree. Continuing to run, he managed to catch up with the screaming Rabia.

"Rabia! Grab this branch!" he shouted as she entered a widening area of the stream. If she couldn't remain near the water's edge, there would be no option but to jump in and save her.

"I-I...caaaaaan't!" screamed Rabia, but barely audible over the sound of the rushing water. She was being pulled away from the edge of the water, her body suffering an onslaught of icy chills. Sikander, who had been taught to swim back in University Public School, didn't hesitate now because he could see that the problem would only worsen if he couldn't reach her within the next half minute or so.

"Hang on!" he cried and jumped in wearing his qamees and shalwar. She hadn't moved too much farther from the edge and within several seemingly interminable seconds he grabbed her arm, as the two of them slid down the slope. In a stroke of luck, an eddy caught them, pulling them back to the edge. As soon as it did, Sikander reached for

and grabbed a bush branch with his right hand, arresting their motion while holding on for dear life with his left hand to Rabia's wrist. Slowly he got one leg around a larger part of the bush and with himself secure, pulled Rabia close enough to the water's edge to let her gain her own footing to use her free hand to grab the bush. Once Sikander was sure he had her secure, he let go to extricate himself from the water with Usman and Saleem's help. Saleem, who had never learned to swim, also reached out and helped his sister out of the water until she could lie down on the solid bank. The two of them lay flat on their backs gasping for breath and shivering in the warm air.

"Are...you...al...right...Ra...bia?" gasped Sikander staring skyward, his wet chest heaving and visible through his soaked qamees.

She nodded while panting, unable to utter anything. By now Noor had also caught up with them along with Ejaz and Abdul Latif. Noor took off her shawl and began wrapping up Rabia both to guard her modesty and to dry her off. Sikander meanwhile was able to get up and took off his qamees, hoping to dry himself in the open air. Although the water evaporating from his body chilled him, it allowed his skin to dry in the warm sun.

"Rabia!" said Sikander, now catching his breath. "Rabia, you need to pay attention to what you're doing instead...instead of just chatt...chattering," he uttered as his jaws and teeth vividly illustrated the meaning of the word. He tried holding his composure while dressed only in his soaking wet shalwar pants, his qamees held in front of him guarding his own modesty while still shuddering. She looked at him admonishing her and could do little else but giggle nervously while shivering under her mother's shawl. Rabia was laughing at the comic absurdity of Sikander's appearance and her considerable joy at not having drowned. The laughter was amplified a moment later when she recognized the absurdity of her *own* appearance. It didn't take much for Sikander to follow suit.

The rest of the onlookers watched with curiosity, relieved and thanking Allah for the safe rescue of Rabia, and seeing that all would surely soon be well, they decided not to ruin their objective for the day and walked back up the slopes toward the spot where the lamb was being cooked, helping Rabia and Sikander to dry off under the sun as they did so.

Razya and Hinna waited, holding up their hands for eyeshades against the sun's afternoon glare while staring toward the upcoming troop and straining to see the cause of the commotion. Finally everyone was back together, recalling both the danger and the comedy of the experience as Hinna added her chador to the task of helping Rabia recover. Usman felt more than a little guilty at having led Rabia to get carried away with what he was saying when she lost her balance.

The hot tandoori lamb meat was a big help in getting the two water brats back into some semblance of normality. Rabia had set her clothes to dry in the sun while remaining wrapped up in shawls. Sikander's qamees became wearable in about a half hour.

It didn't take long for the anxiety to give way to nervous humor and for the others to start joking about Rabia's chattering nature almost getting her killed. Sikander couldn't help staring at Rabia, dealing with the taunts of her brothers and cousins, and for the first time he felt as if he recognized in himself the same feelings that Ejaz had mentioned. He glanced across to catch Ejaz's eye and saw him already gazing in his direction with a penetrating stare and a serious smile. Without further discussion with his friend, Ejaz had at least one question answered.

He was not alone. Razya was clear, having noted for some time that Sikander was "eligible," and now, in order for the most recent experience not to seem improper, well, one could do worse than propose marriage between the two of them.

Rabia, meanwhile, had not let go unnoticed the debt she owed Sikander. But in this moment what she felt was not like one who owed a debt, but a deep sense of caring for the one who had cared for her to risk his life. She wanted to be with Sikander and couldn't explain to herself precisely why. Why was she feeling this strange feeling when it was surely the same Sikander that she'd laughed and joked with ever since she lost her shyness to him all those months ago? But for now it didn't matter, and as they sat through the rest of the afternoon, both Sikander and Rabia tried hard not to let too much of what they were each feeling become apparent to the rest of the group or, for that matter, each other. Sikander would only occasionally steal a glance in her direction and for her part, generally, her glances did not coincide with his. All of this trying, however, was, through its sheer effort, also apparent to Ejaz and Razya, and all they could each do was to hide

their smiles inside themselves until the time came to act. That would no doubt be soon.

The rest of the family was oblivious of these goings on. At least, if Abdul Latif was thinking of such things, he was being uncharacteristically masterful at hiding his thoughts from his face.

The same sentiments that came from the aftermath of the near drowning experience seemed to carry across the group. Ejaz was moved to shift his position slowly closer to Hinna. Her big blue-green eyes were inescapably beautiful and hypnotic, and he found himself experiencing a heightened tenderness toward his new bride with whom he had hardly spent any time. He felt for her patience at letting him be absent without complaint. She, too, had understood the harsh realities of life in Afghanistan and had known that the recently completed mission was not an act of whimsy but her new husband's dedication to a mission in which she believed even as strongly as he. Ejaz saw a charming cheerfulness in Hinna that evoked in him the desire to be away from the family, alone with her to spend time to learn her and be learned by her. They would be spending the rest of their lives together, and being a rare Pathan who was concerned that his wife should express her wishes forthrightly and without fear, he was anxious now to get on with their life-building together.

"Ejaz, would you like some more?" Hinna asked. "Ejaz?" Ejaz stared back at her, not hearing her question as a question but merely having the enjoyable experience of her speaking his name. "Ejaaaz?"

"Hm? Y-yes," he replied as he held out his plate.

The sun sank lower and the warmth began draining out of the air as the mountain shadows to the rear of the family group loomed larger over the northern faces of the Spin Ghar slopes. It was time to clear up, toss the garbage in the stream, and start heading back to the village. It hadn't been the kind of day that any of them had expected but it *had* been interesting.

Ejaz and Hinna ambled a little further behind the rest chatting amiably, eager to be alone again. They were now firmly on a path of mutual discovery.

Rabia and Sikander could not, however, be seen to be doing the same. She remained attached to her mother's side, overcompensating for her inner desires. Sikander also deflected attention from any hint of a

subject of him and her. He began talking about the experiences of Arghandab, at least the less painful ones, such as his fondness for the fragrance of pomegranate blossoms. During part of the stroll, he began a game similar to I-spy. He would say aloud an English word representing something he could see, and any of the rest of the group had to guess its Pashto counterpart. It entertained him to see Rabia winning by appearing to guess the right answer only on her fourth or fifth attempt when in fact, based on what he'd taught her on previous occasions, she had known the meaning all along.

The families reached the village just as it had become dark enough to perform maghrib, and after such a large meal out on the slopes, they went directly to bed after isha.

The following morning, Ejaz walked across to Abdul Latif's house seeking to chat with his aunt. Abdul Latif had gone back to sleep after fajr but Razya was awake and about to prepare a simple breakfast.

"Assalaamu 'alaykum, Aunt Razya," greeted Ejaz to his wily aunt who had understood precisely why he was there.

"Wa-alaykum assalaam, Ejaz. Are you not going to be breakfasting with Hinna this morning? Did you fight with her?" she teased.

"No. No, Aunt Razya. I wanted to talk to you about Sikander."

"Oh? What's he done?"

"Done? Oh no, nothing like that. I just...I...I don't know if you have any sense of this, but don't you think that Sikander might be a good match for Rabia? They're surely both eligible."

Razya pretended to be intrigued. "Hmm...I suppose that could be a match," she responded cannily. "But if it were proposed, how would you feel about it, Ejaz?"

"Aunt Razya, I think you can see how *I* feel," began Ejaz, "I was with Sikander all the way into Pakistan and down to Qandahar. I spent nearly two months fighting the DRA and the Russians with him. I saw how he took poor Usman under his care and I've seen how—"

"Yes...yes, Ejaz, that's all very well, but tell me, have you seen or learned what he thinks of Rabia? Has he told you what *he* thinks of her?"

"When we were going into Qandahar, he let me know how he felt but he truthfully couldn't be sure." *I like that kind of honesty*, mused Ejaz before continuing. "Aunt Razya, *I'm* sure now and I think it would be perfect if you could come up with this idea and approach my mother. She'd naturally consult with me. I'd take the appropriate day or so to think about it and would, of course, agree."

"And what about Rabia? Don't you...need her to agree?"

"Huh! More than you might imagine, Aunt Razya."

"Oh?"

"Well, when I wanted to marry Hinna, I told Uncle Abdul Latif I wouldn't want to marry her on just the say-so of her father or mother. Hinna had to agree, which, alhamdulillah, she did. Obviously, I would wish to do the same for Rabia. I know this hasn't generally been our way in the past, but I also know that we shouldn't simply treat sisters or daughters as livestock. That isn't the proper Islamic way."

"Hmm. Yes." Razya nodded with more than a hint of cynicism. She had time and again seen girls being literally sold to settle their fathers' debts or in payment of a gambling obligation or in the time-honored fashion of swara. Afghanistan might be a Muslim country, but that didn't mean that the Muslims there, or anywhere else for that matter, were uniformly able to separate tribal custom from religion. "Well, Ejaz, as it happens, I agree with you...I can't see what would be so wrong about such a match. It is truly one of Allah's blessings to assist a man and a woman to find each other in marriage. I'll talk to Noor, but you'll need to approach Sikander before I take that step."

Ejaz thanked her, saying he would talk to Sikander as soon as the opportunity presented itself. Razya made it clear that if Sikander's wishes could be confirmed, she would need no more than the week to find and use the "right" opportunity with Noor. With the conspiracy agreed, Ejaz returned home, Razya returned to her preparations for breakfast, and in an adjacent room Sikander rolled over, smiling before returning to sleep for a couple more hours.

Over the next few days, Razya sought an opportunity to make her move with Noor. The moment came when Razya was over at Noor's place looking for some red lentils, being in short supply. As she poured a cup into a small bag, Razya made her pitch. Noor took several

moments to absorb the proposal, posing the obvious but anticipated questions.

"I can be in favor of such a match, Sister Razya, but what about Ejaz? He's the head of the family for me and right now I can't imagine this happening without him consenting."

"Yes, of course, neither can I. Let's hope he's favorably disposed...not to mention Rabia herself."

"Oh, leave Rabia to me," said Noor. "I'll talk to her after you speak to Ejaz."

Razya nodded and the two women parted. Each now believed she was doing something quite noble and each failed to grasp the extent to which she was being leveraged.

Later that day, as the family regrouped for the evening meal, Razya got the nod from Ejaz that Sikander seemed to be willing. That in turn triggered the claim made in a quiet corner to Noor, of Ejaz's consent. Noor was thus cleared to take her cue to speak to Rabia, but in keeping with her full rights as wife of Ejaz, Hinna also needed to be in on things. Since Hinna and Rabia had an excellent relationship, Noor saw an opportunity to kill two birds with the same stone by asking Hinna for her opinion as well as to broach the subject with Rabia.

Later that same evening when Abdul Latif, his family, Sikander, and Usman left to go home, Noor approached Hinna.

"Hinna, I'd like to discuss something with you."

"Adey?" responded Hinna with appropriate Pashto respect.

"You know, Rabia's almost seventeen and should really have been spoken for by now but...well, this accursed war..." Noor fumbled over the words with a nervous laugh.

"Yes. I've wondered about that too," said Hinna. "Adey, have you thought about Sikander?"

Noor looked at Hinna in silence for just a moment with the eyes of someone whose wind had been removed from her sail before responding, "Yes...yes, Sikander, uh—for example." Her suspicion grew. "Do you think that would be a good match, Hinna?"

"I think so, Adey. I talk to Rabia a lot also and I think she might be willing to marry him. I know they seem to argue quite a lot but it's really all in good humor."

"Yes, I notice it too, and besides, Rabia is only seventeen now and that's an age where a girl can be—challenging." Noor declared, rolling her eyes as she uttered the words.

"Perhaps if I talk to her, Adey?"

Noor pretended unawareness about what she was now certain was going on and agreed that Hinna's talking to Rabia might be a better way forward. Hinna presented the case to Rabia to listen to her mother's proposal, leaving the way clear for Noor to exercise her right to present it to Rabia. Listening dutifully and patiently, Rabia took only a moment to accept. Noor "broke" the news to Ejaz. Ejaz pretended to deliberate on the subject for all of about an hour before pronouncing that he thought it was a good match and that Razya and Abdul Latif should in turn be asked to present the match to their charge—Sikander.

The "dance" went on for at least another day by which time all parties agreed to an outcome that both Sikander and Rabia had hoped for all along. Yet, the cultural mores in that part of the world demanded proper protocol be followed over which a few other wrinkles had played out, but in the end everyone was satisfied—with one major exception.

Sikander was sitting on the floor in Abdul Latif's main living room cleaning his Kalashnikov and smiling with anticipation about the prospect of marrying Rabia when Abdul Latif walked in. He had just come from chatting with Razya.

"Sikander?" asked Abdul Latif. "You're proposing to get married to Rabia—and that would certainly be a blessed match—but you haven't discussed this with your parents. I find it discomforting that you might be taking this step without that discussion."

"I know, I know." Sikander assumed a slightly worried look while paying extra attention to his gun and not wishing to make eye contact with his mentor. He paused, staring intently at the weapon as he asked, "Brother Abdul Latif, if I'm making decisions about taking other lives in a time of war, can't I be allowed to make a decision about my own life?" Sikander leaned on characteristic late teenage logic.

"Hm! Well, I'm not sure it is so simple. I mean I...I certainly understand what you're saying but is your response perhaps a reflection of the inconvenience of asking them or is it because you feel there's no need? Wouldn't you also be making a decision about *their* lives? Or are you so 'divorced' from them that it doesn't matter?"

"Brother Abdul Latif, look, I've been in contact with them a few times and I'm confident that they respect my judgment. They've been very supportive of my commitment to the mujahideen mission, so—"

"We still have supply mules going and coming between here and Peshawar and I can arrange for a letter to get to your parents if you wish, Sikander. I can even arrange it so that they can get one back to you. Do you want me to do that?"

Sikander hesitated only for a moment before nodding and admitting to Abdul Latif more explicitly that this was probably not a bad idea. Sikander might have been wise beyond his years but hormones were hormones and it was not easy to overcome the urge to proceed in all haste with a decision that would result in his legitimate union with Rabia.

"W'Allahi!" proclaimed Abdul Latif. "I'll arrange it then. The whole thing will probably take no more than a couple of weeks. Can you wait that long?"

Sikander stopped wiping down the Kalashnikov, finally looking up, slightly embarrassed as he saw a familiar smirk on Abdul Latif's face, which quickly spread into a wide grin.

The arrangement was made and the letter written. Along with the customary inquiries as to everyone's health and well-being, Sikander wrote about Abdul Latif's family, Noor, Rabia, and his wish to marry Rabia together with his desire for his parents' permission. Some men were about to leave for Peshawar to sell captured weapons and return with a variety of supplies. They were pressed into taking Sikander's letter.

About two weeks later, the response came back and as Sikander opened it he read its words expectantly:

Dear Sikander Bettha,

Assalaamu 'alaykum! We are all well here and our hopes and prayers are that Almighty Allah continues to deliver

good health and his protection to you.

We received your letter which came to us from a Pakistan Army captain who said it had been delivered from some Afghans who had come from the village where you are. He would not name the location but that doesn't matter right now.

Sikander, we have never had the opportunity to spend the time talking to you in depth, but we are grateful to Allah to allow this way of reaching you on this occasion. As your father, I wanted to tell you how sorry I am that I was unable to control my anger and unleashed my frustrations on you when I did. Please know that after you left, it upset us very much. We were so worried. We called the police. It didn't do much good and it seemed like all of our lives had come to an abrupt end. A few days later, however, at about the time we suppose you began to fight in the path of Allah, we found that our problems were becoming almost too easy to solve and before long we were given a large piece of business by the Pakistan Army. They even made advanced payments, which greatly helped our situation, alhamdulillah!

That change in our fortunes has continued, by the grace of Allah, and we can only suppose that your choice to fight in his cause is the reason for the reversal of our misfortune.

Sikander paused, looked up, and smiled, simply muttering "Junaid," as he shook his head from side to side before continuing.

Sikander, we learned from your letter that you have found someone that you believe you want to marry. As Allah has seen fit to send you in his path to fight, we must believe that it is his will that you should meet such a girl and we have been impressed with your commitment, which we know must have been the result of finding yourself in the company of equally committed people who are willing to risk their lives fi-sabeelillah.

We trust completely in Almighty Allah and if he has placed you in this place among these people, which we feel he must have willed, then we must believe that the place

and the people are good. Your mother and I give you wholeheartedly our blessings. As a token of this, we are sending some things which we handed to the captain who kindly promised to return to us to pick them up today and take them with him, pack them, and send them to you. We hope everyone will be pleased with them.

Our prayers are with you, Sikander. Do what Allah guides you toward and do it with honesty. We pray you will be with us again and that we can also meet our new daughter-in-law very soon. We love you, bettha!

Allah Hafiz,

Your ever-loving father and mother.

Sikander read the letter to the end and let his hand drop with it as he finished, feeling elation while allowing himself to exhale a suspended sigh of relief. His reaction was not only to the permission he had received but also to learn of the family's situation having abated and of the good fortune that was now coming their way. He longed to be home and was overwhelmed with both nostalgia and joy.

"There was also this," came the voice of Abdul Latif who had greeted the men that had returned. Wiping his eyes with the back of his wrist, Sikander turned around to see a large package having about the same proportions as a Stinger case lying on the floor. It was wrapped up and sealed with packing tape.

Sikander opened one end of the package and saw that it contained gifts from his parents. As he noted that, he felt he should give charge of it to Razya, whose guest he was, and ask her to look through the contents.

Razya's role as the surrogate for Sikander's mother was not lost on her at this moment, and that, combined with her limitless curiosity, made her eagerly accept the task. She carefully separated the items, laying them out on her durree. There was a box of glass and gold bangles, a red embroidered silk lehenga and bodice, four gold jewelry sets of different levels of evident expense and complexity, two pairs of ladies' size seven shoes, three lengths of embroidered silk, a sherwani, seven men's qamees and shalwar combinations, a pair of decorated cream-colored khussas, and a man's silver and gold ring. There were also three recent photographs of Sikander's family.

To each item was taped a small piece of paper on which was written either a name or a relationship. Sikander was to receive the sherwani, the khussas, and a qamees and shalwar suit. The other qamees and shalwar combination suits were to be distributed to Abdul Latif, his sons, nephews, and Usman. The simpler jewelry sets were to go to Razya, Noor, and Hinna along with the lengths of embroidered silk for conversion into qamees and shalwar suits. Everything else was for Rabia.

With the important task of making sure the rightful recipient was to receive each item, Razya tidily set aside everything and, with Abdul Latif's objection having thus been thoroughly addressed, she prepared for an engagement process to begin.

From Razya came a formal appeal to Ejaz as head of the household asking for Rabia's hand for Sikander. Equally formally, Ejaz agreed on condition of acceptance by his mother and Rabia herself. He reported back that such was indeed the case whereupon the engagement was sealed with exchanges of gifts and Rabia, finally, was to be Sikander's wife at some point in the not too distant future.

Rabia handled her new engaged status quite well, especially as it had suddenly showered her with attention and gifts from Sikander's evidently well-to-do and exotic parents. She grew more excited at the prospect of getting married and finally becoming a bride herself while she grew more anxious at the looming separation from the home that had been hers for all her seventeen years.

For the next several months, the women of the extended family busily made preparations for the wedding which Razya had negotiated with Noor to take place at the end of March of 1988. It would be after the worst of the winter and before Ramadhan, leaving plenty of time for celebrations before settling in for a month of fasting. Until that time, everyone would be busy with the planting and harvesting seasons before the winter was upon them.

While they were "only" engaged, Rabia and Sikander held their proper distances from each other as any interaction would now be considered improper without at least another family member present, preferably either her mother or Razya. Their conversations became somewhat stiffer and less familiar. A few times, though, circumstances created situations when the two were alone and able to steal a conversation from under the nose of culture.

One such occasion less than a week after the engagement was when—unknown to Noor—Abdul Latif and Razya had traveled for the day to Anarbagh to meet with Razya's cousins. Noor asked Rabia to go over to Razya's place to borrow some wheat flour. Sikander and Usman were busy with a rudimentary game of chess from small carved pieces of wood. They had learned the game together with Irfan and Saleem when they were in Scotland and, whenever it was played, it recalled fond memories of those evenings of rest and relaxation unknown to them in Afghanistan.

Rabia arrived at the door, brashly wandering in expecting to find Razya and saw that no one appeared to be home.

Aunt Razya won't mind me taking some flour, she assured herself as she proceeded to fill the bag she had brought along. On her way back out, off to the left side of the pantry, out of the corner of her eye, she caught a glimpse of Sikander and Usman sitting on the durree, improvising on a portion of its checkerboard pattern with their makeshift chess pieces. Clearly, both young men had been deep in silent thought when she had walked in without a sound. Now the weight of the bag and her evident struggle with it, betrayed her presence.

Sikander broke his concentration to look up at the same time as she uttered, "Si...Sikander," without thinking. Sikander could see his fiancée holding the plainly overweight sack. He turned to look Usman in the eye and back to Rabia. "Rabia. What are you...what are *you* doing here?"

"Oh, I...I needed to borrow some flour." Barely able to lift the sack, she rolled a glance and tilted her head to point to it.

"I see," said Sikander wondering how to prolong the conversation. "I...um...I..." he paused and looked back at Usman who had by now already understood that their game would not be commanding Sikander's attention for a while. Offering to withdraw to a different room, he swiftly acted on the offer, not waiting for a response.

"I...um...don't suppose Sister Razya would mind," offered Sikander meaninglessly while it bought him a few more seconds to conjure up a more intelligent comment. Rabia didn't bother with a verbal agreement and simply raised her eyebrows briefly with the tiniest hint of a rolling of her eyes to signify her acknowledgment of the fumbling obviousness of Sikander's words. She too was now standing

expectantly, alluringly, waiting for his next—hopefully meaningful—utterance.

"You know I...I hope you liked the gifts that my family sent across," he offered.

"Oh, yes...yes, they're very beautiful and um...I was surprised at the way the shoes—Sikander? How, how did you know my size?" The issue hadn't registered with her previously.

"I didn't. It was just a lucky...I mean, I...my mother would probably have guessed and expected that we would let them know somehow if the shoes didn't fit." He shrugged. "What about the lehenga and the jewelry?"

"The lehenga was just beautiful. I never saw anything like it...but I haven't tried it on as yet. I, uh, I didn't think it would be appropriate."

"Oh?" asked Sikander, genuinely surprised.

Now Rabia wore the nervous smile. "Well...you know...it's a wedding outfit, so I wouldn't want to try it on just—"

"Actually, Rabia, it's...um...for the engagement, I think."

Rabia's face lost some of its nervous tension as she immersed herself in Sikander's warmth toward her. "Sikander, you're charming but you know...you don't *say* charming things...you're just...just charming when you don't know what to say." Her eyes creased as she shook her head from side to side, wearing a wry smile. She pursed her lips and, realizing that the awkwardness of the moment could become a problem, bid him salaam as she began walking out.

Sikander was afflicted. Smitten. He was not in any doubt now about the enjoyable aching reported to him by Ejaz and wondered how he would manage without his fiancée for so long. But in the moment, he quickly checked his mind from drifting off as these same sentiments propelled him to stand up and offer to carry the heavy bag of flour. He hurried toward Rabia and reached out his hand.

"Let me get that for you, Rabia!"

Her eyes, looking askance to meet his, creased again as a radiant, knowing smile appeared on her face and she willingly handed him the bag. Stepping to one side, she gestured, with a ceremonious

wave of her arm, for him to lead the way to her house. To preserve decorum, Sikander took the bag within ten meters of Noor's house, handed it to Rabia, and walked back to Razya's place turning his head once or twice to steal more glances of his fiancée's departing form while he could.

Sikander's feelings of lovesickness were assuaged briefly whenever family gatherings took place, and even though he was only able to converse less intimately, just being with Rabia was a satisfying experience. The sensibilities toward avoiding an "incident" were, however, quite serious and the family had to maintain propriety in such matters or risk considerable loss of prestige if a scandal were to break loose. One thing Sikander could do, though, provided a senior member of the family was present, would be to teach Rabia common English words and phrases.

She had always been an excellent, attentive pupil and was now committed to making him be her success story. Besides, she enjoyed paying him more attention than the subject matter of their interaction officially warranted. Perhaps it was just her vivaciousness and dedication to building a successful life together. Perhaps it was even anxiety through witnessing her recently widowed mother going through her own torments in the aftermath of widowhood. No, a husband was not an asset to be taken lightly and could be gone without warning in any number of ways. She would not be caught napping in making sure he would survive and prosper, and if that meant pleasing him by learning English, then she would give it her all for that reason alone, quite aside from her own considerable appetite for the language.

With the harvesting season and poppy planting in October, Sikander was not challenged to be busy. During this time, he grew closer to Usman who continued opening up to him. They loved to play chess and Usman had assembled an increasingly formidable repertoire of opening moves that would often confound Sikander. Usman was now winning about one in four of their matches and Sikander simply— though inaccurately—put his own loss rate down to the distraction of thinking of "his" Rabia.

The winter of 1987 into 1988 had set in and promised to be more bloody than in past years. The ordinary course of the winter was to take the fighting down several notches as the weather allowed the mujahideen to regroup, while preventing serious losses for the DRA and

Soviet forces. However, that year, based on the enemy losses during the spring and summer and the Soviets' now stated aim of withdrawal, the mujahideen commanders including Hekmatyar, Khalis, Haqqani, and Massoud were convinced that concerted pressure applied via ambushes on Soviet and DRA forces would cause a final commitment to exit their country once and for all. There was little left to fight and die for as far as the rank and file Soviet soldiers were concerned. Perhaps one final winter push by the mujahideen would be enough to drive them into accelerating their withdrawal and persuade them to come to terms with what was now widely acknowledged as a foreign policy and military debacle both inside and outside Soviet circles.

A special campaign was put in place whereby mujahideen could rotate in and out of the now bitterly cold mountain country to press through with ambushes at times and places not previously experienced by the DRA or Soviets. Abdul Latif and his few men did engage the enemy for Jalaluddin Haqqani once during that winter. The results were inconclusive and Sikander remained undeployed out of concern for his "groom-in-waiting" status and the strong desire among everyone not to put Rabia into an early repetition of her mother's fate.

March finally came and the preparations for the wedding had been underway at an elevated level of intensity for at least a month. Sikander's needs were well handled by Abdul Latif and his family, including his increasingly close friend Usman, while Noor and Hinna banded together to make their demands of Ejaz and Saleem, to perform whatever errands they chose to declare as necessary, to effect what would have to be a perfect wedding for their sister.

The wedding itself proceeded with much ceremony in the village of Laghar Juy. Abdul Latif was an elder and that counted for something with his family being the surrogate for the groom's. The gifts that had made their way over the mountains from Sikander's parents were all put to use adorning each of the family members. Sikander was sorry for the absence of his family from Peshawar, but that was simply the nature of the situation.

For her part, Rabia, always a glutton for new experiences, could not have been more enthralled. In truth her pleasure did not simply stem from being the very beautiful focus of all attention. That was, of course, a given. It was something else. A wedding was in every way a consummately optimistic act. With all the progress that had been made

against the Soviet occupation, a new dawn seemed to be breaking. A new era of optimism was being ushered in and people were registering that fact together with its promise of a positive impact on their lives. The wedding underscored all these sentiments, evoking in everyone a sense of joy that reached far beyond the ceremony's boundaries.

In any case, Rabia was in love with Sikander and he with her. The wedding having taken place, they could now freely express that love in all the beautiful ways that Allah had enabled.

Chapter 10
Home

L IKE AN EXCEPTIONALLY thoughtful wedding present for Sikander and Rabia, the best gift of all came from Switzerland. On April 14, 1988, less than a month after their wedding and less than a week before Ramadhan, Pakistan and Afghanistan, with the USA and the Soviet Union as guarantors, signed the Geneva Accords. All parties accepted several provisions, but chief among them was a Soviet timetable for a complete withdrawal from Afghanistan to begin the following month and end on February 15, 1989.

Everyone in Laghar Juy and throughout the country was overjoyed at the news of the Russians' timetable for departure, and the people finally expected to see a new norm emerge for the country—one that might recall the more peaceful days of King Mohammed Zahir Shah's Afghanistan. What would unfold was clear to no one, but it surely held the promise of being better than the last nine years. With this in mind, Sikander and Rabia determined that the time had come to make a move.

It was customary in most South Asian cultures for the bride to move in with the groom's family. For Rabia this was barely a challenge of about fifty meters from her mother's place, which was increasingly bearing the hallmarks of Hinna's gentle hand and paving the way for the daughter of the family to go and start her own nest in whatever part of the world that was to be. Now going "home" was a matter of returning

to Razya's place and "visiting" meant going to see her mother, brothers, or sister-in-law.

However, it was obvious that this arrangement was only a proxy for the real one which lay over the mountains back in Hayatabad. The war was essentially won and Russia's puppet, Najibullah, would no doubt get toppled pretty soon, so there was no better opportunity for Sikander to re-establish life where it belonged—in the suburbs of Peshawar.

On the morning of April 15th, in celebration of the announcement of the coming end of the Soviet occupation—news of which had taken just a day to reach the villages—Razya had invited Noor's family for breakfast. Abdul Majeed and Abdul Rahman were on a land mine clearing mission about five kilometers downstream of Laghar Juy in the fields surrounding the villages of Hindrani and Kalajat and were overnighting there.

Sikander sat cross-legged across from Ejaz on the durree. Usman was next to Abdul Latif and Razya. Noor was between Ejaz and Saleem. Breakfast of halwa, pooree, and spiced chickpeas was laid out in splendor on the durree by Hinna and Rabia, before they sat down beside their husbands.

"Brother Abdul Latif," began Sikander. "I've been thinking that with the Russians committed to leaving we ought to be able to consider living a different way now. One which reflects that the war is indeed in our past, and that we've turned our backs on such a brutal way of life."

"Very well put, Sikander. Our warrior poet!" said Abdul Latif as he looked around the room with his creased, crow's-feet eyes, grinning.

"I've decided it's time to go back to Pakistan with Rabia as soon as possible," continued Sikander. Not trusting he could get his explanation out there if he hesitated, he launched into a hurried rationale. "It's been nearly two years since I left home and I really want to see my parents and brother and sister, and I want Rabia to be introduced to them, too. They haven't even seen her pictures."

Sikander was deep in the heart of in-law country and there was no way that the subject could be easy. The others around the room began digesting his revelation. All knew that the subject would come up sooner or later, but it was upon them now and no one had an adequate

response beyond the silence beginning to fill the room, threatening to burst its walls. He felt compelled to continue.

"I also can't thank you and your wonderful, gracious family enough for all that you've done to help open my eyes to a world I would never have been aware of. However, Brother Abdul Latif, as you've become like a father or a big brother to me, I have to beg your leave and that of Sister Razya." Sikander combined the gasp from failing to manage his breathing effectively with a sigh of relief at having finally discharged the announcement.

Abdul Latif pondered a while before starting into his answer.

"Sikander," he began. "Sikander, I am not sure even where to begin, but of course, we all...understand the need for you to return to your people and your family. We're proud to consider you a part of our family and we will—so long as I have breath in my body—be proud to call you a son."

Razya, always the calming influence in crisis, felt compelled to say something. "Sikander, you've always been a pleasure to have around and I've enjoyed your wise words and your courage to fight for what you believe in. It makes me feel...no matter where you'll be, you'll always want to protect Rabia. Please...go with all our blessings for both of you."

The unfolding conversation drove Rabia to direct an anxious stare toward Noor while her two brothers and new sister-in-law studied her intently. Feeling embarrassed at the way this discussion was turning out, Sikander sought to adjust its course.

"I...we...haven't committed to a time yet, but it would be appealing to arrive in time for the start of Ramadhan. That should be about three days from now, shouldn't it?"

"Ramadhan!?" sprang forth three voices in unison.

"Well, yes," said Sikander, unable to imagine how better to explain it. "That would mean leaving tomorrow if we can move quickly and without much to pack."

Noor, whose head had hung low since the start of the conversation, allowed herself to meet Rabia's persistent, and now evidently pained and apologetic gaze. The swelling body of liquid in Noor's eyes ran out of space, trickling down her otherwise motionless

face. Yes, she had given her daughter to this adopted son of Abdul Latif. Yes, one day he would no doubt return to Pakistan, but the same gift of victory now being savored by her people was to be the ironic trigger for the bittersweet taste of the inevitable departure of her daughter, her baby, from her daily life.

"Adey," Rabia uttered, intending quiet reassurance, while watching her mother's emotions unfold. Rabia understood the expression she was witnessing—it was primal; woven into her mother's psyche from the day her mother had been born; activated but held in silent reserve for this very moment since the day Rabia had been born.

"Adey!" Rabia broke down sobbing on her mother's familiar shoulder. Not that she wanted to stay; she was keen to go with Sikander. This was simply to be the down payment for their rapidly approaching but emotionally expensive departure.

Though permission was being sought as a matter of courtesy to the host, no one had any doubt about how this would turn out.

"We'll take you there."

Abdul Latif shifted to the subject of "how" instead of the much weightier questions of "if" and "when," both of which seemed in all fairness to be resolved by the look in Sikander's eyes and, curiously enough, thought Abdul Latif, in Rabia's. No one could hold it against Sikander to want to return. Rabia was now his wife and that was that.

They made ready immediately after fajr the following morning, after more tearfully resigned farewells in which Sikander's own eyes would not be persuaded to remain dry, much less Rabia's. Husband and wife, together with Abdul Latif, Ejaz, Hinna, and Saleem, set off up the slopes and on toward Takhto Kalay each riding a mule with two more mules in tow carrying provisions and gifts intended for both Hinna's family and Sikander's.

Just before noon, they were safely in Takhto without undue worries, given the subdued hostilities in the immediate aftermath of the Soviet withdrawal announcement. They were, as usual, warmly welcomed by Azam and his family. Abdul Latif repaid the welcome by delivering a few gifts of clothing for Azam's wife from Razya. They lunched with Azam and his family before moving on, so that by early afternoon the group had passed Showlghar and Chenar. By dusk, they were on the plain where Hinna's home village was situated. Throughout

the afternoon, Hinna visibly displayed her anticipation as she neared her maternal home. Rabia, meanwhile, was increasingly leaving hers behind. It was not lost on either of them as they chatted along the way atop their mules, whenever the terrain was smooth enough to enable anything resembling conversation.

"I don't know how I'm going to adapt to Sikander's family. What if I make some mistake or they don't like some of my habits?" Rabia, revealed more than a little of her apprehension. "Hinna, you must have had some of the same feelings when you were on your way to Laghar Juy, didn't you?"

"Hah! Yes, I did Rabia!" Hinna laughed. "Some of the things I'd imagined were truly absurd, I must tell you!" she continued. "I suppose it's the natural thing when a new bride is moving to her in-law's family, but you know what helped me was to remember that my mother-in-law must have gone through the same experiences."

"Of course that must be true, but do you believe that by the time we enter their family they still remember those times?"

"Possibly not, but that doesn't mean you can't remind them," explained Hinna.

"And how would you do that?" Rabia probed, although she had already begun formulating ideas as to how to answer her own question.

"Oh, different ways. Sometimes I'd simply see that your mother had a moment to chat and I...I'd ask her how it was like when she first moved into your grandmother's home. It helped to ask her to relate some of her own stories, especially the funnier ones. Once we'd had those conversations, I found that Aba'i was a little more willing to see my own situation differently—with some sympathy."

"Hm...it sounds like a good approach, Hinna. Did your mother teach you that?" inquired Rabia. She began to wonder that if it had indeed been the case, how could her own mother have shortchanged her on such advice?

Hinna nodded but qualified, "Not all of it. But make no mistake, Rabia," she cautioned, "there'll be times when what you do will be so alien to your mother-in-law she'll want to teach you the family's way. It might be something you were taught to do by your mother a certain way. That'll be when you won't necessarily see why the other way is

better. It might not even be something serious or important but somehow, I suppose it's what makes us who we are and when tiny matters have to be different, well, I don't know…it's just harder."

"So, how did you handle that?" Rabia could see—perhaps for the first time—the depth of wisdom in the young woman who was now mentoring her.

"Again, different ways. I can't even really say I've finished. It's just been a continuing experience. One thing you shouldn't forget Rabia, and what really matters to me, too, is that you truly do have a warm family and that makes it worth the extra effort to be a part of it."

"That's kind of you to say, Hinna. But what about the teaching situations? What kind of different things did you do there?" Rabia, as insatiable as ever for information, continued probing.

"Well, you know, sometimes it would be the same approach. I'd ask your mother if her instructions for how I should bake bread or when to bring out the water during a meal were things she'd learned at her mother's home or picked up after getting married. The answer didn't matter really. My asking her was the important thing. It made your mother remember her situation in my place and understand mine better."

Rabia was in awe. "Hinna, I had no idea you were so well prepared to become a daughter-in-law!" she declared, laughing along with Hinna. The mirth continued in fits and starts, but it soon crossed Rabia's mind how the experience had distracted her from her own feelings of separation from the only family she had known. The distraction itself was immediately terminated by this very thought, and her laughter acquired the new companion of a mild frown signaling a growing sense of nostalgia. She held back her sadness as best she could and tried changing the subject.

Rabia gazed at Hinna and then up the trail toward Ejaz, remarking to herself how lucky he was to have stumbled upon such a treasure. Her wand-yaar had to be studied for everything she could possibly reveal about adult life. Indeed, the wand-yaar had now turned into a solid "khowr."

"Hinna?" continued Rabia, spending Hinna's seemingly limitless patience with her driving curiosity. "Tell me about Ejaz…" She raised

her eyebrows adding a gleam in her eyes and a slightly mischievous grin. "What do you make of my big brother?"

Hinna lowered her gaze, knowing her mule had no need of her vision at this moment, and smiled. She let the moment pass as her face and silence conveyed all that needed to be said. It was Rabia's cue to scale back the questioning.

The question, however, did launch a myriad trains of thought for Hinna. She had truly found a wonderful, considerate, but courageous person who had stepped up to be the family's father figure after his own had passed away. He'd been burdened in a very real way by the awesome legacy of his father's martyrdom and met the challenge in every way he could. He'd been sensitive to Noor's situation, joining as she had the swelling ranks of Afghanistan's widows. Hinna admired him for all those things but also the way he quietly and privately cared for her, his wife of just about a year. Though she hadn't let on as yet and it would be another three weeks before she could be certain, she believed strongly that she might now be expecting their first child. That made her feel even warmer toward her husband, who had relieved her immensely by returning from the Arghandab campaign with just a minor injury.

As the group finally entered Hinna's home village, the late afternoon sun stretched the mountain shadows over the plain while silhouetting the travelers. They remained unrecognized by the posted lookouts until they were almost upon the village. But all was well and they were allowed to move on, finally coming to rest at Yaqub's house. The household spilled out onto the dirt street as soon as they learned who it was and once the mules had been taken care of, the party moved indoors.

Gifts were unpacked and delivered to Hinna's family. They likewise offered yet more gifts for Abdul Latif's extended family as well as the newlyweds. As the travelers began to unwind for the end of that day, Hinna felt beyond happy. On her face a completely new expression of hushed contentment had taken hold. She was back—back among her parents and siblings. Rabia watched the expression emerge and recognized its cause instinctively. It made her think of how to revise all her understandings of her sister-in-law that had hitherto been borne of an "in-law" setting in Laghar Juy. This, she thought, is the real Hinna, and again she directed her gaze toward Ejaz, understanding what

Hinna's inner beauty had meant to her brother when he had first laid eyes on her.

All of this preyed on Rabia's mind as she searched for some ideal formula for integrating into Sikander's family—some way that she might adapt Hinna's masterful approach to her own situation.

Having unpacked and intending to stay at Yaqub's for Ramadhan, Ejaz and Hinna were thus transformed—as soon as the following morning—into hosts for the remaining travelers. Hinna proudly prepared breakfast, serving nihari, paratthha, and a semolina halwa. It was a substantial meal but would soon be digested once the four remaining travelers mounted their mules and set off again. Abdul Latif finally and reluctantly rose to begin the journey for the rest of the day with the intent of reaching the Torkhum Road before nightfall; if they were lucky enough to find the Pajero there, then perhaps they'd continue directly to Jamrud. The distance was not far but the going would not be easy.

The travelers made ready and the mules were packed. Now it was time for Hinna to part from Rabia and for Ejaz to say his farewell salaams to his sister and his fellow mujahid and newfound brother-in-law, Sikander. The girls hugged and sobbed as they understood their mutual role reversal. Rabia's already well established bond with Hinna had grown stronger on this trip. They were the only women and provided company and comfort to each other. It hadn't been quite the same when everyone was busy while the men were in Arghandab. She let Hinna's arms fall away and wiped her face with her dupattha before turning around to face Ejaz.

Ejaz had always been a calm and deep force. He could handle himself as well as many and better than most mujahideen. He was tough and battle hardened, not given to outbursts or displays of wanton emotion. Yet, in parting with his little sister, all he could do was sob, his shoulders hopping up and down. He gave Rabia a big hug and passed the palm of his hand over her head in blessing her, much as her father would have, as she too cried with her head buried in his chest and arms. Rabia was four years younger than him and he had been her protector. He had been a source of solace together with her uncle, as both men had done their level best to prevent her from feeling the full pain of losing her father. Besides, Ejaz simply loved her as his little sister.

Saleem looked on, unsure of how he would respond when he, too, would be saying salaams to his sister in Hayatabad. Abdul Latif's adam's apple likewise betrayed his unwelcome anticipation of having to leave behind his only niece in just a few days' time. But he had been in this world long enough to know that this was indeed the way of the world and there wasn't much that he could do about it.

Making frequent rearward glances and waving their arms to the family standing outside Yaqub's home that morning, the four remaining travelers rode off. Eventually they made it to the edge of the plain and climbed up to the northeast taking the switchback trails over the pass into the last valley leading to the Khyber Pass and the Torkhum Road not far from Jamrud. By early evening, not saying much of anything on the way, they reached their familiar stopping point. When they arrived, there was already a group of mujahideen heading back over the mountains to Khost awaiting any travelers that might be coming in from the west with mules. Sikander saw the Pajero outside and warmed to it like an old friend. It was now considerably well worn and as dirty as ever.

On this occasion the vehicle had been driven there by one of the Khost-bound travelers and the expectation was that someone from Arif's place would drop by to pick it up later. Sikander had only an inkling of how to drive a vehicle. Abdul Latif was a self-confessed mobile road hazard behind a wheel, and there was no question of Rabia being able to do it. It was time for Saleem to do the very thing for which he had come along on the journey.

The vehicle took the rough switchbacks with ease and delivered significantly more comfort to its occupants than the otherwise loyal mules had been able to do. This was Rabia's first ride in any automobile since she had been nine years old when her father, a much better driver than Abdul Latif, had taken his family in a fellow mujahideen commander's captured old GAZ-69. From the little she could remember now, there was no comparison with this air-conditioned but filthy vehicle, though it did seem to have more than a little aroma of the charss that was so widely smoked in these parts.

Soon they arrived at Arif's place around the back of the house and Abdul Latif struck his crusty fist on the thick sheet metal outer gate to announce his presence. A servant by the name of Abdullah, trotted to the entrance, recognized Abdul Latif, and duly let the Pajero back into

its home, explaining that Arif was away and would be back shortly. Everyone piled out as Abdullah helped unload the vehicle.

This was not an evening for discussions of war or other planning in the basement, so Abdullah showed the group into Arif's ground floor living room, where comfortable sofas lined its walls with coffee tables next to each sofa. In the middle was the large Persian rug, with its striking gumbad design, so familiar to Sikander from his past phone calls. Rabia looked at the rug and found herself studying its pattern, thinking of Hinna—the accomplished rug weaver—and feeling the emptiness from the absence of her traveling companion.

A small table to the side of one of the sofas was where Sikander remembered he had used the phone, which was still there, expectantly staring back at him. The room was air-conditioned, making it comfortable by comparison with Noor's mud-brick house that relied on thick walls and the shutting out of daylight to achieve some measure of shade and cooling.

The four of them remained seated, taking a light refreshment offered them by the servants while awaiting the arrival of Arif. In an uneasy silence, shifting around in their seating postures, they waited for twenty more minutes when the sounds of another vehicle, a horn blowing, and the grease-hungry gate swinging open could be heard one after the other. Moments later, as Arif Saiduddin strolled into the room his relaxed jaw rose in a smile, and his eyes brightened up as if being lit from inside. He approached Abdul Latif with his arms wide open, hugging him profusely along with Sikander and Saleem.

"Assalaamu 'alaykum wa-rahmatullahi wa-barakaatuhu, Brother Abdul Latif. This is a surprise indeed. What brings you here this evening?" he asked. "I had received no word," he noted as his face began losing its smile, contorted for a moment, then adopted a frown which was all too familiar to Abdul Latif and only slightly less so to Sikander. Sikander glanced sideways with a slight wink and a barely noticeable shake of the head to Rabia, re-assuring her that this was not serious.

Arif began processing the failings in procedures that must have been responsible for this unacceptable lapse. Abdul Latif entertained himself for just a moment longer with Arif's boyish nonsense before intervening to let him know the purpose of their journey on this occasion.

Once again Arif's face lit up but this time his mouth opened to let his bearded chin drop as his eyes darted over to meet Sikander's. He grinned as he took everything in and pronounced his thoughts for all to hear.

"First of all, Ramadhan Mubarak to you all and to Sikander and uh...Rabia?....I wish you much barakah and a long and happy life together, inshaAllah!"

"JazaakAllah!" came the reply from just about everyone in the room.

Arif seated himself at the sofa next to Abdul Latif and said, "Alright, you're here now and we should organize a special welcome under the circumstances, don't you agree, Sikander?" Sikander made the customary plea for nothing special to be prepared and the customary apology for arriving unannounced.

"Oh, that's alright. It's really nothing," countered Arif, as was equally customary. "So, Sikander, I suppose that a call home will be in order?"

"It would be very kind of you to let us use your telephone. We'd like to prepare our family for our arrival tomorrow, inshaAllah."

"Yes...yes, of course! Let's do that after dinner and isha, shall we? Then I suggest tomorrow morning after suhur your family will have the time to make all the necessary preparations for their new bahu!" Arif's eyes gleamed while his lips creased into a warm and knowing smile.

"Brother Arif, we'd prefer to ride to Hayatabad. Would that be possible tomorrow in the Pajero?" asked Abdul Latif. "We have a few errands to complete and I could also call Junaid to meet us there if that's alright with you."

"Brother Abdul Latif, w'Allahi! You shame me by even asking. The vehicle and a driver will be yours for the day tomorrow, and let me know when you want to make arrangements for returning. I'll be sure to get the mules organized."

"Arif, you're a kind man and you'll indeed be remembered as one of the people that thanklessly did so much for our resistance," responded Abdul Latif, "and inshaAllah, your reward will be in heaven."

The travelers ate dinner, prayed isha, and when all the food had been cleared, everyone except Rabia and Sikander went downstairs to Arif's large meeting room.

To her great delight at being so stimulated, Rabia took in the visually splendid setting of Arif's living room. Her head swiveled constantly as she mentally noted the fabric of the drapes, the items of small furniture dotted around the room, the bookcase against the wall in front of her, flanked by two intriguing, evocative, and colorful Gulgees, though of course she had no idea of their value nor of the fame of their creator.

As much as Rabia was reading her surroundings, Sikander was reading her. He wondered how she would feel about Hayatabad as he picked up the phone and dialed home. The phone barely rang once when it was immediately answered by Javed.

"Hello?"

"Assalaamu 'alaykum, Abba-jee!"

"Sik...Sikander! Sofie, come here; Sikander's on the phone. He must be back in Pakistan!"

"Abba-jee, I'm actually not so very far from home and I received your message and all the wonderful gifts and—"

"Bettha, when are you coming home? Did you go ahead with the wedding? Is our bahu with you? Is she there?"

Javed was barely able to contain his questions, while growing more audible to Sikander were the footfalls of his mother over their marble tiled floor as she, too, approached the phone.

"Here, Sofie," said Javed handing the phone to his wife.

"Sikander?" Sofie said, her voice quivering.

"Yes, Ammee-jan, it's me and I've come back to Pakistan. I'm coming home...we're coming home!"

Despite her considerable skills at holding her poise for most matters of social interaction, Sofie had almost no such abilities when it came to her children, and while struggling valiantly she wept silently, unable to speak and equally unable to hide her condition over the phone. Sikander waited patiently, choosing to allow the silence to do its job. When she could muster the ability to speak, she continued,

"Sikander, bettha, we've...we've waited so long for those words. Where are you? When will you be here? Did you receive what we had sent you, and what about Rabia? Where's my bahu, bettha?"

"Ammee-jan, here's my...here's your bahu, Rabia." Sikander motioned to Rabia to approach and speak.

"Rabia?" came the voice over the line in as gentle and inviting a manner as Sofie could find.

"Assalaamu 'alaykum, Adey," responded Rabia.

Recognizing the cue, Sofie switched to Pashto. "Rabia, my dear n'zhowr! How are you? How's Sikander treating you? Does he look after you? Oh, I'm so impatient to...I'm so..." Sofie could not continue in her state and handed the phone back to Javed. Rabia did the same for Sikander.

"Rabia?" asked Javed.

"No, Abba-jee, it's me. I'm not far from home and inshaAllah we plan to be home tomorrow by mid-afternoon. Abba, we did it with the Russians. We're kicking them out! This was what we talked about at school and now it's actually happening!"

"Sikander, I'm really proud of what you've done and become, alhamdulillah! I know your education was important, but it can be resumed. Allah guided you to answer his call and you took it, bettha. I'm so proud of you. I...I can't wait to see you both." Choked with emotion, Javed was unable to proceed.

The conversation barely lasted a moment longer as Sikander softly said his salaams and put the phone down, gazing at Rabia. She was looking slightly upset and down at the floor in front of her.

"What? What is it, Rabia? Rabia?"

Rabia was thinking about her mother and brothers and how, shortly, she would be the "outsider" in the house with her uncle and brother no longer there to protect her. Having heard his mother now, she imagined the pain Sofie must have felt when Sikander had left them almost two years ago. Sikander took her out of the living room to rejoin Abdul Latif, Saleem, and Arif.

"Everything alright?" asked Abdul Latif as he saw a hint of dampness under Rabia's eyes.

"Yes, everything's alright," assured Sikander, not wishing to draw attention to Rabia's state just then.

The visitors were shown their rooms with Sikander and Rabia given prime choice. Too tired to do anything else, it wasn't long before they fell asleep.

About an hour and a half before sunrise, everyone awoke to participate in the suhur for the first fast of Ramadhan. As travelers, it was optional for Abdul Latif and Saleem and questionable for Sikander. Rabia, however, had been in her monthly cycle for the past five days and was therefore unable to fast or pray in such a condition. She would make up for the lost days after the end of her cycle.

The three men chose to perform the fast regardless of their travel status, while Rabia discreetly joined her husband for the suhur. She would simply avoid the niyyah, making solemn pronouncement of fasting intent after the suhur, which was the normal way to commence fasting each day.

They filed into the dining room off to the side of the living room. Abdullah had laid out a sumptuous suhur spread. Rabia's face lit up at not only the food's appetizing aroma but also the beautiful way it had been presented. Part of her was again cataloging her experiences in Arif's fascinating home with a view to replicating some aspect of them at some time or other in her own future "nest."

After suhur, everyone freshened up and changed. Sikander had made sure that all of Rabia's clothes and jewelry, with just a few exceptions left at Noor's place, had come back with them on the mules. By about midday, the zuhr prayer was performed and the vehicle packed once again. Saleem, thankfully, was no longer asked to drive in the busy streets of Peshawar now that Arif's driver, Zaffer, was at their disposal.

The time came to leave for Hayatabad. Zaffer drove the Pajero back down Warsak Dam Road onto the GT Road. At Takht Baig Chowk, taking the left fork to stay on the GT Road, they made the turn to the right past the Industrial Estate and into Hayatabad. As the huge Zarghooni masjid loomed ever larger directly ahead of them, a wave of memories rushed through Sikander and his heartbeat picked up its pace as he was almost home. His head swung to the right and left as he

strained to discern any meaningful changes in the neighborhoods he had called home until almost two years ago.

The streets are a little quieter, thought Sikander, but then he remembered that in Ramadhan, that would likely be accounted for by the fasting and slightly slower pace of life. Perhaps it was also his recall that had expected a bigger contrast with the naturally slow village life to which he had become accustomed. Before long, the vehicle was on Lalazar Avenue after which it turned to the left past the Zarghooni masjid where the asr azaan had just begun booming from the bullhorn loudspeakers. Only five minutes later, Zaffer drove the Pajero into J-block and pulled up outside Sikander's home with the black metal gate and red brick building behind the creamy white stucco wall.

Arif's driver sounded the horn and a young man came to open the gate. Sikander barely let the vehicle come to rest inside the short covered carport beyond the gate when he hopped out and greeted his brother.

"Jameeeel!" he cried as he hugged his brother warmly.

Jamil reached out to grab his long-missed brother and enveloped him, verbally incapacitated and overwhelmed by his elation. After half a minute, he was finally able to utter "Bhai-jan!" He turned his head toward the rest of the house and shouted out, "Ammee! It's Sikander bhai! He's home! He's home!"

Tentatively, Rabia, Abdul Latif, and Saleem stepped out of the Pajero as they took in the peaceful seclusion. Despite the home's warm, inviting quality they felt a little reserved at Sikander's "home turf" advantage after having things the other way around for so long.

Rabia wore one of her less flamboyant outfits due to the sensibilities of Ramadhan, but she took care to avoid any soiling of her nice clothes by picking up the hem as she stepped forward. At that moment Jamil exclaimed in Urdu, "Bhabhi!"

Rabia was unfamiliar with the word and as he uttered it, though puzzled, she was sure of its seemingly friendly meaning simply by seeing her clearly overjoyed brother-in-law. In short order, everyone moved away from the Pajero and approached the entrance to the lounge.

"Sikannnderrrr!" hailed a voice from eight meters away. Greeting her son warmly, Sofie approached Sikander and pulled him close to her bosom. She absorbed his presence with her motherly love, uttering silent prayers of gratitude. While doing so, her eyes met Rabia's, forcing a fresh smile upon her face as she reached for her new daughter-in-law and, without the slightest hesitation, laid her hand over Rabia's head, stroking gently before pulling her in closer to herself to convey her acceptance and welcome. Sofie would have to come to know her better for this feeling to transform into genuine heartfelt love, but there was no reason not to expect that to happen soon.

Abdul Latif and Saleem remained watching the scene uneasily. Though of course they were both welcome, they felt the stiffness of being first-time visitors and of not belonging.

Sofie looked up and, seeing them, sensed their combination of pleasure and discomfort. Apologizing, she released the two newlyweds while drawing her dupattha further over her head, and invited the men to come into the lounge to take a seat. Before they moved, Sikander began the introductions.

"Ammee, this is Abdul Latif bhai and Saleem bhai. They have been the ones who took me in when I was confused and sleeping in the masjid. They saw to my needs and with only...a little pressure, helped me to decide to fight for their cause, alhamdulillah!"

Regaining some of her composure from the emotion of the past few moments, Sofie gestured to the two of them to proceed into the lounge. Sikander felt more than a little loyalty toward Abdul Latif and Saleem, but now transforming into their host, he followed them awkwardly in while Rabia was led by Sofie as she was still trying to determine how to embrace being in her future home yet still very much feeling like a guest. She abandoned the attempt. It was too soon and too big a transition for her to make, and as soon as she did let go, she became much more at ease.

"Where's Abba-jee?" asked Sikander while casting a loving stare at his mother that lasted longer than the question had warranted. She had seated herself next to Rabia. Jamil sat between Abdul Latif and Saleem, while Sikander was seated next to his mother on the opposite side to Rabia.

"Sikander, your father was prepared to be here all day but at noon he got called away to deal with a customer who could not wait, bettha. He so very much wanted to be here for you but—" Sofie shrugged wistfully, "his customer was inflexible."

"A customer *is* a source of a living," Abdul Latif remarked, attempting a constructive comment, as Saleem sagely nodded.

"Indeed, Brother Abdul Latif, indeed," acknowledged Sofie with a polite smile but—she wrongly believed—with much more meaning than Abdul Latif could have known given the family's crisis of a couple of years earlier. Abdul Latif, however, had known of the crisis since the day he first met Sikander.

"Javed should be home soon; he called just before you all arrived and I know he doesn't want to be away from home any longer than absolutely necessary." Sofie's mind switched gears as she realized the time. "Please pardon the question, but may I know if you are fasting today?" she asked as delicately as she could. It was not usually polite to inquire about a person's state of fasting during Ramadhan.

Several affirmative and equally polite responses came back, clarifying the absence of any need to play host with water or light refreshments, but prompting her next question. "And does anyone need to pray asr?"

The men nodded while Sikander went to check the prayer room behind the lounge, seeing if all was in order. Indeed it was, as was the rest of the house, in obvious anticipation of his own return, he mused. Re-entering the lounge, he indicated to the men to proceed into the prayer room. As the men prayed, Sofie managed to direct more focus on Rabia and studied her admiringly. Rabia had a natural beauty, she noted, and she mentally rehearsed dressing and decking her in jewelry as a young girl might imagine playing with a doll.

"Tell me, Rabia, is this your first time in Pakistan?" Sofie asked.

"Yes…yes, it is," responded Rabia shyly. Rabia's personality was deeply submerged at that moment, awaiting permission from the layers of her consciousness that governed her etiquette and reserve to allow them to melt away. That was not to be for at least another two days.

"And how does it feel?" asked Sofie, hoping to elicit a little more than conversation-killing affirmatives and negatives.

Her mother-in-law's presence, the strange surroundings, and her new status as bahu of the household intimidated Rabia. The difference between them and the mud-brick homes of Laghar Juy was difficult for her to fathom and overwhelmed her village sensibilities, though she bravely dealt with the schism. While doing so, she was filled with loving admiration for her husband for never having succumbed to drawing arrogant comparisons between their two worlds.

"I...haven't seen very much yet, but what I have seen seems to me to be very pleasant. Sik—," she hesitated to pronounce his name, coming to an etiquette crossroad. She didn't know if wives pronouncing husbands' names was an accepted or frowned upon behavior and while thinking about this, her memory mercifully recalled Sofie's own reference to her husband by his given name. "Sikander had told me many things about Pakistan and you, his parents and brother and sister." Rabia paused, supposing that this had been quite enough to be uttering without so much as inviting her mother-in-law to speak.

"Rabia, please relax. This is your home, you know. You are not our guest but our...new daughter." The word seemed to be just the cue for Sameena to enter the lounge. She had been in the shower taking far longer than was reasonable to get herself ready for the family homecoming during the entire commotion of Sikander's arrival.

Sameena was a slightly precocious fifteen and had started developing rebellious tendencies around her mother, but today the adolescent was on her best behavior as she too was filled with a sense of well-being that emerged from knowledge that everything was in its proper place. Besides, she was curious about her new sister-in-law.

"Oh...uh, Ammee-jan, and...Rabia bhabhi? Assalaamu 'alaykum!" she offered, looking in Rabia's direction while delivering her customary greeting.

Rabia nodded gracefully while serenely smiling at Sameena. Sameena held the potential to be a person she might come to befriend as someone closer to her own age. "Wa alaykum assalaam, Sameena," she said, having made the trivial deduction of identity from Sameena's opening remarks.

"Sameena, do come in and sit down beside your new bhabhi!" said Sofie, to which Sameena responded without issue. As she

approached Rabia, Sofie excused herself for a moment as she made a hurried attempt to reach Javed on his office line but without success.

Returning from the short asr prayer, the men filed back into the lounge to sit down in exactly the same places as before. Sameena promptly got up from her seat and exclaiming "Bhai-jan!" she rushed over to hug the brother she hadn't seen in almost two years. As Abdul Latif and Saleem looked on, instinctively stepping aside to make room for the reunion, Sikander pulled Sameena toward him and being substantially taller than she was, his bearded chin rested over her head as he held her and granted a tear to roll down his cheek. His lament was over a time missed seeing his sister embark upon her journey into womanhood.

With the greeting between brother and sister concluded, Sameena resumed her place next to Rabia with more warmth than before. She, too, was filled with expectancy over the possibilities that a new relationship, with a female companion of similar age, might offer. After some harrowingly turbulent times, the family ship was finally looking to settle upright.

"Sarwat!" Sofie called out loud. In a few moments Sarwat, who had obviously replaced Sairah as the family maidservant, came into the lounge and was asked by Sofie to start final preparation of that day's iftar.

"Brother Abdul Latif and Saleem, we've made complete arrangements for you to stay with us for as long as you like but at the very least for the next few nights after your long drive," offered Sofie, ignorant of their precise modes of transportation. Having dealt with matters of feeding, it was time to turn to the next issue of housing her guests.

"Your offer is kind and generous, Sister," said Abdul Latif. "We have accommodations up in Jamrud, however, and we probably ought to be returning soon."

"Oh, we won't hear of such a thing, Brother Abdul Latif," Sofie insisted. "You must stay with us at least tonight. Please, it would be our great honor and you can no doubt spend some of the night talking about your experiences in the war with my husband who will certainly be very interested."

"If you insist," Abdul Latif replied with slight but appropriately deferential dip of his head, "it would be we who would be most honored." He turned to Saleem to discuss what should be done about Zaffer and the car that Arif had generously lent them for that day only. They could not afford to ignore the numerous demands routinely being placed on the vehicle, and it would be wrong to impose upon Arif. "We, uh, have to return the car to our host in Jamrud. We—"

"Oh, please don't worry about that," assured Sofie. "We can supply you with our own car and our driver if you need transportation over the next day or so. If you need to tell your driver to return to your host, please feel free to do so."

Abdul Latif indicated to Saleem to take care of releasing Zaffer and before long the Pajero was on its way to yet another mission. Saleem returned to the lounge and everyone indulged in small talk. A quarter of an hour later, Javed arrived. The absence of any unfamiliar vehicle left Javed with no way of knowing if his son was indeed back or not.

As soon as Sofie heard the vehicle pull into the carport outside the house's lounge, she went straight for the door to greet her husband with confirmation of Sikander's arrival. She hastily explained who else her husband should expect to find in the lounge and that Javed should be on his best behavior as she dusted off his business suit and adjusted his tie, neither of which he was accustomed to wearing.

Thus prepared, Javed eagerly entered the lounge as he was about to see his son after so long and his bahu for the first time. He hardly had any opportunity to get into the room when Sikander, Abdul Latif, and Saleem were already on their feet.

Sikander stepped forward to embrace his father.

On this occasion, even uttering the commonly used "Abba-jee" was more than Sikander could handle and he simply grabbed his father around his chest to give him a long, silent hug. Javed, for his part, was only able to voice "Sikander!" He hugged his son back and, overwhelmed with joy, he simply repeated silently to himself his thanks to Allah for returning his son to him unharmed and for giving his son the elevated stature from having fought and won in an honorable jihad against the Soviet Empire.

A minute of this wordless embrace elapsed when Sikander finally let himself go from his father, allowing an introduction of the two other men in the room and, of course, Javed's new daughter-in-law. Abdul Latif, more relaxed now that the head of the family was home, greeted Javed warmly and offered several highly complimentary comments regarding Sikander's character, intellect, and strength.

Finally, Sofie gestured to Rabia to stand up and be blessed by her father-in-law, which he did with full propriety. A genuine delight at the fact of being a father-in-law radiated from Javed. That day he felt very blessed that Allah had brought him and his family to that point.

Not long afterward, everyone gathered for the iftar, which being on Sikander's first day back, was highly auspicious. Ordinarily Javed was not an extremely religious man, but he was what he himself might have described as God-conscious and with his son back home, he felt it necessary to make a positive gesture to his Creator. In line with custom for thanking God in such situations, the Hayatabad butcher's shop was asked to slaughter two goats and the meat distributed among the local indigents as well as at a refugee camp outside Peshawar.

After iftar, Javed excused himself to go to the Zarghooni masjid to participate in that night's taraweeh. Instinctively, the rest of the men elected to join him.

Walking into the Zarghooni masjid's large, sonorous prayer hall, Sikander managed a glance at Abdul Latif and Saleem to acknowledge this place of their first meeting almost two years earlier. They had been unfamiliar, strange men then and now they were family. They had seen many adventures together—witnessed death together and faced mortality together. They were beyond family in any ordinary sense of the word. Abdul Latif and Saleem mirrored Sikander's glances. The prayer was complete in about an hour and a half and the men walked home.

The following day Abdul Latif and Saleem took time to go out to Jamrud market and Jumma Bazaar to buy various provisions and sundry items to take back home. They also managed to meet up with Junaid. The war was not technically over, and much had to be done even after the last occupying Soviet soldier departed. The two men came back in time for iftar and once again went to the Zarghooni masjid for taraweeh before spending the last night of their visit with Sikander's family.

That evening, as Sikander and Rabia settled in, Javed was able to sit with Sikander, Abdul Latif, and Saleem and listen with intense fascination about their war experiences, particularly of Batawul, Scotland, and Arghandab. Others in the family would periodically pop into the lounge to listen to parts of the story while keeping busy with their own chores as Abdul Latif led the discussion of every topic but the Stinger.

After the usual suhur the following morning, Abdul Latif and Saleem had come to the moment neither wanted but had to confront. The mood was jovial enough as the food was laid out and the solemn niyyah to hold a fast was undertaken by all present, now including Rabia. For their own parts, Rabia and Sikander steeled themselves for the moment of parting.

Inevitably, the baggage was brought out into the dew-filled dawn air and set down on the patio bricks near the carport. The bricks were still warm from the previous day's heat Sikander noticed as he walked out of the lounge entrance door in his bare feet.

The early morning aromas were as rich at this time as the bird song was cacophonous, and apart from a slowly brightening and broadening band of bluish white and red near the eastern horizon, the rest of the sky was dark with stars still visible, though a pale reflection of the spangled splendor of the Spin Ghar nights. At this time in the morning, having yet to reach its first quarter, the moon was below the horizon, busy delighting the other side of the world with its beautiful new crescent.

As fajr had already been completed, there wasn't much more to do or say except the salaams of farewell. The brave faces and attempts at good humor were pushed all the way until the vehicle was loaded and the men had only to get inside to depart. Rabia looked at the long face of her normally cheerful and caring uncle. He had no daughter and leaving young Rabia with her new family was a totally new experience for him. The anguish at leaving his surrogate daughter behind was eased significantly, however, by the fact that he had let her go into Sikander's respectable and well-to-do, God-fearing family. Saleem, despite his resilience at the other partings en route, also wore a glum expression. The other family members were engaged in helping with either packing a fresh round of gifts being sent by Sofie back to Laghar Juy or the travelers' own recently obtained supplies.

"Now Brother Abdul Latif, please do remember to come back with Sister Razya and the rest of your wonderful family," said Javed, and turning to Saleem, "The same for you, young Saleem; you need to bring your family too."

Following on his heels, Sofie turned to Abdul Latif. "Brother Abdul Latif, please also convey my letters to both Noor and Razya. I am really longing to meet them!"

"Rest assured, Sister," responded Abdul Latif, not quite bringing himself to feel comfortable pronouncing Sofie's name. "I will definitely not forget to deliver your gifts and messages. Please make du'a for us to have a safe crossing back to Laghar Juy." Smiling but with a slight quiver in his lips, he faced Sikander and tried to say something but just couldn't quite do it so he simply shrugged, giving Sikander a giant hug and wiping the dampness from his own eye. Finally, Abdul Latif's eyes met Rabia's as he gently brought her head to his bosom with his hand, as she too engaged in a futile attempt to say something while holding back a flood of tears. The flood won out and she remained that way throughout the farewell until the last of the hugs had been distributed and the men entered the vehicle and were on their way. The small family group stepped outside the iron gate in the dawn air and waved until the car turned to disappear from their street to make its way to Jamrud.

Their departure allowed Rabia and Sikander to move on in their own hearts. Rabia had already begun to adjust herself to being in the place she would now call home. Sikander, meanwhile, home at last, felt safe and able to relax in a way he hadn't experienced for a very, very long time.

Home. The word acquired new depth and breadth in Sikander's mind. He wanted to swim in its welcoming warmth. It was a warmth that penetrated the coldest, darkest recesses of his consciousness— recesses which even in the short span of his life thus far had needed to make room for memories of conflict, hatred, dismemberment, death, and friends lost, now each an integral part of his being. Unlike a necrotic limb, however, they could never be amputated from his psyche.

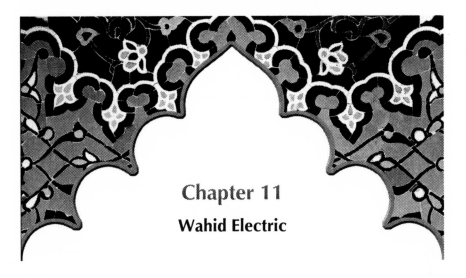

Chapter 11

Wahid Electric

R AMADHAN CULMINATED IN A truly joyous 'Eid-ul-Fitr. The joy was magnified by the commencement just a few days earlier of the first of the major troop withdrawals by the Soviet Union from Afghanistan on May 15. Life would hopefully have a chance to start afresh in Afghanistan very soon. The Soviets were leaving Najibullah Ahmadzai in charge as the nominal President, but most people didn't give him good odds at surviving many weeks beyond the last Soviet troop departure. They were wrong.

Back in Pakistan, the situation for refugees hardly improved around Peshawar. They were still amassed near the city at places like Nisar Bagh to the northwest and Azhakhel to the east. They needed basic facilities, which were hard to provide, and even the facilities needed for the army of NGO and foreign aid workers engaged in relief operations were lacking. From a business point of view, Javed was busier than he had been in a long time. In fact, in the almost two years that Sikander had been fighting in Afghanistan, his company had quadrupled in size with over a hundred employees, mostly focused on expansion into different towns and cities across Pakistan as well as on procurement of new products from Taiwan, South Korea, and Hong Kong. Their electric pumps, motors, and generators were always in demand and not simply to meet refugee camp needs.

Pakistan's electricity grid was less than adequate to the demands of its exploding population and load shedding was a normal daily

occurrence. Generators were essential items for most businesses, even threatening viability if not installed, and Wahid Electric Supply Company was in a strong position to capitalize on this growing trend.

In early June of 1988, Wahid Electric completed a move to a new larger wholesale supply facility in the Industrial Estate area to the northwest of their Hayatabad home. Javed, with his son now safely home, was a transformed, optimistic businessman.

At home, Sikander and Rabia were in the process of settling in and the family had begun readjusting itself around the resumed presence of its elder son and the new arrival of Rabia. For Sikander, it also meant reconnecting with his friends from school and, though not to the same degree as before, with Hamid. Sofie had maintained a good relationship with Rubina, and the family was still in the same residence in Hayatabad. Hamid had finished his last year at school, landing his much desired PAF commission, and he was about to start his second year at the Pilot Academy in Risalpur, near Nowshera, which was luckily not at all far from Peshawar. Sikander pondered the possibility of going up to see his old friend and taking Rabia with him, but it was just one of countless thoughts that crossed his mind when he considered reconnecting with the people he had known yet hadn't seen in so long.

Rabia had to work to find her place in the family unit, applying much of what she had picked up from Hinna together with her own considerable instincts. Her inquisitive nature quickly helped her lose her shyness, particularly around Sofie and Sameena. This was most effective when the conversation revolved around Sofie's life and experiences, focusing, as Hinna had advised, on Sofie's first days and months as the wife of Javed. Predictably, these conversations worked very well to heighten Sofie's own sensibilities of the pressures and challenges of being a "bahu" when she had first joined the household of which she was now the matriarch. Like all new relationships, though, it had its ups and downs and there were certainly episodes when sparks flew as a result of some trivial aspect of Rabia's habits in, for example, style of food preparation or cleaning up. However, it could have been a lot worse if the family had not had Sarwat as their maidservant to do most of these things, most of the time.

"I can't understand your mother," Rabia would say after being taken down for some failure or other, such as setting the tableware improperly. "She could simply tell me how to do it correctly, but she

shows me her frustration and looks at me as if I'm not from this earth for having failed to be born with the knowledge!"

Sikander would simply shrug and declare that he was powerless to replace his mother. It was a feeble attempt at humor at a time when it was least needed. On the occasions when Rabia chafed at his not taking her seriously enough, he would further feel compelled to remind her that though it might be technically possible, he also had no intention of replacing her.

Whatever the level of humor, Sikander was indeed truly in love with his wife. He had known her now for exactly two years and her personality, beauty, and intellect were a perfect match for him. It would be nice, though, he thought, if she could just dial down her Shinwari temper a notch. Especially when crossing with his Yousufzai mother, or they'd have to find a way to work around it.

As time passed, the flare-ups grew short-lived and became more infrequent, as deep down, both women enjoyed each other's company and held more than a modicum of respect for each other's intelligence. In Sofie's case her patrician background demanded respect, whereas with Rabia, while it was a substantial leap from Afghan village to upper middle class Peshawari society, her quick wit was readily apparent to Sofie. Intriguingly, the number or rules in village society might have been greater and potentially more complex, but the rules of middle class society life were simply different and required her to follow a steep learning curve. Progress was rapid, however, as Rabia rarely let an important piece of information get past her, and it was equally rare that she forgot anything she had already learned. Above all else, Sofie and Rabia knew and trusted that each loved Sikander very much.

One aspect of Rabia's arrival which was admittedly a pure bonus was her innate ability to act as a bridge for communication between Sofie and Sameena, as she would often be the honest broker and represent each point of view to the other for most situations. Most of all, the resulting female triangle operated so that each of them could rely on an independent view from any of the other two as to how the third might react on any given issue. At the very least, it had the effect of improving relations between Sameena and her mother.

By July, as Sikander re-entered the rhythms of living in Peshawar, he decided to return to his schooling in whatever way he possibly could when school resumed in September. Seventeen-year-old

Jamil had done very well and brought home excellent exam results from University Public School. The same, however, could not be said of Sameena who had lost a worrying amount of ground in her English, mathematics, and science scores. Although she performed well in fine arts, it would not be adequate to get the kind of A-Level results required for a shot at a high quality career. On Sikander's advice, Sofie determined that Sameena's pursuit of art interests would be suspended unless she agreed to a summer tutoring program; despite protestation over the potential interference that such tutoring might bring into Sameena's social calendar with her friends, Sofie would not be importuned. Javed was worthless when it came to interventions of this nature as he was too busy tending to the source of the family's income. With the matter settled, Sofie set about looking for a female tutor who could provide the supplemental education needed.

About a week later, the tutor, a local teacher named Maryam Reza, came to the house. After a preliminary visit to iron out matters of scheduling, fees, and other administrative issues, the first full session of tutoring began in earnest. Twenty minutes into the very first session, which took place in the dining room and was intended for Maryam to gauge Sameena's proficiency, Rabia happened to be coming down the stairs when she heard Sameena reading hesitantly in English. It was a passage from Rudyard Kipling's *Jungle Book*:

> "...old when he was caught, that makes him nearly seventy—a ripe age for an elephant. He remembered pushing, with a big leather pad on his forehead, at a gun stuck in deep mud, and that was before the Afghan War of 1842, and he had not then come to his full strength."

Rabia slowed her usual avalanche-like descent of the stairs to a much reduced pace, out of curiosity. She was in any case in no particular hurry when the exotic language emerging from Sameena's lips caught her attention at the point where Sameena came to the word "Afghan." Rabia stopped to hear what might be the subject that Sameena felt the need to use the name of her people. Being unable to understand English beyond the few words Sikander had taught her, of course, meant that this had to remain a mystery for some time to come. The smattering of knowledge she *did* possess only made matters worse as she frustrated over the fragments of understanding she could extract,

which were too small and few in number to be reliably assembled into meaning.

As she listened to Sameena reading slowly, with Maryam's frequent corrections in the Pashto that Rabia herself could readily understand, Rabia thought about how she longed to be educated and able to speak English like her husband. She had a natural curiosity about the world and when admonishing Sameena or Jamil was fond of quoting from the Holy Qur'an about how human beings have an obligation to explore the perceivable world and see the signs of God's will in all of existence. But right now, as she listened, she was feeling her own frustration of not knowing what the author who had felt the need to mention the Afghans in his book was actually talking about.

"Sikander?" asked Rabia that night. "Sikander, don't you think I should learn to read and write English just as you can?"

"I...um, yes, you know I've...since almost the day we met but...uh, what brought this up, Rabia?" stumbled Sikander. Though failing to answer his wife, he was curious nonetheless.

"Well, I mean, it seems to be what a lot of the world uses...and...I don't know, I think it would be a good idea. Do you see any harm in it?" she asked, unwilling to hear an answer other than the one she wanted.

"Of course not. No...in fact, I would have wanted you to learn very soon anyway. I was also thinking about Urdu too."

"You were thinking about—?" asked Rabia, slightly surprised by the subject even registering with Sikander. "You never mentioned it to me, Sikander. What, exactly, did you think?"

"Well," he said now feeling nervous about the depth of any hole he might have begun to dig, "I like the idea. I mean...it shouldn't be hard to find a way to get Maryam to fit you into her schedule to coincide with the times she has to come to the house anyway."

"Yes. *I* was thinking something similar, too!" professed Rabia, getting excited at the prospect. "And I...I could even work with Sameena so that we could help each other, though I can't imagine how I could ever catch up with her."

"Oh, if she slackens off like she'd been doing at school, and knowing how you devour information like a hungry tiger, I'd say it might take—a week?" Sikander laughed.

"Sikannnder!" retorted Rabia, wounded for not being taken seriously. "Don't you *want* me to learn?" She threw a pillow at her husband, feigning a frowning indignation but unable to suppress a reluctant chuckle as she recognized herself in his comment.

There was, of course, the simple but necessary formality of obtaining Sofie's permission as matriarch to go ahead with learning English, which was unhesitatingly given and the arrangements were made to organize Maryam's time. After each one-hour lesson with Sameena, Maryam's attention was directed to Rabia in Sameena's presence. It improved Sameena's understanding also to have her be involved in teaching Rabia as the two fed each other's progress in Maryam's absence.

After the first faltering steps with the alphabet, which in any case had been taught to her by Sikander back in Laghar Juy, Rabia began reading elementary children's books from the series Clifford the Big Red Dog, and over the next three months she progressed to more complex materials. She also prized her Sixth Edition Concise Oxford English Dictionary, which on occasions she read for simple recreation. It made Sikander's life a little more miserable as he was often called upon to explain the meanings of the words used to describe the meaning of yet other words in the dictionary. On rare occasions, it revealed his own incomplete understanding of the language and each time it did, she took the opportunity to tease him.

As the weeks passed, Rabia's grasp of the subject and her sharp mind made the going easy, and relatively soon, she found it appealing and useful to watch some of the English language segments on the Pakistan TV channel. Even more interesting for her was picking up the Dawn newspaper as it arrived daily at the Khan household. She enjoyed reading it privately in a corner, moving at her own pace. Reading the paper, she also constantly encountered lifestyle cues from its numerous articles and advertisements.

✿

In the small back room of a house in Peshawar, an organization that had been instrumental in funneling money and recruiting non-

Afghan mujahideen to fight the Soviets was embarking upon a transformation into something completely different. It was called Maktab-ul-Khidmat and it had been founded by a Palestinian called Abdullah Azzam and his former protégé, Osama Bin Laden. Azzam wanted the organization to use its funneled wealth to establish a purely Islamic state in Afghanistan. A third member, Ayman al-Zawahiri—previously of the Egyptian Muslim Brotherhood—was in favor of fighting a global Islamic jihad against anyone opposed to the establishment of a pure Islamic political entity. This included attacking corrupt rulers of so-called Muslim countries. With a Soviet withdrawal now in sight, the debate had come to the forefront and it was no surprise that arguments became more heated. Bin Laden leaned in the direction of al-Zawahiri.

❧

Rabia was lucky in being able to remain in some form of rudimentary contact with her family back in Laghar Juy. On his frequent trips to Peshawar, for supplies and weapons, Abdul Latif was sure to visit his niece. It was August 1988 when during one of his trips that he, Sikander, Javed, Sofie, and Rabia were sitting out in the back courtyard of the house, chatting about how the fight against Najibullah's government was dragging on in Afghanistan when Jamil came running out from within the house.

"Come quick! There's been an airplane crash. It's Zia. He's…Zia's dead!"

"*What!?* When!?" asked Javed.

Everyone proceeded hurriedly into the TV room and stood in a semicircle around the screen. Reports were being relayed of the deaths of Zia-ul-Haque, much of the Pakistani military high command, the US ambassador Arnold Raphel, and US brigadier general Herbert Wassom in a PAF C130 in Bahawalpur. Not much remained of the crashed aircraft with very little information as to how the crash occurred and what would be happening next. In the absence of facts, Abdul Latif's mind raced and though he still had enough of it left to recite under his breath the customary Quranic ayah for a Muslim's passing, he was feeling paralyzed. A moment passed when thoughts of calling Arif came to him. At the very least, he needed to see if this would mean any change of plans going forward.

"May I call a friend?" he asked Javed, who nodded with his gaze still fixed to the TV news reports, while glancing briefly at Sikander and tipping his head as if to indicate that he should show Abdul Latif to the phone and stay with him if need be. Moments later a call was placed. It took eight attempts to get through due to the phone network being overwhelmed by traffic stemming from the news. Finally, he reached Arif who clearly sounded distraught.

"Brother Arif, I couldn't *imagine* it." Abdul Latif heaved. "What will happen? With us? With the effort to fight the Soviets and the government forces? Do you think they'll see this as an opportunity to change their minds and stop their withdrawal?"

"Brother Abdul Latif, I...I can't really say anything right now. They appear to be treating it like an accident, but several things haven't been learned as of yet from what Junaid is telling me. All he can say is that they've lost a lot of top officers and it'll take time to recover."

Sikander and Rabia entered the room naturally curious to learn what all this implied for the mujahideen.

"What about getting supplies back?" Abdul Latif pressed. "Zia was our main supporter and he was the one who argued with the Americans that helped—"

"You'll have to wait a few more days than planned, Abdul Latif. We're just working things out right now and it's too soon to understand what happens next. Call me in about five days when the dust settles."

A deeply worried Abdul Latif let the handset almost drop onto its cradle. All he could do was extrapolate—Who did it? Who would come to power? Would they be interested in the Afghan issue? He felt as if his head would explode with the questions that were streaming into his consciousness but finding no path of release, accumulating instead like the burgeoning contents of a simmering volcano.

Sikander and Rabia felt powerless to help her poor uncle other than to gesture to him to come back into the TV room. They returned and sat down. By now the news wasn't new, repeating to the point of being unnecessary. They switched off the TV and blankly looked at each other.

Generally, the mujahideen had an extremely high opinion of Zia. He had been the holdout on the Geneva Accords which, over his

objections, his Prime Minister, Muhammad Khan Junejo, had gone ahead and signed anyway. Most people believed Junejo had been dismissed a little over a month later for just that reason. For Abdul Latif himself, Zia's death was undeniably a blow which he had still to come to terms with. Still in a daze, he joined the other men, leaving the TV room to sit in the lounge while the women proceeded into the back of the house.

Javed tried to analyze the events in more detail. "They said that the plane was almost bobbing up and down and the pilot was not in touch by radio. If there was a problem with the aircraft, they would surely have heard something from the pilot, some distress message, wouldn't they?"

No one could confirm or deny Javed's question but the conclusion it presaged was obvious. If the pilot did not communicate with the ground, then he was likely harmed in some way. That would possibly mean sabotage. Certainly not a missile, as all the reports they had heard pointed to the aircraft being intact at the time it flew hard into the ground.

Whatever the truth, the Pakistani pastime of formulating and promulgating conspiracy theories went into overdrive and Rabia, who was certainly distraught at the news, took to reading as much as possible in the following days by checking the Dawn newspaper stories.

Zia no doubt had his fair share of enemies. The Bhutto family had lost their leader at his hands. The Soviets could hardly have been more pleased with his death since it was his instigation that enlarged existing American support for the mujahideen and turned the tide against them. The Movement for the Restoration of Democracy had been frustrated at the numerous false starts to elections only to be set aside for continuation of Zia's martial law and dictatorship. The list of Zia haters also included the Indians, always handy candidates for Pakistani political conspiracies, and even Mossad, the Israeli secret service, which was believed at some level to have infiltrated the ISI. It was a long list and time might tell what the real facts were, but not quickly.

After several days, the political scene became clearer. Mirza Aslam Baig was now the highest ranking military officer and everyone held their breath until he declared that the country's elections would proceed as scheduled in November. The aging Ghulam Ishaq Khan was

sworn in as President and the country hunkered down for the parliamentary election process to begin in a much more unfettered way than any candidate had imagined just a few days earlier. Abdul Latif was once more in touch with Arif.

"Brother Arif, do you have any better information now? We need to be going back, but we have to know if anything's changed from either the ISI or the new command or the government. Are the Americans still behind us?"

"Abdul Latif, I do have some information now. We're still fully committed to the mujahideen. Junaid has it on highest authority within the ISI that the effort must not be interrupted and in fact, we have to consider planning a large campaign against Najibullah's forces because it won't be enough to have the Soviets gone if he's still in power. The mujahideen need to be assembling a government."

Abdul Latif could not disagree with the rationale and confirmed with Arif that they would be receiving the necessary weapons and supplies together with the support to return via mule using one of the usual routes. He took his leave from Javed and Sofie, made his usual salaams to Sikander and Rabia, and returned to Arif's place where his men were, though unusually, none of the sons or nephews had been able to come due to the need for harvesting and planting in Laghar Juy.

With the election now in full swing and the country's news more intense than ever, Rabia continued through this period watching TV and reading Dawn almost incessantly, while quickly gaining on Sameena in her grasp of English.

By the end of August, life had settled down in the aftermath of Zia's death. Sikander had attempted to arrange a return to University Public School, but it proved too complicated. Instead he opted to take tutoring, which worked out well, allowing him to become better acquainted with the family business while being prepared at home for his A-Level exams. He routinely discussed business with his father, which pleased Javed immensely. There was a new maturity and confidence, each born of experience, that Javed could clearly see in Sikander, which contrasted with the well meaning but naïve young man who had stormed out of the family's lives two years earlier.

Rabia became steadily more proficient in English but as an additional bonus, the simple act of living in Pakistan meant that she also picked up more than a smattering of Urdu.

Meanwhile, in Afghanistan a new mission had taken shape. Defecting former DRA General Abdul Rahim Wardak, now with NIFA, planned an operation to cut the Jalalabad-to-Kabul road as a prelude to attacking Jalalabad from the Torkhum sector on its east while cutting resupply opportunities for the DRA out of Kabul on its west. Younus Khalis's HIK forces, Gulbuddin Hekmatyar's HIH, and Burhanuddin Rabbani's JIA had all joined in a loose coalition with NIFA in an attempt at a coordinated attack, which required several hundred tons of supplies to be ferried by mule across from Pakistan. The operation was codenamed Operation Arrow, or "Ghashay" in Pashto. Acting as part of the HIK, Abdul Latif and his sons and nephews frequently traveled back and forth to help supply the operation throughout September and early October, which in turn meant equally frequent visits to meet the always welcoming family members in Hayatabad.

In these times, Rabia was proud to demonstrate her advancement in reading and speaking English as she read the newspaper and translated as best she could. It had the desired effect of garnering respect for herself with Ejaz, Abdul Rahman, and Abdul Latif. On the next occasion in early October, Saleem accompanied Abdul Latif and the two of them were dropped off from Jamrud as usual early that evening. Although Saleem was genuinely happy to see his sister after several months, when they greeted each other and she approached him, he seemed to present a certain distance that she had neither experienced before nor expected. He simply passed his hand over her head in an act of almost fatherly blessing. He also had a significantly larger beard than before, looking very much the proud Afghan mujahid rather than the warm and loving brother she remembered.

Dinner was served with the entire family together and when it was over, Javed and Abdul Latif took to the lounge to chat as was common during such visits, with the two men experiencing a growing rapport between each other.

"Brother Abdul Latif," began Javed, "how's the Soviet withdrawal going? Do you see any difference in life in Laghar Juy?"

"They're proceeding, but make no mistake, Brother Javed, Najib's like a fishbone in the gullet," replied Abdul Latif with more than

a little disgust. "The DRA isn't simply melting away and we'll either need to drive up their desertions or defeat them, or both."

"We'll continue to pray for you and your efforts and hopefully the current buildup will accomplish its objectives," responded Javed, being appropriately vague.

After dinner, Saleem, Rabia, and Sikander proceeded into the TV room only to chat, while Sofie joined Abdul Latif and her husband.

"Saleem, you seem quiet this evening. How is everyone at home? Is aba'i well?" began Rabia. "And what news of Ejaz and Hinna?"

"So many questions, Rabia!" Saleem observed. "We miss those at home. It's too quiet without you. Aba'i is fine and yes, she does miss you very much and looks forward to when you might be back. Sister Hinna and Ejaz are also at home. Hinna's expecting as you know, and has to be careful with herself these days."

"Ah yes," responded Rabia glancing briefly at Sikander, "the baby's due in—December? It must be too late for her to come back to her parents until afterwards, right?"

Saleem nodded. Rabia paused for a moment, then looked down in thought briefly before raising her eyebrows beaming. "Brother Saleem, I've been learning English, you know, and I can now read newspapers. Would you like me to show you?"

"It's uh…late right now, and I have to perform isha and get to sleep. Perhaps in the morning, Rabia?" responded Saleem, rising to excuse himself.

Rabia waited until he was well on his way to his room before voicing her concern. "Sikander, did you notice Saleem's behavior?"

"Yes. He didn't seem to be his usual self. He's normally quiet but I'm sensing maybe he's become more religiously stern, listening to some of his earlier comments, Rabia. When Ejaz was here last time, he'd mentioned that Younus Khalis had visited Laghar Juy to offer his encouragements to the mujahideen. He took some of the young men along with him supposedly to give them more guidance in the way of Islam. Saleem and your cousins were among them, but somehow Saleem seems to be more deeply into this stuff."

"Well, he seems quiet. That's all. If he's more properly following Islam then that's fine. Maybe we can learn something from him too."

"Mmm...maybe."

Seeing that they were alone in the room, Rabia moved up behind the seated Sikander and stooped down to put her arms around his neck as she lowered her head next to his. "Have you thought about children, Sikander?" she asked, wearing a broad smile.

"Mmm? Yes—" he replied, smiling back while laying a hand on her forearm, "but we have a lot of time. I've just turned twenty and you're still in your teens, so what's the hurry?"

"Oh, I'm not saying right now, Sikander! I was just...asking." Unable to let go of the smile, she added a cocked eyebrow to her expression and in her signature tone of undisguised sarcasm said, "Come on, let's go back to the lounge and...join the adults?"

The point not lost on him, Sikander smirked as they walked over to the main lounge where Abdul Latif, Javed, and Sofie were sitting.

"Ah, Sikander, I've been talking to Abdul Latif and we agree that it would be helpful to send over one or two diesel pumps and a turbo-generator so that they can create a reservoir and generate electricity from it for parts of the village," pronounced Javed, clearly pleased with himself and his small contribution to the mujahideen effort.

"Will you be able to take such things with you on this trip, Brother Abdul Latif?" asked Sikander. "It seems like a lot for something unplanned."

"True enough, but it could still be done the next time we come, if the equipment could be disassembled into components that could be quickly reassembled. That way the mules will be able to handle it."

"That's excellent then," remarked Sikander, impressed with his father's generosity. Before long the conversation drifted into small talk and petered out as everyone finally went to bed.

The following morning, Rabia wanted to show Saleem how much progress she'd made in her English lessons by reading from the Dawn newspaper's headlines and other stories. Saleem offered a polite compliment to her for improving herself but reminded her to guard her modesty.

"Well," she pouted, mortified. "I'm not exactly parading in the streets." She was obviously disappointed at Saleem's less than delighted reaction to her efforts.

Sensing where the conversation might be headed, Sikander attempted to change its course. "Rabia, why don't you read something else from the newspaper?"

Fueled by her irritation over the previous subject, Rabia began once more to read, reporting that Benazir Bhutto seemed to be ahead of the opposition in the running for the election due to be held in November. With a sigh of exasperation at the demands on his intervention, and anticipating the probable fallout from a conversation about women and their role in politics, Sikander stepped in once again to change the subject.

"How's Usman doing, Saleem?"

"Oh...he's doing well; he's become virtually another son to Uncle Abdul Latif and still helps in missions. He and I make a good Stinger team and we miss you for that role Sikander, though I'm happy to say we've become a lot less busy lately."

Sikander's redirection of the conversation had done the trick.

Abdul Latif and Saleem left that morning to ferry their cargo of weapons and supplies across to Afghanistan for Operation Arrow. Javed, Sikander, Rabia, and Sofie saw them off, wishing them well and praying for their speedy, safe arrival and victory.

November came and after the first week, word came that Operation Arrow had been an outstanding success. General Wardak had managed to destroy two bridges over a four-kilometer stretch of the Jalalabad-to-Kabul road, with a large contingent of vehicles and soldiers stuck between the bridges. After a lull, the mujahideen attacked in force and overwhelmed the DRA forces with more than five hundred of their soldiers dead, more than two hundred captured, not including almost a dozen captured officers. They lost over forty tanks and APCs, and several other light and heavy weapons were captured along with the prisoners.

A little more than a week later, Benazir Bhutto won the election and was duly sworn in as Prime Minister. Life continued largely unchanged until February the following year when the last of the Soviet

forces officially departed. Najibullah continued in the central government and mujahideen forces continued to hammer away at the DRA who now had to manage without any Soviet help. Mujahideen progress was much slower than anyone would have believed as the DRA began to operate more effectively as a fighting force, perhaps out of the knowledge that success or failure was truly down to their own competence without the Russian crutch.

Meanwhile, Javed's business met with continuing success and Sikander began, with more serious involvement, to learn the details of Wahid Electric Supply Company's operations. He had been to the company on several occasions after coming back to Pakistan and learning more was clearly important to Sikander. Javed was happy to indulge his son's wishes. The man who now stood before him had proven leadership potential, and what better than to lead the family's company?

"What are we buying and selling? What about prices? Where do we buy from? What kind of customers do we have?" were among the numerous questions on Sikander's lips when Javed had Sikander accompany him to the warehouse. Sikander's personable nature allowed him to build relationships with the people who worked for his father.

Munir Anwar was a forty-two-year-old Punjabi who had migrated up to Peshawar in the mid 1970s. By all accounts he seemed like a dedicated and hard-working person and had quickly won the confidence of Javed, who subsequently put him in charge of buying and accounting, as well as hiring and firing of the lower level clerks and handlers working at the warehouse. The sales department was the responsibility of Javed himself and another employee named Rehan. Javed handled the large accounts while Rehan managed the counter staff for walk-in business and small accounts.

The business process was fairly simple. There was a warehouse. It distributed electrical goods such as motors, pumps, switches, and generators. Goods came from such overseas locations as Hong Kong, South Korea, Taiwan, Singapore, China, Japan, and several European countries. Less expensive products, mostly from Punjab and Sind were also distributed by the company. Wahid Electric obtained locally produced items directly from manufacturers and imported foreign-made products from larger scale distributors in Singapore or Dubai.

Contractors, government agencies, and the military were the usual buyers and their purchases were typically no more than one or two items of any given type. Goods were picked up from the port of clearance for overseas items and trucked to the growing number of outlets owned by Wahid Electric in the NWFP and northern Punjab.

As for pricing, Javed typically doubled his cost, giving him fifty percent gross profit, which covered his overhead and returned a decent net profit if volumes could be maintained. With most of his suppliers he had terms, and the vast majority of his business dealt with cash buyers. This gave him considerable room to maneuver as long as he didn't do any other crazy deals like depending on the honesty of the Kabeer brothers of Dubai.

Sikander was sharp-witted enough to understand the numbers and the overall business concept but felt weaker in his knowledge of the company's products. So he took to spending his time with either his father or Munir—largely responsible for purchasing—to try to understand more about the products.

Munir, a portly man, always wore a qamees and shalwar to work. He ate well and it was easier on his stomach to be able to loosen or tighten his ezarband as needed. His desk and office were littered with catalogues and he was constantly on the phone negotiating with suppliers over price, hunting down stray shipments, arguing with customs officials, barking at trucking companies, or sorting out space for incoming deliveries. He could do all of these things in English, Punjabi, Pashto, and Urdu. Sitting across the desk from Munir and having a conversation with him was like trying to cross a busy highway. Each comment or question had to be delivered or received in between all the other things competing for his attention.

"Munir, why do the different types of switches vary in price so much?" asked Sikander, or "What's the difference between an AC motor and a DC motor and why do people want either kind?" The answers likewise came back in manageable packets of meaning, interrupted by a phone ringing, the conversation on the phone itself, the resumption of the answer, back to the phone, and so on, until eventually it was reassembled as best it could be, back in Sikander's head.

As long as being on the phone buying, negotiating, arguing, or organizing shipments wasn't super critical, Munir would tolerate the young Sikander's questions as he was obviously the owner's son and no

doubt set to rule the company one day. In little more than two weeks, Sikander formed a grasp of the purchasing side of the business and felt ready to engage his father with questions regarding it.

"Abba-jee, have we ever considered getting some of these products from America?" or "What about avoiding Singapore or Dubai altogether to buy direct from factories?" Some of his questions were still a little naïve but many others had merit.

Javed had himself become a much more mellow personality since Sikander first left home and was happy to spend the time answering Sikander's questions, but most especially he enjoyed asking Sikander for his opinion on just about anything.

Following the Soviet Union's withdrawal in February, came the departure of most of the non-Afghan mujahideen, most notably Osama Bin Laden who returned to his native Saudi Arabia, though he was frequently in and out of Pakistan.

In the back rooms of the small house in Peshawar where the Maktab-ul-Khidmat had routinely convened, things had not proceeded well for Abdullah Azzam. There was increasing acrimony between himself and al-Zawahiri over the matter of the future direction of the Maktab's resources, and Bin Laden had generally been swayed by al-Zawahiri, despite his long-standing friendship with Azzam. Al-Zawahiri argued that with the coming end of the Cold War and America emerging victorious, the new threat to the realization of an Islamic state was none other than America itself, hitherto the staunchest ally of the mujahideen. He further argued that if an insignificant disorganized band of mujahideen could prevail over a vastly superior foe, it could only have been by the will of Allah. Therefore, standing against America in the aftermath of the Cold War should be approached with the same zeal and conviction about ultimate victory as was the case against the Soviets. Al-Zawahiri's fiery rhetoric appealed to Bin Laden.

On November 24, 1989, Azzam and his three sons were killed on their way to an evening prayer at the local masjid. The killings were accomplished with anti-personnel mines and regardless of whoever was responsible, al-Zawahiri's ascendancy with Bin Laden was assured. Having lost its co-founder, Maktab-ul-Khidmat was absorbed into a new organization whose aim was very much along the lines al-Zawahiri had

articulated, namely a global jihad aimed at establishing an Islamic state. It was called the Base—in Arabic, "al-Qaeda."

Al-Zawahiri's position seemed vindicated when the United States did indeed virtually abandon Afghanistan as a place no longer worthy of attention or expenditure once the Russians left. The Soviet Union was on its way to imploding and there didn't seem anything to gain from an elevated presence.

In August of the following year, however, a seismic wave shook the political globe, with even greater aftershocks that would reverberate for well over a decade. From under the sleeping noses of the world's most sophisticated intelligence communities, former US ally against the Ayatollahs of Iran, Saddam Hussein of Iraq, chose to lay claim to Kuwait by military force. His troops barreled into the neighboring and largely defenseless country to the great alarm not only of the United States but also Saudi Arabia, whose oilfields were now a stone's throw from Saddam's reach.

Bin Laden immediately launched an appeal to the Saudi royals to allow the mujahideen to come and defend Saudi Arabia. The Saudis, however, were either pressured to accept US assistance or picked them out of preference, and to Bin Laden, the prospect of unbeliever soldiers occupying what he considered Muslim holy land was anathema. It turned into full-fledged enmity, whatever negative feelings he might have had until then toward America for its recent abandonment of Afghanistan. Bin Laden's own sensibilities as to the sacredness of Arabian lands might well have been fueled by the pivotally historic role played by the giant Saudi Bin Ladin Group in maintaining, refurbishing, and expanding the facilities in Makkah and Medinah. The company had been founded by his father and the contracts for Makkah and Medinah were a large part of the source of the family's immense wealth. With it came a deep sense of responsibility for his family's being essentially the caretakers of the epicenter of Islam. Whatever the cause, his anger was manifest.

The Gulf War was quickly prosecuted with Saddam being pushed back into Iraq—his gilded cage. But success against Saddam was of minor consequence to Bin Laden. The presence of US troops on Saudi soil made him implacable and continued to add fuel to his fire, while more firmly cementing his embrace of al-Zawahiri's global jihadist vision. He swore to end the situation.

Following the Gulf War, in 1992, Bin Laden's animosity toward the Americans and the house of Saud was so strong and openly vocal that he was forced to leave Saudi Arabia. At the invitation of Omar al-Bashir's government in the Sudan, he moved al-Qaeda to that country and began in earnest to set up operations for al-Qaeda attacks on US interests until such time as the US pulled out of "Muslim holy lands."

That year, Afghanistan saw the start of its next period of turmoil. With warlord Abdul Rashid Dostum switching sides to the mujahideen, Najibullah's government finally fell. Najibullah himself tried to leave Afghanistan but was blocked, so he returned to Kabul seeking refuge in the UN compound with his brother. It was at this time that Afghanistan slid progressively into civil war, as no single power base was strong enough, or well coordinated enough, to form a strong unifying government.

Abdul Latif now lived the more normal life of a local village elder. He had successfully organized the construction of a reservoir upstream of Laghar Juy and had set up one of the generators that had been provided to him by Javed. It created a small amount of electricity delivered by wires precariously run over makeshift pylons to allow electric lighting at night into many village homes.

Relentlessly, the civil war strengthened its grip on Afghanistan, and with the exception of the far north and the Panjshir Valley leading into Kabul—still tightly controlled and unified by Ahmed Shah Massoud—the rest of the country had become the province of lawless warlords. Its first small ripples began to be felt in Laghar Juy and had even crept into Abdul Latif's and Noor's families. Abdul Majeed and Saleem had become more and more radical. Ejaz, Hinna, and Abdul Rahman, who was now married to Sabiha, the niece of Azam of Takhto Kalay, were much more traditionally—though still by any external measure, conservatively—Sunni. Rifts between the family members were apparent but had not led to anything catastrophic. A certain "cordial tension" persisted in the air on matters of religious stricture.

Based on the ability to buy products effectively and to supply them reliably, especially in trading with the Pakistan government, Javed managed to continue a steady path of growth for the Wahid Electric Supply Company. It entered the 1990s as a fast-growing, politically well connected and financially strong company with offices in Karachi,

Lahore, Gujranwala, Rawalpindi, and Quetta along with its headquarters in Peshawar.

By 1992, Sikander was twenty-three years old and a thriving, reasonably well educated young executive who, in preparation for taking the helm someday, was becoming more confident with his own developing management skills. Rabia had meanwhile become proficient in English and Urdu and liked to chat with her husband in English, very occasionally catching him out with errors. She had become a young Peshawar society woman, though neither she nor Sikander diluted their own orthodox form of adherence to their Islamic faith.

Jamil had enrolled in the Lahore University of Management Sciences and was working toward an MBA, which he hoped would serve him well in the family business. Sameena had grown into a beautiful nineteen-year-old and, having successfully completed her A-Levels, had been admitted to an undergraduate program at the London School of Economics to study International Relations and History. At last, all those hours of catching up under Maryam Reza had paid off during the summer of 1988. She was now also engaged to be married to Wasim, the son of a senior army officer living in Islamabad with the wedding set for September of 1993 following completion of her bachelor's degree.

It was a routine October day in 1992 when Sikander was in his office at Wahid Electrical Supply. He had nominally become the manager of human resources and labor relations for the company, from which position he and his father felt he would draw useful insight into how the company functioned without risking too much direct and immediate damage from any mistake he might make. In any event, he would not be hiring or firing anyone in management without recourse to his father, so risks from that perspective were reasonably well managed.

That morning, he had been down at the material handling area at the back of the warehouse dealing with a minor labor issue when, on his way back to his office up the stairs on a mezzanine level overlooking the warehouse floor, he was about to pass by one of the guest offices for people visiting from other company locations around the country. No such person was visiting that day—Sikander would have known about it—yet he heard a voice using the phone in that office. It was recognizably Munir's and although Sikander had heard the voice many times before, the tone was markedly different on this

occasion as Munir seemed—quite out of character—to be struggling in his attempt at swaying the person on the other end of the line, lacking all of his familiar self-assured and commanding tones. Moreover, Munir wasn't in his own office, which aroused Sikander's curiosity.

"...Yes, yes, I'll get it for you, sir; you don't have to worry but please...please be patient. It will not take much longer and then I'll be done and you will have what you want," continued Munir.

The odd nature of the location from which he was making or taking the call and the almost plaintive tone in his voice made Sikander remain to continue listening. His time as a mujahid made him instinctively but unnecessarily hold his breath for a moment and watch his step to remain noiseless and undetected. He stood upright in a relaxed posture overlooking the warehouse floor but close to the part of the guest office which was a solid wall. This would attract the least attention from any passing warehouse floor employee who would simply assume he was looking at floor activity.

Munir continued to speak: "...yes, you really *should* believe me. Just have a little more patience and our business will be done," he offered nervously as his words traveled through the gap in the not completely closed door. At that moment, Sikander, who could not have been seen through the glass door from his position next to the office's solid wall, saw the door open slightly from some air movement, following which he heard it close as Munir clearly wanted the privacy but only now had noticed that the office door hadn't originally been closed. Fortunately for Sikander, Munir didn't think to check outside before closing it.

The conversation, though still audible, was too faint to make out and Sikander gave it a moment before calmly turning to his right and continuing along the mezzanine gangway past the office upon which he had been eavesdropping, past Munir's own office, and on to his own.

He took his seat and began grabbing and stroking his beard while contemplating what, if anything, all this might mean. Munir was a solid hand in the business and not one to be challenged on an empty basis. If it turned out to be an innocent matter, then Munir's loyalty might be compromised by his probable indignation at an accusation. This was, after all, Pakistan, where indignation at the slightest provocation was in plentiful supply, while trustworthy employees were

not, as Sikander had grown to learn firsthand in his nominal role at Wahid Electric.

Sikander came up with a plan. He wouldn't confront Munir on this matter until he had something concrete. He would also keep it from his father who might get anxious at the possibility of losing Munir and maybe do something Sikander couldn't predict. He was thinking like a mujahid.

Over the next several weeks, Sikander systematically explored the possibilities without revealing his motivation, examining different kinds of transactions, all in some way or other involving Munir. He began with purchases, checking the product quantities against purchase orders. Moving on to sources of supply and verifying the legitimacy of sources, he could find nothing untoward. Everything seemed to check out, so without attracting suspicion from Munir, he also began watching the man more carefully. Other than the occasional use of the spare office for phone calls, he could not put a finger on anything in particular. It was late November when reluctantly, Sikander decided on one last step. He placed a call to Arif, who happened to be in Peshawar.

"Hello?"

"Arif bhai, Assalaamu 'alaykum, it's Sikander from Hayatabad. How are you, old friend?"

"Wa alaykum assalaam! Alhamdulillah, I'm fine. And how are you, Sikander? It's so nice to hear from you. To what do I owe the pleasure of this call?"

"Arif bhai, I have a favor to ask of you. I don't know how to reach Junaid bhai, but if it's at all possible, I need to ask him for some information which will help me in potentially solving a problem. I can give you my number and if you simply ask Junaid bhai to contact me then you won't need to compromise your knowledge of his contact details. Can you do this for me, old friend?"

"Of course!" replied Arif. "And I'm sure Junaid won't mind you having his contact information, but I'll call him first just the same. Is everything alright?"

"Yes...yes. Nothing serious. I just need some information to be checked out."

The main business done with, they exchanged a few more pleasantries before concluding the call.

About a day later, Junaid called Sikander's home. Arif had been true to his word.

"Assalaamu 'alaykum, Sikander. How are you, mujahid? It's been quite a while since we last spoke!"

"Wa-alaykum assalaam, Junaid bhai. It certainly has been a while, my friend, and I must apologize that my next contact with you has to be in the form of a request for a favor after all that time—"

"Oh come on now, Sikander! What can I do for you?" interrupted Junaid.

Sikander elaborated the details of Munir Anwar for Junaid, hoping his friend might use his access and contacts to do some checking.

"No problem, Sikander. I think it should be fairly straightforward, inshaAllah."

"JazaakAllah, Junaid! We should get together sometime. Call me again and we'll do that," Sikander sincerely suggested before the conversation ended.

Two days later, Junaid called, and after the customary greetings, he began with a question.

"Sikander, what exactly do you pay Munir?"

"Er...about twenty thousand rupees a month," replied Sikander. "Why?"

"Well, your man Munir is either stealing from you, getting another income from someone else, or is independently wealthy. Or all three!" Junaid joked. "He's routinely banking between fifty and a hundred and twenty thousand rupees a month and paying out of that account in similarly large sums."

"What!?" uttered a stunned Sikander. "Brother Junaid, have you any idea how he might be doing that? Or any other information you think is important?"

"As a matter of fact I do," replied Junaid, enjoying the moment. "Munir appears to be a director of several companies and many of them seem to be suppliers to you. My guess would be that he's redirecting

purchases from suppliers into his own front companies and using them to supply Wahid Electric. You're paying just a little bit too much for each product and he's pocketing the difference at virtually no risk, since he wouldn't have to buy anything that your company isn't already committed to buying. If you go direct to the source or the manufacturer, he won't be able to take advantage of this skimming."

"Hmm...Brother Junaid, can you name the companies?"

Junaid supplied the names and Sikander noted them down. It would now be a matter of going back over the purchase transactions to see if those names appeared as suppliers to Wahid Electric and that would be that.

At the office the following day, Sikander initiated his detective work. Sure enough, the names started popping up on the suppliers lists. Over a couple more days, he went through actual purchase transactions and saw the products being purchased. Scouring over historical information, he found other genuine suppliers not on Junaid's list and saw in many cases the same products but at lower prices. The case was made and Sikander decided to take the proof he'd assembled to his father the following day after wrapping up a few loose ends just to make his case airtight. A sense of pride came over him as he imagined Javed being truly impressed at his unearthing Munir's secret disloyalty, while further adding to the trust Javed would be placing upon him in future.

It was December 3rd. That evening, Sikander and Rabia had been invited to Hamid's place. Hamid had married Afreen, the daughter of an electronics retail business owner, and the four of them were good friends. Hamid was also a flight lieutenant and by all accounts it seemed he would soon become a squadron leader. That particular evening, Sikander was not his usual easygoing self as the matter of Munir continued to gnaw at him and he wondered how he would broach the subject with his father. By the time the evening was done, it was late as Sikander drove home with Rabia.

"Something wrong?" asked Rabia.

"Hmm? Oh...no, not really. Why?"

"Well, Sikander, you seemed...distant...this evening, and I might add, right now too," noted Rabia using the English word for distant. Sikander sighed, confessed himself to be preoccupied with a work issue, and apologized for spoiling Rabia's evening. The couple

returned home well after midnight and clearly too late to discuss anything with his father.

After a fitful night, Sikander overslept, leaving Javed to head off to work without him. It also blew Sikander's chance to introduce the topic of Munir at breakfast. *It'll have to be at work*, mulled Sikander. *Still, I suppose that's the right place anyway. No sense upsetting Abba during the morning commute.*

Sikander was no more than ten minutes behind Javed. He parked the car in the front lot and with a spring in his step in anticipation of the task ahead, he strode through the glass entrance doors at the front of the building.

Sikander was taken aback by the scene confronting him. People were milling around the office reception area forming a small crowd. Puzzled, he stepped up to them and as he worked his way past them, his heart began racing in anticipation of something dreadful. Too many of the onlookers were mumbling for him to discern anything coherent and while wading through the throng, his anxiety received another jolt as he heard the unmistakable wail of a siren growing louder as it approached the premises, eliminating all doubt about its intended destination as it stopped abruptly. Frenzied, Sikander quickened his pace, pushing people aside to allow him to pass until he, too, stopped abruptly.

Lying on the floor of the reception area encircled by onlookers was Javed, pale and motionless. His collar button had been opened and his necktie loosened. A glass of water was on the floor next to his head. Rehan was kneeling by his side. All Sikander could do was to kneel down to join him and hold up Javed's head. Detecting no motion, he nonetheless clung to the hope for an outcome whose expectation his rational mind had already abandoned.

"He…he greeted me just coming out of his office and was about to go through the warehouse entrance door when he…just stopped suddenly and staggered to let the wall support him!" Rehan's eyes were red with realization. "Just…just slid down the wall all the way to the floor! I asked for a glass of water…held him in my arms until his eyes—" Rehan lost the capacity to continue as he choked on what he was trying to describe.

Briefly the hope in Sikander's mind increased as medics approached but, as they asked Sikander to step aside for them to work on Javed, he could see the look on their faces, responding to the absence of life in Javed's eyes. They tried mouth-to-mouth resuscitation and pumping his chest to try to restart his heart, but to no avail. After listening closely to his chest and placing a mirror over his mouth and nose, the lead medic stood up heaving a sigh. Sensing who Sikander was, he laid a hand on his shoulder, telling him quietly that it was over. Javed had passed on.

"We can't say for certain, but it could be a heart attack, a brain hemorrhage, or something else," said the medic. "I don't believe we could have done anything more. It was Allah's choice to take him back—he had to go."

"Abbaaaa!" cried Sikander, holding his father's lifeless torso in his strong but presently useless arms. "Abbaaahaa," came the soft anguished cry as he gazed down upon Javed. The moment paved the way for a mighty rushing torrent of thought. Thoughts of all those times that were, and those that might have been. Sikander pictured the pain he had caused from leaving home and the guilt that Javed would have taken upon himself. He pictured Javed's hopes for the future. Hopes that his spirit had casually abandoned. He pictured the way this day might have finished and the way it was now destined to finish, but most of all, he stumbled into a new fascinating and terrible insight. The doors to his father's experiences and memories that had been thus far wide open for all of Sikander's own life had, in a single moment and without warning, slammed shut. All those memories, those experiences, the stories of Javed's youth and earlier years, had now vanished into oblivion, beyond the reach of all existence. Gone.

While he sat on the polished foyer floor with his head in between his knees, Sikander's paralyzed mind was unable to register any awareness of his father being placed on a gurney. He stood up, eyes streaming tears as he watched what used to be his father, a real thinking person as early as that same morning with a past, a present, and aspirations for a future, now heading on its way to a process. An object, unable to embrace the slightest engram, much less comprehend its own condition. It was a body. His father's dead body.

The medics covered the body and removed it into the ambulance which then, more slowly than for its arrival, made its way to

the Khyber Teaching Hospital, on the GT Road, barely a kilometer from Sikander's old University Public School. It took Sikander another minute before he could reconnect with the scene.

He vainly tried to imagine something, anything that might be invoked to rewind the last hour in some way. Surely just an hour might be possible? From outside himself he could see himself reaching out to that ambulance and it being pulled back toward him in time. He could see it happening. Why couldn't it be so? Time's callous forward march would not be persuaded. His struggle was for control where none existed.

Acknowledging the finality of the moment, his lips reluctantly moved to utter the ayah from the Qur'an most often recited for such an occasion: "Inna lillahi wa inna ilayhi raaji'un." Except perhaps in dreams and sometimes nightmares in the coming days, there would be no rewinding.

Everyone was told to go home and the Wahid Electric Supply Company was closed. A notice was placed on the doors indicating the business's temporary closure and providing a phone for emergencies, to be routed to Rehan's home number.

"Javed had a short but a good life, Sofie. Allah's will is surely always supreme. Have patience, my poor dear. Have patience," counseled Rubina.

Sofie sat in her disheveled condition listening to her friend but unable really to connect, staring instead into empty space, in sharp contrast to the bemoaning lament of earlier that day when Sikander had returned home with the awful news. Rubina assured her that Javed had been lucky not to have been a long-term invalid or otherwise a burden on the family.

Sameena and Jamil were home anyway as both their universities were on break for the holidays. They were young for the loss of a parent and had a hard time handling it. Each would alternate between uncontrollable sobbing and periods of somber interaction with the numerous extended family members and neighborhood mourners who had accumulated at the family home. Several of them brought food, as was the custom upon a death so that the immediate family was spared the task of thinking about food preparation.

The whole family had earlier been to the hospital to view Javed's body which had been wrapped up with the exception of his serenely relaxed face. For all the world he looked as if he would be waking up at any moment. For Rabia, Javed had been in every respect the ideal of a father-in-law that she might have wished for, and she too was distraught. But she was also a source of great strength and comfort to Sikander and the rest of his family at this dark time. Her short life had already shown her enough death to have stiffened her resistance to its occurrence, though without draining it of all feeling or meaning.

Following the custom of Islamic burials, the funeral arrangements were hastily made within twenty-four hours. The family had long held burial land at the Charkhana Cemetery in Peshawar's Gulberg district. Javed's body was laid to rest right next to his parents, Shahnawaz and Nazeera.

Sikander was now the head of the family. He had to come to terms with all that this implied. In front of him lay the completion of Jamil and Sameena's educations and organizing both their marriages with of course Sofie's matriarchal involvement, but financially at least and in some other important social respects, Sikander had succeeded Javed. This in turn elevated Rabia's station in the family, though Rabia was far too thoughtful a person to make an issue of it. About ten days after Javed's funeral, a delegation of Abdul Latif, Razya, Noor, Abdul Rahman, Ejaz, and Hinna, accompanied by Adam and Azhar, their two sons, came across by bus over the Khyber Pass as it was now relatively easy to do, even though a civil war raged on in Afghanistan.

As the mourning drew to a close, and coincidentally the new year had begun, life had to get back into a semblance of normality and the day came for Sikander to go to work at the Wahid Electric Supply Company. He had been thinking about this day ever since his father died, recollecting his imaginings of how that day would revolve around confronting Munir about his deceits but ended up unfolding in the tragic way that it had. It was time now to finish what he had set out to do then, but this time there was no one else that needed to be convinced. He was the "maalik" of the company and could decide whatever he wanted.

He walked into the building a little later than his father would have done in order to be sure that the employees would be there when he arrived. Instinctively he had a different demeanor as he hesitatingly

reached for the doorknob to his father's office. His father's full name was still painted on the door's glass with the word "Chairman" written underneath. As he opened the door and looked across to the far end of the office, he slowly approached his father's chair and sat in it with reverence. His nostrils picked up the now faint but unmistakable fragrance of his father's aftershave, which Javed had assiduously applied every morning. Sikander sighed. His eye's moistened as they had done many times in the last week, while he wiped his face with the palm of his hand.

He sighed once more, but this time with steely determination. He would show Javed's spirit all that he, Sikander, could now accomplish with his father's legacy, and with that realization, he asked his assistant to summon Munir.

Munir showed an appropriate level of remorse for Javed's death as he had done all along in its aftermath. He passed a few remarks about how Sikander reminded him of Javed. Sikander was not in the least bit interested in any of these sentiments now. It was different when Munir was at the house offering condolences, but this was work and Munir had a loyalty problem that had to be dealt with.

For his part, Munir felt lucky that the man whom he had been defrauding for the last couple of years was now gone and in his place an inexperienced twenty-something was in charge. It would be plain sailing and he would be able to deal with his gambling debts more easily than before and maybe even pocket a profit on the side.

"Munir bhai," began Sikander. He used the Urdu expression for brother as a necessary mark of, in this case unwarranted, respect for one who was older. "I've been going over our purchases of the last several months or more and it seems we have been switching suppliers from older more traditional sources."

Munir wasn't sure what to make of such a comment, being wholly unprepared for it. "Sup-suppliers?" he feigned.

"Suppliers." Sikander nodded. "I've noted that we used to use Pak Industrial Motors and then about—eight?—months ago in that case..." Sikander looked down intently as he flipped backward and forward through the purchase ledger, largely for theatrical effect, "yes, eight months, we appear to have switched to Punjab Imports for more or

less everything below ten horsepower? What caused us to do that, Munir...bhai?"

"We...uh, we...we were being given better terms I think on that one Khan sahib."

"Really?" replied Sikander. "Well *that's* interesting. Because when I contacted Pak Industrial, they described to me their prices for this power range and even now they appear to be lower than what we began paying eight months ago to Punjab Imports when we switched to them. I mean, the difference isn't very much but consistently it's there. And I'm talking about the same product, same brand. Everything's the same...except the price."

"Oh...I, uh...Really? I'll definitely have to look into that," responded Munir. Even his relatively dark face was now assuming the color of a beetroot as he awkwardly adjusted his sitting posture.

"Yes, well, Munir...bhai, I must say I wonder who would be running a company like that with consistently uncompetitive pricing. I mean, I would like to know what they were thinking to be charging us a premium when virtually every month since switching to them we've been steadily growing our volume. Don't you agree?"

Munir nodded affirmatively without saying a word.

"Why don't you look into it, Munir bhai? And come back to me with a full report—*today*."

Sikander delivered his demand with raised eyebrows while drilling holes behind Munir's eye sockets with his stare.

"I...uh, I'll see to it right away!" Munir got up to leave with the hint of a deferential nod, feeling in that moment that he might himself be literally following in Javed's footsteps sooner than he had ever imagined.

"Thank you, Munir bhai!" Sikander dismissed Munir with a final request, "Oh, and please close the door behind you."

Sikander was pleased with his first command step. He was sure that Munir would resign within the week and was wrong by only four days. An hour after leaving Sikander's office, Munir left a sealed envelope addressed to his new boss at the reception desk. It contained his resignation. He calmly walked out of the building, never to return.

Sikander thought about his new situation. He would have to project the leadership qualities that his new job required and for some reason this realization made him think about the old days when he was learning so much from his mentor, Abdul Latif, and his boys crossing the mountains or fighting the Russians. Somewhere in those experiences were surely the lessons he might draw upon—lessons he would need as the barely twenty-three-year-old leader of a two-hundred-person organization spanning seven cities across Pakistan in 1993.

Sikander never opened Munir's letter.

To the great delight of Sofie, by November of 1993, Sikander and Rabia became the parents of a healthy baby boy, Ayub. It was almost a full year after Javed's passing, and whether it was real or simply the emotion following Javed's death, Sofie insisted that there was something of Javed in Ayub's eyes and lips. Sikander and Rabia couldn't see the resemblance, but if it brought solace, there was no harm in that.

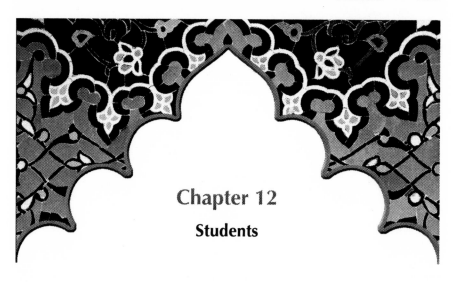

Chapter 12

Students

B Y 1994, PAKISTAN SWUNG BACK to returning Benazir Bhutto into office, continuing the country's flirtation with a period of ping-pong democracy. In neighboring Afghanistan, however, the situation was different. The country—if this part of the world might ever warrant such a label—had all but fallen apart. Warring factions abounded and had become destructive, ethnocentric fiefdoms where each local warlord was a brutal law unto himself, backed up by his paid militia, while terrorizing the local population.

This was no less true in the villages near Qandahar, and from one of those in particular, called Singesar, a one-time member of Younus Khalis's HIK by the name of Omar was reportedly prevailed upon to come to the aid of two teenage girls who had been kidnapped and raped by one of the local warlords. Omar raised a small force of about thirty students from the local madrassahs and, armed with a total of sixteen rifles, set out to arrest the warlord. They captured the man, shot him, and hung him off a battle tank barrel for all to see.

Word of this incident reached Pakistan. Benazir Bhutto saw in these students a force quite different from the warlords, seeking it seemed, to bring order to the country. On what some might describe as "advice" from the ISI, supported in turn by the CIA, she sanctioned financial support for the movement to bring order and security particularly to some of the more important truck routes through the south of the country.

Encouraged by the Pakistanis, Saudis, and Americans, and empowered by their funds, this group of students and their swelling numbers, both within Afghanistan and Pakistan, became known as the Taliban, a label meaning "students" in Pashto and derived from the Arabic word, *talib*, meaning "student." Their leader came to be known as Mullah Omar.

The Taliban held to an austere and essentially concocted form of Islam, which could best be described as a blend of the Deobandi school out of India and the ancient Pashtunwali tribal code which pre-dated the arrival of Islam to the region. Moreover, it was implemented through the influence of mullahs, who themselves had not undergone the degree of formal scholarly Islamic education that would have qualified them to dispense knowledge and learning with anything resembling a traditional form of "ijaazah."

A puritanical regime took hold, whose most visibly evocative actions included the curtailment of the freedoms of females above the age of eight. Demands were made for women to wear burkhas. Schools for older girls and women were abolished on the premise that it was impossible to create an environment conducive to females being educated without significant modifications to village, town, and city infrastructures to assure separation of the sexes. Modernity was shunned and education in the modern sciences and technology was widely considered a gateway to the sinful ways of the west.

The Taliban attracted numerous former mujahideen, including several of Younus Khalis's former people, such as Jalaluddin Haqqani, and reached into most villages to a greater or lesser extent.

Abdul Majeed and Saleem were exposed to more of this kind of teaching than the others in the family and seemed to be more clearly committed to the Taliban cause. Many of their fellow villagers, including in this respect Abdul Latif and the rest of his little clan, welcomed the Taliban's ability to restore a semblance of peace and order, putting the local warlords in check. However, soon after accepting them in their midst, came a fear of the Taliban's increasingly harsh authority.

Within Abdul Latif's extended family, things came to a head in Laghar Juy in September of 1995. Ejaz and Hinna were on their way back to Noor's place with their boys Adam and Azhar, after a stay of a few days with Hinna's parents. Hinna wore what most Muslims in the

world at the time would have considered a conservative dress style, but because part of Hinna's face was visible, it did not meet with the requirements of Taliban rules of dress. Saleem had returned from Pakistan having spent over a month in a madrassah just outside Peshawar and had become vocal about such matters. He was at home with Noor when the family walked in.

Ejaz offered his salaams in the usual fashion. Noor responded warmly while Saleem remained quiet, gazing down at the floor in front of where he was sitting.

"Saleem?" probed his older brother. "I've just offered salaams to you and after we've been away for so many days I'd have expected to receive a greeting at the very least. Why are you being disrespectful to me, your elder brother? Saleem?" Ejaz pressed, hearing no reply. Still, his tone wasn't yet hostile. After hesitating, Saleem opened up.

"Brother Ejaz, I've been very troubled lately...especially so now. I've had my eyes opened to all the things we don't correctly observe in the following of Islam and...and that makes us either...it makes us apostates worthy of being put to death." Saleem was visibly upset with his own conviction of what he had just uttered.

"*Death!?*" exclaimed Ejaz loudly. "What are you talking about? Have you lost your mind?"

"My mind? No, not my mind, but I've been...*we*...*we've* all been on the path of losing our *souls* and I ask you, I beg of you, brother, before it's too late. Adopt the true teachings of our beautiful religion. Only that way can we...can all the calamity that we...we've suffered as a people ever be rectified."

Ejaz tried reasoning with his brother. "Saleem, we...we aren't rejecting belief. Yes, we may be doing some things in ignorant ways and indeed we should learn more, but this...this Taliban practice...it's not Islam. I'll grant you they're well intentioned...but they're misguided ideas put forth by so-called mullahs who haven't even completed their own educations. Are you simply finding fault with the way we dress or walk or talk? That's what you believe protects or harms a soul before Allah?"

"Our women have been commanded to guard their modesty," insisted Saleem. "I look at...at Hinna...and see that she's ignorant of this requirement. The day will surely come when she'll be punished for this.

She'll be punished for walking in the streets of the village shamelessly alone—"

"*Saleem!*" interjected Ejaz, angrily raising his hand. "Have a care how you talk about my wife!" He paused to let himself cool down before continuing more calmly. "We...we *do* observe the teachings of Islam. It's our faith...our belief. You *know* that. The injunctions on hiding the face in its entirety have no precedent in Islam except for the wives of the Prophet, may Allah's blessing and peace be upon him. Look, the Qur'an is quite clear. Let me show you." He stood up to reach for the family's Pashto-Arabic version off a narrow alcove high in the wall where reverence demanded it be kept, free of risk of desecration by falling or careless handling. He opened it to Surah 24, Ayah 31 and read out in Pashto:

> "And say to the believing women that they should lower their gaze and guard their modesty; that they should not display their beauty and ornaments except what (must ordinarily) appear thereof; that they should draw their veils over their bosoms and not display their beauty except to their husbands, their fathers, their husband's fathers, their sons, their husbands' sons, their brothers or their brothers' sons, or their sisters' sons, or their women, or the slaves whom their right hands possess, or male servants free of physical needs, or small children who have no sense of the immodesty of sex; and that they should not strike their feet in order to draw attention to their hidden ornaments. And O ye believers! turn ye all together towards Allah, that ye may attain Bliss."

Out of respect, Saleem remained silent listening to the complete verse before responding, "Yes. I, too, am familiar with this verse, but if you could hear Mullah Omar, whom I met in Peshawar, tell you what lies underneath this and the information in the authentic hadith of the Prophet, peace be upon him, then you'd understand how you misread these words."

"How? How did I misread them, Saleem?"

"Well, for practical application we *have* to look at the many hadiths of the blessed Messenger of God, may peace be upon him, that declare that a woman must cover herself completely and not expose her hands and face."

"But as you know, Saleem, direct reference from the Qur'an is always acknowledged to supersede hadiths. I quoted directly. Nothing in this verse refers to covering the face."

As was invariably the case, the debate continued inconclusively, but Saleem was clearly the more tormented of the two about what he perceived to be the evil effects of living outside the complete guidance, in his view, of the Qur'an and Sunnah. What helped him to this view was the certainty of the turmoil in his country at the time, with which no one could argue, and the equal certainty of one who "knew" that a collective national departure from the "straight and narrow path" was most assuredly the cause.

Unfortunately for Ejaz and Abdul Rahman, who experienced similar sentiments from Abdul Majeed, the Taliban were winning out on this and other debates. They had the backing of force, including such international financial backing that it in turn required. In effect, the people of the villages bought protection from the evils of warlords in exchange for fear under the Taliban who stepped up their severe threats of punishment for what they deemed improper behavior.

By 1996, with the Taliban closing in across the whole country except the Panjshir Valley, their armed presence was the norm in places like Laghar Juy and from that point forward, things would never be the same. On the positive side, there was a dramatic reduction of abusive behavior such as robbery on the roads and trails, and the Taliban even targeted the production of opium by declaring it unlawful and enforcing the ban with a modicum of success.

Abdul Latif, now sixty, was designated a village chief and council member but without any real influence. He was deeply troubled over the rifts in his once unified and cheerful family and wasn't able to intervene with any authority, but he also couldn't bring himself to abandon his beloved village and his children and grandchildren.

Abdul Rahman and his wife, Sabiha, and their family kept to themselves while the same was true for Ejaz, Hinna, and their children. Razya and Noor were both confined to their homes unless a male member of their respective households could be available to escort them. This was not especially onerous, as they had generally observed this principle, to a practical extent, for most of their lives. Having to wear the head-to-toe burkha was quite a different matter, as was being forced into any behavior relating to their personal dress and day-to-day

conduct, however much they may have agreed or disagreed with it. To them, how they dressed was less important than who determined it. It was simply a matter of freedom. To such people, men or women, what was compulsory behavior in Islam was something to be imposed upon oneself and not the job of a legal code. To Razya, Noor, and Hinna, it didn't *lack* the essence of being compulsory. For them, the locus of compulsion needed to be internal instead of external.

It was not long before Ejaz and Hinna decided to leave Laghar Juy and cross back over the border into Yaqub's village where technically, at least, they would be in the slightly more liberal Pakistan with much less of the puritanical influences of the Taliban. At the time they took Noor with them. She complained bitterly that her departed shaheed, Abdus Sami, would never have accepted Saleem's attitude toward his mother when he had admonished her roughly about stepping out of the house alone for a moment. She returned about a week later unable to live away from the village of her family and late husband.

Despite the implication—by the simple fact of scale—of greater modernity and sophistication in towns and cities, women's lives in places such as Kabul and Jalalabad fared much worse than in villages. Professional women in roles such as doctors or teachers were dismissed in large numbers and driven underground or confined to their homes. Schools for girls were closed pending a "restructuring of the infrastructure to allow older girls to get to school out of sight of any male observers." No one believed that this would ever be practically realized. The Taliban did not actually have any principle objections to girls' education. They simply had no proposals for any acceptable way of delivering it.

It was during the turbulent ascendancy of the Taliban that Osama Bin Laden's Saudi citizenship was revoked owing to his issuing several open verbal rebukes toward Saudi King Fahd for having promoted the Palestinian-Israeli Oslo Accords. Finally, after a series of botched attacks on Egyptian leaders, he was ordered out of the Sudan in May of 1996.

The Taliban, well on their way to assuming control of all Afghanistan except the Panjshir, were only too pleased to welcome back the "Arab-Afghans" of al-Qaeda and with them, Osama Bin Laden, whose friendship with Mullah Omar began to blossom.

During this time, it was possible for Rabia and Sikander to pay visits up to the Aka Khel mountains and villages once they had learned of Ejaz and Hinna's relocation. They enjoyed taking Ayub with them and letting him play with Adam and Azhar, while the parents debated the politics of their two countries and the world at large. Rabia was expecting her second child and in June of 1996, Qayyum was born.

By September of that year, with the exception of Ahmed Shah Massoud's militia and the Panjshir Valley territory it held in the north, the country finally succumbed to the Taliban. One of their early actions after having captured Kabul was to seek retribution for Najibullah's excesses. Although he and his brother had taken refuge in the UN compound in Kabul, Taliban forces summarily dragged them both from the compound, executed them, and hanged their bodies from the frame of a traffic kiosk. This form of execution and corpse-display became the gruesome trademark of Taliban retribution for others to beware.

By the end of 1996, four years had passed since Javed died and ten since Sikander had first joined the mujahideen. Now, with his brother Jamil helping him, Javelin, a contraction of Javed Electrical Industries—renamed in honor of their late father—was on its way to becoming one of the larger national wholesalers of electrical products in Pakistan. Javelin was a major supplier to the military and to the private sector, which had begun under Nawaz Sharif to participate in a program of infrastructure development throughout Pakistan.

Osama Bin Laden—having no confusion about his global jihad mission—reactivated training camps all along the Pakistan border from near Qandahar up to Nangarhar, readying his jihadist recruits from all over the world, but in particular from Saudi Arabia. The standing evil of American troops in the holy "land of the Haramain" was absolute anathema and had to be opposed by militant jihad as far as he and his followers were concerned. Over the previous several years, Bin Laden and others had been persuaded about their particular version of Islam, a specialized and narrow branch of Salafism, labeled by others as "Takfiri." This was based largely on the teachings of one-time Egyptian

intellectual Sayyid Qutb who in turn drew his conclusions from the eighteenth century teachings of Abdul Wahhab.

Abdul Wahhab himself had been a follower of the medieval polymath and scholar, Ibn Taymiyyah, who was known to have articulated highly conservative views about the "pure" form of Islam. Qutb was a member of the Egyptian Muslim Brotherhood that had tried to assassinate Gamal Abdel Nasser of Egypt. He was executed by Nasser in 1966 after a lengthy jail sentence.

Going beyond conventional Salafism, Qutb's interpretation held that all so-called Muslims who had departed from what he believed were the strict forms of practice established from the period of the Prophet and his immediate successors—the "salaf" period—were in a state of "jahiliyyah," or tacitly embraced ignorance and opposition to truth. As a result, they were to be considered apostates, for whom, according to interpretations by twentieth century scholar Maulana Maududi, punishment by death was permissible. This gave rise to a number of political movements generally labeled "Salafist" who sought political change based on these principles. Though himself not a Salafist, Maududi's and others' opinions on apostasy gave license to followers of Salafist ideology to kill people they deemed to be ill-professed Muslims, without compunction.

By contrast, several other Muslim scholars had written on the impermissibility of killing even professed apostates, much less those determined as such by the judgments of an extremist few. A more subtle middle ground of opinion also existed which held that apostasy was not itself grounds for a death penalty, but the active promulgation of a non-Muslim way of life by an apostate was, as this could be likened to treason given the absence of a separation of church and state in an Islamic conception of a Muslim state. However, for the Salafists holding the "death-to-any-apostate" view, such reasoning had no merit. They were therefore referred to as Salafi-Takfiris, owing to their pronouncement of "takfir" on other Muslims, effectively declaring them kafirs. Ayman al-Zawahiri was from the Muslim Brotherhood and his Salafi-Takfiri ideology had consolidated its grip over al-Qaeda in the near seven years since its emergence out of the old Maktab-ul-Khidmat.

The takfiri line of reasoning effectively granted permission to commit terrorist acts in which indiscriminate killings generally followed, since even if they involved killing of Muslims, they would likely be

"apostates" and worthy of death. The 1993 World Trade Center attack was arguably the first act committed by this movement against the United States. However, the attacks that really drew initial world attention under the al-Qaeda banner took place five years later in early August of 1998. They involved the bombings of the American embassies in Nairobi and Dar-as-Salaam, which put Osama Bin Laden on the ten most wanted FBI list in the USA. Two weeks after the embassy bombings, President Bill Clinton ordered cruise missiles to be launched from the Arabian Sea toward several locations along the Afghan border with Pakistan where Bin Laden's training camps were located. Yet none of the attacks killed him or any of his close deputies. Meanwhile, similar attacks on Sudan hit what the Sudanese claimed was a pharmaceutical plant producing about half of Sudan's pharmaceuticals capacity, while the US alleged that it had been a chemical weapons factory.

When the news reports in Pakistan made public the US attacks on Afghanistan and Sudan, Sikander was shocked and could not imagine that the United States that he had loved from afar could take such a step against the very country it had been helping only a few years earlier. He rationalized that the precision of the weapons meant that the US was at least being careful not to incur unnecessary deaths and that the Afghans in general were not the targets but rather the terrorists of al-Qaeda. Sikander did wonder, though, how the Taliban government of Afghanistan would view such a blatant attack on acknowledged guests. The ancient code of Pashtunwali and its melmasthia tradition was deeply rooted in the Pashtun culture. Allowing anyone to attack a guest was a mark of great disgrace upon a host and a seriously embarrassing exposure of weakness, the like of which would be hard to live down. This was the case no matter how unruly the guest might have been. Retaliation to such dishonor was therefore imperative in order to avoid the dishonor being complete.

As 1998 rolled into the following year, Javelin continued to do well as it broadened its supply sources while adding more locations around Pakistan. Sikander generously carried on his father's tradition of ferrying electrical equipment to help expand upon Laghar Juy's reservoir and generator setup. He was approaching thirty, and in the prime of his life.

Through Javelin, Jamil increasingly demonstrated *his* managerial skills. To his credit, Jamil had spearheaded the implementation of a rationalized database system for their product catalogue and for order processing, billing, shipping, and receiving. The system greatly reduced the scope for employee fraud and reduced inventory carrying costs by enabling the business management to be better informed.

At home in Hayatabad, life was good for the most part. Jamil had married Kausar, as had Sameena, to husband Wasim, by whom she now had a young daughter named Rukhsana. Rabia was a constant companion and close friend to her widowed mother-in-law. Whenever Sofie indicated a desire to go out, meet with a friend, or go shopping in one of Peshawar's many bazaars, Rabia and often Kausar would be the willing companions. It wasn't at all hard since Rabia, herself vivacious and excited by interacting with others, loved to shop, especially for things that would enhance their home's décor, but especially of the part of the family home she had now fully adopted as her own.

The U-shaped configuration originally conceived by Javed and Sofie for their house was more than superficially aesthetically driven. It was a direct reflection of their ideals of having the families of both sons living under one roof together with the parents for as long as each would live. Sikander was to have the north wing and Jamil the south. Sameena of course would be moving to her in-laws and the family would thus be set up for a whole new generation to come. Indeed, the pain of losing Javed was very much lessened for Sofie by her emerging brood of grandchildren. She could now play with and dote upon them and she especially enjoyed shopping for them.

Sofie did, however, often reflect wistfully upon Javed's hard work having led to no such reward for him, as he had not seen a single grandchild in his lifetime. Ayub, who was almost six, went to school in Hayatabad where the different phases of development made it something of a pleasant, if now sprawling suburb of southwest Peshawar. Ayub and Qayyum were looked after by an Afghan nanny named Atiya; like many such people in her situation as a refugee out of Qandahar, Atiya spoke perfect Pashto, acceptable Urdu, and more than a little Farsi.

With the continuing success of Javelin, Sikander provided financial assistance so that Abdul Rahman, Sabiha, their two children, Sadiq and Sohail, together with Ejaz, Hinna, and their now three

children, including the newly born daughter Riffat, could all migrate into Pakistan, leaving Laghar Juy permanently. Abdul Majeed and Saleem had become full-fledged members of the local Taliban and enforced their version of Islam with vigor. Much to Rabia's regret, however, the older generation refused to leave Laghar Juy. In a bid to get them to change their minds, Rabia and Sikander decided to make a direct trip into Afghanistan, taking with them Ayub and Qayyum who had so far not seen their maternal grandmother. This time they traversed the rough roads in their own Pajero over the Khyber Pass. Sikander had a soft spot for Pajeros, this being his second since his father had passed away.

It had been many years since Sikander had been into Afghanistan and he had imprinted in his mind a scene he recalled of the last time he had been in Laghar Juy. He had left it behind, climbing up the slopes on mules toward Takhto Kalay eleven years earlier, looking ruefully back at the village he would not see again for so long. A village that had transformed him from a boy to a man.

Hinna, Ejaz, Rabia, Saleem, and Abdul Latif had been with him on that mule ride into Pakistan. Even though he knew that things were very different now, his own memory had morphed into a romanticized echo of itself and he could not imagine any change in that image despite the intervention of so many years and all the turmoil and conflict that had gone on since.

The vehicle wound its way up the Torkhum Road toward Landi Kotal and as the road turned north and split apart its northbound and southbound lanes, Sikander could just about recognize the compound into which he had been driven. Beyond it up the hill stood the house from which he had departed to walk across the mountains, leading Neela, the roan mule, thirteen years earlier. Now, for the first time despite his living in such proximity to this famous mountain pass into Afghanistan, he was finally traveling along its entire length. Having passed Landi Kotal after some dramatic and breathtaking switchbacks, the vehicle entered the small town of Torkhum on the Afghan side of the border.

At this time, the Taliban were heavily supported by Pakistan's government and Nawaz Sharif had wholeheartedly upheld the tradition. Accordingly, people coming out of Pakistan were generally welcomed, though the Taliban were naturally suspicious and were not giving any

concessions to their strict codes of dress for women, which Rabia had to abide by. She had already donned her royal blue burkha with the embroidered top and crocheted meshed viewing panel, through which she would have to peer while out in public.

One benefit of these times was that highway robbery had all but vanished as the Taliban's strictures held that all punishments for crimes be vigorously deterrent and not simply "fitting" the transgression. Not much earlier, this lesson had been learned the hard way as evidenced by the hanging of severed limbs by the roadside with a label identifying that their erstwhile owners had been highway bandits. Robbery of this kind dwindled to a fraction of the levels under warlord rule almost immediately. Sikander and Rabia could take their children in safety toward Laghar Juy.

Once they reached Batawul, about halfway between Torkhum and Jalalabad, they drove off the road toward Anarbagh where there lived an uncle of Razya's, an old man called Zubair. Sikander parked the Pajero, looking for anyone with an apparently official capacity. A small throng had gathered around the vehicle, mostly out of curiosity, and the closest of them peered inside. Although Rabia was a child of these parts, she had already spent long enough separated from her native culture to feel uneasy at this level of attention. Finally, two Taliban youths approached the vehicle, brushing aside the others. Sikander explained his name and purpose. He let on that he had fought against the Russians together with people from these parts years ago and was looking for Zubair. The interaction proved effective as one of the youths offered to direct him to Zubair's meager home. Once there, the youth stepped out, calling into the house asking for Zubair and a moment later the somewhat surprised old man walked out.

"Assalaamu 'alaykum, Uncle Zubair!" Sikander spoke a little more loudly than normal, hugging the man warmly. "I'm Sikander Khan, who had come here many years ago to fight the Russians with Abdul Latif and his sons and nephews. Abdul Latif...He's married to your niece Razya. Do you remember me?"

"Wa-alaykum assalaam!" responded Zubair, acknowledging the mention of his niece and her husband from Laghar Juy, but having difficulty remembering Sikander.

"We're here as the guests of Abdul Latif and would like to be shown the way to his place if you would please guide us," asked

Sikander. Although Sikander had been reasonably familiar with the general area surrounding Laghar Juy, he had never come in by the road route out of Torkhum and was in any case looking for the bound protection of melmasthia, which would all but guarantee safe passage for him and his family to Abdul Latif's house. His use of Abdul Latif's name and of the "guest" word acted like a switch, transforming attitudes and confirmed the harmlessness of the visitors while binding their hosts to protect and safeguard them.

"Sikander Khan! You are most welcome, brother. We shall be pleased to guide you to the house of my niece, but first please sit with us and have some chai."

It would have been grossly impolite to refuse. The higher a guest's station in life, the more important the host would seem to his neighbors and others in the village. This fact was not lost on Zubair and with the Pajero in full view of his neighbors, he simply wanted to savor the moment for as long as possible.

After tea, Zubair asked one of his neighbor's sons, a young Taliban by the name of Tayyab, who himself had a cousin in Laghar Juy, to escort the family. Covered in her burkha, Rabia took the backseat of the vehicle, so no issues of impropriety presented themselves. Within an hour, the Pajero was driving up the rough sloping streets of Laghar Juy and finally reached the familiar stretch in the higher elevations, where Abdul Latif's house was situated.

Tayyab got out of the vehicle and made the unnecessary indication of Abdul Latif's home toward which Sikander was already beginning to stride. To avoid any allegation of even temporary unaccompaniment against Rabia, she remained close to Sikander's side, though keeping a small but appropriate distance from him, holding the two young boys' hands on each side of her. Once it was clear where the family needed to go, Tayyab bid his salaams before strolling down the slopes a few hundred meters to his cousin's place to spend the night.

Sikander strode carefully into the house and started to call out, "Assalaamu 'alaykum? Is anyone home?"

"Who is it?" came back the voice. It was after maghrib and Abdul Majeed had just completed the sunset prayer. He was walking out toward the entryway of the mud-brick house when he came upon the family, a sight that took him aback.

"Abdul Majeed! Don't you recognize your relatives anymore? It's me—Sikander!" Sikander laughed and tried hard to reconcile his last image of Abdul Majeed with the one he now confronted. Standing before him was a tall Afghan, wearing a black turban with broad white stripes and black qamees-shalwar outfit, not very different from the one worn by the young man who had escorted Sikander and his family out of Anarbagh.

"Sikannnderrr! You…"

Grinning broadly, Abdul Majeed approached Sikander to deliver a big engulfing hug. Sikander returned the gesture and the two of them held it together for a good fifteen seconds. Behind Sikander, Abdul Majeed could see Rabia in her burkha and the two boys.

"Ahh! Ayub and…Qassim?" He looked quizzically toward Sikander, certain only of his uncertainty over the younger boy's name.

"Qayyuuum!" the three-year-old offered enthusiastically.

"It's Qayyum," affirmed Rabia from behind her burkha.

"Qayyum! That's right." Abdul Majeed turned to face Rabia but kept his gaze lowered as he acknowledged her politely. Sikander observed how like Abdul Latif his son had now become. A fact which was more apparent from studying Abdul Majeed's gestures and facial expressions than simple looks alone.

"Rabia! It's been such a long time. Welcome! Welcome! Please, sit down while I call Aba'i and Abaa and…Fatima, my uh, my wife. They're in the back finishing up with salaat-ul-maghrib."

"Fatima? Your wife? When did this happen, Abdul Majeed, that you didn't invite me to your wedding?" Sikander asked indignantly, being half-serious about it.

"Ah…" Abdul Majeed raised his eyebrows and lowered his head while keeping his gaze fixed upon Sikander's eyes with a hint of shame and a smile. His face was asking for his friend's forgiveness. "I…I…it all happened pretty quickly with my uncle's cousin's daughter; we didn't even have an engagement," he answered meekly as he shrugged.

Realizing he would never actually get to see Fatima's face, Sikander nodded politely and returned the smile, then turned to Rabia. Through the mesh in her burkha he could see her returning his glance

before facing Abdul Majeed squarely for not having told her or her husband of the wedding.

"No, Brother Abdul Majeed, you don't get off so lightly with your cousin! There'll be a badal for this."

Though half-serious also, Rabia recognized that this time of reunion was not a moment for displays of acrimony, but she was genuinely cut by the lack of her involvement in her cousin's wedding.

"Abaa! Adey!" called out Abdul Majeed, clearly pleased at the arrival of Sikander and his family and the respect being shown for his beliefs in the manner of their arrival. "Come and see...Sikander's here...Faaatima!"

Abdul Latif and Razya were not long in coming out and although her age permitted her to have no burkha according to even the strictest interpretation of the Qur'an, Razya was wearing it just the same. Fatima followed not far behind.

"Sikannnderrr! Raaabia!" cried out Abdul Latif. "W'Allahi, so good to see you after so long. Oh, and look...you have your boys with you mashAllah, w'Allahi Sikander, they're just like you!" Abdul Latif hugged Sikander tightly and turned to his niece, stroking the top of her burkha but clearly seeing from the shaking of the fully covered figure that she was crying. He glanced at Abdul Majeed, who immediately understood his cue to leave them for a while. Fatima followed him, not having uttered a word other than a brief salaam.

Once they were out of the room, Rabia was able to remove her burkha in front of her uncle. Unlike Abdul Majeed, he was "mehram" to her. A woman needed a veil in front of a non-mehram, and in this part of the world, the interpretation of "veil" was resolutely the burkha.

The weeping didn't stop. It simply spread around the room as it was more than related to the joyfulness of reunion. Somewhere among these tears of joy had crept in those of lament for the sad demise of what was once a vibrant, united village. Its energy had once faced down and beaten an immeasurably better equipped foe. Now it had become dark and riven by fear, under the repressive strictures of a force bent on protecting the soul, with the threat of physical violence, if need be, to administer that protection.

Were any souls protected? Who could say? Yet whatever the effects on individuals, the greater these efforts were, the more elusive any soul for the place as a whole proved to be. Indeed, Laghar Juy was now truly soulless, and into that emptiness, the spirit of Abdul Latif's own family seemed to be draining away as manifestly as the stream waters flowing through the village. Such a loss merited mourning and their individual psyches understood this even as their conscious minds did not.

For all the repression and fear, inherently Abdul Majeed and Saleem had not transformed into bad men. Neither had many Taliban. For most Taliban, their love had not vacated them as if they were some sort of undead. They had simply concocted for themselves an entire system of guiding principles which led them to a behavior whose outcome, at least in their conviction, would result in a better society. They were not to be compared with the greedy, murderous, raping warlords that had preceded them. The Taliban were, in a very real sense, a reaction to them; for them, the demands of a secure, orderly, and peaceful society comporting with their own perhaps unique precepts of Islam's requirements left little room for personal liberty.

Of course, as ever with the human species, when given authoritative sanction to administer with impunity, even saints could turn into sinners and there were clearly elements of the Taliban who appeared to revel in their meting out harsh punishments for any infraction.

"Where's Usman?" asked Sikander, wondering whatever had happened to the young man he'd brought back from the Arghandab campaign.

"Ahh...Usman!" Abdul Latif pursed his lips and raised his eyebrows as he nodded. "It would have been a couple of years ago that he left the village and got married. He's somewhere in Khost again, his birthplace, you know."

"Oh? Do you hear from him?" asked Sikander, disappointed.

"Sometimes," responded Abdul Latif. "Must be at least a year since the last time." He shook his head wistfully. "When you think about all that he and his family went through, it's a wonder he's as cheerful as he is. We miss that around here."

After a few brief moments, with Rabia having donned her burkha again, Razya called Abdul Majeed and Fatima back into the room and asked them to join herself, Abdul Latif, and the visitors to visit Noor and Saleem.

The group readied themselves, leaving the vehicle by Abdul Latif's home, and walked to Noor's place. Noor was inside and before the men entered, Abdul Latif called out to indicate to Noor that she should prepare herself for non-mehrams, as was now the requirement.

After hastily making such preparations, Noor indicated that Saleem was not at home but that all was ready for the group to walk into the house, which they did.

"Aaaadey!" moaned Rabia as she ran toward her too-long-unseen mother.

"Ya-Allah! Raaabia! Rabia my dearest...Oh dear girl, it's been so long!" The two women, each wearing a burkha, hugged each other and shook as they sobbed. Their surreal sack-like forms, wobbling as they did, forced Sikander to suppress the urge to chuckle at the comedy of the image. Its tragic elements, however, weren't far behind and the urge abated as quickly as it had arisen.

After half a minute, Sikander approached and lowered his head to be stroked in an act of blessing by his mother-in-law. While this was happening, his two young sons were brought into the room holding their Taliban Uncle Abdul Majeed's hands. Looking upon them, Noor wept with renewed impulse as she stretched out her hands to draw them closer.

"Assalaamu 'alaykum," said Ayub knowing only that this was the right thing to do to please the grown-ups in the room.

"Asslamlikm." Qayyum, knowing even less, struggled with so many syllables. Nonetheless, the words they had each uttered earned them tight warm hugs from their grandmother as she continued to weep joyfully at finally having an opportunity to meet them.

For several minutes, the commotion continued with the excitement of reunion and of Noor seeing her grandchildren. As it died down, the family sat cross-legged on the floor in relative peace.

Rabia, society wife of a wealthy Peshawar businessman, fluent speaker of Pashto, Urdu, and English, wearing her burkha, retreated to

the back of her mother's mud-brick home and began preparing tea on a crude charcoal stove. For her, the physical experience was a key of familiarity, unlocking with each passing moment numerous happy memories of her childhood and teenage years, even in the face of war, as the fiery young girl who would lick other peoples' minds dry of information. As the water was heating, she gazed at the walls, into the backyard, and just about every other direction around her, drawing more memories from the slightest visual cues as she allowed them to envelop her with their maternal warmth. It was worth a smile.

Abdul Majeed left the house to look for Saleem, who was out patrolling the locality to make sure everyone's behavior remained within religious limits. He had been hand picked by regional authorities of the Ministry for the Promotion of Virtue and Prevention of Vice to serve this role for Laghar Juy. Twenty minutes had passed when the two of them entered the house and with a broad grin Saleem warmly embraced Sikander, his onetime Stinger class fellow. Saleem appeared much as he had done on the last occasion that the two men had met in Pakistan. He offered his condolences at the passing of Javed some six years earlier and sat on the floor beside Sikander, chatting about how things had evolved over the years at Laghar Juy. Naturally, his focus was on the law and order that had finally arrived, and on how the opium growing was now a thing of the past. He was also genuinely thankful on behalf of the village people for the supply of the means to generate electricity that had been kindly donated by Sikander and his father before him.

Sikander was wise enough to know not to get embroiled in an ideological debate with his two young Taliban friends and hosts. He simply wanted to reconnect with them and to try to persuade Abdul Latif, Razya, and Noor to come back with him to Pakistan. That conversation started after dinner.

"Brother Abdul Latif," began Sikander, eyeing the former warrior intently. "It's really great to see you again after so long. I know that most of the resupply runs to Nangarhar have stopped now since the Americans have left, but we still need to see you from time to time, you know."

"W'Allahi, Sikander, I understand and I truly would like to get over there but circumstances just don't permit it. Without the resupply

runs, I have no sponsorship, no transportation. I'm truly sorry that I don't have the means to come."

Sikander gazed upon the aging face, understanding something of the hurt that Abdul Latif undeniably felt from not having the freedom to come and go to Pakistan as he did before. The fearsome Taliban rule had reduced this man to a fraction of his former stature and robbed him of much of his dignity. Sikander was clear that whatever proposal or suggestion he might make, it would have to be sensitive to Abdul Latif's need to preserve what was left of that dignity.

"Well, brother, what if I could let you—borrow?—my vehicle. Would you be willing to come? If I were to arrange it to be delivered to this village for your use to come and go as you please. Would that be a way to solve the transportation problem?" Sikander didn't wait for an answer. "Look, I know that driving isn't something you like to do, so why not bring Abdul Majeed or Saleem, and of course Aba'i? We need you too. We need you to be with us at least some of the time as our children grow. Would you do that? For us?"

"Sikander," Abdul Latif replied hesitantly, "what you've said tonight, what you've done today in coming, it...it's truly wonderful that you thought to do this and I would love to come and visit you in Peshawar. Even frequently. But please understand, Sikander, we cannot leave our home in Laghar Juy—"

"Brother, we understand that it will only be for visits and we won't ask you to abandon your sons or village—" interrupted Sikander.

"—because we're committed," continued Abdul Latif as if without interruption, "to Abdul Majeed and Saleem, who are also our children and whatever they do, whatever they think they want to do, they'll always be our sons. Your offer with the vehicle is very kind," he replied, indicating, without formally saying it, his acceptance. His sense of "badal" was working hard to rationalize how to achieve an "exchange" for the enormous favor offered to him and it was hard for Sikander to convey to Abdul Latif how much he and Rabia saw the mere act of being visited as the greatest favor possible.

"Adey, what about you? Won't you also please join us and your grandchildren? At least some of the time, Adey?"

Rabia's plaintive gaze into her mother's eyes—a gaze unseen owing to their burkhas, but absorbed all the same by her mother—

elicited yet more quiet tears from both of them. She began blotting her cheeks with the fabric of her burkha, promptly telegraphing wet patches and with them, communicating eloquently what was passing through her mind.

Noor was too overcome in her own burkha to do more than nod slowly, and with each nod, her head landed in a slightly lower position as if ultimately destined to hang in shame or sorrow. She motioned with her head to go into the back and to have Rabia join her where the burkhas could be removed and they would be able to embrace and interact with the intimacy that the situation deserved. They moved to the back with Razya and Fatima joining them.

Rabia embraced her mother and once more with Razya, finally turning to Fatima to do the same. Noor was, of course, only too pleased to have the opportunity to visit her only daughter and her family, so the conversation was quickly over on that matter. It cheered Rabia to get past the point and with it, her inveterate curiosity could be unleashed on an unsuspecting Fatima. She needed to know everything about Fatima with no detail left unvisited.

The conversation meanwhile continued in the main room between the men. "Do we not get invited?" asked Saleem, half-seriously.

"Yes, of course!" replied Sikander. "As I mentioned, at least one of you will need to come to drive the vehicle but both of you must come whenever possible." After about another hour or so of lengthy but careful and therefore harmless conversation, it was time to perform the isha prayer and prepare to retire to bed. Sikander and Rabia combined maghrib and isha.

The following morning, the extended family regrouped with the women again donning their burkhas after separately eating breakfast and joining the men. The discussion resumed about having the Laghar Juy relatives come to visit Sikander's family in Peshawar, but it would have been unseemly on this trip to drag off the senior relatives in the Pajero without any forewarning. It was therefore agreed that the vehicle would be sent back after two weeks, and Saleem would bring back Abdul Latif, Razya, Noor, and Rabia, who, as Sikander had just learned, had without much difficulty been persuaded to stay at her mother's place with the children and come back with them all. While slightly annoyed at learning this fact only now, he understood that he could not

be an agent of their continued separation after so long and acquiesced meekly.

"Are you going to be alright here? You don't have a lot of clothes with you. And the children? Will they manage?" After agreeing to their stay, Sikander held out some hope for a good reason to emerge that would encourage everyone to see how inadvisable it might be. He really didn't want to be without Rabia and his boys.

"Clothes?" asked Rabia, picking up on his question with cold sarcasm. She spread slightly apart her gloved hands and allowed her head within her shuttlecock burkha to tilt down and then up. She was still glaring back at Sikander through the burkha's mesh while lowering her hands back on her lap before redirecting her stare more meaningfully in Abdul Majeed's direction.

Sikander remained silent and Abdul Majeed shifted his stance awkwardly as he and Saleem independently glanced around the room to see who else might be turning to either of them to ask why all this was necessary.

"Well, it's settled then. Tomorrow I'll return to Peshawar and we'll be sure to send back the Pajero for you to come back with it in about two weeks. You can push everyone to get ready, Rabia, as I'm sure only you can!"

The following day came and knowing they would be seeing each other in a couple of weeks, Sikander drove away in the Pajero after picking up Tayyab. When they arrived at Anarbagh, Zubair arranged an escort to the Khyber Pass border, after which the escort returned by taxi to Anarbagh.

The two weeks went by slowly for Sikander, but he busied himself through the passing days. Finally, having sent the Pajero with a driver, the family group returned a day later to Sikander's relief and delight. The Pajero, though technically loaned to Abdul Latif and his family, was in effect a simple gift and Sikander, who certainly had no need to worry about the cost, procured a newer one within the week.

Abdul Latif and the family could now come and go as they pleased. It was also not long after this that wireless GSM cell phone service became available in Afghanistan and with it, direct immediate communication with Laghar Juy became possible. This allowed making arrangements for trips to be much easier, although despite cell towers

being in Kabul, Jalalabad, and along the approaches to Torkhum, the service was far from reliable.

♠

Five hundred kilometers away from Sikander and his family, down in Tarnak near Qandahar, Osama Bin Laden had been the target of American retaliation in the prior year, and in the midst of his Taliban hosts, his sense of a need for badal was all the more heightened. In giving vent to it, Bin Laden began to develop plans to seek that badal. Two plans emerged. The first was directly aimed at the source of the Tomahawk missiles that had attacked the camps—namely ships in the Arabian Sea—which had particularly angered him for having been launched from within his own home territory. He appointed Abdul-Rahim al-Nashiri and Abu 'Ali al-Harithi to formulate such a plan.

The second plan was a dusted down redesign of one presented to him about five years earlier by Khalid Sheikh Mohammed in Pakistan. The argument had been that Khalid's nephew Ramzi Yousef's attempt at hitting the World Trade Center in 1993 had been too ineffectual. With a different approach, those and other landmarks could be hit successfully. Such an attack would not only exact revenge for the missile attacks but also strike at American prestige. The proposed approach would use aircraft as cruise missiles. In 1995, the plan had been casually entertained but not at the time taken seriously. Now Khalid had modified his plan to use passenger airliners and even had a non-US component targeting Asian locations with hijackers who would not be able to obtain US visas. Bin Laden asked Khalid to put the plan into action, to find the hijackers that could be relied upon to execute it, to organize whatever flight training and logistics that might be necessary, and to deliver a body blow to the United States of America.

Meanwhile, in May a major flare-up of tensions between India and Pakistan arose when a Pakistani initiative to make a surprise move against the town of Kargil—just to the south of the so-called Line-of-Control in Kashmir—was made. The advance was ostensibly by irregulars and local mujahideen seeking liberation of Kashmir from Indian rule but was heavily backed by units of Pakistan's regular army. The conflict lasted until August of that year, resulting in all initial gains made by the offensive being given up under a torrent of international condemnation against Pakistan's allegedly brazen move. By making it appear to be an opportunistic land-grab by Pakistan for Kashmir, India

managed to deflect attention away from any legitimate claim being made by Kashmiri separatists that might have caught the attention of the international community.

An embarrassed Prime Minister Nawaz Sharif was blindsided by the Kargil offensive and claimed only to learn of if from an irate Indian Prime Minister, Atal Bihari Vajpayee. Sharif was especially embarrassed in light of the Lahore Declaration of earlier that year in which India and Pakistan had agreed to seek a peaceful resolution of the Kashmir issue, which had dogged relations between the two nuclear armed countries since their independence from the British in 1947. His generals had different ideas.

Indeed, only four generals had conceived of the plan and knew about its details and one of them was a friend of Sameena's father-in-law, Omar Khan. He had come to know Omar from the time he and Omar had been SSG officers. The general's name was Parvez Musharraf and he was now the Army's Chief of Staff and Chairman of the Joint Chiefs. Sikander had met Musharraf much earlier, on occasions when Sameena had invited Rabia and himself to come to one of Wasim's family functions where Musharraf had also been invited. At that time Musharraf had held the rank of major general.

In October of 1999, General Musharraf was on a PIA flight back from Sri Lanka when Nawaz Sharif, the Prime Minister, tried to remove him as Army Chief of Staff and replace him with Ziauddin Butt. Sharif ordered that the flight carrying Musharraf should not be allowed to land in Karachi but to land instead at Nawab Shah. From the aircraft—which was now circling Karachi due to the countermanding from onboard and running dangerously low on fuel—Musharraf managed to contact senior army officers, urging them to intervene with their own coup. The urging worked and Nawaz Sharif was summarily removed from power, while the generals ordered that the airliner be allowed to land, with barely minutes of fuel on board. Musharraf disembarked and assumed the position of the country's Chief Executive, effectively terminating once again the country's most recent tinkering with democracy.

It was during the aftermath of the coup that Sikander had been invited to an evening dinner at his mother's cousin's place. The cousin's name was Zainab and she had a son, Salman Khan, who lived in Durham, North Carolina, with his French-American wife Sabrina. Salman had established a small software business in 1988, which was

prospering. He was a clean-shaven slim young man of thirty-three years wearing thick eyeglasses, and he was on a short visit to see his mother in Peshawar while on his way back from a business trip to Nagoya. He spoke English without an accent but enjoyed much of his native Pakistani traditions, including relaxing in a traditional shalwar and qamees combination. Sikander found him intriguing. He moved closer toward Salman, introducing himself and the blood relationship between them.

"Brother Salman, how long have you lived in the USA?"

"Mmm...a little over sixteen years, Sikander. Why?" he responded.

"Oh...I was just curious." Sikander recalled his yearning to visit the US one day or even live there. It had, if anything, increased as a result of the original help given by the US to the mujahideen, even though recent developments resulting in the missile attacks in Afghanistan had dampened his feelings a little. "I've always wanted to visit that country and maybe...maybe live there one day. Do you enjoy living there?"

"Sabrina and I *love* living in North Carolina. It's a beautiful place, especially in the spring and autumn. The people there are very friendly and it's a welcoming place for someone with any brains, if he or she knows how to put them to use. Actually, Sikander, the US is one of the few places on earth where if you can offer something of value, you'll usually find someone who recognizes and pays for it. It's also a great place to raise children, but before considering a move, why don't you visit first and see if it is the kind of place you imagine it to be?"

Rabia's ears pricked up and her attention was drawn to the comment about it being a good place for child-rearing. She tuned herself out of her ongoing conversation, giving all the appearance of listening while in fact paying attention to the dialogue between Salman and Sikander about three meters away at the far end of the room. It wasn't really difficult as Sikander and Salman were going at it in English.

"—want to live there, they have some pretty tough immigration rules and laws. You'll need a green card. If you have close family, it can be done but it's a pretty long wait. It's easier if you have a job that requires you to work there or better still, if you invest money and set up a business, though I don't remember how much and what all the rules

are. In some way or other, all of these can work," said Salman. "But you do need a good immigration lawyer to help you."

"Do you discuss Pakistan and Afghanistan over there, Salman?"

Sikander was curious as to why the Americans had left Afghanistan to fend for itself after the Russians had left, despite having provided so much money and weapons.

"You mean among ourselves, the expatriate Pakistanis, or generally with other local people?" asked Salman.

"Either way, I suppose. It seems no one in that country is too concerned about what happens now that the Soviet Union is basically done."

"I'd say that's about the measure of it Sikander. I mean...that scale of assistance wasn't out of generosity was it? It was simply a matter of winning the Cold War and once in their minds that was done, Afghanistan was no longer an important part of the world. No oil. No gas. Perhaps some minerals...but really, mostly problems." Salman suspended a shrug until his point sank in.

"Yes, I see what you're saying, and what about the people in the country from this part of the world? How do the Pakistanis you come across in the USA discuss Afghanistan?" asked Sikander.

"Actually, to tell you the truth, I don't think we generally discuss much beyond the prospects for Pakistan now were back under the...'generals' again." Salman smirked with raised eyebrows. "We also like talking about how the Americans are really the ones pulling the strings and that the country seems to be governed from the American embassy!" Salman chuckled cynically.

"Perhaps I'll try visiting sometime soon," remarked Sikander. "I'll have to see what the visa process here in Islamabad looks like and if...if I have to, will it be alright to use you? As a sponsor, I mean. Just in case? I've heard that everyone needs a sponsor."

"Sure! We'd love to have you come and visit us. We could even make a vacation out of it and go and see some of the places I have to admit we haven't even seen yet. If you bring Ayub and Qayyum, Sabrina and I have our own little boy and girl; we could probably try going to Disney World. I'm sure you and the family would enjoy it very much, Sikander."

Sikander smiled, turned his head slightly, and adopted a vacant look as he tried to imagine the places mentioned in the conversation. His only meaningful reference was from his recollections of Applecross, whose name and location other than its being in Scotland, he still didn't know, but which seemed as exotic as Salman had described America to be.

Thinking about it for only a moment longer, Sikander determined that it was time he finally delivered on his long-standing promise to himself. He would visit America.

Chapter 13

Enduring Freedom

B Y THE RECKONING OF MANY, a new millennium rolled in on January 1, 2000. Along with giant sighs of relief at the continued operation of virtually all key software throughout the world, dispute raged over whether or not another a year had to pass before the new millennium could be considered to have started. Whatever the merits on each side of the debate, Osama Bin Laden had a different conflict on his mind. Three thousand kilometers southwest of Peshawar, on January 3, 2000, a guided missile destroyer called the *USS The Sullivans* was moored in the harbor of Yemen's port city of Aden.

Named after the five Sullivan brothers who had lost their lives in World War II, the ship was a member of the mainstay Arleigh-Burke Class of US Navy destroyers. Each was a launch platform for the US Aegis weapons system and related radar. In direct retaliation for the earlier missile attacks launched from such ships on Afghan training camps along the Afghanistan-Pakistan border, Osama Bin Laden authorized a plan to attack such a destroyer, banking on the fact that they commonly harbored in Aden. With the USS The Sullivans stationed there, the attack was set in motion and a small boat, filled with explosives, approached the ship.

Before it reached its target, however, with its heavy burden, the draught of the boat was much greater than was safe, and the waves lapping over its side caused the boat to begin taking on water, further

adding weight, rapidly exacerbating the problem until the vessel sank, leaving the destroyer unharmed. Although he was disappointed, Bin Laden was not about to give up on the plan. He needed a bigger boat. With such an amendment in mind, Bin Laden had his people draw up a new plan for repeating the attack at the next opportunity.

As the year wore on, Sikander and Rabia saw more of Abdul Latif, Razya, and Noor. On two occasions, even Abdul Majeed and Saleem managed to come across the border to meet their nephews and more of Sikander's family. Saleem also finally married Amina who, by all accounts from Rabia, was a regally beautiful girl from Jalalabad, although Sikander would never see her due to her burkha. Fatima, meanwhile, had given birth to a baby girl, named Latifa, after her grandfather. With cell phone communication possible, the family began to interact more often, and the Pajero was put to extensive use bringing family members back and forth.

Coincidentally, exactly one year to the day since General Parvez Musharraf had been in power, another US Aegis destroyer, the USS Cole, was moored in Aden harbor for a routine refueling. At 10:30 am, it began to take on fuel. Less than an hour later, a small boat approached the vessel, laden with approximately a thousand pounds of high explosives; even though it was headed straight for the Cole, rules of engagement at the time did not permit the crew of the ship to open fire on the boat. Below decks, just as the crew was lining up for lunch, an enormous explosion blew into the galley and other decks, creating a gash of a dozen meters by twenty meters visible for all to see. When the mayhem finally settled down, seventeen US sailors had died and thirty-nine had been injured.

Less than a month later, Americans went to the polls and amid much controversy about the count, following a Supreme Court ruling on the matter, George W. Bush was named America's forty-third President. When Bush assumed the Presidency the following January, and later received briefings on al-Qaeda, he declared that he did not want to respond to al-Qaeda one attack at a time and was "tired of swatting flies."

At about the same time, Khalid Sheikh Mohammed was well on his way to completing plans for what was then called the "planes

operation" within al-Qaeda. During the prior year, he had been working with Khalid al-Midhar and Nawaf al-Hazmi as two of the intended hijackers that would likely be able to get US visas together with members of a recently arrived group out of Hamburg, Germany, led by a young man called Mohammed Atta. Bin Laden selected Atta to be the overall plot execution leader while Khalid was named as the planning leader. An elaborate system of communication between the two was established with Ramzi bin al-Shibh as the primary go-between.

It was common for Al-Qaeda to use the code word "wedding" for any terrorist attack. Before long, what was loosely known as the "planes operation" received the more official title of "The Big Wedding" within al-Qaeda planning circles. With the key operational details worked out and teams identified, the members of the hijack plot required to pilot Boeing 757 and 767 aircraft were sent to different parts of the USA to obtain flight training—in some cases, only refresher training—on airliner flying.

In Afghanistan itself, skirmishes and heavy fighting had become a routine occurrence between members of the Northern Alliance and the Islamic Emirate of Afghanistan's forces, the latter being the national designation for the country conferred upon it by the Taliban. Despite the fighting, there was a relative state of peace in Nangarhar Province and until this time, although it had become a lot tougher, Sikander and Rabia still saw their extended family about once every other month. But a fatal blow was dealt to this form of family interaction when in July, the Pajero, which had by now seen some rough times, rolled to its final resting place, with a broken transmission. There was no straightforward way to bring it back immediately, so the families made do with the often patchy cell phone system. It was a poor consolation relative to the travel, and Rabia felt particularly troubled at having no convenient solution to allow the personal visits to continue. In early September, succumbing to much exhorting and scolding, Sikander promised his wife that as soon as he had a free moment he would look into the problem and see what might be done.

Following several days of heavy fighting, forces of the Northern Alliance led by Ahmed Shah Massoud conceded some districts in Kapisa Province. It was September 8th, and Massoud moved back to

Khwaja Bahauddin in Takhar Province. While there, on the following day, he granted a media interview. Despite claims of being a Moroccan-born Belgian, the reporter was in fact Tunisian and had brought a stolen camera with him filled with explosives. The explosion killed the cameraman immediately and an initially injured Massoud died within the day after emergency hospital treatment failed. The reporter was also injured, though he had no doubt expected to die. Any such expectation was met when after being captured he allegedly tried to escape and was shot and killed.

Two days after Massoud's death, despite reported warnings from Jordan, Italy, Israel, Pakistan, and others as well as several alerts popping up from within US security and intelligence circles throughout 1999 to 2001, the US was caught by surprise on September 11, 2001. Even George W. Bush had received a detailed Presidential Daily Briefing on August 6, 2001, suggesting that Osama Bin Laden was "determined to strike in the US."

At about a quarter to seven in the evening of that day, Sikander was at home in Peshawar, settling down to relax with a copy of *Electrical Construction & Maintenance Magazine*, while Rabia and Sofie were in the lounge playing with the boys. Sikander had just begun reading when he heard the unmistakable sound of screeching tires followed by loud banging on the steel doors providing access to the home's carport and front patio.

"Open up! Open up! Hurry!" called out a frantic voice from outside. It was Jamil returning home after staying late at the office. He was expected back around this time but with far less commotion. Kausar heard him and hurried to the gate to let his car in. As soon as it was feasible, Jamil drove through the opening not waiting for it to be completely open. Slamming the door of his car after spilling out, he ran into the house, calling for his brother.

"Excuse me?" exclaimed Kausar. With her ego bruised, she followed her husband who had all but ignored her upon his arrival as he barreled into the dwelling. His additional failure to acknowledge her exclamation simply piled on the injury.

"Sikander bhai! Sikander bhai!"

Sikander put down his magazine and headed out of the lounge to find out what the fuss was about when, gasping for breath, Jamil bumped into him.

"Sikander bhai...CNN! Switch on CNN!"

"Jamil, what is it? What's happened?" asked an alarmed Sikander.

"Please, bhai-jan! Just turn it on. Turn it on...there've been attacks in America...World Trade Center in New York. Hit by aircraft!"

"Jamil!" Sikander had barely absorbed his brother's words. "Calm down! An airplane hit the World Trade Center? Why...why do you say it was an attack? Couldn't it just have bee—"

"Bhai-jan, I didn't say *an* aircraft, I said *aircraft*! There have been two planes flown into the two towers and now there's smoke pouring out of both of them and...and oh God! The people in there!"

"Alright. Alright, come on."

Flanked by Rabia and Kausar, Sikander and his brother hurried into the TV room. Kausar's indignation at having not been acknowledged upon opening the gates quickly evaporated as she began absorbing the gravity of what appeared to be unfolding. Likewise, sensing something was amiss, Sofie picked up the children, handed them to Atiya, and asked her to get them to bed. She too proceeded to the TV room. By now the TV was on and tuned to CNN. As the picture took shape on the screen, news anchor Carol Lin had been describing a third aircraft—this one having impacted the Pentagon—while the video image cut away from the studio to a street in New York as people were screaming and running from the buildings.

At that moment, the unthinkable happened.

Slowly, surreally, the south tower started sinking into the ground as if a giant trap door had been opened beneath it by some evil, unseen hand. What had a moment earlier been a pall of billowing black smoke streaming away from the building was now replaced by a giant inverted mushroom cloud of dense gray smoke and dust followed by debris and paper. Millions of pieces of paper—some laden with meaning, others with meaningless doodles scribbled during a dull meeting rudely interrupted just an hour or so earlier, yet others blank, vacant, and simply awaiting meaning, but now acquiring one neither imagined nor

imaginable. It didn't matter now. They descended fluttering and wafting, like so many white autumn leaves into the ghastly, unrelenting gray accumulating rapidly below.

The dust engulfed everything on the ground, blotting out the sun and the lapis lazuli beauty of that fateful New York sky. About half an hour after the first tower fell, now all too imaginably, the north tower followed suit in a near carbon copy collapse. All that remained was air in the space where two buildings with over seventeen thousand people in them had been standing just a couple of hours earlier.

The family remained pinned to the TV for almost the whole night. Early talk show hosts, commentators, and various experts began reflecting that all signs pointed to al-Qaeda and Afghanistan.

By the early morning in Peshawar, which was still the evening of the 11th in Washington, George W. Bush delivered a speech on national TV, which was seen live throughout an increasingly worried world, including Peshawar, and the most alarming point came when he uttered the chilling words:

"...We will make no distinction between the terrorists who committed these acts and those who harbor them."

Even though by now they had lost a night's worth of sleep, the family members in the TV room glanced anxiously at each other when Bush completed his speech.

The attacks resulted in almost three thousand lives lost from over eighty different nationalities. They had the additional effect of liberating the US government to do whatever it felt was needed to address the threat of al-Qaeda and, to whatever extent American interests were otherwise at stake, to pursue the adventure anywhere in the world that circumstances might dictate. Speculation mounted about counter-attacks on Afghanistan or potential raids to seek out and perhaps kidnap or kill Bin Laden and his entourage. Whether the USA wished to be back in Afghanistan or not, it would indeed be back—and this time, directly. Inevitably, its actions would hit home for Sikander and his family.

Sikander and Rabia began increasing their cell phone contacts with Abdul Latif whenever they got the chance just to be sure that things were alright, but communications grew even more patchy than normal, and due to circuit overloads, calls were often dropped. From what he

and Rabia could learn in snippets of conversation, Abdul Majeed and Saleem were heading off to join other Taliban to the west of Laghar Juy up in the Spin Ghar region. The Tora Bora caves were well fortified and supplied, so that would be among the preferred locations. Before they left, Sikander tried to impress upon them to avoid any place likely to be a known target for American attacks. At the time, Sikander imagined an American response involving more Tomahawk cruise missiles, similar to those following the embassy bombings. Abdul Rahman and Ejaz were both on the Pakistan side of the border with their families and Sikander tried to persuade Abdul Latif and the rest of them to come back. Yet Abdul Majeed and Saleem remained undeterred, refusing to hear of such a move for themselves as they felt this would be a gross dereliction of duty to their fellow Taliban brothers.

All consternation focused on the likely US response as American public opinion now squarely anticipated that it would be comprehensive and would inevitably result, contrary to Sikander's naïve hopes, in more than simply another round of cruise missiles at a few training camps. In Peshawar, as elsewhere, this was the only subject on people's minds and lips.

Five days after the New York attacks Sikander was in the office mulling over the likely scenarios that might well be unfolding in Pakistan and Afghanistan over the coming weeks and months. The talk around the place was incessantly about how terrible the attacks had been, how years of bad US foreign policy had created the monster that had attacked it, how this would affect life in Pakistan, how India might capitalize on the situation, and, of course, how everything had been secretly organized by the US government anyway. The existence of the Project for the New American Century and its neoconservative adherents received wide exposure in Pakistan as further evidence of the "conniving ways of the Americans." Indeed conspiracy theories were ripening just about everywhere, from society functions to sports events to local kebab and paan shops, and were part of the entertainment in just about every taxicab ride in Peshawar. Whatever the station in life of any individual, he or she always seemed to have the inside knowledge of what the Americans had really done and how the whole thing on TV was more or less staged.

It wasn't long before Sikander himself was drawn into one such discussion with Jamil and Rehan. He caught them in a conversation

vying with each other as to whose theory was more Machiavellian, each seeking to outdo the other's supposed insights into what was really happening in the corridors of power in Washington, Islamabad, London, Riyadh, and New Delhi.

"They wanted to create another Pearl Harbor for themselves," declared Jamil. "Now they can pretty much do as they please and everyone in their own country will be too frightened to stop them."

Rehan nodded fiercely in agreement. "This has to be the work of the CIA. No doubt about it. And pretty soon—"

"Pretty soon you'll run out of conspirators and conspiracies, Rehan!" interrupted Sikander's voice from behind him.

"Khan-sahib! I...I...didn't—" stammered Rehan.

"Oh relax, Rehan. I didn't mean anything by it. But you know, it seems to me you people are talking about the wrong thing. At least right now, instead of discussing how these things came about, we should be trying to understand how they'll unfold and what options we have, and I'd begin with the facts on face value before inventing plausible unproven conspiracies."

"Meaning?" asked Jamil.

Sikander looked at his watch, glanced over the mezzanine balcony, and saw that there was a lunchtime lull in customer activity in the sales section. He motioned to Rehan and Jamil to follow him into his office.

Sikander was filled with anxieties, not least of which were for his in-laws and his own considerable investment of time and risk to life and limb when fighting with the mujahideen. It had been for their country's freedom, yet Afghanistan was in so many ways also *his* adopted country. He *needed* this conversation. The two people in his presence seemed to be engaged in the subject anyway, so they would have to do.

Sikander ushered them into the office and motioned for them to take seats. While turning back around and peering out of the doorway, he called out to his assistant, "Naseem!"

"Sir?" she replied from beyond his office.

"Naseem, bring in three cups of tea, will you, and bring a snack with them if you can. Semosas will be fine or simple egg or chicken sandwiches. Thanks!"

Sikander ambled back into the office, sitting down on his swivel chair behind a desk piled with paperwork.

Rehan and Jamil sat slightly ill at ease at being pulled in to the office basically to indulge in what at most other times would have been seen as idle chitchat. But that was no ordinary day.

"So, the way I see it," began Sikander, "the starting point is to accept that it will surely be only a matter of time before the Americans come in force."

"Huh! Let them try. They'll have the same experience as the Russians! Easy to get in, hard to get out!" scoffed Rehan.

Sikander studied Rehan for a moment or two longer than the point might have warranted. Rehan was an honest, hard worker with a heavyset build, a tar-colored mustache, and broad black eyebrows with slightly greasy hair—in sharp contrast to his brilliant white dress shirt and red tie. He looked every inch a Pakistani white-collar worker.

He was a superb salesman and had a strong patriotic streak in him, but he had little idea how the Russians' fate had unfolded over ten years ago and absolutely no idea about what it took to achieve. With the briefest hint of a frown, Sikander allowed himself a staring smile, swiveled in his chair, and returned to what he felt was the subject.

"Al-Qaeda is the target that has to be destroyed. This much is clear," he began. "It will require at the very least the key leaders such as Bin Laden, Atef, and Ayman al-Zawahiri, and everyone else alleged to be connected to the attacks in New York to be surrendered to the US."

"Yes, but—" began Jamil.

"—but the Taliban being the Pashtuns that they are," continued Sikander, "the Americans would fare better squeezing blood from stones before expecting them to hand anyone over."

Jamil nodded and Rehan swung his head from side to side which in any other culture but the subcontinent would have meant negation, but here it meant "no doubt!"

"Melmasthia is alive and well even though we're now in the twenty-first century. And the Pashtunwali code isn't going away. It has, after all, been around a lot longer than Islam in Afghanistan."

"In any case," Jamil chimed in, "they're also itching to remove the Taliban, so despite what they say, they probably don't actually want the Taliban to give up Bin Laden. If I were them, I'd be doing as much as possible to push this...this Mullah Omar into a corner and leave no face-saving option."

Sikander nodded.

"So, a plan involving a Taliban surrender of al-Qaeda would need either an impossibly deep rift to turn one group against the other, or else a devastation of the Taliban along with al-Qaeda. Now, I for one can't imagine, even it were to work, a quick enough campaign that would cause the desired level of rift between al-Qaeda and the Taliban, which means that any plan with a short-term expectation of al-Qaeda's destruction needs also to entertain the Taliban's ouster from power, which, as you so aptly point out, Jamil, is what the Americans want anyway. And that requires two more things."

Becoming more engaged with this reasoning, as Sikander clearly appeared to have given the subject some thought, Rehan couldn't help forming a frown of curiosity. Sikander began to answer the unspoken questions.

"The first thing would be to cut off their sustenance, and the second would be the installation of a credible alternative. And don't forget, no one in their worst nightmare would be willing to stomach a return to the time of regional warlords and the lawlessness that came with that. I don't think even Bush wants that."

"So, to dislodge the Taliban—" resumed Jamil, thinking aloud.

"—means to focus on Pakistan, historically the Taliban's primary source of support," Sikander said, completing Jamil's point. "Look, the Russians and Iranians are hardly likely to jump to the aid of the Pashtuns, and pretty much all of what they get from the Saudis comes through Pakistan."

Jamil and Rehan began extrapolating the implications of Sikander's words as their faces betrayed the effort.

"Hmm...so we should prepare for being attacked as well then," offered Rehan, nodding slowly.

"No. *No!* Well...I hope not!" Sikander couldn't dismiss such a notion entirely. "I'd have to suppose that the US would turn to Musharraf and ask him—very convincingly—to block support for the Taliban. They'd want us to stop supplying them and to block their escape from Afghanistan...or at the very least the escape of al-Qaeda people."

"How might they do that?" asked Jamil.

"Oh...a big carrot, and a big stick."

Sikander began drifting from well-reasoned thinking into more speculative realms. He needed to pause in order to do more thinking aloud.

"Yes...yes, I suppose I'd be making offers of big aid payments to Musharraf, and Pakistan generally, and I'd be telling Pakistan that if we don't acquiesce, we should expect to be bombed, or maybe more likely that India would get a signal that the US would look the other way in the face of an Indian attack on us...though I think with our nuclear threat, the India card would be a tough one to play and a very high risk card at that."

"Yes, but if an Indian attack on us were to happen..." Jamil began building on Sikander's thoughts, "No doubt they believe Musharraf would have to respond to such an attack, which would pave the way for America occupying Afghanistan while being very unfriendly toward a Pakistan pre-occupied with protecting its eastern front against India, and who knows, maybe even cross Pakistan's western border in pursuit of their mission."

Sikander wasn't completely ready to agree with Jamil. His thoughts shifted to other factors. "Even China wouldn't want to be crossing the US right now, so we can't rely on the Chinese to hold off an Indian government advance or help us if they get a strong US signal to remain out of it. And a Pakistan struggling to deal with an Indian offensive will be a Pakistan unable to support the Taliban."

"Actually, if the US wants to direct Pakistani effort away from supporting the Taliban, it won't need an Indian attack," observed Jamil. "It would just need a credible threat of one."

"Meaning?" asked Rehan.

Sikander filled in. "Meaning that some incident could be arranged which would spark a massive response from India. They would move several divisions up against the Pakistani border. Musharraf would have to respond and as long as things don't spill over into a nuclear conflict, the stalemate alone would sap his resources, leaving little or nothing to support the Taliban," explained Sikander.

"So what do you think should happen next?" asked Rehan, feeling more gravity in the situation than he had at the beginning of the conversation. Before anyone could answer the proposed query, Sikander heard Naseem rapping on the glass pane of his office door as she let herself in with a tray of tea and sandwiches.

"Thank you, Naseem. You can set it down over there." Sikander pointed to a credenza. She acknowledged, set the tray down, and left the room quietly. Sikander walked over to the credenza and poured the tea. He passed the plate of sandwiches to Jamil and Rehan and continued as he took one for himself.

"I think Bush should probably convince Musharraf that any other strategy than wholehearted support for the US, including the use of Pakistan for transporting large amounts of equipment and supplies into Afghanistan, will be suicide." Sikander paused as Rehan and Jamil nodded.

"How will Musharraf be able to sell that to the public here and, more importantly, to his generals?" asked Rehan.

"With plenty of sweeteners both for the country and the generals, Rehan. In all cases, though, I don't think there's a way to avoid a large attack on Afghanistan, and if the Northern Alliance people can put something coherent together, I'd be backing them with men and materials if I were Bush."

Three days later, President Parvez Musharraf openly announced his decision to join the US on the Global War on Terror. He basically had no choice as he himself explained, because Pakistan could ill afford to have a concerted US/India axis against it.

While seemingly obvious as a decision, in the words of Deputy Secretary of State Richard Armitage, "it would be onerous" in its

consequences. What had been until that moment a concerted Pakistani policy supporting the Taliban against the Northern Alliance had to be reversed abruptly, and that was something that deep loyalties between the interface people on both sides would certainly not permit. There were hundreds of Pakistani military personnel in Afghanistan, generally in the role of ISI military advisers. Moreover, nearly seven years of propaganda to the Pakistani public—working to see the Taliban in a positive light—had been a success and could not be undone in a heartbeat.

Whatever the considerations, any doubt about a possible attack by the US was finally put to rest when George W. Bush made things crystal clear in his speech of September 20th less than ten days after the New York attacks:

"The leadership of al-Qaeda has great influence in Afghanistan and supports the Taliban regime in controlling most of that country. In Afghanistan we see al-Qaeda's vision for the world. Afghanistan's people have been brutalized, many are starving, and many have fled. Women are not allowed to attend school. You can be jailed for owning a television. Religion can be practiced only as their leaders dictate. A man can be jailed in Afghanistan if his beard is not long enough. The United States respects the people of Afghanistan—after all, we are currently its largest source of humanitarian aid—but we condemn the Taliban regime. It is not only repressing its own people, it is threatening people everywhere by sponsoring and sheltering and supplying terrorists.

"By aiding and abetting murder, the Taliban regime is committing murder. And tonight the United States of America makes the following demands on the Taliban.

"Deliver to United States authorities all of the leaders of al-Qaeda who hide in your land.

"Release all foreign nationals, including American citizens you have unjustly imprisoned.

"Protect foreign journalists, diplomats, and aid workers in your country.

"Close immediately and permanently every terrorist training

camp in Afghanistan.

"And hand over every terrorist and every person and their support structure to appropriate authorities.

"Give the United States full access to terrorist training camps, so we can make sure they are no longer operating.

"These demands are not open to negotiation or discussion. The Taliban must act, and act immediately. They will hand over the terrorists or they will share in their fate."

A few days later, Pakistani people, particularly followers of the Jamiat 'Ulema-e-Islam, began a march toward the Afghan border in support of the Taliban and al-Qaeda.

During the same period, Sikander was constantly connected to some news source or other—CNN at home, the local radio in his car, or the same CNN channel on a TV he had installed in his office.

Two and a half weeks after President Bush's pronouncements in front of a packed joint session of the US Congress, US CENTCOM commander General Tommy Franks had his detailed plans for the Afghanistan invasion locked and loaded. Most of the world, sympathetic to the US national tragedy, stood fully behind a mission of ousting the Taliban regime and catching the al-Qaeda leadership to bring it to justice.

It was late on October 7th when Sikander and Rabia were watching TV, as they had now almost become compelled to do. With them were Jamil, Kausar, and Sofie. This time, they were glued to the set when in front of their very eyes, reports came in of attacks having begun. At ten o'clock that night in Peshawar, George W. Bush was back on American national TV to announce that Operation Enduring Freedom had been launched.

Though their minds had been prepared for something like this, no one expected it to be that night and everyone was deeply anxious. Rabia could only think of her country and her people back home in Laghar Juy, but especially of her Taliban brother and cousin who were now the avowed focus of American rage. Through a messy contortion of circumstance and logic, their deaths would become a matter of American policy. She arose and trudged into the quiet lounge, sat on a sofa, and with her forehead nestled against her arm on the sofa's armrest, began sobbing uncontrollably.

Sikander had paid a short visit to the bathroom when she left, and just as he was about to resume his seat, he looked around to see her missing. He asked where she was, but no one had been paying enough attention to know. He was worried for Rabia and didn't want to her to be alone. He didn't need to see her to know what she must have been going through, but he did feel the need to be with her. Stepping out of the TV room Sikander proceeded to the only other place where she was likely to be. Entering the lounge, he could see Rabia weeping more than hear her, as he sat next to her, laying a hand gently on her silently bobbing shoulder without saying a word. She didn't acknowledge him to begin with, but after a while she picked up her head and leaned into him to seek a solace he was powerless to give.

"Rabia. Rabia, I'm sure they'll be alright. The Americans have smart weapons. They won't attack the general people. They know who they're after. We should pray for everyone there. That's what we can do."

"Why?" cried Rabia. "Why couldn't you have fixed the car, Sikander?" she pleaded through her sobbing. "Why didn't you go there and bring them back?"

"Rabia, I...I..." How could he now tell her that he'd simply been too busy and that he obviously had no idea that terror attacks in New York were about to transform their world. "I'm sorry, Rabia."

Sikander pondered his options. Paralysis didn't come easily to him and he was, after all an intelligent, experienced individual. Surely there was something he could do. After pausing for a moment with her head in his arms, he finally pronounced a decision he felt would alleviate things. "Rabia, I'll get them. I'll go back and get them. We managed to get across the mountains before when the Russians were there. I can do it again by mule if I can get in touch with Ejaz and Abdul Rahman. Let me...let me try to get them back now, Rabia."

Rabia was clear about Sikander's culpability in failing to do anything about the vehicle. However, she was also the mother of two children and lady of a household. She had seen the debilitation caused by widowhood from her mother and to some degree Sofie. She had a keen sense of risk and this did not seem like a good idea. Besides, she loved Sikander. Rabia broke instantly from her sobbing.

"Sikander, *no!*" she said emphatically. "We've no information. You heard Musharraf say how Pakistan was now solidly in the Americans' camp. It's too risky!"

Sikander looked upon his wife's strained but still beautiful face. He was relieved that she had managed to regain her composure from this little interchange and more than a little pleased she was able to focus on his well-being. "Rabia, I don't want to do anything crazy either. Look, if it makes you feel better, I won't do anything unless I can dig out either Arif or Junaid to see if they can tell me something or maybe even help me. I won't go without their help. How's that?"

Rabia paused. Her quick mind was considering the possibility of getting through with ISI help, which even she knew would probably add considerably to any likelihood of success. "Do you...do you think you can *do* that?" she asked, wiping her tears with her dupattha.

"I can certainly try..." promised Sikander. "I *can* try."

The following morning, he entered his car and turned on the radio. His hunger for information was insatiable and he couldn't be without the news for a mere moment. The news was not good. In Peshawar, along with other towns and cities across Pakistan, widespread rioting was reported as people protested the American attacks on Afghanistan. In many quarters, Bush's newly launched Afghanistan campaign served to confirm suspicions that the New York attacks had been staged. In Quetta, someone was even killed during rioting and Sikander wondered what he might encounter just getting to Arif's place. He decided to call ahead first on Arif's cell phone.

"Assalaamu 'alaykum, Arif?" he began. "Are you in Jamrud?"

"Wa alaykum assalaam, Sikander. I am indeed in Jamrud. Troubled times, eh? How goes it with you, old friend?"

"I'm fine, Arif, but, well, you know what's going on over there and I'm very worried about the family in Laghar Juy. Listen, I left them a vehicle, oh...about a year ago and it's uh, broken down so they can't get back and join us here in Peshawar, which is really what we'd like with all that's happening."

"Hmm...yes...yes, I see but...well, you know what President Musharraf is saying. I don't see—"

"Oh, screw what *he's* saying, Arif!" retorted Sikander. "Arif, we need to get back there to help them get out. They're my friends and relatives! They're *your* friends! We have to do something."

"Alright! Alright, look uh, let me call a few people and see what can be done. Where are you, Sikander?"

"About to park in your backyard."

Arif came out to meet Sikander while making an up-and-down examination of Sikander's black Pajero.

"Good taste in automobiles," he muttered as the two of them hugged briefly before stepping indoors.

"Well, here I am. Let's make the calls," Sikander prodded.

The two of them entered Arif's living room. Just as Arif reached for the phone to dial, however, it rang.

"Hello?" inquired Arif.

"Arif? Arif, is that you?" came the voice over the line.

"Yes?…Yes this is Arif. Who's this?"

"*Aaaarif!*" exclaimed the voice. "It's *me*…Junaid! I have to come and see you!"

Arif cocked his chin up and rolled his eyes in the direction of Sikander. "Junaid? Junaid! Assalaamu 'alaykum wa-rahmatullahi wa-barakaatuhu! It's funny you should say that because sitting here with me is, guess who?"

"Listen, Arif." Junaid did not have the patience for a guessing game just at that moment. "We have to talk; we're getting all kinds of conflicting messages here about us and the Taliban. I have a mission to plan with you."

"Come on down to Jamrud, Junaid bhai, and we can talk, because right now I have Sikander sitting across the room from me and he's of the belief that he has a mission to plan too."

"Sikander? There? With you?"

"He certainly is, but listen. Why don't you come straight over and we can talk?"

In about twenty minutes, the three of them huddled together in Arif's basement. The old map of Nangarhar was still stretched out with

numerous pencil marks, names, and other tidbits of information scribbled copiously over it, and no small number of stains of one kind or another.

"Junaid," began Arif. "You've known Abdul Latif for years. His son and nephew are Taliban that you and the ISI have supported for at least…what is it now? About seventeen years, isn't it? Since they were just barely…teenager mujahideen…you called them, right?"

"Yes," sighed Junaid impatiently. "It's been at least that long."

"Well, brother, it looks like we need to put another mission together for them. This time it's not about helping Afghanistan or kicking anyone out. It's about rescuing your friends. Do you hear what I'm saying?" Arif adopted the transformed and serious look on his face that only he seemed to be capable of.

"Arif bhai, I…I…yes, we do have to do that, but we have a bigger issue to deal with. Please, just hear me out, will you?" responded Junaid. "It's coming from the top brass here in Pakistan. They have many assets on the ground over there which, with our literally having to switch sides, is creating a really awkward situation for us. Just a week ago, we were arming, equipping, and informing the Taliban on how to move against the Northern Alliance. This week, we have to help the Northern Alliance commander kill the people who were our friends last week! Do you hear what *I'm* saying?"

Hearing Junaid's words and realizing their enormity, Arif and Sikander both began imagining what he had in mind and how they themselves might be useful.

"Proceed," said Arif, having thus been subdued by the scale and significance of Junaid's mission.

"We have a situation developing where we're going to try to get out as many of our own officers and as many of their Taliban contact people as we can during an open window which Musharraf is negotiating with the Americans. He's got a direct communication going on with Cheney's office and he's telling him that if he doesn't get his ISI people out of Afghanistan, his prestige with the Pakistan Army is destined for the crapper. That'll destabilize Pakistan into an unholy mess, which even Cheney can see is not what anyone wants right now."

"How will you do it?" asked Sikander.

"With the Americans behind the Northern Alliance, the game is going to be over I'd say in—six?—ten weeks at most? So, we're going to establish a spot where we can assemble our people before the Northern Alliance can get there and see if we can airlift them using Six Squadron's C130s, while getting the Americans and the Northern Alliance people to hold their fire for as long as a few days or nights until we're done. Musharraf is trying to keep the American focus on the ISI contingent as being the real purpose, but he's willing to let others slip on board if they can make it there in time."

"So you're saying we should aim to get our own people to that spot at the right time and they could be lifted out to Pakistan?" asked Sikander.

"Indeed I am, sir!" said Junaid as he raised his eyebrows and assumed a tight-lipped smile.

"Do you have any idea where?" asked Arif.

"Qunduz. The Americans will try to build an in-country airbase from which they can launch other sorties. Both they and the Northern Alliance will focus on winning Mazar-e-Sharif—the locals there are anti-Taliban anyway—and once that's done, they'll be able to secure Qunduz airfield and create a safe corridor all the way to the Pak border. That'll allow us to fly in and pick up our people without concerns of being shot out of the sky."

"You mean the Northern Alliance and Americans will just stand by and watch an airlift of their enemies take place? Doesn't sound very likely."

"I know it sounds strange, but Musharraf is playing it just about right I'd say. He's convincing them that his ISI are critical assets and he'll be toppled if they get killed over there. We think the Americans understand this and are going to—yes, maybe reluctantly—go along with it."

"When does all this happen?" asked Sikander. "I have to get over to Laghar Juy now, don't I? I mean, if those people have a shot at coming back through that route, it's going to take days to make it to Qunduz."

"Right now we're looking at sometime in mid to late November. Wherever the ISI advisors are with the Taliban, we're telling them to fall

back in the direction of Qunduz, if they have to vacate any territory. Our estimate, working with the American plan, is that mid-November will be when we'll be able to come in."

Sikander was getting a glimpse of the business of war. He could see the innumerable contradictions and cross currents that made moral certitude only feasible in the outermost wrappers within which this war had been packaged and presented to its financiers, the American public. Behind the wrapper, it was a filthy, rotten, shit-ridden affair. Still, on this occasion those same moral dilemmas were working for him and his family, so he wasn't going to question them too rigorously. He simply shook his head slowly as he took it all in.

He studied his old friend Junaid, whose real name he still didn't even know. Junaid was almost fifty years old and probably a lot further along in rank than he let on, but he would always be Captain Junaid to Sikander. Every time Junaid and he met, some new insight into the man became apparent and this time was no exception.

"So, what about getting to Laghar Juy? What help can you get me, old friend?" asked Sikander. He was now clearly addressing the right person.

"Well, the reason I came here is that we'll need to organize getting across while the Americans are still playing the game with remotely launched weapons from the Arabian Sea or that Indian Ocean island they have...what is it?"

"Diego Garcia," proclaimed Sikander matter-of-factly. He'd been glued to CNN for so many days it hadn't been hard to come up with that.

"Yes...Diego Garcia," confirmed Junaid. "They have submarines and the Carl Vinson aircraft carrier, which leaves the Northern Alliance—our new allies—down to just their own troops and weapons plus the CIA special activities people and other military special ops fighting the Taliban. While they're still busy getting the Taliban out of the major cities, we have our chance at taking some people with enough mules and other supplies to get to Qunduz. That way we'll be able to help our people either to use the mules to travel over the passes or to get them on to Qunduz for airlifting in November."

"What about vehicles?" asked Sikander.

"If it has wheels, it'll be blown up," deadpanned Junaid. "They'll treat anything mechanized as either Taliban or Northern Alliance, and depending on where they are, they'll even risk friendly fire if they aren't where they believe their friends should be or can't generate the right IFF codes from the transponders that the CIA will have given out."

"So, when do we leave?" asked Sikander.

"On October 26th. There are a lot of logistics to organize, but that'll be a few days before the full moon so we should have plenty of nighttime light," replied Junaid. "We're going to a place just outside Torkhum. The Americans won't be hitting anything coming into the country from Pakistan just yet, so we can take vehicles in with us. But we'll need to let them come back as we pick up mules from Torkhum, because we can't go any further with wheels."

The men picked themselves up from their conversation around the map and got ready to leave, when a lingering question struck Sikander. "Er...Junaid bhai?"

"Mm?"

"It seemed when we were talking just now that you might be coming?"

"Yes, that's right. Why?"

"Well, you...you hadn't gone across when we used to do this with the Russians; why this time?" Sikander was genuinely curious.

Junaid looked down for a moment before reconnecting. "Iqbal, my uh...my son. He's over there with the Taliban." Junaid began answering the question he could see forming on Sikander's face, "Oh, I was all in favor of him going over there at first. Learning something from them, you know? Huh! He'd been really into the American thing—jeans, T-shirts, and baseball caps—and it warmed my heart that he got interested in his Deen. But then he...he started to write things to me. Sikander, I didn't recognize him anymore." Junaid couldn't restrain a quiver in his voice. Simply recalling that Iqbal was a member of the Taliban had clearly heightened the fear he felt for his son's life. "He's...he's been there for the past four years since they took control of the country and well, now he's in trouble. Sikander, I can't leave his rescue to others when I'm in a position to do more."

Another new fact from the depths of Junaid's complex persona had just bubbled up to the surface for Sikander. He wanted to ask more but he could see this wasn't an easy subject for Junaid, so he let the matter go.

"One last thing then," continued Sikander. "Should we meet here as usual and if so, when?"

Junaid looked at Arif to get his cue. "Let's say at 1900 hours on the 26th," Arif suggested to nods all around. The three parted, each lost in his own uniquely brewing anxiety.

From Arif's place, Sikander drove to his office. It was on his way home anyway and he needed to let Jamil know of his need to be away for maybe a month or more starting from the 26th. In the time available they would work together to prepare for Sikander's absence. He revealed nothing of the airlift mission or any other potentially risky information. He simply explained he had to travel to Afghanistan, with the ISI, to bring his in-laws safely into Pakistan. Jamil, while apprehensive about Sikander's going, knew it wouldn't be worth bothering to try to dissuade his brother, given Rabia's family situation.

When he finally reached home in the late afternoon, Sikander stepped out of the black Pajero and into the lounge. Atiya was there with Qayyum.

"Where's Rabia?", he asked.

"Oh, Khan-sahib, she went to pick up Ayub from school and should be back very soon." Atiya returned her attention to Qayyum. She had laid out some children's English elementary reading books to entertain himself. Sikander slumped into the sofa and lay back with his head against an arm, inhaling a long, slow, deep breath and exhaling a short, complete sigh. He turned his head to see his young son playfully turning over the thick glossy cardboard pages and making simple sounds while looking at the pictures.

What a world! thought Sikander. *What a crazy, stupid world.* His gaze had fixed on Qayyum and his obliviousness of the madness into which the world had run itself. Qayyum's world was simple. It was beautiful. The people who'd created the book he was thumbing through were happy, beautiful people. They were Americans. How could things have unraveled to the point of their becoming indiscriminate targets for nineteen Saudi fanatics believing that heaven lay on the other side of

their acts? How could they have decided that an entire country, already hard-pressed to eke out even a meager existence, should now bear the brunt of the cost of seeking out the criminals, simply because their government refused to turn them over without presentation of evidence? He loved America and hated what she was now doing to him, his family, and his adopted country. In that thought, not having slept well in the past few nights, he dozed off.

"Sikander? Sikander? Sikander, wake up," came the voice as Sikander began to stir.

"Hm? Oh..." murmured Sikander as he began accumulating consciousness. It was Sofie who had awoken him. "What...uh...what time is it?"

"It's six in the evening, Sikander. You fell asleep. It's time for something to eat."

Sikander positioned himself upright and as the fog continued to clear, he said, "Ammee-jan, I...I can't eat right now. Tell Sarwat to hold on and leave the rotthis for a little while longer. She can heat up the food later too. Where's Rabia?"

"She came home with Ayub. She's asleep too...in the bedroom. I asked Atiya to take Ayub and Qayyum away so you wouldn't be disturbed, bettha," she said in her soothing motherly tone as she retreated into the kitchen to ask Sarwat to delay serving dinner.

Sikander yawned and rubbed his hair vigorously to speed up recovery of his consciousness and proceeded to his bedroom to wake up Rabia. He needed to tell her about his plans without delay.

"Rabia? Rabia, wake up. Rabia?" he prodded her and slowly she too regained consciousness, asked the same questions about the time, and finally sat upright on the edge of the bed.

"I think we have a way of doing it, Rabia!" said Sikander when he was reasonably sure of her alertness. "I think we can get your family out!" he continued, waiting for some kind of response.

"Sikander you *can*? When? How?" she asked in a tone that betrayed her depression and lack of recent sleep.

"I can't explain it all, but it does involve me going over to Afghanistan soon," he explained. "I'll probably need to be away for four to eight weeks."

Feeling the weight of Sikander's proposed plan Rabia became more alert and involved in the conversation. "Sikander, what…what do you mean? Why that long?"

"Look, I really can't explain it all to you, but you should know I'll not be going in alone and the operation is being carefully planned."

"Are you sure about this?" asked Rabia anxiously and with a hint of suspicion.

Sikander nodded and put on the most convincing smile he could, hoping he would infect Rabia with it. She returned a forbearing look. Deep inside Rabia wanted desperately to believe that a plan based on the kind of assistance that Sikander had previously discussed might work. But she knew her husband well enough to know that he wouldn't try to deceive her, so if he had a plan, it meant he'd obtained the kind of help that it demanded.

"Then I'll just have to trust you, won't I, Sikander?" Rabia uttered, as her eyes narrowed and she, too, formed a smile, a little more involuntarily than Sikander's.

Optimism began to regain its familiar grip on her and with it came the urge to give Sikander a warm, loving embrace. They had dinner and retired to bed, deliberately avoiding additional TV that night. Lying in the relative darkness with just a nightstand light to illuminate them, Sikander felt a tenderness from Rabia which he'd been missing for several days, as the tension leading up to this war had taken its toll. At that moment, Rabia was more relaxed than he'd seen her in a while and gazing upon her face in the low light, he was once again smitten by her ordinarily irrepressible beauty. His wife had returned to reclaim herself. Having each slept for a couple of hours already, and with a burgeoning profusion of pheromones in the room, they were in no mood to sleep.

October 26th came and Sikander was probably better prepared than on any previous crossing, albeit some years older. A few days before the appointed date, he and Junaid met again in the Jumma Bazaar where Junaid handed him a specially prepared map with an accurate representation of roads and waterways but most importantly the topography, which for any mule-bound journey was indispensable. He studied the map, intently figuring out options until he felt he had been as thorough as possible. Now that the day had finally arrived, he gathered up some cash, put a few simple belongings together, including

the map, and hugged his family passionately, especially Rabia, before driving himself to Arif's place, leaving his vehicle in the back lot.

Junaid was already there with several others whom Sikander had not seen before. There were also two vehicles. On this particular mission, itself one of several similar missions going on over the next few days, a total of twelve men were to travel and the intention was to split up into six teams of two with specific coordinates from which to draw escapee candidates. The ISI teams leaving that evening were to go to Nangarhar, Lowgar, Wardak, Paktia, Ghazni, and Bamian provinces, respectively, to take their ISI brothers up to Qunduz. Sikander was to join them but obviously had his own agenda with Laghar Juy.

As of that moment, American bombing campaigns were still making their way through specific targets that would disable the Taliban ability to wage much of a war or even mount a meaningfully coordinated defense. Early warning radar installations, command and control facilities, airfields, and aircraft on the ground were all targets.

The two vehicles left that evening for the border at which they arrived by just before eleven o'clock that night. Security from the Afghan side was virtually nonexistent. Clearly, there didn't seem much point in preventing people from coming into the country, and in any case, communication with Kabul was dead with the phone lines disabled.

The men piled out of the vehicles and connected with another ISI officer who led them into a small place outside Torkhum where forty-eight mules awaited them. The vehicle drivers turned around and sped back to Landi Kotal while the teams split up to proceed to their designated locations. For Sikander, at least, it was not difficult since they were already in Nangarhar. He joined up with another officer named Iftekhar who had been introduced to him back in Jamrud as a lieutenant in the ISI.

Junaid headed to Wardak where he believed his son was located and with him went another of the officers. As Sikander was not in that team, he had not been introduced to the officer by name. Even so, Sikander gave Junaid and his companion a comforting hug and went on his own way with Iftekhar.

"We need to get off the road tonight, Sikander," said Iftekhar. "We'll try to remain about ten kilometers to the south of the main road

and my mission is to get to Ghani Khel, then to Nadir Shah Kot and Shahi Kot to pick up our people and move them up toward Qunduz. You can separate and take two mules with you and go on southwest from Nadir Shah Kot to Laghar Juy. Try to gauge the situation and if you feel you can come back this way or over the pass near Showlghar with your people, then do it. Otherwise, we can meet up again at Qunduz. Bear in mind," he warned, "the Americans and Northern Alliance presence is going to increase sharply once they get a major air base, whether it's Qandahar or Mazar-e-Sharif or Bagram near Kabul. Once they do, you can expect a lot of attention on the border regions with Pakistan, which is why we've set this thing up for Qunduz in the far north. Any questions?"

Sikander was a little tired but he got the picture and didn't have any serious follow-up questions. *This Iftekhar's a buttoned-down fellow,* he thought. *Probably doesn't have much experience in being on this side of the fence.*

In any event, the two needed to avoid making any more noise than necessary with plans to travel at least a hundred meters apart so as not to attract attention as potential Taliban. The moon was bright as predicted, so it wasn't hard to track Iftekhar sometimes from right behind him, sometimes from the left or right.

Once in a while they could hear jets flying overhead; some were clearly very high altitude bombers. At other times, they could hear Tomahawk cruise missiles whizzing across the countryside at barely a hundred meters off the ground, each relying on a triad of GPS, terrain contour, and visual scene matching to deliver destruction unerringly to its selected destination. Error in selecting the right destination was a wholly different matter.

At just after three in the morning, they both arrived into Ghani Khel with their trains of four mules each. Iftekhar asked one of the night watchmen about his contact, an ISI lieutenant named Imran Sarwar. The watchman knew Imran and took the two men to where he was staying, waking him up to meet them. He in turn led them to his safe place where they could rest. They slept for a little more than five hours, following which the three of them, together with a Taliban from the village, left for Nadir Shah Kot.

It didn't take long for the four men to make it to Nadir Shah Kot and as soon as they did, Sikander made ready to leave them so he could

proceed to Laghar Juy. They met up with another two Taliban and an ISI man. Sikander wasn't to be traveling with them so there were no introductions. Finally the moment arrived for Sikander to split up from the rest of the group. Iftekhar reminded him that to be lifted out, Sikander and his relatives needed to be at Qunduz no later than November 17th. Sikander took his two allotted mules and bid the teams salaams as he turned southwest to go up to his old adopted haunt, which was a little more than thirty kilometers upstream following the local stream all the way.

That evening Sikander stopped at a house in a small village called Jabeh where he introduced himself as the young brother of Abdul Latif of Laghar Juy, explaining that he was looking to be put up for the night under the protection of one of the villagers, a man by the name of Gul Baz, who had heard of Abdul Latif but confessed to not knowing him. Still, he was generous enough to offer an evening meal, a place to rest, and breakfast the following morning. Having thanked Gul Baz for his hospitality, Sikander continued his mule trek all the way to Laghar Juy, but when he arrived at Abdul Latif's house, he saw no immediate sign of life.

The men are no doubt off embroiled in the fighting, thought Sikander. "Sister Razya!" he called out. Arising behind the main room's doorway leading from the rear where she had been preparing a small early evening meal, Razya recognized the voice and hurriedly emerged, without donning her burkha, to meet Sikander. She simply pulled her dupattha over her head a little more than normal as she rushed to embrace him. The hug was tight, and though longer than might have seemed normal even under such circumstances, Sikander reciprocated warmly.

"Ohhh...Sikanderrrr!" she cried softly and again let herself go pretty much as she had done when he and Rabia had returned with the Pajero. He lowered his head and allowed himself to be blessed with a stroke of her hand.

"Sister Razya, where is everyone?" asked Sikander. She looked down and slowly raised her eyes with a forlorn expression. "Sis...Sister Razya, what?"

"Sikander! Oh...Sikander! My Khan. He's...he's gone, zwey!"

"Gone? Gone where?" asked Sikander, his conscious mind clinging to improbability while the expression on Razya's face eloquently proclaimed the needless nature of such a question.

"We couldn't get word out to you. Allah took him back, almost two weeks ago," she stammered as she described the event that had turned her life on its head in the midst of the bombing and all the other evils of the time.

"Abdul Latif! Inna lillahi wa inna ilayhi raaji'un!" cried Sikander. Amid all the turmoil, his mind simply hadn't been prepared for such an eventuality. He couldn't contain himself for the loss of his surely indestructible old friend. "What happened?" he asked, hardly able to apprehend the fact.

"After the bombs started to fall again, you know, Sikander, his heart simply broke. He had seen so much fighting, so much killing. After all the hope when the Russians left, he was so sure that we would finally have peace. But now, with the family all split up and the latest attacks from America, he...he just didn't have the heart to continue living any longer."

"So, you mean he just...sank into a depression?" asked Sikander, still unsure of what Razya was saying.

"You know, Sikander, he wasn't the same after the boys joined up with the Taliban. It just wasn't the way he had always believed the Deen of Islam should be practiced," she began explaining while regaining her composure and wiping her tear-stained cheek with her dupattha.

"Yes...yes, I know about—" started Sikander.

Razya didn't wait for him to finish. "He...he was praying salaat-ul-fajr and it must have been after the last sajdah..." she gazed into the distance and shook her head slowly from side to side, "he...he just stayed there, sitting in tashahud without moving. It was as if Allah had decided he should return to him from within the middle of prayer, may Allah be praised and may he bless him. It even took a while for me to...discover." Razya heaved a sigh before continuing, "Sikander, you should have seen the people who came to his funeral. Even eighty-year-old Younus Khalis was able to come, along with Jalaluddin Haqqani from Khost and many others, but getting word back to Pakistan

was...well, with the bombs and everything and the boys out with the Taliba—"

Her eyes creased, closing tightly as the pain of continuing was clearly too great. Sikander felt a counterintuitive and slightly embarrassing sense of joy coming over him as he processed the manner of Abdul Latif's death in his own mind. It gave his grief immediate pause, neutralizing it like a soda would an acid, providing something to hang on to.

"That...that's so beautiful, Sister Razya. For Abdul Latif to have had such a graceful departure from us all. It's just so beautiful. It was a truly enviable death! Yes...enviable." It was the only word Sikander could think of as he heaved a sigh while his heart felt as if it had run out of space within which to beat. "Is he...buried near here?"

"I believe so," said Razya, wiping her face again.

"You...*believe* so?"

"The Taliban wouldn't let women come to graveyards."

Sikander permitted himself a brief moment of relish at the fact that this ill-informed idea of Islam that had been imposed on the sweet people of Afghanistan might well be drawing to a close. "Sister Razya, where's Abdul Majeed?" he asked.

"He's gone. He's gone," she replied.

"Gone...where?" Sikander asked guardedly, almost primed for even more revelations of death, while realizing that Razya was becoming a little too overwhelmed to be much more coherent.

"He...they...they both went up into the mountains. They'll almost certainly be in Tora Bora now, and...Allah...protect themmmmm!" She started wailing uncontrollably once again. "I've heard bombs being dropped up there...So loud. So *loud*..." Razya continued to cry as Sikander held her head against his bosom, comforting her as best he could. After briefly letting her drain her emotion, he asked about Noor, Fatima, and Amina. She replied that they were all safe and that Fatima and Latifa, Razya's young granddaughter, were in the back of the house while Amina was at home with Noor.

Sikander picked himself up, feeling as if his own weight had doubled as he did so. He paused and sighed for a moment before telling Razya he'd be back shortly.

He walked over to Noor's house and met with her and Amina. They too were distraught at the absence of any men in the household and that their younger son, Amina's husband, was on the run in the mountains. Sikander knew the rough location of Tora Bora and thought about whether it was worth trying to go up there to bring back Saleem and Abdul Majeed in time to depart for either Qunduz or a tough trek back to Pakistan through the mountain passes. But before going too far down that road, he needed to know where Abdul Latif had been buried.

Eventually, he found a young man who was evidently not a Taliban, at least not at that moment. He asked the man the whereabouts of Abdul Latif's grave. As he began pointing, Sikander interrupted and asked him to take him there. The man obliged and they walked about two hundred meters to the rough graveyard. It wasn't hard to see the relatively fresh, unmarked rectangular mound of dirt.

Sikander raised his hands with the palms facing upward and the young man with him followed suit as they both recited the Surat-ul-Fatiha. Sikander recited a few more prayers and finished up with Surat-ul-Ikhlas, following which he picked up a fistful of dirt from near the grave and tossed it onto the mound. A solitary tear rolled down his cheek. He stood a moment longer staring at the grave's mound, seeing not the mound but the grinning face of Abdul Latif Khan waking him up for the fajr prayer in Hayatabad. That image, inexplicably to Sikander, recalled the words he had heard so often in the last few weeks: *Enduring Freedom*. As they came ringing into his consciousness, he replayed in his mind Razya's description of his longtime friend's blissful departure from this world. He'd left them all without warning and was now in a place where his freedom from all injustice and oppression, all want and need, would indeed be enduring.

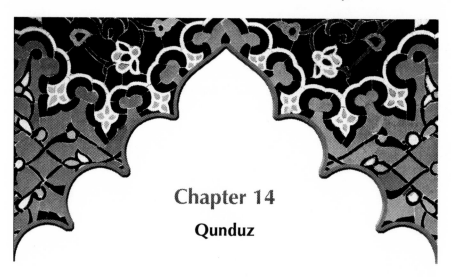

Chapter 14
Qunduz

THE NORTHERN ALLIANCE pursued its slow, steady, but relentless advance toward Mazar-e-Sharif. Though not so much in that area, most of the initial pounding of Taliban targets elsewhere in Afghanistan was unending and effective, and neither the Taliban nor the al-Qaeda Arabs knew what to do.

An initial wave of selective bombing had been successful in taking out any possible assets that might have enabled the Taliban to mount a systematic, coordinated defense. Once Taliban communications were subdued, attention shifted to direct attacks on those ground forces that had yet to surrender to the advancing Northern Alliance troops. As of the start of November, the first phase was still in full swing, while targets of opportunity, especially vehicles perceived to be supply trucks carrying oil and other important commodities into or around Afghanistan, were systematically attacked. Oil tanker trucks seemed to be a favorite among the F-18 pilots from the Carl Vinson and the Enterprise, but generally any form of vehicular traffic incurred a sizable risk of becoming a target.

Sikander spent a few days organizing the women of his family in Laghar Juy for the upcoming travel, but before that journey could begin, he had to get up to Tora Bora to find Abdul Majeed and Saleem, whom he hoped to persuade to take to Pakistan with him.

As he readied to set off, standing outside Razya's house, Sikander asked Noor and Razya if they had any specific indication of where the men might be.

"When they were leaving here, they had said they would be going toward Tangi Khola, right by the caves," said Razya. "If, on the way there, you ask people to point you in the right direction, understand that it's also called Karo Khel," she added.

"Ah...I think I know that location. It's about thirty kilometers from here, isn't it?" he asked.

Razya and Noor shrugged as they didn't know in detail. Fatima came out of Razya's house having overheard the conversation and, speaking through her burkha, she described the general direction.

"Brother Sikander, to get to it you would have to stay close to the mountains and head due west to Ghoshtara. From there you could pick up a dirt trail, which will continue in the same general direction tracking the foot of the mountains and take you through Harun Baba all the way to Payenda Khel. At that point you'll need to leave the trail. It will turn north, but you will need to continue west to cut across to Tangi Khola. That would put you right at the base of the mountains where the caves are a little higher up. There you will come to a clear path to get up to them and I'm sure you'll find plenty of Taliban to help if you use my husband's name."

Sikander looked back at Fatima, as she peered through her burkha. "JazaakAllah, Sister Fatima."

Fatima nodded, acknowledging his thanks and wished him "Khuda Hafiz."

Mounting a mule and with the second one trailing him, Sikander headed out of the village, up the lower slopes, and then west to Ghoshtara. At these elevations he made about ten kilometers an hour and in less than two hours, he was already leaving the trail at Payenda Khel. Throughout the journey, he heard the distant rumblings of explosions. Looking up, Sikander could see the cloudless sky etched by numerous vapor trails generally running southwest to northeast and then arcing back in beautiful white loops or turning slightly to go on to the northwest. *A beautiful heavenly signature authoring such hellish devastation on the ground*, Sikander mused sadly. The mountains added

their own ghostly echo to the rumblings coming from as far away as Kabul and Jalalabad.

Sikander managed to get about three kilometers along the westward trail when he felt his mule tense beneath him, spooked by the noises, although this was rare as these animals had spent virtually all of their short lives thus far being familiar with the din of battle. Clearly the Americans were using something quite different from the Russians to try to obliterate the Taliban.

He decided to dismount and go ahead on foot when he saw a band of black-turbaned individuals heading in his direction. They were carrying AK-47s and had RPG launchers strapped to their shoulders as they headed toward him. Sikander on this occasion was unarmed so he proceeded with caution, believing he might easily be mistaken for a local anti-Taliban tribesman, which might not be a good thing. As they neared, it was clear that the troop was dejected and weary. It was also clearly too late for Sikander to hide; he had no choice but to brave it with them. He couldn't have been a threat, being quite evidently unarmed. In the midst of these concerns his furrowed brow suddenly relaxed.

"Ha! Abdul Majeed! Saleem!" cried Sikander, relieved to see the two men he had been seeking walking among the troop. They in turn recognized him and Saleem raised his weapon in the air in a gesture of acknowledgment as a weary smile crinkled his face. Sikander knew that these men must have seen and endured some serious bombardment along with its devastating and memorable effects.

"Sikander!" cried out Saleem. "What are you doing here, brother? You should be safely in Pakistan right now with your family."

The three men stopped while the others in the troop moved on, oblivious to the encounter. They were quite clearly too drained to be arrested by anything but a direct imperative.

"I was on my way to Tora Bora to look for you two. I've come back to Afghanistan to try to get you both out of here with your families. But what...what about you? Where have you been? Combat?"

"If you'd gone to Tora Bora you wouldn't have found us," noted Abdul Majeed. "We're on our way back from Jalalabad and we came straight up following the brooks and streams toward the hills to get out of the open country up north."

"What were you doing in Jalalabad?"

"We got word that there had been some kind of attack on America and they were going to attack Afghanistan because they said al-Qaeda attacked them and we wouldn't turn over Bin Laden to them!" said Saleem.

"That's about the sum of it," replied Sikander, noting the remarkable succinctness in Saleem's grade-school explanation.

"You've heard that Ab...Abaa died?" Abdul Majeed asked.

"Yes, I also heard how he died and probably why he died, may Allah accept his soul in peace. I found a young man to show me his grave, offered a Fatiha, and I'm just coming from there."

"It was the second day after he was buried that we decided to head up to Tora Bora because that's where some of the early bombing had been going on, but then we heard about major conflicts up north from Taliban fighters coming down our way, so we decided to see if we could join the fighting up there. We were on our way to Jalalabad to rest before proceeding north," continued Saleem. "There'd been so much bombing, Sikander! So many bodies, cars, trucks, buses on the road blown to pieces or burned out with bodies looking like charcoal in them! What's going on? They want to catch some criminals, yet so many men, women, children, and animals have to die to let the Americans have their badal? That isn't badal!"

"Yes I...I know it's...insane. Totally insane," Sikander looked down as he shook his head sideways. "Just imagine, Saleem. If everyone in the whole world was insane, then who'd be left to call us insane? We'd all think we were normal and continue living crazy lives...like we appear to be doing right now." The usually levelheaded Sikander's frustration mounted.

"The Northern Alliance forces were trying to take Mazar-e-Sharif and we needed to block that," said Abdul Majeed. "As Saleem was saying, we'd stopped in Jalalabad on our way to help defend Mazar-e-Sharif when hell came to earth! It would have been about the 11th of October and everywhere we looked, there were bombs raining down on us. They hit Majpoorbal Village and the Sorkhrod masjid. A couple of days later it was Jalalabad again. After about three more days they kept coming and hit Morgai and Gere Khel. Then I distinctly

remember on the 18th a missile just wiped away a family in a truck trying to flee Jalalabad."

"So what made you leave and how did you end up here?" asked Sikander.

"For several days there was no more bombing so we decided that with the bombardment we'd seen, we would have little chance of making it up north. We uh, thought to return to our families and see if there was a way out of this hell, and when we met up with some others coming out of Kabul, we all decided to track back closer to the mountains. We were actually just coming through Tangi Khola about an hour or so ago. From a distance it seemed like on this side of the Spin Ghar there was no action so that's why we chose this way around," Abdul Majeed explained.

"Well, if either of you want to ride on mules, I have these two here and I'd say we have to get moving. I'll tell you more when we get back," explained Sikander.

The three of them trekked back to Laghar Juy, taking turns riding a mule with about a half hour of walking at a time for the one on foot. Reaching Laghar Juy early that evening, they were warmly greeted by the women. It was the first night in three that Abdul Majeed and Saleem used a bed.

The following morning, November 4th, after everyone awoke, Sikander approached Abdul Majeed and Saleem to confer with them, bringing all the women to join in the decision making to come.

After a meager breakfast—provisions having been difficult to obtain lately—they gathered round sitting cross-legged on Razya's durree to hear what Sikander had to say.

"I've come with the help of the ISI," he began. "Now, understand something. Officially, Pakistan has sided with America and is...um...fighting the Taliban." Sikander paused to let this fact sink in, especially with the men.

"Huh! If I'd known that the whole country would be getting bombed because we didn't let the Americans have Bin Laden, I would have sided against the Taliban," Noor proclaimed bitterly, her head aimed straight at a sheepish looking Saleem. "You've brought nothing but hardship, and now this! For what? All because some poorly

educated mullahs convinced you of their own crazy Islam! We could have been in such a better position!" she said as she started shaking in her burkha with tears that prevented her from continuing. She had boldly voiced what Sikander felt, and he reflected on what he might have said and when he might have said it, to be effective in setting his two good friends on a different path. What material from which source would have convinced them of a different meaning to Islam than the one they had embraced? He could think of several such occasions but checked himself, as this was not the time for such reflections.

"Adey, we have to make some important decisions. The main thing is to remain alive until the madness can be stopped or burns itself out."

"So what are you proposing, Sikander?" asked Saleem, anxious to change the subject.

"Well, I did say that this was the official position…but the Americans have been persuaded by Musharraf that he can't just switch sides and abandon his ISI staff here without being toppled by his own generals. They agree and have cleared the way for an airlift. Pakistan will be flying large transport aircraft into the country over several nights beginning around the 15th and going on till about the 17th of the month. The intention is to evacuate their people."

"Evacuate? Where from?" asked Abdul Majeed.

"That's the bad news. They are going to be using Qunduz," replied Sikander, waiting for acknowledgment before moving on.

"You mean…all the way up *north*?" asked Saleem.

Sikander glanced briefly downward and nodded, looking back at them, his lips stiffening.

"Well, that has to be at least two hundred and fifty, maybe even three hundred, kilometers from here!" exclaimed Saleem, suspending a shrug. "How are we going to do that? We need to make a solid twenty-five or thirty kilometers a day."

"While bombs are raining on us," added Abdul Majeed, his bent knee and interlocked knuckles under his chin, propping up his weary head. Sikander glanced in the direction of each of the women, unable to see their expressions but aware of them staring at him intently.

"There's another option," he offered cautiously. "It'll mean crossing the high passes more directly toward Pakistan like we've done in the past, but with all of us, we'll require more mules than the two we have. The distance is a lot shorter and we could stop by where Ejaz lives. We should get cell phone coverage once we're on the Pakistan side, and I could arrange to get Arif to pick us up."

"There was bad weather two days ago," observed Razya dryly. "A few of the women were discussing it while you were gone yesterday and described how their men had been trying to get out that way and couldn't get through."

"And if that's true and we take the chance trying it, then we'll have to turn back and will need to travel even farther from there than from here directly. Meanwhile we'd have wasted valuable time. I think we should all discuss it and decide," Sikander suggested, his eyes scanning the room.

At first no one responded, and he waited uncomfortably for an answer. Finally Saleem spoke. "I...suppose...if we were to get more mules, we could use them for either choice. What, if anything, do you know about the American bombing? Is it likely to remain over the big cities or are they going to try to block the mountains as well?"

"I don't know." Sikander shrugged. "But given where we are, I don't think we can risk the mountain route when I know whatever Junaid has said is unlikely to be a lie or a mistake. After all, I did come into Afghanistan with him and several others. I would recommend taking mules up to Qunduz. We could travel along the outskirts of major roads, being sure to stay out of sight, and break up into two or three groups. Their missiles will be likely be programmed to attack major facilities, so we should keep as far from such threats as possible. That would leave us exposed to their fighter aircraft, which tend to be the ones going after small groups and convoys, but I think if we're not in vehicles it should help."

"What about Northern Alliance? How will we avoid that problem?" asked Abdul Majeed.

"As far as I recall, they are either in the Panjshir north of Kabul and being met by Taliban ground forces, or they'll be much further north, going after Mazar-e-Sharif. It is a risk," admitted Sikander, "and if we come across them we could surrender to them, appealing to their

being fellow Muslims. We certainly wouldn't want to risk our women and Latifa by engaging them with our weapons."

"May I be allowed to speak?" Amina's voice emerged from behind her burkha.

Sikander glanced toward Saleem who did not stir and while maintaining his eye contact with him, Sikander asked her to continue. "Sister Amina, we all need to be free to speak here. Please, say what you want to say," he encouraged, turning to listen to her.

"I believe we should go with you to Qunduz and pray to Allah. He will be the one to protect us and get us there, if we truly believe in his power. Our wits are to be used until we have exhausted them. At that point, salvation lies in recognizing that all outcomes belong to Allah and we have to be at peace with his decision, for the fates of all of us belong to him."

No one could disagree and Sikander turned back to lock eyes with Saleem, but Saleem's head was tipped down and eyes closed as he took in his wife's words. He was consumed by a guilt at having been a party, in whatever small way, to the calamity now befalling all of humanity. What his wife had said, in a manner betraying a wisdom beyond her years, but without openly insulting her husband, simply made them all understand that.

After Amina had spoken, the rest of the group seemed to coalesce in agreement on the Qunduz route and Sikander felt as if a plan to get to Qunduz could now be described to them all, but first he wanted affirmative agreement.

"So, is there anyone who still wants to take the mountain route?" he asked. No one answered. "Qunduz it is then?" he asked and slowly, Razya at first and then the rest began nodding in agreement.

"Alright, there are eight of us including little Latifa. We should try to get at least another eight mules. That will gives a total of ten. Latifa can ride with one of the women, so we'll use seven for riding and rotate three with whatever light baggage we want to put on them. Now, where can we get extra mules?"

"There's a village not far from here...about fifteen kilometers. It's called Sharkanay, in the general direction of Anarbagh, and I know

someone there who normally has mules. A lot of people have been leaving the villages so there may be some available," Saleem suggested.

"Fine. So, two of us should go with the mules we have. Abdul Majeed, can you come with me?" asked Sikander.

"Let's go as soon as possible so we can be back this evening," Abdul Majeed urged as he nodded.

Following the briefest of preparations, the two of them rode off with Sikander borrowing Saleem's weapon for the ride. They made good time into Sharkanay, stopping en route for zuhr prayer, then sought out the man who had the mules. He had six. Sikander had been wise enough to bring both Pakistani rupees and US dollars. He knew the dollar would be the more fungible, but right now he preferred to offer ten thousand rupees which the man gladly accepted. The mule trader also explained that they might find more mules in Kamkay Kalay, which would not be a significant detour on their way back to Laghar Juy.

The two men led three each behind them in a train back along the path, but this time more slowly. They stopped in Kamkay Kalay and found the other mule handler who took a further five thousand rupees for the two available, despite much argument from Abdul Majeed.

Trailing four mules each behind them, Sikander and Abdul Majeed stopped briefly for asr before riding on. By sunset, they returned with their mission accomplished. Surprisingly, thought Abdul Majeed, the bombing had not come into this area in a very intense way just yet, though probably because the Northern Alliance had no value for any remaining local targets at the time.

The bombing until then had in fact been of two kinds. One was to deny any meaningful air defense counter by the Taliban, while the other aimed to hit Taliban ground forces where they presented significant opposition for the Northern Alliance. The attacks in and around most cities had been to strike the former types of targets, which, once demolished, removed the need to continue attacking until or unless it was in support of the Northern Alliance's ground forces.

However, such air defense facilities as their might have been, were often determined from information dating back to the Soviet era and were typically located in populated areas. Moreover, there seemed little distinction in bombing priority between old or disused facilities and functioning ones, largely due to the use of satellite imagery or aerial

photography without adequate ground-based human intelligence, resulting in so-called collateral damage with many more civilians killed than the American government had acknowledged in its own news briefings.

Whatever the circumstances governing these choices, the result was that in Nangarhar Province for some days there had been hardly any new bombing attacks and Sikander and Abdul Majeed had been spared the need to dodge the bombs.

As dawn broke on November 5th all plans had been made ready for the family to start heading out. After fajr prayer, Sikander asked everyone to reconvene in Razya's home for breakfast and to discuss the route and other details. When breakfast was done, with everyone still sitting around the empty space in the middle of the durree, Sikander reached into his qamees's deep side pocket to pull out the tightly folded map handed to him by Junaid, getting everyone's attention as he spread it out.

"We should all understand how we're to get to Qunduz, but particularly Abdul Majeed and Saleem, in case we have to split up or anything should happen to us," explained Sikander as he began to describe the route.

"We'll proceed back the way we came the day before yesterday from Tora Bora," he said, glancing toward Saleem and Abdul Majeed. "Once we get to Tangi Khola, we'll head northwest toward Wazir and take the trail north out of Wazir to Zor Bazaar and then, staying near the trail, we should arrive in the bottom of the valley at Baghwanay. From there we have to turn west to Ghare Kala and once again north at that point to be able to cut through a gap in the mountains as we get into Laghman Province. If we keep following that trail for about nine kilometers, it will take us to the main Jalalabad-to-Kabul road."

Sikander paused for questions and comments. Abdul Majeed and Saleem were the critical ones and they needed to understand the route so that any splitting up of the group would still leave a semblance of the plan in place.

The two men seemed to be clear, as this was territory with which they had at least some familiarity.

"Where next?" asked Abdul Majeed.

"We should have an easier time of it along that road but we need to stay well to the north of it because vehicles on it will be targets. We need to follow it west toward Kabul but leave the road at Sorubi, near the lake of the Naglu Dam. At that point we turn north to follow the lake's eastern shoreline and pick up the Nejrab River going north. That country is relatively easy going until we get just south of Nejrab itself, where we need to take the trail across the mountains into the Panjshir Valley. We then have to follow the Panjshir River until we come out to the north of Bagram near Mahmud Raqi right here," explained Sikander pointing to the map. "From there we'll cross over to Charikar. At that point, we'll pick up this main northbound Kabul to Mazar-e-Sharif highway, which will also take us through more mountain passes to Pul-i-Khumri. As before, we'll stay at the riverbank level and not on the road. At Pul-i-Khumri, we have to take the eastern branch of the road toward Baghlan and from there to Qunduz."

"You seem to have this option very well covered, Sikander!" remarked Razya.

"Sister Razya, this was the plan I entered the country with when I came with the ISI people."

"So how about timing?" asked Abdul Majeed.

"Good question, Brother," replied Sikander. "Here's how I see it. I think we can get to Baghwanay by the end of today—yes?" He looked for confirmations and seemed to get no objections.

"Right. So, from there to the lake at Sorubi should take us to the end of tomorrow, November 6th. On the 7th we need to get about two thirds of the way along the Nejrab River. By the end of the 8th we ought to be in the mountain pass on our way to Charikar. The 9th should see us in Charikar. We ought to make it as far as the Salang Tunnel by the 10th, and for the 11th we should be at about where the road takes a sharp turn to the west, right here," Sikander pointed, "and on the 12th I'd like us to be at Pul-i-Khumri. If we allow a couple of days from there, we should make Qunduz by the 14th. The actual airfield is to the south of the city on the east side of the main highway, so we won't need to go quite as far as the city itself. We need to be on the tarmac at the airport in order to be lifted. I'm going to suggest that we approach it under cover of darkness while the Taliban are still in control of the city. If they also control the airport then that will be fine but if, as I suspect, by then the American offensive has put a siege on the city, then they or the

Northern Alliance will have control of the airfield and we'll still be in a position to leave based on Musharraf's arrangement. Either way, we need to get there in time for one of the PAF flights that come in. If we're really lucky, Junaid will be there to confirm our legitimacy, but in any case, he gave me documents I should be able to use if need be."

The family was impressed with Sikander's apparent grasp of the map of Afghanistan. It remained to be seen if that grasp extended to understanding the real terrain and what he had described in terms of realistic goals. The going implied about twenty-eight kilometers each day, which seemed like a feasible distance if the animals could be rotated appropriately and were kept well watered and fed. Indeed, the plan's maximum use of river valleys and the green zones surrounding them would afford some level of protection and requisite fodder for the mules.

With these matters understood and gone over more than a few times with Abdul Majeed and Saleem, the troop set off from Laghar Juy. For Abdul Majeed's and Razya's benefit, and with Razya's insistence that there would be no wailing or moaning, the family made a first stop once again to offer the Fatiha prayer over Abdul Latif's grave. Saleem and Abdul Majeed were too weary to try to oppose the women's presence and were told by a confident Sikander that the schools of Islamic codes of behavior where women were excluded from visiting graves had only arisen from early injunctions against such visits due to the older Arab tradition of hiring women to visit graves to lament the departed in as dramatic a fashion as possible. However, most scholars agreed, as Sikander pointed out, that as long as such behavior was not indulged in, grave visitation by women was acceptable and encouraged and had many sound hadiths to support that view.

By mid-morning of November 5th, they visited the grave, offered the Fatiha, and were on their way. Razya and Noor wept softly inside their burkhas as they occasionally stole a glance back upon the village which had ironically been a haven in war and a place of family strife in such peace as there had been in Afghanistan since the Soviet defeat. A palpable sense of sundering felt as if it was coming from within their very beings. Their memories, hopes, dreams, and yes, even their fears—all the things that had defined who they had been up to that moment—were being left behind to become just so many piles of mud-bricks and rubble.

Stand watch over it, Khan, my love. Stand watch over it as you did so well in life. We have to leave you now, but it will always be your place. Yours until Qiyaamah! mulled Razya to herself, weeping softly as her sorrowful ride took her out of sight of the village for the last time.

Apart from the bomb blasts that could be heard like rumbling thunder in the distance, though unclear as to location, the going was relatively quiet. Sikander, however, being generally skittish, felt the need to add an extra caution.

"Remember Andy and Simon?" he asked of Abdul Majeed and Saleem. Saleem nodded without saying much. "Well," Sikander continued, "that's how effective the deception can be, so we really have to be watchful of any strangers, especially if they're not alone. I suggest we group in such a way that Abdul Majeed, you lead with Sister Razya behind you and Aba'i behind her. Fatima can come next and then you, Saleem and Amina. Fatima will of course be carrying Latifa and she'll be in the middle of the group. Saleem, if you keep the spare mules with you, I'll float from the front to the back and stay no more than about half a kilometer apart from you. Just watch for my signals for when it's safe to keep coming forward. After a while we can switch duties."

"Sikander, what if we're separated for any reason?" asked Saleem, betraying a tone of apprehension in his voice.

Sikander thought for a moment. "We'll just have to hope that doesn't happen, but if we do get separated, then at least each of us men knows how to proceed and where to get to."

Nothing of major consequence took place on the first day as they easily reached Baghwanay in eight and a half hours, taking frequent rests by the side of the numerous streams. They found an abandoned mud-brick home in which to spend the night. Luckily scavenging from another nearby abandoned home a discarded box of matches with three unused sticks in it, Noor lit a fire to supplement their blankets and keep them warm that night.

Early the next morning the group entered the narrow pass that would lead them north to the Jalalabad-to-Kabul road. As they neared the road in the afternoon, they were stunned at the number of bomb craters and debris they had to navigate around, as well as at the wreckage lining the road into the distance in both directions. Overhead, an occasional jet could be heard screaming, prompting them

instinctively to take whatever cover they could, although the fact that they were openly visible and not in vehicles probably assured their survival—at least for now.

By evening that second day they had made good progress along the main highway and left it to go north into Sorubi. Another largely uneventful day had ensued, though they could still hear the distant rumbling of bombs exploding in Kabul.

As the third day came along, they were headed up the Nejrab River Valley, remaining as planned close to the water's edge and venturing only toward the road if an impassible obstacle made it worth the risk. Progress was again good as all the bombing activity seemed to have either died down or was now too far away to be heard. Either way, the hideous sounds had become inaudible, and with the noise not dominating anyone's consciousness, the group did have some time to chat while en route along the Nejrab River. On one such occasion, as Saleem took his turn to ride out in front, Sikander decided to ride between Noor and Razya.

"Sikander?" asked Noor. "You know, I never got the opportunity to thank you for thinking of us," she said. "JazaakAllah."

"Adey," responded Sikander. "How could it be otherwise? Rabia and I, we...we miss you and the rest of the family immensely ."

"Yes...I suppose that must be true, but aren't you blaming us for not having accepted your offer to come and stay in Pakistan when you asked us to?" she suggested inquisitively.

"No...no, Adey! Not at all! I understand the attachments that we can all have with where we were born and raised, and besides, who could possibly have known that things would come to this? The very people who helped us to rid the country of Russians, then abandoned us and now—" Sikander had to pause as an F/A-18 screamed up the Nejrab Valley like a large hungry eagle looking for its daily morsel, "attack us," he muttered while craning his neck skyward and just barely following the streak of metallic death flying off to the north.

"How are Ayub and Qayyum?" asked Noor, preferring to ignore the jet. Hers was an act of defiance more than indifference. She was sick of having her reactions dominated by external events and was determined to behave how she wanted for a change.

"Oh, Adey, if you could see them now!" said Sikander proudly. "Ayub is going to a nice school and doing very well. He's definitely Rabia's offspring, if you understand my meaning."

Noor and Sikander chuckled in unison. "Qayyum has Atiya, his Afghan nanny to look after him and he's just started to look at picture books."

Noor could see how much love flowed from Sikander for his two children, and that made her reflect on how her own love could not be diminished despite her strong disapproval of the ways of Saleem as a member of the Taliban.

By the end of November 7th, Sikander and the rest of the group were almost at the northernmost end of the Nejrab Valley just to the south of the village that shared its name with the river, and they were slightly ahead of schedule. Latifa was a remarkably easy child to bring along and didn't do much complaining aside from being scared at the passing aircraft overhead as they often came very low up the valley.

As long as we remain close to the riverbank, we won't look like a military troop, thought Sikander. He also realized that ironically the bright blue shuttlecock burkhas were probably of great value in telegraphing to pilots that theirs was a family, a non-combatant group, and no threat to anyone. The night was cold and even though they took shelter in a natural bluff against any wind coming down the valley, they lit a fire and took full advantage of their blankets.

The sun rose on November 8th, coming over the crest of the far side of the river valley. Once it cleared the ridgeline, the air warmed in its presence. The group had not been going for very long when they came upon the trail leading up into the hills to their west, which was to be their passage into the Panjshir Valley and thence west to Charikar. The pass was more like a narrow ravine of about four kilometers in length leading up out of the Nejrab Valley. At the western end, past a saddle in the hills, was the Panjshir River that coursed westward ahead of them, while in the opposite direction, after a large sweeping bend to the south, the same river led back to Sorubi, forming another feeder river running roughly parallel, to the west of, and alongside the Nejrab. Like the Nejrab, it drained into the very same lake at the Naglu Dam. Its pass was fairly steep to begin with but quite passable after about half a kilometer, and although a few switchback paths had to be taken, they were soon up on the high ground and gazing back, for the last time,

upon the beautifully green valley of the Nejrab, its waters meandering calmly in ironic contrast to the turbulent time and space through which they flowed.

Sikander assumed the scout role again, putting him out in the lead by about half a kilometer. Abdul Majeed talked with Fatima while Razya handled Latifa on her lap. As the terrain had become somewhat rougher, there was considerably more bouncing than previously. Latifa giggled every time the two of them bounced together on the back of the mule and Razya laughed with her, partly in play and partly because she could do little else. The amusement didn't take long to infect the rest of the group.

"Do you see how happy she is at these saddest of times, Abdul Majeed?" asked Fatima from within her burkha.

"Yes, Fatima, of course I do," replied Abdul Majeed, picking up the wistfulness of Fatima's comment.

"Do you think if she knew how life will be like for her she would want to continue?" asked Fatima.

"How do you mean?"

"Well, let me see—she would get to the age of eight and then you would bring her out of all meaningful contact with anyone and she would be kept at home without any schooling. Am I right?"

"Yes...and...no," replied Abdul Majeed. "Let me explain. We Taliban have not been against girls getting educated. We simply wanted it to be in a way that doesn't involve girls going unaccompanied on their way to school in full view of boys. Islam prohibits women from traveling unaccompa—"

"Not quite, Abdul Majeed," interrupted Fatima. "What Islam says according to most traditions is that women must not travel unaccompanied for journeys lasting more than a certain time—that by tradition works out to be a little under eighty kilometers or if the interpretation is generous then whatever distance is covered in three days and three nights."

"So what's your point?"

"My point, dear husband, is that there was never any need to restrict girls from going to public schools. It ought not to have been a problem of accompaniment when such a school could hardly be

expected to be more than three days away from a girl's home under any circumstance."

"Hmm...but the 'ulema say that the rulings are for any amount of time, and not three days and nights," protested Abdul Majeed.

"Not all or even most 'ulema have come to that destructive conclusion, Abdul Majeed," Fatima persisted. "And that misunderstanding is going to cost our people dearly when the present generation of girls grow up. They will be women with no idea how to impart any wisdom or knowledge to their children." Fatima launched into her final jab. "And that's what we imagine will be the ideal outcome for our daughter in this world, is it?" she asked scathingly.

"But Mullah Omar has said—"

"Oh, please do not call him that, Abdul Majeed," retorted Fatima impatiently. "He himself vigorously denies being a mullah and openly acknowledged that he did not finish his own schooling at the madrassah. That's *why* you people call yourselves the Taliban...not the Mullahs."

Abdul Majeed fell silent. He would sooner have faced a Russian helicopter at that moment.

By nightfall, the group, remaining intact and in increasingly good spirits, reached a point about ten kilometers north of the sprawling Bagram air base. They had left the Panjshir Valley and were thankful that they hadn't encountered Northern Alliance troops, whose traditional stronghold was in any case in the northern part of the valley far from where the travelers were.

As November 9th emerged out of the night and dawn began to spread its familiar crack in the blue-blackness of the sky, the group arose to perform the fajr prayer. In the distance to the southwest, not quite as far as Bagram, painted over the gradually emerging horizontal vista lit by the rising sun was a pillar of dense smoke that in the windless morning air stood vertical and undisturbed—an eloquent, thick, black exclamation mark providing a terminal punctuation to the collective scream of a war-torn landscape. Its dot was a burning oil tanker.

Another bomb. Probably last night, thought Sikander. It was too far away to tell where this "target of opportunity" had been and Sikander made a spirited effort to resist the urge to process the bomb's

inherent tragedy in human terms. Instead he tried to imagine a driverless gasoline truck winding its way to Bagram and being "taken out." He tried. He failed.

Surreally, Sikander found himself dissecting time. He imagined the moment at which the explosion would have taken place and how the wave of pressure would have started to buckle the metal of the truck. He imagined the last moment of consciousness of the driver and the one before that, and the one after. He imagined how the driver's rapid vaporization would have denied him any awareness or preparation for his own incipient oblivion. By some grotesque measure, the driver might thus have been considered "lucky."

Before the image could settle too far into his consciousness, they were on the move again. Abdul Majeed took the point duty. Sikander resumed his position between the two matriarchs, while Saleem kept Amina and Fatima company. The thunderclap explosions resumed and the entire group wanted to keep moving so that the sound might weaken and hopefully disappear altogether. But as long as they were simply traveling west to reach the main highway, Kabul remained to their south almost a constant forty kilometers away and would continue to dog them with its rumblings.

When he could break himself away from thinking about the bombing, and to help take his mind away from it, Sikander would discuss with his companions what life was like back home in Peshawar. He liked to describe his parents and especially how much he'd learned from his father after returning from Afghanistan near the end of the Soviet occupation. He also took pleasure describing his business in which Noor, in particular, seemed interested, though such interest was rooted firmly in her concern for the source of her daughter's financial security. Indeed, as he had begun to describe the intricacies of dealing in electrical switchgear and how expensive it could be to warehouse, Noor succumbed to her curiosity.

"How much money do you make in a month, Sikander?"

Sikander thought about the question for a moment. In upper middle class Pakistani society, patterned in many respects on Western cultural norms, this was not a common question and would certainly have seemed rude. Yet for more down-to-earth people the question was not at all intended to be jarring or insulting and was considered in some

senses about as polite as asking one's health, being merely an extension by such reasoning into asking about financial health.

"Adey, I...uh...suppose I could never say that I make quite enough!" he replied, emitting an unconvincingly nervous laugh while trying to deflect the earnestness of the question with his own plainly unskilled humor.

Noor wasn't buying it and persisted, becoming puzzled as to why Sikander would not be open about answering such a plain and simple question. Relenting, Sikander revealed his income to her and once he did, she became at once pleased and quiet. Sikander could not, of course, observe the former. The silence accumulated as he finally caved in.

"Adey, did I describe too small a sum?" asked Sikander.

"Ha!" Noor erupted in a laugh, which she was clearly unprepared for. It was a sound Sikander had not heard for long time. "Sikander, I'm sure it's enough! Quite sure!"

He went on to describe his brother and sister and the house where he lived. After about an hour of this line of discussion, the origin of Rabia's curiosity was plain to see. He had never experienced such discourse with Noor, having only seen her in the light of being an all-too-recent widow. What could he know of her personality from before then? Rabia and Noor were probably much more alike than he had imagined.

They arrived just north of Charikar ahead of schedule and now the main highway was almost upon them, running from left to right in their field of view from their slightly elevated vantage point. Behind it to the west lay another range of mountains, abruptly putting a stop to the gently sloping plain on which they had been traveling. To their right, their eventual direction for the following day appeared decidedly imposing as there, too, the land rose very sharply, creating a seemingly impassable north wall. Before long, they reached the highway. Evidence of recent military activity was visible as more burned out wrecks of vehicles dotted the length of the road at various intervals. Their number bore compelling testimony to the killing that had occurred in this war during what was hardly a month since it began.

"Behind those mountains is Qunduz. Soon we'll have completed half the journey and, alhamdulillah, we should still be

getting there ahead of time," announced Sikander to everyone. "It's time to stop for this evening and maybe pick up some lamb kebabs from a local shop or stall."

The road seemed important enough for more than one enterprising Afghan street peddler to be trying his luck with the elevated pedestrian traffic. The group lost no opportunity to stock up whenever they came across a fruit or vegetable stall.

As morning broke on November 10th, after fajr the group turned once again to the north, tracking parallel to the main road out of Kabul. As planned, they remained at least half a kilometer to the east or west of the road and rarely saw vehicles puttering up or down the once busy national artery. The bombs over Kabul were relentless, but thankfully, their noise finally began to abate. Having made their turn to the north, Kabul receded steadily behind them. Their luck held up and they made it, tired but unscathed as far as the Salang Tunnel by day's end.

The rest of the trip, although presenting challenging terrain, remained relatively uneventful until they approached Pul-i-Khumri arriving, as planned, on November 12th. It would take just another two days beyond that and they would be done. Pul-i-Khumri was a modest sized town spanning about five kilometers along the main road leading to Qunduz. There was a fork in the road at that point and the west branch led to Mazar-e-Sharif and beyond, while the east branch would take them along the Qunduz River to Qunduz itself. There was only one problem. Now that they were approaching the capital of Baghlan Province, they would be firmly in Tadjik country and could not assume they would be safe. The Tadjiks were generally the enemies of the predominantly Pashtun Taliban and though the territory was still nominally under Taliban control, hostility simmered beneath the surface. Most of the locals spoke Dari but Pashto was also generally spoken. None of the travelers spoke Dari.

Sikander, Abdul Majeed, and Saleem discussed options for slipping through the town. Certainly a group of three men, four women—in which two were older women—and a baby could hardly appear less hostile. The extra three mules carrying a light load would also not seem out of the ordinary. With Afghanistan being one of the most heavily mule-populated parts of the world, this was among the most common ways of getting around with any personal belongings in tow.

The challenge was to recognize and avoid forces of the Northern Alliance and not to get captured or killed simply for the fact of being Pashtuns.

"An easy thing will be to put away the black turbans, brothers," said Sikander. "I have my pakol with me to wear, but I only have that one. I suggest we go bare-headed until we can find a shop where I can go in to buy a couple of pakols for each of you."

Then he confronted what he thought would be the biggest challenge to the men. "We should also get the women to remove their burkhas and wear dupatthas. But...in respect for your wishes, we'll ask them to keep them hanging well over their heads."

Abdul Majeed and Saleem looked at each other without saying a word and turned to face Sikander. Saleem's nod of agreement was barely perceptible while Abdul Majeed sat motionless on his mule. Sikander did not try to confirm the sale but acted as if he'd closed it. Standing on principle on matters such as dress and headgear would be pointless. Their lives might depend on it and even the Taliban were generally comfortable with the widely held position among Islamic scholars that all behavioral prohibitions were suspended to the extent necessary for survival. The matter was for the conscience to decide on each occasion as to whether survival was indeed being threatened.

Their challenge lay in the possibility that the town might not yet have pushed out the Taliban, and having adopted the garb of the Tadjiks, they might ironically confront a zealous Taliban religious policeman.

"If we find a Taliban who challenges us on these matters, I think you should let me handle the questioning, Sikander," said Abdul Majeed. "If need be, I'll persuade him to understand the truth of our situation and he should be sympathetic."

"I don't think we'll be getting that kind of problem, Brother Abdul Majeed," said Saleem. "The Taliban are too busy focusing on Mazar-e-Sharif right now, and besides, the Tadjiks here have strong and fairly liberal views about women. I think I remember learning that Pul-i-Khumri is the place where Ayesha Bibi—or was it Bibi Ayesha?—was from. Do you remember her? She was a mujahideen commander when we were fighting the Soviets, and I think if I remember correctly that she

might have had about a hundred mujahideen men or more fighting under her leadership."

"As you mention it, I do remember her name but I didn't know that she was from here," replied Abdul Majeed.

"Of course, those for whom women are simply property to be kept locked away until needed would have difficulty with that. Would they not?" asked Fatima pointedly of her husband. Abdul Majeed simply raised both eyebrows as if to acknowledge a modicum of validity to the question, but he knew better than to be baited by it, particularly by the scathing wit of his wife.

"Instead of you both traveling bare-headed, let me go ahead and try to buy those things and see who's running affairs in Pul-i-Khumri if I can," said Sikander. "Then maybe we'll be able to make sense of how to get past the town."

Everyone agreed and Sikander rode into Pul-i-Khumri to look for hats and shawls.

The rest of the travelers decided to sit by the river as it was reasonably far from the road at that point and they had seen enough to know that they did not want to be near vehicular traffic. "It's a lot quieter up here," said Razya to Noor.

"The Americans must be focusing on Kabul and Qandahar right now," observed Abdul Majeed.

"Maybe, but I think Mazar-e-Sharif and Qunduz up here are important too," added Saleem.

By late afternoon, just as their conversations were increasingly about what might have happened to Sikander and whether they should or shouldn't leave without him as had been planned before their journey, to their great relief they spotted his silhouette returning. Bobbing about on one side of the mule, apparently held within Sikander's own clenched fist were three small plastic bags.

When he finally reached his companions, the contents were distributed leaving a beige pakol for Abdul Majeed, a brown one for Saleem, and the cream colored one that Sikander had to begin with. The women discreetly removed their burkhas and put on chador shawls, which were also quite warm to wear. Sikander had bought the same thing for the men. The weather was cool but bearable at that moment,

and the chadors would help. However, during the night when the temperatures fell significantly, they would prove to be an invaluable addition to their blankets.

This was the first time Sikander saw either Fatima's or Amina's faces, and in a highly awkward but equally instinctive fashion, he nodded and smiled at each of them before casting his gaze elsewhere. He felt as if this was the very first time he had met them and reflexively responded the way he did. Abdul Majeed wasn't looking in a direction to notice, but Saleem was. He deflected the issue and thought to ask about Sikander's experience.

"How is it in the city, Sikander?" he asked.

"It's hard to say, Saleem; I didn't see any Taliban but I did look out for how the women were dressed and walking about. Judging by that, it seems that the Taliban have mostly pulled out of there, which is good news and bad news. Big bushy beards will also attract attention, so I bought the chadors to wrap up in and cover our chins. They'll help us to remain warm too," he explained. "I *will* say, however, that the people at this end of the town do seem more relaxed. How it is when we get further north I don't know and I can't say where we will or won't come across the Taliban," Sikander cautioned.

Finally, Sikander took out the third bag and without opening it lifted it up and wearing a grin, he proclaimed, "This place has pretty good fruit and vegetables."

The group completed asr and resumed their onward progress. It soon became dusk and after another pause for maghrib, they made the decision that reaching the north side of the town was probably wise so they continued to move in the darkness, which they hoped would provide some cover against suspicious eyes. Latifa spent a lot of the time trying to peer out of Razya's chador which was engulfing her, and she became frequently irritated. The strategy of passing her back and forth between Razya and Fatima just to keep her from throwing a tantrum seemed only partially effective, so the group decided after making about three kilometers of headway to the north side of the main part of the town to rest up in a secluded cluster of trees among open fields between the Qunduz River and the main road from Kabul, close to a point where the Qunduz River made a large sweeping turn to the east and about halfway to Baghlan from Pul-i-Khumri.

The following dawn, they awoke after having spent a refreshing but—more remarkably—quiet night out in the open. As the first red light of dawn struck upon the faces of the mountains ahead and to the west of them, which themselves defined the boundary followed by the Qunduz River, they became bright red beacons, while the rest of the area on the valley floor was still quite dark. The group performed fajr, ate some dried fruit that Sikander had brought back with him, and moved on while the day was still breaking. The task was simply to follow the straighter of the road or the river, which usually worked in opposite senses. Where the land was flat, the river had many bow-shaped zigzagging bends, but the road was relatively straight. Where the land was craggy and hilly, the road switched back and forth while the river ran quickly and more straightly through the slopes. Riding atop mules, it was not too hard to negotiate many slopes fairly directly, but sometimes they would have to make switchbacks.

The going was good until they made it past Baghlan to Char Shamba Tipa, a tiny tribal village to the south of the point where the river led into about ten or twelve final kilometers of canyon country before opening out onto another plain south of their destination. As the group approached the north side of Char Shamba Tipa, they came across a sight they had never seen before.

Dotted around the landscape in groups of three or four were Taliban foot soldiers cutting across from the west to enter the same canyon. It took a while to confirm the nature of the scene, for in the distance they appeared as if they might have been soldier ants. Sikander estimated that there were at least several hundred that he could see, but perhaps more than a thousand.

"We're probably coming upon escaping soldiers," Sikander observed. "They don't look like they're gearing up for a fight from the way I see them walking. In fact, I can make out some people limping."

"My guess is that they're all trying to regroup in Qunduz, which means that Mazar-e-Sharif must be a losing battle against the Northern Alliance troops and CIA," noted Abdul Majeed. "We should probably still go carefully. I get the uneasy feeling we're being watched and made ready to be ambushed."

"Yes, and some of them might also be the ISI people and Taliban who are supposed to come out through the airlift," replied Sikander.

"Meanwhile, I suggest we dress in a manner more appropriate to these people," came Amina's voice. She was already donning her burkha and the other women followed suit.

Abdul Majeed and Saleem put on their turbans, leaving the pakols in place and wrapping the cloth around them while also leaving the customary half a meter, or so, hanging loose over the shoulder. Sikander remained the way he was—without a turban.

They proceeded cautiously up to the canyon and converged on the rest of the mass of Taliban. Abdul Majeed decided to engage some of them in conversation, if only to establish his own Taliban credentials and to learn of their situations. He rode ahead a little distance to catch up with them and, seeking out a relatively weary looking group of three, he approached them on his mule, dismounted, and asked a few questions in Pashto.

"Assalaamu 'alaykum, brothers. Where are you all coming from?"

"Wa 'alaykum as salaam, we're coming from Mazar-e-Sharif," replied one of the them.

"What happened? Why so many going to Qunduz?"

"It was Dostum and Atta Mohammed Noor's people. They rushed the Imam Bukhri Bridge, taking the military base and the airport. We were then attacked by a larger force, including some Americans that all but forced the fight to a retreat by our own fighters. So we decided to pull out and pull back to Qunduz. We're regrouping there," he said. "If we have to die there then so be it. But until then, we'll be fighting those Tadjik haraamzadas who sold their souls to the Americans!"

Abdul Majeed rode back to the group and let them know what he'd encountered.

"We should probably try mingling with them until we get to the airfield," Sikander noted after a moment of consideration. "It's about fifteen kilometers from the far side of the canyon and we might make it there by dark."

They joined the rest of the group and moved along a little faster than walking pace so that by the time they were out of the canyon, they were close to the front of the throng. None of the escaping Taliban was in much of a mood for conversation. They were anxious about being

trapped in the canyon, or more generally about Qunduz being the place where many of them might face the end of their lives. Some of them no doubt thought that their salvation lay at the end of this walk if they were, for example, among the ISI or their sponsored Taliban. In any case, they had no inclination to chitchat with the group from Laghar Juy.

As night fell, some of the men decided to keep walking while others opted to bed down. The canyon walls progressively spread apart, widening the floor into a flatter valley as the Qunduz River underwent a large S-bend before resuming its northerly track toward Qunduz. With the increased separation between the canyon walls, Sikander noted how the wind that had been channeled into sometimes quite strong gusts was now far more docile. The mountains were behind them and with the wind dying down, the group found a natural weather-shielded cove where they could take their rest for the night.

Morning broke once again. It was November 14th and they were within eighteen kilometers of the airfield. As usual, the morning fajr prayer was completed, this time with a healthy gathering of twenty to thirty travelers, after which everyone collected their things to load up on the mules and proceed once more. As they were about to set off, a voice called out from about ten meters away. "Sikander!"

Sikander was not sure who had called out his name and looked around. With people and faces everywhere, he was unable to place the sound.

"Sikander!" called the voice again.

This time Sikander did catch the eye of the one who had uttered his name. Despite the garb, Sikander could see it was Junaid and with him was a young man who appeared to be in his early twenties, who Sikander correctly guessed must have been Junaid's son.

"Junaid, you old tiger! Assalaamu 'alaykum!" exclaimed Sikander as the two moved closer to greet each other. Seeing them, Abdul Majeed and Saleem, both grinning, rushed across to where Junaid was standing to greet him and his son, who was introduced as Iqbal Junaid Khan. With formalities out of the way, the rest of the Laghar Juy group was also introduced to Junaid and his son. Junaid didn't take long to raise the obvious question about the missing Abdul Latif.

Sikander held his breath for a couple of seconds and released a great sigh. "Junaid, I'm afraid he passed away about a month ago, about a couple of weeks before we came in from Pakistan."

Junaid's eyes widened as they darted across to meet Abdul Majeed's gaze. "Oohhh...Inna lillahi wa inna ilayhi raaji'un. Abdul Majeed, I'm so sorry! *So* sorry to hear that! We've lost a great, good, and kindhearted man whose concern was for his people!" Junaid was visibly shaken by the news. "I must pay my respects to your mother. Where is she?"

"JazaakAllah for your condolences, Brother Junaid. My mother is over there..." Abdul Majeed replied, pointing to where the four women and Latifa were standing. Junaid approached the women and asked for Razya whom he had never met and who, due to them all wearing burkhas, needed to identify herself. Upon calling out to ask that she let herself be known to him, Junaid expressed his great sorrow at learning of his friend's death and expressed his pride in having known a man of Abdul Latif's stature as a genuine hero for the Afghan people.

Razya thanked him for his remarks and was pleased to learn of Junaid's long-standing association with her late husband, which she promised him she would try to learn more of, if time and fortune permitted. Junaid turned back toward the men now regrouping with their women. Sikander, Abdul Majeed, and Saleem briefly shared the story of their experiences from leaving Laghar Juy to arriving where they currently stood.

"I heard from some of these people that they're coming out of Mazar-e-Sharif, and it looks as if they've been doing so for several days now," said Abdul Majeed.

"That's right," acknowledged Junaid. "The first lot came out on pickups, SUVs, and flatbed trucks. Naturally they moved more quickly and it didn't take them long to get to Qunduz. What you're looking at today is almost the back end of this group. Sikander, you remember I mentioned that we need to be in Qunduz airfield no later than the 17th?"

"Yes?"

"Well, today is the 14th and we should be arriving into Qunduz by this evening, inshaAllah. We'll have to wait around until tomorrow night because that's when the first of the PAF C130s will be flying in.

My information is that the arrangement with the Americans is to keep a flight corridor clear until the night of the 17th and after that, we're on our own. They've been told it will be ISI and Pakistani military advisers, but we're trying to get others out too."

The group, enlarged by Junaid and his son, began moving again. Junaid and Iqbal had been traveling on foot but were now able to ride two of the spare mules. There wasn't much further to go and the mules had done their jobs admirably, so rotation was no longer important. By the afternoon of the 14th they finally managed to make it to the airfield. A single runway—number 11 at the southeast end and 29 at the northwest end—lay sprawled across a plateau, accessed from its western end by a service road that led east out of the main Qunduz-to-Kabul road, up a small ravine, and onto the airfield plateau.

The scene they confronted was one of a few hundred people, mostly men but a few women and small children who had gathered at the airfield. Arranged at the back by the few buildings at the airport were the pickup trucks, SUVs, and flatbeds that had been used by evacuees. Nearby, several mules were tethered to whatever was convenient and to each other. Sikander and his companions dismounted. He and Junaid took the mules to where the others were and motioned to another spot out on the apron of the airfield as a rendezvous for everyone. Abdul Majeed, Iqbal, and Saleem escorted the women and Latifa and found a place where they could lay out their blankets and chadors to sit on and later sleep upon. It was late afternoon of November 14th. They had safely made the long, difficult journey to Qunduz, and with days to spare.

Chapter 15
Sheberghan

FROM THEIR POSITIONS IN THE distance on the high ground on the south side of Qunduz, as well as high on the ridges and peaks that walled the canyon on the way in, members of the American Special Forces and the Northern Alliance fighters looked on at the steady flow of Taliban, Uzbeks, Arabs, Pakistanis, and the smattering of others as they filed north through the canyon, up the main road, and into the airport entrance. Clearly they weren't simply the Pakistani ISI and military advisors caught by the recent change of sides by their government, as had been promised to Washington when Musharraf had secured the safe passage. As far as the onlookers were concerned, these evacuees would just as soon have slit their throats, and they were infuriated at having been commanded not to engage the enemy. But orders were orders and these had come from the very top in Washington. However, as soon as the last flight was done and the last evacuee loaded, the soldiers had no confusion about what they would do with whoever was left behind.

Sikander and his companions had hurried to Qunduz airfield over the last ten days. Now their mission was to wait. The adults in the group generally understood that it was better to have arrived too soon than too late, but poor Latifa was definitely not pleased about the ordeal and her tantrums were her way of sharing her displeasure with the adults. The women made spirited efforts at comforting her, but in this crowded, high-risk gathering of Taliban, ISI men, and diverse

nationalities including notably one or two highly suspicious looking blue-green-eyed pale-skinned Caucasians among the crowd, it was hard to remain unaffected by the frequent wailings of a single infant.

Meanwhile, Junaid diligently searched among the crowd, identifying the ISI officers among the thronging evacuees, gathering them together to help organize things including the rest of the crowd. Sikander was pleased to see Junaid bring Iftekhar along to reintroduce to Sikander and his fellow travelers. Compared to the prim and proper soldier Sikander recalled from their first meeting in Jamrud, Iftekhar looked the worse for wear. He had been into Kabul looking for his evacuees and had seen intense bombardment of the city over the past couple of weeks. Even so, he was appropriately cordial.

The evacuees were to be organized into groups corresponding to airplane carrying capacity. Each group was to consist of a hundred and twenty-five to a hundred and thirty individuals, which resulted in six groups as of that afternoon. For fully equipped paratroopers, the C130 could take on about ninety-five, but without a soldier's full complement of accoutrements, the aircraft could handle over a hundred and twenty swarthy, well-fed soldiers. The evacuees were neither swarthy nor well fed.

Two C130s of Pakistan Air Force Number Six Squadron were set to take off from Gilgit and Chitral, land at Qunduz and fly to Peshawar to unload into a processing facility. From Peshawar, the aircraft would return to Qunduz and shuttle back and forth until the target evacuees were extracted, or the "safe passage" window closed.

The Americans did not wish to have a large contingent of Taliban in Qunduz, whose siege was due to begin shortly, and they had authorized a hard stop for the safe corridor a minute before midnight on November 17th. This would take place about a day after the start of the siege that would apply to the city on the 16th, while leaving another day for the airlift to be completed. Anyone left behind after that, be it at the airport or the city, was, within the upcoming week, about to have the same luck as a Thanksgiving turkey.

After determining which of the ISI officers would act as the leader for each group, Junaid headed back to Sikander and his companions. It was forty minutes before sunset.

"Sikander!" called out Junaid, as he ran over to them.

Sikander, who had been chatting with Saleem and Abdul Majeed, turned around as he heard his name. The enlarging silhouette of Junaid was painted over the orange sky with the bright halo of the low sun behind him. Sikander put his hand to his forehead for shade to try to get better eye contact with him.

"Junaid, what's going on?" asked Sikander as Junaid breathlessly approached.

"After maghrib we're organizing everyone into plane-loads of a hundred and twenty-five at a time and asking them to stay together. When the airplanes come in tomorrow, there'll be no time to lose and each group will be boarded in sequence. The flights ought to be about an hour and a quarter or so apart."

"Sounds like it makes sense, Junaid bhai; what group are we in?" asked Sikander.

"The bad news is we're in the sixth group, so after the first plane takes off, which we expect to be around ten in the morning, we should have just over six hours to wait to board our flight, right about asr time," replied Junaid.

"Actually, that news isn't all bad, Junaid. If I leave right after fajr, at say seven in the morning, I'll be able to get to Qunduz, sell all our mules, and come back on my own in time for our flight."

"How long do you think it will take?" asked Abdul Majeed anxiously.

"Well, the city's about seven or eight kilometers from here. With all these mules in tow, I should get there in about an hour and a half?" he proposed as the men nodded intently. "If I can get them sold off in say two more hours, that would bring me up to ten thirty in the morning. I have nothing else to do so I should be able to ride back on my own in less than an hour if I push hard enough, which would get me back here for zuhr prayer time at the latest. If it takes a little longer with selling them, then let's allow another two hours and I'd still be back before two thirty in the afternoon with maybe two more hours to spare."

"Hmm...sounds like a good plan, Sikander, especially as the cease-fire seems to be holding and we have guarantees on it," observed Junaid. "And even in the unlikely event you're delayed for any reason,

you'll still have another two days of airlift left. That should be ample reserve."

As the afternoon wore on and the sun descended almost to the horizon, people all around the airport apron began straining to find the new crescent moon. At this time in its monthly cycle, it would be setting very close to and shortly after the sun. It had extra importance as it would mark the start of Ramadhan, 2001, if seen.

In the final moments of sunset, there was a shout from one of the bystanders who had climbed onto the main building's rooftop. He had seen the crescent and began pointing it out very close to the ridgeline of some hills about twenty kilometers away. Aside from the canyon cut by the Qunduz River, the plain on which the airport was located, continued all the way to the west up to the hills. At that distance the hills hardly occupied one and a half degrees above the horizon. It was an ideal location from which to be searching for the Ramadhan moon crescent.

As the other people in the crowd began to see it too, there was a cheer and a moment of solemnity as people raised their hands in prayer to wish for blessings in this most troubled of Ramadhans in recent times. Sikander and his family group each did the same and when the prayer was over and everyone had wished each other a blessed Ramadhan, there was a quiet lull as people thought about all that was going on and how uncharacteristic of Ramadhan the events unfolding around them were. Many quietly rejoiced the prospects of being out of the place in a few hours or at most a couple of days. Others ruefully reflected on all that they were now walking away from, including their friends and relatives, some of whom had been killed in only the last few days.

In Qunduz, the direction to face Mecca was a virtual perfect alignment with the November setting sun and moon, so all they had to do was line up in rows to face the moon as they had been doing a moment earlier.

The azaan was called for salaat-ul-maghrib, after which the group simply rested. Razya began to reminisce on the exploits of her late Abdul Latif with Junaid and was pleased to be able to fill in for herself some details of his life while he had been in Peshawar on those many trips that he had made. Junaid was truly saddened to have learned of his friend's death and knew to a certainty that when Arif would find out, it would be major blow for him too.

The time for isha prayer came shortly afterward and upon completing it came the customary nightly taraweeh prayer of Ramadhan. The following day was to be the first fasting day under ordinary circumstances, but as the people in the airport were all in a state of travel, it was permitted to suspend the fast and many of them elected to do so.

Under the night lights of the airfield, after taraweeh was finished, everyone fell asleep under their blankets and chadors.

Morning broke and those holding fasts had already awakened and taken whatever food they might have brought with them for their suhur meal, following it with the intention for a fast. The fajr prayer was conducted again in jamaats for each of the designated groups of a hundred and twenty-five or so people at a time. As soon as it was finished, Sikander and his companions felt their stomachs growl in hunger as the dried fruit from Pul-i-Khumri was all they had eaten, the last of it having been consumed the evening before. Like most people on the open tarmac nestled under blankets and chadors, Sikander did not feel inclined to sleep after the fajr prayer was done.

"Let me see if I can also pick up some food while I'm in Qunduz," proposed Sikander to the rest of his friends. His idea of going into the city now sounded better, with the rest of them being as hungry as they were.

"How much do you think you'll get for the mules, Sikander?" asked Abdul Majeed out of curiosity.

"Oh, I think nine of them could fetch at least two thousand rupees each. I'm sure they'll be in demand if a siege is about to happen."

"First let me write you a confirmation note to admit you back in here this afternoon," offered Junaid. "And just in case we have to leave, you'll still have it to show the other ISI officers here. It's a precaution." Junaid hastily wrote out a letter signing it with his own pseudonym of "Junaid," rank, and serial number, advising Sikander to be sure to show it to the ISI officers standing guard at the airport entrance as he left and again upon his return. Junaid also promised to make sure the ISI people there would know to admit him if he should, for any reason, return after their flight group had left.

"If we do split up, we'll all be regrouping for a while at the air base in Peshawar so we can wait for you there if that happens," he explained.

"Very good. Let me see if I can be back before noon."

He imagined he would be selling the mules to some Taliban unit in all probability. He had never made a secret of not liking the Taliban very much. However, he had given them leeway in his own mind at times based on their having been poorly educated, often orphaned youth who had been misguided into an overly austere understanding of Islam with which few Muslim scholars had ever agreed. He understood something of their situation and in the final analysis, they were fellow Muslim human beings.

Aware of the pressure of time, Sikander returned to where the mules had been tethered, mounted his own, and took the others behind him out to the entrance of the airport. He explained what he was doing to the ISI officers at the entrance, who made way from him to ride out. Taking the airport connector road to the main Qunduz road, and now confident with all he had seen so far regarding this ISI evacuation, he decided to use the actual road instead of tracking parallel alongside it. It did not take as long as he'd imagined to ride into the city itself.

Qunduz was an ancient city, once visited by Alexander the Great en route to his conquest of Bactria, a fact noted by Sikander the first time he recalled reading about it in school in Peshawar. It had registered with him that he'd been named after someone so illustrious, and however childish it might now seem, he was once again feeling some form of soldierly affinity with the great conqueror.

Although Qunduz was a Taliban stronghold, it had a mixed population of Tadjiks, Uzbeks, Pashtuns, Hazaras, and others. Qunduz was also a city on edge, awaiting its fate. Countless conflicts in the past had demonstrated what a bad idea it was to be on the losing side in this part of the world.

As Sikander rode in with the mules ambling behind him, he asked some Taliban about where he might buy or sell mules. They pointed him in the direction of a livestock bazaar on the east side of the city about a couple of kilometers away. He rode on to reach the small open air market on the main road out of Qunduz toward Khanabad.

The livestock vendor, an Uzbek, examined the animals and offered a thousand Pakistani rupees for each, which Sikander knew was an absurd opening bid. He bargained a while and eventually the two men settled on twenty-two hundred rupees, which for the nine mules on sale netted Sikander almost twenty thousand rupees in cash. Considering the circumstances, Sikander felt upbeat at having seen the mules dealt with appropriately and being able to go pick up some good food to take back with him to the airport.

He turned back on the Khanabad Road toward the center of the city where he saw a bakery which seemed acceptably enticing, given his state of hunger from the previous evening's meager meal…if one could call a single serving of dried fruit a meal. As with every other bakery, the aroma of freshly baked bread was alluring. Sikander had no difficulty stopping to pick up enough bread, kebabs and chickpeas to make up for his and his friends' relative abstinence of the last few days.

Having performed his last mission of the morning, Sikander duly mounted his lone mule one more time and headed down the main southbound thoroughfare back toward the airport. As he rode atop his mule, he rolled up a naan around a kebab and ate it, quickly abating his hunger.

He had covered about half a kilometer thinking, for most of that time, about everyone back at the airport, picturing them all anxiously anticipating the growing drone of the engines of the aircraft that would soon be arriving on this beautifully sunny and brisk morning. While in the middle of imagining such a scene, his euphoria was interrupted by a sharp stinging sensation below his left shoulder blade near the middle of his back and almost immediately afterward he could feel himself losing his balance—followed by his rapidly eroding consciousness as an unrecalled blackness engulfed him.

Junaid gazed at his watch for the fifth time in as many minutes. It was three thirty in the afternoon. All day long the C130s had been coming in and going out just as planned. The sixth group was next and by now everyone in the group, hungry and tired, was consumed by mounting anxiety for Sikander. No one could fathom how he could have been delayed or lost. No one wanted to contemplate the worst imaginable outcomes.

"What's keeping him?" exclaimed Junaid to Iqbal, Saleem and Abdul Majeed as all four stood peering intently at the airport entrance on the far side, craning their necks to see if they could get a glimpse of a solitary rider on a mule, but without success.

"Brother Junaid," said Noor, standing up to join them, "why isn't he back yet? What do we do if he doesn't come back in time?" she asked nervously.

Junaid let out a sigh as he afforded himself the time to turn his head toward Noor while Abdul Majeed, Saleem and Iqbal remained on the lookout. "We'll have to leave without him, Sister," he said, but recognizing that she needed some hope for her son-in-law, he went on to tell her how there were still two more days of airlifting and that she shouldn't worry.

"He's probably had a much harder time of selling the mules than he was expecting and...Qunduz is...well...a big city, so maybe he's just gone from place to place," he suggested, doubting his own words.

With Noor wearing her burkha there was no way that Junaid could have seen her skeptical eyes. He didn't need to, as it was clear how deeply worried she was, and he hadn't told her anything to alleviate her concern. Noor had known Sikander for over fifteen years and she understood him to be resourceful and intelligent, so whatever he was having to deal with, at least for the moment she drew more solace from this knowledge than from anything Junaid could say to her. While she pondered several awful possibilities, Junaid walked over to one of the other ISI officers about twenty meters away, who was waving his arm over his head with a two-way radio in his hand.

Noor felt the hand of Razya gently weigh on her right shoulder as she looked down, feeling herself losing the battle to hang on to an optimistic expectation.

"Noor," said Razya, "it's no good imagining the worst. We should be praying for the best for Sikander and that he makes it safely to Pakistan." Fatima and Amina also rallied round her but their combined effect was to invite Noor to unload her feelings and burst into tears.

Suddenly, their worries multiplied as, looking out low in the southeastern sky, one of the others in their flight group cried out, "It's here!" after he'd seen the gleam of the afternoon sun's reflection

momentarily bouncing like an orange flashbulb off the windshield of the approaching Hercules. Almost immediately thereafter the black dot of the aircraft's growing silhouette against the sky could be seen by all who were eagerly anticipating its arrival. By that time Junaid was on his way back to the group from his chat with the radio bearing ISI officer.

"Why isn't he back? *Why?*" demanded Noor as she started sobbing. Junaid's face revealed everything he was thinking, yet he didn't want to volunteer any answers as this was not the time for white lies, half truths, and platitudes.

"What? What's the news, Brother Junaid?" asked Razya, when he returned to the group.

"We just have to hope and pray, Sister Razya, that Sikander's alright and can make it for this flight which is, I have to admit, looking close to impossible, but it could be he's on one of the others in the next two days. Right now we have the choice to stay or go and I recommend that given the dangers here, we should be going, or at least *you* all should."

"Dangers?" asked Noor anxiously while trying her best to control her tears.

"I've uh, just learned that the Northern Alliance and Americans are turning on their siege this evening and...well...that there could be fighting tonight in Qunduz," said Junaid, exhaling heavily.

Noor didn't say anything as her still figure inside the burkha kept her head pointing in the direction of Junaid for a good five seconds before it lowered, succumbing to the crushing weight of realization that they would indeed be leaving without Sikander.

"You said *we* should all go, Brother Junaid?" asked Saleem.

"Saleem, I have to stay here for him. The siege starting this evening will be on the city itself even though people coming in from south of the city, as we did, can still get into the airport. I'm afraid he's going to have a tough time making it through. But if he can and does get through, we'll be here for him for up to two more days."

"Well can't you—can't we—go look for him?" asked Abdul Majeed. "We can miss this flight, too, can't—"

"*No!* Abdul Majeed, we can't go to look for him," said Junaid more firmly. "None of us can. The forces surrounding the city won't

permit it and that'll put us all at risk. No, Abdul Majeed, Saleem, and you, Iqbal—you three have to take charge of this group and see yourselves through to Peshawar. Look, I'll write down the address of Sikander's home and you should find any way to get to it by taxi—otherwise, Iqbal will be able to help. Once you're there, I'll either bring Sikander with me if he makes it through, inshaAllah, or at the very least I'll tell you whatever I learn after I return. I'm...I'm sorry."

Junaid lowered his head to one side only imagining the expressions on the women's faces. He tried unsuccessfully to offer them hope by describing the many possible causes of Sikander's delay and the possibility that there was still a good chance that he would make it back on one of the many remaining flights.

Iqbal stared at his father who assured him that with or without Sikander he would definitely be coming at the very latest on the last flight out two days from then. Junaid looked in the direction of Abdul Majeed and Saleem with a plaintive expression to get their cooperation on his decision. Reluctantly, Abdul Majeed nodded as he gazed downward, frowning and consumed by guilt; guilt of having been so blinded into following the Taliban into a path of self-destruction; guilt of losing everything that had been accomplished in bringing some semblance of peace for a few years in Afghanistan. Above all else, it was the guilt that his cousin-in-law and good friend who had risked his life to help him come back as part of a family might actually now be paying with his life for this to happen. He began to choke on his feelings while bottling them inside.

The droning of the C130's engines grew louder as the aircraft approached the airfield at a steep rate of descent. Its wheels finally touched down, and almost immediately, the pilot reversed pitch on the giant propellers, bringing the aircraft to rest in less than five hundred meters. The pilot cleaned up the wings, retracted the landing flaps, and made the turn toward the apron. As soon as he did, the people of flight group six were asked to stand up and given directions to form a four abreast line, about thirty deep and head toward the now opening rear ramp door. The aircraft would not be powering down, as the intent was to be out of there as soon as loading was complete, so the pilot feathered the propellers to a flat pitch, which minimized any blast from them that would potentially hinder boarding.

"No...no! Sikander, zweeeey!" wailed Noor, as she began to resist being escorted, but Abdul Majeed and Saleem did their utmost to reassure her that this would be the best thing they could do right now. Shouting over the noise of the engines, they finally prevailed upon her to come with them and join the rest of the women.

Junaid looked on as the last of the passengers boarded the ramp and after a few moments, the giant door started to close. He couldn't see his own group as they were too far into the aircraft to be seen from outside, but he waved nonetheless. He said a prayer of "fi-amanillah; Allah Hafiz" to them as the pilot reset the pitch, throttled up, and taxied all the way to the far end of the runway to a point only a little further away than where the aircraft had touched down less than twenty minutes earlier. Finally, it lined up on the runway, and as the pilot went to full throttle, the aircraft lurched forward, gathered speed, and was airborne within seven hundred meters. Junaid watched as the Hercules gained altitude and headed in the direction of the sun before making a giant sweeping arc back to the east.

The moon was another day older, its crescent more visible and beautiful that early evening, as with each passing day it moved a little further from the sun and set a little later. Junaid hung back for the two remaining days and nights. Finally, when the last flight from Pakistan came in, he offered a prayer of hope for Sikander and with a heavy heart boarded it, continuing until the last minute to hope for that solitary figure riding on a mule to come galloping into the airfield at its southwestern entrance. The hope remained unfulfilled.

✿

Slowly, Sikander peeled open his eyes as he equally slowly regained consciousness. He did not know how long he had been unconscious or where he was. All he could see was the beautiful crescent of the moon through an opening in the wall to his upper right. He lay on some kind of crude bed.

At first Sikander could barely recall what he'd been doing, where he'd been going, and just about anything of the moments leading up to him feeling the pain.

Yes, he thought. *The pain. There was pain involved. What was it? Where?* He tried to move and as soon as he did, a searing but quickly familiar pain made known its presence in the middle of his lower chest.

As he tilted his head forward, he could see he had been bandaged crudely with signs of blood at a point just above his right fifth rib. Immediately he rolled his head back down, still reeling from the pain he had felt a moment earlier. Another pain came into focus behind his head and below his left shoulder and then another all the way down his left side. He cursed the consciousness that was putting him through this agony as he realized its cause as being a gunshot wound.

After a few moments the pain associated with his minor movement subsided to a level he could just about handle. His attention began to turn to whatever he might be able to recall and while trying, he again looked toward the sky through the open window and began to focus on what he might be able to see.

The moon blinked, as a solitary eagle owl flew across its crescent. It caught Sikander's attention. He began to think about the relative darkness in the sky and studied the approximate size of the crescent. It must have been about the third or fourth night of the moon. *Where am I? Who shot me? Will I survive? Survive! Yes! Have to survive! Rabia...children...have to get back. Back to where? To Pakistan...to Peshawar.*

Slowly, steadily, the threads of his memories began to weave the fabric of awareness back into an increasingly coherent whole. *I was returning, returning to...to the airport to...to...make the airlift. Yes. It was the 15th when the crescent had just been sighted. The crescent. Something's wrong...it must...it must be two or three days old.*

A new and dreadful realization swept over Sikander. The beautiful moon had proclaimed an ugly, simple, and inescapable truth. It had to be around November 17th or 18th, which meant that he had missed his ride out of Afghanistan.

As the realization's ramifications came coursing through him, his spirit sank into a bottomless emptiness and he couldn't help silently weeping while he began to worry about his situation and what might now be happening to him. *Cease-fire...there was a cease-fire! I shouldn't have been shot! Who did this? Who singled me out? Why?* Sikander protested as if to some invisible referee that the game hadn't been played by the rules.

The strain of all these thoughts and questions were too much for him as he again felt the sting in his lower right torso. He felt the need to

lie back when finally it dawned on him that if he was in a bed, someone must have put him there. Someone who wanted him alive. Yet he was feeling too exhausted to analyze why, and he fell asleep again.

💬

The bright daylight was visible through the window but the sun must have been elsewhere in the sky, which was a bright blue at this time. It could have been morning or afternoon, but as it seemed that it was the light that had woken him up, he imagined it was probably the morning. While he was contemplating the time of day, Sikander heard voices approaching and getting louder as they were clearly headed for whatever room he was in. He didn't feel concerned. If they were the ones who put him there, then he was supposed to be alive. If not, then he didn't mind dying right then. Besides, he was in no shape to put up a fight.

"...recovers by the time the siege is done," said one voice.

"His wound luckily didn't hit anything major," said the other, who spoke with the confidence of one who was knowledgeable. "But his blood loss *was* significant," he qualified. They spoke in Dari and Sikander had no idea what they were saying.

The voices came into the room as the door swung open. Sikander pretended to be asleep and then to stir as if the noise of the two men's arrival had been the cause of his awakening. He looked at them and saw that one of them was balding and probably in his forties, wearing a dark brown qamees and shalwar. He had some instrument or piece of plastic in the upper breast pocket of his qamees and was carrying a plastic bag in one hand with what looked to Sikander like it might be bananas along with some other fruit. The other man was much younger, in his twenties, and was sporting a Kalashnikov with a bandolier around his body. He wore a cream-colored pakol similar to Sikander's own.

"Who...who are you? Where am I?" asked Sikander instinctively in Pashto. His throat was parched and he was weak with hunger.

"Ah! Finally you awaken. We were hoping you'd be awake by now," remarked the older man, switching to Pashto and in a reasonably affable tone. He seemed pleased, which was probably a good sign, thought Sikander. "Huh! You're lucky," he continued. "You were hit by a sniper whose bullet went through your back and missed most

everything! Just a little part of your left lung was impacted. I had to plug it for a while to prevent the lung from collapsing, but it's going to heal. You still need to get rest but you're young and strong so it shouldn't take many days, perhaps a week, to at least be on your feet." While pouring some water from a nearby bottle into a glass that had been set by the side of Sikander's bed, the man continued, "I'm Dr. Atiq Mohammed, and this is Rashid Ehsan. You're in Qunduz. Here, let me help you drink this." The doctor sat by the bedside and helped Sikander to slake his thirst.

"Wh-why am I here? I mean...aside from the shooting?" said Sikander, feeling already tired from uttering these words.

"You may not know this, but Qunduz is under siege by the Northern Alliance. You were found on the street, bleeding but alive. We had driven the Taliban further back into the town where several thousand are holed up. We're in some kind of negotiation to get them to surrender," he said, "but you know, the message doesn't reach everyone all the time. You must have been hit by the Taliban thinking you were one of us. We thought the same thing initially, which is why we picked you up and treated you."

"What...what do you intend to do with me?"

Rashid Ehsan exchanged a glance with the doctor and then back at Sikander. He pulled out a piece of paper from his own qamees's upper breast pocket. As he unfolded it to read, it seemed vaguely familiar to Sikander.

"We found this on you," said Rashid, and as he proceeded to read it, Sikander knew this was Junaid's letter to gain him re-entry to the airport a few days earlier.

"What does that mean for me?" asked Sikander.

"It means that you must be Pakistani ISI or at least an associate and that you were attempting to get out of the country with your Taliban friends," said Rashid. Inexplicably, Rashid had a smile on his face suggesting little concern or even indignation toward Sikander, which even in his condition, Sikander found slightly puzzling.

"Huh! Taliban friends!" remarked Sikander with whatever disgust his injury allowed him to assemble, while he turned his head away from the two men to face the wall to his right.

"You being...Pakistani, and not having left on the airlift, means you're the...uh...the subject of this..." said Rashid cryptically but to sufficient degree to get Sikander to turn his head back to focus on him. Rashid held up another piece of paper. It was a leaflet of some sort which had been written in Pashto, with a message suggesting a sizeable reward for handing in non-Afghans who were more than likely Taliban or al-Qaeda fighters.

Sikander read the contents and cast his eyes back toward Rashid and then Dr. Atiq. "What does this have to do with me?"

"The Americans are looking for Pakistanis, Arabs, Chechens, and others who have been over here helping the Taliban, and unless you had left on one of those flights over the past three days, you will be considered one of these people. That means you're worth...um...almost five thousand dollars to us, especially if we can deliver you alive to the Americans when we meet up with them."

"But I'm *not* a Taliban!" protested Sikander, feeling his strength sapping away. He was too weak to mount an argument much less a fight about his status.

"Look uh...Sikander Khan," said Rashid as he re-examined Junaid's letter which had named Sikander, "that kind of money is just too large to ignore. If you are innocent for the Americans, then they will let you go. If not then, well...then you will have to deal with consequences, but to us you are worth five thousand dollars, regardless."

"What will you do with me?" asked Sikander.

"Like we said, we're going to be delivering you up to the Americans to collect our money, but first we need to get you back to health and wait out the siege," said Rashid.

Sikander looked at him for a few seconds and then back toward Dr. Atiq. He could not quite come to terms with a bounty hunter doctor and yet here was one staring back at him and seeing in his return to health a pecuniary benefit quite different from medical fees. Such were the products of war, thought Sikander, immediately consumed by his sense of revulsion.

"Look, you're weak and you must be very hungry. We've brought some fruit. It'll be best if you just take a little of it right now."

Atiq took out a couple of bananas. They were the miniature variety and he peeled a couple of them, leaving them by the side of Sikander's bed next to the water bottle. Finally, he set the bag with the remaining fruit down on the floor next to the table before leaving the room with his partner who locked the door behind them.

By November 22nd, Sikander was able to sit upright on the bed, but it was still a challenge to stand without a supporting surface. However, he could slowly maneuver himself to the wall where the open air window was located, and peering outside from the window, he could see he was about four stories off the street level without a hope of being able to escape through the opening. Atiq and Rashid made typically two visits each day, bringing food and drink while also tending to his wounds. Sikander seemed to be progressing better than Atiq had expected.

In Qunduz city, negotiations were going on between the Taliban and the Northern Alliance. The Taliban, who had suffered hundreds of losses through simple desertion or defection to the Northern Alliance in Qunduz, were in a corner. Their reasoning had been that to avoid massive casualties and damage to the once historic city, surrender was the only feasible outcome. The Taliban offered to give themselves up in exchange for safe passage back to their homes and safe escort out of Afghanistan for the non-Afghan combatants. On November 22nd, the Taliban surrender negotiations were complete and a force of some five thousand Northern Alliance troops made its way to Qunduz from Mazar-e-Sharif to accept the surrender while also taking the foreigners into captivity. This would leave the Taliban holding just one major city in Afghanistan, namely Qandahar.

On Saturday, November 24th, the fighting in Qunduz was essentially over and the Taliban surrendered en masse from deeper inside the city. At this time, Sikander was up on his feet and able to walk with minor assistance. His wound had not completely healed but the process was well underway and with a doctor, albeit motivated by less than ethical ideals, he was speedily coming back to recovery.

All day on the 24th out on the street Taliban and other al-Qaeda fighters were being herded into groups, bound and immobilized. A large force of between three and four thousand had surrendered mostly without a fight, expecting to be eventually sent home. Sikander himself was still held in custody by Rashid and Atiq. He tried to get a sense of

what was going on outside by periodically going up to the window while also exploring any possibility to effect an escape. The room was locked from the outside and he was in no physical shape to try to break down the door. In a curious way, Sikander did not seem to mind being a captive. Perhaps it was the courteous—albeit ill-motivated—treatment he had received or perhaps it was his own sense of needing to rest before attempting anything risky. As the day drew to a close, it was possible to see that several new prisoners had arrived on the street, while several had already been taken away. That evening when the two men brought dinner up to Sikander, Atiq began to prepare him for his impending departure.

"You'll need to get ready to be sent to Mazar-e-Sharif, Sikander Khan," explained Atiq.

"When?"

"You've probably seen that they've started the transportation of prisoners and that will continue tomorrow, but the operation will be carried out throughout the next few days."

"We'll delay your transfer until the last day, considering your injury," added Rashid, in an attempt to keep Sikander relatively calm. Sikander dropped his head, knowing that argument was futile but a thought came to him.

"Look, do you know who I am?" he asked.

"Yes, you're a pro-Taliban Pakistani who is with the ISI," said Rashid.

"No! That's not correct. I'm Sikander Khan, a Pakistani, it's true…but I'm…I'm a successful businessman based in Peshawar. I married an Afghan woman many years ago. I was a mujahid with your people against the Russians more than ten years ago. I came back to retrieve and bring to Pakistan my wife's family and…and we had come to Qunduz for the airlift you already know about. I just came back to the city to dispose of some mules and then I don't know who shot me…so…so you see? I'm not the kind of person the Americans would be interested in. Besides, if you let me out of here and help me back to Pakistan, I could give you twenty thousand dollars." Sikander paused to see if the carrot he had just dangled might brighten any eyes.

Atiq and Rashid looked intently at Sikander and then toward each other. Atiq responded, "Mr. Sikander Khan, you might well be who you say you are and by your own admission you're a Pakistani. The rest doesn't much matter. The Americans are looking for Pakistanis and they will pay. We can't take the chance about your story. Maybe the Americans will understand and believe you and let you get home. We just want to be paid."

Sikander did not try to make too much of an issue. Though he had never been there, he had a sense of familiarity with America and Americans. He could handle himself in English, so he felt that as long as he could survive to the point of being handed over to them, then perhaps his two captors were right. He would just have to be patient, and with that thought, taking the now bearable pain, he completed his isha prayer and went to sleep. The following day, November 25th, was a virtual repeat of the previous day for Sikander.

❧

At a vast, ancient, Persian fort called Qala-i-Jangi, just outside Mazar-e-Sharif, in north-central Afghanistan, November 25th was to be far from a repeat of anything, even by the standards of the latest conflict. Being a fortress, Qala-i-Jangi was an ideal choice to house the Northern Alliance's newly arrived prisoners. On November 24th, the previous day, several hundred Arabs and Pakistanis had surrendered to Abdul Rashid Dostum's troops under the assumption that they would be questioned and repatriated. Instead, they were imprisoned and made ready for questioning by American interrogators.

The new prisoners had evidently not been searched and had concealed weapons with them. They had even used them to kill two of General Dostum's officers. Even so, no security protocol was in place. On the 25th, they and more prisoners newly arrived from Qunduz were questioned about how and why they joined the Taliban and why they were there. At that moment, several of the prisoners jumped their questioner, CIA Special Activities Division Officer Captain John Michael Spann. By all accounts he fought them off first with an AK-47, and after emptying it, with his pistol until it too emptied. As the prisoners kept on coming, he fought hand-to-hand until he was mobbed by them, scratching and gnawing at him until he died. His partner, Dave Tyson, pulled out his AK-47 and also emptied it on the assailants. Unsure of the extent of the prisoners' armament, the rest of the Northern Alliance

fighters, together with Tyson and some news crews who had been there to film the prisoners, took refuge in the northern part of the fort.

In Johnny "Mike" Spann, the American Global War on Terror suffered its first combat casualty, and the CIA headquarters at Langley, Virginia, had yet another star—its 79th—carved into the wall of fallen heroes and painted the customary black. It would later lighten with age and match the gray color of its neighbors.

Qala-i-Jangi had been well known to the Taliban and they had made for the weapons armory at its southern end, which enabled them to take control of virtually the entire southern half of the massive nineteenth century fort. In the northern part of the fort, Tyson managed to use the TV news crew's satellite phone to call the US embassy in Uzbekistan asking for reinforcements. American air strikes were called in over the southern half of Qala-i-Jangi. In addition, a Soviet era T-55 tank moved into the fortress compound and fired on the southern half. Several bombs were dropped on the armory but the prisoners were doggedly persistent.

The following day, the 26th, which was to be Sikander's day of arrival, the battle of Qala-i-Jangi raged on. Northern Alliance soldiers directed their mortar fire at the southern end of the fort and again called in close air support. By nightfall, so-called "smart bombs" were dropped but in a confusion over coordinates, one close air support team called in bombing on its own coordinates by mistake, killing and injuring several Northern Alliance fighters as well as injuring four British Special Forces personnel. By late that night, two AC130 Specter gunships circled overhead firing into the armory, setting off several explosions whose fires continued to rage well into the night.

Back in Qunduz on the morning of the 26th, Rashid and Atiq returned for Sikander and woke him. He had gone to sleep after performing the fajr prayer as it was now fully ten days after having been shot and he felt he could handle it. The recovery had been progressing well. Sikander was also more at ease with the idea of surrender to the Americans. He had heard many stories during the civil war from Abdul Latif that taking prisoners was not a well developed concept among either the Taliban or the Northern Alliance, and several cases of surrender followed by massacre had been reported on both sides.

While Rashid held the gun on Sikander, Dr. Atiq tied his hands behind his back with a scrap of bandage cloth. The two of them marched him carefully down four flights of stairs and onto the street. As he came out, similarly bound Taliban prisoners were still being brought into the street and made to sit down on the ground to await transportation. Those of them who were not Afghan were to be transported separately to be sure that as high value captives they would not get mixed up with the others.

Rashid continued holding guard over Sikander while Atiq began interacting with a Northern Alliance fighter who was seemingly in charge of transporting the prisoners. Sikander could see that Atiq was being paid by the man and he judged that he, Sikander, was being sold for transportation, presumably at some discount to the five thousand dollars but enough to make them free of him so they might go about their own business. Transportation was now someone else's problem. Sikander had become a traded commodity.

Shortly after, the man approached Sikander, his boots kicking up dust in their wake. Barking something in Dari, he grabbed him by his arm and pulled him toward the street among a gathering of what were plainly non-Afghan prisoners, including several from Pakistan. Sikander never saw Rashid and Atiq again. Strange men, who had treated him well to get him to health so that they could sell him, as if he had been livestock.

The Northern Alliance leaders in Qunduz had already arranged for shipping containers to be used to transport prisoners to the jail at Qala-i-Jangi fort. They had been using them since the surrender a few days earlier. Over a dozen containers were lined up alongside each other. Sikander could see the Taliban prisoners being herded into each one, and only when crammed full would the doors be closed and sealed. There must have been at least two hundred in each of the long containers, Sikander guessed. Although the negotiated commitment not to shoot the Taliban was being adhered to, packing them into containers in that manner was highly likely to be deadly to many of them over a three hundred kilometer trip. He wondered how they might fare on that journey. Finally, he himself was shoved into a container with the forty-three other prisoners of his own group which at that count seemed unbearably bad, given that the container was smaller than the others.

As the container doors were closed and sealed, the space became immediately dark with the exception of thirteen large caliber bullet holes in the metal from which white spots of daylight were visible. After a few moments, he could make out the others' faces from just that small amount of light. They were all dark and silent, awaiting their fate. After a few metal-on-metal banging and clanging sounds, the container was lifted into the air and maneuvered to bring it over the trailer on which it was to travel. Everyone groaned as the container lurched and then they could feel it sway like some evil fairground ride, until finally it came to rest and they could hear it being secured to what could only have been a trailer. Sure enough, before long, with a jolt, the truck began moving. Sikander was finally leaving Qunduz.

The truck proceeded out from the south side of Qunduz back to Baghlan and Pul-i-Khumri. Every bump in the road seared Sikander's wounds. About ninety minutes into the ride, the air in the container became stifling. The men inside were burning oxygen faster than the thirteen tiny holes could replenish it and before long a sense of imminent panic began brewing. Sikander asked aloud if anyone else spoke Urdu, Pashto, or English. Almost everyone was able to answer positively and Sikander proposed that they establish turns where each man would place his mouth over a hole for five minutes. That would allow each person to make it to a hole with about twenty minutes between turns. Meanwhile, to consume the least possible oxygen, he told them that they would have to sit perfectly still, not panic, and breathe slowly.

Some of the Pashto speakers could also speak Arabic and communicated the same information to the Arab speakers. Thus the group organized themselves along the lines he had explained, taking turns breathing from the bullet holes. It crossed Sikander's mind how the other container travelers who had been packed with much greater crowding would have fared. His mind wandered off into a macabre guessing game of how many would die with the same number of breathing holes to get to a number that could survive with the accumulating dead no longer needing oxygen.

The truck ride was an unrelenting, black hell. With no warning of impending bumps or turns, every experience was a surprise and the occupants of the container had to endure hours of unsettling tossing and

swaying, especially while the truck was moving through canyon country.

Finally, having arrived at Qala-i-Jangi, the men in the container could hear sounds of gunfire, heavy weapons, and bombing. It seemed fearsome yet strange to each of them. They could only imagine what might be going on, but nothing they could imagine was comparable to the raging battle there that night. As he approached the ancient fort, the truck driver could see the angry tracer rounds raining down from the circling AC130 gunships and hear the battle proceeding from ground level behind the twenty-meter high walls of the fort. Every so often the night's blackness was punctuated by bright flashes silhouetting the fort's walls.

"Qala-i-Jangi," Persian for "fortress of war," was sadly living up to its name far beyond the scope ever imagined by its creators. Guards had been posted at the perimeter two kilometers away and that was where the truck carrying Sikander came to a rest.

"Foreigners from Qunduz," declared the truck driver with about the same matter-of-fact tone as if he'd been describing a haul of rice.

"You can't bring them here now," came the response from the Northern Alliance guard.

"What then?" asked the driver testily. He was tired and in no mood to mess around. With all that he could see going on, compliance wasn't difficult, but he still needed new direction.

"Wait there," said the guard, who disappeared for five minutes to talk on the radio before coming back.

"Sheberghan. You'll have to take them to Sheberghan," said the guard. The prison there is accepting these types of prisoners now. American Special Forces are there right now and they'll know what to do with your cargo."

With that, the driver rolled up the window, reversed out of the fort area, and drove on. He cursed the guard, cursed Dostum, then Bush and Bin Laden for his need to remain awake to take his haul another eighty kilometers from Qala-i-Jangi.

Inside the container, in the pitch blackness punctuated by thirteen faint whispers of moonlight, Sikander heard moans and groans but the container had become quieter than he had been used to earlier.

He himself was parched and struggling to remain conscious. He also feared that his internal wound might have reopened as he could feel a wetness on the front of his qamees. Slowly, the whispers of light from the eleven day-old moon coming through the thirteen holes turned to an orange-pink before becoming white as, finally, the day began breaking.

The sun was up when the truck finally came to a rest at Sheberghan prison. The door seal was broken and the doors swung open.

The scene confronting the Northern Alliance fighters and the American Special Forces soldiers, was much like moving a rock and finding all kinds of disgusting insects scurrying in response to the sudden change in their environment. The men, a term which could barely be applied to the creatures inside, were lying and sitting, some on top of others, some asleep with their heads against the metal walls of the container. Out of the truck came the stench of death, urine, and other indescribably foul smells. Sikander could see blood smeared over the front of his qamees. It looked like another prisoner had bled from a wound as he could tell that it was on the outside of his qamees. Several bodies were lying around with their eyes in a glazed and ghastly open stare.

The guards themselves took a moment to get over the shocking sight and began dragging the prisoners out of the container.

"That's all?" asked one of the American paramilitaries, quickly covering his nose and mouth with his one free hand.

"Yes," replied one of the Uzbek officers with him. "These are from Qunduz. They should have been deposited at Qala-i-Jangi, but well…you know what's happening there."

"Yeah, raghead bastards!" uttered the American and he told the others to drag all of them out and take the dead and dying out into the desert southwest of Sheberghan to bury them. "Take the walking ones inside. We'll hold 'em here until we figure out what to do."

"Come down! Come down!" yelled the guard to the prisoners in broken Pashto. Finally, Sikander stepped out in the light and was almost blinded by it as the sun was now high in the sky. It was probably about eight-thirty or nine, he thought.

However brief that moment of fresh air, Sikander savored every millisecond of it. He was barely able to move and as he walked toward the building into which they were all being led, he began to cough and saw a fresh stain forming on his qamees. This time it was from inside. He staggered for a while and was caught by an Uzbek guard as he began sinking to the ground.

"He needs attention!" said the guard looking in the direction of the American soldier. The soldier paused for a moment, then walked slowly up to Sikander. Being a Special Ops soldier, he had a Kalashnikov which he used to lift up Sikander's qamees, he could see there had been a wound and a dressing. He rolled his eyes to the left, tilting his head briefly in the same direction, gesturing to the guard to walk Sikander over to the prison hospital.

The battle of Qala-i-Jangi continued raging throughout that day and into a few more. Eventually some eighty-five surviving prisoners from among the hundreds that had been brought there surrendered one more time as they were without weapons, ammunition, and food. Now they were systematically being flooded while occupying the basement of the armory in the fort. It was from this group that the so-called American Taliban John Walker Lindh emerged with a wound to the leg and was taken away back to the USA for recovery, detention, and trial.

From the moment Junaid had shown up at Sikander's home without him, everyone was plunged into anguish over the fate of the head of their household. The pleasures of Ramadhan that had been the norm in prior years could not be enjoyed and everyone was consumed by their concern for him. Friends and extended family members would often come around to console the family. During this period Junaid was frequently back and forth to visit them. Being connected to the ISI, he had a grasp of things which provided a source of comfort to Sikander's family. Besides, it was easy for him to do as he, too, lived in Hayatabad.

Not long after his return to Pakistan, Junaid went up to see Arif in Jamrud. Arif was a good man with his ear to the ground for all kinds of news and information that wasn't to be found on CNN or the BBC. He was disappointed to learn of Sikander's disappearance, but like many people who knew Sikander, Arif seemed to believe that the young man's resourcefulness would probably see him through. He was,

however, devastated to learn of the death of Abdul Latif. The two had known each other for more than twenty years, right after the Soviet invasion back in 1979. Still, he marveled at learning of the manner of his death, which he, along with just about anyone else who heard of it, could only describe as "enviable."

A week passed and the news coming out of Afghanistan was grim. The uprising at Qala-i-Jangi was all over CNN, for at one and the same time it revealed the death of the first American combat casualty and the emergence of John Walker Lindh, the American Taliban. A less well-known fact was that the uprising and the many subsequent deaths in the container loads of prisoners both largely involved prisoners from Qunduz.

Junaid was at Sikander's home visiting when CNN first broke the news about the battle of Qala-i-Jangi. Rabia asked Junaid to interpret the meaning of what she could see and hear. She could not watch it without almost becoming catatonic with fear from imagining the worst things happening to her beloved husband.

"It's a massacre!" said Junaid. "It looks like things got out of control in the prison yesterday, where the Taliban captives had surrendered, mostly from Qunduz. Several…uh, several hundred Taliban have been killed and things remain unresolved. The battle's still going on." Each word pierced his soul.

Sikander, why did you have to listen to me!? Ya Allah, bring him back to me safely—I beg of you—please, please bring him back! Rabia half prayed and half wept quietly as her two young sons looked on. They missed their father too, but it was hard to watch their mother cry and berate herself, often openly. Unable to continue, Rabia arose to go into the lounge. Junaid and Sofie followed.

"You know, we don't know anything about where he is, whether he left Qunduz before the surrender. Even if he remained, he's a strong enough and intelligent enough person, Rabia," said Junaid reassuringly. "He'll get himself out of trouble…don't you worry now."

"Junaid bhai! What can we do? What can we *do*? There has to be *something*!?" cried Rabia.

Sofie, standing behind Rabia, placed a tender, supportive hand on her daughter-in-law's shoulder. "Rabia?…Rabia, Junaid bhai's…he's

right. We have to be patient and pray to Allah who listens even more intently to worthy individuals in Ramadhan. Pray for his safe return."

"Sameena's here," Jamil called out from beyond the lounge where they were all seated. He and his wife Kausar were just leaving the TV room when Sameena drove in through the front gate together with husband, Wasim.

"Assalaamu 'alaykum!" she called and came into the lounge to sit with the others. Sameena had met Junaid on one of his earlier visits and acknowledged him on this one too. She saw Rabia with her wet cheeks and approached her. They hugged.

"Rabia bhabhi!" offered Sameena. "Look, I may have some good news," she added cautiously, speaking in English. Her time studying at the LSE, coupled with the near constant use of it in her father-in-law's family home, made it her preferred medium and she felt a certain bond with Rabia through the language.

Rabia's whimpering halted as she wondered what news Sameena might have and how she might have it in relation to Sikander.

"What do you mean, Sameena?" asked Rabia, calming down slightly.

"Well, you might remember my father-in-law knows Gen…um…President Musharraf well and he saw what had happened in our family and thought to ask President Musharraf if he could pass along the query about Sikander bhai."

"What do you think can be done, Sameena?" asked Sofie, trying to get more clarification. Overhearing this, Jamil also entered the main lounge.

"I'm not exactly sure, but let's say, for example, that he was captured. From what I'm able to learn, there seems to be a priority among the Americans to interrogate Pakistanis and, Junaid bhai, I think you had said that he had a paper signed by you, didn't you?"

"Yes, I did…" said Junaid as he was beginning to catch on to what Sameena was getting at. "I did, and if they found *that* on him, at least it could confirm he's one of Musharraf's own people who failed to make the airlift. Perhaps if they take him into their custody there might be a chance to find him and have him returned to us, inshaAllah!"

"How do we get the process in motion?" asked Jamil.

"We already have. Abba-jan—Wasim's father—has already contacted Musharraf, so please continue to pray for Sikander bhai to be alive and to return soon." Sameena panned the room to make eye contact with just about everyone.

Now all they had to do was wait and monitor the news as well as the back channel via Wasim's father. Throughout this time Sofie was a pillar of strength. She just knew her son was alive. The knowledge had integrated itself deeply into her being.

Rabia, already upset at having learned a week earlier of her uncle's death, had now to wait for news of her husband with a gnawing hope. A hope that yielded no permission to be experienced without exacting the full price of reflection upon the terrible consequences of not being fulfilled.

Chapter 16

Jahannam

THE TAPPING OF SHOES AGAINST a hard concrete floor were the first sounds Sikander heard when he regained consciousness. The air was notably fresh. There was something important about that freshness, but Sikander couldn't quite recall what it was. As his consciousness began to take shape, however, it was the air's essential contrast with what lurked in his memory that triggered those recollections. He was at once overcome by his own foul memory of that dark day of being in a black container with a growing number of corpses and the dank air. Sinister, stifling air—not worthy of the name. Sikander wept into his pillow on the hospital bed as he thought of young men, foreigners, mostly from Pakistan, who knew nothing of local customs and traditions, who had surrendered themselves in the naïve expectation of being dealt with humanely. The weeping was not like any ordinary crying he could recall. It was not even conscious. He could barely focus on a reason for the tears as they kept emerging like a lava of emotion. It was as if his mind and spirit were draining out of him—draining into the pillow along with his tears.

Sikander had no sense of time or place. His consciousness was adrift without anchor in either dimension. It hadn't been possible for the container occupants to overhear the new instructions given to the truck driver during the night, and he had no capacity to have grasped the contents of any signage as he spilled out of the container the following

morning. He struggled to move his head and saw that he was in some sort of hospital ward where other beds were visible beside his own, lining the walls on all four sides. Men were lying helpless with horrific injuries. They included amputees and people with splints and casts on their limbs. He could see that the hospital, such as it was, was very crude and as he formed this view, his mind drew back into a modicum of focus as he could now also recall having been let out of the container and feeling euphoria from merely having survived.

Guards were noticeable at the entry swing doors to the ward. Later that morning, a nurse came delivering a simple meal of buttered bread and onions and to change the dressing on his wound.

Wound. Yes, I...have a wound. He remembered feeling fresh blood oozing out of it as he was leaving the container.

"Where are we?" he asked the nurse. She had a troubled look on her face and paused for a moment before looking up and to her left and right to see if anyone was within earshot. When she saw that all was clear and that the guards couldn't hear her, she whispered, "Sheberghan...Sheberghan prison hospital." Sikander thanked her for being a fellow human being.

Sikander had been in the hospital for two days before regaining consciousness or at least waking up. He had been deprived of much sleep on the way from Qunduz and had suffered blood loss as well as general weakness from the now two-week-old bullet wound.

Once he was able to sit upright, he began to take in heavier foods and feed himself. On December 2nd, about a week after arrival at the hospital, Sikander was finally visited by two American guards. Unlike Special Forces paramilitaries, these people were uniformed soldiers. One was a first lieutenant with name tag Bryers and the other was a Captain Valdez. He had slightly darker skin, which enabled Sikander to recognize the man as Latino based also on what he saw of the name. Sikander guessed he was probably the same age as himself.

Valdez was a thickset individual of about a hundred and eighty-five centimeters. His narrow eyes and slightly downturned mouth at that moment conveyed a look of great earnestness. Bryers was a white Anglo-Saxon with a long thin face and the slightest hint of freckles. He could not have been much more than twenty-two, thought Sikander.

Valdez turned to Bryers. "Is he coming?"

"He's on his way, sir."

Sikander didn't want to volunteer his own knowledge of English until he could be confident he was talking to someone who might be able to control his freedom. These people looked like preliminaries to him so he remained silent.

A few moments later, another man, also in a US military uniform, emerged from the swinging doors. His name, somewhat surprisingly to Sikander, was Khan and he looked like he was probably of Pakistani origin. Sikander could not be sure, but it seemed as if he was a second lieutenant in rank and about the same age as Bryers.

"Okay, let's get this thing rolling, Lieutenant Khan. Please ask this prisoner his name, where he was captured, and why he was there."

Khan translated the request into Pashto. *Well look at you…you might have come from anywhere as far afield as India to Afghanistan,* reflected Sikander while inwardly acknowledging the seemingly accurate translation of the questions. Sikander thought about whether or not to begin talking in English. He decided it would look bad if he left it until much later. It would seem he'd been playing with them and they didn't look like they were in the hospital ward wanting to be played with.

"My name is Khan. Sikander Khan. I was shot in Qunduz. I was brought back to health by some Northern Alliance people who sold me to one of yo…your buyers. I have been in Afghanistan since the end of October as I had come to help get my in-laws out of the country once you people had started to…bomb this country."

Valdez's eyebrows lifted reflexively as he looked across to Bryers and then made eye contact with Lieutenant Khan. The young lieutenant didn't say anything. His gaze was fixed on Sikander with a look of disdain, as if to ask why Sikander and his ilk were so bent on bringing such a name as theirs into disrepute by being affiliated with terrorists.

"Well…looks like we have a brother or cousin o' yours, Khan!" said Valdez, smiling. Khan didn't respond and Valdez waved his head in the direction of the doorway while also rolling his eyes that way, as if to point the way for Khan to leave the room, being no longer required.

"Okay, okay...seems you can speak my language, Mister Khan. What about the Taliban and al-Kayda?" he asked, strongly mispronouncing the name.

"Captain...Valdez. Captain, I came to arrange for my in-laws, my...my wife's extended family to come back with me to Pakistan out of harm's way. None of them are Taliban or al-Qaeda. They were from a village called Laghar Juy, which is south of Jalalabad in Nangarhar. We spent over ten days walking and riding by mule to get to Qunduz from which the Pakistani Air Force arranged for some people to come back to Pakistan. It was...it was Musharraf—" he paused to regain the strength to continue. "It was Musharraf who had arranged the airlift with your Vice President Cheney."

"Mmmhmm..." responded Valdez. "And how come they're gone and you're the only one around? You came for them but they couldn't wait around for you? Sounds like your in-laws are like mine!" Valdez allowed himself a mischievous chuckle amid the seriousness all around him, while glancing briefly back toward Bryers for affirmation of his humor. "You people!" said Valdez, shaking his head from side to side. "Your stories just seem to get more and more fanciful. I have to hand it you. But...Mr. Khan...from where I'm sitting it sounds like bullshit. You understand bull...shit?" asked Valdez, separating the word into its components as he leaned his torso over the edge of the bed, his face mere inches from Sikander's.

Sikander gave a slow, cautious nod of acknowledgment as Valdez dug deeper. Valdez straightened, pondering for a moment.

"Okay...suppose you're right and you did come like you said..." he shrugged. "Why didn't you stay with your fellow travelers?" he added, in a sideways headshake that joined the still suspended shrug.

"I...I had taken the mules on which we had ridden into Qunduz, expecting to sell all but one of them and return to the airfield to my people with some money and food so that—"

"Food? Hmm..." cut in Valdez. As Sikander nodded cautiously once more, Valdez resumed his grilling. "Mr. Khan, shouldn't you have been fasting? I thought it was Ramadan. Don't you all have to be fasting? And even if we leave *that* aside for a moment, if you were going to fly back to Pakistan, why did you need food anyway? Didn't you

think there would be any on the flight? How long could the flight have been anyway?"

Sikander was overwhelmed with the barrage of questions.

"You know, Mr. Khan, it isn't sounding very convincing! You hear what I'm saying?" asked Valdez.

"Oh...no, for Muslims who are traveling it isn't obligatory to fast," replied Sikander. "And we had last obtained food in Pul-i-Khumri which had been a couple of days earlier, so our need was from hunger from the journey—before Ramadhan had started."

"Hmm...we can check on that, but I have to tell you, Mr. Khan, or...whatever your name is...you're not making a lot of sense right now. I mean, you're picked up with a bullet wound, you're in a major hotbed of fighting where the largest surrender of hostiles in this whole war has taken place. You're from the largest group of non-Afghan hostiles—the Pakistanis—and you're giving me this...this story about rescuing in-laws from some...village hundreds of miles away! Please. Do us all a favor and start telling me something I can hang my hat on."

"Look, sir, I'm Sikander Khan. I have a business in Peshawar called Javelin, and—"

"Peshawar? Peshawar did you say? Okay. Let's suppose that's true. Tell me, Mr. Khan, you said your in-laws were from a village in Nangarhar? How did you ever find someone to marry all the way out in the middle of nowhere south of Jalalabad?"

"It's the truth...sir," replied Sikander, resignedly.

"Oh...the truth," replied Valdez in mock acceptance, standing back and looking down his nose as if he had absorbed something of significance. "Well, let me reiterate—you're in Kundooz, you're with none of the people you say you were traveling with, you have a bullet wound in you, you've confessed to being Pakistani...shall I go on, Mr. Khan?" asked Valdez pointedly.

Sikander had no reply.

"Look, Mr. Khan, I'd like to help you out of this predicament if you're indeed telling me the truth, but so far you haven't given me anything to believe in," said Valdez with seemingly genuine concern that the right thing be done. Again Sikander could offer nothing more or different from what he had already told them. Valdez paused for a

moment hoping for something, anything to take the interrogation into a different direction but eventually he sighed in resignation.

"Okay, he's sticking to his story...for now at least," Valdez shrugged. "Bagram." he pronounced simply, while signing something official looking presented to him by Bryers. Sikander's immediate future looked bleak.

It was December 7th. In exactly two months, the American led and backed Northern Alliance forces, which by themselves for five years had no answer to the Taliban rule, now held the north of the country. Meanwhile, the Eastern Alliance under Hamid Karzai, having marched into Qandahar after the battle of the bridge at Sayd Alim Kalay, held the remainder. The war to remove the Taliban was all but done.

Sikander was moved out of the hospital having once again made good progress with the attention he had received and was now placed in a single cell. He felt the cell to be a blessing compared to the seared memory of the hell-trip out of Qunduz.

Valdez never came back to talk to Sikander and at first Sikander was curious as to why he was no longer of interest. It took him a while to realize that he'd only been subjected to an initial screening, and as his screening officer hadn't been satisfied with the answers he was getting, the more "expert" facilities of the Bagram Collection Point, as it was then called, at the giant Bagram Air Force Base, were to be used.

Unfortunately for Sikander, the answers he had given to Valdez were far from satisfactory and Valdez's report simply wrote up this particular prisoner as "unconvincing, uncooperative, wounded and captured in Kunduz—requires further interrogation, English speaking Pakistani, Profile—strong match for al-Qaeda or Taliban."

On the 15th of December, Sikander was picked up from Sheberghan and taken in the back of a ten-ton truck down to Bagram. He was hooded and bound and had ear muffs to isolate external sounds so that apart from the jostling of the truck he had an eerie nauseating feeling of being inside himself. Any sense of freedom he might have had from taking in the air or even the scenery that would otherwise have been visible out of the back of the truck was not to be his to absorb.

He was his own prison cell.

After about eight hours of riding in the back of the truck, Sikander, still bound, hooded, and muffed, was led by a hand gripping his arm to make small shuffling steps imposed on him by the shackles on his ankles, and taken into a much hotter place. He could not see it but it was one of the vast hangars, built originally by the Russians like the rest of the entire base when they had invaded in 1979.

Once inside, he was separated from other prisoners but still in shackles, and led through a concertina wire clad cage being used as a sally port to get into a larger holding pen. Sikander was highly dazed and disoriented. He had imagined it was still some time in the afternoon and that he might be outdoors. When the hood and muffs were finally removed, he could see it was dark outside through some windows in one of the far hangar walls.

Immediately he was made to strip naked and received a full body cavity search. He was also photographed. With his clothes back on, he was taken to his holding cell.

A month passed. Sikander still awaited some indication from anyone about his condition. Finally, on January 8, 2002, he was visited by an interrogator.

"Mr....Khan...yes, you...Khan? From what I see here, you understand me, don't you?" Sikander looked up at the officer. He was a major with "Duke" written on his name label.

Duke was in his late thirties and looked like a person who cared about his appearance. His BDU was a little more prim than most others that Sikander had seen. His noticeable Farragut, Tennessee, drawl made him sound almost affable with just about everything he uttered. He was a career soldier, loved his job, and was looking for this war to make his next mark on his résumé to be noticed by his chain of command.

"Major Duke," said Sikander, nodding. "Yes, yes, I can understand what you're saying."

"Gooood!" Duke responded, wearing a grin. "That means we're going to be able to communicate and it will always be better for you if we can communicate." Duke's tone was both amiable and engaging. He began shuffling through some papers containing what looked like a printed report, and without looking up to make eye contact with Sikander, Duke continued.

"Mr. Khan, I want you to understand something. Things don't look too good for you from the information we have. If you want to avoid a very bad future, you're going to need to provide us with a more convincing story than what you've been trying to sell so far." Duke glanced up at him while wearing a convincingly sympathetic and worried frown. "You understand me?"

Sikander nodded.

"Okay—says here you were over looking for your family? Why? Where are you from originally?"

"Major Duke, the report is incorrect. I hadn't said I was looking for my family. They were my in-laws and in fact I had already found them and had helped them to a safe evacuation out of Qunduz airfield by the Pakistan Air Force in the middle of November, right at the start of Ramadhan."

"Uhuh...um...how'd you get shot?"

"Specifically? I don't know. I'd just returned from selling the mules we'd used to travel to Qunduz from a village south of Jalalabad. I'd just come out of a bakery, picked up some bread that morning, and...and was heading back to the airport when I was shot."

"What morning...do you remember the date?" continued Duke.

"Major, I recall very well that it was the morning of the 16th of November. You see, it was the morning after we'd seen the setting of new moon from the airport, marking the start of Ramadhan."

"And where was your family at that time? How come you weren't with them? How come you went into Kundooz when surely you must've known that the place was surrounded?"

"I...I had the understanding that we had three more days before there would be any fighting in Qunduz. I felt it would be safe to take the mules into the city and sell them. I was going back to the airfield to rejoin the family when a bullet struck me from behind. The next thing I remember there were two Northern Alliance people, one of them a doctor...yes...a...a doctor Atiq...who treated me for the injury and they held me prisoner so that they could...sell me, and they even showed a leaflet from your military which promised thousands of dollars for turning people...al-Qaeda...people in to your forces," replied Sikander.

Duke hastily wrote something down before continuing. "Hmm...how do I know you weren't found as an al-Kayda fighter, shot by the mujahideen, and then turned over to us?"

Sikander thought for a moment how Major Duke had used the word for the mujahideen. That's what *he* had been. Now he was being positioned in Duke's mind as one outside that circle and in fact as its enemy. He surprised himself with his own level of resentment at such an exclusion by this non-Muslim soldier, when he, Sikander, had done so much and endured so much to have earned the distinction of being called a mujahid.

"I...I...can't answer that, sir," replied Sikander. "I don't know how to prove I'm not a member of some organization."

"Oh...it's not a good idea to get cute with me." Duke delivered the threat in an advising tone, quietly, but effectively, conveying his supressed anger. Sikander didn't continue. The major launched into a more direct form of interrogation, his demeanor changing to a more aggressive one as his questions were short and designed to drive a certain pace in the conversation.

"Okay...let's go over your history...born where?"

"Pakistan, Peshawar."

"Where's your home address?"

"It's in the suburb of Hayatabad to the west of Peshawar."

"What do you do for a living?"

"I run a business called Javelin in Peshawar. We sell wholesale electrical products."

"Mmhmm...Where'd you go to school?"

"University Public School, in Peshawar. Not far from—"

"Father, mother, names?"

"My father was Javed Wahid Khan and my mother...my mother's name is Sofie Khan."

"Brothers? Sisters?"

"Yes. I have one brother, Jamil, and one sister, Sameena."

"Uhuh...When did you finish high school?"

"I...I didn't finish, sir. I left before completing high school so that I could fight against the Russians. That's what brought me to Afghanistan in 1986, and it...it's how I met my wife."

"Wife's name?"

"Rabia."

"Children?" As major Duke grilled him, Sikander's gaze lost focus and his mind began drifting off, thinking about Rabia, Ayub, and Qayyum. It had been months since he'd seen them and he wondered what they must be going through at that time.

Suddenly, Sikander felt a sharp crack over his head causing him to reel in pain from the blow he had just received. He couldn't reach with his hand to soothe the pain where the blow had struck as his hands were manacled.

"Children," repeated Major Duke in a more forceful and menacing tone devoid of question.

"Yes!" cried Sikander. "Two boys!"

"Names?" asked Duke.

"Ayub and Qayyum."

And so the questioning went on without reaching any particular point where it might seem obvious where Duke was taking the matter.

"Well now...I guess we both understand each other, don't we?" Duke went on as Sikander nodded slowly in response. "See...Mr. Khan, I don't want to tell you that you've just told me a pack of lies. I want to begin by supposing everything you told me was true. Suppose you do have your business, your wife, your kids, and all the other things we just went through, but suppose also that you felt like coming back to Afghanistan because you hate America and Americans and...just maybe suppose you'd seen—" Duke shrugged, "CNN...in Pakistan, and thought...you know? I should go over there and help the al-Kayda folks against these nasty Americans. Now how would I know—just from what you've told me, mind you—that you didn't do that?"

"I didn't. Until now I have always liked America. America had helped to make it possible for me to fight the Soviets. I never met with any al-Qaeda people, I don't agree with their views. I..." Sikander could think of nothing else to add.

"Mmhmm...sure. Do you know how many people that love America I've met in the last ten days? Any idea, Mr. Khan? You're a non-Afghan. You're a self-confessed Pakistani, caught in Kundooz, coincidentally, the very area that the Taliban and al-Kayda people had retreated to. Most of the non-Arab, non-Afghans came from Pakistan, from all walks of life, I might add, and now...now that you've been caught? Huh! Why, you *love* America! Now what I want is the truth. I want to know all the details of any plans you're aware of. I want to know dates. I want to know places. Names of people you were with. Names of leaders. What do they have cookin'? Where are they hidin'? You understand what I'm sayin'?" demanded Duke in his less practiced drawl.

"I don't have any al-Qaeda connections. I never met any of them. I don't know how to convince you of that!" pleaded Sikander.

"Well..." said Duke with a snickering sigh as he shook his head, "Mr. Khan, I can't spend all day with you. I figure you know that. I'm not gettin' your cooperation and there are people who know how to do this way better than I do. You'll be seein' them soon enough!"

The new year rolled in and Ramadhan was long finished. There had been subdued 'Eid-ul-Fitr celebrations in Pakistan not only due to the war going on in neighboring Afghanistan but at the same time, major tensions had resurfaced between India and Pakistan on their mutual border with massive troop concentrations involved. It was in the aftermath of an attack on the Indian Parliament where several policemen, a gardener, and the six attackers had been killed. Lashkar-e-Taiba and Jaish-e-Mohammed were two militia groups that had been named by the Indians as responsible, and customarily, Pakistan was accused by India for having sponsored them and provided safe havens for their training. The Pakistani leadership continued to insist on the legitimacy of the Kashmiri people's separatist movement, which these two organizations had, originally at least, been fighting for. Most people agreed, however, that they had recently become much more focused on Islamist militancy than on achieving a new political reality in Kashmir.

Finally in mid-January, Parvez Musharraf gave a speech to suggest that extremism would be combated within Pakistan but that Pakistan still claimed full rights to Kashmir. This seemed to help defuse the tensions and there was, for several months, a stand-down by both

sides. In these times, however, as Rabia, Sofie, and the family at large all waited, Sameena could bring no word of any development from President Musharraf. He was too busy avoiding a nuclear conflict with India to think about tracing Sikander among the numerous prisoners being processed from all over Afghanistan.

✿

"Get up! Get up! Get up!" barked a staff sergeant while striking a stick on the bars of the cage in which Sikander was being held. It was the 11th of January and Sikander had just gone back to sleep in his cage after performing fajr, when he was roused abruptly. He had no difficulty obeying, as anything else was impossible. As soon as he sat upright, he was carefully brought out of the cage, shackled at the ankles and manacled at the wrists, and made to sit with his shackles also tied to a chair while his head and beard were shaved.

"You can't have hair on your head or a beard where you're going," said the solider doing the shaving, none too carefully. "Can't risk the lice." Once the shaving was complete, he was forced to strip naked and again given a full body cavity search. While he winced at the pain, it took all of Sikander's effort to suppress his reactions. He had long since learned not to pass comment or reveal a reaction to any treatment. Anything resembling a reaction added significantly to the risks he faced of a brutal retaliation and would clearly only add to a soldier's satisfaction if humiliation had been the intent and he was to receive confirmation of it being felt by the prisoner. However, not all soldiers were the same during his time at Bagram, and Sikander could clearly discern differences in ethics and moral values between them. But it was noteworthy how as time passed by with little sanction against misbehavior toward prisoners a general drift toward more sadistic tendencies became noticeable.

After the shaving and the strip-searching, he was re-dressed while tight fitting goggles were placed over his eyes with black tape over the glass panes, which was also used to seal his view of anything around the edges. Over his mouth was placed a surgical mask, and earmuffs were put over his head. His hands were wrapped with mittens while the manacles were removed so that they could be reapplied with his hands behind his back and his legs remained shackled. In this condition he was brought outside of the building.

The engines of the C-141 Starlifter idled as it awaited its cargo with its gaping loading ramp down. Sikander, linked apparently to at least one other prisoner in front and one behind him, was forced to stand still while an officer patted him down over his entire body, seemingly keen to inflict just a little more pain. When all was clear, he could feel something being written on his forehead using some kind of volatile ink marker. Finally his head was covered entirely by a large black hood.

Once again, Sikander recalled the eerie feeling of being imprisoned inside himself. He was jerked along as the chain between himself and the next detainee slackened and tightened though it was only vaguely possible to detect the cause. A disembodied hand appeared to have grabbed him at the elbow and began dragging him forward while preventing him from falling from the awkwardness of the shackles.

Finally, Sikander and his fellow detainees were made to sit on the floor of the aircraft. Webbing straps were passed through everyone's arms and likewise with their legs and ankle shackles in such a way as to fix the men and stop them from bouncing around inside the cavernous twenty-one-meter-long hold of the giant transport. Sikander could barely feel anything and his arms and legs started to become numb. Shortly after takeoff, the aircraft underwent several maneuvers and each was a fresh source of pain. The pain subsided when the airplane assumed a straight attitude and climbed out to cruise altitude. After approximately fifteen hours, Sikander again experienced excruciating pain as the airplane landed.

Two months earlier, on November 13, 2001, George W. Bush had issued a Presidential Military Order on the treatment of detainees as Illegal Enemy Combatants, a concept not mentioned in any of the articles of the Geneva Conventions. White House legal counsel further went on to advise the President that the Geneva Conventions did not apply to such detainees, even Taliban detainees who, they argued, came not from a state but from a "failed state." The theory establishing the significance of this distinction was not argued. The November 13th PMO essentially handed the President the right, without recourse to any other authority, to designate, incarcerate, and eliminate anyone on the strength of a "determination" of illegal combatant status. The agility it

afforded the administration seemed like a worthwhile value in light of most people's fearful resentment of the provision of due process to suspected terrorists.

Added to this was a further theory that the US Naval Base at Guantanamo Bay, Cuba, while under the control of the United States, was not sovereign to the United States and based on this was outside the reach of the US courts. As a result, any detainee believed or declared by Presidential order to be an illegal enemy combatant was subject to indefinite detention in a place under US government control but not sovereign US territory, out of reach of judicial process, capable of being dealt with in any manner whatsoever, while having no legal recourse to challenge such detention or treatment.

Back in 1994, a camp facility was created at the naval base in Guantanamo Bay to house Haitian migrants as part of Operation Sea Signal. At the south side of the base, several camps, beginning with Camp Alpha and then Bravo, Charlie, Delta, and Golf were constructed. When more were constructed on the north side, the naming began from the other end of the alphabet, beginning with Zebra. From among these camps on both the north and south sides of the base, the American government decided to establish a large scale permanent facility for holding and questioning detainees captured in the Global War on Terror. As a temporary facility, Camp X-ray was hurriedly prepared while the larger Camp Delta was redesigned for more permanent use. X-ray was to be pressed into service almost immediately, using concertina wire and chain-link fencing, with tents for guards and specially constructed concrete floored units with wood and metal roofs about two and a half meters square, for detainees. Meanwhile, Delta—which involved a lot more construction activity—was to be made ready by April of 2002.

By order of the Secretary of Defense, Donald Rumsfeld, two Joint Task Forces were set up by US Southern Command. JTF-160 was created to manage and handle detainees, and JTF-170 was created to interrogate them. JTF-160 was composed largely of Military Police units while JTF-170 was composed of intelligence-gathering personnel comprising what was called the Joint Interagency Intelligence Facility at Guantanamo.

✿

By the second week of January of 2002, everything was in place for prisoners who had been picked up in Afghanistan and held for questioning at Bagram to be brought over to Guantanamo's Camp X-ray. Sikander was among the first batch to be made ready for the transfer. He had plainly failed to convince anyone that mattered that he was not a member of al-Qaeda or Taliban. As he was a Pakistani caught in Qunduz by the Northern Alliance, he was highly likely to be an illegal enemy combatant who was probably injured during fighting against the Northern Alliance and was therefore not difficult to designate. The likelihood was so high that no military officer would risk his career on a benefit of the doubt.

As Sikander was taken off the airplane, he could hardly feel anything. He was led, although it seemed more like being dragged, into a waiting vehicle, which drove from the airfield to the north side of the giant base. Once out of the vehicle, he was again hauled in the direction of the barbed and razor wire fencing that defined the perimeters of Camp X-ray. Eventually, the goggles, face mask, earmuffs, and mittens were removed and he took several moments to get used to the light. When he looked around, he saw that he was among about thirty other people and the lights were shining brightly in the room.

"Face the front!" came an order over a loudspeaker and a second later came another one in Arabic, in Urdu, then Farsi, and finally Pashto.

"Remove all your clothes. You are being prepared for admission into Camp X-ray. This is a place where there is no law. We are the law. If you obey our law, you will be treated well. If not, you will be punished and dealt with severely!"

The message continued in multiple languages. After it had finished playing, a guard came into the room using his rifle to point the way for the prisoners to move to their left into another room. Sikander could see he was being guided into a shower room. As soon as he trudged into it, he was accosted by a powerful smell of some sort of chemical, possibly a disinfectant, which gave way to the rush of water over his naked body. After five minutes, the shower was done and a guard appeared with towels. Sikander was handed one in which to wrap himself before he had the wrist manacles, belly chain, ankle shackles, goggles, earmuffs, face mask, and mittens put back on. He was then

taken to yet another room where he received a small pile of things to carry.

As he followed the train of men carrying these items, another soldier called him over and told him—but more demonstrated to him in gestures—that one more time he was to receive a full body cavity search. When the search was complete, the soldier motioned to Sikander to move to a bench by the wall.

"Put this on," he commanded, handing Sikander a vermillion jumpsuit. The soldier pointed him in the direction of a cubicle with no door where he assisted Sikander in putting on the jumpsuit, releasing only those restraints that were necessary, one at a time to enable the clothes to be applied to each limb. After dressing, he was taken to see a physician who gave him a medical examination, including measuring his height and weight, checking for lice, performing a blood draw, and taking of DNA samples. Lastly, a full dental examination was performed and when all the admission procedures were complete, Sikander was finally led to an isolation cell in Camp X-ray where he was to stay for a period of thirty days having no contact with anyone else. Sikander was now firmly under the control of the JTF-160 MPs and they knew their way around prison and prisoner management.

With the Geneva Conventions ruled by the Bush Administration as inapplicable, the MPs of JTF-160 had nominally at least to work with standard operating procedures which were themselves continually evolving. Those procedures included starting any internment with thirty days of isolation. By contrast, the Geneva Conventions stipulated that solitary confinement was exclusively for prisoners after committing infractions and not before. Alone with his dark thoughts for those seemingly endless days, Sikander learned the nature of solitary confinement and why the Geneva Conventions were so vocal about its use.

✿

Paralysis had become the norm for life in Hayatabad. Sikander's absence had seen to that, and while he could not be simply forgotten by any means, everyone tried to work through it as best they could. Abdul Majeed and Saleem were introduced to the workings of Javelin and began to help in sales and warehousing. Jamil did an admirable job of managing things under the circumstances and began getting to know both young men. But it rankled with him still that the two of them had

been a part of the cause of the troubles. He started to spend more time with them and would often take them back to the Zarghooni masjid to listen to some of the more enlightened Sunni speakers who were manifestly not in the pro-Taliban camp. Neither did they subscribe to some of the austere, harsh interpretations of Islam that had come to be associated with the Taliban.

Saleem became particularly interested in the teachings at the madrassah nearby and began to acquire a sense of the depth of Islamic knowledge and learning that was possible. He gained new insights into how life could be expressed in much richer terms than simple lists of the "do's and don'ts" which had seemed more characteristically the Taliban way of thinking. Moreover, he could see that such behavioral requirements and injunctions were meaningless unless wrapped around a deeply spiritual core set of beliefs and convictions, and the pursuit of these began to engage him more and more as time went by.

Seeing such a change, and at the encouragement of Fatima, Abdul Majeed followed suit and soon, the men began providing informed opinions about Islam that resonated with most of the rest of the family's thinking. They began to understand more deeply the importance of education to both men and women. They learned about the relative empowerment of women that was originally a cornerstone of Islam in contrast with the primitive era of ignorance in the Arabian Peninsula before it, and, to a large extent, the resumption of many of the old pre-Islamic misogynistic tendencies in much of the Muslim world centuries after the initial wave of Islam's spread. Saleem so excelled in his abilities to read and understand the "Tafsir," or detailed analysis of the Qur'an, that he enlisted in a program of learning to become an 'alim—or qualified knowledgeable one.

By early February, the tensions between India and Pakistan that had flared up at the end of 2001 at last subsided to a simmer, much to the relief of a Bush Administration that was looking for Pakistan's undivided attention in its own campaign in Afghanistan. President Musharraf's attention was thereby a little more available to focus on other matters.

As the month went by, no new developments came through for Rabia regarding Sikander. However, on the weekend of February 22nd, as Sofie and Rabia were watching over the children in the lounge, their attention was abruptly shifted to the slamming shut of a car's doors. It

was Sameena and Wasim and they had arrived at Sikander's house with news.

"Ammee! Rabia! Come quickly! I have some news!" called out Sameena.

"Sameena? What is it?" asked Rabia anxiously, not daring to hope for too much.

"Rabia! President Musharraf conferred with Abba-jan and asked for more detail but especially a photograph," she said. "The more recent the better."

"A photo?" repeated Rabia. "I don't have a recen—wait!" she exclaimed, her heart quickening.

"I remember him putting on a suit and tie for a company photograph back in August for the Pakistan Day celebrations. That should be in our room, or if not, there's sure to be a copy at the company!"

"Can you get it?" asked Sameena.

"Jamil bhai! Jamil bhai!" called Rabia. Jamil was in his own bedroom when he heard the call from below.

"Coming!" he called, quickly putting on his qamees.

"Jamil bhai, it's a new development," said Rabia, trying to remain calm. "We've been asked to provide a photograph so that we can confirm that our Sikander is the correct person." Rabia's demeanor blossomed into one of radiant hope from the knowledge that something as concrete as this was being done and yes, it was only a photo but it seemed like a major step in the right direction.

"Jamil bhai, you have to go to the office, open it up, and confirm that there's an August 14th—Pakistan Day—staff photograph that Sikander had taken. You were in it too, remember?" recalled Rabia.

"I do remember it," admitted Jamil. "Actually, there's no need to go to the office. I've got one in my room."

Rabia urged him to get the picture and hand it over to Wasim who was patiently waiting to be able to do his part. The photograph was retrieved and brought down. Wasim took it confidently and assured the family he would do all he could to expedite processing of the picture and to pursue the matter with President Musharraf.

✤

After the thirty-day period of isolation, it took a few more days for the interrogators under the JTF-170 to get to Sikander, and when they did, the same questions about personal details, history, siblings, parents, schooling, and so on were among the many things that Sikander had to repeat. He did not realize it at the time, but under the joint task force several different agencies had both rights and reasons to interrogate him.

Interrogations were never pleasant. Sikander had really only one thing to hide. Saleem and Abdul Majeed *had* been members of the Taliban. It helped him to understand that with all the interrogations thus far, he had not been driven to elaborate on this. He had convinced himself that his captors were interested in hard-core al-Qaeda and Taliban leadership and not two misguided young men. Likewise, Sikander knew Abdul Majeed and Saleem well enough to know that they were not interested in fighting the Americans prior to any occupation of Afghanistan. Equally, neither of them was interested in al-Qaeda's views mostly because even for them, there was little if any interaction with al-Qaeda and they did not agree with whatever principles they had understood al-Qaeda to hold. They were firmly in the mainstream Sunni camp whereas al-Qaeda, though avowedly Sunni, was steadfastly Salafist and Takfiri with no compunction about killing Muslims by declaring them to be apostates for not taking up the use of lethal force against Israel or America.

Sikander had likewise felt that the Taliban had never formulated an agenda of rabid anti-Americanism. Indeed, they had been helped into power by the Pakistanis and the Americans. The State Department had been warm to their ascendancy. It struck Sikander as especially ironic that now, because of their Pashtunwali code and immutable sense of obligation to protect seekers of such protection, namely al-Qaeda's leadership, their entire country was in someone else's hands and they had been criminalized by the very people who helped them to power. Indeed, captives such as himself were now held to be below the rank of criminal. At least people being tried as criminals had the rights of *habeas corpus* and a presumption of innocence until proven guilty beyond reasonable doubt. Being neither designated as lawful combatant nor alleged criminal meant that detainees such as Sikander were not to be afforded rights under criminal law nor the protections of the Geneva Conventions. It was the system's way of saying either "we're incapable

of making mistakes" or "the wrongful loss of a few people's liberties are worth the preservation of those of the many."

There were two specific measures of a detainee's behavior at Guantanamo—compliance and cooperation. Compliance was demanded and meant the absolute absence of anything like defiance toward their captors. The mere hint of a failure of compliance was grounds for punitive action. If a rule was broken, the offending prisoner was then the subject of a beating by the Immediate Reaction Force, or IRF, whose personnel were typically assigned the duty in a roster so that all MPs were given a taste of this role. To be "IRF'd" was the dreaded consequence of any failure in compliance, and for punishment, MPs would typically burst into the cell, five at a time, and engage in any or all of a number of styles of physical beatings but very loosely based on the standard operating procedures laid down for such disciplinary interventions. The degree of adherence to these procedures was largely down to the personalities of the individual MPs. Since failure to adhere to them was generally without consequence to themselves, those MPs inclined to indulge in sadistic pleasure took advantage of the opportunity on each IRF'ing occasion.

While in Camp X-ray, Sikander was placed in a cell resembling an open cage. Its walls were constructed from a form of chain-link wire and the cover was made of a combination of wood and metal. The floor was concrete and otherwise, the cage was open to the elements. Small creatures like spiders and scorpions were able to come and go, and there was no privacy. He was there alongside other prisoners, each in their own sub-unit of the overall cage structure. From time to time, the detainees would be let out for a few minutes of walking exercise.

During one of these breaks, Sikander got his first taste of what it meant to feel the wrath of the IRF. The detainees were called back from break and Sikander took about a minute longer than allotted. When he walked in, the IRF arrived in full riot gear. The first MP rushed him with his shield and forced him to the ground. He held Sikander's head. The second and third came down with full force on his arms, and the fourth and fifth each took a leg, beating him and then shackling him. In that condition, they then picked up his torso while pinning his legs to the ground and pushed his torso hard down onto the ground. He didn't have a chance to react and was unconscious for at least half a minute.

When he came to, he was made aware of his infraction and warned not to repeat it. Such punishments became part of life at Camp X-ray.

As he recovered from his punitive ordeal, in a state of near delirium, Sikander cast his mind back to the numerous moments leading up to his arrival in Guantanamo where he might have weighed the risks of escape differently. He began to fantasize about jumping out of the fourth story window in Qunduz, while he was still injured by the gunshot wound. He thought of feigning death and being buried in whatever grave had been used for the ill-fated Taliban prisoners who had died on the journey from hell in the container. He imagined what it might have been like if he had disguised himself as a medical staffer walking out of the prison hospital in Sheberghan, or perhaps if he had snatched at an unwary guard's gun in Bagram.

Of all the things Sikander had imagined up to this point, being captured and taken into custody by the Americans had been the most likely—in his mind—to result in reasonable treatment.

Americans!

How different these people were from the humane, God-fearing people he'd come to learn about that had been of so much help during the Russian occupation. How far they seemed from the open society that his Aunt Zainab's son Salman from Durham, North Carolina, had described, with his family vacations, his SUV, and his Yosemite photographs!

Sikander could often hear the cries and screams of fellow inmates in pain after having been subdued by the IRF MPs. It didn't seem to matter if they were in a non-threatening position. The MPs would do their worst anyway. Alongside such punishments they would either withhold or give CIs—comfort items. These could be flip-flops, more clothing, or less clothing with a minimum being boxer shorts. They could go all the way to board games for highly compliant prisoners. Achieving compliance was all about breaking the detainee spirit. Curiously, though, the detainees were given Qur'ans to read and were allowed to pray five times a day and were also allowed to re-grow their facial hair. The Qur'ans were, generally speaking, treated with respect. Each would be slung inside a face mask and left to hang from the bars of the cage, though Sikander did hear of occasions where MPs had abused the Qur'ans in despicable ways.

If being given the IRF treatment for a failure of compliance was bad, the kind of treatment meted out for a failure of cooperation in interrogations was generally worse. It was not long after the first round of interrogations that Sikander was again taken for questioning in mid-February. He had just been held over in a preparatory room in which the air conditioning had been turned up fully to the point of being almost icy cold. He had also been deprived of sleep for the last twenty hours when finally he was brought into a light-filled interrogation room. In the room was a male interrogator and a female as well as two MPs. The male was wearing a US Army uniform while the female seemed to be from the US Navy.

Captain James A. Mahler Jr. was the lead interrogator. He had a gaunt looking face and short curly hair. He wore rimless glasses and his thin mouth with lips barely visible betrayed no hint of ever having smiled. Tired from lack of sleep, Sikander could nonetheless somehow sense that this man had put himself in a state that required discarding some of his own humanity—a state which, among other things, permitted him to operate with a perversion of logic in grasping cause-and-effect as it related to detainees. Such logic allowed that the mere act of being interned in Guantanamo was its own evidence of guilt. For Mahler, Sikander was yet another personification of al-Qaeda—a surrogate for all those "bad guys" out there that must be hated because of what "they," or more accurately "their kind," did in New York a few short months earlier. He was one of the "worst of the worst." He had to be. He was in Guantanamo.

While Sikander was shackled to his chair, Mahler began by going through what Sikander assumed might be his prior interview records. He didn't ask him the usual questions.

"When did you last meet with Shareef?" asked Mahler.

Sikander didn't understand the question and supposed he may have misheard Mahler. "I...I didn't hear the question," said Sikander in his relative stupor.

Mahler peered over the top of his eyeglasses and made the briefest eye contact with each of the two MPs in the room, while calmly uttering the single word "Down." Immediately, Sikander felt himself being lifted off the chair by the armpits. That motion was no sooner complete when he felt a single knee pushing forcefully behind each of his own, causing his legs to bend while his torso was still being held

from under his armpits. The two MPs brought down Sikander's torso with him now on his knees. Pinned in place with the MP's knees behind his own, his torso was rapidly slammed against the floor. Keeping their knees dug into the back of his, they forced his own knees to press into the floor.

Sikander howled in pain. After a short amount of time, the entire procedure was repeated and then finally, he was picked up again by the armpits and dropped into his chair.

"It will cost you this treatment if you fail to listen to my questions, Mr. Khan," said Mahler softly. "When did you last meet with Shareef?" he repeated.

"I...have...no...idea...who...who that is," Sikander replied, his eyelids tightly closed in a grimace as he gasped initially to utter each word.

"I'm referring to Jehangir Mohammed Shareef. He's an al-Kayda coordinator for west Peshawar, Mr. Khan," said Mahler.

"Look...truly I...I don't know who you mean. Maybe he used a different name?" offered Sikander trying to avoid an unnecessary act of violence once again on the mere misunderstanding over an alias.

"Hmm..." Mahler seemingly resisted the temptation to repeat the punishment of a moment ago. "What about Qureishi? Let me clarify...Atif Masood Qureishi? A lieutenant colonel in the ISI? When did you last meet with him?"

"ISI? Sir, I...I only know one officer from the ISI. It...it was from my time as one of the mujahideen, but I last saw him in Qunduz airport in mid-November before I was injured and captured. He had come over from Pakistan to...to help recover ISI people who needed to be...to be...picked up when Musharraf changed sides..." replied Sikander, barely holding on to his coherence.

Mahler looked across to the Navy woman. From what Sikander could tell, she was not beyond her mid-twenties. She was a lieutenant and he noted that in her own way she was also beautiful, bearing something of a resemblance to actress Nicole Kidman whom he had seen in several movies in Peshawar. She opened a folder and pulled out a picture, handing it to Mahler. He examined it briefly before placing it

in front of Sikander's face. Sikander took a moment to focus on the picture and shifted his gaze to make eye contact with Mahler.

"Do you know this man?" Mahler asked. The man pictured was in a full dress Pakistan Army uniform together with the cap, but the face in the picture was unmistakable.

"Yes...yes, I do. He's the person I mentioned previously. His name is Junaid. Captain Junaid is what I have always called him," said Sikander.

"Well, you should know that he's a lieutenant colonel in the ISI and his real name is Qureishi. Atif Masood Qureishi," said Mahler. "When did you last see him?"

"As I told you, he...I...I left him at the airfield at Qunduz when I...when I went to sell the mules. He was the one I left my in-laws with. He...he...I've always known him as Junaid," Sikander shook his head sideways, still in a daze.

"Well, he's working for al-Kayda, Mr. Khan. What does that make you? Huh?"

"al-Qae—I...I don't know what to tell you," pleaded Sikander, weary but alarmed. "I-I've only met him in Peshawar except the last time when he...when he traveled with me. He told me he was going to get his ISI people out of Afghanistan and offered to help me get there too, so I could get my wife's family across into Pakistan when the war started. He...he split up from me to recover his people while I...while I went to my wife's village. We met up again near Qunduz and he took charge over the family while I went to sell the mules."

"Now that's more the kind of talking we want from you, Mr. Khan. Lieutenant, see to it that Mr. Khan gets a toothbrush and flip-flops. You see, Mr. Khan, when you cooperate and answer our questions like this we can treat you quite well," said Mahler.

"But...but *you* knew more than *I* did. How was this helpful?" Sikander was genuinely bewildered.

"Never mind that, Mr. Khan. Now, tell us what you know about any planned attacks on the US. Tell us what you know about people already in the US; other al-Kayda agents, people in Pakistan that you know in training camps. Tell us what they're planning, Mr. Khan," demanded Mahler and this time his tone was much less cordial as his

face grew more intense and his lips were tighter than ever as he bent down lower to approach, but not quite meet, Sikander's eye level.

"Plans? Agents? I-I...don't have any idea about any *plans...*" Sikander answered.

Mahler straightened up and once more looked up at the MPs, muttered the word "Down," and again, as if it had been a well choreographed ballet movement, they repeated the routine which brought Sikander up off his chair and crashing down onto the floor. This time, however, all the pain from the previous drop came back to torment him. Sikander screamed, unable to bear the pain. Within a few seconds he was lifted back up by the armpits and dumped into the chair.

"Tell us what we want to *know*, Mr. Khan. *Make it easy on yourself,*" demanded Mahler, emphasizing each word.

"I don't know! I...don't...know! I've told you what I know!" screamed Sikander, following which he let his head hang limp. Mahler and the Navy woman looked at each other.

"I'm leaving this shit-can and taking a cigarette. These guys are leaving with me," said Mahler, and lowering his head toward Sikander's as he had done before, with a tone of disgust and a smirk he softly uttered, "I'll be back."

Mahler and the two MPs left Sikander alone with the woman in the Navy uniform. After the door closed behind them, Sikander heard the woman's voice for the first time.

"Dirty business, this," she said. "You think we like doing this?" Her face had a business-like pleasantry, as if she might have been making an appointment with a customer. All of Sikander's upbringing about being polite, and especially so in female company, urged him to respond with politeness. It was very difficult, and these people knew it, thought Sikander, to remain focused on where he was and why he was there. Besides, whatever mental faculties he had left at that moment were now absorbed by the thought that Junaid had been a member of al-Qaeda. He fought hard within himself to recognize that Mahler's claim might not be true.

Sikander said nothing in response to the woman while she continued, but he did now note that her name badge said "Alexander."

The slightest hint of a smile occupied the corner of his lips for less than a second as he considered the irony of being held in captivity by a woman of this name.

"You know, we usually get the information we're looking for. It seems such an idiotic thing to go through the agony that it must be for you, only to cave in and give us the information in the end. Don't you think, Mr. Khan? I mean, why not behave like civilized people? Why get into all this...all this...physical stuff?"

"Huh!" sighed Sikander. "Tell me...tell me what you'd like me to say..." he asked wearily and then screamed, "*Tell me!*"

"Oh...everything you know and nothing that isn't true," she advised, unfazed by his volatility. She approached him more closely and started caressing his hair with her soft hands. Crouching down to be able to whisper into his ear, she said in an alluringly quiet voice, "Tell us everything we want to know, Mr. Khan. We'll show you our...appreciation."

Sikander sensed the fragrance of the Amouage that this woman was wearing, which coincidentally had been one of Rabia's favorites after she had moved to Peshawar. He decided to use the fact to recall Rabia, forming and focusing on an image of her while he resisted the urge to react to Lieutenant Alexander. His Muslim sensibilities demanded that he be repulsed by such a move, even though physically, she was impossible to ignore. But whatever he felt, he neither expressed pleasure nor revulsion. Just no reaction, which in his dazed and sleep-deprived state did not require a lot of effort.

Mahler came back, having tossed his cigarette butt on the floor outside the interrogation room. "Well?" he asked Sikander, while looking across at Lieutenant Alexander.

"I can't tell you what you're asking for..." said Sikander. "I can't...I don't know."

Mahler gave an icy glare back to the MPs and having glanced at the Navy lieutenant and seeing the hint of a slight, slow side-to-side shaking of her head, he gave the MPs the indication to get Sikander back on his feet and drag him back to his holding cell.

Sikander was all but unconscious when he was almost hurled in the cage, bumping his head against the far side wire wall. The ache didn't matter now. He just needed to sleep.

When he awoke, he could see other detainees scrutinizing him. He raised his hand to feel his slightly swollen lip and a cut on his forehead.

"Interrogated?" asked a voice from across the aisle which separated his cage from the adjacent set of cages. It was a young man who spoke English with a British Cockney accent.

Sikander nodded.

"Yeah, I've had that treatment too, man. They don't hold anythin' back, do they?"

Sikander shook his head. He had little desire and less ability to speak.

"It makes them really happy if you tell them something. Makes 'em feel like what they're doing's really workin', you know?"

As the morning light improved, Sikander could see the man across the way. He was well built, similar to Sikander though perhaps a little shorter. He was also wearing a white skullcap. Being a dedicated adherent of Deobandi principles the man wore his jumpsuit pants well above his ankles. Sikander was a bit more alert now and when he looked across, he saw the young man looking back at him. "Assalaamu 'alaykum!" said the man. "I'm Fareed."

"Wa 'alaykum...assalaam," replied Sikander with hardly enough energy to get the words out.

"How are they treating you?" asked Fareed.

Sikander, with his legs on the floor and his body resting against the wire wall of the cage, simply rolled his head the other way as he let out a short sigh. It told the young man asking the question all he wanted to know. Sikander turned his head back to look at Fareed. "I'm Sikander."

Looking down, Sikander was drawn into examining what those two words might now mean. Who was he? He couldn't ground himself in this insane string of events that had befallen him and he wondered if

this was just the beginning of perhaps a rapid slide toward insanity. How could he possibly be the man he supposed he was?

I can't be the person that ran away from home while a teenager, fought alongside the Afghans, trained in Scotland, fought the Russians, built a business in Peshawar...No! Another part of him overruled this nonsense. Of course he was Sikander.

Sikander felt himself drift into and out of a belief that his past was only imagined and, for that terrifying moment, he felt as if he'd always been a detainee. More terrifying still was the glimpse his psyche was offering him of the possibility of such feelings lasting for more than just a moment. *No!* He had to remain in control He was Sikander. He had to remain Sikander.

"How...long have you been here?" he asked Fareed.

"Not sure," replied Fareed, gazing wistfully skyward. "It wasn't long after the Americans came into Afghanistan. Sometimes I think it was too soon after the New York attacks. God...who would do somethin' like that, eh? Who would have the balls to calmly get on a plane, slit the pilot's throat, and fly it into a building, man?" He shook his head in disbelief.

"They picked me up and did terrible things to me, man! I think they felt that...they just needed to throttle somebody, anybody who might look like they could've done somethin' like that. They were probably competing with each other for who could get the most revenge. God!"

"You don't sound like you're from Afghanistan or Pakistan," noted Sikander, becoming more in command of his faculties.

The young man smiled, though it was barely observable across the shadowy cell. "I'm not. I'm from England. Just north of London actually. I grew up there."

"Really? Are you...were you...al-Qaeda? Taliban?"

Fareed didn't answer that question. He couldn't trust Sikander with whatever the truth might have been. He just looked down at the concrete floor of his cage.

"How did you get to Afghanistan?" probed Sikander.

Fareed continued averting his eyes downward, paused, and then heaved his chest in a silent chuckle until he had to wince at the pain involved in doing so and began describing his journey. "I was eight when I came with my mum and the rest of the family. We lived in Woodford. I actually studied reasonably well and y'know, I got some pretty decent grades and I went through all that school stuff and I was going to university," explained Fareed.

"Really? Which one?" asked Sikander, still fighting the pain of speaking. He'd heard of Oxford, Cambridge, and London—among one or two others.

"City. City College, in London," replied Fareed.

Sikander acknowledged without letting on that he had never heard of it. "What did you study?"

"Huh! Computer science," replied Fareed with a wistful grin. "But I didn't finish the program. I just wanted to get out and about, get out of England and y'know...see somethin'."

Sikander managed to nod. "I...as a matter of fact, I didn't finish school either."

"Really? Hmm...well anyway, I was actually in Germany, y'know, when I was struck by a car. It was serious. I almost died! Well, technically I think I did...you know how when your heart stops?"

Sikander nodded, becoming a little more fascinated despite his physical state.

Fareed continued. "I dunno, I think that was what turned me to think about Islam. I mean, I wanted to know more so when I came back to England, I started going to this masjid in London, and because I knew a bit about computin', I helped them build a website."

"And then?" Sikander's curiosity grew.

"And then, well, they liked what I'd done for them and y'know, that sort of made me feel good. I decided I'd go over to Afghanistan. Get some training. I wanted to be a soldier for Islam."

"Hmm," acknowledged Sikander.

"So it would have been right after Bush got elected—or appointed—dependin' on how you want to look at it..." Fareed almost chuckled, "that I went off to Afghanistan and...y'know...I went to some

camps. But that was long before those attacks on those buildings. Man, those attacks!"

Sikander continued acknowledging.

"So, after the attacks, I was fightin', because all we'd had until then was bombs, bombs, and more bloody bombs rainin' down on us! But then those Northern Alliance people, they caught me in Qunduz and held onto me. I'm sure they were well paid for turnin' anyone over to the Americans."

It was quite clear that Fareed was defiantly anti-American and, it seemed, a fellow-in-misery for having been picked up in Qunduz and sold to the Americans just as he had been. Sikander shared his own story with Fareed. Fareed was visibly upset and it was all that Sikander could do to calm him down and warn him not to direct his anger toward the prison guards or interrogators, as that might land both of them, but certainly at least Fareed, into serious trouble with resulting injury.

Sikander and Fareed periodically talked to each other and the conversations usually boiled down to a pretty damning critique of how the American government had responded to the attacks of September.

A few days later Sikander was hauled back in for questioning and the treatment was repeated with more names being given to him. Always it would be Mahler with the MPs accompanying him, and more often than not Lieutenant Alexander. Each time she was in the room, she would be left alone with him and usually try something soft, seductive or sympathetic to get Sikander to reveal new information. However, as usual, Sikander, ignorant as he was, could not tell anything of al-Qaeda plans, and as usual, whenever he was judged to be uncooperative, Mahler would see to it that the MPs got their "exercise."

As the year crept along, the temperature started to climb in Guantanamo. On a hot day in the middle of March, as Sikander lay in the sweltering heat, MPs arrived to "escort" him to the interrogation block where Mahler was waiting. Sikander almost welcomed the likely respite from the heat that the interrogation would provide and was steeling himself for having to repeat his usual denials. But the questioning on this day took a different approach. Mahler, joined only by the MPs, was not interested in his knowledge of other possible al-

Qaeda members but to understand Sikander's own makeup as an al-Qaeda terrorist.

"You say you've been trained to use Stinger missiles? Must've been quite an experience. Where? Where were you trained?"

"Captain, I was trained somewhere in Scotland but I don't know where."

"Scotland? Hm...and how'd you get to Scotland?" asked Mahler.

"I...I was transported in a PAF Hercules to Qatar and from there to...whatever location it was in a British Hercules."

"Describe the place," asked Mahler.

"It was hilly. There was plenty of water to the west where the sun would set. There were islands across the water and they had their own hills. It was a long time ago. I...I don't remember many of the details," replied Sikander.

"Any more?" asked Mahler.

"Any more..." repeated Sikander thoughtfully. "We...we were in some sort of camp with cabins and they took us in a helicopter, which I remember had two rotors."

"How many of you were there?"

Sikander paused to think while remembering how risky such a pause might be. "There were...there were perhaps fifteen to twenty of us...no, it *was* fifteen, because we were put into five groups of three."

"Remember any names?"

Sikander again thought carefully. "I...I remember some people...yes," he replied.

After about a couple of seconds of waiting, Mahler prodded, "Well?"

"There was Irfan who had a brother...uh...Usman," said Sikander, "and there was Abdul Rahman and Saleem, my wife's cousin and brother."

"Where did Irfan and Usman come from?" asked Mahler.

"I remember Khost is what they said, but Irfan was killed by the Russians at Arghandab after...after saving my life," replied Sikander, reflecting on the experiences of that day.

"Hmm...touching. And what about the other guy...Usman?"

"After Arghandab, we brought Usman, who was about twenty, back with us to our village in Nangarhar...near Jalalabad. He...he had nobody. No family. The rest had been killed by the Russians years earlier...we...my wife's family offered him a place to st—"

"Where's he now?"

"I don't know, but—" Sikander, fearing retribution for not knowing, quickly continued, "but on...on one of my earlier trips back to the village a few years ago, I was told he had moved back to Khost. I haven't seen him since the Russians left in 1989."

Mahler paused for a while and stood, hovering over Sikander's bound form. Speaking in a calm, almost soft voice, he began again. "Y'know, Mr. Khan, I've just two more years in this job. Two more years of active duty." He paused for a moment. "I used to have this friend...a really good buddy of mine. We were neighbors. He and I would spend weekends sometimes going hunting or simply working in each other's garage workshops. Or just chilling out at a local bar. Anthony—Tony we called him—Tony DeLea." Mahler shook his head and smiled wistfully. "Only...he's no longer a buddy of mine. You see, he...he was blown to bits in September. The guy barely had a chance to know what was coming. Take a look at this..."

Unexpectedly Mahler pulled out his wallet and from it a picture. He held onto it tightly from a corner as he brought it closer to Sikander's face.

"See him? He's the one on my right after we went duck hunting together in Virginia. You know, he has...he left a wonderful wife and a sweet little daughter. Darling girl. Only eleven when he was killed on 9/11. See him, Mr. Khan?"

Sikander nodded and rolled his eyes to look back at Mahler.

"Now how do you expect me to live with myself if I don't see to it that justice is done? How can I face that girl again? Hm?" By now Mahler had pulled back the picture and replaced it with his hot breath on Sikander's cheek.

Sikander was tempted to give Mahler a philosophical response but didn't dare risk it for another beating for "being cute" and therefore "requiring discipline."

"I...I suppose you have to go looking for the ones who did those things...Captain."

"Well, you got that right, Mr. Khan. You got that right. Yeah...I have to go looking." said Mahler, wearing a cynical smile, which changed abruptly into a sharply focused frown. "So, you going to help me with that...or are you going to be getting in my way by not telling me everything you know?" Mahler nearly shouted the last couple of words.

After all that questioning about his past, Sikander's heart sank as he was brought back full circle into the rut of answering who he knew and what plans he knew about. He hesitated. He didn't want the terrible beating again.

"Captain...I...I...just tell me what you need me to say. I don't know what to say. I don't...Oh! Nooo!" moaned Sikander as once again he was given the treatment as soon as the MPs saw Mahler's eyes lift up to meet theirs with a slight nod. This time he didn't even bother to utter the customary "Down." command. The MPs knew precisely what his eyes and slight nod had asked for. Immediately following the nod, Mahler stood upright and turned his back on the scene to let the MPs do what they did. It was his small way of disowning their action while being responsible for it.

When he could speak again, Sikander had to ask the question that had never left his mind since eternity began, back in the middle of November. "*Why?* Why are you doing this to me?"

The MPs were about to repeat the punishment when Mahler put his hand up to indicate for them to wait a moment so he could answer Sikander's question. "Mr. Khan," he replied in a tone suggesting that the question was curiously surprising. "I'm doing this for my country, for Tony...and all the other Tonys out there and their families. And I'm doing it because...I'm a Christian and I know what you ragheads with your murderous, pedophile, brutal, woman-hating Islam are trying to do to this world." His words were soft, penetrating Sikander's ear, and as he uttered the last of them, Mahler gave his signature nod to the MPs who repeated the punishment once more.

Mahler was frustrated with Sikander's unproductive interrogations. From one interrogation to the next, something about Sikander continued to rankle with him. By now Sikander should have cracked. From the circumstances of his capture, it was hard to see how Sikander could be anyone other than a pro-Taliban or al-Qaeda terrorist who was now putting on a show. Yet Sikander was giving him nothing. He even imagined that Sikander had been trained to behave in ways that would invite torture precisely to be able to validate the claim of having been tortured in any court of international law or public opinion. *If they want to play that game,* thought Mahler, *well, then…I guess I should oblige the bastards.*

Eventually, though, Captain James Mahler was forced to conclude that after such "harsh interrogations" and, given Sikander's background, he was not knowledgeable about anything related to al-Qaeda. Sikander's value as a source of intelligence looked dubious. Throughout the whole time, he had not provided anything more useful than the corroboration that he had met the person whom he had known as Junaid but who was in fact Atif Masood Qureishi of the Pakistani ISI.

Sikander regained consciousness to find himself back in his open cage and feeling like a sack of broken bones. He had no idea how long he had been there. Fareed was gazing at him. As soon as he saw Sikander stir, himself sore from similar treatment earlier, Fareed cursed their captors under his breath. "Haraamzadas!" Since this was clearly a derogatory comment—whose meaning even the guards by now understood—it was punishable by being IRF'd. Sikander didn't have the energy to agree with him. He had to use everything left within him to remain focused on hanging on to his own identity. It was slipping away from him.

On April 28th, some three hundred of the Camp X-ray detainees were told to pick up what few CIs they had in their possession and be ready to move into a new purpose built facility. This was to be their "permanent" place of incarceration, which had been constructed at Camp Delta. The remainder were moved the following day. When the detainees were taken round to the south side of the naval base, they were led in the usual goggles, earmuffs, and shackles packaging that denied them any sense of who or what was around them. They were transported in a windowless van and finally dropped off at the newly constructed buildings, being housed in enclosed cells. Camp Delta was

a much larger place, accommodating the swelling ranks of the detainees. The camp had a banner on its entry gate with the caption "Honor Bound to Defend Freedom."

The perimeter of Camp Delta was made from chain-link wire fencing, which had earned it the nickname of "The Wire." To Sikander, however, this was "Jahannam"—a name ingrained into the Muslim psyche as the unrelenting, eternal punishment earned after a misspent life—from which escape was impossible.

Chapter 17
Family

C AMP DELTA WAS MORE organized and less basic than Camp X-ray. Though they were still austere, the cells were covered and more comfortable. Exercise was possible in a better organized fashion, and after Sikander's troubled initial experiences, he had learned how to behave as a compliant and cooperative detainee, though he continued to maintain no knowledge of al-Qaeda individuals or plans. He had eventually admitted that his wife's brother and her cousin had been Taliban members but that they had returned to Pakistan and, as he described it, had been disillusioned by the movement even before leaving Afghanistan. At least he had convinced himself that such was probably the case from what little he had observed en route to Qunduz.

Sikander was now living in relative ease and could play games, interact, and eat with fellow detainees. He was in a sub-camp of Camp Delta, named Camp 1. Nearby, whenever he was out exercising, Sikander could see construction going on. *They plan to keep many more people here*, he noted sadly. Fareed had also been moved out of Camp X-Ray, but Sikander hadn't seen him in a while. It was during this time that he also received visits from the International Committee for the Red Cross and through them was finally able to get a letter out to his family.

He realized now that for as long as he had been suspected of being an al-Qaeda operative who had fought actively in Afghanistan, he

had been treated as highly uncooperative and had been therefore denied access to ICRC personnel.

Now at last, as it was approaching five months since he had been brought to Guantanamo, Sikander was able to write to his wife. He chose to write in English, thinking at least his captors would acknowledge his cooperation with their censorship objectives and if they were going to labor under the illusion of deriving intelligence value from it, then English would make it all the more easy for them to see that they would be wasting their time.

Dearest Rabia, Assalaamu 'alaykum!

Rabia, I miss you so much. I miss you and the children and Ammee-jan, Jamil, Sameena, and everyone else. I miss you all. You are receiving this letter to let you know that I am alive only by the grace of Allah. I am being held in an American camp at Guantanamo and the Americans have the mistaken belief that I have been a member of al-Qaeda or the Taliban. After I left Junaid and the family at Qunduz, my dearest, I was shot in the back but again thanks to the grace of Allah, I was not killed and was able to recover. However, I was captured and handed over to the Americans. I have tried to explain to them that I was strongly against al-Qaeda and the Taliban, but until now they appear convinced otherwise. Rabia, please find a way of getting me help with lawyers or do whatever else you can, my dearest, but please help!

Wasalaaam, your life companion and loving husband,

Sikander

✿

It was May and it was hot in Peshawar. After much flurry over obtaining a photograph four months earlier, no one seemed to know of any efforts that might have been made to locate Sikander or determine his condition, and Rabia and her family had become despondent. Deep down inside Sofie was always sure that her son was alive, and even though she missed him terribly, it was as if she was getting her reassurances directly from within her spirit, connected as she felt it was, to his.

Rabia, being more grounded in this sense, was up and down, sometimes believing with great conviction that Sikander was alive and at other times being consumed by gnawing doubts. Noor would often help, possessing the same demeanor as Sofie. In fact, Noor and Sofie

had become good friends and aside from the tragedy that had befallen her daughter, Noor had reason to feel good about Saleem's turning toward an "informed" understanding of Islam and his reconnection with Ejaz and Hinna. With a healthy steady income from Javelin, Saleem and Amina soon found a rental home that they could afford in another part of Hayatabad, while Abdul Majeed and Fatima opted for a move on the other side of the Industrial Estate closer to Jamrud. Abdul Rahman and Sabiha were also up in the Jamrud area where Abdul Rahman had opened a small convenience store in Jamrud market using money that Sofie had loaned him in Sikander's absence. He was assiduous in paying it back on, or ahead of schedule and was beginning to prosper.

There was an army camp near Jammu in Indian occupied Kashmir. On May 14, 2002, gunmen arrived there and opened fire, killing thirty-four people, mostly wives and children of Indian Army officers serving in Kashmir. Four days later, Pakistan's ambassador was expelled from India. Two day later still, clashes between India and Pakistan killed six Pakistani soldiers and an Indian soldier, and civilians from both sides. The Kashmiri separatist leader Abdul Ghani Lone was assassinated on the following day, and on the day after that, India's Prime Minister Vajpayee ordered his troops to prepare for war.

Meanwhile, Musharraf had let it be known that he would not rule out the use of a nuclear first strike against India, and from May 24th going on for a few days, Pakistan carried out a series of missile tests.

In parallel with the run-up to the tests, the situation deteriorated to the point of the US and other countries asking their non-essential citizens to leave India before the end of May. Even the Russians who tried to mediate couldn't make headway. In early June, an Indian Unmanned Aerial Vehicle was shot down inside Pakistan near Lahore. Finally, in mid-June, amid mounting international pressure, Musharraf made an important "gesture" speech to the effect that violent extremists and terrorists would not be supported from Pakistan in the future. India moved back its naval vessels from blockading Karachi and the tensions seemed to wind down.

During this period, it was impossible for Musharraf to focus on much else than his country's standoff with India. But by the middle of June, immediately following the gesture speech, things began to open up.

✤

It was a blistering June day. The doorbell rang at the Khan residence in Hayatabad. Sofie heard it and asked Jamil to answer, as he was the only male about the house at the time.

"Yes? What can I do for you?" asked Jamil upon opening the metal gate.

A man claiming to be from the International Committee of the Red Cross in Islamabad presented himself. "We have information about a Mr. Sikander Khan and would also like to leave behind an item of mail from him. May I enter?"

Jamil was stunned by the man's claims and could do little else but comply. As he let the man in, he called to his mother and Rabia.

"Ammee! Rabia bhabhi! Please come quickly! There's...there's news from Sikander bhai!"

Sofie was in her sewing room putting together some small items of clothing for Ayub and Qayyum. Rabia, trying both to read Dawn and watch CNN simultaneously, clung to the slim hope of learning any news that might have any bearing on her husband's probable fate. Noor was sitting with her daughter. When Rabia heard the words from Jamil, she too sprang to her feet, hurrying into the main guest lounge with Noor close behind, trying in vain to keep up with her daughter.

All but Rabia took their seats. Too anxious to sit, Rabia wanted to stand to hear what had happened to her husband. The man in a gray Western-style suit was clearly from the sub-continent. He looked every bit his forty-eight years, and as he too sat down, he retrieved a pair of black-rimmed reading glasses and a note of folded paper together with a sealed envelope from his inside jacket pocket.

"Assalaamu 'alaykum! I'm Yusuf Mirza." he began with a smile. "I represent the International Committee for the Red Cross and I wanted to let you know that the ICRC has located someone by the name of a Mr.....Sikander Khan who is presently a detainee at Guantanamo Bay in Cuba. He was—"

"Ya Allah! Tera shukr hai! Alhamdulillah! Oh, I *knew!*" cried Sofie. Rabia almost dropped onto the sofa with relief and whispered a prayer of thanks for this good news.

Yusuf turned in her direction "Might you be..." he looked down at his now unfolded notepaper and back up again, "um...Mrs. Rabia Khan?" asked the ICRC officer.

She nodded, unable to speak at that moment.

"Ah! Good, good. I have information that your husband has been held on suspicion of fighting for al-Qaeda...or the Taliban." His eyes darted up over the rims of his glasses toward Rabia. Rabia immediately put a hand to her lips, as did Noor and Sofie. They were pleased and apprehensive at the same time. Unable to suppress the joy of knowing he was alive, they were nonetheless concerned for what incarceration at Guantanamo might mean in the face of such baseless charges.

"He has written you a letter which I have here for you." Yusuf held it out to Rabia.

"How is he? When will he be released?" asked Sofie. "I've heard on CNN that they don't have to release anybody when they're in Guantanamo! Oh...Allah have mercy!" she exclaimed at the thought of permanent incarceration.

"Are you his mother?" asked Yusuf, while Sofie with her fingertips still over her lips nodded as she kept her gaze toward the floor in contemplation of the awful possibilities for the future.

"I...I do understand you must be going through a very difficult time...but I recommend you find a lawyer...one who is a US citizen and who can perhaps make a case for Sikander to be released. Please understand, however, that the ICRC doesn't intervene in this matter. We only make sure that prisoner treatment is consistent with standards for humane treatment of such prisoners, and although we have no power to force any change we do publicize any mistreatment we may come across," he explained.

"Oh...and uh, we're also able to make deliveries of mail and small packages between families and prisoners if you wish. I'd be happy to answer any questions you may have, if I'm able, but please understand I'm not the one who meets with Mr. Khan—that would be done by my colleagues from the USA."

Sofie was not quite sure what to make of the man, but the news about her son being alive was at the very least something she could now

hold on to. Noor found it difficult getting past her own harrowing memories of the departure from Qunduz in the afternoon of that fateful day in November. It was as if she was desperately trying to return to that moment and intervene upon history—intervene in whatever small way possible, as one might to divert the course of a train on a railroad track. But this train was long gone. She imagined one of them—herself, Junaid, Saleem, or Abdul Majeed—persuading Sikander not to go into the city. They could have said something to hold him back—anything...anything that might have resulted in a different unfolding of events. How far things had unraveled from just that small error! Here she was in Peshawar with her daughter and there Sikander was in Guantanamo, a staggering thirteen thousand kilometers away, suffering who knew what indignities. All for the price of a few mules and something to eat! She began weeping silently out of anyone's view.

Rabia accepted the letter from Yusuf frowning quizzically while turning to look away from Yusuf and wondering what she should do now.

"Mrs. Khan, I...I can stay if you wish to write a reply, or I can come back if you wish," said Yusuf. "Visits to Guantanamo by ICRC people in that part of the world normally go about every ninety days, so there isn't any rush upon...I mean...I meant...I'm sorry, I didn't want to suggest that...um...."

Yusuf thought about what he had just said. It had often seemed to him how oddly meaningless all norms of the passage of time became in these situations. There was "ordinary time" and there was "prison time." For most prisoners in detention, nothing ever seemed to happen quickly.

"Perhaps it's better if you come back," said Sofie, seeing that Rabia was unable to say very much. She wanted to read the letter in private.

"Ammee-jan," said Rabia, turning to Sofie then glancing at Noor. "I think I need to go into my room to read this letter alone and then we can talk about what we should do."

Rabia had few illusions about a quick solution. She had hoped before and seen the hopes fizzle out into nothing. She did not want to have those feelings again, not at the moment as she was preparing to learn of her husband's condition and thoughts. While everyone else

remained in the lounge, she went to her room and perched her shaking form on the edge of her bed, opening the letter slowly, not daring to expect anything. She put the envelope to her nose to see if she could catch any scent of him. Anything...anything that would connect her with him at that moment would have been welcome. She read the letter.

Once Rabia was finished with it, her hand fell on her lap still clutching the paper. She looked away and dropped her body back onto her bed with her face down on her arms and cried. *Why? Why? Why is this happening to us, to me, to Sikander, to all these nice people in my family?* she thought. *Oh...if he'd only married some respectable girl from a local family, he'd never have had this trouble! How could this be happening?*

After a short while, Rabia was able to regain her composure and came back down into the lounge. It was obvious to the others that she had been weeping, but at that moment, she had little concern for her appearance.

"Yusuf's gone. He promised to be back again tomorrow so that you can write back to Sikander, Rabia," said Sofie with a half-hearted attempt at a smile. "We thought it would be best that way. Look, Rabia," she offered, "until just now, we had no idea where Sikander was or if he was even...even alive! We have to take heart from the news of his well-being and whereabouts! We have to take this test from Allah and come through. He wants us to make an effort now. Let's not fail that test. Right?" Sofie tried to get Rabia to focus her sharp mind on some idea or approach that might make sense. Rabia listened politely but her mind was already ahead of Sofie.

"Jamil bhai?" she asked.

"Hmm?"

"Jamil bhai...you...remember we sent in that picture not long ago to President Musharraf's office?"

"Yes, of course I do. We gave it to Sameena to pass along through her father-in-law to the President," he said. "It didn't seem to do any—"

"Well, perhaps we couldn't expect much of anything..." interrupted Rabia. "because we couldn't point Musharraf in any particular direction. Do you think that things might be different if we

could convey to him the entire circumstances of what had happened but especially the knowledge of where Sikander is right now? He might feel he has something specific, might he not? Wouldn't that be a good reason to take things up with the Americans? I'm sure they would listen to him in such a matter, wouldn't they?" she asked, betraying a less than complete certainty.

"Hm…" replied Jamil. "I do see what you mean, Rabia bhabhi, but I…I don't have any idea of what to do specifically. We should probably chat with Sameena. Would you like to go there now?"

"No, I have to take care of the children just now, but could you call her perhaps and ask her to come over?"

Jamil called Sameena who was at once excited to learn of the news about Sikander. She agreed to come that evening to discuss what could be done.

❧

June in Guantanamo was hot and humid. Even as early as ten-thirty in the morning, the heat was oppressive as Sikander walked outside during an exercise break. These days, he was subjected to less of the ill treatment that he had received from Captain Mahler. The interrogations no longer continued in their earlier manner. The new people seemed to be more humane and though he didn't know it at the time, those he had met with most recently were from the FBI making their own efforts to connect the dots between people of interest for them all the way from Pakistan to al-Qaeda operatives potentially still "sleeping" in the United States. One thing Sikander *had* given them was the name of his mother's cousin's son, Salman Khan of Durham, North Carolina. That was basically the only person Sikander could say he knew in the USA. During their interactions with him, Sikander's FBI interrogators seemed genuinely impressed with Sikander's own sense of concern that no new terror attacks take place.

While the interrogators were somewhat more bearable now, the disciplinary punishments meted out for the slightest infractions were quite a different matter. And though Sikander had to learn the hard way from the early days that, for example, it was highly dangerous to damage or even write on a polystyrene cup, being US government property, it always pained him to learn of yet another detainee paying a high price for lessons of that nature. Certainly Sikander was well aware

of all the punishments handed out to other less cooperative inmates, or perhaps simply newcomers getting the full "harsh interrogation" treatment while they were still disoriented. One particularly galling example was when a detainee had lost his clothing privileges and was down to boxer shorts. In the air-conditioned space he was cold and wrapped himself in his prayer rug. The next day it was taken away from him for having been "misused."

But on this day, walking out in the hot sun, he could smell the Caribbean air in his lungs and life in this "Jahannam" felt bearable. On such occasions as this exercise walk, shackled though he was, Sikander often paused and thought back on his life and tried to gain a perspective on what was truly important to him. The captivity had a crystallizing effect on his understanding of where he stood in relation to his circumstances.

If he couldn't have material prosperity, he could value family relationships. If he couldn't have family relationships, then he could value personal liberty. If he couldn't have personal liberty, then perhaps he could value human dignity while in captivity. If not human dignity, then maybe he could be allowed to value self-respect, and if not even self-respect, then at the very least self-awareness. He was who he was and he wouldn't let go of that no matter how hard *they* might try to dispossess him of it. That was non-negotiable, prisoner or no prisoner. Alive or dead. On this day he was deep in such thoughts.

In every respect over the past six months he had lost all but the last of these things, and in realizing that their very absence from his life was the best evidence of their worth, Sikander smiled. It was a smile of resignation and yet also one of realization of a deep and cosmic truth about himself and how he would henceforth value things in his life. On top of this came the realization that his essential self amounted to no more and no less than the sum of his values and the behavior toward which they would guide him. And that would be as true if he never left Guantanamo, as it would be if he was ever to return to his beloved Rabia, their children, and the rest of the family in Peshawar.

Trudging along, taking the heat that perhaps others might not bear, taking the pain on his ankles and yet still wearing the hint of a grin, Sikander had what people called inner peace. With this, he was mentally in a place whose perspective also gave him new insights about his captors.

He looked at them as people trapped in their own circumstances. By now he had come across several guards who were genuinely nice people with integrity and honor. Some of them were forced to behave in ways which were clearly against *their* values and natural inclinations. They could be distinguished from the more sadistically zealous ones, and perhaps worse still those that had simply let themselves go. They were the ones behaving as if they were principled humane people, but who found the permissive environment too severe a temptation, succumbing in short order to a new behavioral norm of inflicting wanton hardship and cruelty upon the detainees. All this was, of course, in the face of much loftier ideals of humane treatment codified in numerous memoranda and operating manuals. But that didn't matter so long as there were no real sanctions on misbehavior.

Sikander felt a genuine sense of concern for such people, for in his mind, their circumstances formed a more cruel prison to them than anything they could fashion to confine him. At least he was aware of his situation. Unlike him, they had lost themselves and would probably spend a long time if not the rest of their lives dealing with this self-inflicted destruction of their own souls, ultimately searching for ways to repair themselves long after he would either be physically healed or dead. Consciously or unwittingly, they would be searching. He even found himself wishing them luck, not with disdain but with a genuine sense of concern. In his mind they would be striving for an insight already in his own possession.

The walk was finally called to a close and Sikander shuffled quickly back toward the building containing his cell. The rest of the morning was spent making progress with a copy of *Grapes of Wrath* that had been brought to him on the trolley cart that was euphemistically called the "library." The day so far had been thankfully free of interrogations and he had made it as far as lunchtime. He had slowly fallen into the habit of marking time in half-day increments and always indulged in a moment of self-congratulation for having survived or avoided interrogation for every such half-day that passed.

By lunch he was with some fellow inmates with whom he had built a reasonably good rapport because of his ability to speak at least Pashto, English, and Urdu. Sikander had by now also picked up a smattering of Arabic, causing him sometimes to ponder the irony that

his long-standing wish to learn the language so that he could better understand the Qur'an, was, to some degree at least, being fulfilled in this, of all places. Like the vast majority of Muslim children, being non-Arab, he had learned how to read the Qur'an in Arabic, but without understanding the language. It was akin to learning litanies in Latin with little grasp of what was being said.

While he was at lunch, a guard came into the noisy gray room and called out his name. "Khan? Sikander Khan?"

Sikander turned around and stood up lifting his arm. "Yes, sir!" he called out, instinctively understanding that delay was unwise, while his spirits sank over the probability that no self-congratulation was likely for the second half of the day.

"This way!" said the guard without any further clarification.

Sikander caught up with the guard who stepped back to make sure he followed Sikander. With the guard's direction, he moved along to his cell and as he was about to walk into it, the guard indicated to him to keep walking past it. His heart sank even further, quickening its pace.

Sikander had no idea where he was being taken and his concern mounted with each step. This was not normal. Anything not normal usually ended up being painful. Although on the verge of panicking, Sikander retained enough of his faculties to understand he was about to enter a place into which he hadn't been since moving to Camp Delta almost two months earlier. After a brief trek down a few more hallways, he was led into another building which certainly wasn't one that he could recall ever having been used for interrogation.

The soldier indicated to Sikander to hold out his arms and as he complied, trembling with dread, the soldier unlocked the wrist manacles. He did the same for the ankles and the belly chain. Sikander's hands and feet were free to move. "Take these and put them on," said another soldier handing him a short-sleeved shirt, a pair of pants, some regular socks, and a pair of simple slip-on canvas shoes.

"Why? Wha—" began Sikander when he was interrupted.

"Please put them on, Mr. Khan." The smooth, silky voice coming from somewhere behind him, belonged to a woman who stood to the left of the doorway, not initially noticed by Sikander when he'd

walked into the room, too concerned about what was happening to focus on anyone but the soldier who had escorted him there. "You're going home."

You're—going—home. The enormity of these three words subconsciously confounded Sikander so that he could not immediately absorb their meaning. As if he could see the features on a maddeningly familiar face, while remaining unable to assemble them into a memory of the person's name, Sikander grew frustrated for several seconds struggling with simple comprehension. Finally, his deeper psyche relented, granting permission to his conscious mind to embrace the sentence as a whole. Sikander began wondering if this was some new and elaborate trick to fool detainees into saying something that they might not have otherwise said. Again he looked around the room, landing his gaze back upon the evident owner of the voice.

She was slim, about a hundred and seventy centimeters tall, and beautiful. About thirty years old, guessed Sikander as his attention landed on her straw-colored hair tied in a ponytail with a crimson velvet bow. She carried herself with a certain poise, and in her prim light gray tailored jacket and skirt with crimson camisole and matching shoes, she would have been more easily imagined stepping out of a Wall Street doorway than handling a detainee release process. She smiled at Sikander again. It was at once innocent, acknowledging, and deferential.

For all the peace he had found in himself and for all the resilience he had accumulated in the face of the oppression he had experienced, at that moment, Sikander found this woman, this beautiful, attractive woman, more annoying than he had ever imagined anyone might cause him to feel. It wasn't her fault that she was being so incongruently pleasant. That was possibly just her nature. It was her comprehensive disconnect from the pain and suffering meted out to so many seemingly undeserving people in this place, this place of pain from which, it now appeared, he was simply to step away. Her smile underscored her detachment from the kind of lives being led just a few meters away, giving her cheerful mood a distinctly grotesque quality in Sikander's mind. For him, she was the consummate metaphor for the contemptibly unaware yet attractively innocent American public—a public that had a reputation for a sense of fairness and magnanimity but which was now surely too afraid or too oblivious of what was going on

in its name to intervene against the actions of its government. And here they all were, every one of them—a montage of American humanity, in the guise of this young woman!

The woman offered her right hand, introducing herself.

"I'm Dianne Drummond. I'm from the US State Department and I'm here with Department of Defense orders that authorize your release!"

Dianne's renewed smile simply added to Sikander's irritation with its orthodontically radiant quality. He was inwardly shocked at the anger coursing through him. It was as if the all the rage that had built up inside him, but suppressed for fear of certain violence at the merest hint of it, was now free to be spent with the abandon that one might have with the proceeds of a winning lottery ticket. He had to exercise more discipline upon himself at that moment than he had ever felt the need for in all his life. Lingering fear—fear of being IRF'd—was helping him succeed, though just barely.

Uttering no words, but with lips quivering angrily, Sikander, not moving his head, slowly lowered his gaze to the soft and slender outstretched hand, stared at the hand for a moment, and then lifted his eyes back again to meet hers. Dianne responded by lowering her hand while clearing her throat from the awkwardness of the moment and continued, directing Sikander to a small windowless office where he could change in private. A few moments later, wearing the clothing given to him, Sikander emerged from the room.

Sensing his anger and understanding only most of it, Dianne indicated to the soldiers to stand outside the entry doorway as she closed the door behind them. At the same time she offered Sikander a seat and now, with a slightly more serious look on her face, she pulled out some papers from her briefcase. Sikander took the moment to study her further.

Aside from being beautiful, Dianne—a native of Ridgefield, Connecticut—had all the regal confidence of a Katherine Hepburn. She knew who she was and would not be easily upset. She would approach things at face value, giving the benefit of the doubt. Sikander could also detect something of a steely persistence. *Whatever her job at the State Department, she can't possibly be doing it at this moment!* he thought. *They could surely not have actually hired people for such a role. No,*

she has to be a career diplomat, he imagined, as the job needed all the diplomacy that any human being might ever need to muster.

"Mr. Khan, President Musharraf has intervened on your behalf and confirmed your status as not being a combatant but the owner of a bona fide business in Peshawar with no record of plotting or acting against the US government. It hadn't been done earlier because no one knew you were here. According to this, you had been identified as missing in the region of Kunduz by an officer of the ISI, but no one knew your whereabouts."

Sikander was still speechless and he stared back at her as if she was from a different planet. Though she clearly belonged to the same species, indeed she was from Earth. Guantanamo was the different planet.

"What...what am I...where am I to go from here?" he asked, genuinely curious.

"After I complete the paperwork here, you'll be taken in a vehicle to the other side of the bay where we have a State Department jet waiting to take you to Peshawar," replied Dianne as she finally started having an effect in soothing Sikander's sensibilities and he began to regain control over his inner self.

"The...uh...thing with the handshake...I'm sorry," he said, and before Dianne could respond, he continued without making eye contact. "Muslim men aren't really supposed to touch a woman they aren't married to."

"Mr. Khan, I respect your beliefs, and I'm sorry I wasn't better informed when I offered you my hand."

"The men...the...the other prisoners...will I be able...is it possible for me...for me to say my salaams and farewells to them?"

"I'm afraid not, Mr. Khan," she replied with a note of sympathy. "As you've now been officially released outside their controlled space, you have no standing to be allowed in."

Sikander pondered the rejection and its ironically laughable rationale. He was not to be allowed into a place he had been forcibly kept for the past five months. Nonetheless, he felt that not saying salaams and farewells to fellow inmates was a small price to pay for gaining freedom, and he was sure that any of *them* would feel the same

way. Dianne left the room to go back outside and promised to be back in a short while.

By four o'clock that afternoon, some two and a half hours after Sikander had been pulled out of lunch, Dianne returned to the room and asked him to come with her and an MP. They stepped outside.

Outside. it was a palpably powerful concept from which Sikander's sense of manifest estrangement was foremost in his consciousness. Outside was a state of mind and not any place in particular. Whether indoors or outdoors, while incarcerated, Sikander had, since the previous November, been "inside."

Parked outside the building was a gleaming black Chevy Suburban. He was asked to sit in the middle row of the vehicle next to the MP while Dianne sat in front. He obliged and the vehicle was on its way to the airfield. Sikander was in a cold sweat. Right next to him sat an MP. Sikander wasn't wearing a prison jumpsuit uniform. Neither was he shackled nor manacled. It was simply hard for him not to feel uneasy about being where he was and he made sure that he kept enough distance on his part of the seat to avoid contact while the vehicle maneuvered round bends and corners.

Finally they arrived at the airfield, went through a clearance process, and drove up to a white Gulfstream IV with the United States of America Department of State seal proudly displayed near the entrance door that was itself open, revealing the unfolded entry steps to the aircraft. It was fueled, checked out, and ready for departure.

A soldier opened the Chevy's door for Dianne and another did the same for Sikander. At the aircraft, another official looking civilian joined the two of them and introduced himself as Lee Carver. He was, by what Sikander could tell, a more junior staff member than Dianne and probably worked in her department. Carver had the task of making sure the logistics from arranging the aircraft to organizing clothing to meals en route, and the meet-and-greet at the destination, were all in place and that nothing would go awry for the trip. He held out his hand for Sikander as Sikander shook it tentatively.

When all three of them, a flight attendant, and the flight crew were aboard the airplane, the door closed. As he heard it seal off all sound from the outside, for the first time since he had been captured Sikander was overwhelmed with the urge to believe that he was indeed

leaving that terrible place. Yet he was conditioned for surprises and not ready to give up on the possibility of a twist yet to be revealed. Was it real? Dared he to believe that finally he was done with his ordeal and that there might indeed be escape from "the Wire?" Sikander looked around inside the aircraft cabin. He sat facing forward. Opposite and facing him was Dianne, while Lee Carver took his seat across the aisle from him on the left side of the cabin. Behind them Sikander noted that there was also a long leather couch and was struck by the opulent wood and leather finishes all around him that stood in sharp contrast with the austerity of just a few hours earlier that same day—an austerity to which he had grown accustomed.

He heard the engines rumble to life and kept his gaze fixed on the door. *Any moment now!* he thought. His mind filled once again with expectation and dread, drilled deeply into him by the conditioning of his imprisonment and interrogations. Dashed hopes were, after all, a powerful force for breaking any spirit. *Any moment now!* The engines would wind down, the charade would be over, and he would see an IRF team bursting through the airplane door and start one more time that awful procedure of pinning him to the floor while an interrogator spouted out unanswerable questions all over again. Perhaps it was going to be Dianne, or maybe someone yet to come into the aircraft cabin. He also imagined being interrogated on the flight and that it might just circle over Guantanamo for an hour or two and then land again with some critical information extracted from him and him languishing in his cell once more. They might try any of these things, and it might be painful, but no, they weren't going to *surprise* him. He would be ready for them.

Dianne stared sympathetically at Sikander and could see he was in a dazed and disoriented state. He needed time to catch up with events and perhaps this journey would help him begin that process in the next several hours.

Unusually that day, a steady breeze poured in from the east, which meant that the airplane was soon taxiing out to runway 10 and lining up. The tower clearance was given and with the flaps set to the required twenty degrees for takeoff, the pilot throttled up the engines, released the brakes, and rolled down the runway, taking the aircraft aloft into the east. As it climbed out steeply, Sikander looked out of the

large elliptical window to his right. How a place of so much agony could look so beautiful was itself a marvel.

The Gulfstream passed over the narrow inlet that formed the opening of Guantanamo Bay. The narrowness of the inlet was what made it such an excellent naval harbor. Once they were over the other side, wooded hills sprawled below them and with the sun high in the sky, looking out of the window, Sikander could see that they were now flying just to the north of Camp Delta maintaining their heading. He looked down at the camp and was suddenly oppressed by a sense of guilt. He was leaving, but for several hundred people down below, already rendered obscure by simple altitude, the endless night of despair would continue.

Taking in the scale of Camp Delta from the air, Sikander wondered how many people might be incarcerated there. *How many people might indeed be dangerous terrorists posing a threat to the United States?* he wondered. There had to be many, surely? It might have been his way of easing his sense of guilt from being released, but he imagined at least *some* evil people who would do anything to kill. Kill Americans, kill Muslims, kill him. He harbored the hope that "legitimately" detained inmates who truly posed such threats were in the vast majority in Camp Delta, that his capture as an innocent, an aberrational error, was the rare exception. Still, evil or not, there was no justification in Sikander's mind for the extra-judicial treatment being meted out to inmates in the hell he was flying over now.

"Mr. Khan, may I call you Sikander?" said Dianne as Sikander nodded in acceptance. "Sikander, perhaps you'd like a drink of tea or coffee? Or perhaps you'd like to sleep?" Sikander looked back at her as he simply uttered the words, "Sleep...yes, sleep." Dianne passed a quick glance at Lee who asked the flight attendant to provide some blankets for Sikander.

The flight routed off the eastern seaboard of the United States before making a descent into Halifax Shearwater airport in Nova Scotia. Sikander awoke to prepare for the landing. He had been in a deep sleep and it was almost as if his body, having not permitted itself such a luxury with all the anxieties of his captivity, was now greedily demanding all it could get. It was payback time and Sikander's consciousness had to pay.

The aircraft stopped for about forty minutes to take on fuel. A fully fueled Gulfstream IV was good for about seven thousand kilometers including reserves. The Atlantic crossing required a full load. With the day drawing to a close, the beautiful sleek jet took off once again, its white paint reflecting the orange glow of the sunset. It was bound for a small civilian airport called Baginton, near Coventry, in England. On this occasion, everyone was asleep. With all the sleep he had taken during the previous day, Sikander awoke earlier than the other two as the thin line of orange and blue heralding a new day could be seen through the large windows of the aircraft. Like a broom sweeping across the horizon, the daylight began brushing away the night, and before long, as they made landfall over Stranraer, the June morning illuminated the land beneath them. Small emerald fields bounded by black dry stone walls and punctuated by towns, villages, and roads were visible through the broken cloud cover. By seven in the morning local time, the jet once more started its descent.

Dianne arose to wash and freshen up while the flight attendant brought Sikander coffee and bread rolls. Lee and Sikander followed suit. They didn't say much to each other as the aircraft came in over Coventry from the north, touched down, and taxied across to a point just outside a small hangar where it could be fueled once again. With clearances already established by the State Department, everyone stepped out of the plane as the refueling took place. They walked across to a comfortable waiting area where they sat for about an hour looking through magazines. This was the general aviation part of the airfield and the facilities were somewhat rudimentary, but clean.

With refueling complete and fresh clearances obtained, everyone loaded back on the aircraft to complete the last legs of the journey. They were to fly to Amman and from there to Peshawar. During the next leg of the flight, as everyone was now fully awake, Dianne chose a seat next to Sikander and from her briefcase pulled out several pieces of paper. She read one of them in depth and looked back at him.

"Sikander, we traced your capture back to a Dr. Atiq Mohammed in Kunduz, and he confirmed your story of how you'd been shot and how he had treated you for that wound. We also received direct representation from the office of President Musharraf that you

were not an al-Qaeda or Taliban fighter and that you had gone missing after delivering your family to Kunduz airport."

"All of this is what I had already told everyone who ever interrogated me," replied Sikander.

"Yes, you…um…didn't say that your were actually *with* the ISI. Why not?" she asked.

Sikander paused for a moment and thought about how to answer the question. He did not want to risk being returned to Guantanamo. Perhaps this had been important in Musharraf's persuasion of the US government to release him. Since it was not true and denial seemed awkward, he chose to be inscrutable. "I was only asked about being a Taliban or al-Qaeda and my interrogators didn't seem interested in much else," he replied.

"Sikander, it's okay. We're taking you home and you don't need to be concerned," said Dianne. "Look, I have this letter for you also. It's sealed with the US State Department seal on both sides, and it must remain that way. If you ever have the intention to come back to America, then you'll need to deliver it in this sealed envelope along with whatever paperwork you put together with your visa request."

Sikander took the envelope. He had no jacket so he folded it and put it in his hip pocket. He didn't want to do much talking at that moment. He wanted to think about what Dianne had just told him, but was prevented from doing so by the next thing to be revealed to him.

"Sikander, when we land, we'll give you a few other documents, but before you leave us, we'd like you to consider providing us with…intelligence."

"Intelligence? What kind of intelligence?"

"We know Peshawar is something of a hotbed for Taliban sentiments and al-Qaeda members and sympathizers. We've spent a lot of time, trouble, people's lives, and money securing Afghanistan against the Taliban and their support for al-Qaeda. We need people like you, in your position, to let us know if you hear anything, see people, say, with an Arab background, or foreigners maybe buying suspicious items or asking suspicious questions. You yourself have claimed to be against these organizations. Wouldn't this be a good way to prove it?" Dianne's brow wrinkled plaintively.

Sikander thought for a moment. *She's being clever.* He certainly had no love for al-Qaeda and yes, he had professed a concern for the misguidedness of the Taliban. If he reported on such things, he could manage it in his conscience and yet he detested the thought of helping the Americans after what had happened to him. On reflection, though, at that moment on the State Department's airplane, it didn't seem like a good place to be foreswearing the possibility of assisting them. It was tactically wise to accept the notion but in order to make the acceptance more credible, he decided to offer some resistance.

"Miss...Drummond?" he began.

"Mrs. Drummond. Actually, I'm widowed, but you can call me Dianne."

"Yes, uh, Dianne..." began Sikander, working through the ripple of sympathy passing through him from her surprising little revelation, "as you correctly noted, I had been captured and delivered to your people for being a non-Afghan. You didn't, however, mention that your people paid money for me. In not trying to escape from my initial captors, I had imagined that it would be better to be delivered to the Americans than Dostum or his cronies and at each step, I avoided thoughts of escape until I was with the American soldiers. I was taken against my will to Guantanamo where I was...tortured..." he paused to take a breath. It seemed the one word had consumed a lungful of air just to prepare and utter. "And beaten by...by your people. It's good that the error has been recognized after almost seven...seven months of hell. Why would I not wish simply to go back to my life and try to forget what you have done to me, try to rebuild my life but also rebuild my sense of who I was? Why?"

Dianne paused and gave him the most sympathetic smile she could. It was clearly a skill of hers. "Sikander, we're genuinely regretful of your treatment. We know your government is trying to help ours despite popular opposition, but you must know, more attacks on the United States will not go unanswered. Don't you want to help avoid such killing?"

Dianne had a compelling persona. Along with her undeniable physical appeal, her personality was by every measure also radiantly beautiful. But for the draining experience of Guantanamo, Sikander was a man in his prime and the effort to resist her and to resist staring at her or scanning her shapely form bordered on exhausting. Unable to meet

her alluring gaze for long, he cast his eyes down, thought for a moment about her proposal, and gave a grudging nod coupled with a lengthy sigh. "What would I have to do? How would I communicate with you?"

"You'll need to contact a person at this number in the American embassy and, Sikander, please don't share that number with anyone." Dianne handed him a business card which showed a business called Pakswitch Limited with a managing director by the name of Azam Shah.

"After the city code, when you dial the number using every second digit and then start back from the beginning with the digits you missed, you will be dialing a dedicated line at our main number in the embassy in Islamabad, but it will route in fact to Washington. Anyone dialing the number as it's written will get a busy signal."

Sikander was impressed by such a simple security tactic as he put the card in the breast pocket of his shirt.

"Dianne…I'll consider it," he said and then leaned back in his seat to take in the moment. A moment where his once most desired place to be, America, was asking him for his help after treating him so badly. Of course, he was under no illusions that he would somehow make the difference between success or failure in America's war. But he was amused at the notion.

The day moved along at a fast clip. The sun was already low in the sky by the time the flight soared over Istanbul and it was dark upon reaching Amman. As the aircraft landed, Sikander peered through the window of the jet to see that it was raining. He had never been to Amman. The jet parked near the VIP lounge—a facility in its own dedicated building—and armed with umbrellas taken from the Gulfstream's closet, the travelers disembarked to proceed quickly inside. The lounge was a study in opulence. Beautiful warm lights lay recessed into the periphery of Rojo Alicante marble floors, each of them bathing bush-hammered Jerusalem Cream limestone walls from below, teasing shadows out of the naturally undulating stone surface with their shallow lighting angle. Persian rugs lay over the rest of the floor surrounded in turn by cream leather sofas and a pampering level of service. Cold cuts, sandwiches, hot and cold drinks, and pastries were constantly being served on sparkling silver trays.

The State Department certainly has friends in Jordan! thought Sikander. He wasn't wrong. An hour after the landing, with night

drawing on, they departed once more and were airborne for the last leg to Peshawar.

About five hours later, the aircraft began its last descent and now for Sikander it felt very real that he was finally to be landing at the place at which he ought to have arrived almost seven months earlier. He wondered who would be there to meet him. Clearly no one was going to be terribly interested in advertising the American government's obvious error in taking him, he reasoned, so it would be a low-key affair.

It was just after four-thirty in the morning local time and the day was beginning to take shape. The door of the jet finally opened with the steps unfolding from it and after a moment to clean up, Sikander, Dianne, and Lee stepped out into the early morning Peshawar air.

The birdsong was raucous. A faint aroma of bougainvillea was apparent but initially mixed in with the kerosene smells of the Gulfstream's jet engines. The bougainvillea won out, becoming more distinct and stronger as they walked further away from the jet. It was a smell which Sikander hadn't experienced in a long time. Other aromas from morning street hawkers' preparations of chickpea curry, nihari, warm naan breads, and semolina halwa were all evident in abundance. They were welcoming him back and in their greeting came the flooding recall of the home town to which he had now returned. Long awaited and long overdue.

The three travelers had walked five meters from the aircraft when Sikander noticed about twenty meters in front of them were two white Caucasians who Sikander supposed were American embassy staffers. Behind them was a black Chevy Suburban with dark tinted windows. But standing about three meters to their left, to his great surprise, was Junaid, or Atif Qureishi, depending who had to be believed.

Sikander relented to the unwelcome recollection of an interrogation months earlier. He couldn't help seeing Junaid in a different way. He couldn't be sure who this man was, but as the doubts rolled around in his mind, he began to recall that at all times Junaid's behavior had been extremely honorable and the only source of his suspicion had been his tormentor in Guantanamo. He allowed himself a smile as he approached Junaid with his arms stretched out and they embraced. Had Junaid simply been a Pakistani ISI officer here to

welcome back a fellow officer from a long absence it would have been one thing. But these two men had last seen each other expecting to reunite in four hours—four hours that had transformed into practically seven months.

"Sikannnderrr! Mere bhai! I'm so sorry! So sorry for what you've been through, friend. It must have been an awful, terrible nightmare."

"Junaid...Junaid, I...I..." Sikander had no words for the moment. Unable to express himself, overcome by his rapidly changing situation, he was meeting his long-standing friend of sixteen years.

Dianne Drummond and Lee Carver stood beside each other looking on at the reunion. Eventually Sikander let go of his friend and turned around to face his two traveling companions. He approached Dianne, wiping his face into a more presentable condition. As he neared her, he could see the emotion of the moment had not been lost on her and much of the effort of applying makeup inside the airplane had gone to waste as she too dabbed her nose and eyes with a paper tissue she had hastily retrieved from her handbag. Sikander met her gaze understanding in that moment that regardless of any sentiments she might have professionally fabricated throughout their brief encounter, she herself *was* the real thing. His recent ordeal had done nothing to dampen his gentlemanly instincts as he felt compelled to offer an apology for his hitherto largely unrevealed rage during their initial encounter.

"Dianne I...I'm sorry."

"Sorry? Sikander, what...what for?" she sniffled in genuine surprise.

"I was cold and behaved badly toward you when we met, while all along you've tried to do your job—and I must tell you that you do it very well, Dianne. I shouldn't have taken out my anger toward your military colleagues on you. I was just...just filled with so much of it I couldn't...well, I don't know if I'll ever be able to forgive what they did but that's no excuse to...to—"

"Sikander, it's okay!" said Dianne in her velvet voice, quickly repairing her mildly dented composure. There are all kinds of people everywhere. Among Afghans, Pakistanis, Americans...and I...I just don't want you to believe that we're all the same. We're not. Go now, go." Dianne emitted a crying chuckle. Perhaps by peering into Sikander's

soul for a few hours, she had grown to see what a monumental mistake her government had made. Perhaps the thought of him returning to his family reminded her of the tragic loss of her own to a car accident. Who could say? But the thought did prompt a fresh urging from her.

Lowering her head slightly to her right and in command of her faculties once more, Dianne continued, "Go to your family, Sikander. I can see you love being back in your country and I only hope one day maybe you'll get to experience the country that *I* love...inshaAllah," she finished her remarks with the invocation of God's will over all things as she knew Muslims liked to do. With that, the simple utterance of the words "Allah Hafiz!" to Sikander was all that was needed and after an additional glance in the direction of Junaid, with Lee following her, she joined the other two men who had been silently waiting to get into the SUV. They were soon on their way driving back to Islamabad where she would be debriefed about, at the very least, having accomplished a mission of getting Sikander's acceptance of providing intelligence to them.

Once they were gone, Sikander walked back through the airport buildings with Junaid, who had all the clearances necessary, and got into Junaid's car. Sikander had no luggage and before long the car was on its way across Peshawar to the west side into Hayatabad where a large family gathering awaited him.

The air in Sikander's home had been electric ever since word had reached Sofie and Rabia from Sameena about President Musharraf's quiet intervention on Sikander's behalf. It had been a week now since they had heard that all necessary steps were being taken to secure Sikander's release. Elation turned into outright euphoria when it was learned that Sikander was due to arrive the following Saturday. Junaid had been informed to connect with his ISI colleagues to be sure he could be present to receive Sikander as soon as he disembarked in Peshawar.

Preparations at the house were akin to those in a society wedding, with beautifully colored lights strung over the exterior walls and the large black metal gates, giving the place a festive feel. The hanging patterns formed swags running two or three meters across and repeated all the way around the roofline of the house and on the front gates. Even though the morning light had firmly established its foothold on the emerging day, the hanging lights were stunning to look at.

Jamil and Kausar, of course, lived there together with Rabia and Sofie. Visiting them were Sameena and Wasim with their daughter Rukhsana; Ejaz and Hinna with Adam, Azhar, and Riffat; Saleem and Amina; Abdul Rahman and Sabiha with Sadiq and Sohail; Abdul Majeed and Fatima with young Latifa, the little traveler who had come back in the airlift from Qunduz. The three matriarchs—Sofie, Noor, and Razya—were also there. All the children were being supervised by poor Atiya, and amid all the welcoming mayhem in a household that had lived in quiet dread of the worst news for half a year, was Rabia who was at that time, of all times, in her bedroom and in a deeply pensive mood.

What would this experience have inflicted on my poor Sikander? she wondered. How might it have changed him? Would she be getting back the same man she had grown to love? The father of her children? As these questions floated around in her mind, another part of her came out in front and demanded to take control, insisting that none of these questions mattered. If they could just get back together and start rebuilding their lives, everything could be fixed. They would get through this. It had been a long hellish ordeal and now that they would be together again, they would get through it. Rabia was a determined woman. She would be his source of strength, and he hers, so that they could scale the rest of the mountain of their life and reach its summit together.

Rabia was also contemplating how she would have to adjust to his being around the house again. She was apprehensive about the scars he might be carrying back with him and what they might mean for their relationship. As she was deep in thought in her bedroom and the hubbub and commotion was going on downstairs, there was the honking of a car horn from outside the newly painted black metal gates followed by pandemonium as suddenly everyone personally felt the need to be the one to open the gates.

Rabia could tell from just the changes in the noise and the car horn that Sikander must have arrived. It was about the right time. The family had been told to expect Junaid and Sikander for breakfast and it was now seven in the morning. No one had gone back to sleep after the fajr prayer out of sheer excitement. All of the non-resident family members had arrived the day or evening before and had been put up for the night by Sofie. Blankets and other forms of bedding were all over the

house as people had slept on beds, sofas, and the floors, all in accordance with their relative standing in the family hierarchy.

The car drove through the gates and as the doors opened, Junaid got out, dashed around to the other side, and opened Sikander's door for him to step out. As soon as he did, everyone mobbed him. There were plenty of floral garlands, which were customary under such circumstances from all the women in the family to lay around Sikander's neck. Sofie approached him, put her arms around him, and simply wept for joy that her son was back home safe and sound. Noor was next and all the blame that rightly or wrongly she had piled upon herself for having left him behind in Qunduz now erupted and she apologized emotionally to Sikander.

"Sikander, Sikander, I'm so sorry you had to endure…Oh zwey! We had to leave you there. My poor boy!" she continued weeping.

Finally, Rabia could be seen descending the steps and one by one, as the rest of the family noted her coming, they quieted down. Silence crept upon the room as voices died down looking on as Sikander and Rabia laid eyes on each other. From behind Rabia came running nine-year-old Ayub, who with a simple joyful shriek of "Abba-jee!" ran up to his long missing father and wrapped his arms around Sikander's legs hugging him that way, almost tackling poor Sikander. As Ayub tightened his grip, Sikander winced from some of the residual scars due to repeated injuries to his knees during the IRF interventions back in the Wire. Trailing Ayub by only a few seconds came Qayyum.

"Ayub! Ayub. Oh! And Qayyum!" cried out Sikander as he tried to pick both of them up. "Look at you! You've grown so much!" His health was not what it should have been at that time and he had difficulty with the task. Rabia was taken aback by Sikander's loss of weight. He had become a pale reflection of the man she had last seen leaving for Afghanistan in October.

While Sikander struggled with his two sons in his hands, he looked back at their mother. Rabia had a shy, knowing smile on her face. With all those present it would have seemed in bad form for her to leap upon her husband and profess her sorrow at his absence, her immense relief at his return, and her boundless love throughout. In such company, everything would have to be accomplished with looks given and taken between each of them. But living in the society they had for

all their lives, even elaborate communications could take place with just the eyes.

His spoke of the torment, the terrible times anticipating the pain and suffering, the despair, and the moments of peace. They also spoke of the love that had survived without injury out of the expectation of just such a moment sometime or other in his future. He had not known when or where, but he had known it would happen.

Hers spoke of the added anguish of not knowing his whereabouts and whether he'd been alive or dead, of contemplating widowhood, having witnessed that fate befall and dominate the experience of her mother over the last decade and a half and, more recently, her mother-in-law. They spoke of her love for him and of the anticipation of learning that he was alive and then hoping upon hope for some way, any way, of getting him back.

The day was a joyous one and Sikander enjoyed the company of his relatives and his friends, but all the while, he was unable to shake out of his mind the torment that his fellow inmates would be feeling from their strained existence in Camp Delta and from not knowing if, or when, a release might be in the offing. As the festivities carried on, he would periodically take on a vacant stare as he imagined himself hearing screams in the distance that would get louder in his mind like a ringing bell getting closer and closer until it drowned out just about everything within his world of the here and now. Whenever that happened, he could be seen briefly touching his temple before reconnecting with the events going on around him.

Sofie and Rabia had, at different times, each noticed these moments. On one occasion it was at the same time and they instinctively exchanged glances, understanding that much work lay in front of them if, beyond recovering him physically, they were to succeed in getting Sikander back mentally.

When nightfall came he went to bed with Rabia and although there was much that he wanted to say and do, he was too tired to remain awake after his long flight and the intense day that had followed it, and with such a comfortable bed, he drifted off to a much-needed sleep.

About an hour and a half before fajr, Rabia was awakened by the muffled sounds of Sikander's voice. He was moaning and crying out "Uuuuhh! No! No!"

The moaning grew more forceful until it broke through from somewhere in the underground of his consciousness into a full-blown scream. By now, Ayub and Qayyum arose in the room next to theirs and were crying from fear of the monstrous noises that they had just heard. Being together, their fears were feeding off each other and no one was there to comfort them. Again he screamed. "No! NooOHHH! Aaaaaghhhh!"

"Sikander! Sikander! Wake up! Wake up, Sikander!" pleaded Rabia as she shook him gently at first but more vigorously to try to pull him out of his nightmare.

Sikander awoke, breathing heavily as if he'd just been sprinting. "Uuh! Uuh! Oh..." he gasped as he became aware of his bedroom and his wife and that what he had been experiencing was just a nightmare. While he had left Camp X-ray and Camp Delta, they were unwilling to leave him quite yet. But with all that was possible with the cruelly creative capacity of the subconscious mind, the experiences of Guantanamo and the ride to Sheberghan haunted him in hideously embellished caricature. He gripped Rabia tightly. He hugged her close to reassure himself that he would do anything to avoid losing what he now had back in his possession.

"Rabia...Rabia. Sorry," he offered in a loud whisper.

She didn't need it and stroked the wavy mane of hair that he had allowed to grow before being whisked away from Guantanamo. Rabia's soothing reassurances did nothing to prevent Sikander from recognizing what had been done. They both arose and entered the adjacent bedroom to comfort their two children. A single nightlight was plugged into the wall outlet next to their bed and against the remaining darkness the mutually hugging family was silhouetted.

From the south end of the master suite over the front of the house looking across to the north wing of the courtyard, Sofie, having hardly slept that night, could see into the children's' bedroom and the silhouetted family in a huddle. She was looking at one branch of the generation to follow her and could see the love that was present in that room. It made her feel happy for the future yet sad that she was to

continue this part of the family's journey and her own path to her twilight years without her late husband. Her son was back, though, and right now that was all that mattered.

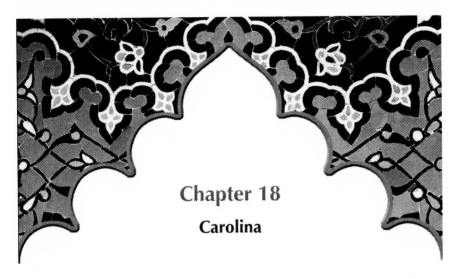

Chapter 18
Carolina

SIKANDER HAD BEEN HOME for almost six months since his release. Although the nightmares continued, he consulted a doctor who prescribed some behavioral therapy and antidepressants. With the start of 2003, he was already down to fewer episodes, despite the occasional compulsion to get away from uniformed men like soldiers and police.

On the positive side, such as there was, Sikander had done a lot of introspection during his now seemingly short captivity and found that it had done a remarkable job of ordering the priorities in his life. While, perhaps as a product of his father's genes, he had enjoyed all aspects of conducting a business, he would never put that above looking after his family and his inner sense of groundedness. His adversity had acted as a mirror to his own soul and had taught him a great deal about who he was. That was valuable and never to be forgotten.

Rabia was expecting their third child and despite being a Pakistani male in Peshawar, Sikander did many unexpected things to help Rabia rest and relax while he ran simple errands, like taking the children to school and shopping for essentials.

As much as Sikander had endured his own transformations during his experiences in Guantanamo, his in-laws from Afghanistan had gone through theirs. No longer were they the village dwellers of Laghar Juy. They lived in or near some of the priciest suburbs of

Peshawar. This sometimes made for light comedy at their expense, as entrenched villager habits appeared amusingly incongruent within their modern living circumstances. Noor and Razya had always cooked in a crouching position seated on their low patthras. Those were now discarded in favor of stand-up stoves and sinks and the like in the kitchen. Whenever Sarwat was absent or sick, they enjoyed stepping in to fill the void, but still had to get used to standing upright while cooking; the novelty did have a certain appeal to them. Rabia had had her own issues with such changes, but the older women just took longer to get used to doing things this way. Going to the bathroom was another such experience in its contrasts with the village style of carrying out the same task.

Not long after Sikander's return he and Rabia had decided that apart from a brief visit to the office with Jamil to meet everyone there, he wouldn't return to work until he truly felt well enough to make a difference. Although the business had not done much growing, Jamil had run it competently and had, if anything, become more capable for it. He was a more cautious young man than Sikander, and that had been just fine in Sikander's absence. But after two months, the combination of cabin fever, his wife's and mother's tendencies to want to overfeed him to help him regain his weight, and his general interest in managing the business left him anxiously waiting at home for Jamil's regular evening reports. Sikander wanted to be there in the thick of things. Besides, Ayub, who was almost ten, and Qayyum, seven, were quite a handful around the house and it was problematic to try to make business phone calls with the noise of their playing, arguing, and fighting going on in the background.

Sikander, meanwhile, having brushed with Americans in one manner while in captivity and, to a small degree, in a more positive way on his journey back from Cuba, had resumed his interest in things American. The family was invited to many friends' homes—including Hamid's. Hamid was a squadron leader now on his way to becoming a wing commander and enjoying it thoroughly. Whenever they visited, Sikander would always be called upon to recount his story about how he had been shot, captured, sold, and taken to Guantanamo, though he was reticent to talk about his actual experiences there. He felt it might be dangerous and it was in any case embarrassing to talk of such things as torture in polite company.

The news from overseas was not good. George W. Bush was now seemingly committed to a campaign to "finish the job" begun by his father more than a decade earlier. The neo-conservatives in his team who were in high places, particularly in the Department of Defense, were all itching for a reason to invade Iraq on the strength of "proof" of that country's program for development and production of weapons of mass destruction. This mission to "do something about Iraq" was pitched and packaged for public consumption inside visions of a free democratic Iraq whose narrative might have been lifted from newsreels of the liberation of France in World War II.

Sikander was taken by the way in which narratives could be subtly directed by the choices of words. Having seen the effects of a daisy cutter bomb, he was struck by the sheer "approachability" of its name. It surely had to represent something on "our" side. It didn't seem to matter that everything within half a kilometer in all directions would be obliterated. The obliterated things would be bad things, and mass destruction wasn't the "intent," so this could never be called a weapon of mass destruction. He wondered if it had been in the Iraqi arsenal how it might have been labeled by the American political system and media.

Sikander understood how American public opinion could also buy into this "legitimacy of honorable intent." He could recall what he thought was probably its defining moment when more than a decade earlier, video pictures of precision laser-weapons delivered to a designated room in a targeted building were shown by American generals during the first Gulf War. Americans could feel at ease with the knowledge that even if civilians were going to get killed by their tax dollars, it would all be with the spirit of minimizing unintended deaths and for the greater good. He resented how the Bush presidency had seemingly chosen to ride a wave of fear within the populace, which further seemed to be granting free rein to the administration to erode liberties while making whatever belligerent moves were necessary to eradicate choice enemies, especially those lacking a nuclear threat. To Sikander, Saddam Hussein had come squarely into the line of fire for Bush's agenda. He had become a target of political opportunity.

Sikander avidly consumed news and editorial opinion from several sources, including those found on the Internet. His firsthand experiences in Guantanamo permitted nothing less, and he began in his own mind to believe that it was only with an incurious, sedated popular

media that the Bush Administration could set about making a clear and present threat out of Iraq and Saddam Hussein. He was struck by the ease with which it seemed to be possible in a modern democracy.

There were the unimaginative attempts to link al-Qaeda with Saddam's regime. There was also the use of public threat levels, which, as far as Sikander could see, accomplished virtually no changes in public behavior but whatever changes in levels of anxiety were desired. They became an effective way to deliver the message to the jittery American public that something or other was a threat to world peace and stability. For now, Saddam was a useful personification of that "other." He had, in his previous eviction of weapons inspectors, heightened the threat by further failing to provide evidence of the absence or dismantling of weapons of mass destruction.

A British government claim that Saddam Hussein already possessed the capability to launch such a weapon within forty-five minutes of forming the intent simply fanned the flames. But Sikander was clear that there was no denying that the Bush agenda was greatly assisted by the cruel, heartless, and brutal regime of Saddam. He was by all accounts a terrible individual who needed to be brought to justice. In the first months of 2003, the preparation of the country to go to war in Iraq, which in Donald Rumsfeld's terms would indeed be unlike Afghanistan in being "target rich," was well under way. General Tommy Franks had put together his plans, and after much debate with Rumsfeld about the levels of force necessary to accomplish the mission, Franks had now about as lightweight a force as he could safely take into Iraq.

Bush is simply picking a target that has plausible culpability. An imbecile can understand that the rabidly secularist Saddam could never be an ally of the Salafist, jihadist Osama Bin Laden, thought Sikander.

During the run up to the war, Sikander and Jamil began discussing the Bush agenda for Iraq one evening. Jamil was half inclined to agree with Bush's policy on the matter of regime change even though he, too, detested the President.

"Saddam is, after all, the cause of the previous Gulf War and in any case a pretty unsavory character, so why do we care about a rationale for the impending invasion?" he argued.

"Yes, Jamil, but it isn't as simple as going in and taking out Saddam, is it? I mean this...this WMD thing is just today's rationale. It

can be adjusted as the need arises and the mainstream media can certainly be called upon to do its patriotic duty to convince the American public of whatever message the administration needs to convey," Sikander noted cynically. "Besides, Bush needs this to get more public support as his re-election campaign is about to get going," he added. "The problem in all of this will be that the people who will be killed or injured won't have a grasp of the reason why the American taxpayer would be seeking their deaths. Do you suppose that a family failing to escape a stray bomb would care that the bomb was being dropped in pursuit of the same family's need for freedom and democracy? Do you suppose they would care that they weren't the intended victims?" asked Sikander, feeling a genuine sense of disgust at what was about to be unleashed, as his emotional momentum was getting the better of him. "And as for terrorism, how many new terrorists do you suppose are going to be spawned by the unintended death of a father, mother, brother, or sister? Do you suppose the surviving family members will see these events as accidents and applaud the honorability of America's motivation?"

Jamil rarely saw this side of Sikander and began feeling a little intimidated at the anger simmering inside his brother. He did his best to unwind the topic and disengage.

"Look, Sikander bhai, I agree with your view about a war in Iraq. I was just making the comment about Saddam. Surely you agree that a regime change would be a good thing?"

Sikander thought for a moment. "I do agree, Jamil, but do you have any idea of how many regimes have been changed without a war since World War II? Don't you suppose that the Americans could organize covert operations to infiltrate Saddam's government or military and assassinate him? I do understand that they are probably more concerned with the aftermath of a removal of Saddam, and maybe just killing him and departing isn't such a good idea, but do you see any effort going into that even now? Surely the same power-vacuum issue will be there whichever way Saddam is removed?"

With that, Jamil gave in and changed the subject before he was "rescued" by Kausar, who asked if he wanted to join her for an evening stroll as the weather was cool and pleasant. American foreign policy was clearly a touchy subject for Sikander.

It was early in the morning on the 18th of March in Peshawar when President Bush issued his ultimatum speech to Saddam and his two sons to leave Iraq within forty-eight hours. As the day drew on, the news spread throughout Pakistan that Bush was actually going to do it. Most people in Pakistan felt that he was capitalizing on the "teach-em-a-lesson" mentality that was rampant in the wake of 9/11.

Sikander got a call at the office—a call that was quite unexpected.

"Assalaamu 'alaykum, Sikander! It's Junaid."

Sikander perked at the sound of Junaid's voice after so long. "Wa 'alaykum as salaam, Junaid! Nice to hear from you again."

"We just got word that Bush has made the anticipated ultimatum to Saddam. It's virtually guaranteed that there'll be a war within a couple of days."

Although it was not good news from his friend, Sikander truly appreciated the conversation. "I already heard. The office is buzzing with the news. It certainly looks like war, doesn't it? What do you think will happen?"

"Let's talk about it tonight. Will it be okay if I come over this evening?" asked Junaid.

Sikander accepted and called home to Rabia to let her know and tell Kausar and Sofie. Rabia was three months pregnant and it wasn't the best time to be asking her to prepare for surprise guests.

Junaid came to visit that evening. The news channel anchors had already wheeled in their retired generals to comment on the rich array of technology gearing up for the clinically precise delivery of death. Weapons systems were being described in intimate detail as the world watched, riveted to their TV screens. Intriguingly to Sikander, the descriptions only reached the point of describing the "delivery" of the weapon and rarely into how the killing was accomplished after the delivery.

It had been a while since Junaid had been in touch with Sikander. After having dropped his friend at home on the day of his momentous return from Guantanamo, Junaid had visited only a few times. That night after dinner, he, Jamil, and Sikander sat in front of the TV to watch CNN and the BBC, looking to see if anyone could reveal

anything truly new. They had seen President Bush deliver his speech at least three times and decided that for that night, at least, there would not be much, if any, new information. Jamil excused himself and went to bed.

"Bush is the most dangerous person on earth right now," Junaid remarked.

"Hmm..." responded Sikander. "Do *you* think that Saddam should stay?"

Junaid shook his head. "No, I don't think he should stay, but I don't think a US invasion and the death and destruction that it will cause is the way to get him to leave. Besides, the Americans aren't so naïve as to publicize the real agenda in their foreign policies. We wouldn't. Why should we expect that they would? Look at what's going on with the media there."

Sikander generally agreed with Junaid's assessment on the invasion but was curious to learn more about Junaid's comment regarding the media. "What do you mean?" he asked.

"Sikander, the media has been buying its way into politics for a long time now. They've needed favors. Take, for example, what's happening to their local TV and newspaper market regulations. Hearings conveniently opened on the question of consolidating local media ownership, which personally, I would have argued would narrow local markets' access to diversity of opinion."

"Well, we have pretty narrow diversity here in Pakistan, Junaid."

"Yes, and we could do better and probably will. But that's the country that holds itself up as the beacon of democracy—a...a model for the world to follow. Yet, here we have an administration about to enter a war that it needs to sell to the public. They open these hearings and now media owners will toe the line and maybe get the reward in a few months. Oh...and it can't hurt to have the son of the Secretary of State be in charge of the Federal Communications Commission. The media companies have made all the right financial contributions to the politicians to buy those favors. Why would they now be critical of the providers of those same favors?" he asked cynically. "No, they understand what kind of food the American public needs to be consuming right now and they're feeding it to them. And when the

fighting starts it'll be pure amphitheater. What about you, Sikander? You of all people should understand how deceptive they can be."

"Speaking of that...Junaid, I know you're with the ISI, but can't you trust me—your old friend—enough to tell me your real name?"

"We...we *weren't* actually speaking of that, Sikander," responded Junaid pointedly.

"Hmm," uttered Sikander, contemplating Junaid's elusiveness.

Junaid looked at him and thought about the pain and suffering that Sikander had been through a little more than a year earlier, much of it because he had helped Junaid and his son make it out of Afghanistan. Junaid was approaching LPR or "leave pending retirement" now and he couldn't see much harm in letting Sikander know his name. He would think about it.

"You know, you might not believe it, Junaid, or should I say...Atif? But the Americans seem to know quite a lot about you. Or they believe they do."

Junaid's eyes met Sikander's with a pokerfaced stare.

"Relax, Junaid!" Dismissing the seriousness of his own comment, Sikander continued, "What? Do you think I'll be revealing that without your permission? What do you take me for? The Americans told me your real name is Atif Masood Qureishi, according to the interrogators I was put in front of."

"Well..." said Junaid, pausing to think about what he had just learned. He held his breath for a second, then let out a sigh. "My name isn't Junaid. That much you know, Sikander. It is indeed Atif Masood Qureishi and I'm...I'm now a brigadier ranked ISI officer."

"I see. Tell me, Junai—uh...Atif?—tell me, is it true that you're connected with al-Qaeda in some way?" Sikander was too far into this whole thing to back out now.

"No! At least not now," he confided as he looked up at Sikander. "It was 1991, when Iraq overran Kuwait. We and the CIA had helped Bin Laden to come into Afghanistan when the Russians had been there. Osama didn't do much by way of fighting," Atif shrugged, "but he did provide a convenient source of untainted non-US money in the wake of the whole Iran-Contra controversy, and I'd say ultimately he trained maybe upwards of thirty thousand non-Afghans to fight. After

Saddam's Kuwaiti adventure, Bin Laden pitched to the Saudis to let him lead the effort to protect Saudi Arabia's own oil fields against Saddam and they refused. They wanted the Americans to do it for them as did the Americans. He warned them that the Americans might never leave, but certainly they wouldn't leave in years, and he went away angered when they rebuffed him. I *had* been a member of Maktab-ul-Khidmat, the predecessor organization to al-Qaeda, but no…I'm not a member of al-Qaeda today, Sikander. Frankly, I'm not surprised that the CIA believe that I am. As for me, I already had that conversation with my chain of command, oh…maybe eleven years ago, and they understand what the facts are. If your captors put this theory to you, I'd say they were baiting you or their intel is worse than I thought."

Sikander pondered Atif's comments and wondered what, if anything, would have been different about his experiences in Guantanamo if he had known this information.

"Well, Atif…I certainly hope you know that you can trust me to keep this in full and strict confidence?" Sikander looked for acknowledgment. He had pushed on this occasion and hoped he would at least get some credible answers. He certainly hadn't wanted to stake their friendship on the issue.

Atif nodded and smiled resignedly. His alter ego was established almost twenty years earlier while the Russians were gaining the upper hand in Afghanistan and he couldn't see how any damage could be done now. It hadn't been mission critical to keep the use of "Junaid" as his name, but he had kept it with those who had grown accustomed to using it.

The two of them continued a while longer, sipping tea and discussing the world after Saddam and the world after Bush, but in particular, the world of Pakistan.

The war began on schedule. Forty-eight hours after the ultimatum had been given, a cruise missile had been targeted to hit a house where Saddam was reportedly spending the night. What followed was what the Pentagon and the media pushed as the campaign of "shock and awe," which was an aerial bombardment of the usual command and control positions with a focus on preventing the Iraqis from mounting a coordinated defense against both airborne and ground attacks. Ground forces would soon be advancing on the country and air superiority was a military requirement if those troops were to remain

well protected. The media mostly played along by allowing itself to be safely embedded within the US troop units. Its effect was to cause bonding with the troops and to report empathetically with them for the most part. Above all else, the administration had no desire to allow televising the return of body bags with grieving relatives. They were sensitive to such imagery undermining the administration's intent to wage war in its own chosen manner and timeframe instead of being driven by public opinion.

Sikander could only watch and in his own way, as a former mujahid, admire the speed with which General Franks' battle plan largely unfolded into a ground troop advance into Baghdad. From then the US Administration began its long and slow process of getting in and out of a quagmire with its mix of achievements and calamitous blunders. Among the largest of the blunders was the absence of a meaningful plan for handling a large-scale evaporation of the Iraqi military, which morphed into a number of sizable and deadly guerilla forces, giving the Americans and their coalition partners a continuing irritant for years to come.

Ayesha was born in September and her arrival made Sikander feel as if his family was now complete. Saleem had delivered Noor to the family home to be with her daughter for the month or so before the birth and to remain with her for at least seven weeks afterward. That was customary and no one in Sikander's family had the slightest issue with it. One effect of Ayesha's birth was that Sikander would find any excuse to come home early. Ayub, now almost eleven, and seven-year-old Qayyum were over the moon at having a new little sister. Noor was likewise delighted at this near perfect replica of her own family.

Perhaps it was simply the passage of time or perhaps it was the arrival of Ayesha. Either way, for Sikander it had been a long time since he felt any of his once frequent anxiety attacks or experienced his awful nightmares, and while he could not eliminate the physical and mental scars altogether, he had virtually reconstituted himself physically, though bearing the obvious effects of being over thirty. Importantly, his inclination to a short temper on discussing what he continued to believe was a badly thought through plan to attack Iraq began to simmer down. Aside from being an adorable baby girl, Ayesha was, with her arrival, therapeutic for Sikander.

During the Christmas break of 2003, Salman Khan was visiting Pakistan from his home in America. Salman's own business was doing extremely well with his image stabilization software. Among other uses was one for remotely piloted or unmanned aerial vehicles. These UAVs had grown in popularity among the Americans as a tool for carrying out reconnaissance and eventually, with modified wings and increased structural strength, they were able to launch laser-guided Hellfire missiles typically against ground targets. The Predator drone represented the most advanced form of this type of platform. In fact, Salman's software solution was used extensively throughout several civilian and military applications.

While he was in Peshawar, he invited Sikander and his extended family over to a dinner party at his aunt's place.

"Salman, it has to be close to—what?—four years ago when we met?" Sikander asked.

"Has it really been that long, Sikander bhai?" responded Salman with a "time-certainly-does-fly" shake of his head.

Salman had become curious and interested to meet Sikander since his release. He often got into discussions, all cordial of course, with his American friends and colleagues about the nature of the war with Iraq and where America was headed. He looked forward to hearing Sikander's perspective.

"What news from America?" asked Sikander, quickly qualifying his broad question with, "The war, I mean...what do they think of what's happening with the war?"

"It's a good question, Sikander," said Salman. "Muslims in America are generally okay, though there was a time right after September 11th when it was pretty scary with the occasional brick through a masjid window. Now things have settled down on that front, I think we have a country that's pretty split about the Iraq war. Things haven't been going well and Iraq looks as if it's heading for a mess... or it's already there. They were all for the Afghanistan war, but with Iraq it's a lot more muddled. They haven't found WMDs, and now they're all backpedaling into claims about the evil dictator and the need to remove him and Iraq's need for freedom. Saddam was caught two weeks ago, so I suppose any discussion about WMDs can be swept under the rug, God

bless them," he said chuckling cynically while shaking his head with pity.

"Yes...God bless them indeed, Salman." Sikander thought about God blessing America. "Tell me, Salman—do you think the God that created the cosmos and managed all of existence for maybe tens of billions of years has formed a preference for blessing America, which has existed for a little more than two hundred of those years? And what would that mean anyway? Would that mean that if he even cared about nations instead of human beings, he would pick America over others? And if so, why would he not want to bless Iraq, Afghanistan, or Pakistan at least as much as America? Maybe more if the need is greater. Is the American concept of God that the people of these countries aren't worth as much to him as Americans are?"

Salman had no idea what to do with such a barrage of questions, so he tried a different kind of response. "Sikander, I recall when we met last, we talked about your possibly coming to America? It seemed to me then that you had a lot of love for the country and maybe even a desire to live there. Your...questions suggest a seeming dislike of it and I wonder if that's the case. Of course, I, uh, know about Guantanamo, though I...I can't say that I could even begin to understand *that* experience, but it wouldn't be hard to see how it might have, well, changed your perspective?" proposed Salman.

Sikander pondered Salman's response. "Salman bhai," he said with a hint of a smile, "I...think I still like America and what it stands for and the kind of place it seems to be..." Choosing his words carefully, he tucked his lower lip under his upper teeth while hiding them with his upper lip. "I believe the American people are letting themselves be led down the wrong path right now. But you know there is one thing, Salman. I have to say that I believe among all countries in the world, America is probably still the most capable of identifying and correcting its mistakes most quickly. That's a huge asset that's worth hanging onto."

Salman nodded in agreement and reflected on the hope that things might change for the better.

"My question about God blessing America was more...academic than judgmental," clarified Sikander, though hardly convincingly.

"Hmm...Sikander bhai?" asked Salman, pondering Sikander's last comment. "How did it feel to...to—"

"To be in Guantanamo?" Sikander could see Salman struggling with the obvious question. Salman chose not to refute Sikander's guess. "You know, generally I don't get into that discussion. It's genuinely painful and I uh...I used to get nightmares about those days so often that it required psychiatric therapy with drugs to get on top of that. Alhamdulillah I'm not using anything like that now, but to...to answer your question, I can easily tell you how utterly ghastly and how unlike the nature of your own descriptions of your adopted country that experience was."

Sikander proceeded to describe not only his own ordeal but also the things about which he had high confidence were going on with other detainees. There were reports of much worse treatment than he had experienced, and what he felt most strongly about was the absence of any kind of legal framework to govern the manner in which detainees were being treated. Regardless of the detail to which Sikander felt he could go, he never mentioned any soldiers' or prisoners' names. It helped him to submerge the memories in his day-to-day recall by not attaching names to the experiences. But, he thought, if a military sadist wanted a vacation where he or she could delight in delivering torment with no judicial consequences, Camp Delta would be a hard place to beat.

At that time neither Sikander nor Salman had heard of extraordinary rendition.

Throughout this conversation, Jamil listened on in amazement at some of the things that he was hearing for the first time and Sikander often gave him glances during the narrative simply to suggest this was not something to repeat to others. Sikander made a mental note to himself to warn Jamil more explicitly that he shouldn't tell their mother or the other women who at that moment were in a different lounge while this conversation had been proceeding.

"And what about business in America, Salman?" asked Sikander, changing the subject.

"Right now the economy has hit a bit of soft spot, probably because of the war, Sikander, but generally I think that we're in pretty good shape. Money is cheap and I personally can't complain," replied

Salman. "Sabrina and I are building a new home just outside Durham and you should come and spend some time with us when you get the chance."

"Hmm...yes. Thank you, we'd like that, but what about business in general?" asked Sikander. "Do you find it easy to carry on in business? Are there big issues with conducting business in the USA? How does it differ from here, if you can even answer that?"

"Sikander," replied Salman with a curiously peaked eyebrow, "are you thinking of doing business in America?"

"Actually Jamil and I talked about this and we feel that we're only going to be able to take the business so far within Pakistan, while America is of course a vast market for electrical parts as well as perhaps other related products. I mean, I don't think we'll be selling 'Made-in-Pakistan' electrical products there anytime soon, but 'Made-in-China' is a different matter."

"Other products?" asked Salman.

"Yes, you know, general electrical items?"

"Sikander, it's certainly a big place and a big domestic market, but your best bet would probably be to find a troubled cash-poor player in electrical products, a national distributor or regional wholesaler who could perhaps be bought."

"Bought? Yes, of course, bought. How would we do that, Salman?" Sikander pressed.

"Well, you'd obviously need to try to search for these types of companies. There are publications that list such opportunities, but you know, increasingly I'm finding the Internet to be powerful for this sort of thing. I just use Google or Yahoo! and type in what I'm looking for and it usually comes up."

"Yes, I've used Google," acknowledged Sikander, making a mental note to himself to pursue that option to the fullest. "So what would we do if we found such a company?"

"Well, if you have their contact information, just make a call," replied Salman. "Otherwise try to work with specialty companies that work in the general area of preparing companies for sale."

"And how would we go about doing that?"

"Oh, the same way as with the target company. Google and Yahoo! would work just as well for that," replied Salman. "By the way, Sikander, there is a cash sum, about a quarter of a million or so I think, which if invested to create jobs allows the investor the opportunity to become a resident without a green card. It's some kind of visa program. You might want to try calling the embassy here, or...check on Google," he chuckled.

Jamil took note of Sikander's inquiries, though he was not really concerned that this might be any more than an exploratory conversation. Regardless, it was certainly intriguing.

"Well," said Sikander, "there might be a time when that looks interesting. Salman, I think you know our business well enough. What we might want to do is to buy a national distributor in the USA through which we could take advantage of our Chinese manufacturer connections and increase volume beyond the small levels that can be supported here in Pakistan. The lower costs will make us more competitive in Pakistan too."

"Yes...yes, I get it. Well, it sounds very reasonable. I'll look out for an opportunity like that, but it's such a big place. Do you have any location preferences?"

"I think either coast, Chicago, Detroit, or Houston would make sense for our kinds of products, but you might want to check that out too. If we're buying an existing distributor, then presumably all the sales and other data will be available in their accounts, right?"

"Yes, that should certainly be the case," replied Salman. "But I think I'll begin with North Carolina or Virginia since I know that territory fairly well," he added.

The rest of the evening proceeded easily without much by way of controversial conversation. After about another hour and a half, Sikander, Jamil, and the women were on their way back home in the latest Land Cruiser that Jamil had bought in breaking away from the Pajero tradition. Rabia, Kausar, and Sofie had fallen asleep in the car as they headed back across Peshawar to Hayatabad.

"Were you serious about doing the US investment, Sikander bhai?" asked Jamil, breaking the monotonous silence as they drove.

"Fairly serious," replied Sikander, "but what do you think about the idea, Jamil? I mean, pricing in this country is pretty much the same for everyone, so it's all a matter of cost control. Thanks to you, we have some of the best information systems and operations to keep our fixed costs down, but we still have to pay what we pay for the products. China's now dominating the manufacturing sector and if we get economies of scale by expanding overseas, we'll be bringing the product costs down in the Pakistan market as well."

"For me, the logic's fine, Sikander bhai, but I'd say it's down to execution risks and any hidden problems that we might not see in any acquired company. But are you sure you want to do this in America and not, for example, Europe? I mean...with your...your..."

"My experience? Hm! No, Jamil, I'm not sure," smiled Sikander, "but it's worth considering further, don't you think?" Sikander was being rhetorical. "Yes, it *is* just one possibility, but I like it because it's a single, large market in many ways, so even after buying a regional wholesaler instead of a national distributor, we might be able to expand across the country more quickly than across several European ones."

"We should talk about it again," suggested Jamil.

Weeks and months passed and from a work point of view, although nothing became of Sikander's thoughts about a presence in America, he worked diligently on the supply side to conclude more lucrative deals for product sourcing, particularly in China. He traveled to Shanghai on more than one occasion and was impressed with the pace of development there. It reminded him of similar developments also underway at that time in Dubai.

The Shanghai trips made an impact on Sikander as he could see what education and human development could accomplish, and now that he had a young daughter, his thoughts frequently turned to providing the best in education and opportunity for the children. In this he had no argument from Rabia. On several occasions, he discussed setting up in the US and Rabia seemed interested, though she was obviously concerned that he might be at risk if he put himself in their clutches once again. She had a fairly positive view about the country but wasn't sure about Americans in general.

"Rabia, I don't think that should be a risk, but if it makes you feel any better, I do have what that State Department lady, Dianne

Drummond, gave me when I was brought back to Peshawar," explained Sikander. "She said it'll make it clear to the visa section at the embassy in Islamabad that they should grant me clearance or, at the very least, that they should ignore that I'd been wrongly held in Guantanamo. She also told me that I wasn't to open the letter so, I suppose it *is* slightly mysterious."

"Sikander, if you think it's the right way to build Javelin, then you should do it and trust in Allah to clear away the obstacles," said Rabia. "I certainly like the idea of my children getting their schooling in America or England, but if America is the right place to be for business, then I'm with you."

Life in Pakistan continued largely as before with its ongoing challenges, but over the next two years, Sikander's business grew substantially. When customers were interested in large purchases, he would occasionally get involved, and in one or two cases he came across such purported buyers who spoke Urdu or English in strange accents. For those cases, Sikander had kept the business card that Dianne had handed to him upon leaving him in Pakistan and he dutifully called the number if he suspected the proposed buyers to be nefarious. Whatever information he had, he passed on to the contact person who gave the obviously fictitious name of Mr. Flintstone. Each time he would thank Sikander, take down the particulars, and ask Sikander to continue to go about his business.

From a business point of view in Pakistan, Sikander's heightened sense of understanding of human motivations and perspectives led him to be able to see into a buyer's or seller's mind to understand what they really wanted and negotiate the best deal. He had a good handle on taking negotiations to the limit and was in a strange way thankful for having personally grown through surviving his brutal treatment a few years earlier. At least he *thought* that was the reason, but who could say?

Javelin acquired or opened smaller entities in the surrounding area, but more importantly, the company moved aggressively to expand in its established cities and added several more. The company imported a greater diversity of products while also acquiring a few local manufacturers, which gave them significant cost advantages where customers weren't looking for name brand products—just the lowest price. In Pakistan, refrigeration and air conditioning markets were large

and these too needed compressors and pumps that Javelin could supply. The combination of the risk-taking Sikander with the meticulous and cautious Jamil worked extremely well.

By 2006, Javelin was on target to generate revenues of nine million dollars and had been floated on the Karachi stock exchange as the nation's premier wholesaler in its class. The flotation placed a market value equivalent to over forty million dollars for their company and netted the family the equivalent of sixteen million dollars in cash from selling forty percent of the company into the public markets.

Being thus flush with cash, together with having a meaningful stockpile from years of successful operations, Sikander and Jamil agreed that Salman, with whom they had been in regular contact, should make inquiries once again for a target for acquisition. His original inquiry had fizzled out as Sikander's focus had shifted to product supply contracts, but he was dutifully back on the prowl again. Sikander's lawyers provided him with the easy-to-fulfill conditions of the E-2 visa for the United States of America while Salman found him a counterpart attorney in Durham who would handle the immigration process once a company had been earmarked.

After about two more months of searching, Sikander finally received a call from Salman.

"Sikander assalaamu 'alaykum! It's Salman."

"Hey, Salman, wa-alaykum as salaam! What news?"

"There's a regional distributor based in Henderson not far from where we are. They're called Carolectric Corporation and are doing about ninety million dollars in sales. The company has three hundred and fifty people and is looking for cash because an eighteen-million-dollar bond is maturing soon. The owner is an older man. He's seventy-two, and none of his three children wants to stop their careers to buy his company from him or run it. They'd rather inherit the sale proceeds when he dies," explained Salman.

"Mmhm...And what's he looking for, Salman?"

"I think he'll agree to a deal. Here's what I propose. You need cash and financing of ninety million dollars. For the company, your offer should end up at seventy-two million. We could try going out with a lower number like sixty-five million, but I think he'll settle at seventy

to seventy-two. Having paid him for all the stock, you would issue yourself eighteen million dollars of new stock and put that much in cash into the company—you'll need that cash to pay their bond. Allowing for his probable tax liability, he'll be walking away from this business with anything from forty to fifty-million. At his age that's an okay deal if he can stop working, avoid the hassle, and just retire," explained Salman reading from his notes. "Oh…and one other thing, Sikander. He said if does sell, he doesn't want to act on this until at least September."

"Do you think we can obtain the finances, Salman?" asked Sikander.

"I think so," said Salman. "With the proper US deposits and bank guarantees, I think it should be possible. You should have cash from the recent flotation of Javelin. I'd say it would probably work if you brought in around twelve to fifteen million dollars of your own money and finance the rest. There's plenty of profit to support debt payments and if you use surplus profits to expand the business, then you could probably accelerate the settlement of the financing."

"Okay, assuming the numbers work, how do we take it further?"

"Let me look into it but, Sikander, understand that a deal at this scale is big enough for us to be using specialist law firms and accountants obviously."

The men agreed on a plan of action. Sikander discussed it with Jamil who agreed subject to his cautious mind's need to review the hard numbers. They called a meeting of the Javelin board to put the offer formally together through a new company to be established in the USA specifically for this purpose. Salman would arrange the company formation and Jamil would coordinate putting the money into it. That would provide the necessary balance sheet for bank financiers or private equity firms to come in and arrange the desired combination of debt and equity financing.

April came and Sikander proposed that the family make the trip and try to experience more of the country than they had heard about in the media. They would take a vacation and it would give them a chance to get firsthand experience of the place. It would also be a test of whether Dianne's official letter would prove to be of any value or not. He filled out and submitted their applications—as required by the US Embassy—to the SpeedEx office in Peshawar and waited for approval.

Sikander included a note with the application referring to his having a sealed letter from the US State Department for the attention of the embassy personnel. He also included a photocopy of the envelope showing the State Department seal and noted that he would make it available in person should the application make it as far as an interview. Not surprisingly, it did.

The interview was scheduled for six weeks later and Sikander planned to travel in late July after school was done for Ayub and Qayyum. The State Department letter—though Sikander didn't know it—simply contained an official request to admit Sikander and his family into the United States and to acknowledge his history of detention at Guantanamo but requested officials to ignore it as an unfortunate error. Sikander and Rabia were interviewed and visas were issued for the family in June.

Once the way was paved for admission into America, Sikander had his office order the necessary tickets. The date was determined and with the intention of being away for four weeks, they left on July 20th on a PIA flight from Islamabad to Jeddah at around eight in the evening, spending much of the night in Jeddah's airport, following which a Saudi Arabian flight leaving in the morning of the 21st took them to Washington, DC.

The eleven-hour flight out of Jeddah left around nine in the morning and Sikander with his family traveled in the first-class cabin. Relaxing in his seat, he looked around and couldn't help recalling the flight on which he had been bound, hooded, and shackled before being placed in the back of a USAF Starlifter to be hauled away to Cuba from Afghanistan. It made a difference to him that he sit by a window seat and be able to look outside.

At almost two-thirty in the afternoon, a little more than half an hour before the scheduled landing time, the aircraft began its descent. The sun was shining beneficently on the east coast of the United States. Sikander was sitting behind Ayub with Qayyum in front of him dwarfed by his seat. Rabia was across the aisle from Sikander with Ayesha in the next seat over. With his window seat Sikander wanted to catch a first glimpse of the country that he had once longed to be able to visit, and for reasons he could not quite explain to himself, despite all the experiences of the intervening years, his yearning was still very real.

The approach to Dulles on that clear July afternoon enabled Sikander to see cars, trucks, buses, and trains going about their daily business. He was on the right side of the aircraft and as it made its long sweeping turn to the right before lining up for Runway 1 Right, he could see in the distance the Washington monument and the Capitol building.

All those people down there. All that civilization, thought Sikander. These are the people that al-Qaeda is trying to annihilate and these are the people now doing their level best to direct their political, military, and financial resources to annihilating al-Qaeda.

From up there they didn't seem deserving of anything other than to be left alone to pursue their lives. That, of course, was far too simple an insight to reflect the deeper realities of world politics. Who controlled resources? Who produced them? Was the "American way of life" that he could see represented by the vehicles and people going about their business down below actually possible without requiring the trampling of other interests elsewhere in the world? From what Sikander understood, certainly the neo-conservatives presently in power seemed to believe it wasn't possible, being only able to envision the world in terms of such resource control conflicts, requiring in turn that America retain the upper hand with an iron fist. In Sikander's mind, such people had completely missed the important role of ingenuity and its ability to render traditional resources—or the means of producing them— obsolete.

As Sikander pondered the beautiful afternoon scene, with the Capitol building in the distance and ordinary life proceeding throughout the panorama, it seemed to acquire an emblematic quality. In it, he could see the dichotomy of the decent, good-natured, and charitable American and the inherent selfishness of the sanctified "national self-interest" that had resulted in the uncharitable projection of power around the globe on the charitable American's behalf.

The family didn't face any issues getting through customs and immigration and before long were in the terminal building looking for their luggage, some currency exchange, and the rental car.

About four and a half hours passed with one coffee stop as jet lag kicked in. After a few twists and turns off the highway and into one of the pricier suburbs of Durham, at about nine in the evening the rented Range Rover's navigation system made its final and welcome pronouncement: "You have arrived."

The family was warmly received by Salman, his wife, and their now three children each of comparable ages to Sikander's. A few of Salman's and Sabrina's friends had been invited that same evening just to meet the new arrivals. Sikander and his family were beginning to feel as if morning had broken, so it was not too hard to handle the visitors and still remain awake. After a light meal and small talk about the state of Pakistan at the time and about American policy, the local guests left and Sikander, Rabia, Salman, and his wife Sabrina remained sitting in the family room with Salman and Sabrina's children fast asleep but Ayub and Qayyum playing with the games and toys to which they had been introduced upon their arrival. Their internal clocks hadn't quite adjusted just yet. A final evening cup of green tea was served and the four of them chatted idly for a while.

Rabia could not help noticing the way the home had been decorated and furnished. She saw the possibilities for how their own home in Hayatabad might benefit from some of the same design ideas. Sabrina adroitly noticed Rabia's curiosity.

"Let me give you a tour, Rabia," she offered, and the two of them gladly went on their way. The house was not small, and Rabia had much to talk about, so it took a while for them to return. While they were away, the two men chatted about Carolectric.

"The deal's basically defined, Sikander, but it's good you'll be taking some time to meet with the people there. The owner is a Mr. Gordon Elmer and he's eager to meet with you. He doesn't want his life's work to be destroyed by someone who won't, for example, preserve or improve the private company culture or who might strip the company of assets and try to maximize the short-term gain."

"Likewise, Salman," acknowledged Sikander. "You know we're looking for a real presence in the US and to drive down overall product costs to benefit our Pakistan business too."

Salman noticed Sikander flagging. "Look, in a few minutes it'll be Saturday morning. You can rest up most of the weekend, I can introduce you to friends, or we can go sightseeing. You don't have to decide right now. You need some rest. We'll be ready to go into Henderson on Monday and the appointment is set for first thing in the morning."

Sikander and Salman chatted about a variety of other non-business related topics and before long their wives were walking back into the family room.

"...they're cherry, which is quite popular in this country, Rabia," explained Sabrina as the two of them ambled out of the kitchen. The tour was complete.

The family was shown to their rooms. Ayub and Qayyum were to share a bedroom with Salman and Sabrina's son Isa, who at that time was asleep. Ayesha would be sleeping with Ambar and Meena, the latest addition to Salman's family, but not that night, as Meena was too young to find herself waking up with a total stranger, so Ayesha was put in with Sikander and Rabia.

"It's an impressive home, isn't it, Rabia?" asked Sikander.

"Yes, it is. I like the way our bathroom is laid out. It must be nice and bright in the daylight. I saw a window in the ceiling," she noted.

"Hmmm..." said Sikander as he dozed off into a much-needed peaceful slumber.

The weekend was relaxing—a perfect refresher for them all. On Saturday, Salman and his wife set up a brunch buffet in the kitchen. They had invited more guests over, including a neighbor or two, and the conversations were warm and friendly.

Sikander could see much of the allure of living in this country and the individually genteel nature of the people. What was it, he wondered, about conflicts that made people see others as simple caricatures of reality—demon or human? The human *we* against the demon *other*. *We* would always be multifaceted, multi-dimensional, and complex. The *other* was always simple to grasp and one-dimensional, composed only of the evil that propelled it to seek *our* annihilation. What was it that made individually good-natured people like these fuse into a militarily collective intent with often such heartless and cruel results? These thoughts constantly prowled Sikander's psyche but always gained ascendancy when he could see the positive images of America and the Americans around him.

The conversations were polite and generally, the neighbors who were all white Caucasians except for one African American couple,

exhibited concern for the state of things in Pakistan—about poverty or lack of access to good education or health care. Their opinions, though loosely valid, seemed genuinely only informed by the likes of TV and popular press and lacked the nuanced understanding that conversations of that nature warranted in order to reach beyond being the polite pleasantries that they were. Still, to Sikander their concern, however incompletely- or ill-informed, did seem genuine.

The two families went out to the Eno River State Park just to unwind on a beautiful Sunday afternoon, taking a light lunch snack with them. With the lunch finished, a stroll was in order. Sikander picked up Ayesha in his arms while Rabia let Ayub keep an eye on Qayyum. Ayesha and Qayyum had been suitably bribed with an ice cream cone and Qayyum was reasonably well trained to walk along with his big brother or the adults and not wander off.

"Can we live here?" Ayub asked thoughtfully.

"You'd like that eh, Ayub?" asked Sikander as Ayub nodded fiercely.

"Me too Abba-jee. Are we moving here?" chimed in Qayyum.

"We'll see. Maybe..." replied Sikander in classic parentspeak, and that seemed to buy some silence from them for the time being.

"It's so silent, there's not even a hint of traffic," noted Sikander to Rabia.

"Yes, and so beautiful! So many trees, they go on and on!"

"Would *you* like to live here, Rabia?"

"America you mean? Or here in Durham?"

"Well, I guess we haven't seen much of anything else. I was just curious how you felt about the country."

"Umm...let's ask that question after the four weeks are over. I must say, though, I've found the people to be a lot more friendly and pleasant than I'd imagined." Rabia had come to America with her own notions of American anti-Afghan and anti-Muslim sentiments. She wore a hijab and had half expected to be pilloried for allowing herself to be "oppressed" from the moment others laid eyes upon her, and though there might have been such sentiments in the more crowded places, people generally left them alone or were outright pleasant.

"Yes, I have similar feelings about the people but we have to wait and see. I've experienced a much darker side and this is helpful for me," Sikander replied.

Rabia could see Sikander absorbing the environment and the novelty of the experience. It *was* stimulating. She could also see he had doubts and was clearly hoping that this trip would help put some of those to rest. And who knew? Maybe also some of his demons.

"SubhanAllah, though, Rabia!" exclaimed Sikander. "America's beauty *is* breathtaking. I'm reminded of the feelings I had when I was in Scotland before I knew you very well. Whatever that place was, I'd still love to take you there someday."

The families returned to Salman's house and in the evening Sikander and Salman went through the facts and figures of Carolectric in preparation for the meeting to be held the following morning with Gordon Elmer and Chief Financial Officer, Glen Seymour.

Monday morning came and Salman drove Sikander to the offices in Henderson close to the Virginia state line. They were welcomed into the reception area and ushered into a well-appointed conference room. In the meeting room was Gordon Elmer and Glen Seymour. While nothing had been inked as of yet, they were anxious to avoid starting a rumor about the company being for sale. Elmer warmly put out his hand and offered it to Salman, whom he had met previously, and then to Sikander. The same was done by Seymour and business cards were exchanged in the ritual that custom demanded the world over. The men were shown to two of the fifteen leather-backed seats that punctuated the periphery of a large elliptical table beautifully finished in a Carpathian elm burl veneer. A video projector hung from the white ceiling panels and aimed at a point on the wall where a screen could be electrically rolled down if need be. As Seymour and Elmer took their seats, they began by formally welcoming the two visitors. Elmer examined the business cards and continued with an icebreaker.

"Khan and...Khan? I know this is a common last name, but are you two related?"

"Actually we are, but not as closely as you might imagine, Mr. Elmer," responded Salman. "My mother and Sikander's mother are cousins, and before you ask the next question, their maiden names were

also Khan and each of their husbands' last names is, or in Sikander's case, was, Khan. So, as you might imagine, it's not a really functional last name," he explained with a subdued laugh. "In fact, Mr. Elmer, it's really not a name as such—more a designation of ethnic origin. Sikander and I are Pathans, which virtually automatically means we're Khans. With migrations into western culture, it's simply come to be adapted to serve as a last name."

"Interesting. Well, in any case, Mr. Khan and um, Mr. Khan, welcome to Carolectric Corporation. We're truly honored to have you visit us today and we'd like to offer you a short presentation about our company, but before we do, can we get you something to drink? Tea? Coffee?" asked Elmer.

The visitors responded affirmatively, and tea was brought in and poured into bone china teacups while a plate of cookies was placed on the table in front of the two men. The screen was lowered and the presentation proceeded, with the men from Carolectric describing their business in some detail and pausing courteously to answer questions raised by Sikander and Salman, all of which were acknowledged to be "excellent," "great," or "good." They described the history of the company, the type of products it distributed, the customers they had, the number of employees, how they handled goods, and how they dealt with warehousing and transportation. They also went through copious financial detail, particularly focusing on the recent past and their projections and assumptions for the next five years.

When the presentation was complete, Sikander congratulated them on providing a thorough description of the business. "Mr. Elmer and Mr. Seymour, I must say that *was* a comprehensive presentation. I'm still absorbing much of what you've described..." Sikander paused for a moment to gather his thoughts following which he counted out on his fingers what else he thought he needed. "Can you please provide me with a hardcopy of your material, the names and contacts of ten of your top customers from whom we can take references, a list of who you think are key personnel in the topmost level of management, and references from your largest suppliers?"

"We'd be delighted to provide you with all of those things but, uh, may I call you Sikander?" asked Elmer.

"Of course, and this is Salman," said Sikander as he acknowledged the request.

"And please call me Gordon and this is Glen. So, Sikander, could you give us some sense of your timing and proposed finalized terms on our deal?"

"Actually, we prepared a proposed term sheet which explains everything," answered Sikander as he pulled out three sheets of paper from his briefcase and handed one each to Gordon and Glen while keeping one for himself and Salman to share.

"We're thinking that Carolectric would issue eighteen million dollars of new stock to a company we would form here in North Carolina. That company would also buy all of the Carolectric stock held by the present shareholders for seventy-two million dollars. The transaction would be financed at fifteen million of our own money plus seventy-five in financing. It's all there on the term sheet."

"Yes. Well, that all seems to make sense," said Gordon. "And Salman here had forwarded us the figures previously," he continued. "So that leaves us with how you propose to *operate* the compa—"

"Gordon, I've already understood from talking with Salman," Sikander interrupted, "that you have certain strong feelings about how the company will be managed or operated. I, uh, understand your expectations and there'll no doubt be differences of objectives and philosophy, but I can assure you I would not be paying this kind of money to disturb something which operates as well as your company does already. That's why we're looking for information about your key managers. We'd like to incent them to remain with us after you sell. Aside from that, we're looking for a US presence and an ability to obtain discounts at larger volumes from our Chinese sources, some of which you also use. These volumes can be combined with our Pakistani operation, which is presently much smaller than yours. So you see? We're really not interested in chopping the thing up to sell off the parts."

"Well then," responded Gordon as he looked across to Glen. "I think we should get you all the certified account information and the other things you asked for so you can start your due diligence. Meanwhile, we can't let you leave without a tour of our local facility here in Henderson."

"Of course! We're looking forward to it, Gordon…please lead the way!" responded Sikander enthusiastically.

The four of them proceeded out of the boardroom and Gordon stopped by his assistant's desk. "Julie, I need you to put together a couple of packages for me," he said as he proceeded to itemize most of the things that Sikander had asked for. He left out the key manager information, it being too sensitive a request. As the tour began, he told Sikander that the management summary would be sent to him directly via e-mail.

The tour itself revealed nothing untoward but gave Sikander some new ideas for automating certain functions in Javelin's warehouses. Meanwhile, he continued asking intelligent questions to expand his growing knowledge about the company. As it was late July, many of members of the management team were not physically present, having already gone on their summer vacations. A few were, and Sikander enjoyed meeting with them, while the agreement with Gordon was that he would be presented as a potential customer to keep the proposed transaction confidential. When the tour was over, they went back to the office where Julie had already completed assembling a package for each of the two visitors.

The visit was wrapped up. They said their good-byes and drove back to Salman's house where Rabia had gathered their luggage so that the family could begin the rest of its vacation.

"I really want to see the natural parts of this country, Sikander. I know there's Disney World and Las Vegas and places like that, but I've seen many books and magazines that talk about the national parks. I would really like to see some of them," Rabia pressed.

As the children had different ideas when it came to Disney World, a compromise was reached and the vacation began with Disney. For Rabia, Yosemite and Sequoia were the high points, and Sikander was taken by just about everything he saw, but there was one place he definitely had to visit—the place that had thrust him into the experiences that had such a shaping influence on who he had now become—New York City. He needed to see "Ground Zero" where the World Trade Center twin towers had once stood.

Sikander gazed out at that nondescript space; the epicenter of a geopolitical tsunami whose waves had spread out from this spot, and on that terrible day swept up and transformed so many lives across the globe, including his own. He found himself searching the scene for explanations and in that sense the place was devoid of any. It was just

there. New York, of course, had a lot more to offer for a first-time visitor, but none seared his memory like Ground Zero. Throughout the trip, people had been delightful and though, as a whole, better off financially, they weren't inherently any different from his own people.

A month passed and the family flew back home. Due diligence was completed and Sikander had little difficulty arranging the financing. Electrodis International was formed as the locally acquiring company after it had been sufficiently capitalized, and by September of 2006, it owned Carolectric Corporation. The transaction was formally completed a week before Sikander and his family—this time with Jamil—returned to Henderson. In Sikander's case, he and his family arrived on the E-2 visa based on his control of the company's investment in Carolectric while Jamil traveled on a business visitor's visa. Everything was set for an orderly transition of control.

With a slightly theatrical flair, Gordon Elmer had arranged a symbolic ceremony to "hand over the keys" to the new owners and as a matter of continued but private symbolism for Sikander himself, the date of Monday, September 11th was picked for the event. Sikander had already arranged for an apartment in Henderson, which would give Rabia time to research the local real estate and pick either a lot for construction or an existing home. Jamil chose to stay with them.

About a month earlier, Gordon Elmer had held a meeting with his direct reports to confirm that he was going to step down and a transaction was going ahead in which Electrodis International would be buying Carolectric. He had been honored by a special retirement party at the beginning of September and was back that Monday to participate in the ceremony; as it was so recently after Labor Day weekend, all the other key management and staff, having taken their summer breaks, were also present.

As the new owners, Sikander and Jamil arrived and were met at the reception foyer by Gordon. He took them over to a lineup where he introduced the seven senior management team members that Gordon had previously identified and detailed to Sikander as key people. Sikander and Jamil came to the lineup with Gordon and shook each of the men's hands warmly but simply gave a slight nod of the head to the women as part of their observance of not touching women with whom they held a non-mehram relationship.

Gordon Elmer made a speech to the assembled staff to introduce them to the new owners and what it had meant to him to have formed Carolectric and how much he'd valued having them as employees. He also said a few words about how everyone could rely on the new management to continue in the best traditions of the company. As he wound up his speech, he turned to Sikander and Jamil.

"Mr. Khan, we'd very much like now to give you the keys to the company." As he uttered the words, a door leading from the warehouse to the right of the reception area swung open and a man came through grinning cheerfully while holding a golden key about a meter long. He strode over to where Gordon, Sikander, and Jamil were standing.

"Being a key, we thought it would be best if it was presented to you by our Director of Security. Mr. Khan, please meet Mr. Jim Mahler."

Sikander was listening to Gordon while looking down in the stance of someone politely absorbing what was being said. As Mahler's name was mentioned, he looked up reflexively. His knees felt as if they had turned to jelly and his complexion, though already light by comparison with most Pakistanis, became paler than anyone else's in the foyer. He broke out into a sweat and suddenly felt cold.

Jim Mahler's grin also lost much of its force, but he seemed to hold it together, albeit his eyes were about ready to pop and his heart hadn't beaten this fast in over four years. His grin descended into a warm smile and about a nanosecond later, it became a plastic one.

Sikander stopped himself from falling over by gripping Jamil's arm and after a second or two, he was able to take his own weight. Everyone in the room had their eyes fixed on Sikander and so the only witnesses to Mahler's reaction were ironically Sikander and Jamil, though Jamil did not pick up on the rapid transition of Mahler's smile from warm to frozen.

Slowly, the stiff-lipped Mahler raised the large key, presenting it to Sikander. For the two men, the event had transformed into a theatrical parody—complete with audience—of Sikander's own liberation from Mahler's clutches over four years earlier. Mahler's face, with every muscle held in place, was thus locked in its best efforts to appear cordial. Sikander's expression was likewise sustained by his self-conscious awareness of every pair of eyes in the foyer gazing on him as he too, with his lifeless cheer, held out his hand to pick up the key.

Jamil looked at him to see if he was alright and while that moment dissolved into the next, Sikander's freeze-frame gave way to a recovery of his sense of place and purpose.

"Good...uh...good morning, Mr. M-Mahler," he uttered, before letting out a lungful of air as he held out his hand.

Mahler's hand came out to meet Sikander's. The hands shook each other, devoid of owners.

"Good morning, Mr. Khan," said Mahler, somewhat more in control of his reactions. But then again, he *had* been trained by the best in several faculties, including controlling his facial expressions.

To Sikander, the moment lasted an eternity with all the applause and cheer surrounding him. Finally, still smiling, Mahler stepped back a pace, as not a moment too soon, Gordon gestured that he and Glen, together with the visitors, should come back to the executive suite to complete the formalities.

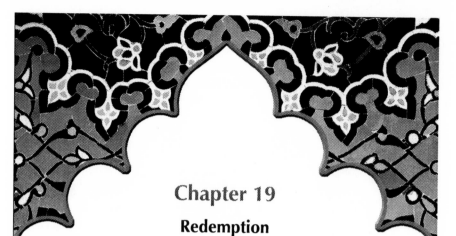

Chapter 19

Redemption

A FTER THE KEY CEREMONY wound down, Sikander and Jamil joined Gordon, Glen, and the other senior management staff in the executive suite. Sikander had not yet managed to shake off the impact of his encounter with Mahler and it dominated his consciousness to the point of impairing his ability to focus on even the simple act of walking. As soon as the seat in the conference room came within reach, Sikander promptly dropped himself in it, trying all the time to mask what was spinning around inside his head. He wasn't completely successful.

"Are you okay, Sikander?" asked Glen. The question further heightened Jamil's anxiety as he had earlier felt Sikander's hand grip his arm in a way he had neither expected nor, for that matter, ever experienced.

Finally seated at the boardroom table, Sikander responded as plainly as he could pretend. "I...I'm fine, I think I was uh, having a dizzy spell. Huh! Jet lag in all likelihood. Please, let's continue."

Sikander had no wish, at least for now, to reveal his prior experiences with the head of security for the company his family now owned. He had a hard time focusing on anything that was being said and allowed Jamil to do most of the running as he thought about the present situation. His pleasantries were on autopilot and he would nod intelligently at the appropriate point, throwing in the odd question to

appear insightful, but his mind was all but consumed by thoughts of what to do about Mahler.

Sikander found himself forced to re-examine his own attitude toward Mahler. At that moment, working for him was the man who had without a doubt transgressed the bounds of decent human behavior while he had been working for Army Intelligence but now, no longer in the Army, he was simply doing his job. He had entered a normal life and was engaged in normal behavior. There had been an invisible wall in Guantanamo that had separated the two men and despite them being physically only centimeters apart, had provided clarity in defining the yawning gulf between them. At this moment, Sikander was on the same side of that wall.

The welcoming meeting was over. Gordon Elmer took a limousine back to Raleigh-Durham and then a flight to Vail, Colorado, the location of his summer home. His retirement had finally begun.

Sikander and Jamil stayed for a while, interviewing the senior management about their current priorities and the annual operating plan that was shaping up for 2007. With that, the day was done and Jamil and Sikander drove back to the apartment. Yet Jamil was troubled over Sikander's apparent unease and needed to voice his concern.

"So, what went on back there, Sikander bhai?"

"Hmm? Nothing. Just...jet lag, I guess," Sikander said elusively, adding an unconvincing yawn.

"I...don't think so, Sikander bhai," responded Jamil, buying none of it. "It looked like something else to me and I think you should talk to a doctor. Have you established one yet?"

"No...we're going to be doing all those things in the next week or two. We still have to locate a house, remember?"

"Hmm..." acknowledged Jamil, sensing that if there was something going on, Sikander clearly didn't want to talk about it. He let the subject pass.

They arrived at the apartment and started to talk through the steps for managing the rest of that week. Jamil wanted to get back to Pakistan before Ramadhan, which was ten days away. Rabia had mastered the stove, microwave, and oven and set to work preparing

something edible but not up to her usual Pakistani or Afghan standard. For that she would need to shop for several specialty utensils.

Sikander was still processing the issue of Mahler as he began unwinding; however, he didn't escape Rabia's ever watchful eye. Rabia loved Sikander dearly. She counted herself all the more lucky to have been given a new start with his return from Guantanamo, and she was compulsively always on heightened alert when it came to the slightest deviation from the norm with him. Her tendency to overreact in this one respect bothered Sikander, as he saw it interfering with any possibility of returning to "normal." But he was sensitive enough to understand her consternation and didn't usually let it get to the point of snapping at her.

"Sikander? Something wrong?" she asked.

"Hm? No."

"Are you sure? You seem a little...distant," she probed.

"It's nothing really...probably just a severe case of jet lag, but I think I'm getting over it now anyway," replied Sikander, trying to give Rabia a lie she could find even moderately convincing. She seemed to buy it and as she processed his comment, he took advantage of the moment to change the subject.

"You know, I need to spend time with the children and just... just play with them. Perhaps that'll help me unwind from the day," he suggested. He didn't wait for an answer from Rabia.

"Ayub, we're looking for a place to live with a good school for you," said Sikander.

"Yes, Abba-jee, I know. I don't suppose we'll find a rare one that does cricket?" asked Ayub. "I'd like to try for a school cricket team if possible."

"Ayub, cricket isn't an important sport in America as I think you know, but they do have others that you'll be able to get into. There's soccer, basketball, ice hockey, American football, and baseball. That's quite a selection, isn't it?"

Sikander could see his explanation failing to register with Ayub, whose obvious desire was for his home country's national obsession.

"How about at home? Do you suppose we could practice cricket at home?" asked Ayub, who at thirteen was just beginning to deal with his own adolescence.

"Hm...I don't see why not, Ayub. I think we can get Jamil Chachu to bring some cricket bats and balls and things on his next trip back here, don't you? There are lots of parks around here, so we should have no trouble finding a place to play or practice."

"I suppose." Ayub shrugged. "When do we start at the new school?" he asked, resignedly.

"Well, we have to get your physical exams done and sort out a few other things, but I'm sure we can get you started within a week or so. We'll get Qayyum into the same school if possible. That'll make life easier for Ammee-jan to take you there and back."

Sikander's comment caught Rabia's attention, overhearing the conversation from the kitchen.

"Oh...I don't think I want to be driving in this part of the world just yet!" Rabia called out. "We'll have to come up with some other answer," she said with a stifled chuckle.

"Actually, Rabia, if you can drive on the streets of Peshawar, it won't be so bad here. You just have to get used to looking in a different place for the rearview mirrors—the rest is natural."

Sikander's attempt to ease his wife's mind was futile.

"Well, if you want me to do that and you don't mind me wrapping the car around a streetlight, then I suppose I could try it," she said dryly.

They performed maghrib, ate dinner, and followed with isha. The children were sent to bed while Sikander, Rabia, and Jamil sat in the apartment living room. Although it was late, the doorbell rang. It was Salman who had come over to check up on them and to enquire as to how the day had proceeded.

"So, now you're a captain of American industry, eh, Sikander?" Salman had a gleam in his eye. "Congratulations to you and Jamil! You've pulled it off and I'm sure your mother will be proud and I'm sure your father—may Allah grant him peace—would have been, had he been alive."

"Thanks for all your help and encouragement, Salman!" said Jamil. "I don't think we would have tried this without you."

"You're most welcome, Jamil. By the way, Sabrina and I would like to invite you all including the kids to our place on Friday evening. Jamil, you're traveling back Saturday, right?"

"Yes, and I'm frankly missing home already. I can't wait to be back. Sikander and Rabia bhabhi, I don't know how you'll be spending Ramadhan here. It's hard to imagine doing that without family and friends."

"Oh thanks!" chimed an indignant Salman, to which Jamil dutifully apologized. "So, how did today's ceremonies and introductions go? Did anyone get much work done?" asked Salman.

Jamil's eyes darted to meet Sikander's as he recollected the slight mishap in receiving the golden key. Sikander was not keen on having the experience dissected either in words or glances, so he held his gaze fixed on Salman, working hard to avoid eye contact with Jamil. This only made Salman feel a bit uneasy as he adjusted his posture reflexively. Sikander moved quickly to prick the rapidly growing bubble of silence.

"Oh, I think it all went rather smoothly," began Sikander, pretending to be lighthearted. "Now that I've seen how this sort of thing is done, I must say I'm a bit giddy with it. I almost feel like starting up on my next deal, but that'll have to wait of course. In fact, Jamil will tell you, I was so giddy that my head even spun briefly while they were handing me the symbolic key!" he chuckled. Finally, Sikander glanced in Jamil's direction to meet his stare, recognizing that Jamil had been looking at him all along, studying him and his reaction to Salman's question.

Sikander could see that Jamil might at last be accepting his story so he moved past the issue to describe the rest of the day: "It was actually quite illuminating to see what all the key executives had to say about their respective roles and their plans for 2007. I'm impressed with their caliber and that should speed up my getting settled into a managerial role. Jamil will handle things in Pakistan and he thinks he can to set up some kind of video link so it'll feel like we're much closer."

They chatted briefly and the subject came round to housing, schools, medical facilities, social security numbers, and driver's licenses. Salman was a huge help in simplifying what appeared to be to both Sikander and Rabia, a complex and daunting task.

"Actually, I think I've found a good school here. It's called Kerr-Vance Academy, which the local people seem to speak highly of," said Rabia. Sikander spun his head and looked back at Rabia, impressed at her initiative. His eyes brightened for a moment while he wore a pleasantly surprised smile. As usual, she read his eyes perfectly. After an hour or so of idle chatting, Salman excused himself, reminding them all of Friday's invitation and left. They were all tired and Tuesday would be a longer day than Monday, so they went to bed.

"Alright, Sikander," began Rabia when they were in the bedroom. "What's wrong?" Her look became more stern.

"Hmm? What do you mean, Rabia?"

"Sikannnder!" she exclaimed. Rabia was annoyed at not being taken seriously enough and this time she would settle for nothing less than the truth. "I can tell when something's gnawing at you and you haven't been yourself this evening. I'm your wife, remember?"

Sikander acknowledged her, taking on a resigned frown. He couldn't let her know. He couldn't let anyone know until he had things sorted out in his own mind.

"Rabia, it's...it's been a long day and I have to be back there in the morning to start running things. I have to decide who's doing what, whether I'd like them to stay or go, and I just...I just think I'm feeling some stress from having to do all these things. You're probably just noticing my anxiety. Can we drop this now?" countered Sikander, hoping the deflection would stick as he suspended a shrug.

Some of it did and Rabia accepted his claims but she wasn't totally satisfied until her intellect stepped in to overrule her intuition and told her it was all probably very innocent. In the time that Sikander had spent since returning from Guantanamo, he'd had several anxiety attacks and perhaps Sikander's own interpretation was accurate or perhaps it was still a lingering effect of his slow recovery. Either way, she thought more carefully about pushing that particular button and let things drop.

That did not do anything to ease her worries though, and she couldn't sleep. Neither could Sikander.

He was unable to decide whether to try to maneuver Mahler out of the company or keep him on. It wasn't so easy to let him go. It would be bad for business and it would look bad to his employees if he were to show up and fire Mahler for no apparent reason. Sikander had absolutely no intention of broadcasting any details of his period of captivity or interrogation unless he felt very safe around whomever he was telling—and even that proved difficult so far. It certainly excluded everyone at Carolectric.

On the other hand, if he was to fire Mahler and even perhaps come up with a rationale, he risked being "outed" by Mahler to the rest of the company out of sheer spite for losing his job. Besides, it just didn't seem right to be losing one's job while having performed it well. Uneasily, Sikander settled on a path of taking Mahler to one side and having an honest discussion with him about the proverbial "hippopotamus in the room" on this matter. If, during the course of the discussion, it became apparent that Mahler was actually not so competent or the discussion resulted in a serious "personality clash," it would leave the way open for a rationalization of his firing. If he came through sounding like he was a professional and could be relied upon, then why risk blowing that up with a firing? thought Sikander.

The following day, when Jamil and Sikander showed up at Carolectric, they went directly to the CEO's office, which had now been emptied of Gordon Elmer's personal items. The office furniture was still in its original place but rectangular patches of brighter color on the walls revealed where pictures had once been hanging and the room, for all its relative opulence, looked sad and unloved.

Julie Barnes, Gordon's executive assistant, remained with the company. Sikander had been impressed with her self-propelled personality and had asked her explicitly to stay on. She found Sikander to be pleasant and courteous and imagined him not to be the kind of boss who would bark orders or relegate her to making the coffee or chew her out for a minor mistake. She was slim with a regal looking elegance of forty-one years. She was in a settled period in her life, which allowed her a generally quiet demeanor and a good sense of humor, coupled with an unimpeachable sense of anticipation of her boss's needs. Not surprisingly, Julie was worth her weight in diamonds

to Sikander and Jamil as they made their first tentative steps. Neither of them could claim much if anything of a grasp of American culture and Julie had lived it. Julie would know.

As a bonus, Julie Barnes was also a valuable asset in helping Sikander with understanding some of the basics of establishing a personal identity within the American social fabric. Nowhere was this more true than in the matter of administrative chores such as obtaining social security numbers and driver's licenses, navigating the myriad choices of health care provision, and finding schools. Furthermore, she could be called upon to perform some of the errands associated with these tasks in a bid to take that kind of load off her boss and allow him to be more focused on issues of running the business. It was a rare assistant who could see performing such services with her perspective.

Before arriving to the US on this occasion, Sikander had sent an e-mail to Julie requesting that she arrange a small sitting area consisting of two comfortable low armchairs and a coffee table placed in a corner arrangement immediately facing the door to his office, which she dutifully arranged. It might have been more at home in the corner of a local Starbucks, which in fact was the concept on which it was modeled, after Sikander had visited a local branch. He liked that informal arrangement in at least a part of the office.

Stepping out of his office to talk to Julie in person about fifteen minutes before 9:00am that Tuesday, Sikander decided to make his first decisions for the day. "Julie, I'd like to go over today's schedule with you. What do you have me down for right now?"

"Sure! Just a moment," she answered as she pulled up his calendar on her screen. "You have the 2007 budget review from 10:00 to 11:30 together with Glen. After that, the plan is to have you go through it with the department heads from noon until five o'clock. Glen asked me to set it up so that you can selectively call each department head and go over their details. You should be able to get through at least the key four or five today and the program continues tomorrow."

"Okay, good. Julie, it's coming up to nine o'clock right now. I'd like you to call Jim Mahler of security. I need to have a chat with him and we won't wish to be disturbed. Meanwhile, please tell Jamil that I'd like him to go over to Glen's office and preview the budget with him. That'll make it easier for us to pick it up at ten o'clock."

"I'll get on it," said Julie, curious as to why Sikander would want such a meeting. The involvement in anything of the ordinary day-to-day business of the company by the security department was usually ominous. If the director of security got involved, that usually meant it was more serious. For him to be meeting the CEO, well, that was about as serious as one could imagine. Sikander meanwhile wanted to be sure that he could place Jamil away from the CEO office without offending his sensibilities by asking him to leave for the sake of Sikander's own privacy. The ruse to get him to sit with Glen was useful in itself but would also help Sikander to meet with Mahler alone. Seven minutes later, he was answering his phone. Mahler was outside his door, waiting.

Sikander couldn't resist the temptation to make Mahler wait. He fumed at the mere thought of the man. After a second or two, surmounting his visceral inclinations and acknowledging that making him wait would be no more than cheap vindictiveness, Sikander asked Julie to direct him in. Mahler stepped into the office, closing the door behind him gently but then boldly, almost menacingly, he strode toward Sikander who sat motionless at his desk. Although not looking very threatening, he put Sikander immediately on edge with his highly unorthodox manner of entry.

"Have a seat, Mr. Mahler," said Sikander flatly. He pointed with his outstretched palm to one of the armchairs at the back of the room. Mahler looked at Sikander and then down at the floor in front of him and back again into Sikander's eyes as if his own had been drills.

"Alright, Mr. Khan. Can we cut the crap?" began Mahler without adjusting his stance. "You and I both know what's going on here and I just wanted to spare us the nonsense." Mahler spoke calmly as he tossed a sealed envelope onto Sikander's otherwise paperless, shiny, dark cherry desktop. On the front was scribbled in blue felt tip "SIKANDER KHAN" in large letters.

"What's this?" asked Sikander, taken aback by Mahler's having unexpectedly taken control over the pace and direction of the conversation. Was Mahler just playing mind games with him? Was he simply switching on his considerable Army Intelligence training, or was he, Sikander, giving Mahler the opening to dominate him by subconsciously communicating submission by some long-buried conditioned reflex from Guantanamo?

"It's my resignation letter, Sikander," said Mahler defiantly, as he remained standing just a meter away on the other side of Sikander's desk and now looking almost down his nose. Sikander stared at the envelope for a moment but did not pick it up. He chose to see it as bait and he was not taking it, once again locking eyes with Mahler.

"Mr. Mahler, please…sit down," he persisted in a more subdued but still firm tone. He resented Mahler having taken the initiative and looked Mahler back in the eye while working hard to suppress some of the anger that was bubbling up inside him.

Mahler paused for a moment, continuing to fix his gaze on Sikander, and then finally and grudgingly broke contact to turn around and stand before one of the armchairs. For all the training Mahler had received in the Army on psychological methods, he was still somewhere deep inside, subject to an instinct to obey an order from a superior. Sikander was not the disheveled scrap of a man in shackles at the mercy of Mahler's slightest eye movement to launch the MPs into their terrible action. At this moment, his hair was combed back and his beard was neatly trimmed—a sort of "Billy Mays" look. He wore an elegant pale blue sweater, a dark blue open-collared shirt, and beige pants with expensive looking shoes. In the best traditions of American culture, Sikander was projecting wealth and power in a country casual package.

Despite his slightly melodramatic attempt at resignation, Mahler struggled with the practical matter of not wanting to be out on the street looking for employment. Something inside him urged him to take an opening, if offered, to have his resignation rejected. Somewhat puzzled by Sikander's demeanor, he took the seat while Sikander came out from behind his desk, joining him and sitting at the opposite armchair.

"Look, Mr. Mahler, I…I wanted to have this conversation because I'd like to make sure you understand that I'm only concerned with your performance and I…I don't…" he took in a deep breath and let it out, as he pressed his lips together before resuming. "No matter what I might feel about our…past relationship, if you're doing your job well here at Carolectric, then that will be all that matters for your employment here as far as I'm concerned. Now the only question I have is, do you have what it takes to stay?"

"You're…serious," said Mahler, admitting a momentary frown and turning what should have been a question into a statement of incredulous curiosity while shrugging and shaking his head slightly but

unable to shake off his puzzlement. Sikander could see some of the tension melting away and took his shot.

"Why wouldn't I be, Mr. Mahler? Do you think I bought this company just so I could have the satisfaction of seeing you fired? Or do you think I paid ninety million dollars because it makes business sense?" asked Sikander. "And if it makes business sense, then why would I undermine that sense by firing someone simply out of spite?" Sikander could feel his urge to vent getting the better of him. "Don't misunderstand me, Mr. Mahler. For what you did, oh…I'd love to act with spite, but then, like I told you in Guantanamo when you delighted in torturing me for saying the slightest thing you didn't want to hear, I'm a businessman. Remember? But *you*…you just turned your job into a…a vehicle that would let you vent your lust for revenge for 9/11. I happened to be available for you to act on that lust under the guise of interrogation. You just did it with at least one wrong person. And…for that matter, you should know that I *did* receive an acknowledgment from the US Government about their mistake in picking me up in Afghanistan."

Mahler gave a cynical unapologetic "humph" and turned his head away, looking to his left out of the window at the far end of the office behind where Sikander had been sitting earlier at his desk. He was clearly wrestling with conflicts, the foremost of which was between the need to avenge the loss of his close friend Tony, on 9/11, and the possibility—though in his mind remote—of having treated an innocent man as brutally as he had.

For his part, Sikander realized that though he had vented a mere sliver of his considerable animosity toward Mahler, certainly nothing resembling "badal," this meeting would go nowhere if he left it at that. He was also mindful of the need to avoid it becoming a shouting match that would be heard outside the office, exposing the controversy. He would have to be more conciliatory.

"Mr. Mahler, look I…I want to respect your expertise. Personally, to whatever degree has been possible, I've come to terms with what happened to me. I certainly don't condone what you did then and…and I really don't know if I can forgive it." Sikander shrugged. "It's a complicated matter for me."

"I was doing my job," asserted Mahler with a lingering tone of resentment, though clearly less intense than before, while he averted Sikander's focus.

"Yes, well, what matters now is how you do your job here. Don't you think?"

"I...I don't understand how..." began Mahler, struggling with what was being said to him. His minimum expectation, thinking about things at length the previous day and night before writing his resignation, was to be fired. Sikander had clearly some strong resentments about his treatment in Guantanamo. Being fired was a "no brainer."

Damn! How did he get released? Mahler struggled mightily to get past this question. Of all the people he'd interrogated, Sikander was among the most likely to be a terrorist member of al-Qaeda. Mahler had been sure of that. Yet here was Sikander, clearly released, thriving, and seemingly objective about the business. Mahler had simply not expected such detachment. He was trained to be suspicious and to crush opposition, not question whether it was real or not. It was his nature to expect others to be similarly driven.

"Mr. Mahler," said Sikander looking down to form his own thoughts much more carefully before re-engaging Mahler's eye, "Look, I, uh, I think a willingness to be cruel and brutal is in me, in you, in us all, really. Civilization—yours, mine, doesn't really matter which," he said, shaking his head. "It's a way of curbing brutality with some kind of code, a...a structure that creates confidence...let's the weak feel they won't be attacked or robbed of their possessions or dignity by the strong. But once a system encourages operating beyond the reach of law, well *then*, as you so amply demonstrated, that brutality will only be limited by the forces at our disposal—no matter *who* we are." Sikander paused but had clearly more to say.

"Was the way I was treated in Camp X-ray your fault? Yes, I think it was, because we're each responsible for curbing our own behavior. But it was also the fault, and continues to be, of this government for condoning or encouraging that behavior."

For a few moments, Mahler's convictions began to fracture. He was confused—unsure of what to think. His expression and his silence made Sikander feel the need to wrap things up.

"Mr. Mahler, we could...we could probably chat about those experiences forever. But for now, can we at least get back to work and just take things a day at a time?" Sikander offered a conciliatory shrug.

Mahler's face reddened with the kind of embarrassment that arises from standing naked before a fully clothed onlooker. It was a look he was familiar with, but only as the onlooker. Sikander had somehow learned more about the interrogator than the interrogator had managed to learn about him, and for Mahler, it felt the same as nakedness.

Something inside Mahler told him to accept the situation and continue with this interesting man, this—Sikander Khan. He was not completely convinced of Sikander's innocence and he didn't care what acknowledgments or Presidential interventions there might have been. He found it hard to acknowledge that his own behavior at Guantanamo might not have had the slightest measure of justification. The cracks in his convictions began to close up again. No, he would stick around and maybe even trap this man in a moment of weakness. After all, he had a pretty good measure of the buttons to push while Sikander had been detained. Mahler would wait it out. However, right now it wouldn't pay to be too honest, he thought.

"Mr. Khan, on reflection and listening to what you've just been saying, well...hm! It might be wiser to stay on...if, that is, you're willing to have me stay." Mahler urged the last few words through his reluctant lips while avoiding eye contact with Sikander.

Oddly, Sikander was the one now feeling awkward after having somehow pushed whatever button got Mahler into a conciliatory mood. He had initially felt fear and then a calm came over him as he released thoughts that unknown to his consciousness had probably been brewing for several years. But now he wanted to bring the conversation to a close, though he didn't just want to push Mahler out of his office.

"Okay, may I, uh, tear up your resignation?" asked Sikander trying to bring the subject back to the ground. Mahler nodded slowly, acknowledgingly, while looking down toward the floor and then more rapidly as he lifted his head to make eye contact with Sikander, confirming his acceptance of Sikander's offer. They both stood up. Sikander walked over to his desk and tore up the envelope, tossing the pieces ceremoniously into the wastebasket. Jim Mahler held out his hand and unlike the previous day with the key ceremony, there was at least the semblance of warmth in it. Sikander looked at it for a second

and reciprocated the gesture while returning his gaze to Mahler. Neither man completely understood his own feelings at that moment, but each had formed his own reasons for why it was worth continuing the uneasy relationship.

As Jim was leaving, Sikander stepped out with him and to draw attention away from his erstwhile visitor, he turned to Julie and asked her to get some wall art that would at least cover the unsightly under-faded patches on his walls. Being an intelligent person, she was still slightly mystified by whatever might have prompted a meeting between Sikander and the company's director of security at this early juncture in Sikander's role as CEO. But before giving it another thought, she began busying herself for about a minute on Google and in less than ten was filling an online shopping cart. Sikander, meanwhile, poured himself a cup of coffee and stood outside his office pensively gazing around at what he'd bought.

"We'll have something by Thursday, Mr. Khan," said Julie with a lift of her lips.

"Hm? Oh...thanks. By the way, Julie, please call me Sikander, Si-kan-der," he said smiling. At that moment he felt lighter, as if the session with Mahler had lifted something of a burden he had been carrying for so long that he had no longer been aware of carrying it—until, of course, it had gone.

Jamil and Glen came over to his office a few minutes later and were ready to start.

"So guys, are we still going to be in business next year?" joked Sikander. Jamil and Glen chuckled as they proceeded into his office.

The week ended with Jamil eager to return to Peshawar. He was pleased with how things had gone, though of course oblivious to the undercurrent with Mahler. The rest of the annual operating plan reviews took place and Sikander had to recognize this as a baptism of sorts, as he had little familiarity with many of the terms and concepts being described to him from a US market perspective, but he was a quick learner. Instead of trying too hard to grasp the details, he leaned instead on his instincts to judge the people working for him as individuals and tried to get a sense of their own grasp of their specific areas of responsibility.

By the end of the week, Jamil was on a plane heading back to Pakistan while Sikander and his family proceeded to establish themselves as legal temporary residents.

During the remaining weeks of 2006 after Thanksgiving break, Sikander and his family began taking root in Henderson, NC. The weather became cooler, but luckily in 2006, no hurricanes hit the continental United States, something that hadn't happened since 2001, when at the height of hurricane season, the nation had hardly been able to focus on the weather. The family found a speculatively built six thousand square foot home not far from the Kerr-Vance Academy. They could certainly have afforded a larger space but neither Sikander nor Rabia wanted to get ahead of themselves. Besides, Sikander personally looked to do great things with the new acquisition before directing the family's wealth toward luxuries. Moreover, neither Sikander nor Rabia were comfortable with the idea of a mortgage given the body of Islamic opinion on the inadmissibility of both the receipt and the payment of "riba", or interest. So they elected to pay for the property outright.

As 2007 began, Sikander felt more direct ownership of the operating plan of the company. It bore his stamp of approval. Meanwhile, Jamil set up a video link with Peshawar, which proved to be highly effective, and the brothers were often to be found conferring or else in family "video fests," always popular with the children.

One evening in early February, out of idle curiosity, while browsing the Internet for information about lithium-ion battery manufacturers, Sikander was intrigued to find one showing up in Scotland. As with many surfing experiences, his attention drifted as he recalled his experiences learning to operate the Stinger more than twenty years earlier. In a flash, it struck him that now with Google, he might be able to search for a location where SAS training had taken place and sure enough, when he compared the names that came up with Google's mapping he was able to see satellite images of those places which had been acknowledged as having served the training purpose. One place stood out as the only location with the correct topography and relative disposition to the water and islands. It was Applecross. As soon as the name appeared on the screen, Sikander couldn't help murmuring it softly. "Applecross"

Some of the names of nearby places around Applecross triggered long-forgotten memories as they came rising to the surface of

his consciousness, places that he and his fellow mujahideen had visited during the bus tour all those years ago.

Sikander decided to arrange a brief vacation for himself and Rabia. It would be a fulfillment of his promise to revisit the place and now he was able to do that. Over the next few weeks, he made the necessary arrangements and without letting Rabia know what he was up to, he arranged for a detour during their next trip to Pakistan, which was due to take place in April. He concocted a story about stopping in London for a few days for a business meeting, which provided a perfect cover for their UK visa applications.

April came. Arrangements were made for the children to stay with Sabrina and Salman until at least Sikander's return, which was scheduled much sooner than Rabia's. Rabia was none the wiser until after they landed in London when he told her that their four-day stopover in the UK was to visit Scotland and that his long-committed promise was being fulfilled. Having flown first class, the two of them had managed to sleep on the flight and were reasonably well rested when they landed.

One more flight from London to Glasgow, where they rented a car, put them within seven exhilarating hours of driving into Scotland's northwest. They proceeded along the west side of Loch Lomond and up the east side of the north end of Loch Linnhe to Fort William. From there to Loch Lochy before heading northwest toward Applecross. The weather alternated between heavy downpours and bright sunshine, but the beauty was unrelenting.

"Sikander, this place is wondrous!" remarked Rabia as her head constantly turned from one side of the scene in front of them to another.

"Wait until you see Applecross," he replied. The day which had begun in London just after sunrise began drawing to a close and Rabia was enchanted by the setting sun amid the clouds shooting shafts of light into the hills, valleys, and lochs of the highlands. By late evening, they parked the car at the Applecross Inn, a charming hotel in a leafy woodland setting at the edge of the mainland looking over the water toward the Western Isles. After a late breakfast the following morning, taking a packed lunch with them, Sikander and Rabia left the inn to explore.

"See over there?" asked Sikander as he pointed out a thin stretch of land to their north. "That's where the camp was I'm pretty sure, and those...those are the islands I mentioned. The weather's perfect with these scattered clouds. Let's just walk around here for the whole day, shall we? We have lunch with us, we can even sit down to enjoy the sunset when the time comes."

"Sikander, it's heaven! The breeze is so sweet I can taste the air! And just...just look at that water. It's like a jewel. A billion flowing diamonds glittering in the sun!" exclaimed a delighted Rabia.

The couple strolled along the water's edge taking in the scenery and the weather. From time to time they stopped to pay special attention to some feature or other. Lunch was taken sitting by the water's edge, and later, as the evening drew on, the sunset obliged by delivering on Sikander's promise. The red halo story from twenty years earlier came to life while they gazed out over the water to the islands in the distance, including among them the enchanted Skye. Sikander basked in the scene and the vindication of his claim of Scotland's beauty that until the trip had acquired fabled stature in Rabia's mind. He made her grant him the accuracy of his claims, which she willingly did. That night was really a belated honeymoon, as there hadn't been much of one in Laghar Juy. But they enjoyed it in every way imaginable, as if it had been their first.

The second day was spent driving around the Isle of Skye after which the two of them returned to Glasgow. From there they flew back to London and on to Islamabad. For the rest of the trip, Rabia stayed behind a few extra weeks to be with her mother and brothers while Sikander was back at work within a couple of weeks. A nanny was engaged to look after Ayesha while the two boys largely took care of themselves, with Sikander typically spending more time at home than usual each day.

Back in Henderson, Sikander's relationship with Jim Mahler was still awkward. Jim had continued to do a competent job but nothing special was being done to try to build a bridge. Not long after he'd settled into the job of being the company's CEO, Sikander decided he wanted to connect with the second level management and he periodically set up either breakfasts with small groups of them or visited them individually in their offices to see what they did and how they did it. After doing this a few times with others, subconsciously giving

himself some practice, he decided it was time to reconnect with Jim Mahler.

The appointment came up and Sikander walked across the building to Jim's office on the lower level. He knocked on the door and got the expected response to come on in. Sikander was immediately struck by Jim's choice of wall decorations and desk ornaments. Jim was a serious hunter. *How predictable and how unpredicted*, thought Sikander as the visual cues around him immediately recalled the picture Mahler had shown him during interrogation, when he wanted to make the point about his deceased friend, Tony DeLea, on 9/11. On the walls hung pictures of different types of shotguns, various certificates, and what looked like prize awards. Behind his desk on a credenza he had three pedestal-mounted gold awards with his name engraved on them and there were two other pictures, including the one with DeLea, showing each of them holding a clutch of bagged ducks after what had evidently been a productive day.

Sikander took a seat and opened up the conversation uneasily. "You certainly seem to enjoy hunting."

"Well, that won't win any awards for astuteness," said Mahler in a feeble attempt at caustic humor. "But yes, I do like to hunt. Ever done it yourself?"

A quiet shiver traveled up Sikander's spine as the mere hint of a question like that was enough to cause Sikander to recall the calm tone of Mahler's questions, which were almost invariably followed by the severe and painful actions of the MPs. He gathered himself together having successfully concealed what had passed through him when he responded. "Not in the sense you might mean, unless you were perhaps counting Russian helicopters."

"Helicopters...yes...Hinds, right?" asked Mahler. Sikander nodded. The topic threw his mind back into a daydream about his experiences in Afghanistan twenty years earlier. He looked away wistfully before catching himself and coming back to the more pedestrian present, but still irrelevant, subject of hunting.

"Where do you go?"

"Go?"

"To hunt."

"Oh, North Carolina and Virginia have lots of places along the coast as well as inland. I like to hunt where I can use a boat blind. It gives me some flexibility and I enjoy being on the water."

"Interesting. I've been a hills and forests person all my life, but I must say I've become attracted to the possibility of boating. Kerr Lake isn't too far from here and it seems like a good place for that sort of thing, don't you think?"

"What kind of boat did you have in mind? I know something about them."

"I'm not sure I had anything in mind, but it seems that something in the twenty-five to thirty-foot range would be a good choice." Sikander was not particularly sure of himself on the subject and at a more basic level, had only recently begun to attune himself to the American units of measure.

"Hmm, that's a pretty decent handful for a boat. You'll probably want to get lessons on it."

"Thanks, I'll look into it..." responded Sikander. "Now, what about security?" he asked looking at his watch. "What would you say are the key areas of focus for you?"

Mahler took a short breath and thought about the question. He wasn't used to being asked about his work by the senior-most executives. They usually took it for granted. It was a little suspicious for him to see the CEO appear concerned about the subject, especially given the historical baggage between these two men. Mahler decided he would offer a straight up professional response.

"We generally aren't worried about intellectual property or espionage or things of that nature," noted Mahler, waving his hand. "But we do care obviously about things like warehouse pilfering, the risk of employees being insiders to a concerted effort at external theft, things like alerting outside parties of shipment arrivals and deliveries or the contents of warehouses, maybe even leaving something unlocked to claim it was a mistake later.

"We also care about computer systems and making sure that all the transactional data is firewalled and we constantly monitor for hacking attempts. You might be interested to know that quite a few of them come out of Pakistan, though most come from China, West Africa,

and the Balkans. A third area of security concern is that we prevent or deter damage or theft of capital equipment, buildings, property, that sort of thing...things like computers, office equipment, and maybe tools on the warehouse floor. Beyond that we're responsible for ensuring that information and documentation is backed up for what's called disaster recovery. Things like a fire or hurricane or massively successful hacking attempt, or even um—terrorist attacks."

"How do you measure what you do as being effective?"

"Each of the four areas of personnel, information, capital asset, and inventory protection has its own set of metrics, which we can judge in relative terms. I have one person in charge of each of them. That way, if we get a theft, for example, of an inventory asset, we can compare that to the total and make a judgment about whether we're improving or getting worse. It's not quite as complete or rigorous as I might be implying right now but it is something I'm continuously working to improve," explained Jim with a little pride.

"I see...and how do you report it?"

"Actually, I collate the information, which is collected weekly into a monthly view, and then report it up to Glen in a quarterly view unless he wants something ad hoc."

"That sounds pretty well organized," noted Sikander, being genuinely impressed. "Jim, as you might recall, I mentioned in December that we should be expanding in this country to support online sales. Tell me, if we were to build a significantly wider reaching Internet distribution capability, what security concerns would you say need to be addressed?"

Jim gave a thoughtful pause before responding. "I guess I'd have to think about it. But off the top of my head, I think we'd need to beef up the TV security systems maybe and inventory recording. We might need to do spot checks, things of that nature. I would strongly urge comprehensive use of RFID tagging. Oh, and we'd need to improve upon, um, employee background checks and vetting processes, especially for certain critical information access roles." Jim was hard-pressed to hold back a cynical smile.

"Hmm...well, please do give it some more thought as I might be coming back to you to take this further. I believe we have to broaden our reach in this country via the Internet," replied Sikander and with

that he got up to leave. The tension, though diminished, was still there between the two of them and Jim's continued cool attitude to Sikander simply encouraged the latter to depart hastily, but as he did so, Jim managed belatedly to sputter out a polite comment.

"Thanks for—" the office door closed, "—stopping by," said Jim, continuing to process what Sikander might actually be up to.

The year progressed without incident and Carolectric Corporation did indeed secure better deals for supply sourcing from China, which enabled Javelin in Pakistan to operate at better margins. Thinking like Pakistanis, the brothers decided they could afford to bring wholesale prices down for the Chinese products and still make acceptable profits. Their competitors were less able to do so and as some of them went to the wall, Javelin either picked them up for rock bottom prices, or bought their assets while letting them fold wherever they found such companies in oversupplied areas of the market.

Ayub and Qayyum had a good year in school and it didn't take long for all traces of a Pakistani accent to evaporate from their English-speaking lips. Ayesha was in preschool, which freed up Rabia to make new friends and neighbors. She sometimes thought about how far she had come from being a poor village girl in Laghar Juy—now a dim and receding memory—to becoming an affluent woman in an up-market North Carolina home speaking highly acceptable English. No work of fiction could possibly have dreamed up *her* unlikely story, she thought.

Indeed, her ability to recount most, if not all, of her history made for fascinating conversation with friends, who also delighted in some of the "cute" mistakes she sometimes made with her language. She did not, of course, volunteer any information about her husband's Guantanamo experience along with her own parallel miseries in that regard.

There were several business and family member trips between North Carolina and Peshawar, though Sikander did not want to risk Saleem or Abdul Majeed coming as visitors, as their Taliban past would probably still have haunted them all the way to US Immigration, even though neither of them had ever fired a shot at American forces. In any case, neither of them was interested in being a designated enemy combatant in Qatar, Jeddah, London, or whatever other intermediate embarkation airport would end up being the focal point for carrying out immigration security assessments. They had no relish to be hauled off, at

the President's pleasure, to Guantanamo in the awful footsteps of their brother-in-law.

Of special note was the housewarming that took place in late May by which time Rabia, with Sabrina's deft hand, had managed to furnish and decorate the new home in an interesting Mughal motif, but integrating modern design elements. Most of Sikander's relatives came from Pakistan for the event, accompanying Rabia as she came back from her own trip. They included Noor, Razya, Sameena, Jamil, Kausar, Sofie, Ejaz, and Hinna and their respective children. Abdul Rahman and Sabiha had not been able to come due to Sabiha being hospitalized for minor surgery.

A few weeks later, after the housewarming guests had returned to Pakistan and with the weather being as close to perfect as imaginable, Sikander held a company barbecue, which allowed him to get to know more of his employees, although it was clear that he was effective at getting out and about while at the office.

Jim showed up to the slight surprise of Sikander and acted properly cordially but not with any deep warmth.

"Ah...Jim Mahler and...?" asked Sikander upon meeting Jim's other half for the first time.

"And Louise," she responded, with a warm smile.

"Ah...Louise," acknowledged Sikander, welcoming her but avoiding shaking her hand out of respect for Muslim sensibility. She caught the hint after barely twitching a muscle to lift up her arm and let it relax just as quickly.

I wonder if she has any idea what kind of a man her boyfriend or husband was five years ago. How did he unwind after a day's work then? Sikander speculated. *Still, he's probably a dear lovable guy right now and who knows? He might not even have known her back in his Guantanamo days.*

The barbecue was a great success, even without the booze, and Sikander got a strong sense that such outings were healthy for the cultural needs of the business. He genuinely felt that it might do some good to repeat them about once a quarter, only with some twists to keep them interesting.

From a work point of view, Sikander was engrossed in the routine issues of day-to-day business decision making. He was frequently on the video link to Jamil and rarely made any move without Jamil's valuable input. They had accomplished at least the first part of their goal for the acquisition and, with Sikander's vision, were looking to larger horizons, having had a glimpse of what might be possible in the US market.

At the time that Javelin had bought Carolectric, neither company had done very much to develop a strong Internet sales channel. That hadn't mattered in Pakistan where Internet purchases were relatively rare. Rather than build out more physical facilities in the US as they had successfully done in Pakistan, Sikander sought to scale the business with one or maybe two ultra-large warehouses which could be placed near the FedEx hub of Memphis and fulfill online orders from anywhere in the country. That would make all inventory available to fulfill any order without being caught with inventory in "the wrong place." They would keep supplying their existing walk-in warehouses with the most popular products, while the central warehouse would provide a lower cost and more scalable approach for the comprehensive product range. As long as customers could tolerate a wait of twenty-four hours and as long as costs of inventory management could be made low enough, they would be able to operate with an overhead advantage, allowing prices to be more competitive than most locally based suppliers. Internet marketing with a good business-to-business brand building plan had to be the priority as far as Sikander was concerned.

Sikander continued maturing his management style of general affability wrapped around a core of steel, which made him resolute when others would perhaps more readily cave. But he never came across as someone who was stubborn. This endeared him to his own management team while his relationship with Jamil—with his strong analytical skills and risk awareness—really gelled them and their company into a serious competitive force. They were still tiny by comparison with much larger international players, but as far as Sikander was concerned that was just a matter of time.

The summer came to a close and just before Labor Day, the children were back in school with Ayesha in kindergarten at Kerr-Vance. That made transportation easy. The weather in North Carolina was still excellent. The first weekend after Labor Day, having left the

children at a sleepover with Sabrina's children, Sikander and Rabia walked along the water's edge at Kerr Lake, enjoying the beautiful weather. It reminded them of Applecross and in some ways even Laghar Juy when the streams would be in full flood.

"There's something special here when the afternoon sun shimmers on the water," remarked Sikander.

"Mmm...remember when you saved me from the river in Laghar Juy, Sikander?" asked Rabia with a gleam in her eye.

"Oh yes..." responded Sikander in mock weariness. "Alhamdulillah it wasn't very deep, though there was certainly a strong current and it was hard to remain standing."

"Yes...but Sikander? What would have happened if it had been deeper?"

"We...we would have not come to know each other," chuckled Sikander.

"What? You wouldn't have stepped in to help me?" she came back indignantly.

"Uh, it would have been hard, Rabia since I...I can't actually swim. I never learned how," he lied, teasing her.

"Well, I think you should learn. I'd have hated to be in the same position with all this water around us now and then discover what you just told me!" she said with a girlish giggle reminiscent of when they were younger. "Sikander, we're truly blessed, aren't we?"

"We are, Rabia. When I consider what we've been through, hm! I can't complain of having had a dull life. Can you?" he asked with subdued sarcasm.

"Hardly! Let's see if we can make it a tiny bit duller, shall we?" They both laughed and each time they seemed to be over it, another glance at each other set them off again. Rabia changed the subject. "You know, Ayub's doing really well at school too, Sikander. I think this was the best move for our children. They have such good facilities in the schools here. Computers, lots of books, art materials, science labs...it's really quite impressive." Rabia reflected upon just another of her many sources of happiness. "You know, you should come one of these days or when they have the next parent-teacher conference."

"Yes, I will, inshaAllah. And I'm pleased that Ayub seems to have taken to baseball quite happily. What about Qayyum and Ayesha? How are they doing?"

"Well, it's probably too soon to say for them but as I see Qayyum sometimes picking up Ayub's books at home, I believe he's learning quickly. His reading and math reports are excellent."

As the sun began to cast a vibrant reddish glow, a million orange shimmering stars reflected off the tiny ripples and waves of Kerr Lake. The couple looked over the lake one last time before finally walking back to their car and driving the short distance back home.

All was finally right with their world.

Since the acquisition, Sikander and Jamil had continued pressing forward with the large central warehouse concept to support online sales, and as far back as February of 2007 they had already decided a purpose built facility would be needed nestled among the myriad other major brand warehouses dotting the outskirts of Memphis International Airport, the huge sprawling hub for FedEx. They weren't the first people with the idea but at least this would be an excellent location from which to ship anywhere in the country.

The plan had been put into action in March and by late November 2007 a modern warehouse facility had been created. What proved special about the design was the high degree of automation that Jamil had insisted upon for the pick-and-place function. Incoming electrical products could be racked in bulk, but the challenge lay in filling an order, with its near random requirement to pick out items from anywhere in the warehouse and efficiently get them together into a shippable package. They would need to be retrieved from well ordered racks and placed in collecting bins with bar codes on them or RFID tags, which would allow the bin and the contents to be tracked to the point of departure into boxes on which shipping labels could be placed prior to shipment. For large, heavy items, road haulage would be the shipping method.

Along with the warehouse was a new marketing campaign to promote the Internet capability, a new website, and plenty of promotional materials to send to virtually all customers everywhere.

The Christmas holiday season was fast approaching and Sikander decided that the senior management should be offered a trip out to Memphis to see for themselves what a marvel of modern automation had been built to support their next phase of expansion. As had happened at the time of the Carolectric acquisition, Sikander felt it important also to have his close family members be there to witness a ribbon-cutting ceremony for the new premises. A block of rooms was booked at the Westin in downtown Memphis. A special senior management party was also arranged, which would take place there not only to celebrate the new opening, but also that the combined company had surpassed the hundred-million-dollar mark for sales that year.

♣

"Come on, kids! Hurry up!" cried out Rabia as she put the final touches on her own packing for the upcoming trip. Sabrina and Salman had kindly agreed, once again, to babysit Ayesha, though she was now getting old enough to be insulted by such a term.

The rest of the family visitors were somewhere or other around the large house—each getting themselves or their loved ones ready. Sofie was so very proud of her sons and what they had accomplished. From the small beginnings in Peshawar with what Sikander's grandfather had started in the early 1950s, this was indeed a major new phase of his legacy and that of her late husband's.

Eventually the whole family managed to rush themselves out of the house and into their respective limousines to get to the airport and were soon on their way to Memphis. The rest of the senior management, VPs, and directors were likewise headed out there during this otherwise quiet period for the business.

That Thursday night, December 20th, everyone was settled in their rooms and suites and everyone was sufficiently tired to fall fast asleep right after isha. The following day at one o'clock in the afternoon, there was to be a brief opening ceremony, a cutting of the ribbon, and then a banquet was all set to be laid out in the warehouse itself.

As Sikander had introduced Jim Mahler to the concept toward the end of the prior year, he thought it would be nice to have Jim fly to the ceremony and point out the various extra security improvements that leveraged state-of-the-art technology for surveillance and data

integrity. Jim's relationship with Sikander had remained lukewarm despite almost a year of reasonable efforts by Sikander. Sikander supposed that this might now be simply the fact that Jim could only defend his behavior in Army Intelligence out of a genuine belief that Sikander was definitely one of the "bad guys" and he, of all people, would not be quick to let it go. However, as he was no longer in the Army, he had no authority to act, especially in the absence of even reasonable cause. So he simply remained at arm's length from Sikander while carrying out his job as best he could, but never losing sight of the possibility that Sikander might still be some kind of al-Qaeda "money-man" or "sleeper" using the company and his position as a cover.

Everyone arrived at the warehouse in time for the opening ceremony and all were received by both Jim and the site manager. Each person was given a hard hat to wear, as this was standard procedure. They were then led inside in two groups, one with Sikander and one with Jamil. Rabia was with Sikander with Ayub and Qayyum in tow. Sikander joked with her about how odd she looked wearing the bright white hard hat with the rest of her black outfit—a black shalwar and qamees with a silver thread embroidered pattern and matching embroidery on a black chiffon dupattha. He even offered a mock apology for there being no black hard hats. Gamely, she embraced suffering the indignity of the problematic fashion statement, but at least she had the comfort of knowing that all the other women were in the same situation.

The warehouse was not drab. Outside was a large retention pond with a fountain and the front of the building was a modern well-appointed office complex for between six and ten offices and a common area. Behind the offices was the main warehouse itself.

It was enormous. One hundred and eighty meters long by sixty meters wide, it was basically a gigantic box, but the interior had been remodeled to handle light-to-moderate-sized electrical products. At the far end was a row of receiving bays for incoming goods and a different row of loading bays for outbound shipments, which would typically be in smaller batches and boxed. There was, for a portion of the space, an advanced picking system to fulfill orders almost completely automatically. Preceding the bays was a packaging area and in front of that, the actual racks of products were arrayed in neat rows. The racking

was a modular type running to a height of over six meters with steel lag bolts holding the racks in place on the concrete warehouse floor.

To a large degree, Jamil provided most of the descriptive commentary and Sikander did pretty much the same thing in Pashto to the sizeable contingent of family members. The tour groups had worked their way more or less in the same sense that products entered, were processed, and left the warehouse and following that flow, they entered the major racking areas.

"Now, as we're walking through this space," began Sikander, "we're warehousing packaged products, like switches, small transformers, motors, and packaged electrical pumps, and these racks are set up so that we can stack to a very large height and still pick products from the top row if need be. Where automation doesn't apply, we still also use forklift trucks. In fact, one is coming this way right now, so I need everyone to step over here..."

Sikander pointed to a spot just behind where he was standing. The forklift operator had cautiously approached the group paying attention so that he wouldn't strike anyone with the vehicle. As soon as he sensed that the danger had passed, Sikander continued. But his attention was caught by the absence of any lag bolts in the flanges at the bottoms of the racks closest to where he and the group were standing. He made a mental note to himself that he would talk to the facilities people to get that corrected in the morning and resumed his role as guide.

"So, in these racks, which have shelving at approximately half a meter intervals, we have a total of almost ten miles or sixteen kilometers of shelves in this building alon—" Sikander had to stop abruptly.

As if in slow motion in front of him, the forklift truck was returning and its driver, paying inordinately more attention to the visitors, had managed to snag the forks in the very racking that lacked the lag bolts. He had been proceeding a little more confidently than he should have been, perhaps even subconsciously showing off to the visitors. The forklift's three thousand kilograms, at even two kilometers an hour, gave it enough momentum to impart a violent jarring motion on the racking and weakened its vertical members, lifting its improperly secured legs off the ground briefly.

Sikander had a sense of what was about to unfold and had already processed that standing in the most exposed position was Jim Mahler. The adrenalin seemed to sharpen his faculties while slowing down the passage of time. Sikander had already subconsciously extrapolated the path of the racking and a potential way to reach across to Jim as well as to bring himself out from the threat of falling objects with only minor injury given his hard hat. Immediately his body lunged forward as he instinctively called out: "Look out!" in the general direction of Jim. Barely a second later, Sikander's strong arms pushed Jim violently to the side and out of harm's way. However, the racking's contents had just begun disgorging from the shelves and a small but heavy switchbox had landed on the floor near Sikander's feet. With his invested momentum directed toward protecting Jim, Sikander tripped on the switchbox, which caused him to fall as soon as he'd pushed Jim out of the way. This all but eliminated any possibility of his protecting himself from the now accelerating onslaught of packages falling or rolling off the rapidly collapsing racking.

Instinctively, everyone retreated even further to avoid the metal avalanche. Everyone but Sikander. The group, including Jim, was horrified at the developing events but most especially as that last section of the racking unit continued descending onto Sikander, who could be seen raising his arms in a defensive but futile posture to afford himself some protection.

Two seconds later, virtually all of the contents of the shelves had rained down on or around where Sikander lay. Hard hat or none, this would not be an easily survived experience. There was utter silence. The entire group of visitors was paralyzed by the horror of the scene but as the shock subsided, the vacuum began filling rapidly.

"Sikander!" screamed Rabia and Sofie together. "Sikander!"

Sikander lay on the ground barely visible through most of the items of shelving, forming a disorderly heap around and on top of him. Mahler looked on and then finally jumped back as did Jamil, Ejaz, and Abdul Rahman and a few of the others to clear things out of the way. Sikander stirred, but clearly not in a very good way. He didn't utter a sound other than just weak gasps.

"Sikander! Sikanderrrr!" protested Rabia as she now ran in his direction. She brushed against one of the other people looking on, which pushed off her hard hat in a single move. She was now looking

down at him under the pile of shelving and contents spread across the floor.

Slowly, Sikander regained consciousness. He was in a daze. He could just barely make out what he could see and hear. Inexplicably, he felt deeply drowsy, barely able to keep his eyes open. In another moment, his crushed ribs and lungs began leaking out blood through his mouth. He was bleeding internally, giving him a drowning sensation.

In a moment he imagined himself to be in water having stepped off—or had he fallen out?—of a small boat. He could see the beautiful girl across the—what was that?—a shoreline? A riverbank? Some sort of water's edge. She was wearing a black qamees and a black shalwar with a beautiful silver embroidered black chiffon dupattha. Her big eyes could be seen looking expectantly at him bending down very slightly, beckoning him with her right arm while calling out, "Sikander! Sikander! Sikander!"

His dream of a night, long ago, in the Khyber hills was coming back to him. Or perhaps he was rushing toward to it. He couldn't tell as he felt himself floating not simply in space but also in time. Floating toward the girl—toward Rabia? Back. Back toward the surface of the water beneath which he was struggling in his attempt to break through. For a moment it seemed he might connect with the girl. She was surely his destiny. She had to be.

Jim pressed his ear to the part of Sikander's chest where he might hear a heartbeat. It was very weak. He checked the pulse while shouting, "Someone call an ambulance!" Two or three cell phones were already open and the process was underway.

"Come on! Come on! Hang in there, buddy! Please...please hang on! Oh my God...Sikander, stay awake! Please! *Please!*" prayed Jim.

In his stupor, Sikander felt himself make it through to the surface at least with his head or mouth. He gasped.

Sikander managed to open his eyes slowly once more. His head was in Rabia's hands while still in his daze, with blood oozing out of the side of his mouth closest to the floor and pooling there. He could see Jim Mahler crouching by his side with Sofie looking on behind, each of their faces twisted in anguish. Into his view from the other side came Jamil. Sikander's eyes moved from side to side and briefly fixed on Jim.

As they did, Jim noticed the slightest hint of a smile on Sikander's blood red lips. He then moved his weakening gaze over toward Rabia and the smile became a little more pronounced before relaxing back to no particular expression.

"Bhai-jan! Bhai-jan! Stay awake. Please hold on! The medics will soon be here!" pleaded Jamil.

Sikander's lips moved very weakly, mouthing nothing anyone could hear.

"Quiet! He's saying something! What's he saying?" asked Jim openly.

Rabia knew what it was.

"He's reciting the Muslim kalimah to himself. 'There is no God but Allah and Mohammed is his Messenger.' It's what we do when we know we're...we're dying," explained Jamil, in a resigned and sorrowful tone, his eyes red with a solitary tear running down his cheek. Jim returned his gaze back to Sikander's face while Rabia still held his head in her hands, weeping.

About three minutes later, the paramedics arrived. They asked what had happened, although the scene revealed much about the way in which Sikander was caught under the falling shelf contents. They could see what had caused the collapse, looking at the now limp forklift truck still enmeshed in what was left of the buckled racking. Sikander's upper body had been subjected to a massive blunt force trauma.

While they were there, one of the medics who had been listening for a heartbeat noted that it had stopped. He prepared his defibrillator paddles. Despite the physical injury and the probable aggravation of the trauma from an electric shock, he had little to lose to try to get a heartbeat going.

Four attempts were made but they proved to be futile and eventually the two men and the woman who made up the paramedic team gave up. The woman looked up and sensing immediately that Rabia was his wife, she slowly shook her head as she closed Sikander's eyelids.

"No...no," moaned Rabia in a soft voice as the awful truth hadn't yet completed its penetration of her dazed consciousness.

"Abba! Abba-jee!" protested Ayub while Qayyum stood speechless but crying as he huddled along with Ayub around his mother, still looking on in horror.

Sofie was now by Rabia's side and she too was in a speechless state. She gripped Rabia tightly and then collapsed, hardly able to breathe. She was quickly intercepted and made to lie down with someone's jacket as an improvised pillow while she began to whimper uncontrollably, still praying for Sikander's survival.

Jamil, Ejaz, and Abdul Rahman, who were all in the US for this special occasion, took it upon themselves to regroup the family and follow the ambulance while Rabia and Sofie rode in the ambulance with Sikander. Sofie rocked to and fro in her seat continuing to pray as Rabia could only look on at her and her beloved husband and weep. The paramedics were reasonably sure he was gone, but that had to be a doctor's declaration so they drove all the way to Memphis's Methodist South Hospital in Whitehaven. Jim Mahler followed in his rented minivan with several of his management colleagues. Within half an hour of arrival, Sikander was pronounced dead, but by then, not even Sofie expected to learn of a different outcome. Still, it wasn't until then that the members of the family uttered the familiar ayah: "Inna lillahi wa inna ilayhi raaji'un."

It was decided, with Rabia's agreement, that in keeping with the Islamic injunctions against delay, Sikander was to be buried in the nearest cemetery equipped for Muslim burial, which was up near I-40 between Galloway and Hickory Withe about forty-five kilometers from downtown Memphis. As far as the family were concerned, this was where Allah had decreed he should find eternal rest and that was that. After the burial, Jamil canceled his arrangements to return to Pakistan as he'd planned with Kausar, and everyone remained at the family home for several days after they had returned to Henderson.

Christmas day arrived in Henderson. A relatively rare but light snow flurry fluttered to the ground as the doorbell to the Khan household rang. Fourteen-year-old Ayub answered the door and standing in the open doorway was the figure of Jim Mahler.

"Hello, son...is your mom home or your Uncle Jamil?"

Ayub nodded and having recognized him from the fateful warehouse visit, he admitted Jim into the home as he also called out for his Uncle Jamil. Jamil came to the foyer and greeted Jim, asking him to come in. He couldn't bring himself to utter the words "Happy Holidays" or "Merry Christmas" under the present circumstances and given the mourning in the home, Jamil was a bit curious about the visit.

"What can we do for you, Jim?" he asked.

Jim looked back with the briefest expression of slight surprise but mostly the look of one who was bearing condolences. "I...I wanted to express my deep regrets and condolences to both you and Mrs. Khan," he said making obvious reference to Rabia.

The surprise element didn't register with Jamil's weary and troubled mind. Looking down, he nodded slowly in acknowledgment of the condolences. He couldn't help experiencing short periods of reflection on some or other part of his life and experience shared with his now departed brother and having to check himself to acknowledge the reality of his brother's death.

"I...I can ask her to come, but in Islam we have something called iddat which means a woman must remain in her home for a hundred and thirty days beyond the death of her husband. She can speak to you but she will be observing the veil," replied Jamil.

"Oh, that...that won't be an issue," declared Jim in a soft near whisper, "and I won't linger. You, uh, you folks must be pretty occupied right now."

"No, no, that's alright, Jim. I'll ask her to come. It won't be a moment," said Jamil reassuringly. After about five minutes, Jamil returned with Rabia wearing a dark gray shawl drawn well forward on her head. Jim noticed how the rest of her clothing was very drab and without any form of ornament. She took her seat on the sofa, looking down and in front of her at a point on the floor while she nodded in acknowledgment of Jim's presence. Jamil sat on a nearby armchair.

"I wanted to say how deeply...saddened and sorry I am that..." he hesitated to take a breath, "...that Sikander died while he, uh, he saved my life."

"Yes, Mr. Mahler," replied Rabia. "It was in his nature to look out for people. Saving lives was something he just did. He...he saved

me from drowning once a long time ago. He was—" Rabia choked a little but after all the weeping of the past several days, she was too exhausted and dry to cry.

"Yes, well, I can certainly attest to that," said Jim looking away as he recalled the events of Memphis. "I brought this." He pulled out a small gift wrapped in a somber wrapping paper and tied with a black ribbon over it. "Please don't open it right now, but...but I think you should have it."

"Oh...uh, thank you," replied Jamil, unsure of how to interpret the gesture, but taking the gift from Jim, just the same.

"I..." Jim began but just as quickly paused to study both of his hosts for a little while, glancing across from one to the other and back again. Finally, he asked a question he only now began to realize needed to be asked.

"Sikander hadn't...told you about me, had he?" asked Jim cautiously while now fully aware of the answer to his own question. He felt a wave of self-loathing overwhelm him. Even now, he was getting more of an insight into the personality of the man whose life Jim had once tried to make as miserable as possible and who had just given up that life to save Jim's own.

"About you?" asked Rabia as she glanced over toward Jamil hoping for some meaning. He could offer none as he too was puzzled. She turned her head back toward Jim but returned her gaze to the floor in front of Jim's feet. "How...do you mean, Mr. Mahler?"

Jim drew his breath and slowly exhaled. There was a crushing feeling in the pit of his stomach and the last thing he wanted to do at that moment was what his soul was commanding him to do.

"Mrs. Khan, Jamil, I, uh...I have to tell you that I used to be at Gitmo and Sikander was...Sikander was...well, he'd been one of my detainees there. I had been his um...interrogator and I...I didn't treat him very well," Jim finished as his eyes reddened and began to leak a tear. With a wavering voice he continued, "I know now how wrong I was and I...I don't have the *words* to say how really, terribly sorry I am."

"Jim, wh-what are you saying? Gitmo? You...you mean *Guantanamo*? When he was being held th—you *knew*

about…you…you knew him from—" Jamil was too incredulous to continue.

Rabia frowned with puzzlement. What *was* this nonsense that she was hearing? It didn't add up. "How could that be?" she thought aloud. "Surely Sikander would… Sikander would have—" At that moment Rabia began quickly recalling the evening of the first day back from the office when Sikander had been handed the golden key. Her eyes glazed and became distant looking while without realizing it, she muttered, "The golden key."

She began dragging out the memory of confronting Sikander with what had preoccupied him and he'd brushed it off with the jet lag remark. As that realization descended upon her, another wave began from the top as she came to understand that the man sitting in her living room, the man whose life her husband had given his own for, was his tormentor in Guantanamo. She broke down and began shaking uncontrollably, putting a hand to her forehead and shaking her lowered head with her eyes firmly closed. She made no noise, simply crying silently.

Jamil had meanwhile come to a similar realization regarding the events of the same ceremony and struggled with his brother's reasoning for not letting him know about the real identity of Jim Mahler. He too, felt overwhelmingly bitter at this moment about the person sitting in front of him having benefited so from his brother's death. Neither he nor Rabia could say anything and Jim began to feel the need to intervene.

"What I did, I…I know it can't make any…God knows Sikander did more than any man I know to prevent it from making a difference," said Jim. "I don't know now if I…if I could ever be forgiven for it. I…I just had to come and let you know how ashamed and, uh…and sorry I am. If there was anything I could do to undo what was done in those days…I'd give my life to do it now."

"I can't ever forgive you for what you did to my brother, Mr. Mahler," said Jamil, no longer able to use Jim's first name and with obvious disdain in his voice while recalling only those superficial details of Sikander's experiences in Guantanamo that Sikander had chosen to share, none of which had included Mahler's name. "But out of respect for Sikander's memory, I'll neither discuss this with anyone else nor use it against you in your job, Mr. Mahler. My brother meant too much to me to taint his memory with vengeance."

"Mr. Mahler...your sorrow and shame will be a matter between you and God, and whatever true repentance you might feel, not toward us, but to God..." came the voice from behind the veil, "and whatever remorse you might deliver to yourself to guide the rest of the life that my...my husband bought for you." Rabia paused to regain her breath. "Perhaps that will be God's way of giving you the chance to understand something more about yourself," she added as a new calm came over her. Her eyes were beginning to open to an insight that her husband had arrived at years ago, during his days at Guantanamo.

"If there's...anything I can do to help—" began Mahler.

"Mr. Mahler," uttered Rabia. "I'll be returning to Pakistan with my children and I will try my best to forget you," said Rabia with a growing tone of wishing him out of her presence.

Jim nodded understandingly as he gazed at the floor in front of her feet. He got up and said in a low voice, nodding a deferential good-bye, "Jamil, ma'am," as he left the room and saw himself out of the door.

Barely a minute after Mahler had left, Jamil remembered the gift that they had been given and he was torn between tossing it in the trash and returning it unopened to Mahler. Without quite understanding why, he decided to open it. Inside was a letter and a small box and Jamil handed both items to Rabia. She opened the box which contained an army medal. It was suspended from a blue ribbon with several red and white stripes down the middle and on the back of the octagonal piece of metal were the words "Soldier's Medal" with the name James A. Mahler Jr. engraved in the area designated for the purpose. She unfolded the paper and in fact it turned out to be two separate pieces of paper. The first was a letter written to Jamil and Rabia which read:

> Dear Jamil and Mrs. Khan,
>
> Words are inadequate to express my sorrow and regret for the loss of your brother and husband, Sikander. In the short time I had known him, I found him to be the most genuinely likeable person I have ever met, despite my own efforts to remain cold and distant to him.
>
> I'm sure you already know I was the man responsible for torturing your husband in 2002. I don't care what the government might call it, because that's what it was and I live

with the regret of that fact every day of my life. A life that Sikander gave his own to preserve. With that courageous act, he spoke to me to say that despite all that I had done, he still thought that my life held value. It was an act that I could personally relate to, as you will see if you read the note accompanying this letter. I think Sikander would have understood why you should have what I've left for you. I am truly sorry and, for what it's worth, I am resigning from Carolectric effective immediately.

Sincerely,

Capt. James A. Mahler, retd.

Rabia looked at the letter for a while longer after having completed it, and without a word handed it to Jamil. She opened the smaller note which was printed on a US Department of Defense letterhead. It was a concise description of an act of heroism on Jim Mahler's part in saving his fellow soldiers and two civilians in a fire at considerable personal risk to himself. At the bottom of the note appeared some language which explained the medal's criteria of issue:

...The Soldier's Medal is awarded to any person of the Armed Forces of the United States, or of a friendly foreign nation, who while serving in any capacity with the Army of the United States distinguished him/herself by heroism not involving actual conflict with an enemy. The same degree of heroism is required as for the award of the Distinguished Flying Cross. The performance must have involved personal hazard or danger and the voluntary risk of life under conditions not involving conflict with an armed enemy. Awards are not made solely on the basis of having saved a life.

As quietly as before, Rabia handed the note to Jamil. For her there was no consoling and it made little impact on her feelings toward James Mahler, though it heightened her sense of Sikander's consummate integrity in keeping the entire matter from her and the family. He had obviously tried to protect their sensibilities in the face of his own decision to keep Mahler.

Jim Mahler had by now stepped into his car. Sitting behind the wheel, he sat motionless next to Louise for a minute, peering at infinity.

Finally, without another word he started his car and drove off. He was in search of something he wanted very badly—something he had seen in Sikander and which had so far eluded him. It was a search his once victim and then life savior had completed years ago, ironically with Mahler's own unwitting but cruel assistance. It was a search for the humanity that, for Mahler, years of hateful corrosion had enveloped and almost—but not quite completely—concealed.

THE END

Appendix A
Glossary

A novel like *SIKANDER* covers a large sweep of geography and culture. Not surprisingly, many terms are used from different languages and the reader generally can get an inkling of meaning from the context in which a word or phrase is used. However, I thought it would be attractive to create a substantive glossary of all the words or phrases that might seem strange to one not immersed in the culture or environment of the novel. Owing to the diversity of settings, I've somewhat unconventionally arranged the glossary to have each word and its language identified, following which is a succinct meaning, and then a more in-depth elaboration for the REALLY curious. If there are uncommon abbreviations, those too are included with "English" in that case being implied rather than stated. Also to make things a little easier, all words are transliterated into Latin alphabet form. Often, alternative forms are widely used and in such cases, they are separated by a semicolon. Where a closely related word exists whose explanation makes sense to provide in conjunction with the original word, they are added alongside the original, separated by a comma.

I am indebted to the kind assistance of Mr. Hamid Sibghatullah for his review of the Islamic terms in this glossary. Any of the nuanced topics could probably each take up an entire book and we have obviously tried to manage the content to a reasonable degree of succinctness. In this regard, as a Muslim, I must acknowledge that several descriptions have been given in the Glossary regarding Islam

and Islamic principles, laws, culture etc. While I have strived to ensure the accuracy of the content, if there is any error then please know that it is not intentional and I seek forgiveness of Allah, Subhanahu-wa-ta-'ala for such error as there may be.

An important theme in *SIKANDER* is the Pashtun tribal code of Pashtunwali. Owing to its nature and to provide a richer sense of the cultural backdrop for Pashtun life, several terms appear in the Glossary which do not appear in the text but are relevant to a more complete understanding of Pashtunwali. All terms which form part of Pashtunwali are delineated as such with the parenthetic reference under the term in question, regardless of whether they are mentioned in the text, or not.

Lastly, there are always many points of view and levels of scholarship which inform the discussion of the meanings of words and terms. I do not profess to be especially knowledgeable about these though I have taken to using research and consultation with others more knowledgeable than myself when the need seemed to present itself. It is highly unlikely therefore, that everyone will agree with my own renditions of many of the meanings and such readers are invited to visit the website for the book: www.sikanderbook.com to offer their own input on the blog pages, or send me an email via the website.

Abaa	Pashto	**Father.** *A term for one's father.*
Abba, abba-jan; abba-jee	Urdu	**Father.** *Term of endearment about or to one's father; with -jan or -jee adds more respect.*
Aba'i	Pashto	**Mother.** *Used to refer to a mother but not to address the mother.*
Adey	Pashto	**Mother.** *Term of endearment directed toward a mother.*
Afridi	Pashto	**A major tribe of the Khyber region.**
Alhamdulillah!	Arabic	**Praise be to Allah!**
'Alim	Arabic	**Knowledgeable one.** *One who is qualified and recognized by the community of 'ulema as having sufficient knowledge of Islam to be permitted to transmit it authoritatively to others.*
Allahu Akbar!	Arabic	**God is great!** *Muslims believe that given the boundless greatness of the Almighty, a simple superlative like "greatest," connotes comparability where none exists. God is incomparable with anything and the normal English translation of akbar is therefore "great," rather than "greatest."*
Allahu a'alam	Arabic	**God knows best.** *Refers to matters of conjecture where the speaker is deferring to the greater knowledge of God and acknowledging the conjecture for being just that.*
Allah Hafiz!	Arabic	**God protects!** *May God protect you. A common invocation at a time of parting. It is often uttered as "Khuda hafiz." In this case, "Khuda," is a Persian word whose Indo-European root is the same as the one for "God." Some Muslims have shunned using Khuda and adopted the use of Allah, but most scholars agree that "God" is an acceptable English translation of "Allah," so a Persian one can be no less acceptable.*
AK-47	Abbr.	**The Kalashnikov AK-47 rifle.** *A Russian made and much copied small arms weapon using a 7.62mm round from a typically 30 round magazine clip.*
Ammee, ammee-jan	Urdu	**Mom.** *Mother as a term of endearment to one's mother; with –jan adds more respect.*
APC	Abbr.	**Armored Personnel Carrier.**

Apostate	English	*One who has relinquished the beliefs and practice of religion.* Most typically refers to Muslims who have turned away from Islam.
'Asr	Arabic	*The afternoon prayer.* The third of the five daily obligatory prayers for all Muslims.
Assalaamu 'alaykum	Arabic	*Peace be upon you!* The customary greeting at the start of interaction between Muslims; loosely equivalent to Hello, Good Morning/Afternoon/Evening.
Assalaamu 'alaykum wa-rahmatullah	Arabic	*A form of greeting which is typically uttered at the end of prayer.* It is directed to each of two angels (on the left and right) ever watchful of, and recording a person's deeds or actions.
Assalaamu 'alaykum wa-rahmatullahi wa-barakaatuhu	Arabic	*Adding beneficence (rahmah) and grace (barakah) above and beyond the normal greeting to people.*
Attan	Pashto	*An Afghan dance.* It is often performed at weddings.
Ayah, Ayat	Arabic	*Literally a Sign of Allah.* It applies to any perceivable aspect of creation, but used most often specifically to mean a "verse," in the Holy Qur'an, all of whose verses are also considered divine Signs of Allah.
Azaan; adhaan	Arabic	*The call to prayer.* Generally it is issued through loudspeakers in modern times to call a neighborhood to the prayer at a masjid. Although Muslims also have various optional prayers they can perform throughout a day or night, the azaan is only issued for the five obligatory prayers according to most Sunni traditions.
Badal *(Pashtunwali)*	Pashto	*Literally a swap or exchange.* It includes, but is not limited to acts of vengeance be they in terms of physical or economic harm to the other party, though always in the spirit of equitability.
Badragha *(Pashtunwali)*	Pashto	*An armed escort for protecting a traveler or fugitive passing through a tribe or clan's geographic boundary, from enemies in pursuit.*
Bahu	Urdu	*A daughter-in-law.*

Balandra *(Pashtunwali)*	Pashto	***Cooperation.*** *Used in the sense where aid is delivered to one who lacks the means to complete a task, such as planting the field. The assisted party typically hosts the providers of assistance with a meal.*
Baraat	Urdu	***The wedding entourage of a groom and his family.*** *It is customary for the groom to arrive at the place chosen by the bride's family for the wedding ceremony and then depart with the bride back to the home of the groom.*
Barakah	Arabic	***Grace or blessings of Allah.*** *Generally it is seen in terms of wealth or well being, though strictly it need not be so. It is also the underlying root of the name Barack as in US President Barack Obama.*
Baramta *(Pashtunwali)*	Pashto	***Similar to bota but with hostages taken from the obligee's village.***
BDU	Abbr.	***Battle Dress Uniform.*** *The BDU was worn by the US Army from the mid 1980's onward and was superseded in 2005 by the Army Combat Uniform or ACU.*
Bettha	Urdu	***Son.*** *The "tth" sound used here is pronounced like an English "t" but with the tip of the tongue rolled back until its underside touches the roof of the mouth prior to release of air.*
Bhabhi	Urdu	***Sister-in-law.***
Bhai	Urdu	***Brother.*** *Used to mean a blood relation but often used as a respectful address to a friend. More common in the "friend" usage culturally than is the word "brother" as used in western cultures.*
Bilga *(Pashtunwali)*	Pashto	***Being an accessory to a theft.*** *Generally evidenced by stolen property in one's possession for which one is held responsible, until or unless he/she makes good the loss, or reveals the source of the stolen property.*
Bota *(Pashtunwali)*	Pashto	***Seizure of property in lieu of an obligation.*** *The seizure is lawfully held until the obligation is discharged. It is similar to a lien but isn't recorded against specific property.*

Burkha; Burqa	Urdu	***A head-to-toe covering for females.*** *It represents the most comprehensive form of practice of veiling. Small holes or a mesh in the facial area allow for limited visibility. The "q" sound here is obtained by pressing the part of the tongue that is in the back of the throat against the back wall of the throat before abruptly releasing it without vocal chord action. As such it frequently appears with no "u" sound following it in words of Persi-Arabic origin.*
Cantonment, Cantt.	English	***The garrison outside many Pakistani and Indian towns and cities.*** *Created and used by the British as a residential area for British army officers, each Cantonment was adopted typically by upper middle class members of native society after the British departed in 1947. The abbreviated form of "Cantt" was often used in place of the full word, as this was how it usually appeared on signboards.*
Chacha, Chachu	Urdu	***Father's younger brother.*** *The Chachu form is usually more affectionate.*
Chador	Urdu	***A large usually woolen shawl.*** *Generally it is worn by men or women as a covering and a protection against the elements.*
Charss	Urdu	***A drug.*** *It comes from the cannabis plant and is traditionally made by hand rubbing the plant leaves but also using other methods.*
Chigha (Pashtunwali)	Pashto	***A posse formed for pursuit of bandits or raiders that have stolen property.***
Chowk	Urdu	***A town or city square or major street intersection.***
CI	Abbr.	***Comfort Item.*** *Small items allowed to the detainees at Guantanamo according to their pattern of compliance and cooperation. The more compliant detainees receive more CIs. Only boxer shorts remain if all CIs have been withdrawn. More clothing, flip-flops and board games represent the other end of the spectrum.*
Deobandi	English	***From the teachings of the Darul-uloom school of Deoband, India.*** *Launched in the 19th century to find a more uncorrupted form of Islam, it has come to be associated with a "puritan" focus on do/don't behavior and missing much of the spiritual aspect of Islam, but this is an outcome of practice and arguably not its essential teaching or philosophy.*

DRA   Abbr.   ***Democratic Republic of Afghanistan.*** *The name adopted by the communist government before, during, and after the Soviet occupation.*

Du'a   Arabic   ***Prayer supplication, specific request of Allah.*** *Unlike salaat, it does not involve physical action of bowing, prostration and sajdah. It is spoken.*

Dupattha   Urdu   ***A lightweight veil or shawl.*** *It is worn over the head without covering the face as such. Sometimes drawn far forward to hide the face similarly to the way a deep hood might be drawn forward.*

Durree   Urdu   ***Floor rug made from thick fabric of cotton.***

'Eid-ul-Adha   Arabic   ***Literally, the festival of sacrifice.*** *It follows the annual Hajj pilgrimage. For a Muslim with the means, an animal is sacrificed and the meat distributed—one third each to one's family, friends/relatives, and to the poor. The sacrifice commemorates the Prophet Abraham's (pbuh) sacrifice of a ram in lieu of his only son. Muslims believe that as it was when he was an "only" son, the son in question was the prophet, Ismail (pbuh), half brother to later-born Isaac (pbuh). The period of the festival is three days and starts about sixty-nine days after 'Eid-ul-Fitr.*

'Eid-ul-Fitr   Arabic   ***Literally, the festival of breaking fast.*** *It occurs on the first day of the month of Shawwal to celebrate the end of* **Ramadhan.** *A small payment of "fitrana," is due upon every person above the age of puberty which is normally collected at the time of the congregational* ***'Eid-ul-Fitr*** *prayer. The celebration includes dressing in one's best clothes and visiting friends and family, giving gifts—primarily to children.*

Ezarband   Urdu   ***Waist-string.*** *A length of crocheted cotton or other commonly available fiber used to form a rope-like drawstring to hold up a shalwar around the waist.*

Fajr   Arabic   ***The dawn.*** *By implication, the dawn prayer.*

Fatiha, Surat-ul-Fatiha	Arabic	*The name of the very first surah of the Holy Qur'an.* *It is also the **surah** that is most commonly recited, being an integral part of each cycle of **salaat**. It is also recited on behalf of a deceased person, most often upon first learning of the death. The act of such an offered recital is also itself commonly referred to as "performing Fatiha."*
Fi-amanillah	Arabic	*[Go] In the protection of Allah.* *A well-wish for the traveler typically used for long or perilous journeys.*
Fi-sabeelillah	Arabic	*Literally, in the path of Allah.* *For the sake of Allah.*
Ghundi (Pashtunwali)	Pashto	*An alliance.* *Usually it is between tribes or clans to serve a mutual interest.*
Gumbad	Persian	*A dome.* *Also used to describe a style for woven rugs in which the central motif is patterned after the interior architectural detail of many mosque domes, containing decorated intersecting geodesic lines and spaces between the lines.*
Gulgee	Urdu	*Ismail Gulgee.* *An internationally acclaimed Pakistani artist from Peshawar.*
Hadith	Arabic	*A narrative attributing sayings to the Prophet Mohammed (pbuh).* *Usually varying degrees of authentication from very sound to weak are applied to such narratives depending on the nature and circumstance of transmission.*
Halal	Arabic	*Permitted.* *It applies to any permitted act such as eating, drinking or earning an income in an Islamically lawful manner. Also applies to permitted things such as foods. Such foods must be inherently halal AND obtained in a halal manner to be considered permitted.*
Halwa	Urdu	*A sweet dish made of different types grains or other vegetables prepared in a typically mashed or paste like form.*
Hamsaya (Pashtunwali)	Pashto	*One who seeks the protection of a village elder.* *Normally it is in refuge from either indigence or blood feud. The Hamsaya enters the service of the protector.*

Haraam	Arabic	***Forbidden.*** *It is the opposite of **halal** and applies to actions and things that can be acquired or consumed such as income or food. A haraam asset or consumable can never be obtained in a **halal** fashion. A **halal** item, however, can be obtained in a haraam fashion which would then make it forbidden.*
Haraamzada	Pashto	***Literally, forbidden-born.*** *Illegitimate, bastard offspring. It is often used as in English as a denigrating epithet but carries more insult than the equivalent word in English may do today.*
Haram; Haramain; Haramayn	Arabic	***Literally a sanctuary or protected space.*** *It comes from the triconsonantal root of "h-r-m," which has meanings of protection, reservation exclusion, and prohibition (see **haraam**). When rendered as a proper noun, it refers to any of the three Holy Sanctuaries of Makkah (Masjid al-Haram, the "Sacred Mosque," which contains the Holy Ka'aba), Medinah (Masjid al-Nabawi – "Mosque of the Prophet,") and Jerusalem (Haram-al-Sharif – "The Noble Sanctuary"). A reference to the combination of Makkah and Medinah is usually expressed as al-Haramayn or al-Haramain where the word ending "-ayn," is a construct for a pair of things, (in contrast with "-een," which signifies a plurality).*
Henna	English	***A vegetable dye.*** *It is dark reddish brown and used to dye hair, skin, and nails in often elaborate patterns.*
Hezb	Arabic	***A group or party such as in a political movement.***
Hezb-e-Islami Khalis	Arabic	***Literally meaning the pure party of Islam.*** *Here it takes the term "khalis," meaning pure from the name of Younus Khalis whose party it was.*
Hijab	Arabic	***Literally any guarding of modesty. Typically, a head covering in which the face remains uncovered but the hair is completely covered.*** *As well as its use by large numbers of modern Islamic women, this form of covering most closely resembles the style used by adherent Jewish women and Christian nuns. Likewise, depictions of Mary, mother of Jesus (upon whom be peace), almost always show a hijab.*

Iddat   Arabic   *A period of four months and ten days following commencement of widowhood and three months if following divorce.* During this period a woman should not leave the home. Its purpose is generally agreed among scholars to establish paternity in case of a woman being unknowingly pregnant after a divorce or loss of a husband.

Iftar   Arabic   *The breaking of the fast.* It may be after an obligatory fast in **Ramadhan** or at other times when an optional fast is undertaken. Importantly, this term is used exclusively for the proper sunset break of the fast only, and not premature termination.

Ijaazah   Arabic   *Literally "permission."* It denotes the permission from a sheikh or *'alim* that authorizes his/her student to dispense religious knowledge or opinion. It is the basis on which one is titled a sheikh or *'alim* (feminine: 'alima) and thereby creates an unbroken chain of transmission for such knowledge dating back to the time of the Holy Prophet Muhammad (pbuh).

Ikhlas, Surat-ul-Ikhlas   Arabic   *Surah 112 of the Holy Qur'an.* It consists of four short ayahs and Its name means "purity," or "refining," which refers to the effect on the soul arising from the acceptance that almighty Allah is one, alone, eternal, absolute, being neither begotten nor begetting, and incomparably unique. It is often recited, commonly in **salaat** and along with **al-Fatiha** in offering prayer for a deceased person.

Imam   Arabic   *A leader.* Commonly, it refers to the one who leads prayers as a matter of routine or just assumes the role on a given occasion.

Inna lillahi wa inna ilayhi raaji'un   Arabic   *Indeed we are from Allah and to him shall we return.* Verse 156 of Surat-ul-Baqara in the Holy Qur'an. This is normally recited upon a calamity or catastrophe occurring in which a Muslim suffers. It has come to be used almost exclusively for when learning of a Muslim's death. Strictly however, it should be uttered for any worry or calamity befalling a Muslim.

InshaAllah   Arabic   *If it be the will of Allah.* Very frequently used to qualify any prediction whose outcome is desirable to indicate that control of any outcome is always in God's hands. Culturally, it has come to be seen as an opting out of responsibility for an action ahead of time and often presages a likely failure to achieve a goal or task.

Isha   Arabic   *The evening prayer.* The last of the five daily prayers.

ISI   Abbr.   *Inter-Services Intelligence.* A Directorate of the Pakistani Intelligence services and the largest of Pakistan's three intelligence services.

Islam   Arabic   *The way of life practiced by Muslims.* Literally meaning peaceful and complete submission, in this case to the Will of Allah. It has the same tri-consonantal proto-Semitic root of "s-l-m," from which the cognates *"salaam,"* and the Jewish "shalom," are derived.

Itbar (Pashtunwali)   Pashto   *Trust.* The basis for dependency on any verbal agreement made in front of a jirga or other witnesses.

Itwar   Urdu   *Sunday.*

Jahannam   Arabic   *The Muslim concept of hell.* A place and/or state of enduring torment.

Jahez   Urdu   *The collection of gifts of money, jewelry, clothes or other useful items given by parents to a daughter for her marriage.* Customary, but not an Islamic requirement, it has gradually become an expectation by groom's families and has widely become seen as a "bride price." Parents typically start assembling a jahez when a daughter is born and add to the collection over the years before a daughter's marriage.

Jahil   Arabic   *Ignorant, uneducated.* It refers to ignorance in a manner typically incorporating the idea of tacit acceptance of such a state. i.e. not blissfully ignorant but willfully so.

Jahiliyyah	Arabic	*Originally referring to the era preceding the arrival of Islam.* It describes a culture which willfully shunned the pursuit of truth and knowledge. It is sometimes used today by some extreme **Salafists** (such as members of al-Qaeda) to criticize a collectively heedless state of mainstream Muslims. Mainstream Muslim scholars resoundingly refute this assertion.
Jamaat	Arabic	*A physical gathering or party.* It can mean not only a political party similar to **hezb**, but also the physical gathering as where Muslims line up for prayer.
JazaakAllah, JazaakAllah Khayr	Arabic	*May Allah reward you.* A form of thanks to an individual. With Khayr or Khayran, it adds the qualifier "well."
Jazaakumullah	Arabic	*The same as JazaakAllah but referring to a plurality of people who are being thanked.*
Jihad; Jehad	Arabic	*Any of four major categories of striving – (a) in self discipline against one's base desires, (b) of the hand (non-military actions), (c) of the tongue (use of argument), and (d) of the sword (military).* Though the latter use is a legitimate one, (much as notions of a "just-war," are articulated in non-Muslim circles), a war as such is better translated as "harb," in Arabic. Indeed, a holy war would be a "harbun-mutaqaddisun," combining "harb" for war and "quddoos," from the tri-consonantal "q-d-s," for "holy."
Jilbab	Arabic	*A long loosely fitting coat.* It is worn over outerwear to cover a woman's more decorative dress and to direct unwanted attention away from the shape or figure of the woman dressed as such.
Jirga	Pashto	*A council of elders.* In a village or potentially larger administrative area among **Pashtuns**. Jirgas frequently dispense justice.
Jumu'ah	Arabic	*Friday.* It is based on the root meaning of togetherness since Friday is a day of congregation.
Salaat-ul-Jumu'ah	Arabic	*The Friday congregational prayer.*
Jumma	Urdu	*Friday and by implicit reference, the Friday mid-day prayer.* It is derived from the Arabic "jumu'ah."

Jumma Bazaar Arabic *A bazaar normally open for Friday typically after Friday prayer.*

Kafir; Kaafir Arabic *One who denies or conceals truth and especially the truth of the one-ness of God.* The element of concealing is central to its meaning coming from the root "kufr"—concealment. It is also a cognate of the English word "cover." It has come to be used to refer to unbelievers.

Kalay; kili Pashto *Village.*

Kalimah Arabic *Verbal declaration.* From the tri-consonantal "k-l-m" —"speak," it means a saying or spoken motto. but refers to one of five specific pronouncements made by Muslims as articles of faith. The most prominent of which, the "tayyabah," is: "There is no God but Allah and Mohammed is the Messenger of Allah."

Kebab Urdu *A ground or minced meat dish.* It is made by grilling, roasting or stewing the meat.

Khan Pashto *Honorific referring originally to peoples of Turkic or Mongol warrior origin.* Very widely used as tribal identity of a **Pashtun** or **Pathan**. In modern usage, it often appears as a last name when aligned to a western norm for naming. The vast majority of **Pashtuns** bear this name as an ethnic identity—including this book's author. It is occasionally used to emphasize ethnicity out of respect and is often delivered in the form "Khan sahib," when addressing one who is a **Pashtun**. The "kh" sound is pronounced most similarly to the "ch" in the Scottish word "loch."

Khel Pashto *A clan. A subgroup of a Zai or Pashtun tribe.* Due to relative immobility in mountain country, Khels have often emerged as confined in single villages and the word has increasingly come to mean "village," in like fashion to *"kalay"* and *"kili."*

Khidmat Arabic *Service.*

Khowr Pashto *A daughter of a sister; niece; "Sister-friend."* It may be as in a sorority or between close female friends but not lesbian.

Khussa	Urdu	***An ornate slipper.*** *Usually it has a curly pointed toe end. Unlike most transliterations, here it is pronounced without conjoining the "k" and the "h" and in fact most westerners would pronounce it correctly with no guidance.*
Lashkar **(Pashtunwali)**	Pashto	***An armed group or militia.*** *In **Pashtunwali** it is formed for a mission such as enforcement, usually assembled and authorized by a **jirga**.*
Lehenga	Urdu	***Ankle-length full skirt typically worn on weddings or special occasions.***
Lokhay **Warkawal** **(Pashtunwali)**	Pashto	***Offering a sacrifice or gift to a stronger tribal entity in return for protection.*** *This can also apply at the level of individuals. An offering (Lokhay) is made and the accepting entity is bound to protect the one requesting protection.*
Maalik	Urdu	***Owner.***
Madrassah	Arabic	***A place of intermediate learning.*** *A school where lectures are a predominant from of knowledge transfer. The term has come to be used to emblemize rote-learning schools, but this is a recent development, and has become a western cultural stereotype.*
Maghrib; **maghreb**	Arabic	***The West geographically and politically. The place where the sun sets. Sunset. The shorter reference to "salaat-ul-maghrib" or the sunset prayer.*** *As with the Jewish faith, sunset marks the start of a new day in an Islamic calendar.*
Maktab	Arabic	***A place where written work takes place and by implication, an office, a primary school, or even a library.*** *The word is very generally applied by context and may even include simply meaning "desk."*
MashAllah	Arabic	***Whatever Allah wills.*** *It acknowledges that any good outcome is the will of Allah and is used to prevent the interpretation of an inflated sense of personal or human responsibility for a positive outcome.*
Masjid	Arabic	***Literally a place of sajdah (see below), or place of worship. A mosque.***
Maulwi	Urdu	***A title honorific given to an Islamic scholar or 'alim.***

Maulana	Urdu	*Literally our master or lord but referring to a human master or lord, never a divine one.* It applies to a person of significant religious authority often seen as such by several generations.
Meerata (Pashtunwali)	Pashto	*A crime of systematic assassination of the male members of a family for the specific objective of eliminating lineage and rights of inheritance.* It is met with strong retribution unless a payment of compensation is made. This can be money in the form of what is called **Saz** or **Swara**. The **Jirga** is used to mediate such moves and if the victims' family accepts the **Saz** or **Swara,** then the perpetrators are free of all claims.
Mehr	Arabic	*The Islamic concept of a financial right accruing to the bride in a marriage, which becomes obligatory for the groom to pay the bride in the event of a divorce or otherwise upon demand.* This stands in contrast to the common practice of jahez, which often results in the groom and/or his family seeking financial benefit from the bride and/or her family. When excessive, this is often termed a "bride price." In most mainstream Pakistani Muslim practice, both the mehr and a modest jahez of usually clothing and jewelry are commonplace.
Mehram	Arabic	*A relationship between sexes where marriage would be impermissible such as between father and daughter.* Non-mehram relationships are those where a marriage would, on the grounds of the relationship per se, be permissible. A woman should be veiled before a non-mehram man. A man should avoid prolonged eye contact with a non-mehram woman. The degree to which this is practiced varies throughout the Islamic world.
Melmasthia (Pashtunwali)	Pashto	*The required behavior toward anyone who is a guest or who is seeking protection of another.* It is a serious dishonor to allow a protected guest to be harmed. Such guests can often include personal enemies but who have nonetheless requested protection.
Mere bhai!	Urdu	*My brother!* A term of warmth and endearment used between good friends. The word bhai has a broader reach than the blood-relation "brother" in English. It is also more informal than use of "brother" in English when referring to a fraternity as in an association or society.

Miswaak	Arabic	*A twig of the arak, peelu or Salvadora persica tree whose peeled bark reveals a stiff bristly core that is used as a tooth brush.* It has been used since ancient times. Among Muslims is significant since it was used and recommended by the Prophet (pbuh).
Mla Tarr (Pashtunwali)	Pashto	*Taking up the cause of an injured party usually against an outsider.*
Mubarak	Arabic	*To be blessed or graced.* Typically offered to others to say "May your good news be blessed" as in 'Eid-Mubarak (A blessed 'Eid) or Shaadi-Mubarak (May your marriage be blessed). It comes from the same root as **barakah**(grace).
Mujahid, Mujahideen	Arabic	*One who is striving in any of the four kinds of jihad.* Plural form is mujahideen but in a western cultural context as with Taliban, the plural is often used adjectivally to describe a singular individual.
N'showr	Pashto	*Daughter-in-law.*
Naan	Urdu	*A flat bread baked in a brick oven by placing the dough against the walls of the oven.*
Nanewatai (Pashtunwali)	Pashto	*Forgiveness of repentant enemies.* Reconciliation.
NIFA	Abbr.	*National Islamic Front for Afghanistan.* One of several prominent **mujahideen** groups organized to fight communist rule and later Soviet occupation of Afghanistan.
Nihari	Urdu	*A meat dish usually served at breakfast time and made from beef shanks and spices.*
Nikaab; niqab	Arabic	*A form of veil which goes beyond the hijab to cover the face except for the eyes.*
Nikkah; nikah	Arabic	*Literally a joining or coming together to make whole.* In common usage it refers to a Muslim marriage ceremony. The legal form of a Muslim marriage.
Niyyah	Arabic	*An intention.* In Islam, all innocence and guilt stem from intent. Niyyah refers to one's intention. Most sins that occur as inadvertent infractions are not considered sins unless the ignorance was unreasonably present. Even so, repentance is a necessary and appropriate response.

NWFP	Abbr.	***North West Frontier Province.*** *One of four provinces of Pakistan, with capital Peshawar. Recently, amid controversy, it has been renamed to "Pakhtunkhwa."*
Paan	Urdu	***A betel leaf used typically folded up and containing stuffing to be folded up and chewed.*** *The stuffing may be of fennel or other forms of flavor, including tobacco according to tastes.*
Paan shop	Urdu	***A shop serving up paans in a variety of formulations.*** *Very common throughout Pakistan and often a focal point for gossip and socializing in a manner analogous to a western bar but usually on a much smaller scale.*
Pakhtun	Pashto	***Same as Pashtun.*** *A large ethnic group covering mostly eastern Afghanistan and the North West Frontier Province of Pakistan. The "kh" form is applicable to northern tribal pronunciations while the "sh" form is normally used in southern parts. For simplicity, the narrative sticks with the easier to pronounce "sh" form.*
Pakol	Pashto	***A woolen cap.*** *Made in the form of a long cylinder with a single open end, whose walls are rolled up to create a brim which grips the side of the head.*
Paratthha	Urdu	***A thin bread made by folding butter into the flour dough before rolling it flat for cooking.*** *The second "h" is aspirated and distinct from the "tth" consonant.*
Partition	English	***The event which created Pakistan on August 14th 1947, at the end of British rule over India.*** *The following day, after Pakistan was formed, the modern country of India was given its own independence.*
Pashto	Pashto	***The language of the Pashtuns.***
Pashtun	Pashto	***Same as Pakhtun.***
Pashtunwali	Pashto	***An elaborate system of tribal law and societal custom.*** *It is codified into several aspects, each dealing with property, dispute resolution, treatment of strangers, protection of victims, and many other areas of law and order. It is generally agreed that this system has been in place for over 2,000 years and predates Islam in Afghanistan.*

Pathan   Urdu   *Pashtun in Urdu/Hindi. The south Asian name for Pashtun.*

Patthra   Urdu   *A low wooden platform stool.* Typically it is about ten centimeters off the floor held up by two short vertical planks as legs and a top plank as a seating surface.

Pbuh or (pbuh)   Abbr.   *Peace Be Upon Him.* A salutation and prayer asking for the peace and blessings of Allah to be visited upon Mohammed (pbuh), the Holy Prophet of Islam. It is considered rude or ill-mannered to fail to offer such a prayer upon the mention of his name or personage. In the written form, it is usually abbreviated thus.

Pooree   Urdu   *A thin fried bread often eaten together with halwa.*

Qamees   Arabic   *An upper garment like a shirt or blouse at the top but extending typically up to or over the knees.*

Qasr   Arabic   *The offering of one of the normal prayers in a shortened fashion as permitted when traveling.* Customarily the midday prayer and the afternoon prayer can also be combined when they are thus shortened. Likewise, the sunset and nighttime prayers may be combined under the same circumstances.

Qiyaamah   Arabic   *The end of days.* The end of the world. The day of Resurrection. The day of Judgment.

Qazi   Arabic   *A judge or one who administers matters of justice such as a justice of the peace might do.* This role is the one called upon to conduct marriage ceremonies.

Qiblah   Arabic   *At any point on earth, the direction that would face the Ka'aba in Makkah, Saudi Arabia.*

Qur'an, Holy Qur'an	Arabic	*Literally, the Recitation.* It refers to the directly revealed divine word of God through the medium of the Prophet Mohammed's (pbuh) utterances while in a state of receiving revelation. It was more than a simple intellectual process of explanation. It was rather a process of independently placing utterances directly into the lips, tongue and vocal chords of the Prophet (pbuh), while infusing his mind and spirit with the total recall and understanding of what had been uttered. The focus on recitation refers to the medium being most essentially verbal even though the content has been captured in written form. It is also why Muslims attach great significance to reciting the Holy Qur'an and not simply reading it silently.
Ramadhan; Ramadan; Ramzan	Arabic	*The Muslim holy month during which fasting is prescribed for all non-traveling, non-infirm, non-menstruating Muslims above a certain age.* Fasting is from before dawn to sunset. It is the month during which the Holy **Qur'an** was first revealed and the revelation requiring fasting is to be found in Surah 2, verse 183:—*"O ye who believe! Fasting is prescribed to you as it was prescribed to those before you, that ye may (learn) self-restraint."* *Fasts that have been excused for the above reasons are to be made up as soon as conveniently possible as and when the reasons no longer apply. Abstinence during fasting is from all ingestible substances, smoking, drinking, food, and sexual activity.*
Ramadhan Mubarak	Arabic	*Wishes of blessings upon another Muslim on the start of and during Ramadhan.*
RFID	Abbr.	*Radio Frequency Identification Device.* A very small microchip that can be incorporated into most products or product packaging to enable ready signaling of product identity, location, and other information when the tag is irradiated with usually nearby radio waves.
Riba	Arabic	*Literally, an increase. Used exclusively to refer to interest or usury in the financial sense.* Receipt or payment of riba is considered **haraam** in **Islam**, and this position is the basis for all appropriately scholar-qualified Islamic finance offerings.

Ricksha; **Rickshaw**	Urdu	*A powered three-wheeled conveyance with a single seat for the driver and a small bench for two or three passengers at the rear with minimal baggage space. Originally, a two-wheeled cart enabling a human runner to transport up to three passengers short distances by holding two long pole-like arms at a point neutrally balanced over the large main wheels of the cart. Subsequently, designs switched to tricycles driven by sprocket-and-chain drives and pedals, but still man-powered. Finally, powered vehicles emerged during the 1960s.*
Rotthi	Urdu	*A flat bread baked directly on an open griddle or tawa.*
RPG, RPG-7	Abbr.	*Rocket Propelled Grenade. (Version #7 with the added designation). A high explosive device, often involving a shaped charge to generate a high energy focused jet of gas and liquid metal that pierces armor. It is typically launched from a shoulder mounted tube, and is effective against armored vehicles such as main battle tanks or armored personnel carriers.*
Sabaz, Sabz	Urdu	*Green, as in the greenery of vegetation.*
Sabaz chai	Urdu	*Green tea.*
Sahib	Urdu	*Sir. Used as an honorific. A mark of respect.*
Sajdah	Arabic	*Prostration with the forehead, nose, palms, knees and toes touching the ground in worship.* Forbidden for all Muslims except toward Allah.
Salaam	Arabic	*Peace. The peace greeting. From the proto-Semitic tri-consonantal form of "s-l-m," which means safe or whole without breakage or damage. The infinitive form in Arabic is "Islam," which describes a state more than the effects of the state—in this case, a state of peaceable acceptance of God will and command.*
Salaat	Arabic	*Ritual prayer which must be performed according to guidelines governing ritual purity, posture, state of mind, and recitation.*
Salaat-ul-fajr, zuhr, asr, maghrib, isha	Arabic	*Each of the prayers of the day are fully described by adding the prefix "salaat-ul-..." in front of the specific prayer as in salaat-ul-maghrib. However, normal usage often drops the prefix.*

Salafism, Salafi   Arabic   *A Sunni sub-sect of Islam. Adherents seek to practice Islam in strict accord with the manner of its practice by the first three generations of Muslims — the "salaf."* It looks for literal acceptance of scripture and avoids an interpretive approach. Salafi is one who practices Salafism. It is often associated with a shunning of modernity insofar as it leads to deviation but such a position in not inherent to Salafism.

Salafist   English   *A term describing any of several movements seeking political change who are alleged to base their motivations on Salafi principles. Such groups are said to include al-Qaeda. Virtually no scholars within the **Salafi** branch of Islam endorse the unauthoritative declaration of **jihad** and the seemingly callous killing involved in terrorism. Neither do they pronounce **takfir** on their fellow Muslims as various Salafist organizations are alleged to do.*

Saz (Pashtunwali)   Pashto   *Compensation for causing wrongful death.* Offered by those acting on behalf of perpetrator(s) to the surviving relatives of victim(s) via a **jirga** and only if acceptable, will it absolve the perpetrator. Saz may be in the form of money or other things of value. It may also be in the form of swara (see below).

Shahadah   Arabic   *The act of testifying. Describes both the taking of the oath to accept Islam, and an act of martyrdom.* The latter is itself an act of testimony to the true articles of faith. The essential quality of the martyr is not the death itself nor the simple commitment to a cause, but the belief driving such commitment being complete and without doubt. A majority of Sunni scholars generally hold that suicidal combat in which the suicide itself is the instrumentality of the combat, is not ordinarily permissible. On the other hand, a certain death but inflicted by the action of opponents, while potentially describable as "suicide," is permissible. Suicidal (or non-suicidal) actions that target non-combatants are also not permissible and there is no theory of collective responsibility applicable to an entire population (e.g. including babies) for the wrongdoing of its leaders. There are no documented cases of the Prophet Mohammed(pbuh) leading or condoning suicide missions, nor sanctioning the slaying of non-combatants.

Shaheed   Arabic   *A martyr. One who has died in **shahadah** fighting an unjust opponent or resisting one. Most generally the death occurs in the fulfillment of any religious commandment in which the effort is driven by strength of faith in Islam. The first shaheed in all Islam was a woman called Sumayyah bint Khayyat.*

Shalwar   Urdu   *A **baggy pant**. It is tied around the waist with an **ezarband** and worn such that the waist and upper portions are hidden under the knee length qamees.*

Sherwani   Urdu   *A **long coat**. Usually it has a tight collar without a lapel, fastened over the throat and several buttons down the top two thirds of its length. It is often ornate and embroidered and worn ceremoniously.*

Shinwari   Pashto   **A tribe of predominantly northeastern Afghanistan and northwestern Pakistan.**

Spin   Pashto   **White.**

Spin Ghar   Pashto   **White Mountains.**

SSG   Abbr.   **Special Services Group.** *An elite special operations commando force of the Pakistan military, similar to the US Army's Delta Force or British SAS.*

SubhanAllah   Arabic   **Literally God is void of all other things.** *This means God is void of dependency or evil. It use is to glorify God's work or acts as when seeing something remarkable.*

Suhur   Arabic   **The meal taken before dawn when it is still dark enough to eat during the month of Ramadhan.** *By instruction directly from the Holy **Qur'an**, it is supposed to be completed before it is possible to discern a black thread from a white one in natural twilight.*

Sunnah   Arabic   **Any act of the Prophet Mohammed (pbuh). The body of knowledge comprising the acts, sayings and tacit approvals of the Prophet Mohammed (pbuh).** *The importance of cataloging this knowledge stems directly from the Holy Qur'an, which declares that the Prophet (pbuh) was the best example of right behavior.*

Sunni   Arabic   **One who attaches importance to guidance from the Holy Qur'an for categoric instruction supplemented by the Sunnah to understand details of how to carry out the instructions of the Faith.**

Surah; Sura   Arabic   *A chapter or segment of the Holy Qur'an.* Each surah has a name which it typically takes from a word or ayah in one of its verses.

Swara   Pashto   *The offering in marriage of a girl of a family of a perpetrator of wrongful death—such as in meerata—to the family of the victim(s) in lieu of saz (blood money).*

Tablighi Jamaat   Urdu   *A party that proselytizes for religious reawakening of Muslims throughout the world.* It is a non-affiliated apolitical movement and is targeted largely toward Muslims to bring them closer to their own faith. It is avowedly pacifist.

Tafsir   Arabic   *Commentary or exegesis of the Holy Qur'an.* The act of interpreting but in non-mystical ways the meaning of the Holy **Qur'an.**

Takbeer   Arabic   *The call to recognize, acknowledge, and pronounce the greatness of God.* Almost always to spur a group of people to call out *"Allahu Akbar"*—God is Great.

Takfir, Takfiri   Arabic   *To pronounce Kufr on someone.* To declare a person to be a **Kafir.** Orthodox Islam frowns upon this practice carried out upon a fellow Muslim once he/she has professed the articles of faith. Takfir is one of the primary forms of justification of carrying out terrorist acts and such people also depart from orthodox Islam in the interpretation of suicide as a legitimate means of military action. They believe that this does result in shahadah—something contradicted by all orthodox Muslim scholars. "Takfiri," is one who engages in takfir.

Talib   Arabic   *Student. In Pashto, the plural is Taliban.* The body of "students" that became a political movement of Afghanistan. Increasingly in western discourse, the label has also come to be applied to singular individuals as in "He is a [member of the] Taliban."

Tandoor   Urdu   *A clay oven.*

Taraweeh   Arabic   *Special prayer during the evenings of Ramadhan.* It focuses on recitations of the Holy **Qur'an** usually resulting in the entire **Qur'an** being recited over the roughly thirty nights of the month.

Tarr *(Pashtunwali)*	Pashto	***A mutual agreement or contract usually governing acts or prohibiting them by mutual arrangement.*** *Violation of the agreement exposes the violator with no recourse if he/she suffers harm from the violated party.*
Tashahud; **Tashahhud**	Arabic	***The seated phase of a Muslim prayer.*** *The posture is one of sitting on one's legs with knees fully bent and hands resting on the upper thighs just above the knees.*
Tawa	Urdu	***A griddle, usually flat or convex on which flat (chapatti or paratthha) bread is made.***
Teega *(Pashtunwali)*	Pashto	***A truce, cease-fire, cessation of hostility.*** *It does not require resolving the underlying cause of a dispute. Breaking the truce invites punitive measures from the **jirga**.*
Tor *(Pashtunwali)*	Pashto	***Gender propriety.*** *For example, prohibition of men touching women or girls to whom they are not married or not **mehram**.*
Tora Bora	Pashto	***Black Dust.*** *The name given to a region of the **Spin Ghar** mountains containing a large complex of caves used by mujahideen and al-Qaeda at different times.*
'Ulema	Arabic	***Plural of 'alim.*** *It is also often used to refer to a consensus among scholars over matters of Islamic knowledge and its interpretation.*
Uzr	Pashto	***An apologetic or sorrowful regret.***
Wa alaykum **assalaam**	Arabic	***And upon you be peace.*** *Traditional response for a Muslim to whoever is offering **salaam** when meeting or starting a reply to a letter/email. Often in written form abbreviated to "WAS."*
W'Allahi; **Wallahi**	Arabic	***By God. By Allah.*** *Often to emphasize commitment to a point, comment or position that the speaker is taking.*
Wahabi; **Wahhabi**	Arabic	***One who is guided by the teachings of 18th Century scholar Ibn Abdul Wahhab.*** *He preached a puritan ultra-conservative form of Islam.*
Walimah	Arabic	***The part of an Islamic wedding ceremony that takes place typically a day after the formal marriage and arranged by the groom's side of the family.*** *Many scholars suggest that it should only be performed after consummation.*

Wand-yaar	Pashto	*Sister-in-law.*
Wasalaam	Arabic	*"...and peace."* A return of a greeting often at the end of a letter, before the signature line in a Muslim's correspondence.
Wudhu	Arabic	*The lesser ablution.* A ritual purification through washing before any prayer.
Ya Allah	Arabic	*Oh Allah.* A direct appeal to Allah. Oh God.
Ya Allah! Tera shukr hai!	Urdu	*Oh Allah! Thanks be to thee!* Thank God!
Yaar	Urdu	*Term of endearment to a fellow male friend.* Used similarly to "dude," in common American slang.
Yusufzai; Yousufzai	Pashto	*A very large tribe of the Pashtuns, mostly residing in Pakistan's NWFP.*
Zai	Pashto	*The generic term for a tribe of the Pashtuns.*
Zuhr	Arabic	*The mid-day prayer.*
Zwey	Pashto	*A term of endearment to mean "Son," in Pashto.*

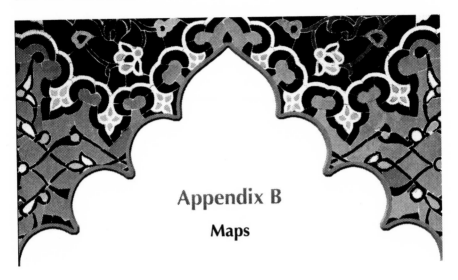

Appendix B

Maps

The narrative of *SIKANDER* covers a wide geographic scope and a few maps have been included to aid the reader in understanding the places of significance to the story. However, although the story ends in the United States, the reader is assumed either to be familiar with US geography or to be easily able to access such information on the Internet and other sources, so US maps are not included. The maps on the following pages are either unique to the story or not easily obtained.

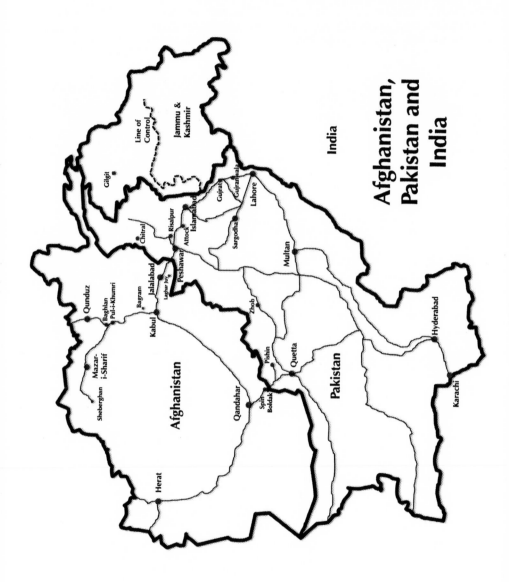

Afghanistan, Pakistan and India

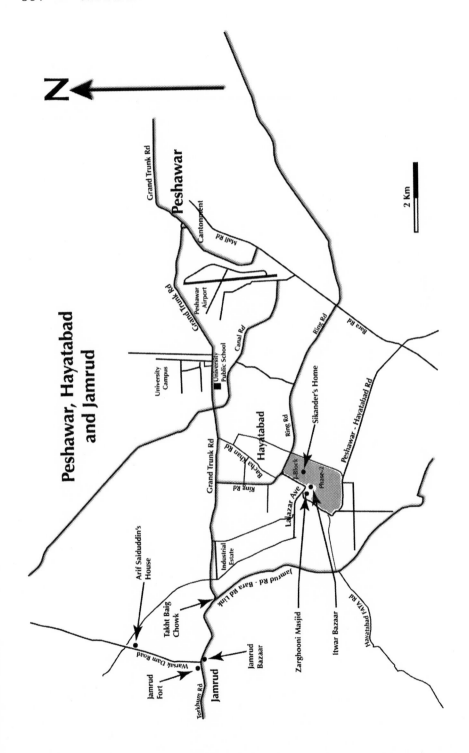

Peshawar, Hayatabad and Jamrud

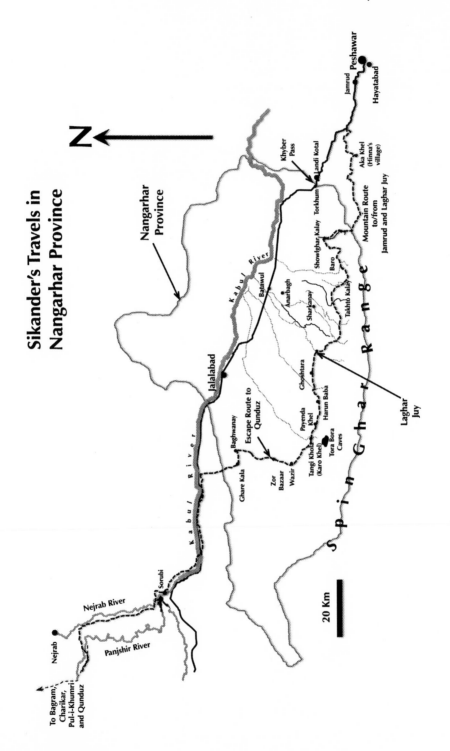

Sikander's Travels in
Nangarhar Province

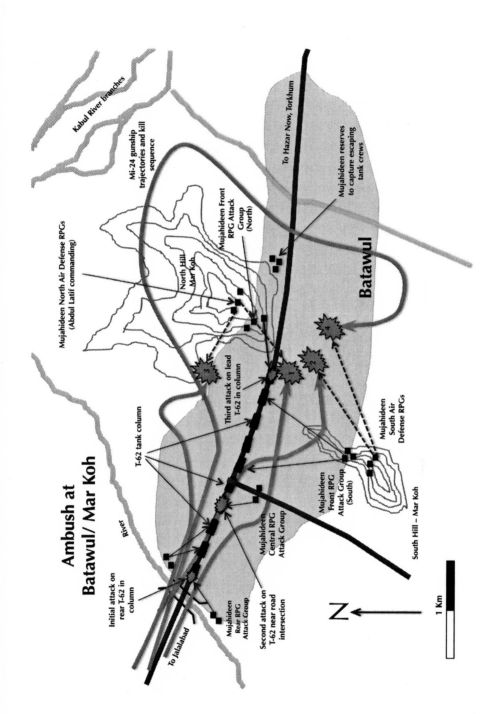

Ambush at
Batawul/ Mar Koh

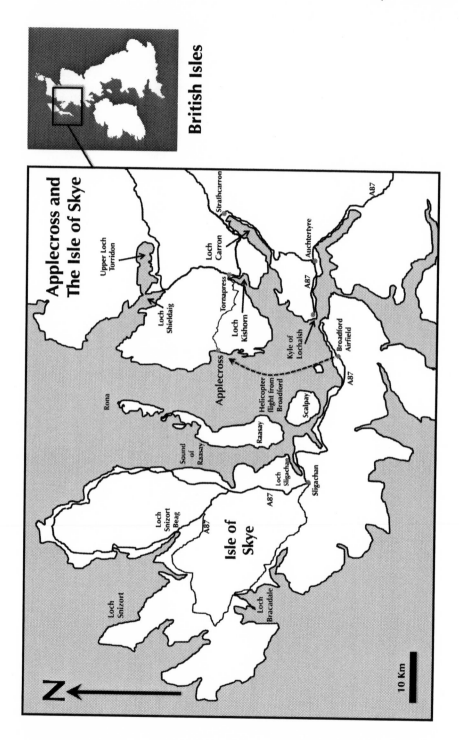

British Isles

Applecross and
The Isle of Skye

Upper Loch
Torridon

Loch
Shieldaig

Loch
Carron

Strathcarron

Tornapress

Loch
Kishorn

Auchtertyre

A87

Applecross

Kyle of
Lochalsh

Broadford
Airfield

A87

Rona

Raasay

Helicopter
flight from
Broadford

Scalpay

Sound
of
Raasay

Loch
Sligachan

Sligachan

A87

Isle of
Skye

Loch
Snizort
Beag

A87

Loch
Snizort

Loch
Bracadale

N

10 Km

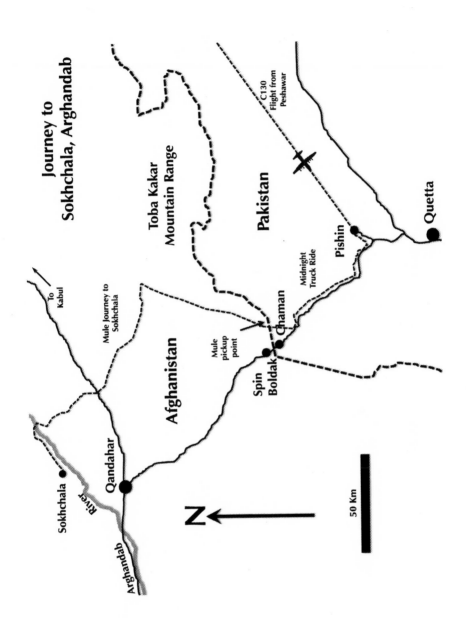

Journey to
Sokhchala, Arghandab

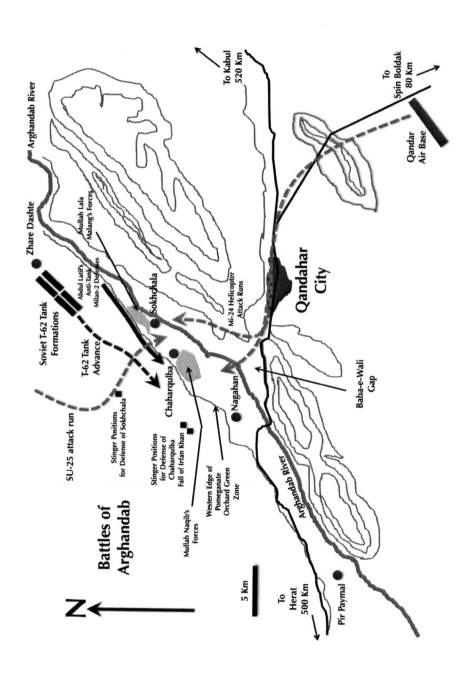

Battles of Arghandab

N ←

5 Km

Arghandab River

Zhare Dashte

Soviet T-62 Tank Formations

T-62 Tank Advance

SU-25 attack run

Stinger Positions for Defense of Sokhchala

Abdul Latif's Anti-Tank Milan-2 Defenses

Mullah Lala Malang's Forces

Sokhchala

Stinger Positions for Defense of Chaharqulba

Fall of Irfan Khan

Chaharqulba

Mullah Naqib's Forces

Western Edge of Pomeganate Orchard Green Zone

Nagahan

To Kabul 520 Km

To Spin Boldak 80 Km

Qandar Air Base

Mi-24 Helicopter Attack Runs

Qandahar City

Baba-e-Wali Gap

Arghandab River

To Herat 500 Km

Pir Paymal

Acknowledgments

Like the story itself, the writing of *SIKANDER* was its own journey, and like all other journeys, both the outward and the inward aspects are often memorable. This has been no different and I would like to thank and acknowledge the many traveling companions without whom *SIKANDER* was going to remain an interesting idea languishing and gathering cobwebs in my mind.

My opening acknowledgments have to be directed to my patient wife Rehana, who tolerated my frenzied life for the first three months of 2010 as I had to get this thing out of me. To her my love and thanks. Next I have to acknowledge my eagle-eyed editor, Pam Guerrieri who was ever concerned with ensuring that the work was as polished as she could make it, often with my impatient voice in the background hurrying her along. Thanks, Pam, for not paying too much attention to that voice. I am indebted to several other readers both professional and otherwise who took the time to pick up the novel and give me a critical sense of the storyline and readability, helping me with their valuable feedback. Special thanks must go to Marcella and Gary DiChiara and their several book club friends, to Jafer and Arshia Hasnain, to Bill Harrelson, Larry Dunn, and to my publicist, Scott Lorenz, of Westwind Communications. In reviewing the Glossary from the viewpoint of its many Islamic themes, my special thanks go to Hamid Sibghatullah who provided many insights and corrections to the often subtle but important points that are made in the Glossary.

References

References have been very important in getting as much of the contextual detail to be as authentic as I could make it. The following have been some of the more prominent references from which I have drawn, but please note, to all polemicists, the references are used for the purposes of contextualizing a fictional narrative and it is not my objective to opine on the accuracy of their content or otherwise. They have helped create the backdrop for a human story, not a political one, and one would be ill-advised to treat this book as a source of reference material on history.

Afghan Guerrilla Warfare in the words of the Mujahideen Fighters by Ali Ahmad Jalali and Lester W. Grau—MPI Publishing Company, 2001

Jungle Book, by Rudyard Kipling—MacMillan Press - 1894

Introduction to Man Portable Air Defense Weapon System—Sub course No. AD 0575, Edition A—US Army Air Defense Artillery School, Fort Bliss, Texas:

http://www.scribd.com/doc/2900214/AD0575A-INTRODUCTION-TO-MANPORTABLE-AIR-DEFENSE-WEAPON-SYSTEM

A Dossier on Civilian Victims of United States' Aerial Bombing of Afghanistan: A Comprehensive Accounting [revised] by Prof. Marc Herold—Whittemore School of Business and Economics, University of New Hampshire.

Camp Delta Standard Operating Procedure (SOP)—Headquarters Joint Detention Operations Group (JDOG), Joint Task Force Guantanamo (JTF-GTMO), Guantanamo Bay, Cuba Effective 28 March 2003

The Stinger Missile and US Intervention in Afghanistan by Alan J Kuperman—Article published in the Political Science Quarterly, Volume 114 Number 2, 1999

Report on Torture and Cruel, Inhuman and Degrading Treatment of Prisoners at Guantanamo

Bay, Cuba—Report by Center for Constitutional Rights, July 2006.

http://www.ccrjustic.org

No Hearing Hearings: CSRT: The Modern Habeas Corpus? An Analysis of the Government's Combatant Status Review Tribunals at Guantanamo (11/17/2006)—Mark Denbeaux et al. (http://law.shu.edu/publications/guantanamoReports/final_no_hearing_hearings_report.pdf)

Second Report on the Guantanamo Detainees: Inter- and Intra-Departmental Disagreements About Who Is Our Enemy (3/20/2006)—Mark Denbeaux et. al.

(http://law.shu.edu/publications/guantanamoReports/second_report_guantanamo_detainees_3_20_final.pdf)

Report on Guantanamo Detainees: A Profile of 517 Detainees through Analysis of Department of Defense Data (2/8/2006)—Mark Denbeaux et. al.

(http://law.shu.edu/publications/guantanamoReports/guantanamo_report_final_2_08_06.pdf)

Plan of Attack by Bob Woodward—Simon & Schuster, 2004

Worse than Watergate by John Dean—Little, Brown and Company, 2004

About the Author

Born of refugee parents from India into the newly created state of Pakistan, in 1952, M. Salahuddin Khan of Lake Forest, Illinois, earned a bachelor's degree in aeronautics and astronautics from University of Southampton, England. He is a management consultant primarily in the areas of product development and marketing. In 2008, Khan was a Co-Executive Producer of a 12-minute short movie called *The Boundary*, starring Alex Siddig of *Syriana, Kingdom of Heaven*, and *Star Trek, Deep Space Nine* fame. The movie dealt with the issues of civil liberties at a U.S. border crossing in a post 9/11 world.

Khan was the co-founder of Salagar Sonics, which produced award-winning self-amplified loudspeakers. His very first product was named one of the "Top 5 New Home Entertainment Products," in 2008 by The Robb Report's *COLLECTIONS* magazine, on whose cover the product was depicted in May, 2008. Between 1998 and 2007, the author served as Senior Vice President and Chief Technology Officer and Senior Vice President of Global Marketing and Strategy for NAVTEQ Corp. From 2006 to 2008, he was also the publisher of *ISLAMICA Magazine*. Before 1998, Khan was the Chief Technology Officer for Computervision Corporation in Bedford, Massachusetts. Khan is a designer, engineer, artist, writer, inventor (he is named on several US patents), and worldwide traveler.

www.sikanderbook.com